C000299442

Adam Mars-Jones has pub   e
and *Monopolies of Loss*), tw   )
and a collection of essays (r
Lightning' has been haile   ls
as a landmark of naturist short fiction (as oppo-   st
fiction).

Further praise for *Cedilla*:

'I was astonished by Adam Mars-Jones's *Cedilla*.' Leo Robson, *New Statesman* Books of the Year

'The most original novel of the year . . . The trilogy, when it is finished, will be a great novel about nothing much – and therefore everything.' Craig Raine, *TLS* Books of the Year

'A beautiful novel.' Leo Robson, *TLS* Books of the Year

'I thought Mars-Jones's last book should have won the Booker . . . I think this one should, too. I loved every crucial, funny, sharp-witted, occasionally wordy, word and would happily trail John Cromer's aware and honest story until he is ninety.' Lesley McDowell, *Scotsman*

'We are clearly in the presence of a formidable talent operating at full strength . . . There isn't a passage here that doesn't sparkle with some well-phrased perception, neatly overturned cliché or freshly minted pun . . . [Mars-Jones] has become over the course of three years one of the most industrious and accomplished novelists in Britain.' Leo Robson, *Daily Telegraph*

'Truly remarkable novel . . . Mars-Jones has Joyce's talent for revealing the absurdity and tender spots of human experience, and a genius for empathy.' *Psychologies* magazine

'Mars-Jones gives his narrator a seemingly inexhaustible supply of dexterous phrases, and rarely does a page go by without at least one line to raise a smile or a laugh – no small achievement . . . [they are] rich and strikingly peculiar novels.' Ben Jeffery, *Times Literary Supplement*

'*Cedilla* is a big book about a big personality. The novel's narrator, John Cromer, is gay, gifted, inquisitive, hilarious, wilful, manipulative and utterly maddening . . . *Cedilla* is an epic novel – not just in scale, but also in terms of its grand philosophical themes and dizzying array of characters – but it's a subverted epic. John is a courageous hero of the spirit, rather than grandiose endeavour . . . Mars-Jones is undoubtedly a wonderful writer and in John he has created a fabulously idiosyncratic character.' Melissa McClements, *Financial Times*

'The happy truth, however, is that reading these books never feels like a chore. Mars-Jones's prose is as springy and sure as John's movements are not. The books' picture of a post-war middle-class family is abundantly comic, but also psychologically astute.' Jonathan Gibbs, *Independent*

by the same author

LANTERN LECTURE
MONOPOLIES OF LOSS
THE WATERS OF THIRST
BLIND BITTER HAPPINESS
PILCROW

ADAM MARS-JONES

Cedilla

{ *novel* }

faber and faber

First published in 2011
by Faber and Faber Limited
Bloomsbury House
74–77 Great Russell Street
London WC1B 3DA
This paperback edition published in 2012

Typeset by Faber and Faber Limited
Printed in England by CPI Group (UK) Ltd, Croydon CR0 4YY

The right of Adam Mars-Jones to be identified as author
of this work has been asserted in accordance with Section 77
of the Copyright, Designs and Patents Act 1988

A CIP record for this book
is available from the British Library

978–0–571–24537–6

For Claude, whose sharp eyes . . .

1 Merry Hell 1

2 Swimming Like a Stone 83

3 Guest of the Mountain 283

4 Dark Ages 407

1

Merry Hell

When I left Vulcan, that self-proclaimed 'boarding school for the education and rehabilitation of severely disabled but intelligent boys', a phase of my mundane education was over. I was now an Old Vulcanian, though not in any hurry to attend reunions – if any were even held.

I had been much changed during my years on those premises. Perhaps you could say I had been Vulcanised, vulcanisation being a process for treating rubber by adding sulphur or other substances in the presence of heat and pressure. Vulcanisation enhances rubber's strength, resistance and elasticity. The description can be made to fit. I (or actually only 'I') had been strengthened and weakened in a complex simultaneous process, fortified and adulterated.

Then gradually the whole world became Vulcanised, in a different sense. A few years later the *Star Trek* series started to be broadcast and became extremely popular. English fans were told that no work was done at NASA on a Friday evening, because staff were required to watch *Star Trek*. They too had to learn what the future would be like.

Some of us loved the graceful shape of the Starship *Enterprise* itself, others coveted the weaponry, those stunning phasers, or the ability to beam down onto planets directly, descending like gods in a cascade of molecules. Others loved the comely communications officer Lieutenant Uhura (of the United States of Africa). No one had any respect for the theme tune – a swoony number which would have gone better with *Come Dancing* – or the nasty nylon trousers worn stupidly short.

I personally was spellbound by the automatic doors on the Starship *Enterprise*, which opened and closed with a distinctive squawking swish.

It was obvious to me that there would be automatic doors in the future, superseding every other sort of mechanism. There would be no more awkward pushing and pulling, no more knobs out of reach. The technology was elementary, surely? No real challenge for a boffin. I wasn't holding my breath for matter transporters or warp drives, but I was confident that there would soon be automatic doors everywhere, swishing open to admit me to privileged spaces, swishing closed behind me to seal off the outside world. I was eager for that future to begin, and I'm a patient person. I have to be, and I'm still waiting.

One element of the *Star Trek* saga threw a light backwards on my past as a severely disabled but intelligent schoolboy. This was the enigmatic character of Mr Spock, impassive and elfin, who came from a planet with the same name as my old school, Vulcan. Technically in fact he was only half-Vulcan, but nevertheless he made us familiar with a number of practices from his home planet, techniques of combat and communication: the Vulcan Death Grip and the Vulcan Mind Meld.

I went along with the general enjoyment of the programme, but I experienced an extra layer of response. To me the phrase 'Vulcan Death Grip' could only conjure up Judy Brisby holding me by the ankles over the stairwell of the school after I had refused a meal of slimy fish, even when she tried to cram the hated pilchards down my throat. The manœuvre as performed by Mr Spock and his kind, though, was a nerve pinch rather than the nerve punches which were Judy Brisby's speciality. It produced unconsciousness without involving pain, a set of priorities for which Judy Brisby would have had no use.

'Vulcan Mind Meld', on the other hand, seemed a perfect way of describing the ecstatic episode in the Music Room, when Luke Squires and I played the melancholy waltz called *Plaisir d'Amour* and were mysteriously played upon in our turn by a poorly tuned upright piano transformed into a blaring Wurlitzer of synæsthetic sensation.

Hip hurdles

In my final interview with Miss Marion Willis, sole Principal of Vulcan, I had made out that Burnham Grammar School was waiting with open arms to shield me from the cold winds of special education, holding out a blanket and a steaming mug of cocoa, to make sure that I was never again exposed to the piercing blasts of winter, as I had experienced them in a frozen turret bathroom of Farley Castle, a folly imperfectly turned into a school.

In fact we weren't quite ready for our encounter, the school and I. There were two hurdles that I had to clear before I could take my rightful place in the state educational system. A perverse way of putting it, perhaps, the clearing of hurdles, since those hurdles were my hips.

Even after I had started being a pupil of Vulcan School I would return every few months to the Canadian Red Cross Memorial Hospital in Taplow (known to initiates as CRX) for the eminent Dr Ansell to give me the once-over. The measuring process no longer included nude photography, as it had done when I had lived in the hospital, and the object in view was explicitly spelled out. She was waiting for me to stop growing. To the untrained eye I hardly seemed to be growing at all, but I was doing it on the sly, and Ansell was patiently waiting for that furtive impulse to spend itself at last.

Usually Ansell spoke to me as grown-up to grown-up, but sometimes she forgot and talked to someone else as if I wasn't there. Even in the days when I was living at the hospital, I had hated the way Ansell would start off in her friendly vein, encouraging me to develop an understanding of my physical situation and a relationship with the medical experts, and then turn to a colleague and say something entirely different, something that was clearly designed to exclude me from understanding. It seemed so rude. On my return visits from Vulcan for monitoring she fell into the same bad habit. So she might say to me, 'John, we're examining your legs in such a lot of detail because when you've stopped growing we can do something about those hips of yours. I'm sure you'd like to sit down properly after all this time!' But then she'd turn to a junior doctor and say something about epiphysis.

Epiphysis. I hated that word, hated and feared it though I learned to say it correctly in my head. Four short syllables, with the stress on the second.

It was being kept in the dark that felt so horrible. There was obviously a reason for it, and I knew what it had to be: I had an extra illness that they weren't telling me about. I didn't just have Still's Disease, I had epiphysis as well, and considering how foul Still's was, *epiphysis* must be much worse, or else they'd tell me about it, wouldn't they?

3

It took me a long time to realise that Ansell wasn't saying anything very different to her junior than what she was saying to me. She was just changing from plain English to technical language. An epiphysis is the growing end of a long bone. Once I understood that, I calmed down and even rather enjoyed the word. There's nothing like a technical vocabulary for conferring the illusion of control. I could see that there were parallels in other parts of the natural world, the growing tips of plants, for instance. It's one of my great regrets that I've never climbed to the top of a coconut tree, to witness the glory of that vegetable epiphysis. Still, who's to say it's too late? Perhaps a fork-lift truck could be commandeered.

Slow frenzy of growth

In my early teens my epiphyses played me merry hell. My legs developed excrescences. Nasty ugly lumps. It began to look as if I had a knob stuck on the outer edge of each leg, to the side of where a working knee ought to be. I thought them very unsightly. I felt they let me down, though I don't have great expectations of this body.

I was almost fond of 'epiphysis' by this time, the word though not the thing, but the same trick didn't work for 'excrescence'. By derivation the words aren't so very different – they both mean something that grows out of something else. Their overtones don't overlap, though. Nice ethereal epiphysis – nasty brutish grotty excrescence.

Luckily my excrescent epiphyses didn't hurt. I thought they did, but I was wrong. One of Ansell's deputies explained that since the knee joint was fully fused and had no moving parts, there could be no pain. In those days it was up to the doctor to decide whether the patient was in pain or not. Personally I thought my epiphyses hurt quite a lot, they weren't just eyesores they were bloody *sore*, but I was outvoted and told otherwise. I had a certain amount of experience of pain by this time, but apparently I could still be fooled like any novice.

The doctor who pooh-poohed my idea that the lumps hurt didn't deny that there were pain sensors in the area of the knee, and also working nerves, he just maintained that there was no movement to set them off. Personally I think that he was defining movement rather narrowly. The end of the tibia was moving all right, in the slow frenzy of growth, blindly pushing against a socket that couldn't accommodate it. Possibly I mean the fibula. But either way – bone grinding against bone. Whatever the explanation, I disliked what I fancied I felt, like the 'faith-healer of Deal' in the limerick. I disliked it more than ever before.

Over time the pain diminished and the excrescences themselves seemed to shrink. Logically this should have prepared me for the idea that my epiphyses had settled down and that my body had done all the growing of which it was capable. I should have been relieved, but I experienced it as a surprise and a worry when Ansell told me that the waiting was over at last. Now it was time to operate.

I wasn't exactly overjoyed. I didn't look forward to going under the knife. Mum was the impatient one. She had been saying for years, 'I can't think why they haven't done the operations yet. Why don't they do them now? They should get a move on!'

I wasn't in a hurry. When I was told it was time for those operations I burst out with, 'But you said it wouldn't happen until I was *sixteen!*' I sounded like a betrayed child, the very thing I wanted so badly not to be taken for. Ansell told me as gently as she could that my body was ready and I should be too. I should be pleased – she said that. There was nothing to be gained by any further delay.

In fact Mum and I were both behaving out of character. We were like clumsy actors with some amateur troupe who simultaneously drop their scripts at a read-through, and pick up each other's without noticing. I was always the one who wanted independence and normality at any cost, and now I was dreading a decisive move in that direction. Mum was convinced that I would never be able to manage on my own, but here she was showing impatience about something that would help (fingers crossed) to bring that about.

For a long moment we spoke each other's lines without finding it strange. The tone of the family drama was remarkably unchanged by the actors going off the rails for a little while, and we soon got back in character.

We made so much of our differences, of course, because we had so much in common. Often the difference was only one of emphasis. For instance, Mum's greatest fear was that she would die, and then there would be no one to look after me. My greatest fear was almost the same. I was afraid that Mum would make me helpless without her, and then die. Almost the same thing, you see, but not quite.

Loving care and domination

My whole grammar-school scheme played into Mum's hands, in a certain sense. Our minds were set on different phases of the future. Grammar school pointed me away from the disabled world, it addressed me firmly to a wider set of possibilities, yes, all of that, except that in the short term (a short term to be measured in years) it didn't. I had made the subtle transition from in-patient to boarder in a disabled school, but now on my triumphant progress towards the main stream of life I would pass through a period of being a day-boy, someone who returned after school hours to the loving care and domination of his mother.

So from Mum's point of view the independence I had promised myself was a cloud with a silver lining – and the silver lining preceded the cloud. There must have seemed every chance that the cloud would simply drift away in its own sweet time, leaving the two of us curled up in its lining.

You might think that having a young daughter would give Mum all the maternal focus she needed. Mum had thought so herself, before the young daughter actually arrived and showed what she was made of. Audrey was no picnic. She was very watchful as a baby, but once she had seen everything she needed to know she started to throw her weight around.

When Audrey chose the womb, as according to the *Tibetan Book of the Dead* we all do (with the benefit of an unobstructed view free of time and space), she must have seen her chance to continue the family tradition of conflict between the generations, as shown by Mum's hopeless struggle against Granny. The day Audrey had her first tantrum she showed that she was already a force fully formed. This was a hurricane that would never simply blow itself out. Local seismographs must have scribbled on slowly moving paper the initial tremors of the Bourne End Fault.

Her behaviour, though, was never quite predictable. Like any sensible volcano, she learned the virtue of long dormant periods, emitting just the odd sulphurous puff to make the villagers in the lava path look up and tremble.

My volatility was necessarily more limited. Mum's thinking started to go in reverse. She began to hedge her bets. Whatever my shortcomings as a son, my huge advantage in Mum's eyes was that I would – surely? – never leave her. She wrote me back into her future, when Audrey started showing how spectacularly unfitted she was to the rôle of the dutiful daughter. My job was to be the bitter consolation of a disappointed life. But only if I let it happen.

Mum hadn't either opposed or strongly supported my bid to escape from Vulcan, but there was no doubt she would be the beneficiary. She would minister to my needs and fall back, unless I was very vigilant, into her old rôle of interpreting me to the world. She would try to be self-effacing and I would try to be grateful. For a couple of years it wouldn't be too bad – but what happened afterwards? No one had suggested any plausible future for me at the end of my education. We were not much further forward than in those days of the 1950s when we looked, she and I, at the uniforms of various careers with a photograph of my smiling face pasted at the back and showing through portholes cut in the illustrations. Since then Dad had suggested I might be an actor, perhaps playing an old lady marooned in a chair who nevertheless bossed everybody about (an immobile Granny, essentially).

Mr Turpin at CRX had suggested I might become a clerk, though it was never clear how someone whose handwriting was the weakest point of his whole academic performance would ever make a go of that. Since then there had been silence about my future. Miss Willis, the Principal of Vulcan, had wanted me to do my A-levels under her ægis, but that was really so that she could point to me as evidence of what the school could do, a sort of high-water mark which would galvanise supporters of the school into paroxysms of funding, not because the academic achievement would usher me into a world of fulfilling work. Or unfulfilling work, come to that.

Mum was the last person to visualise me finding a real place in the world, one that would challenge her monopoly on suffering. She could let events take their course, and rely on their leaving me stranded, with no other options. So I must think of myself as a lodger only.

If I let the waters of home close over my head I would never be heard from again. No door would close behind me with any finality, but no new door would open ever.

The human cloth

The end of physical growth is I suppose a sort of rite of passage. High tide. They measured me at the hospital twice in one day, just for the record books. In the morning I was four foot nine and one eighth inches. Comfortably taller than Edith Piaf. They measured me again at the end of the day – since the spine compresses in an upright position, even an upright position as approximate as mine. At the end of the day I measured four foot eight and seven eighths inches. Still just a little taller than Edith Piaf. She was the lady on the radio who had no regrets (and showed you how to roll the French *r* correctly, at the back of the palate), but wouldn't she have wanted to be a tiny bit taller? I couldn't see that she could object to that – in which case she must have at least one regret, about being so diminutive without the robust excuse of bone disease. This was logical, but human beings, as Mr Spock was not the first to point out, are not logical.

There was logic, though, to the plan laid out for me in my next phase of life, logic in abundance. I would be having artificial hips installed, first one and then the other. There would be plenty of recovery time between. More than the standard period of rehabilitation would be required. I would spend whole months after each operation learning to use my legs. I wasn't starting from scratch, exactly, but the last time I had the benefit of functioning hips had been when I was three. It would be a long process learning to manage such amenities again. For my years of bed rest I had lain down, then gradually I was able to add standing up to my repertoire, but there hadn't actually been anything in between, unless you count lying rigidly at an angle in one wheeled contraption or another. Now whole teams of professionals would be devoting themselves to extending my world of movement. It would be a year-long crash course in flexibility.

So I had a good long time to wait before going to Burnham Grammar School, which wouldn't happen until the autumn of 1967. Educational normality wasn't bearing down on me at any great rate. 1966 was an interregnum, a sort of premature gap year, but I wasn't exactly going to be idle. That gap would be filled to bursting with activity – even if it was largely activity that would be visited on me, namely surgery and physiotherapy. Cutting and then stretching the human cloth. My diary was empty but my days would be full.

The good news about the hip operations was that they were allowed to hurt. Ansell was clear about that. The pain from my epiphyses had been unauthorised. The medical authorities had not accepted its bona-fides. It didn't meet their standards, and they threw it out of court.

Of course pain is unreal, and naturally it's easier to be sure of this when the pain is someone else's, but I felt it was a little presumptuous of medical science to be so selective, to single out my knee-pangs as bogus with such confidence. Now, though, I was going to have some respectable pain, licensed pain, pain that could hold its head up and have its docket stamped, its credentials accepted by the British Medical Assocation.

Ansell didn't use the word 'pain', not out of squeamishness but professional exactness. The phrase she used was 'a certain amount of discomfort'. This would be alleviated briefly with Pethidine and then with Panasorb. Pethidine a strong jamming signal blocking the reception of pain, Panasorb a soothing background hum in the nervous system. Ansell was optimistic, telling me that for the operation to be successful all I needed was a little muscle. And thanks in part to my childhood GP's advice on flexing the quadriceps, that's exactly what I had. I had a little muscle. Bless you, Dr Duckett! Bless your isometric cotton socks.

Physiotherapy, to take place before the operations as well as after, would help to build that little muscle up into a rather more competent bundle of fibres, able to fling my new hip all over the shop, or at least to steer me around nimbly enough.

Artificial hips – arthroplasties – were more or less new technology in those days. Spare parts for the human body! Running repairs. The stuff of science fiction, like the moon landing that hadn't happened yet, like the automatic doors that still haven't. Nowadays everyone's auntie has had hip replacements, but back then people didn't even call them that. Nobody said that I was going to have hip replacements. I was going to have 'McKee pins'.

The idea of mending joints goes back quite a long way. The challenge for those who set themselves to repair nature's failings (above all for the benefit of arthritic patients) has always been to come up with a material that was compatible with human tissue, but strong enough to stand up to the great forces brought to bear on the hip joint. Early candidates included gold, magnesium and zinc, muscles, fat, and pig bladder. None of these cut the mustard. A home-made joint is a tall order.

McKee's breakthrough came while he was tinkering with cars and motorbikes. He thought it was a shame that you couldn't simply replace components in the body that wore out or broke, and he wondered if it might not in fact be possible. His was an engineering perspective, and he set out to solve a medical problem in those terms.

The first operations to install McKee pins were done at the Norwich and Norfolk hospital in the 1950s, but it was years after that before they became anything like routine, and then only in certain cases, rather extreme ones like mine By the time I came to be a possible candidate for the pins, only a few hundred operations had been done. It was still a big step.

The new hip joint would be metal on metal. Partly plastic joints were being installed by Sir John Charnley, but they were still experimental. Metal on metal was tested and predictable. Metal on metal joints had been shown to work well and would last for literally years.

Nothing ages more quickly than progress in medicine. Soon this year's startling new technique resembles nothing so much as a blood-caked saw from two centuries back.

Up to the arseholes in bliss

Mum had her worries and I had mine. Mum was worried about the operations, though she wasn't worrying as an ex-nurse, but as a practising needlewoman. She knew from Dorothy Foot's sewing circle and the skills which she had developed there that sewing three pieces together was always tricky. Two was a doddle, and four not much harder. But three was no joke, whatever the material, whether it was corduroy or human tissue. In the case of actual surgery, a neat piece of darning wouldn't just be a matter of wanting things to look nicely finished off – it would be about securing a strong supply of blood to every part. Arthroplasties weren't plain sailing and they weren't plain sewing.

I wasn't worried about the surgery in store for me so much as the nursing. I would be lying motionless in bed for considerable periods of time. It wasn't the return to childhood confinement that I feared, though it would certainly test that elusive thing, my illusion of making progress in life. It wasn't even my hips that I was worried about – there was no worldly oracle I trusted more than Ansell – but my bottom. I dreaded a return to CRX conditions of bottom-wiping. My worry could be summed up with a quartet of terrible words: Standard Hospital Bedpan Procedure. In my days of bed rest, Mum had been there to attend to me, Mum who was a dab hand with a kidney dish, but she wouldn't be on duty now. Besides, I was a teenager now, too old to be babied in that way, but not ready for the psychic sandpaper of having my tender parts wiped by someone for whom it was the most degrading part of an unrewarding job.

In the end Mum made enquiries. It turned out that the bedbound life was going to be much less of an ordeal in the 1960s than it had been before. Hospitals were better equipped now. There were special mattresses made in three sections. All the nurse had to do was slide out the middle section and place a bedpan underneath. Bob's your uncle and Fanny's your aunt! I would be in heaven, comparatively speaking.

In heaven there is to be no weeping, and presumably no wiping of arses. There isn't much literature about the after-life of bottoms, but there's enough. As Rabelais describes the virtuous dead in the Elysian Fields they're up to the arseholes in bliss, since they enjoy the great privilege of wiping themselves on the necks of live white geese, whose softness (in Sir Thomas Urquhart's version) *imparts a sensible heat to the nockhole*. Something to look forward to, unless you're a goose.

I was moved from Vulcan School to Wexham Park Hospital, Slough, in an ambulance, which wasn't strictly necessary. There was no emergency (this wasn't appendicitis chapter two). If I could survive expeditions in the school's jolting bus then I needed no special cosseting. I enjoyed the ride, though, and managed not to pester the ambulance men for treats or special attention. One of the school matrons, Mrs Buchanan, came with me, just to be a bit of company, a link from the old life to the new, and we had a rare old chat, mainly about books.

For the next year (and more) I would be studying independently, and I had no end of reading lists, including one given me by the English teacher Mr Latham. Mrs Buchanan had her own enthusiasms, and she passed them on. There's no sweeter contagion than a recommended book. She was mad for a writer called J. D. Salinger, whose books had wonderful, ridiculous titles like *For Esmé with Love and Squalor* and *The Catcher in the Rye*. Salinger was right up her street, she said, and she thought he might be right up mine as well.

Tom Dooley

There were no white geese at Wexham Park Hospital to warm the nockholes of the patients, but there was a different sort of exotic creature, something I had rarely seen before in my career as a patient: a male nurse. He was called (can he have been called?) Jack Juggernaut, and he was from Mauritius. Perhaps it was a workplace nickname, or a warping by lazy English tongues of a name considered unpronounceable. The name conveyed his strength, but missed his delicacy. He was certainly strong. Dad was no weakling, with or without jungle training, but my standard of male power was the motorcycle policeman who had once carried me to my seat at the Royal Tournament on an expedition from Vulcan School. He was simply steel. Jack Juggernaut was not – there was a litheness and ease about him. He was also gorgeous in his white smock. Mauritius rhymes with delicious. It could have been horrible to watch that perfect body moving through the halls of the sick, but actually it was glorious. Envy was not a possible response. Wonder carried the day unchallenged. Jack Juggernaut had an enormous dark fruity voice and smelled of vanilla ice cream. Sometimes when he spoke he seemed to hit the resonating frequency of human bones – at least of bones like mine. He was on my wave-length.

Male nurses were a small minority. I assume that I was assigned one to save me the embarrassment which goes with being ministered to intimately by the sex not yours. Of course in my case it caused much more embarrassment than it saved, but in a different key. I wanked myself silly in an effort to keep my fascination with him discreet. Then I could enjoy the sensation of being bathed by this god without causing scandal.

It fell to Jack Juggernaut to shave my groin on the morning of the first operation. I thought I was well insured against arousal, but the touch of his hand summoned up an excitement from the far side of fatigue. He wasn't at all offended by what was offered him, saying sweetly, 'You've got high blood pressure, haven't you? You've got the horn and no mistake. You've got the high blood pressure in your Tom Dooley! Never seen such high blood pressure!'

I was mortified. Mortified mainly because I had been shy and slow on the uptake. This wasn't the first time he had used such phrases. Often enough he had said, 'I need someone to raise my blood pressure,' only I hadn't caught the sexual implication. He had been flirting all along. I'd failed to pick up masses of innuendo, cubic tons of the stuff, and now I'd missed my chances. I'd taken out my frustration on poor Tom Dooley, when perhaps there had been other ways to proceed.

Too late. Now I was going to be immobilised for months while I learned to sort-of-walk all over again, and I had wasted my freedom while I had it. After the operation everything would be different. Flirting would be out of the question when I was back on bloody bed rest. It's not that flirting necessarily leads to anything else, but the whole enterprise is a washout when there's no possibility of going any further. I had been served up delicious Mauritius on a plate and I hadn't even noticed. As the anæsthetics started to take hold I said goodbye to the illusion of consciousness in a state of weary bafflement, as if I was shutting the door on a stray dog that wouldn't leave me alone.

Mystical matiness

While my blood filled up with absence I thought of the only time Jack Juggernaut had actually held me in his arms. Since anæsthetics is (let's hope) a science and not just a series of wild guesses, my weight had to be assessed. It isn't just boxers and jockeys who must ritually be weighed before the big event.

Ever since I had become ill this was an indirect process, since I couldn't stand up on the scales, and supporting me would falsify the results. So now Jack Juggernaut weighed himself, then stood on the scales again with me in his arms, decorously wrapped in a sheet. My weight, of course, was the difference between the two readings.

I enjoyed the idea that my weight was a cosmic unknown, almost on a par with π, not to be apprehended directly but deducible by calculation. I savoured those few seconds in Jack's arms, though I tried to keep my blood pressure low. The body heat blazed through the smock he wore, and I was blissfully cooked in his mystical matiness. This was a perfect moment and would have remained so, even if Jack had a fit of the Aztecs immediately afterwards, tearing my heart out with his large warm hand and throwing it down the sacrificial steps.

There's never a photographer around when you want one, is there? I wouldn't have minded having that moment recorded. A single radiant image to outweigh all the pictures taken of me in hospital over the years. Somewhere in the offices of CRX in Taplow there was a photographic archive documenting the scanty progress of my generation of Still's Disease patients, effectively a rogues' gallery, showing our every deviation from normal posture and shapeliness. We were habitual offenders, backsliders, recidivists, stubbornly attached to the mistakes our bodies made.

I don't remember exactly what I weighed in those days. Not very much, but certainly more than Edith Piaf, since as everyone knows sparrows' bones are hollow and extremely light. And mine are not.

To fabricate the morning

The moment I woke up after the operation I knew something was wrong. Of course, 'waking up' misdescribes what happens after anæsthesia, or any other condition of absence. The world disappears every time we go to sleep, and the ego has to build it from scratch every time, to fabricate the morning. But the world as I reconstituted it in a side ward after the operation wasn't up to the usual standards of realism. Everything was askew and wired up wrong. As I became more aware of what my body was telling me, its messages made less sense rather than more. I wasn't in 'a certain amount of discomfort'.

That wasn't it at all. I was in stark pain, not the suburbs of agony but the main square, in carnival.

I couldn't understand what was happening. It was wrong for me to be having pain on this scale, but that wasn't the half of it: the pain was in the wrong place. The 'certain amount of discomfort' was scheduled for the left hip, but neither of my hips felt any different from the way it had before.

My throat was a different matter, scraped and swollen. It was in torment. When I tried to swallow I almost fainted. I could only think they'd done a throat replacement by mistake. They must have installed an artificial throat, a McKee gullet. Metal on metal. Those brilliant engineers had found nothing better to do than ram a motorcycle exhaust down my throat, still hot from the racetrack.

Everybody knows the scare stories, the scandals of botching. The sweet kidney yanked instead of the rank one, the innocent toes lopped and the guilty spared. Now it had happened to me. I coughed, and clots of blood came up.

Even a newly installed artificial throat should by rights be less painful than this. Perhaps they didn't have the right size in stock, so they made do with what they had, which was far too big to fit the throat space available. The Extra-Large. Then it must have jammed, so they leaned on it until the metal tube forced a passage. They'd gone to work on my throat the way a clumsy burglar forces a lock.

I was rising and falling through layers of dreaming, shunning the surface where the air was so raw but then fearing that I'd drown if I went down too far.

I even dreamed that Judy Brisby, my Vulcan nemesis, matron of monstrosity, had tracked me down at my most vulnerable, sneaking into theatre while I was unconscious and going back to her old tricks of force-feeding. With no pilchards to hand she had made do with a kitchen funnel, and forced broken glass down it.

Force-feeding was of course one of the techniques used on hunger-strikers such as the suffragettes, a form of torture supposedly acceptable because the alternative was starving to death. In my chemical sleep I had been mistaken for a suffragette, when I didn't even want the vote.

These were all good guesses, though I couldn't quite work it out for myself. Previous invasions of my body (appendectomy and so on) had been made under cover of gas. My body was used to that insidious process and raised no objection. I breathed in without protest the fumes of oblivion. Unconsciousness is how we describe it when the body recedes and the Self consults itself in privacy.

This time, though, the approach had been different. The protocols of anæsthesia had changed. This time the somniferous chemical came in through a vein and not the lungs, and my body didn't like that one bit. It retaliated and it sulked. This body passed a vote of no confidence. My throat closed up and I quickly turned blue.

Then there was dismay in theatre. They had to do something fast, but the emergency procedure wasn't obvious or easy. It's a technical point of anæsthesia – if something goes wrong when you're using gas you can just pump it out, and pump oxygen back in, clearing the fumes. You can't do that with an allergen which is already in the bloodstream. You can't just suck it out, any more than you can make a cup of coffee black when you've already poured in the milk. So when something goes wrong after you've administered something intravenous it's action stations. If not panic stations.

Desperate measures were called for, desperate and damaging. The theatre staff had to keep my throat open no matter what. They assaulted me to do it, jamming a laryngoscope down my throat.

A throat lined with barbed wire

In a way, though, I conspired with those who hurt me. For years I had imposed myself on the world by the firmness of my sentence structure. I didn't let anyone take me for a child, though my size might excuse that delusion. Now this successful insistence on adult status worked against me, and I suffered for it. I had managed to persuade the hospital staff that they were dealing with an adult, but the throat they needed to penetrate if they were going to save me was, indeed, child-sized. An adult tube wouldn't go in. There were no child-sized tubes in the theatre. They made do with what they had. They forced the adult laryngoscope down my closed throat, and they brought me back as best they could. With the same fused old hips I'd gone to sleep with, plus a throat newly lined with barbed wire.

All this I learned from Jack Juggernaut in tiny instalments, gradually building up a coherent story. The first thing he said gave only the most general impression. It sounded in his basso croon like something from an ancient blues song: 'Little man, they've done you wrong.' I didn't like being called *little*, but *man* more than made up for that.

I didn't know whether I wanted to be held and not let go, or never touched again. Jack told me my mother was on her way, and I tried to remember that she was really an obstacle to any further independence, but it was too much of an effort. The last thing I wanted to be was someone who cried for his Mummy when things went wrong, but for the time being that was what I was.

When Mum turned up to comfort me, saying, 'What have they done to you, my poor boy?', she was dragging Audrey with her, red-faced and raging.

The way Mum looked was a bit of a shock. She had taken the scissors to her long hair. Short hair had been fashionable for some time, but it had never been her style. We would all take a while to get used to it, even after she had tidied it up a bit.

Her new look wasn't an experiment in fashion but a desperate measure. As a toddler Audrey would only go to sleep if she could play with Mum's hair. She would select a single dangling strand and wrap it round her fingers, holding it close to her face. She would tickle her nose with it, breathing in and out very quickly, releasing and capturing some essence which guaranteed sleep. As Audrey grew and she fitted less neatly on Mum's lap, these demands came to seem less charming.

Eventually Mum started to put her hair up with hairpins, reversing Rapunzel's strategy by winching the magic ladder up out of reach of the suitor below. Audrey only became more frantic to reach the enchanted strands. She retaliated by stealing and hiding any hairpins she could find, so that Mum would be forced to let down her hair. Audrey would bury the pins in the garden.

Audrey may have loved Mum's hair, but she wasn't quite so fond of Mum herself, particularly when Mum withdrew the most important part of herself. Audrey would rage and grieve. Now Mum had been driven to the extreme step of cutting off her hair just to free herself from the fingers that reached for it with maddening possessiveness whenever Audrey was drowsy. And Audrey wasn't happy about the change.

The nurse approached Audrey with a bargainer's smile and said, 'Wouldn't you like a lollipop instead of that silly thumb?'

To judge by the muffled timbre of her voice, Audrey pushed the thumb even deeper in as she gave her answer: '*No.*'

The nurse persisted, with wheedling of a different character. 'A shame for such a pretty girl still to be sucking her thumb.' If I had been able to groan on anyone's account but my own at this point, I might have done it. Audrey was not an easy child to chivvy. She didn't take it well. The comment which the nurse had just passed made it significantly more likely that Audrey would tuck her bouquet under her arm on her wedding day, the better to jam her thumb into her mouth below the veil.

In the short term her response was also characteristic. '*You don't know what's in my garden,*' she said, with vicious emphasis. '*You don't even know I've got a swing!*' At an early stage – perhaps in the womb, where so much is learned – Audrey had developed the knack of winning arguments without going to the trouble of joining in.

I tried not to sob when Mum sat down by the bed in my side ward, partly to preserve some last shred of dignity (some imaginary last shred) and partly out of self-preservation. Sobbing constricted my throat. It aggravated the pain to which it offered the relief of expression.

Dolorific calculus

There's no gold standard for pain, no agreed yardstick. To be truthful, any yardstick would have to experience the pain directly, to flinch and writhe in the very throes of measurement.

Obviously it would be useful if doctors could quantify the amount of pain caused by a particular procedure, so as to compare it with other routes to the same therapeutic objective. Patients might eventually be offered a choice between paths through pain, in which personal preference would play a part. There are those who would opt for the agony-sprint, others for the long haul of sub-acute torment.

Torturers of course could make use of the same figures in their own calculations.

An attempt was made at the University of Uppsala in the 1950s, with the participation of local hospitals, to codify responses to pain. In practice the answers people gave were inconsistent beyond the resolving power of statistical correction. It was impossible to screen out the variables, even after the questionnaires were twice redesigned. Pain itself seems to be mutable, so that sometimes it becomes more intense with repetition, while at other times it dulls into numbness. Flirtatiously the toothache lies low, the moment it has led you trembling to the dentist's chair.

The Uppsala research led nowhere, in the end. It offered a poor return on the krona. So all that remains of the idea is the name of an imaginary standardised unit of pain – the dolor – while the actual project of a workable dolorific calculus was abandoned. So Mum and I couldn't have a conversation, seasoned patient to ex-nurse, on the level of 'Mum, it was agony! It was an 88!' – 'You poor thing, JJ. Childbirth only averages 55 – and I should know!' Our exchanges were much vaguer, with tears on both sides.

Deprived of Mum's attention for those few seconds, Audrey saw her chance of winning it back with interest. She went very quiet, which should have made us suspicious right away, but Mum was preoccupied with soothing me.

Nurses were popping in and out of the side ward every couple of minutes, and Audrey must have taken advantage of one such entrance and exit to slip out herself. So far she only did what any stroppy six-year-old would have done, but in the latter part of the escapade she showed her quality. When Mum had raised the alarm and charged off to lead the search party, she somehow managed to sneak back to where I was. From my position in bed, traumatised and now also upstaged, all I saw was the door of the side ward swinging open and then closed. No head showed at my level. Then a little later Audrey gave a loud and very stagey yawn and stood up, saying she had had ever such a lovely sleep and where was her Mummy? I pressed the bell for a nurse and slowly the fuss died down, with Audrey sticking to her story that she had never left the room. She even said that I had seen her, which was physically impossible, though it also meant I couldn't flatly contradict her story, however little I was tempted to believe her. I could see Mum wavering. It wasn't that she was convinced, she just preferred to think that she wasn't sharing her home with a manipulative little madam.

Audrey was back in a merry mood. She seemed to think the whole thing was funny, which in a way it was. Mum had longed for years with so much intensity to have a daughter. She dreamed of the completion a female child would bring. She had wanted to be so close to someone that they could almost hear each other's thoughts, but now that it had come true she didn't really enjoy it that much.

It was a little breakthrough for Audrey. She had always been a good liar, but now she was an inspired one. She had acquired the knack of being the first believer of her own untruths, letting them radiate unstoppably outwards from that secure core of falsehood.

If Mum really wanted a child who couldn't get away, I was much the better bet – not that I consented to any such transfer of her hopes, but I could see the truth of the situation. Audrey was already a lost cause. She was supremely well armed, with slyness and subterfuge. She exercised charm relatively late in any negotiation, just before the nuclear tantrum of last resort.

Ice cream and jellies all the way

The diet for traumatised throats favoured by at least one of the matrons at Vulcan (a fanatical advocate of dry toast as a healing agent) hadn't reached Wexham Park, or if it had the staff felt too guilty and embarrassed by my particular case to implement it. It was ice cream and jellies all the way, and I didn't need to look toast in the face for weeks.

It took me a week or two to recover from the assault on my throat – slow progress. Another day another dolor. I didn't have all that much incentive to get better, not when I was only getting back to square one. Finally I was pronounced ready for a second go at being operated on. The operation to install the first McKee pin, referred to by others but not by me as my 'op'.

I rather resented the abbreviation. I felt that styling the coming ordeal was my privilege rather than anyone else's. Others should follow my lead and say 'operation', unless and until I gave the signal to authorise the short form. They should defer to me in this matter, since it was the only little bit of surgery in my power.

It wasn't Jack Juggernaut but another nurse who shaved my groin when it became time again. Not that my pubic thatch had made much of a comeback in those weeks. It was still at the itchy stage. I wondered if the change of personnel showed that I was in disgrace for my excitement the last time I was shaved.

The new nurse was the same delicious colour as Jack Juggernaut, and had a lovely faint smile playing about her lips while she went to work. I wasn't worried – that is, I was mildly anxious about the operation but not about the shaving. Later I found out she was Jack's sister. I wondered madly if they had compared notes about Tom Dooley, hardly likely in their culture but something which would nevertheless explain the smile. When she saw him, Tom was dozing even before the anæsthetist arrived with the gas. Naturally it was gas this time.

Mum's warning about how difficult it was to sew together three pieces of cloth – and therefore also of skin – had given me pause, but I wasn't seriously bothered, even after the botch-up of the anaesthetic. I'd seen the excellence of Mum's work as a seamstress. She rose to every challenge, and there was no reason to think that the surgeon was any less skilled. Mum wasn't even a professional dressmaker, just a gifted amateur working for pin money, so it made sense that there should be many levels of expertise beyond hers, Himalayas beyond the foothills where she practised her useful domestic skills. A surgeon operating at a proper hospital must be more than just handy with the scissors and the pins and the needles, with basting and seams. He would be a scientist who was also an artist, a visionary thinker, a Leonardo of the surgical blade. Would my case even be distinctive enough to hold his interest? I hoped at least it would take his mind off the cryptic crossword he had been doing before he entered the sterile area. It would be sad to disappoint a person of such qualities.

I wasn't entirely wrong. The surgeon had skills. He wasn't intrinsically a bodger. Maybe the problem was simply that we were treating the body as a machine, and if the body is a machine then pain is one of the things it produces. The surgeon who operated on me specialised in arthroplasties, in McKee pins, metal on metal. He even had experience in performing them on patients with Still's Disease. So he was a specialist within a specialism. It's just that I turned out to be, once again, even more special than anyone had anticipated.

I was sick to the back teeth of special, but I couldn't make myself ordinary by an act of will or I might have been tempted to try it a long time ago, provided it was on the Ellisdons mail-order catalogue basis, On Approval, your money back guaranteed if not perfectly satisfied.

The worst of the whole darn bunch

I surfaced, by incredulous degrees, from the anæsthetic, into an experience of pain that was beyond anything I had suffered at Manor Hospital, where they tickled the bone with a little hook to get a biopsy sample, or at CRX when Miss Krüger had made us dance for her pleasure. It was worse because it was constant, without modulation. It was some time before I could bring it down into something as mild as an internal scream of betrayal. Ansell had lied to me. Ansell of all people. *Et tu, Barbara!* If this was 'a certain amount of discomfort', then she was a devil who enjoyed making people hurt, who got a thrill out of offering reassurance and then kicking it away, leaving me to dangle on a rope of pain. She was a compendium of all the ghouls I had ever known or heard of: she was Miss Krüger with her invisible pointe shoes of agony, she was Vera Cole wielding her razor on sick boys because she hated to see them suffer, she was Judy Brisby with her nerve punches, she was Anna Mitchell-Hedges letting demons out of their travelling-case. She was the worst of the whole darn bunch because she had seemed so much like a friend.

With the assault on my throat after the botched anæsthetic I had thought my dolor rating, my theoretical Uppsala score, was close to the maximum, but now I had to reconsider my settings. The new sensation was off the scale. Perhaps there came a point, as with my tape recorder, when the needle flicked far into the red and the apparatus began to fail, the signal unrecognisably distorted.

Again I was told that Mum was on her way, as if that was the answer to everything, to anything. I still didn't know what I had done to deserve this black jackpot. I was a dolor millionaire, no doubt about it, and I couldn't help suspecting that they'd done the little man wrong all over again.

Burning spiders in the socket

I had only one consolation as I lay there, with a spouting volcano of agony newly installed in my hip, which I lacked even the power to protect by curling up around, though instinct continued to dictate that impossible reflex. At least the pain was in the right place. The intolerable signals were being broadcast from a transmitter at the proper address, where the left hip was. There was far too much of the pain, and the surgeon had sewn burning spiders into the new socket, he was a hateful monstrous illegitimate brute but at least he wasn't incompetent. He was torturing me in the right place. The left hip was the one chosen for the first operation. The right hip had the benefit of a little movement, but the left was always a hopeless case.

People came in every now and then and spoke to me, but I couldn't take in what they were saying. And sometimes I answered them, but I didn't know what I was saying either. I was howling with pain, and when they gave me pain-killers they didn't kill the pain at all, only muffled the howling. The pain shrugged off the pain-killers, the pain had been inoculated against pain-killers, but at least I wasn't making so much noise and upsetting other patients along the corridor.

Over time I realised that Jack Juggernaut was in my room, smiling and saying something reassuring. 'Don't worry,' he was saying. 'We've heard it all before.' Heard all what before? I didn't understand.

Eventually he was able to get through to me. It turned out that when I started to come round I used every swear word I knew. I didn't know many. I had had very little experience of using swear words, since the time at Woodlands camp when I had learned a useful word and for a few days fucked everything that fucking moved. I had no real feel for the grandeur of the expletive, and there wasn't any artfulness involved in what I howled. I didn't swear like a trooper, I swore like a raw recruit to the world of taboo slang, howling the same thing again and again.

My untutored combination, though, had found favour with those who witnessed my agonies. '"*Fucking buggers!*"' said Jack Juggernaut appreciatively. 'That's downright catchy. Once you've heard it you can't get it out of your mind. We have to watch ourselves round Sister these days. In case it slips out.'

Jack Juggernaut felt the need to reassure me about my swearing because when I wasn't swearing I had been apologising for swearing. I'd go, 'Fucking buggers fucking buggers,' and then, 'I'm so sorry, I'm so sorry.' And then 'Fucking buggers fucking buggers,' the same rough music as before. 'I'm so sorry,' all over again. Jack wasn't trying to stop me from swearing, only from apologising.

Rabble of shits

What Jack Juggernaut told me showed that even when I wasn't fully present in mind and able to control my language, I was ashamed of its foulness. It wasn't just middle-class scruple – there was something else involved. In spite of the dominance of the pain, a part of me remembered that swearing isn't a real recourse for the disabled. You can achieve a brutal short-term effect with foul language, you can make people reel back a bit, but you incur a great loss of prestige over time (and your prestige, however forlorn, is your trump card). It's not remotely fair but that doesn't stop it being true. Whatever goes for women goes twice over for the disabled. A foul mouth isn't ladylike, and it isn't disabledlike either. People will make way for you all right, if you bellow, 'Fuck off and clear a path, you rabble of shits.' The wheelchair will meet no further obstruction – but it's not the best bargain you can strike with the world of your fellows.

Swearing is dirty, and we're above it. That may be the mechanism. Swearing is powerful. We're not entitled. Perhaps the two notions converge in some way I don't see.

Mum took the bus to Slough from Bourne End. We might live on the desirable Abbotsbrook Estate, but we were like poor relations in that prosperous parish, and Mum relied on public transport unless a friend with driving skills happened to be free. She was on her own this time, but she still talked mainly about Audrey, sounding variations on the old theme of I'm-at-my-wits'-end. After Mum cut her hair short, Audrey developed a new obsession – the hairpins she had once hated so much for putting Mum's hair out of reach. Now instead they represented what she had lost, hair that could be worn either up or down. Now hairpins became relics, almost fetishes. She exhumed rusty hairpins from where she had hidden them in the garden, and wore them herself. Finally she insisted on having her own hair cut short, and the hairpins lost their poignancy for her. This whole period of her development was just mourning after mourning – a trailing after symbols that had only ever been symbols of other symbols. This is the pathology of attachments. No wonder psychiatrists are so busy! Sensible religions set out to break attachment before it starts, to nip it in the bud.

Talking to anyone, even Mum, was like trying to concentrate on a chess problem while someone applied a soldering iron to my bones from the inside. Asking about Audrey became as much of an achievement as it would be to work out a dazzling move (*RxKtch!*), with the smell of burning marrow in my nostrils making me want to retch up my empty stomach to the last square inch of its lining.

My wounded hip was reluctant to heal. It was very sorry for itself, and couldn't forgive the insults it had received. After a time it even started to weep. It cried thick tears of pus. I was put on antibiotics, but they didn't help. Finally the command was given to wheel the bed outside, thereby exposing the damage to sunlight and air. The effect was miraculous, on the hip and the whole person. I think the crucial element was actually breeze, the movement of air. The sense that I was taking breaths from a live environment, a larger world that was going about its business without any intention of leaving me behind.

By the time I was moved back to CRX for my rehabilitation I had made a little breakthrough, discovering my own trick for fighting pain. At times when my medication was beginning to wear off, but there were still hours to wait until it was topped up, I found that by concentrating on my breathing I could get a certain amount of relief. The technique may have gone all the way back to my years of bed rest, in which case I was only dusting it off and putting it back into use.

The trick seemed to work differently from the medication. Instead of the pain going away, I went away from the pain. I was practising a sort of home-grown meditation. It was hardly surprising that my method wasn't very sophisticated. Transcendental meditation hadn't hit the headlines just yet – I dare say the Beatles were only just beginning to hear of it. But it was a lot better than nothing, however rough and ready my technique.

Only when I had been transferred to CRX for my rehabilitation, did I get an explanation of why the discomfort had disregarded the promised limits. How my body had failed to coöperate in its mauling as everyone had assured me it would.

CRX seemed to be where I ended up when no one else knew what to do with me. Sometimes I wondered what would happen if I died – would I wake up in CRX on Ward One Thousand, with the tea trolley looming and Ansell doing her rounds, ready with another display of medical words I didn't understand?

When I was installed in Men's Surgical Ansell sat on the bed and came as close to an apology as an authoritarian ever can. 'John,' she said, 'I'm not in the habit of lying to my patients – in fact in the past I've got into trouble for telling them too much of the truth. But in your case, though I didn't lie, I discounted a crucial aspect of your case and seriously misled you as a consequence. My excuse can only be that you – my dear John – are so very unique.' Ansell was teetering on the brink of tenderness, such a joyous novelty that it even interfered with my pedantic urge to point out that there can be no degrees of uniqueness. We're each of us unique, or at least that's the idea we all (identically) cling to.

There were considerate actions as well as kind words. Ansell scrounged up a set of linen sheets from somewhere, for old times' sake. My wardmates made do with cotton, but flaxen whispers lulled this battered body to a threadbare sleep.

Ansell at her softest got through to me. My sense of natural justice, which had become badly inflamed and even infected in the aftermath of the operation, began to heal over at last.

Brimpton or Frilsham

The reason for my swearing, all my foulmouthed groggy screaming, was that from a surgical point of view I was such a special case. One of a kind. It's possible to get just a little sick of being Mr Special.

There was something different about my history. It had been in my medical notes from my first week at CRX – in red ink, by rights – and still it had somehow been forgotten. '*The illness has raged*', as Ansell had said the first time we met, and there was nothing to be done about that.

There had been no point in putting me on steroids so late in the day. In my whole life I had only been put on cortisone for two weeks. No time at all.

All this was on the record, yet had somehow been missed. People always worry about not noticing the small print, but sometimes it's the large print that becomes invisible. It's something that happens when you pay very close attention to a map, until your eye is calibrated to spot the tiniest hamlet with the silliest name (Brimpton, say, or Frilsham), and BERKSHIRE, or ENGLAND itself, looming hugely in widely spaced capitals, eludes you completely.

So we had surprises for each other in the operating theatre, the surgeon and I. He was expecting bones softened up by steroids. He felt entitled to that amount of coöperation from the raw materials of his art, before he went under the flesh to find my bones and save them from themselves. But softness was not what he got, anything but. My bones were hard-core.

I was expecting skilled intervention of a routine sort, a more sophisticated version of a householder changing a plug. It's probably a bit of a fantasy, my idea of the standard operation from which mine deviated so sharply. I seriously doubt whether the pins ever actually *slide* into the bone-putty, with the surgeon hardly needing to bother with his drill – whistling tunefully as he instals the spare part into the machine disassembled on his bench. But my case, at the opposite end of the spectrum, was more abattoir than workshop. It was certainly no sewing circle.

My hip was so dense and so fused that the designated engineer couldn't get any purchase on it. In the end he had to break the bone, in the only way he could think of. That was the surprise my body got in its sleep, the nightmare which made it wake up screaming. The surgeon sitting on my left hip to break it.

He didn't perch gingerly on my hip, as you might mime sitting on a balloon in a party game, since the idea after all was to break it. He had to come slamming down. It must have been more like what happens when schoolboys misbehave in a playground they're too old for. I don't mean the ones who sprint to the swings to exploit the unlimited power of their teenaged bodies, making time stop as they pause at the highest point. I mean the ones who monopolise the seesaw, bucking and plunging wildly until the pivot groans, slamming themselves down onto the seat after being suspended so high above it that you can see blue sky beneath their uniform trousers. It must have been like that in the operating theatre at Wexham Park Hospital, Slough, until the pivot of my hip finally gave way beneath the grimly bouncing surgeon.

I could tell that Ansell was being sincere in her apologies. She took an interest in my diet, recommending wholemilk yoghurt to build me up. Calcium, I suppose, for healthy bones. She tried to get me to gain some weight, putting me on a course of anabolic steroids, making sure I understood that they weren't the same sort of steroids that were prescribed for Still's itself.

Cream of yoga

Yoghurt seemed a very exotic substance to me then, but I liked its grainy sourness from the start. Mum started making it rather than go to all the trouble of tracking it down – yoghurt was hard to find in the mid-1960s, at least in the environs of Bourne End, a town that was no great magnet for epicures. Making yoghurt was hardly a more conventional occupation than taking asses'-milk baths, come to that, but it didn't take long for Mum to get the knack. She would cook the milk, reduce it through evaporation, add the live culture and then leave it in the oven on the lowest setting.

I acquired a real yen for yoghurt, partly because it seemed to me linked to yoga and to yogis, two things that fascinated me. It pleased me to think I was consuming Cream of Yoga in slow spoonfuls. False etymology can be very seductive, but it couldn't help me to put on any weight, and Ansell continued to fret over me.

I don't know how long it was supposed to take a normal case to rehabilitate after McKee pins, or even a normal case of Still's. In my case it took a good six months – and that was just one hip. A fused joint with only a shred of tenuous muscle attached to it doesn't come back from the dead so easily. We were dragging my hip out of the Stone Age and into the twentieth century.

In the short term (which actually lasted rather a long time) my new hip brought total immobility rather than walking power. I was back in the suffocating cocoon of bed rest, after all the trouble it had taken for me to pupate the last time.

Books were my life-raft – or books were the sea on which my life-raft bobbed. My reading lists got me through that time, both Mr Latham's and Mrs Buchanan's. I loved *Pamela*, and it's gloriously long. I pretended to groan at the very idea of long books, but secretly I adored them. My impatience was put on. I was like the child on a journey who keeps on asking, 'Are we there yet?' but actually wants to be told, not 'Nearly, darling', nor 'Pipe down you little pest!', but 'Nowhere near'. We've hardly started.

Even so I took a break between Book 1 and Book 2 to read *The Catcher in the Rye*. If my Premium Bond (I had just the one, a present from Granny) had come up and I'd received some fantastic jackpot (say £1,000), I would have hired someone to make the experience of reading less physically taxing. I wouldn't have minded being read to, though I like to hear a book's voice in my head without anyone else intervening, but an infinitely adjustable human lectern would have been even better, to hold the book at a suitable distance in front of my eyes for hours on end, so I could rest my arm and didn't have to stop reading until my brain itself was tired.

I shouldn't exaggerate. Reading wasn't that much of a martyrdom. Granted, having palms that can't turn and face me is an obstacle to cradling a book as other people do (though it would have to be a light book to be manageable – this explains my fondness for pamphlets). On the other hand, my left elbow being fixed immovable has certain compensations. I can lie on my left side with the elbow tirelessly holding the book open, though these days my left eye tends to lacrimate (without any particular reference to the content of the book) when I hold the position for too long. In those days, though, my tear ducts were in fine fettle, and any crying I did for poor Pamela was properly symmetrical.

Sometimes while I was reading *Pamela* 'Pamela, Pamela' would come on. 'Pamela, Pamela' the song, by Wayne Fontana and the Mindbenders. It's almost perverse, the convergence between pain and the radio. So many songs have reached me through an intensifying filter of bodily distress.

The two Pamelas worked quite differently, of course. Today I could pick up Richardson's *Pamela* and read it afresh, overriding my previous impressions – but 'Pamela, Pamela' is hopelessly porous. I can't hear it except with teenaged ears. It's a magic hanky in which my tears will never be dry . . . A song about growth and regret, really. *When the rest of your childhood forgets as a dream / And the harshness of life dims those peaches and cream*. God-awful grammar, mind you, but still young Wayne had put his finger on something. I was just mature enough to regress emotionally.

Reading is the worst possible mechanism for making time pass. Reading makes time unreal, not by shrinkage but expansion. Look up from your book and be amazed at how little the clock has moved while you entered the stream of mental events. How freely books pour into consciousness. Those books, Salinger and Richardson alike, were doses of atropine instilled into my mind's eye, dilating it to admit a stream of rich blurred images.

There was some startling stuff in *Catcher in the Rye*. One passage in particular made me tense up while I read, though my lying posture made it physically impossible for anyone to look over my shoulder and surprise my guilty thoughts (if I was benefiting from a hired bookholder I would have had to work on my poker face). *He said it didn't matter if a guy was married or not. He said half the married guys in the world were flits and didn't even know it. He said you could turn into one practically overnight, if you had all the traits and all. He used to scare the hell out of us. I kept waiting to turn into a flit or something. The funny thing about old Luce, I used to think he was sort of flitty himself, in a way. He was always saying, 'Try this for size,' and then he'd goose the hell out of you while you were going down the corridor . . .*

Perhaps America was uniquely wicked. Otherwise I could reasonably hope to encounter that sort of thing in the corridors of Burnham

Grammar School, when the next phase of my mundane education got under way at last. I would have to keep my eyes peeled and my wheelchair oiled for every flitting opportunity.

Surly crackle

During my rehabilitation I had to adjust to an unfamiliar style of physiotherapist. The previous physios I had known, the two German ones at CRX, though as different as night and day, poison and balm, had both been what we would now call holistic. Each in her way addressed the whole person. Miss Krüger wasn't satisfied simply with making pain, she wanted to snuff out something essential in the patient. That was her game. Perhaps it really was a game, and she wanted to snuff out her charge's vital spark and then bring it back, as if children were like the Magic Candles in the Ellisdons catalogue which it was so much fun to blow out and watch rekindle after a few smoking moments.

Gisela wanted to make me wholly better, not just the parts of me that lay under her hands. Now I was dealing with physios who took a narrower view than those thorough German ladies. When these ones spoke, it was only to say, 'Again,' or 'One more time.' Or 'Same time tomorrow.' They attended strictly to business and seemed to have been vaccinated against conversation.

My life at CRX had begun on Ward One and continued on Ward Two. Now I had made it all the way to Ward Three, Men's Surgical. Being on a male surgical ward was the first time I had been an adult among adults. The atmosphere seemed very benign, after what I had known before. Once everyone got acquainted it didn't matter that there was no privacy. My wardmates would lend me their newspapers – always the *Mirror* or the *Sketch*, occasionally the *Mail*, which was definitely my favourite. The *Mirror* was physically compact, a tabloid, while the *Mail* was rather larger but not as big as the papers Dad favoured, a happy medium.

They bought these papers from the WVS trolley in the mornings, along with cigarettes and magazines. I found tabloids much easier to manage from a lying position than the unwieldy quality press could ever have been. There's nothing to be gained from reading a high-toned editorial if the recalcitrant unwieldy page keeps falling forward onto your face.

Reading a newspaper not meant for Upper People was a real thrill. Sometimes at home, Mum would buy a *Mirror* out of the housekeeping. 'Let's take a peek,' she said, 'Just to see how awful it is!' Then we would devour it, absolutely devour it. We pored over every page, reading against the clock since the paper had to be destroyed before Dad got home, every shred of it burnt.

When Dad caught me reading the tabloids in Ward Three he was shocked that a son of his could sink so low, but he rallied and tried to bribe me into better habits. 'Tell you what, John,' he said, 'What do you say to having the *Daily Telegraph* delivered every morning? Not just to the hospital, not just to the ward, but right here to your bed? Right into your hand? What do you say?'

My fiscal mind got busy. At 4d a throw, I thought the *Telegraph* a scandalous waste of money. And six issues a week would come to two shillings! I asked for my pocket money to be increased by that amount instead, to seven shillings a week. I pointed out that this gave me the choice of how to use the extra cash. I might buy the odd newspaper, but would certainly make it last more than a single day.

This attempt at striking a bargain was rejected out of hand. It had to be the *Telegraph* or nothing, and so it was nothing. Dad couldn't see that I wouldn't have accepted his offer even if I'd enjoyed reading the *Telegraph*. It would have driven a wedge between me and the men on the ward, who were kind enough to turn a blind eye to my reading just so long as I was discreet and didn't start group discussions about the epistolary novel. They made sure the radio wasn't so loud it derailed my concentration.

I was back in the limbo of bed rest, but the limbo was different and so was I. There is actually no limit to the range of limbos – they're like the greys on an infinite paint card. In various ways the new one was lighter, since I had consented to this period of deprivation and I knew what I had to gain from staying still. There was an end in sight, however distant, a horizon over which rays of unknown wave-lengths would eventually send their light. All the same, I wasn't patient. My body would be seized every now and then with wayward energy, a surly crackle that could only be adolescence.

At various times of life there have been words which have had a sharper significance for me than they did for the world at large. The first word of this sort was obviously 'Granny', not in my family a cloud of lavender-scented sweetness but the inventor of her own style of conversational judo throw, using her opponents' strength against them and leaving them panting on the mat.

The second such word was *librarian*. A librarian for me is a sort of lay magus, broker of knowledge and fascination, and all thanks to Mrs Pavey, the head librarian in Bourne End. She was a melancholy-seeming woman plagued by migraines, but remarkably conscientious. She didn't see her job as passive, a matter of meeting requests merely. She anticipated needs. I think she saw herself as a sort of matchmaker, arranging encounters between books and readers whose affinities weren't obvious. Love at first sight can look after itself. Love at second sight requires careful planning.

So Mrs Pavey would search out books on subjects which Mum told her might interest me, to beguile those long months of rehabilitation, but she was also quite capable of sending something along un-prompted. You could never predict what might turn up in Mum's bicycle basket, in the slightly sticky plastic covers that library books wore in those days.

In Hinduism there's a technical term for someone who has been well on the Path in a previous life and then stumbled. A *yogabhrashta*. The point being that such people are surrounded by helpfulness on their next go-round – just as everyone will be particularly patient with a learner driver who has failed the test a few times.

Isn't this exactly my profile? I've never felt hampered by an *avarana*, a veil of ignorance. I've been beetling after enlightenment from the word go. By 'my profile' I mean increased difficulties but a prodigal scattering of hints and clues, inklings galore, signposts as far as the eye can see.

Come and get me, Copper!

Mrs Pavey got hold of *The Tibetan Book of the Dead* at my insistence, though I must admit I found it a rather penitential read. There was just one wonderful idea in it, which I immediately made my own –

that we choose the womb in the privileged instant between lives. The idea seemed very familiar. That jewel of insight was like the ear-ring which turns up at last in the dust-bag of the vacuum-cleaner. It gave me a sense of relief and restitution rather than new discovery.

A real bull's-eye of Mrs Pavey's was *Gardening for Adventure* by R. H. Menage. Mum made a good pitch for the book. 'It's got a section on sundews,' she said, 'Venus Flytraps, pitcher-plants and butterworts. Mrs Pavey and I felt it would be right up your street. And it would give you and Dad something to talk about, and things to do when you come home . . .' By saying this Mum was recognising a profound truth about the man she had married, that he was always happier and more amenable if there was a project of some sort on hand. Marriage did not fit his definition of a project.

Dad had always been a true botanist, with a disinterested fascination for the workings of nature. He did all the gardening proper, but he regarded the garden as a laboratory as much as a showpiece. Mum's attitude to the plant kingdom was different. She was a kitchen alchemist with no real interest beyond her herb garden.

Usually when people told me I was going to like something, I decided on principle to hate it to bits. This time, though, Mum and Mrs Pavey had got my number. If anything though, the phrase 'right up your street' understated things. *Gardening for Adventure* was so far up my street it had its tongue through my letterbox.

Inactive in bed between my linen sheets, their chaste rustling an audible mark of caste privilege, I was like some winter bulb, dimly thriving, from which little overt growth could be expected. No wonder my mind was attuned to the vegetable kingdom. I was almost part of it.

The introduction to *Gardening for Adventure* got things off to a flying start. It ended, 'By growing the plants described in this book I think you will find that gardening *can* be an adventure – even if the realisation only comes in a police cell after you have been arrested for the possession of opium or Indian hemp.'

I couldn't see what could possibly be so wrong about growing this plant, particularly when the author had explained so carefully how he tended his. On the other hand, I found the idea of sitting in a police cell strangely attractive. When I had been on Ward Two of CRX I had been terrified of moving up to Ward Three, and now I was there I found it wasn't so bad. I was sure I could handle police custody and even prison if it came to that. I was used to institutions – hospitals and schools – and was sure I could turn it all into a game until I had collected the whole set.

There was even a picture of *Cannabis sativa* on the front cover of the book. Combined with the assertion on the back cover that all the illustrations in the book were taken by the author of plants he had grown himself, this seemed splendidly defiant – a gentlemanly way of drawling COME AND GET ME, COPPER!

Mr Menage certainly showed more knowledge of the plant than was common at the time. *The leaves can be made into cigarettes known to the underworld as 'reefers' and hashish is prepared from the exuded resin. Other names given to the plant are bhang which consists of selected dried leaves and twigs, and ganjah (or gunjah) which is the flowering tops.*

About opium he was similarly open-minded ('Many experts state that opium smoking is in fact little more harmful than tobacco smoking – in spite of publicity given to the contrary'). His description of the methods of preparing it for smoking could almost be mistaken for instructions ('It is then placed in the orifice of a special pipe which is puffed four or five times'). Specifying the number of puffs suggested a knowledge more than academic. OVER HERE, FLATFOOT! CRIMINAL MASTERMIND STICKING OUT HIS TONGUE!

I was excited by the possibility of invisible transgression in the allotment, civil disobedience in the rockery. I longed for a criminal record more than anything, while knowing that disability squelched any real possibility of going to the bad.

It was an annoying logic, but I couldn't see any way out of it: I needed to be good in order to deserve to be looked after, but however good I was I would never be as good as the people who looked after me, since they were being 'selfless' and giving up part of their lives to make mine possible. I wanted to be 'selfless' myself, but perhaps I already meant something different by that word.

I was still indefatigably asking the question 'Who am I?', but not getting very far at this stage. I didn't know whether I should feel special or not special at all, part of the broad sweep of humanity or only an afterthought, a slip of the creator's tongue.

'Handicap' was the polite word then, not 'disability'. I had 'a handicap', and so did our neighbour Arthur Foot, but that was only to do with golf. I knew that the word meant a different thing used in that way, but the co-incidence was still rather tempting. It set off new thoughts Arthur had a handicap because he was so good at golf, and a way had to be found for him to play with other people and not beat them every time. Otherwise everyone would soon become bored. And perhaps I was handicapped for the same general reason, to give other people a chance. I could manage to feel worthless fairly often, but the more desirable state of humility seemed to be beyond me.

A stink bomb come to life

There were plenty of other surprises in Menage's book. *Mimosa pudica* folded up when you touched it or blew on it hard – I suppose the name meant that it was embarrassed, somehow – but it didn't react to rain, whether a shower or a downpour. It could discriminate between stimuli. It 'knew' the difference.

Desmodium gyrans, the Indian Telegraph plant, had leaves which moved round and round whenever the temperature rose above 70 degrees Fahrenheit. The movement was very rapid in plant terms, easily visible. The hotter it got the faster they moved. They twirled and twirled until they dropped off, presumably from the equivalent (in the vegetable kingdom) of metal fatigue.

I learned the finer points of parasitism. There are plants which have photosynthetic leaves, like mistletoe, so that they don't get all their nourishment from the host plant – hemiparasites – and there are holoparasites like the dodder we saw on the marshland by Abbotsbrook, with no ability to fend for themselves. There are even endoparasites, plants which live entirely inside the stems of the host, only manifesting themselves as a tiny bud opening into a diminutive flower. Rather like a pimple on your face suddenly turning into a carnation, a buttonhole worn rather too high up. I winced when I thought of that. My complexion was not at its best in those years. When no one was looking I'd sometimes try to burst my pimples with the point of a pencil. It's not a technique I can really recommend, though it's remarkably addictive.

Mr Menage also wrote about *Sauromatum guttatum*, otherwise known as Monarch of the East, and resolved an old dispute. *Sauromatum* was an old friend, though a bittersweet one who had produced a certain amount of conflict. I'd been given one of these bulbs when I was living in CRX, way back when Ward Two was still Ward One. Mr Mole was a porter who thought himself a gardening expert. He told me that it ate insects but I didn't believe him. I knew and loved the carnivores, and this wasn't on the list.

The great thing about *Sauromatum guttatum* is that it's a powerful osmophore – that's the scientific way of saying that it stinks to high heaven. What more could a boy want from a plant? *Sauromatum* was an Ellisdons Stink Bomb come to life. Look after it, keep it warm and it will flower. I waited for the big day, the day of pungent flowering. The girls on the ward duly cringed and coughed and said they needed clothes-pegs for their noses. I enjoyed watching them scream and giggle as they came closer to the source of the stink, then reeled away. The inflorescence only lasts a day or so. Then *Sauromatum* was put back on the windowsill and I forgot all about it. A day or two later Mr Mole took the shrivelled flower and casually prised it open. Inside there were two or three dead flies.

They proved nothing. Absolutely nothing! I hated Mr Mole for saying 'Didn't I tell you so?', for imagining he'd proved his point and had won our duel of botanical expertise. Everyone thought I was in the wrong. It was almost physically painful to know that I was right. Mr Mole was hopelessly unscientific and just jumped to conclusions. When it came to *Sauromata*, he knew sod-all. He had no feeling for them, or he would have asked himself why a plant that – according to his theory – ate flies didn't bother to digest them. It was agony to be dismissed by someone who knew less than I did.

Now, in the same hospital, I finally got the lowdown on *Sauromatum guttatum*. There it was plainly in Menage's book: the plant attracted flies as pollinating agents, not as food. I felt vindicated but also mortified. There had never been any doubt in my mind that *Sauromatum guttatum* wasn't a carnivorous plant. Now I had the evidence – and no one to show it to. I asked after Mr Mole with pretended fondness, but he'd been gone for years, no one knew where. I'm sorry to say that if I'd had a time machine at my disposal at that moment, and only one return trip to make in it, I would probably have used it to turn up with a gardening book from the future, just for the satisfaction of proving Mr Mole wrong in front of witnesses. Of course on the return journey I would have found myself in an unrecognisable 1966, where with the refutation of Mole's Fallacy all ignorance had withered away.

Sometimes Mum brought Peter along to visit me at CRX. Most teenagers sharing a bedroom with their older brother would see some advantage to having it to themselves, but Peter seemed not to think that way. He had never acquired the knack of consulting his own interests ahead of mine. He seemed to yawn all the time, partly with the exhaustion of healthy growth – he too was negotiating adolescence, in a way much more obvious than mine – but also because of his new schedule of early mornings.

We both wanted to grow up and find our own way in the world, but his path was clear. There was nothing to stop him from reaching escape velocity – he was practically on the launch pad already. During the holidays he was doing a paper round! He was earning already. Prepare for blast-off!

We both shared the enthusiasm of the time for outer space and exploration, though we had cried when Laika the dog, first creature in space, died in orbit, trapped in a metal box with none of the smells that she loved. I must have been seven at the time, and Peter five or six. We couldn't understand why no one else was upset – but then we hadn't realised that there had never been a plan to bring her back. Death was part of her mission, as it is of ours.

A thwarting engine

Fired by my reading, I wanted Dad to put up a greenhouse next to the house, so that I could raise specimens of *Drosophyllum lusitanicum* in there. The Portuguese Sundew. One of the few carnivores that likes dry conditions, temperamental, a real challenge. Dad wanted a greenhouse too, but Mum wasn't too keen. Could I mould them both to my sovereign will? It didn't seem likely, since they never seemed to agree about anything. Deadlock was inevitable unless I used subtle strategy.

Dad wasn't easy to handle, even when you and he wanted the same thing. He was less a person in any conventional sense than a sort of thwarting engine. He was strongly counter-suggestible. If there was something anyone wanted, then his reflex was to rule it out, and he found it much easier to come up with reasons against than to wonder why he was so opposed to it in the first place.

It was a curious piece of psychological wiring. If you made any sort of claim on him, he would smack you down. But if you built a wall against him, as Peter and I were busy doing, then a helpless fondness would show through the chinks of it.

For weeks the McKee pin installed at such expense of pain seemed to be a dud. My left hip had no more than a little grudging movement, like a hinge so rusty that nobody can get at it with the oil can. Then I suppose the endless physiotherapy, although painful as well as boring, built the muscle up sufficiently for me to notice the difference. My new mechanical hip changed its tune, starting to make murmurs of competence. It responded, after a fashion, to instructions. It fell into line. I began to be able to sit approximately, not as most of the world sits but to half-sit at a jaunty sideways angle. Sitting with a bit of leaning built into it. This was a welcome change.

Walking was also mildly transformed. I needed a stick to help my balance, but as long as I had that I could get about fairly smartly. Still at a snail's pace, but a limber, youthful snail, impatient to find what was round the corner.

To beguile the tedium of healing the Platonic Librarian of Bourne End worked hard on my behalf. She cast her net widely. Mum had been filling Mrs Pavey in about my foibles and fascinations. She must have mentioned my interest in the occult and mystical, and so various books came along that were attuned to those vibrations. I remember *Psychic Self-Defence* by Dion Fortune, which made me want to join some sort of esoteric Order. But how to find one, and how to know it was the right one? Through Mum I ordered a monthly journal called *Prediction* from the stationer's in Bourne End and pored over the cryptic small advertisements. Of course the occult wave-lengths are jammed with trash. I needed the equivalent of Mum's indispensable consumer guide to pick and choose among the hundreds on offer, a sort of *Which Cult?* The desire to retreat from the world was fierce in me, perhaps because the world seemed to care so little whether I was in it or not. It was the same they'll-miss-me-when-I'm-gone motivation as lay behind my 'suicide attempt' at school.

Mrs Pavey also unearthed books on astral projection and the Tarot. I read the astral projection one first. Hardly surprising that I was drawn to an occult practice that promises so much. I needed no convincing that the physical body was a rubbishy contraption, hopelessly inefficient and outmoded. The book gave instructions for travel in another dimension, no ticket required.

Autofellation

You needed neither driving licence nor working hips. All you needed was 'a dream of knowledge' – a lucid dream, to wit a dream in which you knew you were dreaming. I had plenty of those. It's just that I was accustomed to using them in a rather vulgar way. It turned out I was already an old hand at astral projection, I just didn't project myself very far. To be exact, I projected myself just far enough away from the physical body to get astral cock into astral mouth. Autofellation. On the astral plane I turned out to be remarkably limber. In lucid dreams I became Ouroboros, mystical worm swallowing its own tail. If my tail was good enough for Luke Squires at Vulcan School it was good enough for me. It had never occurred to me before I read the book from Mrs Pavey's library that I could use the same technique to leave the room.

Now, armed with new knowledge, I was ready for some proper exploring. I learned to drift away from the physical envelope through the escape hatch of a dream of knowledge. One night I found myself in a sort of astral maze, opening doors which just led to grey corridors full of other doors, which led to more of the same. An esoteric labyrinth from which there seemed to be no exit, a dreadful place.

Another time I made better progress. I remember leaving the body and venturing forth into the æther. The night sky received me warmly. I looked back, and I could see myself sleeping. The book said I would see a glowing cord linking the astral body and the gross bundle back in the bed, a sort of mystical umbilical, but there was no sign of anything like that. I was untethered. I was a kite without a string. Undeterred I started off into the welcoming void, waiting to feel the astral breeze on my face, to gaze on the placid features of eternity, when suddenly I had a rush of panic. It wasn't a feeling that seemed to belong to me but (of course) a disembodied panic. Then I had the sensation of returning, actually *twanging* back to the physical plane with great force. There was an almost audible snapping of the spiritual elastic. I woke up with a start, re-identified with the gross, inefficient, outmoded body. This wasn't an outcome foreseen by the book I was using as my guide. I took it seriously. There had been no umbilical cord! I had gone exploring on the cliffs of the infinite without being safely attached to base camp. If I had ventured any further I might never have been able to get back.

From then on I stayed put in my sleep. The dream of knowledge seemed to be an unreliable contraption, as much an ejector seat as a gateway to mystical experience. Soon I stopped having the dreams of knowledge, as if I had closed the door on them myself. I was missing an important clue. What I was being offered was something subtler than an escape from this uncoöperative body.

The dream of knowledge, the dream in which you know you're dreaming, is a microcosm or a metaphor. If it's possible to be dreaming but also to know it, then it is possible in 'waking life' to be aware of life's illusory nature. The technical term for illusion being Maya. The guru, the adept, the – as he's called – *jñani* dreams as much as anyone else, but he (or she, though really neither he nor she, since gender is only another of Maya's little notions) always knows he's dreaming. He's awake in his sleep, and in his waking hours he sees through the illusions of life.

I had much more joy from the other book, *The Tarot* by Mouni Sadhu. The book's subtitle was 'A Contemporary Course of the Quintessence of Hermetic Occultism', which was a mystical thunderbolt in itself. I also loved the epigraph, frustratingly unassigned to a source: *Peu de science éloigne de Dieu / Beaucoup de science y ramène*. A little knowledge estranges one from God – great knowledge brings one back into the fold. The moment I read it I recognised this as my own motto. Since then I've seen it ascribed to both Pasteur and Francis Bacon.

My mind salivated when it read the description of the Tarot on the

41

first page of the Introduction as 'a truly philosophical machine'. I read the book all the way to the end, not wanting to admit to myself that I was completely baffled and bogged down. *Privilege Teth: the Adept is in command of the universal therapeutics. This means, that he possesses the art of the absolute criticism (in the mental plane), the art of disinvultuation in the astral, and the use of medical magnetism on the physical plane.* 500-odd pages in that vein. It certainly wasn't plane sailing, on any plane I knew.

Even so I was bewitched, partly by the author's name, and would say it over and over again under my breath. *Mouni Sadhu Mouni Sadhu.* It became a sort of mantra, but it worked the wrong way round, stirring up my thoughts instead of dissipating them. I'm rather embarrassed by the book now, but at the time it nourished me with dark hints and cryptic formulas. I had to crawl through a thicket of obscurities before I could emerge from the gloom and see daylight for the first time.

Gardening for Adventure was partly responsible. Thanks to R. H. Menage I now saw the vegetable kingdom as a place of instructive freakishness, paradox and transgression. His book was a sort of botanical Apocrypha, even a Kabbala. Plants set traps to hunt meat, they fanned themselves when they got hot (*Desmodium*), they brewed deep inside their own tissues the liquors of enlightenment (*Lophophora willamsii*). It turned out that nature didn't bother much with the Laws of Nature, as we so confidently formulated them on her behalf. And that was the part of nature I felt part of, mercury-nature, pumice-nature, platypus-nature, where a metal could be a liquid, a stone could float and a mammal lay eggs.

Milk running down abdominal grooves

Of course I was romanticising my own status dreadfully. The apparent exotica belong to exactly the same order of things as iron-nature, limestone-nature, cow-nature. There's nothing wildly abnormal about mercury or pumice or platypus, they just don't seem to fit the standard categories, lazy preconceptions. There's mercury in thermometers, pumice in many bathrooms, and platypuses . . . well, in the zoo or on television. Even in Tasmania I suppose you don't exactly fall over them, but you might see one if you were swimming in a stream there, and actually if it was a male he might give you a nasty dig with his venom-spur – and serve you right for thinking it was your stream and not his. It's entirely normal for platypuses to be the way they are, that's the point. There's nothing unnatural about lactating through the pores, without benefit of nipples, and having the milk run down abdominal grooves for your young to lick up, it's just not the human style of motherhood. Still, we'd rather treat ourselves to a shudder of wonder than make a little more room in our pigeon-holes.

At the time I was attuned to a cruder logic. Since I was debarred from so many ordinary activities, it seemed to follow that I would have a special affinity for the esoteric. That would balance the cosmic accounts nicely. My bailiwick would be the occult and the perverse.

I thought Mouni Sadhu might have written another simpler book, and pestered Mrs Pavey through Mum until she came up with a much smaller volume called *In Days of Great Peace*, which was more like an autobiography and didn't really engage me. I read about Mouni Sadhu's visit to a spiritual leader in Southern India called Maharshi, whose face expressed endless friendship and understanding, how Mouni Sadhu dissolved into tears which washed away the stains of multiple incarnations and so on, and I thought 'how nice for him' without going any deeper.

Discreet off-stage cough

I must have read the sentence, 'He walked with difficulty, as his joints and knees were affected by acute rheumatism', and yet felt no particular quickening of interest. What else was I looking for, if not a guru with arthritis? The fit was incredibly close, yet I missed it. It was as if I was being protected by a sort of lightning conductor, from premature contact with energy of a high order. I put the book aside unaffected, at least on the surface. In this way a leading player in my life gave notice of his existence with a discreet off-stage cough, waiting in the wings, years before he made his entrance proper.

People value what they pay for. The things they get for free, such as a national health service, tend to be under-appreciated. I wasn't going to make that mistake. Morale is important. I was deeply in debt to a system which was the envy of the world, and I didn't want anyone to imagine they had inserted a metal hip into an ingrate. As soon as I decently could, as soon as there was a chance of being believed, I had been saying how pleased I was with the operation. Despite everything I passed congratulations on to the surgeon who had done the work at Wexham Park – Mr Arden – saying how marvellous it was to have a hip that worked, a hip that didn't just sit there. Modern medical science was wonderful, just wonderful. I was a new person, with my new hip! Hip hip hurray!

But maybe one *Hip hurray!* was celebration enough. When a little time had gone by, I started mentioning that of course the other hip, the one that hadn't been replaced, had never been as bad as the one that had. Which was true, but all the same I was working up to something in my naïvely devious way. It was rather a waste of money – of people's taxes, when you came right down to it – to operate on the other hip, when really I was fine now.

Then Ansell came and sat on my bed and routed my little scheme. She said, 'John, you do know that you're going to have to have the other operation, don't you?' A doctor sitting on a bed in Men's Surgical didn't mean you were dying, as it had when I was on the children's wards, but it wasn't exactly relaxing. I was in for some sort of scolding.

I tried to bluster, but blustering doesn't really work from a horizontal position. It helps if you can loom. 'Well,' I said, 'I was thinking that maybe I'm all right the way I am now.' I was being partly truthful. There's nothing like having a sore new hip that has to be coaxed into the slightest movement to make you fall in love with the good old fixed one. Rigid, dependable, everything a hip should be. 'The physios have been super, and I can do such a lot more now than I ever could. I can't help feeling that there are other patients who have much more to gain from the operation than I do.'

Ansell wasn't fooled for a moment. 'And I don't suppose this is about the pain, is it? The pain that I said you wouldn't have, and turned out to be so severe?'

I didn't have the strength of character to deny it outright, so I just put my head on one side by a few degrees and raised my eyebrows, as if I was considering something that had never occurred to me before.

'Next time at least you'll know what you're in for. And I couldn't in all conscience encourage you to stop now. You've had half the pain already, but you haven't had more than a tenth of the mobility that we can give you with two good hips.'

Hip honeymoon

I gave it a good thinking-over. The new hip worked extremely well. The increase in my ability to live up to my biped pretensions was tremendous. But I wasn't convinced that a second operation would bring about a second transformation. It seemed to suit my gait to have one hip fixed and the other mobile. Would I really be able to manage without a stick after a second operation? Somehow I couldn't imagine a future of walking without aids of any kind, and a stick was a relatively discreet accessory. It could be tucked tidily away when it wasn't needed. I was having a hip honeymoon now, certainly, but it wouldn't last for ever. Sooner or later I'd just have to get on with things, but would a second operation really bring me the life I dreamed of?

I tried to visualise my walking style with two mobile hips. Perhaps my body would go bendy in the middle, if I didn't have the muscle strength to brace myself and hold myself steady in the proper posture. Then I'd be sorry that I'd said yes to the second operation.

After all, who was the one who knew most about the management of this body? I was so sure it was me, when apparently it was the ones who walked around with all their parts well-formed and smoothly functioning. They knew more about the subject than I could ever hope to. I rehearsed my objections to Mum, who said I must take it up with Dr Ansell. Ansell just said, 'We can't have you going through life without being able to walk correctly!' So overall the argument of 'it just isn't on' won the day, despite not being an argument. I voiced my worry about 'going all bendy in the middle' and was told that although that might be the case for a few days, my muscles would soon strengthen up and I'd wonder at my silly doubts. I still wasn't convinced and asked, 'What if I really can't manage? Can't I at least try life with one hip and see how I get on? I feel so well set up . . .'

Dr Ansell had the grace to consult Mr Arden on this point. The message relayed back from him was that if I really didn't get on with a mobile right hip, he could do another operation to set things permanently, 'at any angle you want'.

Somehow I knew that the right hip wouldn't be such a success, and I told Ansell so. 'Don't be silly, John,' she said. 'What makes you think you know better than the surgeon? You're always saying he did a good job on the left hip.' Once the burning spiders had gone to sleep, that is.

'I don't know,' I said. 'I just feel it in my bones.' Then Ansell looked at me with a very strange expression, as if after all this time she still didn't know what to make of me.

Anyway, that was me dished and dashed. In all honesty I couldn't go against the doctor who'd done so much for me. I had to bite the bullet. One day soon I would have to go to sleep in a hospital, knowing that I would wake up feeling like a piece of playground equipment that has been methodically vandalised by people who should know better, trained health-service professionals. Grown-ups. Perhaps this time the anæsthetist would get in on the act. Let everyone have a go, the porter, the lady from the canteen, the whole bang lot. Last one on John's hip's a sissy.

Only one thing made me submit to a second assault, and it wasn't actually reverence for Ansell. I had gone against her in the past, when she had devised walking aids for me that I refused outright, and I could do it again. But until the second hip was done I wouldn't be able to adopt anything close to a conventional sitting posture. I wasn't worried about taking tea with the Queen. I would rely on her, when the time came, to put me at my ease – isn't that her job? But with two working hips, even in the event that one worked less well than the other – as I so confidently anticipated – learning to drive came a lot nearer. Still a long shot but not a flat impossibility.

I quite see the comedy of someone who had always resisted mechanistic accounts of the universe deciding that his life wasn't complete without a car. On the other hand, if I didn't grab the steering wheel with both hands, the joke would be on me for all time. I'd never be able to take charge of my own life. If I didn't make it to the driver's seat then I would never be more than a passenger, dependent on the good will of others. A finite quality, as I had already understood. The people who looked after me had limited stocks of patience, and for all I knew they were more forbearing than most. I had never experienced what it was to carry a burden – and that was the whole point. My only experience of burdens was of being one, and I couldn't claim to have unlimited patience either, in that rôle.

By the time I returned to Wexham Park for my second dose of agony I was armed with new expletives. I didn't want to amuse the staff with amateur swearing a second time. When the pain came I would try, however distressed and disoriented, to invoke the symbolic tetrad as explained in *The Tarot*, represented in the Mysteries of Memphis and Thebes by the four aspects of the sphinx (man, eagle, lion, bull) and also by the four elements. I planned to cry out *Yod Hé Vau Hé*, visualising the seductive shapes of the Hebrew letters in the book. I practised writing them out on the backs of envelopes and leaving them round, just to show that doctors didn't have a monopoly on mysterious scribblings. I too could play that game.

I left *The Tarot* conspicuous by my bedside when Mr Arden the surgeon came to give me his pre-operative briefing. This was a pep talk which didn't leave me with much pep, now that we both knew the flintiness of the material that was waiting for him beneath the veneer of skin. I remember him saying, 'Orthopædics is a fairly brutal business.' He was apologising in advance. He promised he would use the saw wherever he could, and only break what he must of my concrete hip. If he noticed the book he didn't say anything. This was rather disappointing, but it's the sad fact that high professional accomplishment doesn't necessarily broaden the mind. The Top Man in Granny's sense, someone who had soared so high in his medical specialty that he had transcended Dr and become mere Mr again, could still be almost mediocre, viewed in his other aspects. No doubt there were times in my teens when I was downright snooty. I was working very hard to feel superior to the man who planned to crack open one of my hips for the second time.

The pre-operative ritual had changed by the time of my second hip-cracking. It was no longer necessary, apparently, to shave my groin ahead of time.

There was no explanation given. By then I should have realised that explanations were not available on the National Health. It seemed a bit odd, all the same. If it was such a vital procedure last time, then why not now? What had changed? Perhaps I'd gained some immunity from infection along the way. If so, how did they know?

I felt pretty silly asking why I wasn't having this intimate service rendered – as if I was anxious to go under the barber's blade as well as the surgeon's. I certainly had more of a crop of pubic hair than I had had the previous year. My personal experience didn't put me in a position to refute the old-wives'-tale that shaved hair grows back with twice the force.

Fingers in the till of oblivion

There was something I thought I remembered about the anæsthetist on the first hip operation – not the time I had had the intravenous dose to which I was so disastrously allergic, but the second try with gas.

I remembered the anæsthetist having a lovely big beaky nose, a real schnozz, and he said cheerfully, 'I'll just make sure this mask is the right size for you!', slipping it playfully over his own giant conk before fitting it over mine, taking a good old sniff in the process. Was I remembering right? Could that possibly be professional conduct?

Of course anæsthesia distorts perception of its very nature, and after I came round I was too busy trying to surf the waves of pain to be sure of my memories. This time I determined to notice everything, to participate in the experience to the fullest degree and forget nothing that happened, right up to the moment that the mask of consciousness slipped from my face.

I remember the mask itself seeming to grow huge as the gas took effect, and everything becoming unreal and full of echoes. I even think I struggled, trying to kick and move my arms to fight the anæsthetist off.

But it was the earlier bit that was more interesting. This time he didn't say he was testing the fit of the mask, he said he was testing the flow of the gas, but yes, once again he took a good sniff on his own account before it was my turn.

Later, after I had crawled out of the trench of pain into which Mr Arden, summoning up all his professional skill, had tenderly lowered me, I asked Mum about what I had seen. She didn't seem at all surprised. Apparently it's a well-known professional hazard, liable to catch up with you in the long run. Anæsthetists don't exactly fall asleep on the job, but they can't always resist the temptation of dipping their fingers in the till of oblivion.

I think I kept to my resolution of using Mouni Sadhu's *The Tarot* as my own personal dictionary of mystical expletives. I believe I kept 'fucking buggers' up my sleeve for other emergencies. The nursing staff looked at me a little strangely, which was probably no bad thing. I wanted to sound in my agony like an Adept uttering words of power rather than a schoolchild howling.

The man in the next bed when I was installed back at CRX was Mr Thatcher, a nice man who was recovering from having his gallstones out. He had been promised they would give him the stones in a jar, to take home with him when he left. He offered to let me take a look when they did. I was looking forward to it. Apparently there's a lot of individual variation in the size, colour and texture of gallstones. 'Some people,' he told me, 'have just one, but it looks like a mahogany doorknob. Other people just have a handful of gravel.' Somehow it was immediately obvious that he was over towards the doorknob end of the gallstone spectrum.

Glottal-stop gurgle

Most of my conversations with Mr Thatcher revolved around gratifyingly adult subjects: sex, money and alcoholic drink. Because I was anæmic and underweight, Ansell prescribed me a bottle of beer every evening. She had upped the stakes from wholemilk yoghurt. Now it was up to Mackeson to build me up.

I didn't like the beer, it was nasty stuff, but I loved having it. Ansell must have known what a thrill it was for a teenager in a-certain-amount-of-discomfort to be downing beer on doctor's orders.

Mr Thatcher was certainly jealous of my evening prescription, the medicine which came with a bottle-opener, and a nurse to work it.

When my medicine arrived, Mr Thatcher would launch into a lip-smacking rendition of the familiar advertisement for Mackeson. 'Looks good . . .' he would say, in slow tempo and countryman's tones, 'tastes good . . . and by golly it does you good.' Imitating in fact the tones of Bernard Miles, unforgettably frightening Long John Silver on stage and patron of the Vulcan School. Obligingly I would make a glottal-stop gurgle as I swallowed the beer, which was so peatily sweet it did indeed taste like medicine.

I think Mackeson's was one of the first products to fall foul of the Trades Descriptions Act. For a while the company retained the script, omitting only the last four words, so that the false claim went on sounding in the ears of the faithful.

I was aware that drinking stout was a rather *Coronation Street* thing to be doing. That was something else we did, Mum and I, besides covertly reading the *Mirror*, as a way of wincing at the disgustingness of the working classes. It was certainly a different world – in those days the Northern accents were much thicker. When Mum told me with her nurse's knowledge that 'milk stout', which characters like Ena Sharples always seemed to order at the Rovers' Return, was so called because it was thought to promote lactation, I was fascinated. So that was why working-class women were so big up top! But somebody should have told Muzzie and Caroline, posh mother and older sister of my dear friend Sarah on the children's ward, before they over-indulged in the elixir and became so shamingly buxom.

Mr Thatcher had definite ideas about sex. This was at the time when the Sexual Offences Bill decriminalising certain acts between men was making its way, stage by stage, towards reality. 'Homosexuality is a sad condition,' said Mr Thatcher (I held my breath), 'but what can society expect if there are schools with no girls in them? When boys from schools like that come into puberty, they've lost touch with their instincts. They don't know what they're supposed to do.' Co-education would solve that particular problem in a genera-tion. Satisfied, Mr Thatcher moved on to the next social issue in his newspaper.

He himself wasn't married. 'My needs are met by a very special lady, John,' he explained. 'Known her for years. We get on very well. Of course I have to pay, but that doesn't worry me. Just think about it for a moment. People end up having to pay for their sexual business one way or another. No exceptions. Those that get married pay most of all. And it's good to have things settled – I don't like going to different ladies. I keep to the same one. She knows me, y'know. Once you're a regular, her charges are very reasonable. She likes to have things settled too, y'see. Monica says she's fond of me, and I believe her. We have a nice chat and a cup of tea afterwards. We've become good friends. She tells me she wants to take me out to a meal one day, when she's not quite so busy. I can tell you, I'm really looking forward to that!'

Mr Thatcher looked at me rather wistfully. 'We could always meet up after we've both got better and left hospital. We could visit the lady I've been telling you about. If you were with me, and I recommended you, I dare say you'd get a discount. Especially if you've never done it before.' Of course I'd 'done it', just not in the way Mr Thatcher meant – I'd had assignations in school lavatories and music rooms, I'd been pounced on in armchairs and fellated, without my permission though not exactly against my will.

He searched my eyes for any flicker of interest, saying, 'You shouldn't worry too much about the money side of it, John. In fact, why don't you take it as a present from me?'

He really liked the idea of having me as his little pal, but I was getting a bit fed up with people offering me special rates on their prostitutes. What was it that made people think, 'He looks a bit down in the mouth – let's treat him to a working girl'? First Jimmy at the Vulcan School and now Mr Thatcher. I have to say that Jimmy's Minouche, with her cute scrunched-up face, sounded more fun than Mr Thatcher's Monica with her cups of tea and busy schedule. If a similar offer was made a third time I'd get quite shirty, particularly if the downward trend continued, towards the shabbiest drabs and doxies of Slough. Did I really look so helpless? If I'd wanted what they wanted I wouldn't be shy about it, but it so happened that I wanted something different.

Still, the ice had been broken between us, Mr Thatcher and me. I particularly enjoyed our conversations on the subject of money. He said he'd got a tidy sum put aside, but was cagy about how much exactly. Still, when I asked if he could raise £1,000 he looked pretty smug and said he thought he could manage that. I was impressed. I had managed to amass £72 10s 5d over the years, and I liked money very much indeed. That's why I kept it in the Guardian Bank, which had its offices in Jersey. I was a plutocrat in embryo. It was a canny decision to put my funds there, because the Guardian Bank, avoiding U.K. tax, paid 8% per annum. I kept my assets out of the taxman's reach. My money wasn't just saved, it was sheltered, safe from the storms of the business world. It wasn't just in a bank, it was in a *haven*.

Then the news broke on the radio that the Guardian Bank Ltd had been taken into receivership. It was reported the next day in the *Telegraph*, which is where Dad read about it.

I lay in the bed on Ward Three of CRX and considered my newly acquired poverty.

Was the roof over my head about to fall in? No.

Would my food now be stopped? No.

Would I stop getting medicines and nursing? No.

Why, I was even sipping beer that I didn't have to pay for.

Along the corridor I could hear the echoes of Dr Ansell's voice, and I knew she'd be at my bedside in a moment, checking whether I was doing my exercises. She would ask if I was enjoying my Mackesons. I was and I wasn't, but life was good and warm, and I felt as though I was being cradled in an enormous tender hand.

Mum, though, visited in tears because of what had happened to the Guardian Bank. She was literally wringing her hands as she asked, 'What are we going to do about your money *now*?'

I replied that I wasn't going to do anything. Then Dad came in, stiffly formal, dressed for work. Any whiff of crisis made their incompatibility glaring. They didn't seem anything like husband and wife – more like an unhinged widow and the military policeman detailed to inform her of her loss. While Mum went on falling apart, Dad brandished a stiff upper lip that could have knocked down walls.

He advised me to take it on the chin, saying he hoped this setback wouldn't deter me from a future in the world of finance. He even said something about him and Mum helping out if the receiver was unable to recover my money.

I'm sure I was supposed to erupt in tears of joy. I was committing one more crime against the laws of family temperament. Mum wanted more drama and Dad wanted me to hide my shattered feelings behind a mask of indifference. I offended them both in different ways by not really being bothered. I cheated them of any sort of display, either hysteria or stoicism. It didn't sit well with either of them that I took things so much in my stride. Meanwhile the love of money dropped off me like an old scab.

Before he left, CRX kept its promise to Mr Thatcher by giving him the jar with his gallstones in it, and he kept his promise by letting me have a look. It was an ordinary jar with a screw-top, the sort of thing Mum kept in her spice-rack. His gallstones turned out to be more or less in the middle of the range of styles and colours. There were five or six of them, yellow in colour, slightly streaked and glossy. They looked like old-fashioned boiled sweets that had been sucked but not chewed, mint humbugs, perhaps. I wondered what they would taste like, but we weren't sufficiently on intimate terms, he and I, for me to ask if I could pop one in my mouth.

Of course Mr Thatcher was only serving a short sentence at CRX, while I was an old lag. The way things were going, I would be lucky not to become a lifer. Before he left he asked for my address and telephone number, and I gave them with a little reluctance. I didn't want any discounts on suburban courtesans. Perhaps Monica in her turn would be shown the fossilised confectionery cooked up by his misbehaving insides. I hoped Mr Thatcher would have the sensitivity to show her after the act, rather than before.

The law was changing that year, to allow the desires of people like me some legitimate expression. If I selected my partners with great care (screening out under-21s and members of the armed services and Merchant Navy, and one at a time, please), making sure everything happened in private, I could have a sexual life all of my own, within the law. Oh, as long as I waited three years or so without jumping the gun.

I had heard mention among the nurses of a Mr Peever, who had been in the hospital and was 'queer as a coot'. They had to watch him in the toilets. They had to watch me in the toilets, too, in case I fell down, but I realised this was different. He had been loitering with intent – tottering with intent, really – more or less from the moment he could stand up after his surgery. Sister Wright, who smoked eighty Consulate a day, sniggered and said 'Who'd go with *him*?' Well, I would. And wouldn't anyone rather 'go with him' than kiss her mentholated mouth?

I started to pray to Mr Peever in my head, *Please, Mr Peever come back to hospital and I'll go with you. Please, Mr Peever.* I asked as discreetly as I could when he'd been in the hospital and they said about six months previous. And will he be coming back soon? Of course they looked at me as if I was mad. I'd come back to CRX myself after an absence, but of course I was a special case. I had a season ticket, I was a hospital yo-yo. Mr Peever never did come back, or not while I was there. Meantime I broadcast on all frequencies to *Mr Peever, Mr Peever, please, Mr Peever.* I wore a track in my mind with my prayers. We can be flitty together, Mr Peever, just the two of us. Apart from anything else, his name was so perfect, an unimprovable compound of *pervert* and *peeper*. It seemed unfair for God to make such a creature and then withhold him from me. It was a big day when I could finally go to the lavatory under my own steam. That was the proper chapel for my prayers.

Physiotherapy was unrelenting. Eventually they broke it to me that the right hip, despite having the more mobility of the two pre-operationally, would never have the final mobility of the left. I managed to act surprised. Gosh, that's a pity. Nobody remembered that I had predicted this outcome, and I never knew how I knew.

Before the pins I tottered, afterwards I came closer to hobbling. Those aren't technical terms but approximations. My walking also was an approximation. The later motion was sturdier and less precarious. It could cover more ground – but it looked worse. A crutch and a cane advertised the deficiences of what doesn't altogether qualify, even now, as a gait. Strangers have never found my progress reassuring. They look on in alarm.

No one helped me understand the disappointment of the second operation. Perhaps they didn't understand themselves, just shrugging it off as one of those things, but I worked to get to the bottom of it myself. There was a gain of movement in both axes, from side to side and also backwards and forwards, but this wasn't necessarily a good thing. The problem was that I couldn't control the lateral component. However much work we did, the physiotherapists and I, there wasn't enough muscle to support me reliably. All the calculations were correct, but the sum didn't work out as it should have, and I did indeed become bendy in the middle, in very much the way I had feared. The basic arithmetic was off. The sum didn't go 'one successful hip operation plus another successful hip operation equals fully ambulant and permanently cheery chappy, praising the National Health Service with every newly bouncy step'. It went *mobility minus stability equals futility*. I was worse off than I had been before the second operation.

There was no second honeymoon after the second intervention in my bones, since it marked an estrangement, a widening of the asymmetry in my bodily competence. To guarantee my balance I now needed to use my new crutch (with a sort of padded gutter on which to rest my arm) as well as a stick. The right side, the second one to be operated on, was much the weaker, which was quite convenient, since the right arm was the one with enough flexibility to fit comfortably into the gutter of the crutch.

Medical science had over-corrected matters and created new problems. The intermediate stage between operations, with one hip newly flexible, the other still rigid, had actually offered the best compromise and the closest approximation to normal human walking. Dimly I had sensed this at the time, but hadn't been able to overrule the authorities around me. Instead I had agreed to a painful setback disguised as a technical improvement.

I managed never to say 'I told you so' to Ansell or anyone else about the relative failure of the second operation. I'm capable of suppressing my baser self on special occasions, though there's something about my expression which makes people assume I'm constipated when I do, and I had taken enough Senokot on the children's wards of CRX to last me several lifetimes.

I didn't point out that I had been right, and no one ever apologised or repeated the offer of re-doing the operation so as to leave my leg fixed in the position of my choice. I wouldn't have taken up such an offer anyway. I'd learned that there was a tariff to be paid even on a free offer, and I accepted that no amount of tinkering would make my legs keep in step. The whole pattern of my progress (if progress was what I was making) seemed to be one step forward and one step back, which would never be more painfully clear than it was now. One hip forward. And one hip back.

I was still sinking deep roots into *Gardening for Adventure* – Mrs Pavey would only ask Mum for a book back if someone requested it. Despite Menage's enthusiasm I couldn't get excited about orchids at this time of my life, perhaps because Dad was such an enthusiast.

Hobbies were a sort of battleground for us. I loved the challenge of imposing one of my interests on Dad (he being far the most hobby-minded of the tribe), having it supersede one of his own. He in his turn tried to interest me in his obsessions, but I was oddly resistant, so that the net flow of hobbies was in the other direction.

Dad found orchids full of fascination and charm. I went on finding them rather boring – just a load of leaves coming out of bulb-things in pots which sometimes offered you flowers. Perhaps I was working up to a phase of resistance to Dad, and practising on a small scale by rejecting his interests.

If Dad had really wanted to sell me on orchids, he would have told me that they are like ideas. Or perhaps ideas are like orchids. They're born from almost nothing, in sterile conditions – the faintest contamination prevents them from germinating. Then, once started, they depend on getting exactly the right balance of nutrients. They need moisture, but almost more than that they need a breeze. They flourish in the crannies of other plants, not dependent but simply sheltered, in the crook of a tree, say. From a million spores only a few plants will establish themselves – but then they can assume an astounding range of sizes and shapes, from the barely visible (*Platystele jungermannioides*, its flowers barely a hundredth of an inch across) to the towering (*Sobralia altissima*, which can grow nearly thirty feet tall).

I had one particular idea in my head, of all the mental spores, cradled and moistened, scrupulously blown on, which refused to die altogether. After the first hip operation (or rather, between the botched first attempt and the agonising second) Dad had tried to cheer me up, telling me that once my hips had been fixed I would be able to do many more normal things. 'You could travel,' he said. 'Why not? You could even fly, if I said the word,' Dad said.

'Really?' I was roughly as surprised as Wendy Darling must have been when Peter Pan first held her hand and took to the air.

It turned out that BOAC let the family members of employees fly at greatly reduced prices. 'How do you feel about Paris?' Dad asked me.

I didn't feel much about Paris, either way, but I let the idea take root inside me. After that I would remind Dad from time to time of the promise he had made. He hadn't come close to anything as binding as an actual promise, of course, but it did no harm to let him think he had. I jogged his memory from time to time after that, and though he never committed himself in definite terms he seemed to concede that an undertaking had been made to me.

Far more interesting to me than any possible orchid was the succulent known as the Mescal Button, *Lophophora williamsii*. According to Menage, it was sacred to a tribe of Indians in America (the Kiowas of the Rio Grande) who took it as part of their religious rites. I read that slices of Mescal Button were used to replace the bread and wine in church services in Mexico 'as late as 1918', though that didn't seem very recent to me.

The communicants would get coloured visions and coloured emotions and then see the colours of their God. This was really starting to be fun. Mr Menage explained that the phenomenon was caused by a substance in the cactus called mescaline. Researchers who had eaten mescal were unable to describe sensations which lay so far outside ordinary experience. One side-effect was that the drug sometimes 'fixes the limbs in strange, grotesque positions where they remain for a considerable time'. That didn't scare me. I felt sure I was immune. The words 'Mescal' and 'Mescaline' acquired a shimmering aura for me, and I decided that some mescaline tablets would greatly accelerate my convalescence. I wondered if CRX had any tucked away.

The song on the radio every few minutes was Procol Harum's 'A Whiter Shade of Pale', an oddly solemn and gloomy song, more dirge than anthem. I loved it – even before I was told that the group took its name from a pedigree Burmese cat. I loved Burmese cats in their own right.

Nurse Oliveira, a pretty Singhalese girl on Ward Three, was also mad about the song, and wanted to know the words, which were notoriously cryptic. I listened every time it was played, and had soon caught most of them. I wrote them out as neatly as I could and gave them to her. She was thrilled and said, 'Now it's my turn to give you something,' and she wrote something out in her native script. It was wonderful – so much nicer than our alphabet. All those pretty curls. Tendrils and serifs luxuriantly multiplying.

She had another gift for me, a little book which revived my love of such things, the style of mini-book (not even 30 pages) that Dad disparaged as a 'tract'. It was called *The Satipatthana Sutta and Its Application to Modern Life*, a lecture on a Buddhist text delivered by V. F. Gunaratna (Retd. Public Trustee, Ceylon) to the Education Department Buddhist Society, Colombo. It was printed at the Sita Printing Works in Kandy for the Buddhist Publication Society as No. 60 in its series *The Wheel*.

I liked the stress in the little book on *Anapana-sati*, mindfulness of breathing, as a key to unadulterated blissful abiding. As he breathes in a long breath, the Buddhist monk knows, 'I am breathing in a long breath.' As he breathes out a long breath, he knows, 'I am breathing out a long breath.' Ditto with short breaths. Ditto with John, though no Buddhist monk. 'When practising mindfulness of breathing, attention should be focused at the tip of the nose or at the point of the upper lip immediately below where the current of air can be felt.' I had groped my way towards this practice with my breathing games during bed rest, and more recently after the McKee pins.

It was good to be told, too, that the lotus position or *padmasana* was optional ('nowadays rather difficult to many, even to easterners'). And there was ripe irony in being urged to set aside 'a special time for sitting-practice'. Why else was I in CRX? When I wasn't learning to totter again, with two semi-functioning hips, I was learning to sit.

The emphasis on mindfulness was refreshing, and new to me. It made sense to tame the mind by concentrating it on humble processes, to use its strength against itself.

One set of exercises was a bit like spiritual isometrics, to be practised wherever you happened to be, on the bus, in the queue at the bakers, in the doctor's surgery. This was spirituality that demanded no sacrifice, content with scraps of time to do its work. 'You come tearing down in your car and as you approach a junction, the green colour of the traffic lights have just given place to amber. You curse youself, and come to a halt. It is all tension for you as you impatiently wait a seeming eternity until the red colour gives way to amber and another seeming eternity until amber gives way to green.' In those two seeming eternities you can retire into the silence of your self and practise a little mindfulness.

You were supposed to see everything as it was, not as it claimed to be. Be a 'bare observer', not a partisan one. So for instance you would see a banknote as a piece of paper, no more and no less, divorced from the illusion of its buying power. This was an exercise designed to neutralise the workings of imagination, which finds so much more in the world than there is. This was a rather risky piece of chastening in my case, since my life was more or less entirely imaginary. But perhaps that was the point.

Presumably as you got really good at this game you would reach a point where *The Satipatthana Sutta and Its Application to Modern Life* itself became no more than sheets of paper and arbitrary squiggles of ink. Then you could lay the book aside in a state of blissful blankness, the *Nibbana* – curious spelling – mentioned in a text whose meaning had now dissolved in fulfilment of its own teaching. This was the disappearing-ink idea which I had loved so much as a child, given a mystical twist, flowing by capillary action into the Indian Rope that would perform the Trick of fulfilment by vanishing.

Fathom-long carcass

There were aspects of the teaching that didn't sit quite so well with me. Buddhist monks are supposed to reflect ritually on the repulsiveness of the body, from the soles of its feet up, and from the top of its head-hairs down, this 'fathom-long carcass' enveloped by skin and full of manifold impurity. They are supposed to itemise the body's individually repellent elements in their meditation, thinking, 'There are in this body hairs of the head, hairs of the body, nails, teeth, skin, flesh, sinews, bones, marrow, kidney, heart, liver, midriff, spleen, lungs, intestines, mesentery, gorge, fæces, bile, phlegm, pus, blood, sweat, fat, tears, grease, saliva, nasal mucus, synovial fluid, urine.' Curious that synovial fluid hadn't been left out. Did I have any of that transparent viscid lubricant left in my joints, after so many years of Still's?

There were moods when I felt that the task of finding my body (this bag of tubes) repulsive could safely be left to other people. There was one nurse, for instance, Derek, who would sometimes sail right past me, ignoring my requests for help. I knew that nurses were busy people – I had been studying them for years in their natural habitat. They weren't servants, and they weren't responsible for me alone. Still, how hard is it to say, 'I'll be with you in a moment, John'? All the other nurses seemed able to manage it. When he was wiping my bottom, a procedure that didn't give white-goose joy though much improved since my first days at CRX thanks to those slide-away panels, he completely ignored my attempts at chat. Perhaps repugnance came into the picture.

Derek wasn't a physical genius in the Jack Juggernaut class, but he was still easy on the eye. He was blond even if he wasn't tall – well, everybody's tall (except Edith Piaf), but Derek was no taller than many of his female colleagues.

What made being ignored by Derek so wounding was that he was very thick with another young man with Still's. David Webb. I say 'young man', but although at fifteen David wasn't much younger than me he still seemed a boy. He still had a piping voice. I had to admit he looked quite cuddly – it's only now that I see the cuddliness as a consequence of steroids, nothing more or less.

Derek always found time for David, who was blind. So the question for me was: am I too disabled to attract Derek's attention, or not disabled enough? Perhaps it was the bonus of David's blindness that gave him a competitive edge in the nurse-attraction business.

Understandably the question of physical repulsiveness was much on my mind at this period. I decided that simply finding my body repulsive, à la *Satipatthana Sutta*, was too easy to count as a mental discipline. My task was more complicated: first I had to promote my body to equal status with everyone else's, and then despise it along with all the others in its class. I tucked away for later chewing-over a rebellious quibble: if indifference is the goal, then isn't cultivating feelings of disgust an odd way to attain it?

When Derek was chatting to little David, it was as if he wanted everyone on the ward to know about it. He was loud about everything he did. Loudly he cultivated David, and loudly he ignored me.

Nothing he said seemed to be private. One day I heard him boasting about his knowledge of drugs. There wasn't much he didn't know on that subject, to hear him talk, from opium to purple hearts. You could hear him from several beds away. I was feeling very starved of his attention. I may as well admit that. So when I had finally got him cornered I told him I'd heard about this stuff called mescaline, and it sounded just the ticket for me. I tried to whisper to get a nice conspiratorial atmosphere going. I like a good conspiracy – the good ones are the ones that don't exclude me. He was practically shouting, and couldn't seem to catch the name of this funny drug. He wanted to know if it was written down somewhere. I said no, but I wrote it on a piece of paper for him. 'Interesting,' he said. 'I'll see what I can find out.' I was certainly intrigued by *Lophophora williamsii*, but once I had got Derek's attention it was mission accomplished, really.

A snail's eyes on stalks

He came back the next day with a book in his hand and a strange alarmed look on his face. He asked, 'How on earth did you find out about this stuff? It's very hush-hush. Who told you about it?' He looked at me very intently.

I said I didn't remember. *Gardening for Adventure* had got me into trouble, just as Mr Menage had warned, and now I was afraid that the book itself was in danger of being confiscated. I had been silly to be so blatant about dark desires and taboo subjects. Fortunately I realised that if I snapped the book shut straight away, even supposing I could do it discreetly, I would give the game away. So I left it open and said as casually as I could that I'd heard the name somewhere – probably from one of the doctors talking.

Derek picked up *Gardening for Adventure* and ran his eyes over it. My heart was beating hard. The word 'mescaline' seemed to stand out from the page like a snail's eyes on stalks, and still Derek didn't see it. When he shut my book I asked if I could see his book in return. Fair dos. He said no. He wasn't in a hurry to admit that his knowledge was every bit as second-hand as mine – but my book was better than his book. Or at least more broad-minded. His book obviously regarded poor *Lophophora williamsii* as a very wicked piece of vegetation indeed.

Soon after this moment of cosiness I encountered the other sort of conspiracy, the less nice, in the form of a human bubble which sealed me out and left me to suffocate.

As I practised the defective repair which was my walking I became aware of silences on the ward, zones of inhibition which blossomed as I approached. Suddenly membranes of secrets closed in front of me, opened up behind me, like parodies of the automatic doors on *Star Trek*.

In this way I received my birthright, my minority birthright, of paranoia. Information is always in movement and the best way to keep up with it is to move freely yourself. Gossip has a naturally fast pace, it's a game of tag, and there's something very artificial about being included when you can't compete, like a child who's not supposed to feel patronised being patted an easy ball by a grown-up.

Patients on Ward Three would be discussing things in a group but would suddenly hush up when I approached, or even if I stuck my head up from the bed to show I was listening hard. I soon found that the best way of hearing what they were saying was to keep my eye very firmly on my book – *The Count of Monte Cristo* – and not to look up. I felt thoroughly got at until I understood that they weren't talking about me. The conversation was actually about Derek, and I soon realised I wasn't the only one to be excluded from it. The group went quiet when all sorts of people were nearby. There would be quite a gaggle of patients talking about Derek, and then the ward orderly would come in to mop up. By the time he had put his bucket down there would be a pregnant hush – pregnant specifically in the manner of a viviparous fish, say a guppy. The moment the orderly moved on from the ward, that hush would spawn dozens of lively wriggling murmurs.

For two or three weeks I struggled to solve the mystery, and then at last, when two or three insiders were huddled in conspiracy, one of them called me over. He waited for me to hobble over, not letting any impatience show. 'You don't look as if you're the type to grass on a fellow,' he said. 'I think it's time we told you what's what.' He told me Derek's secret. Derek's career was at risk, and everyone was trying to help.

He had a creeping deafness. It had been detected when he was interviewed for nursing, and he was told that he was employable so long as it didn't get any worse. It got worse. It was so bad now that he was all but deaf.

'But that's impossible!' I said. 'I was chatting away to him only yesterday. We talked about all sorts of things . . .' Which wasn't entirely true. The pressure to converse was entirely on my side, and I had always detected a reluctance, which now I began to understand.

'Yes,' came the answer. 'He's become very good at lip-reading. Just watch his eyes when you talk to him again. We're all doing what we can to help him keep his job. Of course if he has to go on night duty he's sunk . . .'

With my new knowledge I tested Derek by mixing up the labial consonants, asking him to bull me pack in the chair, etc. He watched my lips very intently. Perhaps one of the factors in his friendship with David Webb was that he could watch as closely as he liked and David would never notice. It was a strange idea to me, that someone could be invisibly disabled. Part of me felt that if your disability could be kept secret it wasn't up to much. Kids' stuff. There should be a different word for it. Perhaps that was where *handicap* should come in. I was disabled and Derek was only handicapped. He had to work harder to keep up, but he was still in the game.

All the same I wanted to justify the confidence I had been given, and tried my hardest to be on Derek's side. The other nurses did their bit, but they couldn't swap their shifts around indefinitely to help him avoid working at night. When the day (night) finally came that he couldn't dodge a late shift, a staff nurse quietly turned up and spoke to him from behind, and that was that. He was given his cards. Obviously there had been some sort of tip-off, and one of the same people who had tried to help him had informed on him to the authorities. Everyone claimed to be shocked, but I wasn't so sure. Were we really saying that Derek had a right to his job even if he couldn't hear the patients in his care ringing for attention? I found myself reluctantly siding with the authorities.

With an imaginary spoon

One thing at least was clear, with Derek's departure. I wouldn't be getting that mescaline any time soon.

I adored *The Count of Monte Cristo*. A long rehabilitation demands a long book. First hip *Pamela*, second hip *Monte Cristo*. Richardson and Dumas both knew how to play the long game. I wasn't in a hurry. *The Count of Monte Cristo* wasn't prescribed by any reading list but it was still irresistible. I identified pretty strongly with Edmond Dantès. He was gloriously cold and nasty, and we were both stuck – if he had the Château d'If, then I had CRX. Perhaps it's perverse to find your release in an account of someone else's confinement, but that was how it was with me. Dantès was accused of treason and imprisoned – it was almost a disappointment when he got free. And what is juvenile rheumatoid arthritis if not a treason of the body, physical mutiny? My most trusted generals turned against me, leaving me to tunnel my way out with an imaginary spoon.

The only thing against such a big book was its physical awkwardness (or mine). If my human-lectern idea lacked practicality, then I didn't see why the National Health Service, if it could run to linen sheets and bottles of stout, couldn't afford to pay for a reader. Bernard Miles, perhaps, why not? Since he was philanthropically minded (a benefactor of Vulcan) and had a juicy voice, though CRX wouldn't be able to match the fees he got from Mackeson. There would be a certain amount of grumbling from the ward codgers at first, but I was confident that in time they would surrender as wholly as I had. I wouldn't have minded starting again from the beginning. The nurses might not be so happy, since they'd have to pull themselves away from the story to wipe bottoms and save lives.

I wish I'd known then that being read to as they worked was one of the perks traditionally enjoyed by the cigar-rollers of Havana. The *lector* was paid out of the workers' wages. He would start with the daily papers and move on to essays or novels, according to the votes of the workers. Supposedly the workers named a new brand of cigar after the book they enjoyed most of all as they rolled the carcinogenic leaves of their livelihood . . . hence the *Montecristo*. I might have put in a plea for the *Pamela*, but their choice has a lot to be said for it.

The book itself was as close as I have ever come to a big fat cigar, rolled by an expert, delivering the slow-burning pleasure of narrative intoxication. I inhaled it page after page. I blew smoke-rings of pleasure up at the ceiling.

I had an invisible cigar, and since the collapse of the Guardian Bank my money likewise was invisible. Still, I had my evening Mackeson and my copy of *Satipatthana Sutta and Its Application to Modern Life* – so much better as a guide to life than the *Daily Telegraph*. I could even look forward to legal sexual expression only a few years down the road, as long as I could keep my desire for uniforms under control. For now, only the songs on the radio gave a feeling of what I was missing by spending most of the Summer of Love in the Château d'If.

I was relatively indifferent to my surroundings during this period, not entirely thanks to my absorption in *The Count of Monte Cristo*. This was something that made an impression in its own right. I wasn't my usual chatty and forthcoming self. My fellow patients hardly seemed worth the trouble of cultivating, since they were mainly in-patients for a few days only. Why waste precious charm on transients?

My appetite for books had slackened off, and this too was interpreted as a sign of low mood. Of course I finished reading *The Count of Monte Cristo*, but that was different. I was on the last 400 pages by then, so I was really only coasting home. A certain amount of chivvying was set in motion on an administrative level, which took the final form of Ansell sitting on the bed one more time and urging me to cheer up – I was on the last lap, after all, and mustn't lose heart. The second operation hadn't been a roaring success, but I was still much better fitted for life than I had been before the whole cycle of surgery and rehabilitation began.

I'm not sure my mood was really so low – Western culture, uncomfortable with inwardness, tends to interpret it negatively – but I went along with the fiction of depression, smiling wanly and promising to buck myself up.

Of course it's natural, as Dad was always pointing out, for baby birds to be pushed out of the nest by their parents, to fend for themselves. But it's also natural, when it's time to leave any place of safety, for even a senior chick to go back to bed and pull the bedclothes over his head.

Chronic female veto

There was a surprise waiting for me when I came out of CRX the second time, as rehabilitated as I ever would be: Mum and Dad had put up a greenhouse! I was delighted. I showed every shade of appreciation and wonder that the human face can manage. Possibly I overdid it. I didn't know when to stop. I couldn't recognise the point where plausible extremes of joy had been acted out to everyone's satisfaction.

It was an act because I knew quite well what had been going on. My plan all along. I'd been using Peter as my cat's-paw in a campaign of action-at-a-distance, briefing him when he visited me and sending him letters with additional instructions when necessary.

First he had suggested the whole scheme to Dad. The experiment was designed to exploit Peter's standing in the family – I had the idea that Dad was less fully armoured against his second-born than his first-. Dad didn't dismiss the scheme, but he wasn't exactly encouraging, pointing out that Mum would exercise her chronic female veto.

After a suitably calculated interval, Peter was primed to remark that Mum would dearly love somewhere to sunbathe out of the wind. What a shame there was nowhere suitable in the garden . . . particularly as you could divide off one section of a greenhouse – if you had one – and call it a sun-lounge. Was there a nicer word than 'greenhouse', do you think, Dad? Didn't some people say 'conservatory' instead? Perhaps Mum would like the idea better if we used the word 'conservatory'. . .

The vocabulary was a critical element. I thought of using the word 'solarium' instead of sun-lounge, but it was a matter of knowing your market. Dad might enjoy the word, but he wasn't the one with a passion for burning his skin, and Mum would find it intimidating.

Dad said he'd think about it. Maybe it wasn't out of the question. Then the final touch was for Peter to say that Mum would have to be careful not to get sunburn even if there was glass between her and the sun, wouldn't she? I relied on this very oblique hint tipping the scales with Dad.

This was string-pulling in the grand tradition of Granny, although on a humble scale and without real ruthlessness. Everyone was happy, weren't they? I had somewhere to grow *Drosophyllum lusitanicum*, Dad had an indispensable aid to his own more ambitious gardening projects, and Mum had somewhere to bask like a lizard in sunny weather, even on windy days.

That greenhouse was as much my work as if I had slipped out of the body every night, using the handy exit of a dream of knowledge, and dug the foundations with my own astral hands.

I wondered how Granny found the strength to conduct such campaigns on a number of fronts at a time. Yes, I had got my way, and it was fascinating to see that under certain circumstances people could be flicked against each other in predictable pathways like so many marbles, but still I felt depleted and even a little sick.

Peter had had a few Boy-Scoutish qualms about his rôle in the experiment. 'Aren't we being a little . . .?' he asked, and I cheerfully supplied the missing word as 'sneaky'.

It was all very well for him to have high standards, he could wipe his own bottom. I depended on paid strangers or close kin for humiliating tasks and had no prospect of equal dealing, so all I was doing was evening up the odds. Isn't the Boy Scout motto 'Be prepared' anyway? I was prepared to be sneaky. I can claim Homer in my corner, as well as Baden-Powell. All very well for Achilles to be heroic – he's invulnerable as long as he does what his Mamma says and wears his riding hat and his special shoes. Odysseus has to be sneaky to get by.

There was only one detail of the scheme which caused me a little guilt. Dad and I knew perfectly well that the 'sun-lounge' wouldn't help Mum tan, since window glass filters out the short-wave radiation responsible. We were more or less conspiring against her, he and I. We would have needed to fit Vita glass (very expensive) to lend real assistance to her sun-damage project, though this was the heyday of the suntan, its traumatic effects on the dermis unknown or unpublicised, and I can't pretend we were actually looking out for her welfare. I didn't know why Dad got a kick out of putting one over on Mum, but I knew it was so, and that a hint about the screening effects of window glass would give him a final nudge towards the project.

There was no need to mention any of this to the lady of the house. Her happy moods weren't so common that we could risk spoiling them. She pulsated with contentment as she lay there out of the wind on the lounger, basking in placebo sunshine.

Of course we none of us said 'sun-lounger'. Mum's love of brand names had raised this item above the common ruck of loungers. This was the Relaxator.

Mum not only went around recommending products but advertised their disgrace if they failed to perform, denouncing them from her kitchen pulpit. Unable to live up to her mother's religion of the Top Man, she made do with the cult of the household name and the *Which?* Best Buy. Top Thing was a better bet than Top Person – but if a well-known or much-recommended purchase let her down it was a devastating blow, a sort of compound treason-fraud-sacrilege. When a washing-machine got the shakes just out of guarantee (though multiply lauded and endorsed), this was an assault on the integrity of the entire market-place. Hers was a world-view in which trailing threads were always likely to unravel the flimsy *gestalt*, and any little snag could ladder the sheer stocking of her self-belief.

Examples: Kit-Kat (chocolate-covered snack) was on her blacklist because she could never get the wafer fingers to *snap* as crisply as they did on the advert, despite the foil wrapper which undertook to keep them fresh. Kit-e-Kat (cat food) was condemned because it intensified the vileness of feline breath.

When we were slumming it by watching ITV and Kit-e-Kat was advertised during commercial breaks, with a voice asking cheerily, 'Is your cat a Kit-e-Kat?' we would all answer in mock-Cockney accents, 'Then it mustn't 'arf stink!' This was our Bourne End saturnalia – sneering at the common people from our precarious upper rung. The only ITV programme which commanded our full respect, though it was always turned on 'for John', was the Saturday-night wrestling. It was the squirming aspect which spoke to me, I think, not the throwing about – I can't answer for anyone else. I found it utterly thrilling, and was amazed it was allowed in any way at all. I kept quiet but Mum felt free to comment, saying, for instance, 'Amazing to think that all these wrestling positions have names!' One evening a wrestler was pinned on his back with his hands immobilised, so all he could do was push up with his pelvis in the hope of unseating his opponent, busy pushing down in the same style. Mum just said, 'Gosh, Dennis, anybody would think those two were mating!'

The ruddy crutch

It was strange to be home at Trees with my newly adjusted disability (Granny had drummed into us the vulgarity of adorning your house name with inverted commas). The spaces were deeply familiar but had to be negotiated in a new way. As I moved around the house I had new problems of balance to contend with. I could now make reasonable progress, for instance, advancing towards the kitchen sink or the basin in the bathroom, but I needed somewhere to stow my crutch and cane while I used the facilities once I had reached them. No question of putting them on the floor, obviously, so I would lean them against the sink or the basin. Usually the cane stayed put but the crutch, being top-heavy, invariably fell with a scrape and a crash. Then the cry would go up, 'The ruddy crutch!!' Humorous, mock-exasperated. Or rather, expressing true exasperation beneath the mockery of it.

Audrey would repeat the phrase in fun, copying those around her. She must have been six at the time, seven at the most. Mum and Dad seemed disproportionately irritated by the jarring noise, while Audrey's laugh was genuine and delighted, which should have taken the sting out of it. Yet her repetition, though perfectly innocent, was the one I found most wounding. There was joy in it, and the joy that was in it made it so much worse – but I knew better than to ask her not to say it. Audrey's wilfulness was already highly developed, and it was wisest not to alert her to her power to hurt, in case she explored it at her leisure.

When the crutch fell, after the family hubbub had died down, I'd either have to lever it up somehow with the cane or ask for help. Peter would help me very willingly, and Audrey would return the crutch to my possession with exaggerated graciousness, as if it was a prize at the village fête, and she the Lady Mayoress doing the honours.

No one thought of doing anything silly, like attaching a simple bracket to the basin and the sink, some little retaining hook for the crutch to lean against.

It strikes me now how ridiculously easy such a gadget would have been to make. It would hardly test anyone's do-it-yourself skills, but of course do-it-myself isn't an option. Even Peter could have had a shot at it, if he had dared to swim against the tide. All he would have needed was a wire coathanger, bent so that one end curled round the base of one of the taps, the other run to the front of the basin and formed into a hook – into which I could tuck the crutch and still have it handy. Professor Branestawm would have been proud of Peter for such a useful bit of bodging, and so would I. But everyone seemed to prefer waiting for the crash and then raising an outcry. The whole family was oddly attached to my status as a nuisance.

In the kitchen I liked to perch on a stool if given a choice, a privileged position bought with much effort. Perching was always my attitude relative to furniture, I was only pretending to sit out of politeness. I'd need help to get up there, but it was worth it. Perching was my great delight. Of course I had to leave the crutch somewhere, and someone would knock against it, and then the senseless cry would go up, as if in some way it was all my fault. The ruddy crutch. The ruddy family. The ruddy business of being alive.

My sprouting groin

A tube of Immac, procured with much labour from a chemist in Bourne End, had delayed the moment when physical maturity had to be acknowledged, but there was only so much a depilatory could be expected to do. The caustic smell, moreover, was hateful, and I certainly didn't dare use it lower down, though my almost luxuriant pubic hair gave the lie to the Mummy's-little-darling idea, on which tender relations with Mum depended, at least as much as my ghost of a moustache.

Perhaps because of distaste for my sprouting groin, Mum made over responsibility for bathing me to Dad, who almost seemed to enjoy it. He was always drily complimenting me on the excellence of my equipment, which was nice the first time – I so rarely seemed to meet his standards – and rather awkward after that. No teenager wants to be told more than once that he is in possession of a magnificent beast, does he? Not more than a few times anyway, and not by a parent.

Wiping my bottom was a grey area that became a battlefield. In theory this was a job which fell to Dad before he set off for work (I was a reliable morning defæcator), but he soon learned to get an early start so as to leave bog duty to Mum. There was no obvious willpower in the man, yet it was remarkably difficult to get him to do anything he didn't want to do. He didn't seem to have any personal preference until the air around him thickened with an implied course of conduct, and then he generally voted against it.

It's odd, but I don't remember seeing Granny at all during the period of my operations and rehabilitations, but then hospital visiting wouldn't have been her style. She didn't go in for sustained nurture but spectacular interventions. Not for her the weeding and the watering of some humble patch of garden. She would rather just happen to be passing when a hundred-year cactus bursts into the ecstasy of flower, charmingly disowning any credit but letting people come to their own conclusions.

Now and then the trolley which carried the ward telephone would bear down on me, with Granny's precise diction ready to pounce from the receiver, so I had occasional bulletins about her activities. During this period, rather to her surprise, she had made friends with a neighbour in Tangmere. Mere friendship was rather a come-down for someone whose preferred style of relationship was the slow-burning feud. She found a strange sort of nourishment in antagonism, and there was active disappointment for her in soft emotions and smooth dealings.

The mutual benefit of the friendship was that Granny had money but no car, the neighbour a car and no money. All of this may also be part of the explanation for Granny's absence from my bedside, that she and her neighbour were busy motoring to country towns and staying in what Granny never wavered from calling Otels.

At the end of such conversations Granny would say, 'That's all my news, John, and I won't embarrass you by asking you for yours. How could you have any, marooned as you are? And I'm sure the food is terrible. Make sure your mother brings you something better. She has no talent as a maker of salads, as you will undoubtedly know. If she has forgotten how to make the salad dressing I showed her, tell her to telephone me. She has only to ask.'

It's only now that I realise that there is a simpler explanation for absence than either a preference for other styles of charitable act or else her Otel commitments. Ridiculously simple, once the Granular mystique has worn away and you've given the thought permission to occur. Granny hated hospitals, and so she stayed away.

What do people hate about hospitals? The smell. The lighting. Bad tea in the canteen. The fact that death comes calling.

So when people say they 'hate' hospitals, it only means they fear them. Normally Granny embraced hatred with a certain amount of affection, and left the fearing to other people. But during the year-plus of my operations and rehabilitations, it was fear which drove her in any direction but mine, far more reliably than her neighbour's car.

Despite everything I remember the sense of a warm breeze moving through the house, which was partly summer, of course, but also corresponded to a break in the family weather, a climate in which lightning hardly ever flashed but clouds were slow to clear. Tensions never seemed to come to a proper rolling boil, but it was rare for them to stop simmering altogether for the duration of a radiant interlude. It was our nature as a family to seethe rather than explode, and even when we did explode there was no actual violence and very little damage to property. Admittedly Audrey showed signs of being a wild card, who would not play by the established rules that were good or bad enough for everyone else.

Dad had a new job with BOAC, I had a new hip and a crutch whose misadventures seemed to tickle everybody, Peter had a paper round and Audrey hadn't yet devised a hiding place beyond Mum's power to find.

I felt proprietorial about the conservatory-greenhouse (although of course I couldn't say so) and I liked to be parked by it. I was already planning what Dad should grow there, apart from the *Drosophyllum lusitanicum* in whose interest the whole long-distance hypnosis experiment had been conducted.

Love in the key of exasperation

My next project would be to persuade Dad to experiment, in the new greenhouse, with another of Menage's tips, *Musa ensete* – the Abyssinian banana. If we sowed it in spring next year it would reach nearly four foot by early autumn, needing to be transplanted first into a seven-inch and then a twelve-inch pot. By the end of the second year it would be pressing outwards against the panes of the conservatory, and Menage's advice was to get rid of it and start again from scratch. It would be interesting to see whether Dad could be so casual about the fate of the cuckoo in his greenhouse – a plant which would have by then more or less the status of a family member. Then we'd see how good a job he made of rejecting the claims of a vegetable child.

Mum fussed over me endlessly, which I tried whole-heartedly to hate. What do fully-fledged chicks feel when the mother bird regurgitates food down their throats, long after they've learned to feed themselves? Love, I expect, love in the key of exasperation.

She was good at the job. She was more than competent. She wasn't like some of the professionals I had experienced over the years, who had secretly hated the job, or parts of it, and had passed that hatred on. With Mum it was just the reverse. She liked it too much. It would fit her personality and her character (*Heather*) in the Bach herbal system, for there to be one child who never outgrew the need for her. Then she would never need to outgrow her own need. Audrey wasn't the answer to her prayers after all, was in fact showing signs of being a right little madam, while Peter (with that paper round and pub work in prospect) was almost out of her orbit already.

I wanted Mum's life to have meaning – of course I did – as long as its meaning wasn't that she had a tragically stricken son who couldn't manage without her. Unfortunately that was the meaning she had her heart set on.

She was always on my side, but whose side was I on? Not hers. I couldn't afford to be. She was a helper who was also an obstacle. Mum wasn't the alternative to an 'institution', she was an institution in her own right, a one-woman hospice-hermitage yawning to receive me.

Bare observation

I spent a lot of time viewing Mum through the wrong end of a mental telescope, practising the Buddhist vision – *bare observation*, indifferent to the agreed meanings of things – taught by the *Satipatthana Sutta*. What was Mum? Mum was a fathom-long carcass (closer to the fathom mark, in fact, than I would ever be), fat, tears, grease, saliva, etc. More to the point, Mum was the champion of the Relaxator, the Bernina – the sewing-machine – and Sqezy (I was troubled and thrilled by the manufacturer's licence to drop the mandatory *u* after *q*), booster of the Kenwood, the Rayburn, Kia-Ora, Yeast-Vite and Nescaff, compulsive denigrator of Kit-e-Kat and Kit-Kat. The layman's term for this spiritual enterprise is 'hardening the heart'.

When his family spilled out into the garden which was his exclusive province for much of the year, Dad tended to retreat into the shed. Mum's main reason for being in the garden was to pick herbs. She had white paving stones laid in the back plot just outside the kitchen door, in the form of a chess board. Her herbs grew in the black squares, and she could walk on the white squares when she wanted to pick them.

The first thing she did on a picking expedition was to shake her right hand, as if she was holding an invisible thermometer and trying to get the mercury back down to its bulb. When I asked her what she was doing, she explained it was to make her hand go floppy. 'I want to be guided by influences far from the brain,' she would say with a far-away look in her eyes. Her loosened arm would then rise smoothly up and get its bearings. Within a second or two it had jerked decisively towards the appropriate accents to be added to lunch.

Clearly this was herbalist dowsing, yet Mum was horrified when she found out that Peter and I had been playing with ouija boards. I couldn't see the difference – except that regimented herbs don't talk back. But when it was me calling on influences far from the brain, that was somehow sinister and appalling.

In our ouija sessions Peter and I had been having snatches of conversation with two ancestors, Great-Grandpa who designed the Cambridge Divinity School and Newnham College (not to mention bits of Girton) and Mum's Uncle Ted who suicided himself at Jesus College, Cambridge. The ouija board seemed to have a strong Cambridge bias. If it was controlled (Mum's theory) by a minor devil, then it was one that sported a light-blue scarf.

The ouija board was a homely device, nothing more than a glass upside-down on a piece of Dad's shirt-cardboard marked with the letters of the alphabet. It wasn't practical for me to put my hand on top of the glass, so Peter was flying solo. I suppose he might have been cheating, but the messages which came through weren't in his style. Great-Uncle Ted kept saying I THOUGHT IT WOULD BE QUICK, round and round again, and then the astral switchboard seemed to lose interest, saying BLAH BLAH BLAH instead. 'Are you tired?' I asked, and the answer came back, SURE AM, BOSS. After that, no movement at all, however long we tried. Peter seemed disappointed, but I thought this was a good result. A pair of teenaged boys at a loose end had bored the Spirit World out of its tiny mind. Something to be proud of.

We were fairly bored too, on our side of the spectral divide, with Great-Uncle Ted and Great-Grandpa endlessly repeating the same things. Even knowing the ouija board was prohibited couldn't make it interesting indefinitely. There's some forbidden fruit that tastes of nothing much.

One particular song sums up that summer for me. Memory chooses a slice to sum up the whole, but it's no great feat of compression in this case since the record was hardly ever off the turntable. 'Good Vibrations' by the Beach Boys, as radiant and bouncy a song as 'A Whiter Shade of Pale' was strange and riddling.

The record wasn't newly released or even newly bought. It was bought with a Christmas present, but not in a hurry. Peter and I had consulted extensively about it. Mum and Dad had actually given him a book token, in an attempt to enlarge his rather basic library (*Jane's Fighting Ships* and the *Observer Book of Aeroplanes*). I didn't think presents should have strings attached, so I had taken the educational sting from Christmas by agreeing to swap the reproachful token for cash. It was no sacrifice. There were always books I wanted to buy.

I did find it funny that it was Jane who catalogued the fighting ships – it seemed so much more a job for Tarzan. But maybe he was busy picking nits off Cheeta's fur or gathering fruit for lunch.

Soon, of course, with the benefits of his paper round accruing (and lucrative pub work looming), Peter would be standing casually at the counter of a record shop to ask for a single, positively willing the assistant to ask if he had just had a birthday, just so that he could answer 'No' in a faintly baffled tone, as a way of signalling that he was now a man of the world – emancipated from the yearly cycle of presents, rising above the grudging shillings of pocket money, able to plonk down eight-and-sixpence from his earnings as a matter of course, with only a trifling acceleration of the heartbeat at the rash committing of cash to an object that was perishable both in terms of material and its vulnerability to fashion. Those cash-flush days were only just round the corner, but for now expenditure still needed to be carefully monitored, and 'Good Vibrations' had proved a solid invest-ment, vindicating the long period of consultation.

Posh, spinsterly and shrewd

Mum and Dad were predictably incompatible in their tastes for entertainment. Mum favoured light comic songs and routines – her top favourite being Joyce Grenfell, sly, posh, spinsterly and shrewd, because her observations were 'so true'.

Dad on the other hand admired Eartha Kitt, who was sexual and predatory – she even called Father Christmas 'Santa baby', for Heav-en's sake, as if he was no more than a sugar daddy in fur-trimmed pyjamas – yet somehow blatantly for sale herself. No better than she should be, and out for what she could get.

I wonder, though, if Mum had her priorities right. Eartha Kitt was no real threat. If she had turned up in Dad's office he wouldn't have known what to say. He would have looked at his shoes, not her cleavage. Joyce Grenfell, though, could be much more dangerous in her quiet way.

I don't think Mum ever knew that Grenfell was a niece of Nancy Astor's (not to mention a fellow Christian Scientist) and had a cottage on the Cliveden estate. It would have given her the willies to think that Joyce Grenfell might have sat near her in the CRX cafeteria one day, inconspicuous in a little tweed hat and fawn coat, on the alert for intonations and mannerisms. Mum's admiration for the truthfulness of Joyce Grenfell's would have turned to panic. She would hardly have dared to listen to her on the radio for fear of hearing herself transformed in a monologue. It would have been hellish to be on the sharp end of that truthfulness.

When from time to time Dad threatened to buy Mum a record of Eartha Kitt's for Christmas he was teasing, exaggerating for comic effect an insensitivity to her tastes which was perfectly sincere. Like all the men of the era he took something like pride in being a hopeless shopper, clueless and mildly resentful when confronted with a lingerie department, a perfume counter or a high-class confectioner's. Why should he be expected to know what size his wife was, what she liked to smell of, whether she favoured the hard centres or the soft, chocolate plain or milky? These were feminine mysteries and husbands found them baffling on principle. A man who understood his wife's needs would be regarded with something like suspicion. Something must have gone rather badly wrong to produce this morbid state of communication.

Dad despised florists not in his capacity as a male but as a gardener. If Mum wanted to be bought flowers by her husband, she had married the wrong man. In any case, buying her flowers would always have been a perilous enterprise. That whole area was hedged about with superstitions which the most innocent bouquet-giver was sure to trespass onto, let alone Dad. It was unlucky to give lilies, those deathly blooms, or a bunch which mixed red and white flowers. Once when a neighbour gave her just such a bunch for her birthday – carnations – Mum hardly waited to say Thank You before frantically segregating them by colour in different vases so that the bad luck drained away, muttering 'blood and bandages' the whole time. Apparently those were the ominous associations of the ill-starred mixture, though I was mystified by the fuss kicked up. If there's blood, don't you want to have bandages handy?

In the case of 'Good Vibrations' Mum overcame her prejudices, while Dad remained stubbornly attached to his. He violently disapproved of everything about the record, from the barbarous phrase

'Beach Boys' down. It was obvious to him that 'beach boys' were no more than loafers and layabouts. What they needed was jobs. I know Peter could imagine no better job than being in the Beach Boys, but he couldn't quite find the words to say so.

This was a song which really came into its own when the sun shone and the French windows were thrown open. Day by day the volume dial on the household's Bush radiogram crept up, in stealthy increments.

When 'Good Vibrations' was playing, Mum's herb-picking became especially adventurous, with the music pulsing and prancing behind her. She would execute a courtly dance among her plantings in search of the right flavours, like a bee spoiled for choice between flowers. She danced a happy bumbling gavotte around the aromatic chequerboard of the herb garden.

Audrey trotted out from the house and joined in, treating the paving stones as a sort of practice court for hopscotch. Sometimes she lost her balance and trod on a planting, which seemed genuinely accidental, though taking a small revenge on anything which attracted Mum's attention away from her wouldn't have been out of character. She knew exactly how many times she could get away with saying, 'Oh dear, I've treaded on Mummy's parsy,' before she was suspected of systematic trampling. For Audrey in those days, parsley was *parsy* and there was no other herb, hardly another piece of greenery. From her point of view the vegetable kingdom was made up of the holy trinity, parsley, rose and Christmas tree.

Peter would be exercising rather self-consciously in the sunlight with the chest-expander Dad had given him for his birthday, two wooden handles connected with woven elastic ropes. As his powers increased he was supposed to add more of these ropes, clipping them to rings on the handles. Eventually the chest-expander would have six strings, like a guitar, though currently he was stranded at the banjo stage with four – but still, he was stringing and tuning his teenaged vigour as if it was an actual instrument. He was proud enough of his progress to exercise where he could be seen, shy enough to keep the operative area out of sight by wearing an ærtex shirt rather than a singlet.

Even Gipsy joined in the harmonious mood, an ageing dog these days, sedately romping. By now her hips were more or less on a par with my substandard ones, though of course she made no exorbitant demands on them for balance. They held her up without any trouble, it's just that they moved rather stiffly and made her unwilling to risk the blithe jumps of her youth. Dogs' hips don't last for ever. Mine at least had improved with age, thanks to the visionary butchering of Mr Arden.

Sustained hedon bombardment

Dad, of course, retreated to the greenhouse in protest at the din, but gave the game away by leaving the door open a few inches. The elementary particles of sensation had always seemed to stream right through Dad, or to bounce off him. His pain threshold was high, his pleasure threshold higher still. Perhaps this was only the side of him we saw, but we saw a lot of it. It took mighty waves of positively charged experience to provoke the smallest interior ripple of enjoyment. He preferred to go through life without being obliged to provide emotional commentary.

There must be a benefit, for the species if not for the individual, in the refusal of joy. A hedon is the unit of pleasure, just as a dolor is the unit of pain. The hedon isn't recognised by any authority, not even one as marginal as a Swedish university research project. Still, it's logically necessary, even if I just this minute made it up.

Hedon radiation was agitating every molecule of the shed, hedons were pulsing and throbbing like fireflies, tickling the soft palate of anyone within range like inhaled lemonade. Strong California sunshine trapped in grooves of black plastic was converted back into the visible spectrum by the travelling prism, tip down, of the stylus on the family record player. Our English summer was given substance by the American one on the record.

Even Dad couldn't hold out against the Beach Boys for ever. Sustained hedon bombardment day after day, relentless, was bound to find the chink in the shed, and Dad's armour. It took its toll. Dad's resistance was high but he wasn't quite hedon-proof, much (for some reason) as he might want that.

One day he was watering the garden while Mum was playing the song indoors at the usual volume, and I could see for myself how those good vibrations infiltrated the arm that held the hose. Whenever that peculiar passage came round when an unearthly electronic instrument goes OOOWEEEYOOO OOOWEEEE like an ecstatic banshee, Dad would move the hose in luxurious loops and spirals. Random beds and plantings in the garden got the benefit of a more generous, carefree sprinkling, the moisture subtly ionised by Dad's grudging pleasure in the song.

There came a day when I caught him whistling bits of the tune. Dad's was a generation of whistlers. They whistled when they were cheerful and also when they weren't. They whistled their way into the War, and those who came back were still whistling, when it ended, with a fair approximation of nonchalance.

In later life they whistled as they washed the car, as they tidied the tools in the shed, and on their way to the funerals of their contemporaries, though it was always considered poor form to reproduce much in the way of a tune. And now Dad, despite himself, was whistling a song he wanted to hate. I looked enquiringly at him, hoping he would admit to liking and enjoying something that we all loved, but he didn't respond. It would be too much of a loss of face to come clean and admit that not all songs with guitars in them were infantile rubbish. That would mean, somehow, that we had won, if he ever admitted he was just as much seduced by this luminous summer anthem as anyone else.

Intolerable coffee please

There was a similar pattern of behaviour on the rare occasions we went to a restaurant for any sort of celebration meal. Dad would start to rally his troops immediately after pudding, and I would ask, 'Can we have some coffee, please Dad?'

'No point, John,' he would say. 'We'll have it at home where they know how to make it. Everyone knows the coffee here is intolerable.'

'Have you tasted it yourself?'

'I expect so.' Dad didn't enjoy telling actual lies, untruths without any blurring at their edges. He didn't have much of a gift for equivocation, come to that. He was a little better at changing the subject, but I was too fast for him.

'Try to remember. Have you had the coffee here?'

He looked at the corner of the room. 'Possibly not.'

'Then how do you know it's so bad?'

'Experience and common sense.'

'It isn't experience if you haven't experienced it, and it can't be common sense if it's not sensible.'

'It seems I must order some intolerable coffee in order to pander to the prejudices of my son.'

'Yes please, Dad.'

'Waiter! I'd like a cup of your' – the next word was mumbled – 'intolerable coffee, please.'

'Yes, sir. Right away.'

When it arrived he took a small sip. 'What's it like, Dad?'

'Worst coffee I ever tasted.'

'Are you going to leave it, then?'

'Certainly not. Senseless waste. Now put a cork in it, John. Can't a man have a little peace in which to try not to taste his intolerable cup of coffee?'

When he had finished the cup he made a final pronouncement: 'Positively the worst cup of coffee I ever drank or even heard of. Do you want some?'

'Yes please, Dad.' Of course it was delicious. But he'd already given the game away by the way he relaxed as the coffee got to work on him. His look was almost dreamy.

He wasn't trying to be difficult. No one enjoys seeing a fixed idea go up in smoke, an axiom torpedoed. I think it gave him physical pain to change his mind.

Dad got his little bit of revenge for 'Good Vibrations' by commandeering the record player himself, and putting on his own favourite song again and again. Not anything by Eartha Kitt, in fact (perhaps he was more fascinated by the singer than the songs) but a song from a film – 'Moon River' from *Breakfast at Tiffany's*. The song wasn't a single but a track on an album (of Andy Williams singing songs from films), so Dad had to keep returning the needle to the right place on the record by hand, instead of letting it find its own way to the beginning of the song again, as Peter did when he left the repeat lever in the up position. 'Moon River' is a nice enough song, and I was quite likely to find myself humming its tune, but it never saturated the garden the way 'Good Vibrations' did. It didn't have the power to charge Mum's dowsing hand as she picked her herbs, or to make Peter's chest-expanding exercises keep time with its beat (it didn't really have one). After a while Dad would tire of re-positioning the needle, and we would hear other classic hits from the Henry Mancini songbook, and when the whole side of the record finished (with 'Three Coins in the Fountain') the time was ripe for the Beach Boys to storm the turntable all over again.

I knew there was a link between 'Moon River' and Audrey Hepburn, she being the star of *Breakfast at Tiffany's*. My little sister had been named after that demure goddess, and perhaps the idea had been to align her with certain feminine qualities, with neatness and self-control. If so it hadn't taken.

There was a line in 'Moon River' which struck me as being as mysterious as anything in 'A Whiter Shade of Pale'. The song starts talking about two drifters setting off to see the world. Apparently they're *after the same rainbow's end, / Waitin' 'round the bend / My huckleberry friend, moon river, and me . . .*

What on earth was a 'huckleberry friend'? I knew that a gooseberry was someone who stopped two people from being together, but as for huckleberry I was stumped. Dad didn't know either, though he seemed irritated to admit it. Either that or he didn't want me to know what a huckleberry friend was. Perhaps he was afraid I'd ask where his was, if I knew, or want one of my own.

2

Swimming Like a Stone

There was one little thing I had kept from Marion Wilding during our final confrontation at Vulcan, that parting of the ways over incompatible visions of my future. On that occasion I presented Burnham Grammar School as the answer to a disabled boy's prayers, a modern building throughly suited to his needs. In fact it wasn't ideal for a pupil in a wheelchair. Far from ideal. Vulcan had been built as a castle-shaped folly, and was turned into a school for disabled boys in the teeth of its architectural allegiances. Only a tiny lift could be installed, and the inconvenience of this was felt every single day, until the new buildings allowed the dorms to move to the ground floor. Burnham Grammar School wasn't a folly, but it wasn't a sensible construction on my terms. Modern, yes, but lacking a lift of any sort, big or small.

We had been misinformed, before the interview. We had been reassured about the presence of a lift by people in a position to know. I suppose Dad, instead of making the call himself, might have got his secretary to do it (now that he had one) and hadn't briefed her properly. I can see that happening. Take a letter Miss Smith. Oh, and find a school for my son. Yes, Mr Cromer, right away, sir.

So when we turned up for the interview the School Secretary was first flustered and then frosty. What business did we have accusing the school of having lifts? Who had made these false claims of suitability? Burnham Grammar School was strongly resistant to the needs of the disabled, and gave every sign of being proud of it.

Mum looked frantically at Dad, who fished a piece of paper out of his pocket. 'Miss Cornelia Norris from County Hall, High Wycombe, that's who,' he said. Surely information supplied by someone called Cornelia Norris could be trusted? – otherwise the whole world was going smash.

Mum backed him up. 'Miss Norris said there were lifts!' Between them Mum and Dad chanted this formula three or four times. In their own way they had grasped the basic principle of the mantra. Repetition bringing its own meaning.

The secretary wasn't spiritually susceptible to this approach. 'Miss Norris, whoever she may be, doesn't know what she's talking about. There are no lifts on these premises. And never have been.' As if this might in fact be a standard procedure, removing lifts at short notice so as to squash the educational dreams of the disabled. She stalked off into her office, where we could hear her complaining loudly about parents and education officers, and how fed up she was with the whole bang lot of them.

I had already seen the steep and terrifying stairs, and I let defeat slide into my heart. The little flame that had been burning there since that miraculous interview at Sidcot School, when I had been accepted with open arms by an institution to which I hadn't even applied, finally snuffed it. In the case of Sidcot, only Mum and Dad had stood between me and a radiant education, but now they were on my side and still things were hopeless. I felt suddenly tired and said, 'Can we go now? Let's not bother to wait around. Complete waste of time.' I felt rather bitter about it. Dad looked unsure of himself, perhaps because it wasn't in his nature to leave a meeting without being properly dismissed. No shuffling off, no sneaking away. Then before we had a chance to beat a retreat the secretary came out again, with a rather poisonous smile, and said, 'Mr Ashford will see you now'.

Mr Ashford was much more friendly, but also a little dismayed at what we'd been told by Miss Cornelia Norris. He was tall and lean, and he had a distant look in his eyes, something which reminded me of the co-principal of Vulcan School, Alan Raeburn. Perhaps it's a common ophthalmic feature of teachers, produced by a mixture of concentration and vagueness, and the constant repetition required by the rôle.

All tint seemed to be fading from Mr Ashford's face, more or less as we watched. His hair was greying and his eyes were grey already. 'It's a puzzle, certainly. However . . . one thing we do have is plenty

of boys.' He said it again, seemingly pleased. 'No shortage of boys.'
I thought this was a rather tactless thing to say – if the school had
plenty of boys, why would they want another one, let alone a boy who
was lost without a lift?

He meant something different from that. He meant that boys in
bulk would stand in for the missing mechanism. The school had plenty of boys, and the boys would carry me up and down stairs. Two at
the back of the wheelchair, two at the front. If by some misfortune
the boys carrying me lost their grip then other boys, below me on the
stairs, would perform an equally valuable service by breaking my fall,
whether they saw me coming or not. Some girls might end up acting
as shock absorbers too, since the school was co-educational.

'Do you see?' asked Mr Ashford, with a prim small smile. 'The
more that fall over lower down on the stairs, the greater will be the
cushioning effect. They won't *all* fall over and tumble down, will
they? It's elementary physics, and common sense.'

It was lunacy. It was the antipodes of common sense. Each of us
individually may have had doubts about the wisdom of the proposed
system – me, Mum, Dad and perhaps even Mr Ashford – but as a collective we voted for it unanimously. Legally the arrangement must
have been very precarious. If anything went wrong, if I was dropped
and damaged, then there wouldn't be enough lawyers in the world to
break the school's fall. Nothing similar would be contemplated for a
moment now.

Lawsuit virus

The craze for litigation, though, had not yet hit these islands. In
those days hardly anyone went to law no matter what injury was done
them. People trapped under fallen masonry apologised for being a
nuisance, signing away their rights with whichever hand was the less
damaged. Perhaps the lawsuit virus was actually carried by that other
invader, the American grey squirrel. Too late to eradicate it now.

Though I had doubts about the viability of the method of porterage
and mass human-cushioning proposed by Mr Ashford, it wasn't that
I was sentimental about lifts. I can't say I ever cared for them much
as gadgets. In every lift I've ever tried to enter there's been a cheery

chappy who says with a grin, 'Room inside for a littl'un,' when there patently isn't. Perhaps it's always the same man. I may be a littl'un, but when you factor in the wheelchair and (let's hope) the someone to push it, it's more of a littl'untourage. And then I'm perfectly placed, in terms of level, to catch the farts that seem to be forced out of people by the movement of the lift. Is it to do with the change of air pressure, or perhaps a side-effect of claustrophobia?

The full address of Burnham Grammar School was Hogfair Lane, Burnham, Slough. The street name referred to some ancient livestock market, I dare say, but it seemed appropriate enough. We were both taking on something unknown, the school and I, both buying a pig in a poke. On my first day at the school I turned up in the wheelchair. With my McKee pins working smoothly I could now sit down in a wheelchair reasonably convincingly. What I couldn't do, as it turned out, was stay in place while the chair was carried up or down stairs. I perched stably enough for life on the flat but not for the amateurish toting of my peers.

That first day was nightmarish. They couldn't keep the wheelchair level, and if it tipped I would be tipped out, and then the boys and girls who broke my fall would break me in the process. Seat belts hadn't been thought of for wheelchairs back then – they had hardly been thought of for cars. After the first frightening day I had to regress from the Wrigley to a more primitive style of vehicle, back into the prehistoric phase of my life on four wheels. The Tan-Sad invalid carriage from long ago was dusted off – quite literally. I remember Mum disinterring it from the shed and flapping her duster at it in dismay.

One step forward and one step back. Not much of a dance, but that seemed to be what my karma had choreographed for me. I was now independent, in the sense that I was receiving a mainstream education for the first time in my whole life. In other ways I needed more help than I had for quite some time.

I had struggled over the mountains of Vulcan to find myself stuck on a plateau. The Tan-Sad symbolised this predicament – and no one wants to spend his schooldays travelling between classes in a symbol. The Tan-Sad's wheels were fixed, so it couldn't turn corners. It was less steerable than a supermarket trolley, though its wheels didn't squeak. Its great advantage was that it had a broad footplate and so wouldn't tip me out – but it was very unwieldy, and far too heavy to be punted along by a crutch or a cane like a wheelchair. I would always need to be pushed on school premises. No more self-locomotion. No more privacy, or to put it more positively, no more solitude.

I needed to be lifted in and out of the Tan-Sad, like a baby with its pram, a demotion I felt keenly. I wanted a deepened style of relationship here in the mainstream, based on more than wheelchairs passing in the night. So much for being in the swim of a normal education. Already I felt to be swimming like a stone.

Sea of boys

And yet in general terms the mad scheme worked. I never came to serious harm, though the experience of being carried could be terrifying. I got a few knocks from such accidents and I'm sure I dealt out plenty more, but the sea of boys always broke my fall. Ashford was right. They didn't all go tumbling in their turn. Enough hands reached instinctively for banisters to stabilise the toppling tower. Massed pupils acted as a wildly laughing safety-net whenever the Tan-Sad broke loose from its bearers. For everyone but me it was fun and a break from routine, something that schoolchildren crave more than anything. Since then, whenever I see pop concerts on television where the singers dive ecstatically into the audience it reminds me of my schooldays, although it was never by choice that I surfed the crowd in my trundling chariot.

I had been pushed around in the Tan-Sad for years as a child, feeling both conspicuous and invisible, but the new routine made a difference. I was much more self-conscious, of course, as a teenager who was only on those premises because of his fixed desire to be independent. There was another element in play, though. Partly it was the number of people helping, but mainly of course the change of level, the element of laborious lifting, which added something almost ceremonial to my progress from floor to floor. Sometimes when I arrived safely on a landing, and my helpers set me down, there would be a little ripple of applause from the other pupils, as if I had done something remarkable, and though this was nonsense still it made people look at me differently. Naturally the cheers were louder when I was almost dropped, but there was a stubborn feeling of carnival even without a near-disaster.

At the end of each schoolday the Tan-Sad was left in the hall of the school. I would be reunited with it the next morning before assembly, without much rejoicing.

Assembly took place in the big hall. There was a hymn, accompanied on the piano by a plump little lady with a fixed smile, though the minority of pupils who made any noise at all conspired to slow the music right down, stripping it of the slightest claim to forward motion. Roll-call, which was held in the classroom, had a strange element of apartheid. The school was co-educational but not exactly equal in its treatment of the sexes.

The rule was that boys would be called by their surnames, and girls by their first names. The intonations were different too, gruff and challenging for the boys, tender and sweet for the girls. So it would be brusque, denunciatory 'Adams!' for Peter Adams and murmured tentative 'Julie?' for Julie Chandler. A name like 'Valerie' became filigree on the lips of some of the teachers. Valerie was well on her way to becoming a mythological figure. Positively a dryad of Slough.

Even at this late stage of normal education, it seemed that girls were made of sugar and spice (and all things nice), boys of slugs and snails and puppy-dogs' tails. This piece of symbolic theatre was repeated at the beginning of every school day, with girls being cooed over as if they were unique and fragrant blooms, boys marked down as bleak little blobs, no improvement on the fathers whose names they were made to answer to.

Mothering at a lower voltage

Girls were nicer than boys, then. It was official, and perhaps it was even true. Certainly the girls of the school were franker and warmer in their approaches to me – but I was never willingly going to be mothered again. And as far as I could see, sistering was just mothering at a lower voltage. I knew from my years at CRX how easy it was to become an honorary girl, and it wasn't going to happen again. Once in an incarnation was plenty.

Little chatty groups of girls came over to cultivate me. No one quite dared to come alone – but the boys were much less enterprising. Boys were very happy to push or carry the Tan-Sad, and perhaps they had some limited opportunities to spy on me, but I noticed that every now and then a boy would be despatched to ask the girls for information, to find out what I had said and what I might turn out to be like.

There were disordered refinements to the hateful system of roll-call. If two girls had the same Christian name, then one of them would be set apart with a diminutive, so that there might be one Jane and one Janie. If two boys had the same last name, their first initials would be used to distinguish them, but it would be snarled rather than neutrally spoken. The same lips which shaped 'Valerie' so tenderly that you could almost feel the floaty fabric of her dress spat out the initials as though they were bitter pips. The discrimination of tone became extreme when two boys made the blunder of having the same last name and the same initial as well. So it was 'Savage, *Paul!*' and 'Savage, *Patrick!*' spoken with a sort of rage, barely suppressed. How dare twins share an initial on top of everything else! It was asking for trouble.

On my first day I was upset at hearing my surname barked out so baldly. The rasping double consonant at the beginning of *Cromer* suddenly seemed tailor-made for parade-ground abuse.

Ideally I would have reformed the system, but it was more practical to gain exemption from it. I vowed I would become John in the school universally, first in class and then at roll-call. This was a strictly limited blurring of the boundaries: I wanted my name read out at roll-call in the female style, but my interest wasn't in androgyny , only special treatment.

I exploited the physical characteristics of the Tan-Sad, and the way it shaped my encounters with others. If I spoke softly, people had to lean over it to hear me, and then the charm could flow at full pressure. I learned how to sweep even teachers off their feet with the water cannon of intimacy. By the third week every teacher except Mr Jardine was calling me John, and I became John to him by the start of the next term. Only the horrendous Mr Waller stood firm in the face of sentimental pressure. Mr Waller was immune to every strain of personality magic I could come up with. He once logged a formal complaint against me for wearing a coloured shirt. I was the only pupil whose shirts had to be specially made, but I was allowed no compensating fun. It's not as if adhering to the letter of the uniform code would help me blend in.

Of course there was something ridiculous about my quest for Christian-name status at roll-call. For years I had been fighting to be treated as a normal boy, but the moment there was any danger of it happening I threw myself into a campaign for exceptional status.

The day I was called 'John' at roll-call at last, I couldn't stop smiling. I would never be filigree Valerie, but I was no longer denounced as Cromer. I was worming my way into the heart of the place.

Burnham Grammar School gave me what I wanted in the way of education. I don't necessarily mean that it was an educational hothouse, although I have no complaints. The hothouse doesn't suit every plant. The great thing was that Burnham really was a school – a school and only a school. It wasn't anything else in disguise. That was what I wanted. After so much time spent at schools that were really hospitals, or converted tennis courts, or folly-castles, it felt thrilling and holy to be going to a school that was only a school. A school disguised as a school! Glorious double-bluff. To be absorbing knowledge in a building designed, however unambitiously, for that purpose and no other.

I thought, back then, that each phase of my life would make a clean break with the last. In that respect I was like an ignorant student of history, imagining that everyone woke up Victorian one day in 1838. In fact the phases were anything but distinct, with much continuity across alleged ruptures. My ramshackle vehicle trundled across every seeming abyss.

In Hindu iconology there's an image, called the Nataraja, of Shiva dancing in an aureole of flames. His left leg is elegantly, forcefully raised. There are two technical terms attached to this image, *Lasya* and *Tandava*. *Lasya* describes the gentle side of Shiva's dancing, *Tandava* its savagely violent aspect. One style corresponds to creation, the other to destruction. I expect lesser gods are also involved. Hinduism has a crowded cosmology, and there's always room for one more on the casting couch.

It stands to non-reason that creation and destruction are always converging and swapping places – that's what makes it a dance! Dualistic thinking is hard to shake off for anyone brought up on it, but with a little practice the gates of logic come off their hinges and then at last I believe in God the Either, God the Or and God the Holy Both.

At Burnham Grammar I had everything I could possibly want, in terms of visual display. I could see something which I had been missing time out of mind. Horseplay – a sacred thing to me, almost. I couldn't exactly take part in the rough life I watched, but I was sustained by it. Watching was my part in it. I coveted an unruliness I couldn't muster myself, yet I didn't feel excluded. It flowed through me as well as around me. I experienced it as a reconnection. After years in which I never made and hardly saw an action that wasn't carefully considered, I could watch my fellows every day running riot in the spontaneity of their bodies. My eyes filled up with the sights I craved, and my ears were gloriously assaulted by the bedlam din of play.

Cantering compound beast

I was fascinated by the way the boys moved. I loved the frantic shuffle they used when they were late for a lesson but in full view of a master who would tell them off for running. I could see boys dashing along a corridor and turning a corner at full tilt, sliding and scrambling on the polished floor like unshod skaters but somehow not coming to grief – coming to joy, rather. I could watch a boy run down a corridor and leap without warning on another's back. The other boy might stagger, might let out a shout of protest, but instead of collapsing and crying for medical help, as was his right, this victim would grasp his attacker under the thighs and turn assault into piggy-back, sometimes setting off at a canter as a compound beast in search of further collisions, charging with raucous laughter into the ranks of jeering infantry. Cautionary bellows from the staff seemed to be a necessary ingredient of the scene. The uproar would have been much more subdued without their contribution, increasing the pressure of high spirits by keeping the lid on. All this was what made normal education so special.

Mobility is wasted on the able-bodied, just as youth is wasted on the young, which is exactly the way it should be. Even at slower speeds, I saw with wonder that able-bodied boys of my age didn't walk with the scrupulous poise they might have been taught by physios. They took orthodox posture for granted and experimented with every possible variation and perversion on it. They would stand for long minutes at a time on the outside edges of their feet. They would scuff their shoes with every step, taking revenge on their parents for buying footwear which had to renounce any claim to fashionability if it was to qualify as smart enough for school. A flapping sole or a heel entirely worn down on one side was an achievement rather than a disaster. Part of me was horrified by this abuse of shoes, part of me was thrilled.

Some boys walked without touching their heels to the ground for more than a fraction of a second, balanced always on the balls of their feet, though I had no way of knowing if this was an affected showing-off gait which they abandoned when no one was looking. It's never a walking style you see on women, or on men over about thirty. Does that mean that gradually the period of heel contact extends, as the burdens of life increase, until one day that forward bounce congeals into a trudge like anyone else's?

Compared to the way things were at Vulcan, the caste system at Burnham was simple. I existed at the same distance from everyone else in my year, a greater but still uniform distance from anyone above or below me in the school. It puzzled me for a while that an asthmatic boy in my year was treated as if he was made of glass, when I was used to asthmatics as the supermen of Vulcan School, but I soon got used even to that.

After the first week or so, *Savage, Paul* and *Savage, Patrick*, identical twins, more or less monopolised the job of Tan-Sad command. This was unofficial but became a recognised thing. It became their job to manhandle my vintage wagon, recruiting assistants as necessary, and to make sure there was always the required sea of boys beneath me on the stairs in case of a slip-up. I assume they elected themselves for the task by virtue of being a team, ready-made. They had shown their affinity for each other by choosing the same womb, and they coördinated their duties with confidence and even panache.

For the first half of the first term, I found it impossible to tell which Savage was which, but after that I was amazed that anyone could ever muddle them up. There was a period when I got confused if I saw only their backs, but that soon cleared up, and soon I could recognise them from any angle. They were identical twins who didn't look a bit alike, once you could see it.

We would sometimes run a sort of sweepstake. There was money to be made. People would bet on whether I could tell the twins apart from a single body part displayed round the edge of a door. Betting against me was a mug's game. Their hands were genuinely easy to tell apart, not just for me but for anyone, since Patrick played the guitar and therefore kept his right fingernails long, for plucking purposes, and the left ones short, for fret work, while Paul kept his all anyhow. But I could even tell the difference when a bared knee and a bared elbow were offered me round the edge of a door. It helped that scuffling sounds and suppressed giggles behind the door might announce that the body parts on offer were a mixed bag – Paul's knee, say, and Patrick's elbow.

If Burnham was an ordinary school, then it followed that I was an ordinary schoolboy. This was a bit of a shock, though the logic was strong. Nobody before Burnham had seriously suggested that a piece of work I did could be improved in any way. At CRX and then Vulcan I had seemed almost freakishly clever, but then the educational aspect of those institutions was partly ornamental. No one expected us to do anything in the outside world except, possibly, to survive it, so my reputation as a brainbox was fairly meaningless.

School work in my past had a more or less optional status. It was more to keep us happy – which it did, it kept me very happy – than to broaden our world in any meaningful way. At those two schools my intelligence had been on the receiving end, year after year, of slightly alarmed little pats. At Burnham Grammar there was no question of it being treated so tenderly. My brain was pummelled, as if by a relentless physio, brusquely kneaded and squashed until it fought back by gaining in mobility and resource, flexing in the end quite fiercely. It was quite a shock to the system, and the sharpest shocks were administered by Mr Klaus Eckstein.

My interview with Mr Ashford had contained no formal academic assessment, but Dad had mentioned that I liked German. He passed this on as if it might disqualify me in some way, and Mum had chipped in with her own little qualm, saying, 'I'm afraid he doesn't eat meat.'

Mr Ashford disregarded my dietary eccentricity and simply said, 'Then I expect you'll be taught by Mr Eckstein. Quite a character. You'll either like him or you won't.' These formulas reliably indicate unpopularity.

Volatilised mucus

Klaus Eckstein was a portly man, with whiskers sprouting in all directions. He had no small talk. In my first lesson with him one boy tried to lay an ambush by saying, 'My father says the only good German is a dead German.' There was still a lot of this sentiment around, but I was a little shocked to have it spelled out in this way. Eckstein simply snarled back, 'Tell your father he is wrong! Even the dead ones stink.' A horrible, wonderful thing to say, and I was shocked all over again. I didn't understand that there were people who could be described as German, refugees and survivors, whose feelings for their homeland were not sentimental.

Eckstein wore a garment that I'd never seen before, and rarely enough since – a suède waistcoat. He took snuff, tapping the yellowish powder onto a mysterious hollow which appeared at the base of his thumb when he contorted it in a particular way. Then he sharply sniffed up the soft clod of powder. Eckstein kept a hanky handy for the inevitable sneezes, but even· so his waistcoat became encrusted with grains and stains. Suède seemed to be a material perfectly chosen to welcome into its nap a mist of volatilised mucus suspending particles of ground tobacco. The flecked waistcoat and his snuff habit gave him a spicy smell, like gingerbread gone wrong. Perhaps Eckstein thought his snuffbox and waistcoat made him seem like an English gentleman rather than a startling exotic – but what would an English gentleman have been doing on the staff of Burnham Grammar? Such a person would have been no less exotic than Eckstein himself.

Eckstein made a point of being stern and abrasive and rude, but I wasn't going to let a little thing like that deter me from getting into his good books. After his lesson one day, I apologised for how poor my German was, how deficient my general education. This sort of performance I knew to be foolproof: build yourself up and the world will rush to tear you down, but if you tear yourself down the rush is all the other way, to make repairs. Except that Eckstein had not signed up to this convention. He glared and said, 'Indeed. Your German is appalling, as are most things about you. You'll never be much good at it unless you can get yourself to Germany somehow and stay there for a year, a season at the least. A horrible country in many ways, but the only place that foolish English boys can be stripped of their bleat of an accent.'

I tried to take this in my stride, telling myself that the compliments when they came would be sweeter for the wait. Buttering people up had always been my bread and butter, and I wasn't going to be cured of the habit just because I'd been fed a mouthful of dry crumbs. 'I'll try my hardest, sir. And sir? Since *Ecke* is the German word for corner and *Stein* is the German for stone, perhaps you, Mr Eckstein, will be the cornerstone of my German education?' I had been practising this little aria of flattery for days.

He gave a grunt. 'Not unless you dig down into the rubble of what you think you know, and lay some proper foundations. Your accent is *execrable.*' I knew it could hardly be so bad, since the native tones of Gisela Schmidt, star physiotherapist of CRX, throbbed behind every syllable, but I had to salute the mileage Eckstein got from the packed consonants of his chosen adjective. 'You'll never be any good unless you can get yourself to Germany and stay there until it all sinks in.' He didn't acknowledge with his tone that there could be any excuse but laziness for my not heading immediately to Germany, and getting stuck in to the sort of *Deutsches Leben* they don't tell you about in *Deutsches Leben* or any other book, German Life away from the page.

Eckstein belonged to a strange category of teacher, those who can frogmarch pupils to excellence without ever sullying their mouths with a single word of praise. One of his tricks was to say to a pupil, 'With all due respect,' adding with no change of tone: 'which is none.' Following up a standard piece of wheedling good manners with some bad manners all his own. He was extremely unpopular. I loved him from the first.

One bit of regression connected with living at home was my lack of bathroom discipline. I can't fault the National Health Service, which provided me with some equipment at about this time, by paying for a wheeled commode made to my measure. I even remember the name of the man who made it, a Mr Heard. After the trouble he went to, it's only right to commemorate him. It was such a pleasure to have something that really was tailored to my requirements – even NHS hips seemed to be off the peg. I wish Mr Heard had made those! But I was happy enough with my trolley upholstered in maroon leatherette.

As a newly acknowledged normal schoolboy, I came into my birthright of laziness. Schoolboys aren't the most hygiene-minded of creatures. Along with the commode I was the proud possessor of a National Health bum-wiper, an elegant accessory in sculptural terms, a curve of perspex which looked vaguely like a snorkel. I was shown how to use it, but it was a bit of a business and I was happy enough with things as they were.

Mum and Dad, reluctant wipers, weren't so happy. This was an area where they were united for once in wanting me to grow up, though normally Mum fought to hold on to her privileges. Meanwhile I dragged my heels. Re-learning something is very different from learning it the first time. There's no glamour, is there? I knew I could do it, I'd done it well enough before I was ill, so there wasn't a lot of incentive. I'd get round to it sooner or later. In terms of potty-training I was in a state of arrested development, in no great hurry to manage things on my own. This was a time when my personality was made up of plates of artificial maturity and babyishness which were always shearing unstably past each other. This too made me a normal schoolboy.

Advertising homunculus

It was the swimming teacher at Burnham, Mr Marshall, who opened my eyes. He didn't scold, he couldn't have been nicer, but I got the message loud and clear. There was no actual provision for disabled swimming, no extra help assigned. Somebody was going to be neglected, either me or the rest of the class, and for once it was going to be the others. Mr Marshall devoted almost all of his time to me, giving everyone else the dregs of his attention. I'm surprised nobody decided to drown out of pique.

My swimming lesson was really hydrotherapy rather than actual instruction, gentle supported movement in water. It would have taken all the buoyancy aids on hand to counteract the heaviness of my bones (I would have looked like a little Michelin Man, the advertising homunculus composed of tyres) if Mr Marshall had withdrawn his helping hand.

He even dressed and undressed me, and that's how they came to light, the shameful stains that go by the jaunty name of skid-marks. Skid-marks, yes, if you must – but I hadn't been the one at the wheel. So much for Mum's high standards. So much for once-a-nurse-always-a-nurse.

I was struck by a thunderbolt of shame, there in the changing-room. I was about to explain that I didn't wipe myself, but I stopped myself in time. There's only so much of an alibi you can claim when your bum is the guilty party. Admitting that someone else did the dirty work at home would make me seem even less of a grown-up than doing the job, badly, myself.

So belatedly I got to grips with the instrument provided by a grateful Government. It wasn't a picnic – the bum-wiper was a bit of a bugger to use. There was a slit in the perspex into which I was supposed to tuck a length of toilet paper. Then in theory I would pass the snorkel back between my legs, where my arms don't reach, and dab away hopefully at my mucky bottom. With a little paper-folding (though origami was never really my sport) it was even possible to make several wipes with a single length of bog roll. I should make clear that by 'single length' I don't mean a single rectangle between perforations. I'm not a magician! I needed six – four at a pinch.

The whole system was pretty unsatisfactory and first results not impressive. How to put it? The sensitivity of my anal region was more highly developed than the agility of the hands which wielded the tool. I felt sore afterwards but even so I wasn't sure of being clean. If you don't know for a fact that you're clean, then you can only suspect you're dirty.

Gradually I acquired a competence and then an expertise. Even before my performance on the instrument improved, I began to see the virtue of the independence I had so stoutly resisted.

It was wonderful, a fundamental liberty. I had been given the title deeds to my anal zone at last. From now on I didn't have to delegate the upkeep. I had the freehold, full ownership and full responsibility.

In illustrations of fairy stories the wandering hero, such as Dick Whittington, is always shown with his possessions wrapped up in a hanky (always spotted red and white, for some reason) tied to a stick across his shoulder, striding confidently into the future. I've never felt quite like that, but in my mental image the stick is my perspex bum-wiper, and of course the knotted hanky contains a supply of lavatory paper. O for a commode on the open road, and a star to steer her by!

Any fantasy of being the owner-occupier of this body, though, kept running into snags and obstacles. I was still reliant on third parties for a lot of the fetching and carrying, the basic maintenance on fixtures and fittings.

For the first year at Burnham I travelled to school by taxi. The cost was borne by the Department of Education, and the driver was always the same. My personal chauffeur, and my personal porter as well, since he lifted me in and out of the taxi. He hardly spoke, and he had the radio on in the cab all the time. I doted on him. His name was Broyan – *Brian*, obviously, but Broyan was what he said and how I thought of him. Anything working-class was far more interesting than the tedious world of the middle class. I was enchanted by the little I got to know about Broyan, his hobbies, his phobias, and I passed my enthusiasm on to Peter. We were quite the little cult, obsessively worshipping what we decided represented the wonder of the absolutely ordinary, the real. Broyan hated portion-control butter. 'I like a bit of butter,' he would say, 'but I can't stand those little *bitty* bits. It makes me go all shivery just to look at them.' It was the idea of touching the foil that set off the horrors. He had to get his wife (his wife Joanne) to open them and keep the wrappers out of sight. The idea of Broyan going all shivery made me all shivery too.

To give a deep sheen to metal objects Broyan recommended something called 'gunmetal blue'. I thought that sounded wonderful, and so did Peter.

Broyan and his wife sometimes went dancing at weekends. He

was getting used to the new style of dancing that was being done in Bourne End, so different from what he was used to. 'Nobody does proper steps, mind,' he explained. 'Everybody just shakes.' He demonstrated in his seat, writhing crazily. 'They just go roop-ti-toop-ti-toop.' *Roop-ti-toop-ti-toop*. I couldn't wait to pass that on.

If Broyan wasn't really much of a talker, at least he whistled along with songs on the radio, not pushing his lips forward but producing the sound between his teeth in a way that seemed wonderfully earthy. I tried to do the same, practising around the house while Mum rolled her eyes and sighed.

Beta-adrenergic stimulation

My feeling for Broyan wasn't really a romantic thing. I suppose he was the first person that had ever been served up to me on a plate, day after day, in conditions of neutral intimacy. My heart was involved elsewhere, heavily mortgaged. It was yoked to a double star. Paul Savage was a lovely person in his own right, a charmer and a tease. He was also a decoy. It was *Patrick* who was my infatuation. I was head over heels. *Patrick* was in italics permanently. Nothing he did or said could be neutral or unstressed. There were no roman characters anywhere in my infatuated font.

Did either of them know? I think they knew. I mean, they didn't *know*. But they knew. They weren't looking it right in the face, but they weren't in the dark either.

And talking of looking things in the face, that was a strange thing . . . I noticed that I could make *Patrick* blush, but not Paul. *Patrick*'s conscious brain might not have been in on it, but his sympathetic nervous system knew all about my feelings. The facial vein supplying the small blood vessels in the face is very susceptible to beta-adrenergic stimulation. Adolescence is the heyday of blushing, and localised blood volume tells no lies. Every blush is a confession of some little shame, written in the heart's blood.

It was Paul who liked to crack his knuckles. The habit had a ghastly fascination for me, once I understood that it wasn't painful. Imagine having so much confidence in your bones that you would meddle with their safe socketing like that! But *Patrick* must have thought it was a tactless habit to indulge in front of me. He would blush and start to send Paul agitated glances if he saw one hand getting ready to yank at the fingers of the other. Paul would usually get the message, which was a shame. I'd always rather see uninhibited behaviour than something that has been tidied up for my benefit. According to principles that are pure guesswork anyway.

The same thing happened in the larger world of the school. There was a craze, for instance, for boys to stand in doorways pressing their arms outwards and upwards against the frame for a whole minute. Then when they stepped forwards and let their shoulders relax, their arms would rise to the horizontal of their own accord. Their faces wore stupid grins as their bodies were caught out, adjusting to one set of pressures and lagging behind when the situation changed.

If I was around they would tend to stop the game, as if I would rather not see them enjoy it. But why so? Their bodies were no sort of reproach to mine. Why wouldn't I like to see them wandering the corridors of the school with their arms spread out wide, like a band of gormless probationary angels?

It was normally *Patrick* who pushed the Tan-Sad, and Paul who was at the front, and consequently in my line of sight. I had the impression that this state of affairs was engineered by Paul, to keep the object of my interest out of sight, but if so he wasn't too hot on psychology. In matters of the heart there is nothing more persuasive than the evidence of things unseen. With *Patrick* out of sight I could tune my ears to his breathing and even to his imagined heartbeat, and use my specialised knowledge of breathing techniques to inhale his smell through a single discriminating nostril.

Within the limits of unfulfilled desire I could get away with a lot. I could persuade *Patrick* Savage to come with me to the library for private chats, unattended by Paul. School libraries are traditionally unstaffed and deserted, and therefore fertile grounds for sexual experiment, even if (as at Burnham) the library wasn't some gracious suite of wood-panelled chambers but something more like a sliproom, the scanty shelves filled with dog-eared paperbacks and public-library surplus. In privacy, nevertheless, *Patrick* and I would sit together and play games.

We played some exhilarating cricket matches in that library. For me the sound of the game will always be supremely evocative, the lazy air of summer, the sound of a distant mower or nearby bee, the muffled clatter of metal on a laminated table-top. By cricket I mean the handy distillation of it called Howzat, in which the distracting physical side of the game is stripped away. Howzat was essentially a dice game, even though the dice were non-standard shapes. One looked like a primitive garden roller, though its cross-section was a hexagon rather than a circle, the six faces labelled NO BALL, LBW and so on. *Patrick* was a useful cricketer, though Paul was the star, but in this tinned version of the game (the pieces came in a little tin, with a leaflet) I outplayed him on a regular basis.

I would ask *him* to show me his fidelity ring. These were craze objects of the time – compound rings of silver wire, easily tarnished, which fell apart (when taken off the finger) into half-a-dozen linked subsidiary rings, mysteriously and irregularly kinked.

Patrick felt awkward showing me the ring, on the usual basis. Any activity seemed to be inhibited which might draw attention to my incapacities, and my fingers certainly couldn't provide any sort of perch for the ring, but what was *Patrick* going to do, refuse me? When I was at my most pretty-please-with-cream-and-sugar? He pulled the ring off his finger and held it over his palm. Then he dropped it those few inches, giving it just enough of a spin for it to come apart into its connected fragments before it landed. Then he put it back together at top speed, racing through the enigmatic moment when a looping-the-loop movement was needed to make the individual rings nest against each other properly and coalesce into a unit, their kinks unified into a sort of turk's-head motif.

I wasn't satisfied. 'You haven't told me the story. The story is a part of it – you can't show someone the ring without telling the story. You have to do it again.' He sighed and said, 'All right.' He dropped it back into his palm and the one ring became many.

'Once there was a Sultan . . .' – the owners of other identical rings might say Maharajah or Sheikh, we had a very undifferentiated sense of the exotic – 'who gave his wife a silver ring to be sure of her fidelity. Everyone in the kingdom' – if I was feeling mischievous I might correct him with 'Sultanate' – 'knew the ring of the Sultan. Now the Sultan went away on a journey –'

'Was he a Muslim?'

'Er . . . possibly. Why?'

'He might have been going on the *hajj*, you know, the pilgrimage to Mecca.'

'Fine, he went on a pilgrimage. But before he left he gave her this very special ring. Then while the Sultan was on pilgrimage, to Mecca, his wife fell in love with a noble at court. With her husband's deputy.'

'Deputy?'

'Chancellor.'

'"Grand Vizier" sounds better. Go on.'

'The Grand Vizier fell in love with her too, and they went to bed. But before they did, she took off the ring . . .'

'Why did she do that?'

'Because it was her fidelity ring and she was being unfaithful.'

'Why not leave it on, all the same, with someone who knew all about it? The story would work better if she was going to bed with someone who didn't know she was even married – say a travelling lute-player.'

'How is a travelling lute-player going to fall in love with the Sultan's wife and not know who she is?'

'She could go to a concert of his in disguise.'

'And then she says, "Come back to my palace for some Turkish delight?" How's that going to work any better?'

Eventually we'd hammer out a more or less plausible story. If I suggested that a sensible adulteress would carefully slip the ring off her finger and onto, say, a candle, he would agree rather uneasily and then say, rather desperately, that the lovers were so passionate that the candle fell off the Sultana's dressing table. Sometimes I could persuade him to say 'Sultana'. A burst of invention along those lines would cheer him up. The point of all this from my point of view, of course, was to make him concentrate on the narrative – on the Sultan returning so that the wife panics as she tries in vain to reassemble the pledge of her honesty – and not think of his hands while he spoke.

Not all hands are beautiful. I've seen plenty that have made me feel happy with what I've got. But *Patrick*'s hands were both large and handsome. It was part of the mystery of the twins that they should be so broad and well-built. It seemed miraculous that a single wombful could yield such a tonnage, even after a decade and a half's regular feeding.

At the end of the demonstration *Patrick* would return the ring to his finger – the little finger, the only one on which it would fit. Perhaps it really was made for a woman's hand, though there was nothing effeminate about the way the cheap silver gleamed on his adult paw, despite the nails left a little long for extra purchase on the fretboard of his guitar. It was the other, plucking hand which had the calluses on the tips of its fingers.

As he slipped the ring on, I could see the grey-green ghost of its tarnish on the finger. The Sultana herself either had a higher grade of silver jewellery, or gave her hands a good scrub before she risked betraying her marriage vows.

Meaning osteotomy

While I looked at *Patrick*'s hands, he was preöccupied with my right knee, and how bent it was. He asked me if it hurt, and I tried to laugh it off by saying, 'Only when I pole-vault.' He said at least once, 'I don't know how you cope – I could measure that angle with my protractor!' and I admit I winced. His protractor wasn't the relevant part of his geometry set just then. It felt more as if he was sticking the points of his dividers into the unbeautiful joint which jarred his sense of proportion.

I began to brood about it a little bit. My sense of unlovability began to take up residence in that knee. Perhaps *he* (or someone) would only be able to love me back if I did something about its ugly protrusion. 'Something' here meaning 'osteotomy'.

The cult of Broyan made a good stop-gap when I felt ill at ease with *Patrick*. In the early days I sat in the back of the taxi, and then I decided to change things. I took a vow to get myself promoted to the passenger seat, so as to sit by Broyan.

It was roll-call all over again – a major campaign of attrition. When I was given a privilege I wanted to renounce it, but if I was treated equally I pined for my perks. And this time, when I'd got my way, with much wheedling and blackmail (greymail at the very least), I wished I'd left well alone. It wasn't the same at all. Promotion to the front of the car didn't solve anything. My head turns to the left much more easily than the right, so I saw no more of Broyan. What I really wanted to see was his thick neck, which didn't look as if it could turn at all. I found myself wanting things the way they were, before I had shaped them to my will and spoiled the morning drive to school.

I would sit there next to Broyan grieving while he drove, and dully revising my Latin, which wouldn't go in. I seemed to have some sort of specific resistance to the language. Particles of Latin were so compacted they failed to travel osmotically in the normal way across the semi-permeable membrane of the page, and on into the language tanks of my brain. No sooner had I absorbed an irregular verb into my bloodstream than it was attacked and destroyed by the antibodies of ignorance. I had a pack of Latin Grammar cards (Key Facts) which I would wrestle with in the taxi on the way to school, a plastic pack of revision aids in its own little wallet, moderately well tailored to the measure of my hands. The process was satisfactory, but there was no product. Wasn't I supposed to be good with languages? Perhaps it was just German that I was good at. Latin words just lay there on the page supine and senseless.

Everyone else groaned at the very idea of grammar, but that wasn't the problem with me. Mr Nevin had slogged me through all that at Vulcan, and I rather enjoyed it. Grammar was like the algebra of language, except that I could understand it. I could grasp the underlying structure of Latin, but not put flesh on its bones.

I was entered for Latin O-level, but was regarded as very much a borderline case. The set book was *Georgics* IV – the one about bees. By rights I should have been fascinated by this snapshot of past attitudes to the natural kingdom – Virgil, like everyone else until about the eighteenth century, took it for granted that the supreme bee was a king and not a queen. Aristotle installed a piece of polished horn into a beehive so he could watch what went on, without managing to spot that it was a matriarchal society on the other side of that yellowy window.

The exam was scheduled for a Tuesday. On the Saturday night I opened the book for one last despairing bout of revision, and the language looked quite different. It was lucid. It coöperated. Dead language or no dead language, it had come alive. It had only been lying doggo, and it wanted to play after all. The Key Cards shone with meaning in Broyan's taxi on the day of the exam, as if someone had turned on a spotlight on the other side of a keyhole while I crouched to spy on the principal parts of verbs.

In a strange way it was modern teaching methods that had held me back. Previous languages I had learned by rote and repetition, at least in the early stages, whereas Latin at Burnham was taught by stages, through progressive understanding. It's a splendid notion, but I wonder if it suits the brain, really. It's a question of neurology. To learn and understand at the same time is a perverse undertaking, like that silly thing people are always trying to do – what is it, to pat your head and stroke your tummy in a circle at the same time? It's something like that.

I know I've always managed better when I've learned mechanically and understood after the event. Fewer simultaneous mental processes are required. That seems to be the key. It's best if new shapes are allowed to sink into the brain-mush undisturbed. Then they'll pop up somewhere else, in another lobe perhaps, bathed in understanding. Whatever the exact mechanics of my late burst of comprehension, I who had given such ample grounds for doubt earned a 2 Grade and the school's usual response to surprises of this kind, a little flattering sheaf of book tokens.

The witching hour was 4.20

One more thing I hadn't really considered before I started at Burnham Grammar was that a day school only functions in the day. Another sad lapse of common sense, another bit of clever-person's stupidity. The whole point of attending a mainstream school was to be absorbed into a wider world, but that wasn't really on the cards. The problem was Broyan. The magic coach which carried me to the academic ball every morning also came to fetch me, and its summons was imperious. The witching hour was 4.20 rather than midnight, but that was a technicality. Yes, Broyan would wait, but why should he? True, Broyan was employed on a contract basis and there was no meter running except the one in my head (I was very aware that the local education authority wasn't made of money). I could have sent him away but then my predicament, as a young man in an invalid carriage with no way home, would be at least as awkward as Cinderella's.

I was effectively debarred from teenage society by my exclusion from loitering. Teenage society and loitering are two words for the same thing. Without hanging around there can be no hanging together. I did my best to loiter in free periods, but you can't get into the swing of loitering when you're on the clock. In fact I was debarred from taking part not only by the practical difficulties but by my own exhaustion. I just wanted to ride back in Broyan's taxi to Trees, where the cry of 'The ruddy crutch!' could almost sound like 'Welcome Home'.

Unable to build relationships with my fellows at the end of the school day, I couldn't really hope to fill up my schedule at weekends, except with homework. So normally I would badger Dad into taking me to the library on a Saturday. That's where I did my loitering instead, while Dad ran errands. I can't imagine what they were, Dad's errands – shopping wasn't on the agenda for a husband and father of that vintage, except when it came to special errands to select things that women couldn't possibly know about, such as wine.

Dad wouldn't stay when he took me to the library, not being on good terms with Mrs Pavey, whom he described as 'doolally', saying he couldn't understand how she kept her job. It was true that she had her little ways, but none of the patrons minded that. We all have our little ways.

Certifiably insane remedy

Mrs Pavey was a martyr to migraines. Sometimes the pain was so bad that coming to work was out of the question, but more often she struggled in. She always wore a silk scarf – it was part of how she dressed for work – but when the torture inside her head got too much for her, she would blindfold herself with the scarf and lie down behind the counter. Regular users came to know the signs, and would process their own returns and borrowings, tucking the slips into the cardboard pockets and stamping the issue page, taking care not to make too much noise with the stamping machine. I suppose newcomers to the library must have found it strange that the person in charge was lying concealed behind the issue desk, moaning faintly at the slightest sound, but this was really only a tableau expanding on the sign on the desk: *Silence Is Requested.*

Mrs Pavey treated her migraine with a standard remedy of the day. It was an incredibly exotic, certifiably insane remedy, but in those lax days it was readily available. It was called Cafergot Q. A chocolate-flavoured, caffeine-enhanced chewable ergotamine. They looked like sweets, and Mrs Pavey gobbled them down as if that's what they were. When she went to Bourne End surgery for a repeat prescription, our rather flinty GP Flanny (Dr Flanagan) couldn't believe how much she'd got through. Two months' worth in ten days. She didn't make a fuss, since after all in those days a chocolate-flavoured, caffeine-enhanced chewable ergotamine was all part of the pharmacological sweetshop, no more than a quirky flavour of Spangles, latently hallucinogenic. She simply said, 'It's a wonder your fingers haven't fallen off.'

Mrs Pavey was a sweet woman, melancholy-seeming even when her brain wasn't held in its vice of pain. Her skin was oddly creamy and her blue eyes had a lot of grey in them. She lived with her elderly mother, and I never heard a Mr Pavey spoken of.

Sometimes after she had done a particularly inspired bit of truffle-hunting on my behalf, running down some esoteric oddity in the stacks, I would pay her a visit in the library to express my thanks. She would shy away from my gratitude, dismissing it almost, as if she was only doing her job. Which was true, but if everyone did it at that level then 'job' would be a holy word.

One Saturday in the library I came across a book on shorthand, and immediately decided I must master it. I loved the way shorthand looked. It seemed to be an entirely alien language, yet it was still English under the surface of squiggles. When I started to study it seriously I was disappointed to learn that the shapes of related consonants – *p* and *b*, say – were the same, the only difference being thickness of line. Perversely I wanted every sound to be represented by a different shape, which would have turned Pitman into mere hieroglyphics and made huge demands on the memory.

I could never make the pens work anyway.

I transferred my allegiances from Pitman to Gregg, a rival system which did at least use differences of size, if not shape. I got hold of a magazine from the library which promised to teach you eighty new short forms a week. I enjoyed the element of esoteric knowledge, writing words that not one in a thousand people would be able to reconstitute – I suppose it was *Yod Hé Vau Hé* all over again. I didn't really see shorthand as a means of communication, more a cipher with considerable ornamental merits. There was nothing 'short' about it. Everything took a lot longer than if I'd used the uncryptic full-length forms.

It was always against the odds that I could hide an actual object, so my interest was drawn to metaphysical hiding, in other words to secrets. It mattered relatively little that they were secrets everyone knew already, under the heavy disguise of shorthand, or had no interest in, like the arcana (major, minor and downright silly) of the Tarot.

I had turned down all Dad's offers to buy me a subscription to the *Telegraph*, but I sometimes read the paper just the same, if he left it lying around. It's really only my hands which are satisfied with a tabloid. Sometimes I want a broader view than I can comfortably hold. Mum would occasionally fold the paper into a tight little packet for my benefit. One day I read a review of a novel that set whole peals of bells ringing. It was called *The Ring* by Richard Chopping, and it was a story of love between men. Hateful, horrifying love between men. Now that I think about it, the book's title, even its author's name – Dick Chopping! – show signs of campy spoofing, but I wasn't attuned to that then. The *Telegraph* review was full of a mesmerised disgust, and I immediately knew this was a book that would change my life. It was 'savagely frank'. I must read it immediately.

I induced Mum to order this sulphurous book from Mrs Pavey's library, to pick it up when it arrived in stock, and to deliver it to the family home in the basket of her bicycle. Better for so radioactive a volume to be transported in a lead box. I worried that the cover of the book would betray its contents. That would be no way to repay Mrs Pavey for all her thoughtfulness, tracking filth all over her nice clean library.

When Mum gave me the book, I saw that it had no dust jacket, just a plastic sheath over the hard cover, and I wondered if there was censorship involved. Then again, Mrs Pavey might not even have set eyes on the book. Mum told me that she had been having one of her bad days. Her bad days tended to come along in little groups, festivals of migraine.

I quarantined myself from the public spaces of the house and read *The Ring* in my bedroom. If Peter was around then I hardly noticed him. It was a wonderful experience. I don't mean necessarily that it was a wonderful book, but it was a wonderful thing for me to read at the time. I needed a hero, and the central figure of the book gave me one. Boyde Ashlar, 'thirty-four, handsome and not untalented'. A name to savour. He was my James Bond, I suppose. I'd read some Bond books when the craze was at its height, and I'd got something out of them, a sort of second-hand worldliness (which is what adolescents crave, after all), but Boyde Ashlar instantly superseded him. He gave me second-hand romanticism and second-hand self-hatred as well, more than Bond could ever do. What do I remember from the book? Not very much. The hero lived with his hideous bloated mother in separate parts of the same house, communicating by way of a speaking-tube.

I remember one very exciting phrase, about Boyde Ashlar after an unfruitful night out 'returning to his onanistic bed'. I seem to remember that he had a less manly, chattier friend. If ever Boyde caught sight of an attractive man, this friend would say, 'You've gone all cock-eyed, dear.'

Boyde Ashlar gave young men the eye at flower shows – so why shouldn't I? Given licence by a fictional character, my eye contact grew in daring and intensity. I had a few nice looks back, and that was all the encouragement I needed.

There were some wonderful descriptions in *The Ring*, of things far removed from the central situation. The author seemed disgusted by human beings, shuddering at ageing flesh and self-delusion, but he seemed rather in love with nature at its ugliest, or what most people would see as its ugliest. There were quotations from a book about toads and their parasites, for instance, which Boyde was reading. And there was a marvellous description of snails mating. I made the mistake of reading a bit of that to Dad and then he became horribly interested in the book, asking, 'That's absolutely *terrific*! Is it all like that?'.

There's a theory that people with secrets secretly want to be found out. I can't disprove it on the basis of *The Ring*, since I hadn't been able to resist drawing attention to the very thing I wanted kept hidden. I went into reverse, though, the moment my secret was in serious danger of being discovered. I recovered as quickly as I could, and gave the book as grudging an assessment as could square with the fact that I was continuing to read it. 'It started off all right,' I said, trying to sound as authoritative as any reviewer, 'but it's getting to be a bit of a bore. The snails are more fun than the people, really.'

This wasn't the best line to take if I wanted to put Dad off the scent. 'They often are,' he said. 'When you've finished with it, pass it on, will you? And I'll give it a go.'

Which was unthinkable, but I was helpless. I couldn't hide it from him. I had no privacy, either at school or at home. Anyone could get access to my things more easily than I could. I looked miserably at the label that was pasted in every library book in those days, with the message *If infectious disease should break out in your house do not return this book, but at once inform the Librarian. Borrowers infringing this regulation, or knowingly permitting the book to be exposed to infection are liable to a penalty of £5.* In the case of *The Ring* I felt it was the other way about. The book was exposing the household to every germ I spent so much time and energy hiding. And now it was going to shop me to Dad, to expose me as someone whose secret love was not for snails.

Everything spins like a plate on a stick

Finally Mum put me out of my misery by saying, all very casually, 'Do you want me to return that book to the library for you? I could tell Dad someone else had reserved it.' It was a marvellous bit of mind-reading on her part. I wondered, though, if she had noticed, despite not being the scientific type, that my sheets and pyjamas needed changing more often when *The Ring* was in the house. While Boyde Ashlar was on the premises.

'Yes, perhaps that would be best,' I managed to say at last. 'It's really not very good.' Be forgiving, Boyde Ashlar, of the little betrayals of weaker people.

Mum gave a little sniff. 'I read a little bit myself,' she said. Really! Did no one in the family give a thought to my need for privacy? 'It was about a man getting into the altogether and looking at himself in the mirror. Rather silly, I thought.' She must have been very careful about her furtive reading. I always left the book in a precise and particular alignment on my bedside table, and it never seemed to be out of place when I came back.

It wasn't a special precaution for Mum to wear gloves when she took the book back to Mrs Pavey – she always wore gloves when handling library books. Because you never know. A lot of women wore gloves in those days, and this particular mania of hygiene didn't make her conspicuous on her bicycle.

In this way I missed my chance to find out what happened to the thirty-four-year-old hero, handsome and not untalented, of a savagely frank novel of 1967, though I have to say the omens were not good. Boyde Ashlar spent a lot of the book hating himself and his frivolous life, while unable to break free of his obsession with Tex, the masseur at the Turkish Baths, and his involvement with Roddy, a lout with a tattoo of a snake covering almost the entirety of his lithe young body . . .

After reading *The Ring*, playing with myself at night before falling asleep (mental masturbation aided by the pressure of the sheet, mindful to keep my breathing even if Peter was around) became a quite different experience. I was no longer alone. Just knowing that Boyde was probably bringing himself off at the same time as me was a comfort. I knew perfectly well he was only made up, but that didn't diminish him.

I felt that every song, every book and every film – even a school essay – has life in it. It gets some sort of charge when it is written or created, and the charge is renewed by every reader, writer and hearer. Everything spins like a plate on a stick, and every tiny encounter prolongs the spinning.

I used to refuse to leave the cinema while the credits were still running. I'd complain when people walked into my field of vision on their way out that I was trying to watch the film. Dad would say,

'The film's over, Chicken, time to go home,' but I'd sit tight and so would Peter, out of solidarity. 'Somebody's taken a lot of trouble to write all these names down for us,' I would say, while Dad sighed in the dark. 'If it was your name, wouldn't you want people to read it, even if you'd just made the sandwiches? And besides, there may be an extra bit of the film at the very end which is just to reward the patient ones.' Though actually there never was.

If there are levels of reality below us, then it follows that there are levels above, superior to us as we are superior to characters in books, but not themselves absolute. Nothing that possesses characteristics is perfectly real, not even the guru. The guru himself is in some sense unreal – but he doesn't need to be absolutely real to get the job done. When an elephant dreams about a tiger and wakes up in alarm, the tiger wasn't real, was it? But the elephant has been awoken, and that is a real thing.

I was still far short of wakefulness myself at this time, and more preöccupied with lower realities like Boyde Ashlar than higher ones. You could even say that I'd left Boyde Ashlar in the lurch by not finishing *The Ring*. I had neglected to give the spinning plate the full charge of attention to which it was entitled. I told myself that I would borrow the book from Mrs Pavey again after Dad had forgotten all about it, so as to find out what happened in the end, but I never got round to it.

The Red Spot on Jupiter blinks in shock

Eckstein's manner didn't soften as my German improved. Instead he opened up a campaign on another flank by pressuring me to learn another language. He kept me back after one German lesson to make his case. 'You are taking things easy at a time when your brain is still able to absorb new things without difficulty. Absurd! Take advantage of this – it will not come again. You should learn Spanish. Starting *immediately*.

'Here – I'll start you off. I'm about to teach you something you will never forget. My own learning of Spanish was very rapid. My tutor gave me a copy of *Don Quijote de la Mancha* by Cervantes and told me to get on with it. I had to reach degree level from nothing in eight months, and I did. If you decided to learn Spanish, you could get to A-level in a year, very easily. Don't bother with the O-level. It's just a distraction.

'When you leave this room in three minutes' time you will know more of the language than I did when I was thrown in at the deep end with Miguel de Cervantes and his knight.' He walked over to the blackboard, took a piece of chalk and carefully wrote something on the blackboard. It was:

¡ Q u e   t e   j o d a   u n   p u l p o !

Then he stepped back from the board and said, 'You start with the advantage of knowing this charming sentence, which I discovered relatively late in my own progress. When I did, I vowed that it would be the first thing I taught any pupil, if I was lucky or unlucky enough to acquire one. It means,' he said with a deep hissing sigh, '"*May you be fucked by an octopus*".'

The world stood still. The Red Spot on Jupiter blinked in shock. He went on, 'It would be more accurate to translate, "May an octopus fuck you", but such a sentence is not idiomatic in English. It lacks the proper cadence. *Joder* means *fuck*, and is transitive, for obvious reasons.'

When Klaus Eckstein said '*joder*' he used the proper Spanish sound, like a heavy 'H', not far from a guttural German 'ch'. 'No doubt your English teacher will have told you to avoid passive verbs, on the grounds that they are weaker and vaguer. This is an example of the opposite, with the passive construction being the more forceful. And there you are – I have done as I promised. I have taught you something you will never forget. From this day on, you will always have one phrase of Spanish at your disposal. If you do in fact choose to learn the language, not everything will come so easily, but the difficulties are not overwhelming. Now, I have somewhere to be even if you do not.'

I saw that those five little staccato words, those (he was right) entirely unforgettable words, remained on the board, and a wave of fear swept over me. Not entirely selfish fear – I didn't want Eckstein to be compromised in any way, though why was I worried? His unpopularity was already exemplary. He had nothing to fear.

'Sir –,' I piped up, 'shouldn't we clean the blackboard?'

'As I understand the situation, young Mr Cromer, you cannot do so, and I myself . . . cannot be bothered. No one will understand what those words mean,' he added airily, 'and if they do . . . well, who cares? I am here to provide instruction, am I not? Let them learn . . .'

He didn't abandon me quite as brusquely as I feared. He pushed the Tan-Sad roughly to the stairwell, wheezing as he did so, but then summoned up enough breath to produce an enormous whistle which summoned some of the boys with which those premises were so richly supplied.

Orthographical paraçites

Perhaps Eckstein gambled on Spanish attracting me as a language of secrets and obscenities. Presumably the octopus featured in the unforgettable curse because with its eight arms it could quite easily explore a lady and a man at the same time, and still have fingers left over for the eating of its lunch. Eckstein instilled in me the idea that Spanish was a language of adult intimacies. German as I first experienced it was a motherly language, full of lullabies, endearments and diminutives, while Spanish was more of a lover from the start, a fount of forbidden knowledge. German was a familiar hand on the cradle. Spanish was an unknown tongue in my ear.

From then on, at the end of a lesson, Mr Eckstein might mention some virtue or peculiarity of the Spanish language, contrasting it as if casually with German. He thought German and English were both impoverished compared with Spanish in the matter of punctuation, specifically the punctuation of exclamations and questions. In English we would think it very odd if someone only bothered to indicate the end of quoted speech, and not the beginning. ¿So why not apply the same principle to questions? ¡And exclamations! ¿Why not prepare the reader for what is coming? ¡It's silly not to!

Or he might remark that Spanish, unlike German, had two verbs meaning 'to be'. They weren't interchangeable. *Estar* and *ser*. One referred to the merely accidental and contingent, while the other dealt with permanent, existential characteristics. He said that there was a lot more German philosophy than Spanish, but perhaps that was because the Spanish needed less, so much being embodied in their language. When he made these remarks in passing on the relative merits of languages, he didn't address them to me. He never even looked at me, but I realised it was my interest he was fishing for.

He knew what he was doing with these sidelong comments. Ever since I had fallen out with Miss Collins, the tutor of my bed rest years, over the sacred symbol æ, disputed 27th letter of the alphabet, strange forms and symbols had been my chosen playground. If I had been less prudish I would have seen at once that the punctuation of the five-word curse he had chalked on the blackboard was as thrilling as its meaning. Eckstein was drawing my attention to two symbols that were right up my street. *¡If they'd been any further up my street they'd be sticking their tongues* and so on!

I vowed from then on to import these useful symbols into my own essays and letters, in any subject, for every teacher. ¿Wasn't it logical, as Eckstein said? ¿Why should English remain at its historical disadvantage, when help was at hand? Any page of my writing crawled with orthographical paraçites. I didn't much mind that my attempts to Iberiçise English punctuation were invariably crossed out and çingled out for reproach. That's always how the world treats pioneers.

It took me ages to chasten these flourishes and exorcise the cedillas from my *c*s. I loved making those expressive little hooks, dainty curls like stray typographic eyelashes. I wanted to study them under laboratory conditions, magnifying them to see if each cedilla had a little cedilla of its own, and so on down into unthinkable realms of subordination . . . in my mind's eye, my mind's microscope, the inside curve of each cedilla had the dull gleam of something whetted and oiled, like the edge of an infinitesimal sickle.

Little *c*s have lesser *c*s upon their tails to bite 'em / Lesser *c*s have lesser *c*s, and so *ad infinitum*! Unless it might happen that electron microscopy revealed at supreme magnification some final clinger-on, some depender without dependants, the loneliest and most necessary of his kind, his perfect uselessness underwriting a sense of purpose for all the rest.

Eckstein was scrupulous, within the limits of his abrasiveness, to let me down lightly. He explained that although the word cedilla is Spanish and means 'little z', the mark itself does not feature in the modern language, or not in the Castilian master-dialect which was the only one possible to study in schools. I was disappointed but my fondness for the little diacritic held firm. Curaçao was still my favourite drink, of all the ones I had never tasted.

What Eckstein alleged about the absorptive powers of teenaged memory certainly seemed to be true of mine. It seemed to be actively hungry rather than passively registering, and I trained it to do tricks. I threw random scraps to its surplus capacity. I would memorise shopping lists and reel them off to an amazed (or mildly diverted, or not quite bored) audience. Once Dad thought he'd caught me out, until I explained that it was more of a challenge to retain last week's shopping list rather than this one's. I made him dig the old list out of the kitchen drawer and check every item, rather than take my word for it.

Duly mashed

I performed just as willingly with numbers. The trick was to forge associative links – to impose a grammar on numbers, building on their resemblances to creatures or objects. So 2 was represented by a swan, 6 by an elephant's trunk, 1 by a magic wand, and to establish 261 firmly in your memory all you had to do was think of a swan eating an elephant that is waving a wand.

Possibly Mum and Dad thought these hobbies were morbid signs of some sort. They wanted me to make some friends outside school, which in my special case meant 'outside the school buildings', to have things to do in the evenings. And so did I, but their idea was that I should go to a meeting of the Young Conservatives, described by Dad as 'a nice bunch of youngsters'. The Bourne End meeting place of this cult wasn't far away, by the level crossing, within wheelchair range so that I wouldn't need to be delivered like a child to a birthday party.

I agreed, to keep them happy. This was a very abstract display of independence (of 'independence' prescribed by someone else!). I didn't want to go where I was going – I was going there because I could. But I did always love going over the level crossing in the Wrigley, bumping outrageously over the uneven sleepers, almost willing myself to come a cropper. If I'd got stuck and been duly mashed I dare say Mum would never have forgiven herself and the Young Conservatives.

It turned out that their lair was well defended. The only access was by way of a metal spiral staircase. I wasn't having that. I wasn't going to ask someone to carry me up such a frightening structure for the sake of company I didn't want. I went to the Red Lion instead, and drank there till closing time. I can't say I had a whale of a time, but at least I was in a place I had chosen for myself, and someone put 'A Whiter Shade of Pale' on the jukebox. A nice young man in a floral shirt came over to see if I was all right, saying if there was anything I wanted I should just give a shout. I began to wonder if I hadn't stumbled on a 'queer pub' just round the corner from home, hitting the jackpot with my first pull on the handle. What luck! I wouldn't have to go to the extreme lengths favoured by Boyde Ashlar (I had no idea how to find a Turkish Baths, let alone get myself through its turnstile). This nice young man was positively chatting me up. He twinkled at me. Nothing was too much trouble. Then I realised that this lad had found the easiest possible way of impressing a girlfriend with his essential niceness on a first date, bouncing a twinkle at me for her benefit. If I'd been a kitten stuck up a tree outside the pub I'd have served his turn just as well. After that I had no qualms about letting him refill my glass. Pathos has a price, and it was the least he could do. This stranded kitten doesn't come cheap.

Mum and Dad had left the door of Trees open for me as usual. The system was that the door of the bedroom I shared with Peter (when he was in residence), which gave access to the outside world, stayed open except when we all left the house. It stayed open even in cold weather, though on days of actual snow it might be closed when a few satisfying flurries had been admitted. The gain in convenience – the easy flow of unescorted wheelchairs in and out – easily outweighed any inconvenience of temperature. If I couldn't circulate freely myself then I could at least give the air that privilege. It was better than a consolation prize, a pleasurable sensation in its own right.

When I came in that night I was exhilarated out of all proportion to the actual pleasures of my night out. I had mounted an expedition solo, across the tracks and back, over an unknown threshold, and I had come back safe. Peter came in just after me, from his pub job at the Spade Oak Hotel. I sang at the top of my voice while he helped prepare me for bed. I sang 'A Whiter Shade of Pale', inevitably, with particular repetition of the bit about calling out for another drink and the waiter bringing a tray.

Next morning Mum came in beaming to ask about my big evening out. My late-night song recital seemed to indicate a social break-through. She wanted all the details of my evening of Tory glory. It was only when I told her I hadn't gone to the Young Conservatives after all that the atmosphere became suffused with toxins. Mum went quite white. It was one thing for me to engage in alcoholic carousal with Young Conservatives, quite another to do anything of the sort at the Red Lion. That was beyond the pale, and my singing of a cryp-tic Procol Harum ballad suddenly changed from a natural burst of exuberance to a sinister display of drunkenness, though I missed the same number of notes either way. The song might just as well have been 'The Red Flag' for all the legitimate entertainment it provided. Mum's face, at first just ghastly, turned a darker shade of puce, and then she stalked off.

She didn't speak to me for four days. She thought I'd been drinking, and as she didn't ask me outright I didn't volunteer any information. I'd stuck to soft drinks, naturally, being under age. Arguments about my behaviour raged through the house without my needing to par-ticipate, which was often the way. Once I heard the phrase ' – showed a little initiative –' in Dad's voice between two door-slammings. That must have been him standing up for me, welcome proof that he could come through with the goods in my defence when he was really up against it.

Dad was a much happier organism altogether, working in the per-sonnel department of BOAC, than he had been as a sub-standard salesman for Centrum Intercoms, his first job after leaving the servic-es. BOAC gave him back some of the sense of himself he had enjoyed in the RAF. He was a bit of a hermit crab, I suppose, when it came to the world of work. He needed the right sort of job – one with a proper chain of command – to give him a shape and a home. Otherwise he felt defenceless, skulking between shells.

During the school holidays I wanted to make a trip to London, to see where he worked. Joy Payne, best of neighbours, a joy to all and a bringer of pain only to herself, volunteered to drive me. So I phoned him up to ask for directions. Normally Dad enjoyed giving this sort of help. I had once seen him with my own eyes writing page after page of directions, with his fountain pen, for the benefit of some passing stranger. How much keener would he be when he was guiding his own son! I was sure a visit from me would increase his standing in the office.

I spoke to his secretary, who was lovely. We had a good long chat, but when Dad finally came on the line he was very short with me. I had used up all my charm on the secretary, and had no reserves left for someone who sounded much more like a stranger than she did. If I had been a salesman I could have got Dad's secretary to sign up for anything, but from the man himself I got the bum's rush.

Dad was cheerful again by the time he got home. 'I've told my secretary not to put you through again under any circumstances. She'll get fired if she lets it happen again. She should have known better, and now she does. So don't bother trying to repeat today's little trick.'

I was stung. How was it a trick to phone your father? I tried to argue my way out of this unexpected disgrace. 'What if there's an emergency?'

'Such as?'

I didn't have an answer ready. 'Well . . . what if Mum dropped dead?'

'Then what on earth would be the point of phoning me about something like that? Show some sense – phone the undertaker instead. I'll find out soon enough when I get home.'

This wasn't a very tactful conversation to be having with Mum in the room, perhaps. Her smile was a rather blighted thing. It wasn't Dad who introduced the subject of death – I have to put my hand up to that. He certainly capitalised on it.

Sentient luggage

I wonder if Dad did actually have the power to fire his secretary for her insubordination in putting through an unauthorised call from a civilian. There was probably a more complex procedure to be gone through, the equivalent of a court-martial – a court-bureaucratic.

At weekends, obviously, Broyan wasn't at my disposal. If I wanted an outing I had to make my own arrangements. That was where the rail system came in. I was never quite so gone on rail travel as Mum, but I can't deny that it served me well. There was a system, or rather there wasn't a system – which turned out to work much better than any formal set of arrangements could have done. I would simply turn up at Bourne End station and be loaded, Wrigley and all, into the goods van. I was treated as sentient luggage. It was glorious.

I would be asked where I was going, of course, but only so that I could be retrieved and off-loaded at the proper time. No mention was ever made of tickets or fares. This can't have been an official dispensation, I don't think – otherwise, surely, the goods van would have been piled high with wheelchairs and their occupants. And there would have been paperwork. It was just a blind eye being turned, a perk extended, without comment, to me personally. Unless a background murmur of marvellous-how-the-little-fellow-seems-to-manage counts as comment.

The sheer novelty of a wheelchair-bound person having an appetite for unaccompanied travel worked in my favour, I'm sure. Still, British Rail and its employees have access to this mystical truth, if no other: the body is always and everywhere luggage.

On one trip, a very neatly-turned-out guard came to have a chat. He was chummy as well as smartly dressed but I felt deeply uncomfortable about my ambiguous status and blurted out, 'Shouldn't you be making me buy a ticket?'

The guard said, 'I can if you like, but I'd much rather not. You're not in a proper passenger seat, are you? Then if I charged you for your travel, which includes the right to a seat, you could make a complaint that you'd brought your own seat with you and been charged for another one. We could charge you as luggage, but then we'd have to work out what the proper price should be. We might have to weigh you on the platform before putting you on the train, and then there'd be the driver waiting and passengers fretting. All things considering, it's best to leave well alone. Just come along when you want to go travelling and we'll see you right. If it's cold we can always find you a blanket, and if you want a bit of company just sing out.'

At Slough I was duly unloaded onto the platform. I was going to see The Who in concert – which was a ticket that had to be paid for in full. I could only hope to be an honorary parcel on special occasions.

The last thing I heard before I notched the Wrigley into top speed and raced off in the direction of the concert hall was a final refrain of 'Ruddy miracle, that little cripple kiddie', well-meant but a bit lowering. Oi! Less of the cripple. Less of the kiddie. Less of the little.

When The Who started playing I nearly leapt out of the Wrigley in forgetfulness of the body. The noise ripped right through me. It turned me into one big throbbing ear, an ear on the edge of pain. Just as well, really, since I couldn't see a thing. I took up various positions in the crowd as it heaved around me, but either there were people in front of me blocking my view or else I was in the lee of the stage and couldn't see up.

On stage in Slough, The Who were offering a sort of masterclass in non-dualist philosophy. While they were playing, it was obvious that there was only one thing in the universe, one thing in any possible universe, and that was this noise.

Then in a break between songs there was a girl shouting something in my ear. 'John, it's Barbara from school.' I hardly recognised her out of uniform. Barbara Broier in purple tights and a very short skirt. Schoolgirls in particular looked quite different at weekends, though the boys were beginning to run them close, what with bright shirts and bell-bottomed velvet trousers. I was the odd one out, looking much of a muchness throughout the week, in school or at large. 'Can you see anything?' she was asking.

'Not really, but it doesn't matter. I can hear everything.' I could hear my ears bursting.

'It's just Susan and I were thinking . . .' The next song drowned out what it was that they were thinking, but I soon cottoned on when they put it into practice. They were thinking that they could tip the wheelchair backwards a bit so as to give me a view of the stage.

It was a kind idea, but I'm not sure that the girls realised how heavy the Wrigley was. They had seen the twins handling the unwieldy Tan-Sad at school, but the Savages had the benefit of lots of practice, as well as being coördinated almost on the genetic level. The Wrigley had the added weight of its motor. The girls gave me some sort of wobbling view, but I didn't exactly feel secure in their hands. I wasn't even sure the visual side of things, when I got it, added all that much. Townshend the guitarist had a huge conk of a nose, and Daltrey the singer had a huge everything, wild eyes, madly curling hair, giant teeth. Entwistle the bass guitarist seemed to be fast asleep, and my eyes were drawn mainly to the drummer, so dapper and pretty however frantically he pounded his kit alongside the ill-favoured others. Keith Moon. They were playing 'I Can See for Miles and Miles . . .', one of my favourites, admittedly for reasons that weren't strictly musical. *Patrick* played it on the guitar and had shown me how simple the strange-sounding chords actually were, with a single configuration of fingers which he slid methodically across the frets.

I wondered if Pete Townshend the guitarist wasn't mildly disabled. He didn't seem to have much mobility in his right elbow. Instead of strumming the strings in the normal way he would send his arm the long way round, to describe a full circle before it crashed into the strings. He certainly wasn't letting disability hold him back, unless it was part of the show after all.

It turned out that some Burnham boys were at the concert too, and they decided to get in on the act, shooing the girls away from the handles of the Wrigley. Further proof of the irrelevant truth that girls were nicer than boys. The boys would never have thought of my preferences by themselves, but now they wanted to use me as a pretext for showing off in front of my original helpers.

They were stronger, but their handling was much less satisfactory. They couldn't resist joining in with the rhythms of the music, until I felt I was being treated as an extension of Keith Moon's drum kit. When they put me down in a break between songs I scooted off to the side where I could concentrate on the sound, bearing down on me from speakers twice my size, without bothering with the pictures.

After the concert I notched the motor into slow gear because of the crowd. An official attached to the group or the hall said that I should leave by the back entrance. The moment I was out on the pavement I notched the Wrigley into top. I didn't know I was about to pass the Stage Door until it opened in my path. Out came a man with his arm round a small woman who looked Indian. He was so intent on her that he didn't see me at first. Even when he looked up he didn't seem to take in what was bearing down on them. For my part I was more enamoured of my rapid progress than of him. Top speed in the confines of that little alleyway in Slough seemed much faster than the same speed out in the open.

At a late stage of my careering progress I recognised Roger Daltrey. By that stage of his life, he had perhaps lost the habit of getting out of the way for anybody. But then so had I. At that speed, a swerve in the Wrigley would have meant capsizement and disaster. The wheelchair and I would be helpless on the pavement, a compound beetle on its back in Slough rather than Prague. A second before impact, Roger must have realised what was about to happen, and leaped backwards with a yell of 'Hooooo!! What's *that*!?' His look of horror as he lurched to safety didn't improve a face that was always rather too craggy for my taste. I do like a smooth face. The sleek will inherit the earth, if I have anything to do with it.

Of course in my way I was star-struck nonetheless, and would have been happy to report to my schoolmates that the great Roger Daltrey had patted my back and thanked me for coming. As it was, I cheekily called, 'Cheers, Rodge – great show' over my shoulder and kept on rolling. 'Over my shoulder' represents not a physical movement but a sort of boomerang trick of vocal projection.

Prince of the pavement

As I left the scene and headed in the direction of the railway station, the exhilaration of being at large in Slough at the controls of the mighty Wrigley took over, and blew away any lingering cobwebs. The juggernaut factor was high. A tune started up in my brain, and not one that I'd heard played at the concert. Not 'Happy Jack', not 'Pictures of Lily', not 'My Generation'. A classic of the 'sixties, nonetheless, with a lazy swagger all its own. Two finger-clicks, and then a crooned, self-satisfied phrase. Not that I could click my fingers even approximately, but I could hear the sound distinctly and visualise it perfectly well. The fingers are braced against each other until the resistance (technically friction) of the skin is suddenly overcome, and the middle finger slams satisfyingly into the palm (though it is the beginning of its journey that makes the noise, not the end). *'{Click} {click} – King of the Road . . .'*

With the Wrigley, though, I was only a prince of the pavement, minor royalty at best. To crown my independence I would need to learn to drive a car.

We say 'clicking your fingers', but the Elizabethans thought of it differently – there's a bit in *Sejanus* about statues of Jove clicking their marble thumbs. Ben Jonson – A-level set book. Obviously you need them both, the middle finger (is it?) and the thumb. Perhaps this mystical percussion was the first fruit of the opposable thumb. Perhaps we came down from the trees communicating by clicking our fingers at each other. Click click: your turn to do the hunter-gathering today. Click click: I did it yesterday. Click click: Say that one more time and I'm going back to my mother.

After she had been so helpful at the concert I could hardly avoid becoming friends with Barbara Broier, despite my prejudice against girls. She was a lovely person.

Barbara told me that she had a pet squirrel. 'What's his name?' I asked, 'Cyril?' 'No,' she said, looking at me as if I was mad, 'he's called Fred.' She had found him injured on the road and had nursed him back to health. I became very matey with her and was finally invited to meet her Polish father.

She lived in Cookham. Barbara was brainy, polite and well spoken, and it followed that her father was gruff and rather alarming. Barbara was not pretty. Those who have put themselves out to be helpful to me have not in general been pretty. When a pretty person has been helpful it has made a deep impression on me, of which I am rather ashamed.

In general terms I feel sorry for pretty people – they're hemmed in by the possibility of losing face, which holds a disproportionate fear for them since they experience it so rarely. As for which is the consolation prize, good looks or independence of mind, I really couldn't say.

Before I was allowed to meet Fred I had to have a chat with Barbara's Dad. He was in a sense the gatekeeper of the squirrel. He had difficulties with the 'r' sound, which I'm sure exists in Polish, so it must have been some sort of impediment. His r's all came out as aspirated g's. He told me a story about a ghoom in Slough – if you gh-ented the ghoom for the night, that was the end of you. Your throat was slit with a ghazor while you slept. Your body fell down a trap-door and was turned into a sausage or even a ghissole. It was the Sweeney Todd legend, essentially, with some variation in the meat products and the scene shifted to our neck of the woods, though I didn't know the original story at the time.

Barbara had said that her dad liked people who stood up to him, and I did my level best. I said that if people didn't insist on eating meat in the first place such murders couldn't be covered up so easily. Just try passing off human flesh in a cheese omelette or an egg salad and see how far you get. Barbara's dad gave a little bark of a laugh at that, and from then on he took a shine to me in quite a big way.

Offer to visitors we don't much like

I liked Fred the squirrel very much, when I was finally shown him, and wanted to touch. Apparently, though, he was likely to bite or scratch, so that aspect of the visit fizzled out. Before I left, though, Mr Broier offered me a glass of tea wine. I'd never heard of wine being made of anything but grapes and was intrigued. It turned out he made it himself. The process involved spreading yeast on a piece of toast and floating it on top of a mixture of tea, lemon and sugar in a bucket, till it fizzed and slowly fell to pieces. More than anything I wanted to see that.

When I got home, even while Dad was driving me home, I started to preach the gospel of home-made wines. I had Mum running to the library to get books, and recruited Dad to make trips to Boots the Chemists for demijohns and airlocks (they had to be glass, not plastic). I put Campden tablets on the shopping list, along with fruit and raisins. Soon we had flagons bubbling away in airing cupboards, for the initial rapid fermentation. Then we transferred them, in the absence of a cellar, to cooler areas on the east side of the house for slow maturing.

I became too impatient to wait for Mrs Pavey to order more advanced books through the library, and started sending off for them myself. I learned that sugar, being a disaccharide, was alien to the human digestive system, so we should convert it (or semi-convert it) to a monosaccharide. I lectured the household in general and Dad in particular about the unhealthiness of sugar. I wasn't happy about the long-term effects of the first batch we made without converting the sugar, about six gallons of it. We decided that it should be labelled 'disaccharide, suspect, o.t.v.w.d.m.l.' The letters stood for 'offer to visitors we don't much like'.

I made experiments. I took sugar in large quantities, added lemon juice and a little water and boiled it at the correct temperature, testing attentively with a jam-maker's sugar thermometer, until everything turned a pale golden colour. All these verbs of action – 'made', 'took', 'added', 'boiled' and so on – represent acts of delegation. I was learning that Dad could be smoothly enrolled into a practical project. He was only uncoöperative when dealing with people directly, without working towards something definite.

I warned him that the cooking process would continue for quite a while after turning off the gas, but he thought he knew best and overcooked the syrup, ending up with a great pan of molasses which he stoically ate on his cereal and drank in his coffee until it was finally all gone and he could look forward to breakfast-time again.

Finally we got it right, decanted the syrup into bottles and used it as our stock. The new semi-inverted sugar refracted light ninety degrees the other way. The first batch of wine made with it seemed miraculous. The syrup dissolved sweetly into the must, fermentation was smooth and very fragrant. The esters floated off the oranges and fruits, and we were all in joy. From that point onwards we really got going, gaining in confidence and also in ambition. We made wine from rose petals, from clover, from nettles, from lettuce, from potatoes, from rhubarb.

We were perfectionists who would never dream of using pectin to clear a cloudy wine (it bonds to the starch and sinks out in the lees). Without pectin it was virtually impossible to clear potato or rice wine, but the trick could be managed with parsnip, if you had the knack. I seemed to have the knack.

My memory of family life is of a constant thwarting, yet when I came up with such a project Mum and Dad would help me to carry it out. Perhaps I really did have some sort of hypnotic ascendancy over them in those years. I wish I'd known – I'd have worked them harder. Half of what I have done in life has come from hypnotising other people. The other half from hypnotising myself.

With Dad in particular I got on better when we had something in hand, something to generate the slow rhythms of companionship. The books had all said 'If you can bear the wait (the hardest part of wine making!) let it mature for two or three years.' For us that was easy. Making wine was the point, not drinking it. We had so much wine by now that we had to store the surplus flagons in the conservatory-greenhouse-sun lounge, where it roiled in slow motion with the dull excitement of fermentation.

Barbara Broier tried to keep me in the swim with school gossip and school crazes, all the things which tended to pass me by. People wouldn't go to the trouble of filling me in. I can't say I missed it. There's something about leaning over a Tan-Sad (or any other disability conveyance) which is mildly shaming to both parties.

There were riddles which passed round the school like verbal measles. Barbara wanted to be sure I developed immunity like everyone else. So she would say, 'This is a good one, John. *Antony and Cleopatra were lying on the floor surrounded by broken glass and water. How did they die?* Let me know if you'd like a clue.'

'Righto, Barbara. Thanks.'

Then she couldn't leave me alone. 'Have you worked it out yet, John?'

'Not yet. But I'm enjoying not being able to work it out.'

'Shall I tell you now?'

'Not yet, if you don't mind.' It became obvious that she did mind. The suspense of keeping me in suspense was more than she could bear. She was bursting with it. 'Tell you what, Barbara. Why don't you tell me another one? That might make you feel better.'

'Then can I tell you the answer to the first one?'

'I suppose so. Is there a time limit? Am I being very stupid?'

'No, John, it's not that. Don't you want to know the answer?'

'Oh yes, but at the moment I'm enjoying the wait.'

'You're impossible. Okay, here's another one. *A man goes into a bar and asks for a glass of water. Instead the bartender produces a gun from behind the counter and points it at him. After a few moments the man says, "Thank you" and goes out. What's going on?*'

'Oh, I like that one. It's even nicer than Antony and Cleopatra.'

'Well, which answer do you want first?'

'At the moment I don't want either, thanks all the same. I've got a lot to think about, what with Antony and Cleopatra and the man in the bar with the glass of water and the gun. Have you noticed, by the way, that there's water and glass in both puzzles?'

'No, John, I haven't noticed and it isn't important.' Then she stalked off, saying rather irritably over her shoulder, 'Let me know if you change your mind.'

I'm not an innocent. I knew exactly how annoying I was being. Of course, negation is the only, rather feeble, form of power available to me, the disadvantage being that I can only use it against people who are actually trying to deal with me, and who might be felt to deserve better. Certainly Barbara Broier deserved better.

Storming the citadel of speech

But there was more to it than that. I wasn't being insincere, though it was intoxicating to see that everyone, potentially, could be strung along. I did enjoy the puzzles as things in themselves. I was almost ready for some Zen koans.

Try to see your original face, the one you had before your parents gave you birth.

The wind is not moving. The banner is not moving. Your mind is moving.

Does your bean curd lose its flavour on the bedpost overnight?

Eventually Barbara came storming up to me and said, 'For heaven's sake, John! Antony and Cleopatra suffocated. They were goldfish! The man in the bar had hiccups – that's why he wanted the glass of water, to cure them. And the shock of the bartender producing a gun cured them anyway – that's why he said Thank You!'

'Yes,' I said, 'I thought it must be something like that.'

'You mean you worked it out, and you've been torturing me all this time?'

'Not exactly,' I said, doing my most maddening impersonation of serenity. 'I just thought it must be something like that.'

The answer to a riddle, like the last chapter of a detective story, is at best a crowning disappointment. The only consolation is to pass the riddle on, so as to relive your disappointment at one remove. Or to read another detective story. In practice everyone agreed with me (once they had heard those riddles' solutions) that they enjoyed the questions more than the answers, but they seemed to think that sooner or later another riddle would have a satisfying solution, as if there was no general rule involved. As far as I could see, though, questions and answers didn't have much of an affinity. You could even say they were natural enemies.

Home wine-making was one thing I discovered at Barbara Broier's house. Another was Victor Borge's 'phonetic punctuation', which the two of us heard one Saturday on Radio 2, as the Light Programme was now called. This was a classic comic routine in which Mr Borge spoke the printer's marks out loud. We loved it, and started to imitate him. We didn't have the original to consult (or a recording), and I imagine there was a certain amount of drift between the acoustic representations we heard that one time on the radio, and our own repertoire of homage. Our full stop (I can't vouch for his) was a popping noise made with the lips, our comma a click of the tongue, our exclamation mark a downward-whistle-and-pop.

This was a party trick well suited to my talents, the tongue being the only muscle in my body that was perfectly obedient. The underlying idea was also vastly appealing, this Peasants' Revolt of underclass marks, the voiceless ones, socially invisible, storming the citadel of speech.

In time, though, it became a compulsion, and my party trick become more like a brush with mental illness. I found it a real effort to leave stops unvoiced, even when answering a teacher's question during a lesson. The return of the repressed isn't a process that is easy to put into reverse. It isn't a straightforward job to put the lid back on Pandora's Box of punctuation, and that little tic took a long time to die down. It helped if I asked Barbara to sit far away from me in class. Then the hysteria had a chance to die down, though our friendship stalled, rather, with what looked like rejection on my part. Sometimes I would get panicky when she spoke to me, for fear that I would erupt again, a displaced Pentecostalist bearing witness to his molten God not in tongues but spoken signs.

A proper cage of rules

When autumn came the family's wine-making activities tailed off, since fermentation became too slow for good results. I looked around for a new project to maintain our momentum, and suggested that Dad occupy his time by growing mushrooms in the greenhouse. 'It'll give a bit of heat to the plants,' I said, 'And the insulating effect will lower our fuel bills.'

Dad might reasonably have answered, 'When did you give a fig for our heating bills, John, with your taste for leaving doors open in all weathers?' Instead he buckled down to become a mushroom farmer.

It was a funny old psychology that he had. He liked to know what he was supposed to do, which was easily managed when he was at work. Inside a proper cage of rules he could be very unyielding – so that my phoning him at work was a tremendous liberty that must be stamped on and prevented from recurring. But at home he had less sense of running on rails, and at the weekends he was almost grateful to have me organise his time. He tried to get me interested in what interested him, but at this stage I was fairly resistant and it's fair to say that the flow of hobbies was more the other way.

Soon I was giving orders, watching him mixing horse dung, straw and organic composting powder, testing the temperature with a hot-bed thermometer. We bought the spawn by mail order from a local farm which advertised in *Exchange & Mart* and even undertook to buy the crop back from us when it was ready. We couldn't lose.

There was great excitement when we saw bits of the peat casing begin to heave with fungal nodes. Everyone went to look in admiration at the little pearls as they grew steadily bigger. We patted ourselves on the back. All that hard work was worth it.

Finally it was time to pick some of our crop and taste them. 'Would you care for some mushrooms, m'dear?' Dad asked, doing a jovial pastiche of what he imagined was Peter's manner at work. 'They're from Chef's own garden.'

'Yes please, Dennis,' said Mum, and then 'I don't think this is a good one, though, dear. Can I try again?' They were none of them good. We couldn't lose – yet somehow we managed it. Something rather ghastly was eating them before we had a chance. Our fungi had funguses of their own.

I scolded Dad for cutting corners with his fungiculture – he had turned the mass too little, he hadn't been particular enough about the temperature of the hotbed, which was crucial. This can't have been much fun for him. Mum joined in with me in what must have been a horrendous alliance. To be hen-pecked and chick-pecked simultaneously, what a fate.

I was already firmly established as the family's telephone wheedler, and I got on the phone to the farm. 'I'm afraid there's something gone wrong with our crop – do you want to come and inspect it?' Suppressed panic leaked down the line. The response was very clear: *Don't for God's sake bring them here!*

Dad said he didn't see the harm in us paying a visit. Privately I thought we would be as welcome as Blind Pew at the Admiral Benbow, primed to pass on the Black Spot to poor Billy Bones, but I also thought it might be fun to make them sit up and take notice. We took a few of our stricken mushrooms with us, though we left them politely in the car. We were relying quite a bit on the 'knock' effect of the wheelchair. The chair always knocked people back, and then they tended to lose track of their normal behaviour patterns.

Knock knock! Who's there? Abel. Abel who? Able-bodied dismay. I asked the farmer if there was any medicine we could administer to our defective mushrooms.

'Um . . . There's powder I could give you.'

'Will that work?'

'No. I'm not hopeful. Best to dispose of them carefully and start again from scratch.'

All the same, they gave us a huge tray of mushrooms to compensate for the failure of our crop. This was a very welcome knock-on effect of our visit. We were many pounds of mushrooms to the good, though the truth was that we none of us cared all that much for mushrooms. It was the activity that was important, the uniting fever of a hobby, and the mushrooms, like the wine we made, were a sort of side-effect, almost a nuisance which we would have done without if we'd been able.

When both of us enjoyed the product as well as the process, though, we made quite a team. I privately claimed credit for having made the conservatory happen, but I have to give Dad his due in matters of siting and temperature control. He knew what he was doing. The dry, desert half of the conservatory was for Mum, of course, but also cacti (mainly grown from seed) and *Drosophyllum*s to boot, though the first few batches didn't seem too happy. It's a temperamental plant, though, everyone knows that. The dry bit of the conservatory had a door into the garden for when it grew too hot, even for Mum.

The damp greenhousy part, which was kept shadier, had no external door. There was plenty of sun both morning and evening, with shade being provided by the trees, carefully pruned to allow a rich flow of air under their branches and over the greenhouse top. Just the sort of conditions your *Cymbidium* orchid is partial to. Moving patches of sunlight generated a really nice tropical fug, ideal for drosera, sarracenias and (even if it was just the once) an Australian *byblis* which Dad raised from seed.

It all worked beautifully, even if *Drosophyllum* wasn't persuaded yet. I would have liked to convey my appreciation to Dad, but compliments were never really part of our currency, in either direction.

An anarchist commune for seeds

Even after the mushroom débâcle I hadn't altogether lost my touch with Dad. It made sense to go on pressurising him for things, just to keep in practice for when it was really important. In one of his *Telegraph*s, probably a Sunday one, I saw an advertisement for an eiderdown called the Margaret Erskine Dream-Cloud. There was a splendid picture illustrating the virtues of the product. It showed a girl ensconced under her eiderdown, warm as toast, radiantly smiling, despite the ice blocks surrounding her, which seemed to crimp the crust-edges of a strawberry-apple-girl pie.

I wanted a Dream-Cloud immediately. It was the perfect solution to my odd combination of needs, my love of fresh air in all seasons and weather coupled with this body's intolerance of cold. There were various levels of insulating excellence, with goose down at the top. That's what I wanted, goose down and nothing less, and I wore Dad down, though he did some bargaining of his own. It was finally agreed that the Dream-Cloud represented two birthdays and one Christmas. Dad said, 'You'd just better promise that you'll make it last.' That was just like him, to save face by taking a hard line – even after he had caved in.

I read and re-read *Gardening for Adventure*, from its first page to the last, and the ones after that. I've always had a particular fondness for indexes, bibliographies and postscripts – everything that publishers call 'back matter'. *Gardening for Adventure* had something I myself had lacked for some years now, an Appendix, which listed suppliers of plants. Number 17 on the list of 35 was Major V. F. Howell, of Firethorn, Oxshot Way, Cobham, Surrey. There were other suppliers relatively near, but I have to admit I was attracted by the idea of ordering plants from a Major.

Majors have popped up at the edge of my life from time to time – starting with the Air Force colleague and friend of Dad's, Kit Draper, who was officially known as the Mad Major. All of them have been somewhat eccentric, though I doubt if the rank of Major actively generates quirks. More likely it's the highest military position compatible with independence of mind.

I wrote to Major Howell asking for his terms of business. When he wrote back I felt that my choice of him had immediately been vindicated. His 'catalogue' was made up of sheets of foolscap paper. There was an introductory paragraph, and then a bald list of the Latin names of plant seeds he had in stock, typed in capital letters. Major Howell's seed exchange was totally egalitarian. Seeds were seeds were seeds were seeds. Common grass seed might sit next to the most exotic orchids, and the strychnine tree be cheek by jowl with meadowsweet – but only if their alphabetical position dictated that arrangement. In Major Howell's pages, breeding meant nothing, family meant nothing, and size meant nothing. CYMBIDIUM and COCOS NUCIFERA were in hailing distance of one another on the page, although *Cymbidium* is an orchid plant with seed so fine it blows away at the slightest puff of wind, travelling almost infinitely far, and *Cocos nucifera* is a monster.

This was not a conventional business at all but something described as a 'seed exchange', a loving and utopian project. We were already living in the Age of Aquarius, though we didn't yet know it. Rumours trickled across the Atlantic with the news that on the New York stage naked performers mixed with the audience at the end of a show called *Hair*, and in Surrey a military man was running a commercial enterprise as if it was some sort of anarchist commune for seeds.

I passed the list across to Dad, who read through it closely before declaring, 'The chap's obviously potty. Take this item, for heaven's sake . . .' – he pointed out a name on the list – 'it's so darn common I only have to open the kitchen window and lean out and it's almost in the palm of my hand. And *Cocos nucifera* . . . Have you any idea what that is?'

'Is it a kind of palm?'

'Not bad, not bad,' Dad said. '*Cocos nucifera* is a coconut. Nothing more, nothing less. Why buy a coconut from this chappie? I can get a coconut in Maidenhead!'

'I think . . .' I said, instinctively defending the Major's eccentricities, 'the Major is referring to the fact that it may be a mere coconut, but that doesn't stop it being a seed. Why should the poor coconut be banned from a seed-list? A seed is what it is. Aren't you always telling me not to make the mistake of despising a plant because it's common?'

Dad just grunted, but soon his eye fell on something more interesting. There were some fascinating items on the list, in among the common grasses and fairground prizes. There were plenty of *Drosera* species which we didn't have, and soon we were making a shopping list of our own. Dad decided that we shouldn't deprive ourselves of some interesting specimens just because the man was potty. Major Howell had converted me instantly, but it took Dad a little longer to come round. He came to mock and stayed to fill in an order form. Soon the Cromers, father and son, were regular customers.

The introductory paragraph of the list explained how the system operated. All seeds in the list were equal, and as far as Major Howell was concerned one item could never be more (or less) equal than any other item – even if one was the size of a cannonball and the other a sprinkling of dusty spores. So you could choose whichever seed you wanted. As far as I remember these were the rules:

Seeds shall be ordered in units. A UNIT shall be six packets of seed plus a GRATIS specimen. A customer who orders two units shall be entitled to a third GRATIS unit, as well as the GRATIS specimens included in the units themselves.

If you have seed which is not in the list, you may exchange it for any item in the list when ordering one or more units. Major Howell does not give cash for seeds.

A packet of seeds (which might contain many seeds, or a few, or just one, depending on size and rarity) cost 5d, so that each unit cost 3/-. It was all splendidly idealistic but also terribly practical. Dad and I ordered two units from the list. I tried to scribble '*Cocos nucifera*' on the form while he wasn't looking, but furtiveness is not my forte and he found me out. He wouldn't wear it. 'Besides,' he added, 'I hope you realise that the old boy has to pay postage costs. In his eyes all seeds may be equal, but I doubt if the GPO will see it that way. Coconuts are heavy items. It will be expensive and inconvenient for him. And I know exactly why you're trying this on. You enjoy creating maximum inconvenience with everything you do. That's you all over, John! But not this time.' I don't think my psychology was really so complicated. I hadn't wanted *Cocos nucifera* in the first place until I was told I couldn't have it. Then it became a project and the thing I wanted above all others. It's a mental mechanism which has served me well, all in all – it got me walking, didn't it?

When I looked wounded, Dad suggested that we add an extra packet of *Drosera* seed to our order. Trying to get around the rules paid the usual dividends.

I can't say Dad was entirely wrong about me. I was always experimenting, taking things to their limit. Wherever I was I would try to turn my surroundings into a laboratory, whether I was making soapsuds from nowhere in CRX, performing mantras in toilets or creating mouth-vacuums in school-issue Bic Biro pens in Vulcan so that the ink got everywhere. There are only so many ways I can play, and this is one of the best. And to be even fairer than fair, to be fair to myself now that I've been fair to Dad, I think that he was a little blind in rejecting *Cocos nucifera* out of hand. It wasn't long before we learned that botanic samples of the seed are very different from the cultivars in the supermarkets.

Over that tantalising ledge

The seeds arrived. They nearly all germinated. The *Drosera* did particularly well, and soon we had the beginnings of an impressive collection. We were encouraged to order a packet of *Drosophyllum Lusitanicum*, the Portuguese Sundew, the uncoöperative Holy Grail of our carnivorous plant-rearing. Good seed added to Dad's refined gardening technique produced astounding results, and Major Howell's name began to smell like a rose.

If there was a slow submarine detonation in progress underneath the whole established culture, then the ripples had lapped against my wheelchair and I too was restless. In terms of doing things for myself my best bet, perhaps my only chance, was independent motion, even if that meant also losing Broyan. I would have to learn to drive. The Wrigley was all very well for getting me to the railway station and the concert venue, and for menacing pop stars, but I needed a bigger engine if I was to reach escape velocity.

This is a standard teenage urge, but in my case it couldn't be fulfilled in a series of gradual stages. My fellows faced a smooth ramp of choices – driving lessons, borrowing the family car, finally getting their own. I, though, would have needed stilts to reach the pedals of the family car. I would have to do the whole thing in a single mighty flying leap, and I would need my own vehicle from the word go.

Or the word stop. Mum, being a non-driver herself, was likely to be discouraging. Dad was unpredictable, but certainly couldn't afford to buy me a car. I would have to organise an embassy to Granny.

The whole family seemed to be a complex mechanism for frustrating desires – like the machines at fairgrounds which Peter had always liked so much, aligning the mechanical grab directly over a desired trinket, so that it couldn't miss, and then pressing a button, and watching as it did. Or glass cases full of pennies stacked so thickly on ledges that a payout was inevitable. Trustingly Peter would send penny after penny down the chute to trigger the avalanche that never came. And now, despite my poor coördination, it was my turn to work the family machine, to send the grab down towards the elusive prize of a car, or push the necessary funds over that tantalising ledge. If there was no jackpot there could be no driving licence, and my life would never broaden out from the straits I was in.

I thought of making my eighteenth birthday the occasion for an extraordinary appeal to Granny – except that she didn't really recognise the pressure of the calendar. It was actually better to steer clear of landmarks such as birthdays and Christmas, and to give her a stronger sense of her own arbitrary grace. The scratching of the pen in her chequebook made a red-letter day all by itself.

Birthdays had always seemed a bit hollow to me also, if only because mine was always overshadowed by Christmas. Then the last days of 1967 showed me a further deterioration of the festival. Mum was determined to mark the occasion, not with a present but with an attempt to pass on a legacy: her own ancient injuries.

On my big day Mum sat me down and told me something she'd been told in a similarly formal manner. By 'sat me down' I mean formally commandeered the wheelchair and manœuvred me into the sitting room. It's to her credit that she let the birthday unfold a little way before she took centre stage and made her announcement. She could have pinned me down in the bed at first light and passed on the trauma tidings – trauma for her, no more than casual interest for me. I chose the womb, and the womb has its own attachments, which aren't mine.

Before she said anything she offered me a drink. That was standard practice for birthdays – it was family custom, enlightened or corrupt as you choose to look at it, to allow us, when we had passed a minimum age, a drink and a smoke on birthdays. One drink and one cigarette. And not just your own birthday, but any birthday in the family, so Peter too would be given his own ration, invited to splice the mainbrace. This, though, was different.

Live coal burning her tongue

Mum took ages to get going. How hard is it to say 'Happy Birthday, John'? Not hard. There was miles of 'I don't know quite how to say this' and 'I've never found it an easy thing to talk about' before she started to come out with anything significant at all.

'Your grandfather Ivo, my father' – and already there was a sort of gulp invading those phrases – 'went out to East Africa in the 1920s to make his fortune coffee farming. That was where the money was to be made.' This much I knew. Families have histories. People seem to enjoy being ruled by them. Grandpa's people weren't rich, he had married above himself in that way, and this was his chance to equalise things. 'Then while he was away, your grandmother my mother' – these tags of kinship received a much harsher intonation – 'had a . . . love affair with one of the local squires. A great love affair.' I think Mum had left space for a mocking laugh for this point in her speech, but it didn't quite come off. The bitterness in her voice was too stark to be laughed away.

This was certainly new. Not exactly what I wanted for my birthday, but still, a surprise. Not to be sniffed at, though hardly riveting. As she moved towards the parts of the story she found unbearable, she fought to control herself, leaving big pauses and looking right past me. She was making some sort of impersonation of female pluck, as we know it from films of the 1940s. Greer Garson, Celia Johnson – and now Laura Cromer, refusing the easy release of tears. 'When her husband returned, my mother was pregnant.

'Pregnant with me.

'These things happen, of course – they always have. But they tend to be hushed up.

'No hushing-up was done in this case.

'In the Father column on my birth certificate my mother put the truth. She had the name of her lover entered, not the name of the man she was married to. She wasn't going to give the world the satisfaction of making her lie. And she wasn't going to spare me the shame that bothered her so little. Luckily' – and here there was a laugh that did more or less come off – 'Ivo had lost his shirt in East Africa. His hair was still dark, she told me, but his moustache had turned white.' Many families have these tales of follicles blasted by shock, fate's lightning earthed by the roots of the hair.

'Anyway, after his little adventure in the coffee business he didn't have a bean. He was in no position to dictate terms. He depended on his wife's financial resources. He wasn't a hero. I suppose he wasn't a fool. He must have thought – better a cuckold than a bankrupt.

'Better to have a bastard being brought up in your house, even one that everyone knows about, than debts that everyone knows about. Mummy's people cut her allowance to the bone for some years, they never quite cut her off.

'They punished her. They said she had made her bed and must lie in it, but they didn't disown her. Perhaps they even noticed that there was someone else involved who had to lie in a bed she hadn't chosen. That was me.

'They have provided for me in their way, but I was never made welcome. I never felt I was part of the family, and I didn't know why until I came of age. Then my mother was kind enough to tell me. And now I'm telling you. Now you know what my family is like.'

This was all fairly interesting, but it didn't shake me to the core or even blight my birthday. Mum had even cheated a bit. Granny had spoiled her twenty-first birthday, not her eighteenth. From anyone else's point of view, this was all ancient history, a grate of cold ashes, fully raked over, but it was still a live coal in Mum's mouth, burning her tongue, and she couldn't wait another three years to spit it out. She accepted me as an adult ahead of schedule, even if it was only to load me down with the family secrets.

I couldn't feel particularly upset. If I had chosen Mum's womb, hadn't she chosen Granny's? We both had a chance to read the fine print, between lives. There's plenty of time. I asked, out of politeness really, 'Did you ever see your real father?'

'Sometimes. In church. Obviously he'd always known who I was. I only knew about him when my mother told me the story. After that I could feel him not looking at me. If you mean did we ever have a conversation about it, then no. Nothing more than Hello and How are you? I called him Uncle Arthur.' She looked at me a little flatly. Neither of us had touched our drink. 'I expect you need some time to take this all in.'

I didn't think I did. I'd already taken it in, more or less. I had disappointed Mum with the evenness of my reaction. She had dropped her bombshell on the appointed day, and it had been something of a dud. The trauma fizzled, though I managed not to say, 'Is that all?' When Dad came in she said, 'I've just been telling John about "Uncle Arthur",' and he only said, 'Oh yes?', as if this might be someone from her sewing circle. Dad was very good at letting things pass without comment, letting them more or less blow through him, and for once I followed his lead.

I don't even remember what Mum gave me for my birthday that year – her real present was that conversation. She was issuing a sort of certificate of damage. It was official, now, that she had never had a chance of happiness, but I honestly didn't see what it all had to do with me.

There was poignance, of course, in Mum's status. The child of a great love, not greatly loved herself. Much was explained about her – her unending quest to be accepted by her own mother, her eagerness to get married, properly married in church and to acquire the respectability of a wife, since she had been cheated of it as a daughter. I understood better now the way Granny seemed to glide on warm and lofty currents, while Mum was always frantically flapping the middle air.

The period of impoverishment, coinciding with her early life, had obviously left its mark. It was like the period of starvation in the womb when a mother is deprived of nutrients, leaving her fœtus underdeveloped. Granny hung on to her sense of entitlement, but absolutely failed to pass it on.

There was more to the story, which I gradually pieced together. After the coffee fiasco my grandfather Ivo (though of course he wasn't actually my grandfather) laid siege to the marital bed. He laid the ghost of Uncle Arthur, and that was the beginning of Roy.

When there was a legitimate son as well as an illegitimate daughter, mother love was poured out till it ran over. On darling Roy. Not because of his legitimacy, I don't think, though I dare say Granny appreciated the neatness of the stitching which repaired the family's ravelled hem. Everything looked more or less conventional again, and her family's allowance was restored to its original value.

It's just that Granny, from her first breath to her last, preferred men to women, boys to girls. Even if Laura had been loved in the cradle she would have been abandoned in the nursery, when Roy came along to take all the love that was going.

Mum and Roy chose the same womb, but Roy had the better sense of timing. It was a different place by the time he occupied it. As between the claims of a girl who was the child of her great love and a boy – any boy – there would never really be a contest, in Granny's eyes. Mum had done nothing wrong. She just couldn't do anything right.

Granny made things worse by taking in a local boy during the war. There would never be enough boys, and perhaps there was one girl too many already. I began to understand Mum's passionate desire for a daughter, to show at least one female soul that she was welcomed, even if the idyll with Audrey hadn't quite worked out like that.

After the birthday briefing I wasn't supposed to think of Granny as anything but monstrous. Of course she was monstrous! But the nerve it must have taken, to insist on the truth being put down on that official piece of paper. To testify against herself in that stubborn way, insisting on disgrace.

The seeming slope of time

Mum's sense of unbelonging was the great business of her life, but it wasn't going to be mine. I wouldn't let that happen. Never mind that I didn't exactly know what the great business of my life was.

You can't be traumatised by a history whose reality you don't accept. I wasn't yet an informed Hindu, but I had cottoned on to a fundamental concept. Blood isn't thicker than water. Blood is only water carrying a particular charge of deluded affinity.

If I'm not tempted to repeat the family mistakes, there's still a real danger of repeating mistakes made in a previous life. In Hinduism, where there are always (thank God) technical terms for spiritual things, these are called *vasanas*. Ruts of the spirit, liable to churn up the clean sand of a new existence. How can you avoid them if you don't know what they are? You have to work backwards, deductively, from your temptations. It's not an exact science, obviously. If you're bossy in your current life, for instance, this may mean that you were the same way in earlier flesh, or that you were completely under someone's heel – hence the current overcompensation.

If by a great stroke of luck you're both powerless and bossy as things stand, then perhaps you're being given a chance to dismantle your ego's engine completely in these highly propitious circumstances. A brief glance is enough to show that the 'engine' is connected only to the horn, and to the indicators – indicators which only signal a change of direction after the event, feebly claiming credit for having caused it. There's nothing under the bonnet. The steering wheel is as irrelevant as the one on a toy car in a fairground ride. Fixed or wildly spinning, it turns nothing. The whole incarnate vehicle slips serenely on free wheels down the seeming slope of time.

In practice, even before I was able to line up actual driving lessons, I clung to my dummy steering wheel as tightly as anyone. I couldn't trust my guru enough to abandon the I-am-the-doer illusion. My will was all I trusted. I hadn't learned that life is a stolid nag that clops indifferently on, whatever we imagine we're doing with the whip and the reins. It's one of Maya's favourite tricks, her impersonation of a frisky filly to be mastered.

Let the reins go, and there's every chance you'll be bucked into bliss. Hinduism recognises that the last moments of a life have a crucially determining rôle as regards the next. Serenity at the moment of death may not guarantee escape from the cycle of birth and death, but at the very least it greases the wheels for the next go-round and leads to reconciled babies who sleep through the night and hardly cry.

Poor Mum still couldn't do anything right, even when she was trying to set the record straight. She hadn't managed to condemn Granny in my eyes, as she must have hoped. Clearly *Pamela*, all thousand-plus pages of it, wasn't a complete guide to the behaviour of the posh and wayward of the 1920s, but it was the closest thing I had, and it did paint a picture of a world in which the odds were stacked against women. Granny wasn't having that. She flouted the conventions of her day and her class without consenting to be martyred by her own rebellion. She had taken a lover and kept a husband.

I don't know about the ingredients of her motive for having Mum officially registered as an outcast. Was she obsessed with a man she couldn't have, or only with getting her revenge on him? The woman I knew as Granny certainly had a talent for settling scores. Or to put it another way – she trusted antagonism as a sort of bedrock for relationships. It wouldn't let her down.

I'm tempted to see the business with the birth certificate as a sort of one-woman suicide pact – a willed social death that was supposed to take her lover with her, dragging the squire down into the sucking bog of disgrace. She signed her own death warrant on that piece of paper, and then she survived after all, her head above water even if she was floating at a lower level than before. Her luck held, when it turned out she had nothing to fear from her husband. Slowly she came back to respectable life, even to prosperity, and it was only Laura who was left out in the cold and wet.

Perhaps in church, when Mum could feel her real father not looking at her during services, he was really not-looking at Granny. Or perhaps he glared at her during the sermon. I can imagine Granny enjoying that.

Whatever she was in church for, it was hardly the spiritual experience. I dare say she was putting in an appearance out of sheer defiance, as a way of saying, I'm as good as anyone here. I have a right.

It's true that in later life she went to early Communion in Tangmere whenever it was offered, but her agenda was strongly earthbound. She wasn't so much consuming the Body and Blood of her Redeemer as keeping an eye on the set of communion plate she had given the church, in her husband's respectable name, after he died. She never really trusted anyone else's cleaning. So when she knelt at the altar rail her posture was submissive, but if she saw any discoloration of chalice or paten there would be harsh words in the vestry afterwards. It's customary for communicants to close their eyes when they consume the elements, but convention wasn't going to make Granny turn a blind eye to tarnish.

Mum expected me to send Granny to Coventry after her revelations, but that was hardly likely to happen. I wouldn't have made an immediate appointment with Granny out of spite, but I wasn't going to penalise her either, for things that were none of my business. There was no alternative to Granny as the motor of the family finances. No one else was going to help me buy a car. My hands were tied. I had to be in the driving seat.

Bird gotta swim, fish gotta fly. John needs driving lessons to fall from the sky . . .

The next time an invitation came for Peter and me to eat at the Compleat Angler, I decided I would get to work on Granny on the car angle. Peter and I had become more or less used to such hybrids of treat and ordeal. We had learned at least some of the rules, though of course Granny could always come up with new ones. She was a living workshop for the manufacture of social stumbling-blocks.

Granny had recently revised her opinion of Peter. It was Granny who had first proposed that he work as a waiter ('the world will always need waiters, Peter'), but it wasn't his new part-time job which had earned her respect. All he had done was have a growth spurt, but that was enough.

Only the year before she hadn't trusted Peter to cross the road by himself, which would have been funny if it wasn't so embarrassing. Wasn't it supposed to be the other way round, he asked me, young men helping frail old ladies across the street? But now she couldn't get over how tall he'd grown, and kept on saying what a fine figure of a man he had turned out to be. She even started stooping while she was walking with him, to make him even prouder of his new stature.

I'm not sure Peter really enjoyed the fuss, but he certainly got a kick out of being taller than Dad. Dad who claimed five foot eleven but was short of Peter's attested five ten. I was a non-starter in this particular race, but I too enjoyed the twinge of superannuation in Dad's shoulders.

Perhaps it was to celebrate Peter's spurt that Granny offered us a drink on this occasion. By this time, as the birthdays rolled by, Peter and I had sampled most things from the family's scanty drinks cupboard. They were all pretty awful, except for liqueurs which could have proper tastes like coffee, peppermint, even chocolate. Otherwise sweet sherry was the best of a bad lot, until I discovered vodka. Vodka had hardly any character of its own, but was a sort of chameleon which could bring out other flavours. Added to BritVic Orange it provided a good imitation of the much missed Government Orange, the wonderful concentrated juice drink of my childhood.

I knew alcohol was supposed to have a physical effect, but the single measures meted out on birthdays had no effect in my case. They were a complete waste of money. A double vodka did a little something. That was the ticket for me.

So I asked the waiter for a double vodka, and Peter chose sherry. Granny added 'Dry,' before he had a chance to say 'Sweet'. Granny wanted us to order in French, saying this would improve Peter's skills as a waiter – it was clear she had never eaten at the Spade Oak Hotel, where he worked. I managed better than Peter and was praised. He was told he could do worse than model his accent on mine. I don't think she was trying to open a rift between us in any specific way. She just couldn't help herself. As if he needed any reasons to hate me! Or would have needed any, if there had been hatred in him.

Poor Peter became more and more subdued as the meal progressed, while John, deliciously inflamed by vodka, really got into the swing of things. He chuffed out his feathers like a budgie on Granny's finger.

I was trying to think how to turn the conversation towards driving lessons (and all that they entailed) when Granny got her oar in first. 'I wonder, John,' she said, 'if you would care to visit me again next week? We can have a private chat.'

Peter said, 'I expect I can get time off again, Granny.'

'You shouldn't try,' said Granny. 'It's not good to expect special treatment.' As if she had ever expected anything else! 'The world is work, Peter, and you'll be working then. John, you should be able to negotiate the Angler on your own by now. There's only the one small step.'

I understood. Granny was a mind-reader and wanted to spare me the embarrassment of asking a favour in front of Peter. My system still throbbed with vodka in our (non-Broyan) taxi home. I decided that Granny was great fun, even adorable. One of a kind. I enjoyed the grown-up part I was playing, and felt sorry about the bad press she had from Mum and Dad. Why couldn't people make allowances and get along?

Peter must have had the patience of a saint. I failed to notice the cranking up of Granny's trap. I strolled right into it, like the fool in the Waite Tarot deck who saunters to his downfall without a care in the world.

At home I carried on in the same vein, hoping to educate the family. You didn't need to play silly games with Granny, just be yourself unto the end and she would be with you all the way. Mum told Dad that I really did seem to have a way with Granny, some sort of knack. I smiled a little bashfully and said there was nothing to it, really. Piece of cake.

Without Granny, after all, there would have been no Wrigley, and no extension to Trees for that matter. Yet Mum wouldn't admit she had ever done the right thing by her. I pressed her on this point, and reluctantly she admitted that Granny knew how to make Christmas special, not just for the boys she welcomed into the house but also for the girl who had no other address.

Small world of chocolate

The children would write their wishes on pieces of tissue paper and then put them in the fire. Somehow Father Christmas always got the message and left exactly the right thing. One year Mum had asked for 'a chocolate dolly in a chocolate bed', and she had got it. Granny must have taken a lot of trouble to find such a specific item. Perhaps she even had it made, going to the top man in the small world of chocolate sculpture commissions. Disappointment was not something Granny would accept at Christmas time, or any other.

'But how did Granny work the trick?' I asked. 'How did she work out what you had written on the tissue paper?'

Mum went rather red and said, 'She told us that Father Christmas could read all the languages in the world as long as they were spelled properly. So we showed her what we'd written to make sure of the spelling.' That blush told me that she was ashamed of her own gullibility. It had been a long time after the event that she saw through the sleight and the magic. And after that perhaps Granny's credit was cancelled, and she was severely debited for the deception, even in the good cause of a happy Christmas.

As my lunch appointment with Granny came near, I felt sorry for Peter's being excluded, but it made sense for Granny to arrange a private audience. We were the ones who were on a wave-length of honesty and trust. We could see beyond trivial distractions.

Granny greeted me warmly on the day, but when with the help of my crutch and cane I made to edge towards the bar, where we had taken our drinks before, she spoke up.

'I wouldn't wander off too far,' she said, 'now that you don't have Peter to help you. We shall go straight to our reserved table – do you see? They have given us a window seat with a direct view of the weir. How very thoughtful of the management!' Any management which didn't fall in with Granny's preferences was not just thoughtless but reckless. She pushed me firmly to the table indicated.

The menus arrived. Granny opened one and handed it directly to me. She pointed a finger firmly at one page rather than the other. 'Tonight, John, you will order from the *table d'hôte*. Granny is not being ungenerous – it's a matter of style. You may make your selection *à la carte* on any future occasion, on two conditions. You must be able to read your choice aloud in an accent that doesn't shame me, and you must be able to carry on a brief conversation in French with the waiter. The waiters here are invariably charming, and it is good manners to meet them half-way. The last time you treated me to your French conversation it was clear that you need to put in more work. Ah yes, I anticipate an objection! Not all the waiters here are in point of fact French. Indeed the most accomplished is Spanish. The objection has no merit. All waiters speak French. French is the language of good food.'

Lunch was turning out strangely. I had been steered away from the bar on specious grounds, and now Granny's commanding finger had skimmed over the list of drinks, past the temptations of *à la carte* and onto the set menu. I didn't mind the restriction of choice in terms of food – I would be plumping for the omelette as usual – but I was puzzled. What could be the matter with Granny?

I thought I understood. She was well into her seventies, not far from eighty. The mind no longer young, softening behind the steely manner – she had forgotten that I was old enough to drink. And after all, directness was the best policy with Granny. Hadn't I preached a sermon on that text only a little while ago? I said I'd like to start with a small drink.

There were two swans on the river near the weir. They were so still they could have been cast in wax. Peter had told me about a cookery demonstration he had seen once, at which the teacher had made a swan out of molten sugar in the seconds before it hardened, an object hardly less magical than the real thing. I could see little pieces of wood being sucked toward the miniature waterfall of the weir, but the swans seemed unaffected by the current. They must have been paddling their feet like mad beneath the water in order to stay so still . . . which was the true swan, the serene upper gliding or the churning below?

Granny watched the frozen swans with me for a minute, then rapped on the table with her knuckle to attract my attention. The smile with which she had greeted me at the Otel was even bigger now. I had experienced some sort of warning twinge when I saw that first smile – surely Granny never normally smiled like that? Now it had grown alarmingly, and I knew it expressed something at odds with welcome.

'I am so glad you have brought up the subject of alcoholic drink,' she said. 'I'm afraid I'd become so engrossed in watching the swans that I hardly remembered you were here.

'No, John. You cannot have a drink. And nor can you on our next visit.

'You see, on your last visit you ordered a double vodka. Now, ordering a double vodka – a double anything! – is not the way it is done. One does not specify a portion. I myself do not order six ounces of lamb chop and two hundred peas. If there are supplementary questions to be asked, the waiter will address them – that is the whole idea behind their training. The waiter will ask me how I want my chop cooked and I will tell him. Another time, perhaps, you will order a vodka with tonic, and the waiter will give you your choice of measures. That is the civilised time to announce your dipsomaniac preference. Then and not a moment before.

'Some Grannies would have chastened you at the time, so as to nip the habit in the bud. However it would not have been nice for you to feel humiliation in front of the waiter, and of course Peter was there too, and I have never been one to intimidate . . .'

The weight of a stolen crumb

Granny's image faded in front of me and I felt my face going bright red. I hated sodding strong drinks, hated sodding Grannies (and Mums and Dads for knowing better), and I hated sodding Otels like the Compleat Angler. I knew that the real reason she had arranged for Peter not to be there was that he would stand up for me. I wouldn't have put it past him to push me from the scene, even at the loss of a perfectly cooked steak. But Granny picked her fights with care, and stage-managed the bouts to the moment of knockout. Now she had me where she wanted me.

Twigs and straws went on rushing down the weir, and the swans just continued to be – *ser* rather than *estar*, in Spanish terms, inhabiting their essences. My eye drifted down to the sash window near our seat, where there was a gap which delivered a welcome breeze to my overheated cheek. A few ants were scurrying back and forth through it, having found a source of food. They had little bundles on their backs. At that moment I would have given anything to swap places with them, trembling with effort beneath the weight of a stolen crumb. The sound of Granny's voice came back. She was saying,

'So I hope, John, that for the remainder of your life you will never again degrade yourself by ordering a double vodka – or a double anything for that matter . . .'

She was a mind-reader all right. She knew I wanted something from her, even if she didn't know exactly what it was, so there was no risk of her over-playing her hand. She couldn't help herself, any more than a spider can ignore a trembling from the web just because it happens to be the birthday of the fly in question.

I decided my only dignified course was passive resistance. I would ignore Granny. I wouldn't eat and I wouldn't drink. She would find that her lunch guest today was Gandhi in person instead of her rather crushable grandson. When the waiter came and asked if we were ready to order, I went on contemplating the swans. I would live on air, I would eat less than an ant. Granny chose an omelette on my behalf, seeming quite untroubled by my silence, but the moment we were alone again she said sharply, 'There is nothing I dislike so much as rudeness to staff. It is always unnecessary.'

When the food arrived she made the traditional little road across her plate, and I made no road of any sort. Granny apologised to the waiter when he collected our plates, saying that I wasn't feeling well. She said, 'I hope at least that they don't make you eat what he has left!', but this wasn't one of her regular attendants, and he gave her a puzzled look.

Sitting in the Wrigley, while (on the astral plane) I spun cotton to weave a *lungi* in true Gandhi style, I reflected that if Granny had in fact been sensible enough to order two ounces of lamb chop and fifty peas then she wouldn't have wasted so much food, and our waiter would have been spared some enigmatic banter.

Granny's voice broke in on me. 'John, I suggest you choose a dessert for yourself, otherwise you can go home immediately. I never imagined you would be so mulish. All I have done is give you a lesson in good manners, which will pay dividends if taken to heart. At the very least you can speak to me. Mostly I enjoy our conversations.' Too bad, I thought. She who pays the piper calls the tune. When everything she hears has been put on for her benefit then perhaps she will miss the real unrehearsed thing.

A single puddle of beige

Granny ploughed on. 'A young man should have something to say for himself, and I never thought you would be backward in that regard. You seemed positively eager to join me today, and I hope you are not so far gone that you need the lubricating effects of alcohol before you can chat with a grandmother who has been, I believe, of some use to you in the past.'

'I'm just not hungry, Granny.'

'Well, John, to save the appearances I suggest that you order ice cream for dessert. Then if you still don't want to eat, it will simply melt, making it less obvious to the world at large that you are being childishly fractious. I will be spared other people's knowledge that I have shared my luncheon with a very uncoöperative relation. I prefer to do without the sympathy of strangers, which has no value.'

Together we watched the ice cream melt. The Compleat Angler happened to be serving Neapolitan ice on that particular day, so the picture on my plate was of layered colours, pink and brown and white, losing their distinctness as their temperature rose to that of the room. I wasn't sufficiently informed about physical law to know how long it would take, assuming that we both stayed in place to watch, for the stripes to turn into a single puddle of beige.

'Shortly, John,' Granny said, 'I shall be ordering coffee for us both. If you don't take at least a sip of coffee – and the coffee here is no disgrace to the rest of the menu, whatever your father might think – then there is really nothing left to say. I will be sorry to break off my dealings with you, but I have made hard decisions in the past and stuck by them. It would be a mistake to call my bluff. Stubbornness is bravery of a sort, John, but it is a bravery turned against yourself.'

The meal had taken a very miserable turn. When I had locked horns with Marion Wilding, sole principal of Vulcan School, I had been prepared for confrontation and I had been clear about what I wanted from her – nothing. I had even enjoyed the clash. This was different. Granny and I were on the opposite of a collision course. If neither of us bent then we would dismiss each other from our lives with a finality not to be taken back. I began to get a sense of the suddenness of schism, crisis that no one saw coming until it had already undone the seams of the world.

The bitterness of it was that I did want something from Granny. I needed a car, and the lessons which I must have before I could tame it. If I broke with Granny, then I was stuck with Mum and Dad and the suffocation of dependency. This wasn't just about vodka and counting peas, ice cream and coffee. Homeric geography had put in an appearance in a hotel dining room in Marlow, Scylla and Charybdis bursting up through thick carpeting. If I wasn't dashed against the harsh rock of Granny's willpower, then I was doomed to the sludge-whirlpool of life in Bourne End. And from my storm-tossed barque I was counting on the implacable Granitic rock to cough up an outboard motor, so that I could skim away from the entire dismal scene. Why would it want to provide that?

Still, if we were trembling on the brink of rupture, neither of us took a step either further or back. If this was High Noon at the Compleat Angler, at least no one was in a hurry to shoot first. Then Granny found a way to negotiate without either party having to back down. She picked up her spoon and stirred her black coffee. Then she turned the spoon upside down over her diminutive cup, took the cream jug and poured from it carefully over that dainty inverted scallop so that the cream didn't dive into the black liquid but seemed to float on the surface, revolving in spiral scrolls.

Granny had to look at what she was doing, which made me feel that the pressure on me was less. I almost thought her hands were shaking, but I knew better than to consider feeling sorry for her. She made her voice soft when she spoke. 'Ivo, who wasn't of course your grandfather though we call him so, liked his coffee like this.' We had never in our conversations referred to the squire or the birth certificate. Perhaps she simply divined that I had been told Mum's side of events. Granny had the knack of having the last word without even opening her mouth. 'If anything he liked coffee more than coffee liked him, as his adventure in East Africa tended to shew.' 'Shew' was the archaic spelling she used in her letters, and I felt sure that was the form of the word fixed in her mind. 'Even before he left on that silly sojourn I told him that I personally would not consider him a success unless Messrs Fortnum & Mason accepted him as a supplier.'

'The top people,' I managed to croak.

'Precisely. In the event he fell short of his own rather modest ambitions. But perhaps you would like me to add cream to your cup in the same way? The taste is quite different, or perhaps it is the texture which is altered. For some reason a little sugar in the coffee helps the cream to float – and I speak as someone who in the normal run of life abhors sugar in coffee. If I can break my own rules so I'm sure can you. It is something which every young man, however stubborn, should try at least once.'

Somehow she had managed to get me off the hook without budging an inch. Even when she made concessions she held firm. 'Thank you Granny,' I was able to say, 'that sounds delicious.'

I'm not sure it was, really. That style of drinking coffee has never caught on with me personally. Perhaps people whose hands have more control than mine can make the cream flow over a sort of miniature weir of coffee as the cup tips, liquid gliding over liquid, so that the elements remain in suspension within every sip, but I couldn't manage that. The demitasse was light and easy to lift, but its small size made it awkward for me to make it travel the last couple of inches to my lips. I had to push my head uncomfortably far forward to bridge the gap. Still, I appreciated the gesture, if not the treat it delivered. Granny with her coffee spoon might seem to be watching over the separation of cream and coffee, but in another way she was stirring incompatibles diligently together, restoring between us some sort of social emulsion.

Passive resistance had served me well, but I can't help thinking it's most effective when it isn't your only option. After all, Gandhi wasn't strongly built, but he could certainly have given you quite a smack with his *charkha* – his portable spinning wheel – if he had wanted, and he would certainly have benefited from the element of surprise.

Flinging biscuits blindly at the orifice

When we had finished our coffee, Granny said, 'Normally a two-course *table d'hôte* at a reputable restaurant is enough to satisfy even a teenager's ravening belly, but perhaps you are still hungry?' In fact my teenager's ravening belly might be heard protesting its emptiness at some distance. 'I believe I have some biscuits in my room, if that would allay the pangs.'

They might. Granny's preference was always for a room on the ground floor, for reasons of her convenience rather than mine, but I reaped the benefit. She even pushed me there. There was a lip on the threshold of her room, not a true step but a rounded edge of metal which gave her some little difficulty to negotiate.

The biscuits were in the same category of presenting a little difficulty. Biscuits in general aren't the easiest things for me to eat, but if I break them into rough quarters I can get them to my mouth without seeming to fling them blindly at the orifice.

'Unless I'm imagining things, John,' Granny said, 'you had something to ask me. I am trying to find a new way of talking to you, since you are clearly no longer quite the person I have assumed. You don't much resemble your mother, or your father either. Perhaps in fact it is me whom you resemble.' I disputed this but gave no sign. 'Is it about the electric wheelchair? Does it need attending to in some way? Perhaps a new battery is required.'

For someone who had helped to fund my adventures in locomotion she was rather in the dark about the details. Perhaps she thought it was in the shed, on blocks, with Dad frantically tinkering in every spare moment. Perhaps she thought I should make a point of coming to see her in the wheelchair she had paid for, just as she would expect me, if she had bought me a smart tie as a present, to wear it when invited to lunch with her. 'The electric wheelchair is at home, Granny, and it's in perfect working order. This is the old pushing chair which it replaced – it's just that the Wrigley you were so kind as to help to buy doesn't fold up very easily. It doesn't fit in a taxi. I don't use it at school either.'

'Oh? And why is that?'

'I have to be carried up and down stairs in it, and I can't keep my balance in it. At school I use the Tan-Sad – you remember, the trolley thing. You've seen it.'

'You're still spending your days in that baby carriage? That overgrown pram? No wonder you wanted to see me, John. What is the alternative?'

'I'm stuck with the Tan-Sad, Granny, and really I don't mind.' Here it was, then, the only chance I would ever have to make my case, to explain that I was hoping to do without the expensive wheelchair altogether, to trade it in for something with a roof and doors. 'But at the moment I'm driven to school in a taxi.'

'Really? How odd. How do your parents afford that?'

'They don't. The local authority pays.'

'How perfectly extraordinary.'

'Granny, I want to learn to drive myself.'

'Is that possible?'

'I think so.'

'I rely on you to make very sure before committing me to expense. So it is lessons you want?'

'I thought the British School of Motoring would be the right choice, Granny – they're the top people, after all. I also need a car to take the lessons in. It will need to be modified.'

'Well, John, I quite see why you wished to talk to me. Am I to buy you a Rolls-Royce? I believe that is still the top people's car, though I have heard of the Aston Martin for a more headstrong style of person.'

'Neither for me, thanks, Granny. I thought a Mini would be more practical.'

'Quite right. It is rather a stylish little toy, designed by Signor Annigoni, I believe. People seem to be able to do everything these days.' I didn't think the name was quite right, though my information about cars was second-hand, a dilution of Peter's expertise. Even if I had been surer of my ground, I would have been foolish to correct her, not just on general principles but because her mistake worked in my favour. If Signor Annigoni was good enough to paint portraits of the Queen, he might be good enough to build cars for her grandson. 'Why not look into the matter and give me the figures later. You can take it that I am not opposed on principle.'

Then she did something surprising. She took me backstage. She let me watch as she washed her hands and face carefully with her favourite glycerine soap. I say 'let me watch' but I suppose I mean 'had me watch', since she pushed the wheelchair into the bathroom for the purpose. It was strange. She wasn't exactly putting on a show for me. She was showing me what lay behind the show she put on.

She explained that glycerine soap was a vulnerable luxury. It was a fugitive jewel of fragrance which would melt away to nothing in minutes if dropped into a bath. So she was meticulous at the basin, following a drill to avoid exposing the precious translucent bar to running water.

I don't enter a room without being invited or noticed, so Granny wanted me to be there, but if she had something to tell me it wasn't in the words. She was saying, 'You know, John, in the War I couldn't get face cream, so I made my own! I used the top of the milk and added some salt. Everyone said it gave my complexion a glow. Perhaps I should never have gone back to shop cosmetics. Still, it's too late to change now, and they haven't done too badly by me. You just have to follow certain rules.'

She wet her hands and then caressed the lather from the soap like a conjuror, just as I had once conjured bubbles from nothing at CRX. The glycerine bar spun its precious veil of foam. 'My mother, John,' she said, as she anointed herself, 'would have been horrified at the idea of putting soap on the face. She scrubbed herself all over with a wire brush every day – and yes, all over does include the face. She believed it removed dead cells of skin and stimulated the circulation. She got the idea, believe it or not, from a newspaper article about the scandalous Elinor Glyn – but that may be a name that means nothing to you. Perhaps in any case we were both just lucky in what nature gave us. Perhaps we would have looked much the same whatever we did to ourselves.'

After the crisis there was a mood of truce, almost of carnival. I felt that Granny was showing me some of her mysteries, not just about age and beauty and resignation but also the thrift of the rich. Above all she was showing me something she may not have known herself – the secret cost of having had things so much her own way, of making the world dance to her tune. As by and large it had. She dried herself, using the towel with a delicate, rolling motion, like someone blotting a fragile manuscript. Then she said, 'Giving in to the temptation to take a nap is one of the worst vices of those very vicious people, the old. Nevertheless I fear I may yield. I find I am very tired. Let me know of your progress with the Mini people and the School of Motoring.' She phoned reception for a taxi to be summoned, and with the last of her strength pushed me out of the door for collection. It broke the mood only a little to be left in the corridor like a pair of shoes in need of polishing.

Granny wasn't the only one to be feeling tired. I could hardly keep my eyes open in the taxi home. Mum wasn't unkind when I told her about the lecture I had been given about the shame attaching to large drinks, as if I had embarrassed Granny with a fit of delirium tremens at table. Mum didn't rub my nose in it for being so wrong about Granny's character and its workings. 'We did try to tell you what she was like, and now you've found out for yourself' — that was all she said, and I was grateful for the light touch.

At some level she must have been delighted, as she made me a cheese and pickle sandwich, that lunch had contained elements of fiasco. She did look very thoughtful when she heard about the successful part of the day, Granny's agreement to an embassy I hadn't announced in advance, but perhaps only because she thought my quest was hopeless, that the Holy Grail of the steering wheel would always be beyond my grasp.

Mum and Dad discussed my driving scheme a certain amount. Dad said, in my full hearing, 'He'll never forgive you if he doesn't get this chance, m'dear . . . life won't be worth living!' There was nothing I could say to that. Better to keep my mouth shut than to complicate matters, by entering in person a discussion where I already figured as a sort of effigy. I still don't know (as often with Dad) whether he thought he was calming the situation or subtly inflaming it.

That night in our bedroom I told Peter that if there was one thing certain on earth it was that I would never again accept a drink from Granny, though he told me not to be too hasty. For his part he claimed not to be in any hurry to learn to drive. It was hard to believe this, since his mechanical bent was so pronounced, and perhaps there was some renunciation in progress. Perhaps he was giving me a head start, letting me get established on four wheels before he entered the competition, or perhaps he realised that without Granny's help there was no alternative to a long wait.

A little push for the handicapped

It happened, though, that just when I was reaching out to the British School of Motoring, the BSM was reaching out to people like me. They were organising a small campaign, a little push to get the handicapped on the road. There was a specialist unit. When I called the local office I said that I might present 'a bit of a challenge' to an instructor, and itemised the difficulties that made me think so, to none of the usual consternation. It's true I'm rather good on the phone, warm and clear, and can often wangle all manner of concessions. This was different. I wasn't sure that the nice lady at the other end of the phone had grasped the seriousness of my case. I asked her if she had all the details she needed.

'I think so,' she said. 'No movement in knees, one knee fixed out of true, short of stature, some movement in right elbow, limited mobility of neck. Is that the lot?'

That was the lot. I was left feeling disappointingly limber, from a BSM point of view, hardly worth the trouble of special help and a separate initiative. It was such an unfamiliar sensation I couldn't even tell if I liked it or not. 'This sounds just the sort of thing that our Mr Griffiths enjoys. Mr John Griffiths. He'll be in touch.'

Some of my classmates at school, though younger than me, were already taking driving lessons. The Savage twins were trying to get two licences out of a single course of ten lessons, by pretending to be a single person. A single person with erratic performance, able to grasp techniques with impressive speed, only to forget them by the next session.

Their way of going about things was complicated enough, but a lot simpler than the approach I would have to take. I couldn't learn to drive on any old car – I would never be able to manage a gear stick, for instance. I would need to get a car first, and then get lessons – and yet there seemed no point in getting a converted car without some assurance that I would qualify as a driver. That was the problem, and John Griffiths was the solution.

Mr Griffiths was every bit as positive when he telephoned. He would come to Bourne End for a preliminary session to assess my prospects. A home visit! He was certainly an antidote to the mood of stagnation and stultitude which could swoop on that household when the hobbies lost their grip.

He was very jolly and dumpy. From the moment he entered the house it was as if he was preaching a sermon, on the text *Lay down thy crutches and drive*. He was a true believer. As far as I was concerned he was preaching to the converted, but Mum had no faith. She was the one who needed to be won over, and John Griffiths pulled out all the stops. Heavens, how he wooed her!

He came rolling and bubbling into the house in Bourne End, saying, 'We're going to put you on the road with a full driving licence, John, and we're going to help you stay on the road for many happy years. Your First Lesson Is Free and I'm going to give it to you right now.' It turned out the first lesson didn't involve the use or even the presence of a car. Just as well he didn't charge – Granny might have had something to say if he had expected payment for instruction that was essentially mimed.

'We're going to put you on the road, John, but we also want you to bring the road into the house. Yes, into the house. By that I mean that when you go to bed at night you must close your eyes and imagine you're holding the steering wheel in your hand. Imagine the road. Instead of counting sheep as you drift off, count something else . . . What, John? No, not cat's-eyes, don't count *them*, whatever you do! You'll hypnotise yourself if you do that . . . Imagine traffic lights. Imagine road signs. Imagine a policeman holding up his hand and telling you to stop. Spend all your mental time on the road.

'But don't think that you're only going to be driving at night, John! You can bring the road into the house during the daytime too. Mother can help you . . . See here, Mrs Cromer, what's your first name? Laura? Now, come on, Laura, this is what I want you to do with your son while I'm not here . . . Turn round please.' She seemed rather dazed, but she did as she was told.

John Griffiths went up behind her and took her hands in his, till between them they were indeed holding an imaginary steering wheel. Then with a *toot-toot!* and various noises of screeching and skidding (he had a fine variety of sound effects in his repertoire), he started driving Mum from room to room. 'Watch out, there's a cow on the road!' he would say, or 'Not very well anticipated there, Laura, I'm afraid . . .'

The dance started in the kitchen. After they had traipsed outside and back to the bedroom which I shared with Peter, and round again to where they started, John Griffiths was telling Mum what an excellent driver she was. 'After all that driving,' he said, 'don't we deserve a little dance in celebration?' He twirled her round to face him, and the next minute they were waltzing. A minute after that, whether by the sort of signal that only dancers can detect or some welling-up of sensual syncopation, Mum's feet were moving to a quicker tempo and her hips were launching into the distinctive jink of the cha-cha-cha.

I didn't know where to look, so I looked at Dad. All this time he had been sitting in his chair, with the *Telegraph* open in front of him. Even after all my years of Dad-watching I didn't know whether he really was scrutinising world affairs by reading the newspaper, or wearily cursing his witch of a mother-in-law for bringing this plump and waltzing madman into the house.

Mr Griffiths ended up by saying that Mum should do for me exactly what he had just done for her. Dad gave a little cough which probably meant, 'Apart from the ballroom dancing, I expect.' Dad's coughs were Service coughs, messages sent in a dry RAF code far more mysterious than Morse, one that I could never quite tune into. He'd been working for BOAC for a number of years by this time, and still the last word you would ever apply to him would be *civilian*.

John Griffiths formally declared that my physical difficulties were compatible with driving a car, and endorsed my choice of a Mini. It would have to be an automatic model, and somewhat modified, which would be attended to by the BSM nerve centre in London, and then John Griffiths would be returning to give the second lesson. The first practical one. The first real one.

The wounds known to mapmakers

All in all it was a very promising start to my motoring life, though driving lessons seemed to be little different from dancing lessons, and I wasn't an obvious candidate for those. Before John Griffiths left he produced a book called *Your Car: Its Care and Maintenance*. It was published by the BSM and written by John Griffiths, none other. In the front he wrote, in a large and confident script, 'For John – and all the Tomorrows on the Road of Life, from John Griffiths', signed with a great flourishing swash of an autograph. I took a quick look inside the book. There were diagrams of all the parts of the engine, with instructions for taking them to bits and putting them back together again. I told him I'd have a hard job managing that, but he said never mind. 'If you know what goes where, in an emergency you can always tell other people what to do.'

I have to say my heart sank at that. I'd heard it before. At Vulcan I did a First Aid certificate, and the chap from the St John Ambulance had taken very much the same line. Man dying by the roadside? Corrosive poison? Train crash? Nothing to it! Just so long as you know what to get passers-by to do! I seemed to be a sort of human pamphlet or tape recorder, an elaborate device to store information, on the off-chance that I coincided, at the scene of an earthquake or the escape of deadly fumes, with able-bodied folk who had failed to acquire the proper skills.

Still, John Griffiths had given me his blessing. A fresh breeze had passed through a house that could be stuffy in all weathers. Though perhaps it was only Granny, beyond the horizon, riffling through the pages of her mighty cheque book.

The household had been benignly shaken up by John Griffiths' visit. Mum had a bit of colour in her cheeks for once. It wasn't that she found him attractive, exactly. He was rather roly-poly, for all his animation, not most women's cup of tea. But it isn't every day that a woman in her middle years (Mum had been in her forties for a year or two) is chauffeured bodily round her home, under her husband's very eyes, by a man who knows how to cha-cha. The British School of Motoring seemed to have merged, on the sly, with Arthur Murray, who would teach you to dance In A Hurry.

John Griffiths had left a sort of glow with me too. I didn't spend much time looking over the car maintenance guide he had left, but I was fascinated by the design of the BSM leaflet that went with it.

Someone had been given the task of representing the British School of Motoring in visual terms. The result was charming. There was a collage of photographs showing drivers under instruction, and there was an oval space in the middle where a map of Britain had been reproduced. Additional lines had been added to the map, to turn it into a sort of cartoon of a man driving. Britain's bottom was London and Kent – the whole south-east region. His leg and foot was formed by the Cornish Peninsula, whose pronged bit had always reminded me of a two-toed sloth. Anglesey provided the shape of his little hands at the end of reassuringly short arms, and the gear lever was in south-west Wales. Britain's head was northern Scotland – and a very bumpy head it was too. It looked as if someone had taken an axe to the back of the driver's head, striking three separate blows to open the wounds known to mapmakers as the Dornoch, Cromarty and Moray Firths. And still he drove merrily on, despite being so hacked about.

I don't think, now, that there was any intended connection between the BSM's drive to get disabled people on the road and the way its design department had rendered the map for advertising purposes. As an impatient student of the John Griffiths method, though, I didn't doubt it. I saw what I wanted to see, just as everyone else does, and what I saw was a cheerfully non-standard body.

For a few moments here and there, I have been proud to be British. It adds up to perhaps half an hour in total. I have some sort of sporadic identification with the look of these islands on a map. It was the design of the BSM leaflet which dug the foundations of this feeling, by alerting me to the fact that the map of the United Kingdom, if you look at it with an open mind, does look so very disabled. If I was any kind of nationalist, I'd claim that as my country. That's where I'm from.

Silence that tingled with icicles

I had fallen in love with John Griffiths and his ideas of bringing the road into the house, and even into my bed at night. I couldn't wait for the car to be delivered. The visit to the dealership in Slough had been straightforward, if anticlimactic. I said I was interested in a Mini with automatic transmission and was shown a red one. 'What colours does it come in?' I asked. 'Red,' I was told. I wondered why. 'It has to be like that one, does it?' Yes it did. More than that. It had to be that one. This was the one it was going to be.

After that, all I had to do was to trip the mechanism that released the flood of money, by telephoning Granny. While we were waiting for the cheque to clear, Mum and I tried to practise driving around the house once or twice, according to the Griffiths method, but we felt rather self-conscious about it. Our hearts weren't in it. It took two to tango, and not these two. I would get a proper dose of the Griffiths method at our first lesson, which was arranged for the Monday after the arrival of the car.

On the Friday morning before the scheduled lesson the British School of Motoring rang, to say they were sorry to inform us that Mr John Griffiths had had a heart attack and died. Could we give them a few days to make fresh arrangements for me?

John's death hit me surprisingly hard, considering I only met him the once. He was the only person I had come across to date who saw teaching me as a piece of fun rather than a solemn duty. The road was for everyone – he excluded no one from the festival. And hadn't he danced his last dance with Mum? Unless he gave his wife a twirl every time he came in the front door, which admittedly seemed quite likely.

I thought I had better phone Granny at once to tell her about the setback in our plans. Harshly her voice intoned, 'Halnaker 226. Good morning.' A formal politeness that would deter even the most presumptuous of tradesmen. She pronounced the exchange name in the local way, as Hannukah, like the Jewish festival.

I put as much drama and emotion as I could muster into my voice. All that came down the line from Tangmere was silence – a silence that tingled with icicles. Finally, standing in her hallway where the phone was, Granny formed syllables. She sent them as electrical impulses down the wire. The heavy receiver at my ear in Bourne End reassembled those little pulsing packages as 'How . . . very . . . inconvenient!' At that moment I disliked Granny intensely and redoubled my grieving over poor John Griffiths.

I asked God to make sure that John Griffiths had plenty of roads and plenty of cars with unlimited fuel in Heaven, and above all an endless supply of hopelessly disabled pupils, who would benefit from the chance of becoming expert drivers under his care. I felt sad that no one else in my disabled country was marking the passing of this hero, whose heart was so big that in the end it choked him.

The red Mini, with the number plate OHM 962F, arrived in May, on the 11th. It was Peter's birthday, but he was unresentful of any eclipse suffered by his special day. He thrilled along to my thrill. Dad pushed the driving seat as far forward as it would go. Then he fetched cushions. Since the roads on the Abbotsbrook Estate were technically private, I was able to drive a few feet that first day. When the engine stalled I felt relief. I was afraid my heart too would burst from sheer joy, and I would go the way of my master in driving. Death I didn't mind, but I wanted the bits of paper in the proper order – driving licence first. Death certificate later.

After that, of course, it was hard slog. Mirror-Signal-Mirror-Manœuvre: M-S-M-M. What it spells is neck-ache.

The substitute John Griffiths found for me by the BSM was called Colin Chivers. He was no substitute in any real sense. Obviously I was looking for an excuse to take against him from the first, out of loyalty to that dancing-master of the road (not that I ever so much as sat in a car with him), John Griffiths. I didn't have to wait long to be estranged. It wasn't the length of his hair which bothered me, falling onto the collar of his shirt, nor the shirt itself, which had a floral pattern, though both were noted by Mum with muted alarm. It was when I was installed in the car, with the seat in the most forward position possible, the concertina of cushions behind my back, my built-up shoes on terms of distant acquaintance with the pedals, and Colin Chivers said, 'I realise that you have certain physical difficulties, but I'm going to treat you just the same way as everyone else.' Oh really? What a hypocrite. No one else got that little speech, did they? He was already treating me differently, in the very act of announcing the opposite.

I grant him his good points. When he saw the difficulty I had actually gripping the steering wheel, he arranged for a sensible alteration to the controls of the car. He installed a dolly, a sort of twirly knob for me to grip clamped to the steering wheel, which spared me the struggle of undertaking vigorous arm movements in a plane that was hostile to them.

After that bit of modification, Colin didn't have a lot to teach me of what I wanted, which was confidence rather than mere technique. His attitude was consistently downbeat rather than inspirational. One of the first things he said was, 'I never forget that we are putting you in charge of a deadly weapon – I suggest you never forget it either.' Another time he said, 'That's amazing! Take a look at the cow in that field,' and then gave me a good old scolding when I did. I had taken my eyes off the road, in obedience to Granny's advice (never pass up an opportunity to inspect your surroundings – the major cause of driving accidents is boredom) but in violation of the Highway Code. I would have to wait until I was a qualified driver before I could risk enjoying 'the privilege of the view'.

When Granny's cheque ran out (its depletion helped along by the bill for the dolly) I assented cheerfully enough to Dad's suggestion that he should take over teaching duties. I wasn't going to re-apply to the fountainhead of cash, even though I was authorised to do so. Granny was still in my bad books for her coldness and I was sending her at least partway to Coventry (to Bicester or even Banbury) – not that she was likely to notice. Dad had reasons of his own for not wanting to deal with the tyrant of Tangmere.

Meanwhile the Wrigley was sold. The cheque was sent to Granny, perhaps with a cubic millimetre of self-righteousness sharing the envelope with it, though it made sense for her to absorb the proceeds since she had funded it in the first place. There was no point in having two motorised vehicles at my disposal. Enough is enough.

Finally my test date arrived. August the 8th, 1968. Red car, red-letter day. My examiner was a woman who made no eye-contact with me at any point, which certainly made it easier for me to read the name on her clipboard unobtrusively – Cynthia Davies. She looked the way I would have imagined librarians to look – distant, disapproving – if I had never known Mrs [Sophia] Pavey. I had discovered Mrs Pavey's first name, which I loved, but I wouldn't have used it in a million years. I didn't say it, but I mentally supplied it in square brackets.

I'd not met a Cynthia before, and if she had seemed willing to talk, inside the tiny car, I would have asked about that lovely moony name. Turning a blind eye may have been all part of her professional technique, but it was very disconcerting just the same. She was so remote in her manner that I took it for granted that she was going to fail me. My three-point turn seemed to take for ever. The seasons changed while I was wrestling that manœuvre into submission. There was marked precession of the equinoxes.

Later on in the test, while I was doing some straightforward if despondent driving, I heard an odd sound, like a slow puncture. I wondered if a tyre was going flat, and what would happen if it did, in the middle of my driving test. Would the whole farrago be cancelled, so that I had to wait for another appointment, or would I end up reciting instructions from John Griffiths' book on car maintenance while Cynthia got busy with the jack, or hung back conscientiously to let me solicit passers-by?

Cub Scout access to the road

Of course it wasn't a puncture at all. The sound resolved into an articulate hiss: 'sssssSSSTOP!' Cynthia Davies was telling me to make an emergency stop – to stop without warning – by giving me plenty of warning. A Galapagos tortoise would have given less notice of a pounce. Space probes have been launched with a shorter countdown. Even so my reactions were slow and my braking was spongy. I resigned myself to more lessons in suffering from Dad. The harvest called a driving licence would require more of the rain called tears. I couldn't even claim that I had been discriminated against. Cynthia had been more than fair, she had leant over backwards, and still I had fallen short of the required standard.

She still didn't look at me at the end of the test, and when she said, 'Congratulations, Mr Cromer' and told me that I'd passed, it was in a very neutral tone. I didn't feel any immediate triumph. She kept her eyes to herself as she passed across my pink slip. There was still no acknowledgement that she'd seen me in the first place. But then she came round to my side of the car, opened the door and shook my hand very gently, as gently as if I was royalty, and there seemed to be a smile hidden in her face somewhere, near her ears perhaps. Then I made contact at last with my own latent elation.

Mum wasn't so sure. She wasn't convinced that a female driving instructor's pass was valid in law. At best it must amount to a junior entitlement, a Cub Scout access to the road.

Perhaps Cynthia's failure to fail me was based on the assumption that I would make a sensible, cautious sort of driver, who would never get into the sort of trouble from which an emergency stop is the only exit. If that was her thinking, she was far off the mark – tragically deluded. The taste for speed that had been piqued by my racing Wrigley, after the NHS-approved plod of the Everest & Jennings, could now be indulged to the limit and beyond. The weeks on the road between passing my driving test and the start of the new term were a carnival of velocity for me. I may not have broken the 70-mile-an-hour national limit, but I didn't need to take things to that extreme to run risks on the roads, many of them steep or winding (or both) around Bourne End.

It was bliss to be able to explore my environment. There was a choice of roads for me to take as I turned out of the Abbotsbrook Estate. Turning left I would come to Marlow (and the Compleat Angler) and High Wycombe, while turning right would bring me to CRX, Burnham, Maidenhead and eventually London. The left turn seemed naturally boring, the right turn inherently exciting. One factor which may have contributed to this was the uneven flexibility of my arms, which made left turns relatively easy and right ones much more difficult. I gather there's something similar in Proust – the A4155 was my Swann's Way. The other direction, the Guermantes Way leading on to the wider world and its temptations, was the A4094.

One day early in my driving career I made to turn right and handled the turn (if I may say so) beautifully. Unfortunately as I did so the dolly somehow snagged itself inside my shirt. Miss Pearce the dressmaker's dummy at Trees made a contribution to this little crisis – the shirts that Mum made me were now closely tailored, and the dolly snagged between two buttons, effectively gluing my chest to the steering wheel in its full right lock. The result was that after I had reached my desired destination, on the far left side of the road to Maidenhead, the car went on turning, still with full right lock, so that it ended up going round and round, as if I was dithering between Maidenhead and Marlow, Guermantes and Swann, while vehicles bore down on me at speed from both sides, sounding their horns and slamming on their brakes.

I managed to tug myself free, to the detriment of the shirt, and stopped safely facing Maidenhead. It had been a bad moment, though once I had got my breath back I found it oddly thrilling to have been on the receiving end of such a fusillade of horn blasts. A twenty-one-horn salute. Only something tremendous in its iniquity would be tooted so royally, at a time when most drivers didn't lay their hands on the horn from one year's end to the next. Mum and Dad, certainly, regarded the use of the horn as inherently foreign.

I felt I had been blooded, initiated into the rough fellowship of the road, far more truly than by any mere licence. I also had a wonderful new secret to keep from Mum. If she had known about my shirt-sleeve snagging on the dolly, her worrying would really have gone into overdrive.

It was a lovely drive from Bourne End to CRX at Taplow. Because the hospital was at the top of a hill, the road up to it was very twisty and dangerous. It was all as steep and scary as Edie-was-a-Lady Lane, full of witchy presence to Peter and me as children. It took real skill to negotiate those bends, and I had done a fair amount of practice there before I took my test.

When I was a qualified driver I loved driving alone up the steep gradient to Hedsor Hill. Perhaps part of the thrill was being so free, so much my own master, bowling along in a red Mini so near to the hospital where my life had been so confined. I should probably have been practising the *Satipatthana Sutta*, breathing in and out in full consciousness, but my promiscuous mystical reading had given me the idea of identifying with the Creator, on the theory that 'as I think, so shall it become'. Aleister Crowley has a lot to answer for. I was reckless, confident that my luck was a blank cheque which could never bounce.

One time, on the way back down from CRX, I was a little cocky. Going too fast, I misjudged the curve and charged up the bank. The car started to tip up. It almost reached the vertical and came within a whisker of tipping over. I tried to lean the other way. Then my little Mini thought better of its rush towards the orgasm of destruction and pulled back from the brink. I had a bumpy landing and was very much shaken.

I just sat there trembling. My neck hurt. I knew I must put on a good show, though, when I got home. I was terrified that if Mum and Dad found out what had happened they would forbid me to drive, licence or no licence, and all my effort would be wasted. I had to saunter back into Trees Abbotsbrook Bourne End Bucks as though nothing had happened. I couldn't really do much in the way of sauntering, but I tried to imagine I was whistling and had my hands in my pockets.

A secret unless proved otherwise

I couldn't even confide in Flanny our GP about the shaking-up I'd had. Mum was always ganging up on me with her. Flanny disapproved of my being a vegetarian, though at least she pronounced the word properly, while Mum always said 'Vegeteerian', putting a sneer in the middle of the word to match the one in her heart.

The first passenger I took in the Mini was Peter. I was greatly in his debt in the matter of transport. Now I could pay him back for all his weary pushing of the Tan-Sad. Mum never asked for a lift, and I never offered. I did invite Dad to come for a ride, but he said he'd rather wait until I'd had more practice. The vote of confidence was never really part of his repertoire as a parent.

The first two times I had come a cropper in the Mini there were no witnesses. The third time, Peter was with me and we came a cropper together.

The previous accidents hadn't taught me much. That close shave on Hedsor Hill had made me take extra care, but I couldn't keep away from those steep and twisty roads. We were even on the same deadly bend, only this time there was another car involved. For some mad reason, the driver behind chose to overtake, forcing me off the road in the process.

Again I just sat there shaking, but Peter with his flexible neck had recognised the driver from the back of his famous head. Michael Aspel the broadcaster – a hero of his until that exact moment. We knew he lived locally, but this was our first actual sighting.

'Nobody does that to my brother!' Peter said, in a wonderful outburst of fraternal love. 'If I see him in any of the shops I'll give him one!' All the fearfulness instilled in him at Lord Wandsworth had been melted away at Sidcot School. In our hearts Aspel was instantly reduced to the ranks, from honorary uncle to local villain, callous roadhog and reckless menace. From then on we could hardly bear to be in the room when Mum listened to *Family Favourites*.

Peter had to help me wrench the steering wheel round before we could get on the move again. I didn't need to swear him to silence about Michael Aspel's endangering of our lives. By now we had lost the reflex of sharing things with Mum and Dad, and everything was a secret unless proved otherwise.

The first day I turned up at school in the Mini I more or less provoked a riot. My schoolmates surrounded the car and begged to be given rides. My status slumped a bit when I had to transfer from car to Tan-Sad, but my image was certainly boosted overall. If only the school's porterage scheme had extended to carrying me around on school premises, up and down stairs, in and out of lessons, in my nice new Mini! I could have attracted attention, when there was something I didn't understand, by discreetly sounding the horn.

Of course more than anything I wanted to give *Patrick* a ride in the Mini, to share the privileges that went with my disadvantages. Ideally it would have been at a weekend, when with any luck the bond between twins would be weaker. But at some point just before I got my test, near the end of the summer term, the Savages had broken off relations with me – both of them. I don't know who had said what, but one day they just walked past me, and from then on we were classmates only, not friends at all. They didn't push me around any more. Other hands gripped the controls of the Tan-Sad, though there was no hiatus in my transport schedule. The Savages had selected their own replacements. There seemed no anger involved, just a cool shedding of closeness.

The obvious explanation was that Paul had told Patrick about my interest in him being more than amicable. That would explain why the wrong twin blushed on the day of rupture. As he passed me Paul and not Patrick showed the signs of beta-adrenergic stimulation. Adrenalin was binding to receptors on the surface of his responsive cells for once, triggering the enzyme adenylyl cyclase to raise levels of cyclic adenosine monophosphate (AMP). His face was blatant with secrets.

Looking back I almost think myself pathetic for not insisting on some sort of reckoning. I had done nothing wrong. My love was discreet – how could it be anything else? I had no chance of forcing my affections on him or on anyone.

I should have had my say, my day in court. Except that drama needs a stage, and I had none. How could I have made the estranged twins lean over the Tan-Sad to be arraigned, to have a grievance thrown in their faces? I never even looked into Patrick's eyes again. I felt as if I had been clean bowled in a game of Howzat when I wasn't even playing – worse, that I was out lbw. I had never understood how you could be dismissed for something that would have happened, when it hadn't.

Dad had always been convinced that I made the world dance to my tune, but the incompleteness of this theory was beginning to become obvious. I had a tune, all right, and could hear it myself most of the time, but I couldn't make it audible to anyone else, let alone persuade them to dance to it.

To raise a differential blush

After breaking up with the twins I was at rather a loose end in matters of the heart. The new hands on the Tan-Sad were attached to bodies, of course, but there could be no question of my transferring my affections to the newcomers (who took quite a while to achieve the teamwork which had come so naturally to the Savages). It had suited me to be obsessed with Patrick Savage, and there was no obvious substitute. Free adults routinely fall in love with married men, creating obstacles to their own fulfilment. I couldn't exactly reproduce that state of satisfying frustration, but I had come close by developing a crush on one of a pair of twins. It was a sort of insurance policy against anything actually happening. As long as I had devised an insoluble tangle I didn't need to think about whether there was any risk.

On some level I think I knew I was partly making it up, even at the time. The twins were almost always together – they were like the sets of toys advertised in catalogues, with the footnote *not available separately*. Perhaps the saddest words young eyes of the period could fall upon.

Patrick and Paul were effectively a couple already, one which resisted the formation of another. I was a fifth wheel from the start.

Still, there had been a real fascination in finding one human being bewitching, utterly distinctive even from the back or at a distance, and his twin warmly neutral, even though they were genetically and environmentally so close to identical, and I was one of the very select group that could see through the similarity to the difference. It was quite an achievement, while it lasted, the ability to create embarrassment on one face and leave the other unaffected, to raise a differential blush.

My crush on Patrick Savage wasn't a very realistic romantic proposition – or else it was profoundly realistic, if deep down I didn't want things to go anywhere, if I wanted to stay secure in the magic circle of hopeless wishes.

If as the *Tibetan Book of the Dead* informs us, we choose the womb, then twins also choose each other. Perhaps Patrick and Paul were husband and wife in a previous life, and couldn't bear to be parted in the next. Except of course that rebirth isn't a reward but a chore. It's like getting an essay back with *Must try harder* written on it. Or else *Don't try so hard*, which is a much harder instruction to obey.

Every Friday I would go to the garage at the end of the village and buy a pound's worth of petrol. That would set me up for the weekend, and give me five return trips to school. It's strange that I didn't mourn the bewitching Broyan, who was of course rendered surplus to requirements by the arrival of the Mini. Peter and I had managed to lay our hands on some Gunmetal Blue of our own in the end, and drove Mum mad painting absolutely everything with it. Plastic kits, to which it wasn't suited. Doorstops. Any old thing. Mum was mystified by the attraction this smelly stuff had for us.

I don't even remember my last ride in his taxi, nor our farewells to each other. I'd drunk deep of his being in the weeks when I was taking driving lessons in the evenings but was still being driven to school by him, knowing that I was between stages of life, with the Broyan era drawing to an end. Then in the end I missed him as little as I had missed my budgie Charlie after I had given him away. It was time to go separate ways, but I would never forget the meaty smell of him, or his characteristic gestures – the way, for instance, he would move his neck convulsively, as if he was choking, while actually sliding out his dentures so as to cement them more firmly in place. Pink glue from a little tube. Really, my love for the man was slightly mental. What was the most personal thing he had ever said? 'Oh, so you had a birfday, did ya? Meant to get a card . . .' That was our high-water mark.

Klaus Eckstein was a canny creature, and it may be that he sensed my new availability for non-romantic interests, compensatory obsessions. In his campaign of match-making between me and the Spanish language he escalated from hints (you've got so much in common, he was asking about you) to commands (*I've booked a table – don't let me down*).

'Here,' he said at the end of one German lesson, handing me a copy of *Nos ponemos en camino*, 'You'll easily be able to manage the first twenty chapters before the weekend is over, and considering that your work-load is so risibly light, you'll also have time to take a look at this poem. You can write me an essay on it.'

'But sir!' I said. 'I haven't even started Spanish, I don't know if I'm even going to like it or want to do it, and you're asking me to write an essay on a poem I don't understand and haven't any way of translating!'

'Oh, you'll manage,' Eckstein replied. 'It's hardly much of a challenge. I'm babying you, really. I had to move from absolutely nothing to degree level in eight months. You should easily manage A-level in a year. And here's where you begin.' It did sound easy when he put it that way.

'So let this help you get off to a good start,' he added. 'I'll expect to receive your completed essay by Tuesday.' Perhaps he saw panic in my eyes, because he made an uncharacteristic concession. 'Wednesday at the latest.' He was even good enough to lend me some Spanish dictionaries. He carried them to the Mini for me, dropping them in the back with a thud. One big, one medium and one small, the Three Bears transformed into reference books.

'I'll give you one more bit of help,' said Eckstein as I started the engine of the Mini. He was breathing heavily, his internal spaces clogged with snuff. 'The first line of the poem means *At five in the afternoon*. So does the fourth line, and the sixth, and the eighth, and the tenth. So, you see, I've translated almost half the poem for you. Aren't you going to thank me?' I shouted 'Thank you, sir!' above the engine noise, but he muttered, 'I thought not,' so perhaps he didn't hear me.

On the journey back to Bourne End that evening I was buoyed up by the challenge I had been given. I wasn't paying due care and attention to the road. It was pure luck that I didn't come adrift on that deadly curve from Hedsor Hill, pure luck that the arch-roadhog Michael Aspel wasn't going home just as fast and carelessly, demanding right of way as a broadcaster's privilege.

I was downright bouncy when I went in to have my supper. Mum commented that her JJ was remarkably chirpy. And so JJ was. JJ liked having private confabs with teachers, special assignments. I had resisted Eckstein's oblique academic overtures during German lessons, but I had appreciated them just the same. There was an aspect of surly intellectual courtship in the way he pushed me into the arms of Spanish. He never resorted to anything as lowly as charm, but his cantankerousness had its nuances, and I knew he wanted the best for me academically. Now I would have to buckle down and justify his interest, to earn the modified contempt which was the closest he could come to faith in anyone's abilities.

Soon the table in the kitchen was spread with papers and notes, as I grappled with the technicalities of a language that I had only just met, unless you count an inventive obscenity scrawled on a blackboard months before. Mum said that she had never seen me tackle a piece of homework with such determination. And still after two hours I was no further forward, despite having moved from the Baby-Bear dictionary to the Daddy. There are many wonderful short books in the world, but it isn't every book that can afford to be short. A short dictionary is one which has weeded out just those language-flowers which you were wanting to sniff and maybe pick.

Nos ponemos en camino was plain sailing, but the intricacies of the poem completely defeated me. This time I wasn't starting on the nursery slopes of a literature, as I had with German and *Hänschen klein*, with a nursery rhyme tailored to my name and psychology. I was starting on one of the peaks, with Federico García Lorca's 'La cogida y la muerte'. My exhaustion wasn't altogether mental: the whole business of manœuvring books about, consulting one for help with another, disinterring references then returning to where

I started, was something my body rather resented. Not the intellectual legwork but the sheer lugging back and forth of tomes. The armwork.

To start with I tackled the poem word by word, as if I was a translation machine, a language grinder.

> *Cuando el sudor de nieve fue llegando*
> *a las cinco de la tarde,*
> *cuando la plaza se cubrió de yodo*
> *a las cinco de la tarde,*
> *la muerte puso huevos en la herida*
> *a las cinco de la tarde.*
> *A las cinco de la tarde.*
> *A las cinco en punto de la tarde.*

yielded only

> When the snow sweat was arriving
> to five of afternoon,
> when the square was covered with iodine (iodine?)
> to five of afternoon,
> the death put eggs in the wound
> to five of afternoon.
> To five of afternoon.
> To five o'clock of afternoon.

To be fair to myself, I did manage to nudge the poem a little further towards English than that – but Eckstein wanted more than a translation. He wanted understanding in depth – an essay. My excitement collapsed. All I could do was pray for my guardian angel to deliver a miracle of understanding – a forlorn hope, since understanding is what miracles leave grasping. On its own my brain could manage nothing. The cells were stumped.

Mum asked what the matter was, and for once I welcomed her fussing. I explained that I had to write about an important poem in Spanish when I didn't know any Spanish. That my wits were at the end of their tether. Mum didn't say anything but moved quietly into the hall, shutting the door behind her.

There was murmuring on the phone. Then Mum came back to tell me that she had arranged for me to see a friend and neighbour of hers, who lived on the other side of the Abbotsbrook Estate.

'María Binns will see you at eight, JJ. She'll be happy to help you with your Spanish poem.' I must have looked doubtful about someone called Binns being an Iberian scholar, because she added, 'María is as Spanish as it's possible to be. Michael – that's her husband – must like her that way. I made a blouse for her once, and when I saw her wearing it, I thought, "Why did I bother to sew on those top three buttons? They'll never be used."'

So Mum had met this Spanish godsend through the sewing circle. It made sense that the *de luxe* dressmaker's dummy, delivered in error, held on to with a passion and named after the intended owner, Mum's guardian angel (or as close as she would ever get), should have a hotline to a whole network of higher powers. Miss Pearce was sending me along to the top woman, and my prayers seemed to have been answered. My guardian angel would rescue me as long as I put in a bit of effort and drove to meet her myself. The system seemed to work more or less on Granny's principles, making sure I contributed energy of my own instead of coasting on bounty. This is a sound spiritual principle too. As one famous formula puts it, the guru is a mother monkey not a mother cat. She won't pick you up by the scruff of your neck and carry you bodily to self-realisation. You have to cling to her fur.

An attractive, well-turned-out woman was waiting for me at the gate of her charming house when I pulled up in the red Mini. My guardian angel was lithe and handsome and dressed in a black suède skirt and jacket which looked brand new. Her welcome was marvellously warm.

'¡Come in, dear John! I am María Paz.' She pronounced her surname the way someone from the North of England would say 'path'. María Paz Binns – the name had its own poetry, though very far from Lorca's. '¿Can I assist you in getting over this small step? ¡Very good! Now if you can manage OK, I thought we'd spread this poem out on the big kitchen table. ¿Would that be suitable for you?'

Before anything else she offered me a little irregular cake she told me was called a *panellet*. 'If you are going to learn Spanish you must learn Spanish tastes as well as Spanish words. The more Spanish food you try, the better will be your pronunciation. There is nothing more

Spanish than *panellet*. In reality . . . *panellet* is Catalan and not Spanish. ¡So you can start by learning that there is more than one Spain! More than one language, more than one tradition, more than one style of food.' She broke the cake in half and popped my piece right into my mouth. Even in those days I didn't enjoy having people make decisions like that without consultation. It replaces one form of embarrassment with another. It may be decisive but it ain't polite. On the other hand, the cake was delicious. That made a difference.

'Lovely,' I said, and María Paz replied offhandedly that one of the major ingredients of a *panellet* was potatoes. 'Michael won't even try it – catch him, he says, eating cake of spuds.' Michael of course being her husband. 'So you see' – she gave me a very winning smile – 'you are already more open-minded than he.' She might not have thought me open-minded if she'd mentioned the spuds in advance, but the *panellet*'s flavour bloomed on my tongue.

'One more thing about Catalonia . . . there is a special patron saint for the region – you may recognise him. St Jordi? Is he ringing a bell?'

'Not really.'

'He killed a dragon, like the English St George. They are in fact the same person.'

'I never knew that.'

'One saint for two countries. More than two – St George is also patron of Greece and of Georgia. But the official patron saint of Spain is Santiago. Santiago of Compostela. St James the Greater. Saint Jordi is a forbidden saint, thanks to that whelp-of-a-hound Franco. Parents are not allowed to baptise their sons Jordi. Imagine not being allowed to name an English boy George!' This would indeed be a strange embargo, though George was not at the time a fashionable name.

If María Paz had happened to mention that St James the Greater was also the patron saint of vets and of arthritis sufferers, as he is in his spare time, then I might have rocketed off into Catholicism and not taken my present course. There are other saints with arthritic responsibilities (take a creaking bow, St Colman, St Alphonsus Maria de Liguori, St Servatus, St Totnan, St Killian) as well as others who watch over vets (St Blaise, St Eligius), but St James the Greater is the only one to hold down both jobs.

Even without knowing about the broad portfolio of St James the Greater's patronage, I was thrilled by the oppression of the Catalans and the whole idea of a forbidden saint. I would name my first-born Jordi – boy or girl, the name worked as well for either. My first-born, or my first cat.

María asked for the poem and read it in silence. She stopped after a few seconds to light an unfamiliar-looking cigarette, its tobacco oddly dark. She inhaled the smoke through her mouth and expelled it thoughtfully from her nose. Dad smoked as if it was a military drill, a form of exercise for the lungs, while Mum smoked du Mauriers with her nerves (it was never just 'a cigarette' any more than the Relaxator was ever just 'the lounger'). It was easy to think that María Paz drew smoke directly into her brain, bathing her cerebral involutions with the cigarette's piquant incense.

She saw me studying her and asked me if I would care to try one of her cigarettes. 'I know it has a rather acrid pong, but is really very gentle and smooth,' she said. 'I depend on my Ducados. Michael gets them for me from Spain when he goes there.' She wrinkled her nose. 'To be honest, if all I could get was English cigarettes I wouldn't go to the trouble of smoking at all.' Sycophantically I agreed with what she said about English cigarettes. It tickled me that my guardian angel brought temptation as well as rescue, making her a sort of double agent. Surely only the devil would smoke black tobacco.

Thanks to the family's birthday and Christmas protocol, I was neither an addict nor altogether a novice when it came to cigarettes. I accepted her kind suggestion. After she had offered me the packet and while she was still brandishing her lighter, she mentioned that she had a cigarette holder somewhere, which might make my first Spanish cigarette a little kinder on my inexperienced throat. ¡Tactful María! She must have noticed that my lack of flexibility would make it awkward for me to bring a cigarette to my lips. Not impossible, but awkward – a certain amount of the movement would have had to come from the neck. It was really my bones and my blushes she was sparing, rather than my tender throat.

The cigarette holder, when it was installed between my lips, gave me a feeling of baleful sophistication, either a matinée idol's or a Bond villain's. I was Noël Coward or else Goldfinger. With our Ducados safely lit, we began the seminar. I would need all available forms of sophistication to cope with the information my guardian angel had to offer.

'John,' she said, folding her arms. 'No one will ever understand this poem without knowing that Lorca was jomosexual. ¡It is an elegy for his lover, who was killed in the bull ring!'

It's true that on the qwerty keyboard the letter *h* snuggles up to the letter *j*, but María's delivery wasn't any sort of metaphysical typing error. The Spanish *j* converges on the English *h* sound, but is much raspier, as different as *panellet* is different from Victoria sponge or a Ducados from a du Maurier. When Mrs Paz Binns told me that Lorca was *jomosexual*, the Spanish *j* came smokily from her lips with just the same passionate and committed intonation that Eckstein had used, when he told me that 'joder' was a third conjugation Spanish verb.

My modest physical size makes any drug work on me rather powerfully. I think I managed to conceal from my hostess the intensity of the nicotine intoxication I was receiving from the Ducados, though at one point I came close to jabbing myself in the eye with the cigarette holder.

María spoke with passion, reverence and proud humility as she explained the fierce national temperament. Bull-fighting was the heart's blood of Spain. She said the first word anyone should learn in Spanish was *duende*, about which Lorca had much to say. Only with this background knowledge could the reader begin to know the way Lorca had felt about his lover Ignacio Sánchez Mejías.

Background knowledge about Spanish culture was exactly what I lacked, and I was particularly hostile to bull-fighting. ¿How could I not be, when even the jar of Bovril in Mum's larder, that nightmarish concentrate of abattoir run-off, filled me with horror and disgust? Still, by the time she had finished speaking and I had taken a final puff on my Ducados, whose butt I jabbed out in the glass ashtray which she held up for me, we agreed that I understood Lorca very well. Also that I should never waste my time with English cigarettes.

Before I left, I asked María to read the whole poem aloud to me. While she spoke I kept my eyes closed. She made the repeated lines pound in fatalistic rhythm, like a funeral train. My mouth was sour with cigarette smoke, but I could still taste the *panellet*, infusing my saliva with its aromas. I sat there concentrating on María's diction, and the exact flavouring of her Spanish vowels and consonants. There's no way you can be sure in advance that any individual native speaker will be a suitable model for your own accent, but for now I would trust my guardian angel to guide my tongue.

When Mum asked me how my lesson with María had gone, I didn't have an answer ready. I had been so busy mulling over the new flavours I had learned, and the problem of forging within my soul a vegetarian *duende*, that I hadn't remembered to concoct an innocent version of the seminar for parental consumption. I certainly didn't want to mention the sexual secret that María had shared with me, nor my adventures with Spanish cigarettes, so I simply said that she was very nice and very helpful, and had given me some nice home-made cake.

I could hardly have been more stupid. Mum might have been troubled by Spanish cigarettes and the discussion of jomosexuality, but she was certain to feel the threat if I touched another woman's cake. It pierced her in her inner core of catering. She grilled me about the cake's texture and probable ingredients. She was keenly competitive when it came to cooking. Her soufflés always rose and stayed risen, unlike those of some neighbours in Bourne End. She even borrowed a trick from Fanny Cradock by playing an electric fan on the fluffy ramparts of the finished soufflé before serving, to show that it wouldn't collapse. It wouldn't dare.

I said that the cake was low to the plate, as if it had hardly risen or not been made with flour at all. It certainly contained almonds, vanilla, perhaps some orange or lemon essence. I didn't quite play into Mum's hands by mentioning the potatoes. She seemed mollified and snorted that it didn't sound like much of a cake, but I wasn't sure I had fully made amends for my cake adultery in the kitchen of María Paz Binns.

His own costly Bovril

My essay on 'The Tragic Bull in Lorca' was delivered to Eckstein after school the next Tuesday. I had taken a day off sick in order to

179

write it. It was a pretty torrid piece of analysis, fuelled by my anxiety to please my benignly scowling teacher, by the unique smoke rising from the black tobacco of a Ducados cigarette, and by my own abstract desire for the handsome bull-fighter, as long as he didn't hurt the bull. His lithe body now lay twisted and crumpled in the sawdust of the bull ring, the suit of lights stained with his own costly Bovril. It was all very feverish, masochistic and pretentious. I was proud of it.

When I came in after delivering my essay, Mum was making a cake, and almost dancing around it, in an unusually sprightly way.

'What on earth are you doing?' I asked.

'Oh, just trying out a new recipe,' she said. I knew she couldn't be as casual as she was trying to seem. 'I got it from María Binns, who got it from *Ideal Homes*. The entire cake collapsed on her – poor dear! – so I told her I'd give it a try.' She had already baked her cake bases, the bricks as I thought of them, and had mortared them together with her home-made buttercream filling. Now she was mixing something else in her pudding basin. 'It's a chocolate icing which goes all over the outside of the cake,' she said, her voice as light and airy as a meringue. In fact she had just popped a batch of meringues into the oven on a low temperature. It was her thrifty habit to let meringues hitch a lift from the relatively high heat that had been used to bake the cakes. The extra expense was minimal.

After she had beaten her egg whites with the rotary whisk, she would hold it above the bowl of stiff peaks and gently work the handle back and forth about half-way round the circle of its action. If the movement was too fast then centrifugal force would spatter the kitchen with flying froth, but if she judged it properly then she could get a trailing sheet of woven foam to lower itself onto the rest of the whipped whites from the whisk, whose meshing blades were almost clean before they even reached the washing-up bowl.

The kitchen was her pride and her parish, although food in its finished form had little interest for her. She rarely served herself more than a few spoonfuls at mealtimes, and though she hated waste she sometimes left even that untouched. She was always saying she would eat later, and perhaps sometimes she did.

Her soft chocolate icing smelled as good as it looked.

'Would you care to try a bit, JJ?' she asked with a bright smile. 'I know you say you don't like cakes, but perhaps this is the recipe that will convert you!'

She passed me a spoonful of the mixture and returned to her creation. As she picked up her palette knife I noticed that she had now combined her sprightly dance with a færie flick. She was smothering the cake with the soft mixture, and as she worked she danced some more. She kept dipping her blade at lightning speed into a pot of water she had nearby. 'It's important to get only a *thin* film of water on the knife,' she said, and the light flashed on her palette knife as she plied it about. Her blade plunged and scooped, making little peaks and valleys in the edible geography of the cake. I put the spoon into the cave of my mouth to test her offering, nearly fainting as the mixture dissolved back into the nothingness from which it was created, leaving my tongue-buds drugged and exulting in the subtle sweetness of chocolate, with a touch of bitterness pulling on my heart.

'Oh, and there's just one more thing,' she said, ' – before I do the washing-up, of course! – that might interest you, JJ, as a scientist.' She showed me the palette knife, so that I could see that there wasn't a mark on it, in spite of all the sculpting it had done, the wonderful irregular symmetry it had given to the finished cake. I suppose the water she'd been dipping it in had been warm.

I didn't need to say anything, and nor did she. The whole scene had expressed what she wanted to say. The equilibrium of the world had been restored, the proper balance of things. *So much for Spanish cakes that don't even rise! Poor dear María Paz Binns, such a darling, brainy as all get-out – and can't even make a simple chocolate cake from a magazine!*

Irrational fear of Tom Stoppard

Bourne End wasn't exactly a glamorous place, but it was always a desirable place to live, and it was beginning to fill up with go-getters. It had been a big step up socially for Mum after years in RAF housing. Among the other service wives she had been something of a queen bee, but she felt the strain of her new surroundings. She was afraid of being shown up as stupid or tongue-tied. That was why the sewing circle, and the company of women who respected her needle-work, had become such a necessity to her.

Not everyone triggered her reflex of panicked inadequacy. Jon Pertwee the actor, who was a neighbour, had become very friendly – even though he had been guilty of drawing the eyes of the world to the area, a few years previously, by recommending it as a location for the filming of *The Pumpkin Eater*. We could do without that sort of attention, thank you.

Pertwee knew how to butter Mum up, saying what a gem the house was – how had he missed it when he was looking for a house in the area? She must promise to let him know if she ever planned to sell.

He buttered us all up, telling Peter and me to call him Poetry – not Pertwee, which sounded like a baby trying to say *poetry* (he did a killing imitation) but 'Poetry' as a proper thespian would say it, chest out and shoulders back. He was entirely approachable, and younger than we originally thought, since at the time he had his hair dusted grey for a rôle.

Poetry was the life and soul of any party. Mum told us about one riverside gala (she heard about it at her sewing circle) at which Jon Pertwee had rowed an abandoned boat until it sank, then swam ashore fully clothed to wild applause.

I hadn't minded when the film people came to make *The Pumpkin Eater*, being thirteen or so at the time. The only complication of the shoot was that one elderly resident turned out not to have signed the release prepared by the production company. She refused to take direction, and would trot out of her front door (innocently or not) whenever the cameras rolled.

I didn't know that Peter Finch was a film star. All I knew was that I had never seen an adult squat on his heels for so long at a time. He seemed to shift his weight very gradually from side to side. When I asked him how he had learned this useful knack, he explained that he was originally from Australia, and had taught himself by watching the Aborigines there. They could squat like that all day.

Peter Finch offered to give Peter and me a ride in his enormous car, but Mum wouldn't let us go. I don't think she was actively alarmed by his celebrity, it was just the old rule about not accepting lifts from strange men, which applied even to strange film stars.

Tom Stoppard was a different matter. He had moved to Bourne End in the spring of 1968, about the time the Mini arrived. Not just to

Bourne End but to our neck of the woods, the Abbotsbrook Estate. His house was called River Thatch. A thatched house, obviously, with a small drive. A front lawn that was laid out for croquet. A large tree shading the sitting room, which faced the stream. Stoppard lived there with his wife Jose (could that be right, wondered the sewing circle collectively? Perhaps it was pronounced Josie?) and their small son.

A conspicuously clever writer was living a few hundred yards away from her front door, and Mum felt thoroughly undermined. She heard about it through her sewing circle, where tongues darted like needles and neighbours or strangers might be thoroughly stitched up. The news, heard over coffee and biscuits, knocked her right off her precarious perch.

Except with Mum, the famous playwright was personally popular. The young literary lion had selected Bourne End to be his personal safari park. He brought an extra bit of distinction to the area – not that we needed it. The great man did his writing in a Victorian boathouse, also thatched, which stood on a tiny island reached by a narrow bridge.

Some of his neighbours, true, complained about the noise. It wasn't wild Bohemian parties, it was peacocks. They made those cries like tortured babies, and they didn't stay where he put them, on the lawn. When he acquired them he seemed to assume with his playwright's imagination that they would stay decoratively put, like stage props, waving their ocellate plumes. In fact your peacock is a wanderer and a pecker. In India peacocks are common wild birds, celebrated in Hindu cosmology as the resplendent vehicle on which the God Murugan rides. They are experts at catching snakes, seeming to enjoy dodging the strikes of a cobra with its hood raised, to the point where it is widely believed that they 'dance' with cobras.

Mum didn't care about where and how Tom Stoppard did his writing, she didn't care about his ornamental livestock. She only cared that he was on the loose, brainy and philosophical, virtually in her street, certain to make her look stupid if they met. The things that he was famous for, the mental quickness, the cunning jokes, the animation and charm, were exactly the things that gave her the screaming ab-dabs. How would she defend herself? How was she supposed to cope, if she found herself standing next to him in the queue at the butcher's or the greengrocer's? He would grin with his vast white teeth, shake his tousled mop of hair, and subject her to an onslaught of epigrams, paradoxes, philosophical conundrums. He would reduce her to mumbling rubble. His brain would crackle with cleverness and hers would simply short-circuit. She would be humiliated and shown up. She would die, that's what she would do.

The chore of being clever all the time

Dad refused to humour her compulsions, saying she should make more effort to control herself. I thought she was doing her best, myself, and I did my bit to help her along. I said I thought it was very unlikely that famous playwrights did their own shopping. Had she ever actually seen him in the butcher's or the greengrocer's? She insisted that she'd seen him coming out of a shop. She recognised him from a picture in the local paper. If he could come out of a shop then he must have gone in, which meant that nowhere was safe. Which shop was it? The off-licence. He had seemed to leave the premises surfing on a wave of highbrow laughter. I said he had probably only popped in to pick up a bottle of wine to take to a dinner party – he would have been in a mad rush and in no mood to stop and banter. There was no risk of his queuing up for lamb chops at the butcher's. Couldn't she see she was safe?

I could see I was getting nowhere so I changed my approach, saying that it was never wrong to make neutral comments about the weather – it was expected. In fact that was probably why he had moved to Bourne End, to escape the chore of being clever all the time in London. She wasn't reassured, I have to say, but for the moment her nerve held steady. She might adjust the lie of her scarf in the hall mirror for a long moment before she left the house to go shopping, taking a deep breath as if she was about to go on stage, but she made herself do it.

Mum's equilibrium was under threat, but mine was pretty sturdy at this time. Eckstein had read my essay. He had got more than he bargained for, I dare say, but then he didn't know that I had a hotline to Lorca's secret soul in the person of María Paz Binns. 'This is a bit sketchy, John,' he said in class, 'it needs some more flesh on the bones. But the bones aren't too bad.' This faint praise was a deafening accolade by Eckstein's standards, and just as well. There weren't many people I'd let talk to me about bones in that way. 'I take your point,' said Eckstein, 'about Lorca's . . . women . . .' He was signalling pretty clearly that my knowledge of Lorca's most tortured thoughts should remain private. I'm not sure anybody else at school would have been particularly interested.

With Mum feeling so shaky, there was more than enough agoraphobia around. I began to suffer from the opposite condition, and to feel the urge to get out and about, to profit from my new mobility. One weekend I decided I would hurl myself out of the nest good and proper. I set off for London with only the vaguest idea of how to get there, or what I would do when I did. Would Dad draw me a map? He would not. Dad, who was perpetually on the lookout for strangers looking even vaguely lost, so that he could overwhelm them with hand-drawn maps and sketches of landmarks, instructions in numbered paragraphs, told me to use my initiative. Initiative! If Dad had had any initiative himself, he wouldn't have ended up under my orders, growing mushrooms that had a death-wish.

I wanted to find Covent Garden, having fond memories of *My Fair Lady*, and fetched up in Soho instead. At first I thought the women who accosted me in my car were flower-girls like Eliza Doolittle, but they weren't, not quite. They were themselves the flowers they sold, and very good saleswomen they were too. Very friendly, very confident of giving me a good time. There was no talk of giving me a discount, which was a definite sign of progress.

I didn't tell Mum and Dad about the chatty prostitutes, but Peter was fascinated and wanted to come with me on my next expedition. I let him do the map-reading, and somehow we ended up at the Palm Beach Casino Club. I got Peter to push me inside, more or less as a dare. The moment we were inside he said, 'This place is rigged. Everything's crooked.' Under the tacky glamour it smelled of stale flowers and desperation, and I was sure he was right, but that was no reason not to play. It turned out, though, thanks to the Gaming Act, that you had to join the club 24 hours before you played, so I joined on the spot and made plans to come back the next weekend. Peter, not yet eighteen, wasn't eligible to play, but I was all right. Peter could come to push, and watch.

During the week I worked out a system. I didn't want to make a killing, just incremental earnings. Peter had a toy roulette wheel at home, and I cut my teeth on that. The system wasn't very sophisticated, but it either guaranteed small wins or limited your losses. I may even have got it from a book or a film, though I'd like to think I was on good enough terms with numbers to work out something of the sort by myself.

It isn't complicated. You wait, without betting, until either the red or the black has come up three times in a row. Then you put a pound on the other colour. If you lose, put two pounds on. Then four pounds. Then stop.

I didn't do badly, small wins and smaller losses. Peter did notice, though, that any time I won anything, there were men who came round inconspicuously to make a note of what I'd done. It wasn't get-rich-quick – it was more like get-poor-slow, but it was a night out. I made a few pounds and we had fun.

Until Dad got to hear of it. He was fascinated, and got me to teach him my system. He couldn't wait to try it himself, and he wasn't going to take me along with him either. I wish I had held out on him about the address, refusing to give him directions, but he'd have found out another way if I had. All I could do was emphasise that it was crucial to follow the rules exactly. He didn't. What a time for Dad to stumble across his hidden hoard of initiative and spend it all at once!

He lost the housekeeping money and some savings as well, and had to get a part-time job driving a van to make good the losses. He came home very crestfallen and blaming me, saying it was the last time any of us went to that hellhole. Which was very unfair, but didn't make much difference anyway, since Palm Beach Casino was closed down very soon afterwards by the police for rigging their wheels. I didn't grieve. I'd more or less lost interest once I'd proved my system within its limits.

With Dad being a van driver at weekends, the mood of the house lightened. Mum and I found a little hobby of our own, not as ambitious as wine-making or mushroom husbandry. We started to indulge in the gentle art of candle-making. At first Mum resisted the idea, because of the element of danger: saucepans became hot, wax could scald. Precisely what appealed to me about the whole thing. I had to convince her that I was a different person from the callow boy who had scalded a neighbour's child. Finally she said that it would be all right so long as I read out directions and gave instructions, while she took care of the lifting and the pouring into moulds and so on. I tried to look disappointed for form's sake, but this division of labour was exactly what I had in mind. I was delighted.

Fizzy drinks frozen in time

Soon we were ordering pounds of slab wax. We learned to hack bits off without making too much of a mess. Then we heated it gently in a bain-marie, which Mum told me was also the proper way to make custard. In another saucepan, a much smaller one, we melted a little stearin and added dye to it. The quantities were so small that Mum sometimes let me do that. I had the idea from the name that stearin must be a sort of steroid, like the ones that had done so little lasting good to my generation of Still's Disease patients, but couldn't find out for definite.

Mum said we couldn't buy a wax thermometer. They cost too much. We found out the hard way that thrift can be wasteful. Our candles often developed a sort of dandruff, which is what happens when you pour your wax too cool. Other times, when we poured too hot, they became filled with small bubbles so that they looked like fizzy drinks frozen in time. Then Mum's hatred of imperfection led her to change her mind, and we invested in a wax thermometer after all.

I was aware that candle-making was a little bit babyish, even as hobbies go, but I didn't care. No one seemed quite sure what maturity would mean in my particular case, and nobody made it sound in the least bit attractive. Mum had the clearest idea, I suppose – her idea was that I would depend on her every day until one of us died. Which of us? I wonder if she gave that question any thought. Some married couples manage not to, after all. If she died first then I would be well and truly helpless, any independent spark long since extinguished, but if I died first then so would she. She was prone to saying, with ominous tenderness, 'What would you do without me, JJ? You'd be lost, it's as simple as that.' My needs were a handy screen for hers. I would never escape from her loving clutches. Puberty meant that she delegated certain unsavoury tasks, but apart from that there was to be no growing away from her in my growing up.

In theory Dad was all for pushing me out of the nest, that being nature's way, but in practice he dithered, pulling me back from the brink by my tail feathers more often than not. One holiday, for instance, Peter and I heard screams and mechanical music. Our ears had detected the possibility of a funfair, and soon our noses picked up the clinching smells of ozone and candyfloss.

Peter wanted to spend all his holiday money on the dodgems. I wasn't so ambitious. I had my heart set on the Ghost Train.

When I told Dad, he said, 'Negative, John. I can't allow it.' Under pressure he agreed to go on it himself, in case the ride was smoother than it looked. At the very least he would describe exactly what went on, though we both knew that wasn't the same thing at all.

He came out rubbing his head, looking rather pale. I begged him to tell me what had happened, and he said, 'Well, there was all the usual stuff, screaming, cold damp gloves trailing against your face, and then some great rubber thing comes down and donks you on the head. Made me see stars – Damn good job you weren't in there too . . . I couldn't've protected you from something as sudden as that, Chicken. In any case, those tracks jerk really sharply inside there. They could hurt your joints and do a lot of damage. Tell you what, though . . .'

His idea was that it was almost as much fun watching people's faces as they came out of the Ghost Train as it was riding it yourself. There was a place where doors were flung open and the cars clattered out, only to swerve and dash back in again, so that's where we positioned ourselves. Dad said it would be a good way for me to become a student of human nature.

It began to seem that my speciality in life was going to be the theory of things. Theory of First Aid at Vulcan, theory of car maintenance with the BSM, and now the theory of the Ghost Train.

The main thing we learned about human nature was that courting couples, clattering into the open for a few seconds mid-snog, with their hands all over each other, don't much like it when they find they're being watched by a middle-aged man and a teenager in a wheelchair. One boy flashed us a V-sign (not the one that Dad was familiar with, the triumphant one from the War) and for a moment it looked as if the girl was going to throw the remains of her toffee-apple at us, before the mechanism whisked them away again into the darkness full of muffled screams. We pushed off before we found ourselves up on charges. At the time I thought Dad was being un-necessarily hasty – I couldn't imagine ever having a criminal record. I didn't see how I could hope to get my mugshot on the list of Most Wanted. A criminal record was just one more wonderful thing out of reach. I needn't have worried. Karma has been kind – though of course it wasn't all that much fun when it finally happened.

You've gone all cock-eyed, dear

From the start, my desire to drive had overlapped with the desire to find sex. In that respect I was a normal adolescent. The intimacies I had enjoyed in the past, at the Vulcan School, had been laid on in-house. No travel was necessary – it was just a matter of seizing the moment, or of failing to get out of the way. But if I wasn't planning on living in an institution then I would have to stop relying on such windfalls of pleasure. I would have to cater to my own appetites and meet pleasure half-way.

With a car I was able to seek it out, and to take myself to places where wickedness might be found. Someone mentioned that there was a disreputable pub in Windsor, 'louche' if not positively queer, but without further details I couldn't find the sins I sought. I had to rely on instinct. It helped if I imagined there were three of us look-ing for what the world might offer, loitering and looking sidelong at promising strangers (to the extent the neck allowed) in the hope that they might look sidelong back at us. Federico García Lorca, Boyde Ashlar and me. We should really have brought Tennessee Williams along, for a bit of humour and common sense, but we didn't think of that. There just wasn't room enough in the Mini.

In a cartoon my two escorts would have perched on my shoulders, one with a halo on his head, the other with horns, arguing the case variously for risk-taking and the straight-and-narrow. In reality Lorca and Ashlar were both on the horny side, and they spoke with a single voice. Ashlar even had a little shoulder-perching devil-angel of his own, the effeminate friend always ready to murmur, 'You've gone all cock-eyed, dear.' Everything conspired to push me towards bravery and the outrageous.

Only a few months after I passed my test I took the Mini down a side alley in Marlow. It was the louchest place I could find, though I had only the dimmest notion of what I was looking for. I knew that there should be light but not too much of it, preferably coming from the side. There should be a suggestion of neglect or dereliction but also of waiting for something. The picture would be completed by a figure in shadow with a cigarette. Smoke swallowed and then breathed out. Weight being shifted from leg to leg with a sound that only woodland creatures, and I myself, could hear.

The lane was promising. And there he was – a figure under the trees at the end, exaggeratedly at his ease. There seems to be a deep instinct that tells us if an unreadable figure, a figure in silhouette, is smiling. The man came up to the car without hesitation, all business, almost before I had parked, and opened the door. He got in. The Mini's suspension lurched, and so did my heart. Would it manage to keep beating, during what must follow?

For all the encouragement my demons had given me, of course, they left me in the lurch when I needed them most. Boyde and Federico had scarpered. Cowards! After all their bold talk.

The stranger parked himself on the seat next to me. Where else was he going to go? In a Mini intimacy is the only option. His cologne was strong, the smell of his cigarette was stronger. He was chewing gum as well as smoking. I could smell that too.

At first I didn't look at him directly, but I thought that I'd made rather a brilliant catch. He reached over with his hand and gave my hair a ruffle, which was exciting if perhaps a little too much an uncle's action, a liberty but also a dead end. The ruffling hand passed my field of vision on its return journey. The skin tone was darker than mine. There were follicles. There was dark hair on the dark wrist. My heart was going like mad, now that I had achieved what had taken so long to bring about. I had brought something uncontrollable into my life, something swarthy, to sit beside me in the car and turn life upside down. When I shifted awkwardly round to return the smile in the passenger seat, I found it belonged to Granny's pet waiter from the Compleat Angler.

The brain is a standardised organ. My brain was like the Mini I was sitting in, marginally adapted to my circumstances but little different from every other brain. It went on producing the standard responses. That evening my brain supplied me with the most foolish possible thought. *Perhaps he doesn't recognise me.* The staff in my mental press office could come up with no better bulletin than that to paper over the cracks. They should be fired. They should all be fired, and they could forget about references.

Of course he recognised me. *Of course* he recognised me! He might not remember my name, but he knew me all right. I didn't drive into the dining room at the Compleat Angler at the wheel of the Mini, but that didn't mean I was in disguise now. He had known who I was long before I recognised him, and the ruffling of my hair had been indulgent but the opposite of the touch I wanted.

He'd only got into the car for a chance to talk about old times, the splendours and miseries of the waiting life. I felt I could tell him a thing or two about that – the waiting life. 'I see all sorts at the Angler, believe me,' he said, 'and your grandmother is absolutely special. A one-of-a-kind sort of lady. ¿When will she come to see me again? ¿To make her little road across the plate?' His Spanishness was beginning to grate on me, and it was mortifying that I couldn't command enough vocab to communicate usefully. '¡When you next speak to your fantastic grandmother, you must ask her to come to the restaurant again soon so we can play our games and have some fun!'

To rob and murder you

Up to that point it had never occurred to me that waiters could feel anything but contempt for those they served. It was actually rather unbearable that everything turned out to revolve around Granny, in Marlow and the wider world. She'd paid for the car, and perhaps if I asked her nicely she'd pay for her special waiter to come home with me, to be nice to me the way Mr Thatcher's lady friend was nice to him. I didn't want that.

I made a supreme effort and said nothing. I tried to nail my tongue into a corner of my mouth, to stop myself from prattling. I wanted to be excused for a moment from my life's long charm offensive. I wanted this man to reach over across to me without being wooed, teased or hypnotised. I hadn't concentrated on the inside of my mouth so fiercely since the game of Teeth, way back in my early days of immobility, when I imagined living inside my own mouth, wandering through the stalagmites and stalactites set in the smooth pink rock. I was determined not to blurt out some winning wheedle.

I gave him the Cow Eyes, more for form's sake than anything else, just in case there was a chance of turning the encounter in a new direction. The silence in the car began to seem oppressive. Then he shifted and said rather sourly, 'You know, I had your number from the word go, from the first time you ate at my table. Absolutely had your number. And all I can say is – good luck!'

Silence had failed and speech must have its turn. 'What is your name?' I asked, wanting to make him stay. '*¿Cómo se llama Usted?*' I'd have asked him whether he didn't prefer black-tobacco Ducados to bland blond English smokes, but I couldn't muster the vocabulary.

'My name is whatever you like,' he said, between chews on the gum and drags on the cigarette. 'Waiter –You There – Gar*song* – Boy.' Granny didn't know his name, but for some reason that was all right. I was the one who had to stand in for the hotel's whole patronising clientele. Granny was fun and I wasn't. Against such judgements there is no appeal. On the whole I'd have preferred it if he'd just wished me fucked by an octopus. The amiable old multiple-violation-by-gastropod routine.

He took out his chewing gum and pressed it against the dashboard with his thumb. Then he was out of the car, joined a few moments later by another man, who materialised out of the shadows of the louchest lane in Marlow.

It was a setback, undoubtedly. No questing hero minds the odd failure. It's just that there are many reasons for a sexy waiter to climb into your Mini in a dark lane, reasons good and bad. He may want to kiss you, he may want to rob you and murder you, he may want to listen to your garbled rendering of homoerotic Spanish poetry. Any or all of the above – just so long as he doesn't want to talk about your grandmother. That's too much to bear. That's the pink limit.

I left his chewing gum where it was. I could have reached it with a little trouble, but it seemed somehow a meaningful memento. It was impregnated with the cigarette he had been smoking while he chewed, and added a sharp smell to the Mini's interior for some time. It became the crusty relic of an ancient frisson. I let it fossilise.

The idea that a disabled boy might go to a normal school such as Burnham had seemed to be my own discovery, almost my own invention. I had hewn it out of the living rock. The idea that a disabled young man might go to a normal university was an idea that I hadn't dared to propose to myself. Eckstein got there first. He had contacts at Cambridge University, but what on earth made him think I might make a suitable candidate? My essay on Lorca, that's what, feverish adolescent outpouring perfumed with smoke from María Paz Binns's sinister black cigarettes, the devil's gaspers.

Eckstein even came to Bourne End to see Mum and Dad, so as to discuss the idea of my applying to university. This was a huge honour, and I did my best to respond appropriately, showing off horribly on the piano that Peter no longer even pretended to play, giving my all in pared-down versions of unkillable tunes, 'Anyone Who Had a Heart' and 'A Walk in the Black Forest'. He brought along a jar of cheese and marmalade, all mixed up, a russet and ochre paste, which he vowed was delicious. I tried some and liked it, but Mum set her mind firmly against it. It seemed to prey on her mind, as if this was some sinister Teutonic depth-charge lurking in her fridge, and she threw it away as soon as she decently could, claiming it had gone off. As far as she was concerned, it had been off from the word go.

It worried me that my A-level results might not be good enough, but Eckstein reassured me in the only way he knew, by making me feel I knew nothing about it. 'If Eckstein recommends you, that counts for something. I don't say they will take you, but they will give you an interview.' From what he was saying, a set of A-level papers barely scratched the surface of the applicant's abilities. A Cambridge interview was a sort of academic X-ray, which would examine the very bones of my mind and pronounce them sturdy or unsound.

His recommended strategy was to apply early. It made sense to allow extra time for the university to prepare properly for my needs (preferably not by coaching undergraduates in the art of cushioning the wheelchair's falls downstairs). I thought back on the time at Trees before Granny's chequebook made the extension happen – if it had taken years for my own home to begin to be tailored to my measure, then it made sense to give a mere institution as much notice as possible. Eckstein also pointed out with his usual tact, which was none, that with my disordered educational history I had some catching up to do. I shouldn't expect to go up until 1970, when I would be a little older than my university equals.

I still wasn't entirely sold on the idea – the idea of Cambridge, that is. I liked the idea of university. Setting my sights on Cambridge was too much like living Dad's life as he would have wanted it to be. Under the trivial difference of disability, wouldn't the other students be rather like me? There would be a sprinkling of toffs and some working-class boys on best behaviour, but there would be an awful lot of the inhibited middle class, from whom little could be learned. There would also be women, but I can't say I gave them much thought. I hadn't yet had my fill of young male company.

Perhaps there were other places than Cambridge that would have me, even without Eckstein's recommendation. There was a cabalistic instrument called an UCCA form to be filled in. The letters stood for Universities' Combined Clearing Apparatus or something of the sort. I describe it as cabalistic because there were strict rules about how to list your choices, not all of them printed on the form. There were rules behind the rules, and perhaps you were supposed to know them from birth. I believe in previous lives, but I don't think mine were lived at graduate level. When the system was explained to me, with all the things that couldn't be said or could only be said in a particular way, I began to think of Great Britain as one big application form bristling with invisible rubrics, needing to be actually filled out only by those who had been refused in advance.

Got an Egyptian tram-driver instead

By then I had found my other place, the university I preferred in my mind to Cambridge. Keele. Keele was new, Keele was modern. It was 'red brick' (it was even in Staffordshire, where they actually made red bricks), and had only been given the status of university a few years before. Fine by me. It made sense that Keele would suit me better. The syllabus there was progressive, requiring students to study both arts and sciences instead of narrowing themselves in the traditional way. I could almost feel my brain expanding at the prospect. Keele was also likely to place fewer stumbling-blocks in the path of a wheelchair than a labyrinth of ancient learning like Cambridge. Admittedly Burnham had failed to provide anything in the way of lifts, despite being new and modern, but the principle wasn't discredited by a single disappointment.

My motoring map told me that Keele was comfortably further away from Bourne End than Cambridge, and this intensified its advantage. Dad was always talking about the excellence of nature's way of doing things, that birds pushed their chicks out of the nest at the earliest opportunity, but it was clear that in this case I would have to push myself out, against the furious resistance of the mother bird. I told myself that at red-brick Keele I would meet true companions, mates, working-class fellows with brick-dust on their brawny arms. This sort of dream seems stupid right up to the moment when it is fulfilled. Didn't E. M. Forster himself crave union with an English policeman? Okay, he got an Egyptian tram-driver instead, but he seems to have made the best of it.

I also had the idea that Dad wouldn't be jealous if I went to Keele, since it would hardly count as a university in his eyes. Perhaps jealousy wasn't even a factor in the equation. It was never easy to predict what would catch Dad on the raw and what he wouldn't even register.

I wanted to put Keele as my first choice, Cambridge as my second, but that was ruled out of court. Cambridge had to come first, or not at all, though in theory the admissions authorities of Cambridge were airy about the irrelevance of other examination boards' assessments of students, saying more or less *If we wanted A-grades, we could take our pick of the best – but really, it takes something more than the ability to pass exams to make the sort of student we're interested in.*

They could see right through the shallowness of status and ranking. You, on the other hand, were required to pay the proper homage. It was legitimate to put Cambridge second if you put Oxford first, and vice versa, as long as you didn't mind the bureaucratic equivalent of a bloody nose. Nothing good would come of such an act of provocation. It was within the rules – even the rules behind the rules – but it was completely stupid. So the sentence 'I want to go to Keele and find proletarian love, but failing that, I suppose I'll risk complicating Dad's emotional state by plumping for Cambridge', when translated into the language of UCCA, became *1. Cambridge, 2. Keele*. How much was lost in translation? Just about everything. It was as inadequate as my first stab at Lorca's poem.

On top of which, you have to put your chosen college in the space on the form, not just 'Cambridge', so my first choice was *Downing College, Cambridge*. Downing being where Eckstein had studied, and where he had his contacts. *1. Downing College, Cambridge. 2. Keele*.

Keele offered me an interview first, in May. I was surprised when Dad said he'd come with me. I'd be doing all the driving, though, I'd promised myself a real safari. I supposed he wanted to get away from Mum, who was being rather difficult, but I was pleased all the same. He was even taking two days' leave from work. Dad and I only ever seemed to be on the same path for a little while and by accident. I felt that I was basically a nuisance as far as he was concerned. I didn't look beneath the surface. I was content with self-pity and a limited view of a complex man. I didn't try to understand more deeply, by making myself sensitive to undercurrents, or the lack of them. Dad thought I was a nuisance, yes, but he also thought Peter and Audrey were a nuisance. It wasn't personal.

Of course it wasn't flattering that one of Dad's routine words for describing us and our behaviour was 'nauseating', and I had been quite shocked when I learned its exact meaning (when Flanny our GP gave me an injection to help me keep food down when I got the measles at last). So Dad was actually saying his children induced the desire to vomit! It served him right that I passed measles on to him so promptly. But after all, if I had wanted a different father, all I would have needed to do was choose another womb. He was only really part of the fittings and furnishings of the womb of my choice, one of the mod cons if you choose to think of it that way. *Dad en-suite, liable to vomit on contact with his children.*

Dad liked being a father, he just didn't like having children. It's not really a paradox. Family life didn't bring out the best in him, but in whom does it bring out the best, exactly? Certainly not me. I could be a perfect beast on evenings when I had decided to bait him.

Peter and I had different approaches to the adolescent task of annoying our parents. I sometimes had set-piece arguments with Dad at the dinner table, while Peter watched wide-eyed, thrilled by the conflict, waiting his turn in life to be bolshie. I certainly had the edge in argumentativeness, but I was hopelessly tongue-tied when it came to body-language, while he had a whole range of physical options open to him. When summoned to table, he could slouch, saunter, drag his heels, or march with exaggerated precision, as if he was on parade or else about to be court-martialled. He had an equal talent for sullenness and for robot impersonation. At the end of a meal he could always slope off with provocative casualness or scamper out and slam the door.

A plume of intellectual radiation

The best I could hope for was to be so annoying that I had to be removed bodily. For instance I might suggest to Dad that the continental approach to water purification was preferable to ours. Why not buy bottled water for drinking purposes and save yourself the trouble and expense of purifying the domestic supply, which was largely going to be used for baths and washing-up anyway? Dad might say that in point of fact very little water in France went for baths, but I would declare this slander irrelevant and return to my needling thesis. Knowing that Dad's goat would infallibly be got, that his goat was a dead duck from the beginning of the sentence, with the whole idea that anything about France or Spain could be sensible. For a man who had seen much of the globe, thanks to the RAF, and was now professionally involved in moving people round it, he seemed to have no idea why they might actually want to travel. If we granted the superiority of the French way of life in any small detail, then very rapidly every doorknob and handrail would bear the taint of pungent garlic and runny cheese. If the Spanish weren't kept in their place, likewise, there would be bull-fights at Lord's and the habañera would replace 'Land of Hope and Glory' on the last night of the Proms. Everything would become erotic and unreliable.

When tensions at table were reaching a rolling boil, Mum would simply grab the handles of the wheelchair and trundle me out of the dining room. She would camouflage the emergency exit by saying it was time for that programme on television I especially wanted to see. I didn't put up a struggle or try to fight the strong hand which clicked the brake off. I was well pleased with my work. This was as close as I could get to banging the door on my own account, having it vicariously slammed behind me while Dad returned to his pudding, digestive juices in uproar. It counted as a victory. I enjoyed the picture of myself as a junior dissident being hustled from the debating chamber. It was only a year since Russian tanks had rolled over the Czech enlightenment, as decisively as the one which had crushed my Vulcan headmaster Alan Raeburn's legs during his army training, and I was learning to use current events to dramatise myself.

I was a little uneasy about our leaving Mum on her own during our expedition to Keele, though Dad was confident it was just what she needed. Her phobia about the clever playwright had intensified, and at some stage had crossed the border, always hard to define, into active delusion. It wasn't just in shops that she feared the sudden apparition of her nemesis. He might pop up round the corner, with an escort of peacocks making that strangled-baby cry, spreading his own great tail of blue-green wisdom wide, until the sunlight sparkled unbearably on all the eyes of his mind.

She no longer felt safe even inside the house. She could sense, almost hear, Stoppard's brain working unstoppably, while she tried to read her library book. She felt as if that brain was an oversized appliance draining the National Grid, siphoning off what little mental power she could muster. If he made her feel so stupid when he was still (relatively) far off, what would it be like if they were ever in the same room? It didn't bear thinking about – which didn't mean she could stop herself. A plume of intellectual radiation was drifting across Bourne End. And she was the only one who knew about it.

I went to the trouble of laying hands on a copy of *Rosencrantz and Guildenstern Are Dead*, thanks to Mrs Pavey. Having read it, I told Mum with the full authority of an A-level student that it was clever but not *that* clever, but she wouldn't be comforted. She could tell that my heart wasn't in it, or perhaps that only my heart was in it, while my mind dissented. She knew me too well to be fooled by good intentions.

My trip to Keele wasn't optional, though Dad's attendance was. Still, if my long-term goal was trying not to dance to Mum's tune, then I could hardly blame Dad for sharing it. What could I do, in practical terms? I did what I could. I phoned Muriel Foot, the linch-pin of Mum's sewing circle, asking her to look in on Mum while we were away.

Dad was my map-reader for the journey to Keele. He was predict-ably exacting in this rôle, allowing only one stop on the way. He already had a spot picked out. It wasn't even on the direct route, but I knew better than to complain. This was the longest bit of driving I had ever done, and I was knackered by it, but I put up a good show. Finally we arrived at the designated lay-by, and Dad got out, saying he needed to stretch his legs and he'd heard this was a good spot to find viper's bugloss, which you certainly didn't see every day. There was a stile nearby, which he climbed. He practically twinkled over it. I admired the fluency of the movements that put space between us so smartly. He was stretching his legs already.

He was gone for the best part of an hour. It got hot inside the Mini. If I had been a dog he would have left a window open for me, I was sure of that, but then I could crank the handle myself after a fashion.

Suddenly he was back, out of breath and bleeding from scratches on his leg. He was wearing shorts, to be more comfortable on the journey, though of course he would change before we got to Keele into a presentable pair of trousers. He scrambled into the car, shaking and muttering, 'Bloody thorns'. I misjudged his mood by trying to make a joke of it, saying, 'That viper's bugloss must have quite a bite.' He ignored me and said, 'Start the car please John. Let's go.' I started the engine but didn't move off right away. 'What happened, Dad?'

'A bull chased me across the last field, that's what happened. Can we get a move on?' Dad never normally let a little thing like a bull worry him. He'd pushed me past any number of bulls in the past. 'I thought you said it was only people who didn't know what they were doing who got chased by bulls?'

'Never mind what I said, John. Move off. Chop chop. Time's get-ting on. We've got somewhere to go.'

I thought that was a bit rich after leaving me twiddling my thumbs for so long. I was the driver, wasn't I? He was only hitching a lift, and it would have served him right if I had gone on without him. I said, 'I'm just taking one last look at this lovely spot.'

'I must insist that you start driving.'

'Granny always said that I shouldn't waste the privilege of the view. Otherwise I'll get bored and crash.'

'Crash later if you must but drive *now*.' Sullenly I obeyed him. 'Your grandmother, John,' he went on, 'is a surly old witch who has never said a sensible thing or done a useful one.'

'Apart perhaps from buying the car you're riding in.'

That stopped him short, but only for a moment, and then he added, 'Oh, she'll make you pay, never fear. Don't you know that?' I knew that. Afterwards he calmed down a bit, though the earlier sunny mood was in no hurry to re-form.

My bright red charabanc

We were given a good welcome at Keele. It seemed a pretty little campus. It looked to me rather an artificial environment, which didn't put me off, rather the opposite. I quite fancied the idea of being a student of the University of Toytown. It was like a more modern version of the village in *The Prisoner*, a television programme which had many devotees at Burnham Grammar, enigmatic spy drama set in a sea-side resort, with splendid neo-Edwardian charabancs to carry everyone around. I found myself imitating the ritual leave-taking from the series by saying 'Be Seeing You' rather meaningfully at the end of my interview, instead of the conventional Goodbye.

The interview wasn't easy, though, and I found myself getting flustered. My German pronunciation faltered. It wasn't what it should have been. It rather let me down.

The canteen offered not one but two vegetarian options. I was told that if I was accepted I would be allowed to drive the Mini on the pedestrian walkways. All of this added to the seductiveness of the place – my bright red charabanc would have right of way.

There was a Victorian mansion which was part of the complex, with an enormous holly hedge which Dad and I admired. It must have been hundreds of feet wide, thirty foot high and almost as thick.

As we were leaving in the morning, Dad pointed out a disabled student, a girl in a motorised wheelchair. I could recognise the dawdling progress of an Everest & Jennings from some way off. I thought her presence was a good sign, but Dad was discouraging. 'While she's there,' he said, 'you don't have a chance. Not a chance in hell – that's just the way these things work.' I pointed out that if she was a second-year she would have graduated by the time I arrived, but Dad wasn't convinced.

I asked Dad if he wanted to do any more botanical sight-seeing on the way home, but he said he'd had enough of nature for the time being. We made do with coffee and sandwiches at a pub.

Muriel Foot was at Trees when we got there, to keep Mum company. Muriel had been worried, and though she hadn't spent the night she had stayed late that evening and returned early in the morning.

The day before, she had found Mum painting over the inside of a window with whitewash, and it had taken some time before Mum gave any sort of explanation. In fact she was putting into practice one of the procedures recommended in the event of nuclear war. The whitewash was intended to reflect the visible wave-lengths of an explosion, but Mum wasn't thinking in terms of a bomb. She was trying to protect us all against the catastrophic flash from Stoppard's brain.

Muriel tried to think of something else to suggest, to take her mind off things. Mum was willing to be distracted, but only up to a certain point. They sat down to draft letters to the local paper instead, warning people of the danger in which they all lived.

Muriel told Dad she thought Mum was having a nervous breakdown, but Dad didn't give that idea house room. 'That's not how Laura's breakdowns go. If she has the energy to whitewash a window it means she's holding her own.' Which wasn't exactly reassuring to Muriel, or indeed to me. It was news (to both of us, I imagine) that Mum had had breakdowns in the past.

Dad shooed Muriel away. She went without verbal protest – everyone knew better in those days than to come between husband and wife – though the set of her shoulders told a different story. Then Dad threw the draft letters in the bin, poured the whitewash away and made a start on cleaning the affected window. Then he went into the garden to see how things were getting along there in his absence. He paid no direct attention to Mum, but that wasn't the way their marriage worked (to the extent that it did). He had a steadying effect unconnected to any communicative current, and being ignored by him at close range was almost enough to bring her back to herself. To love, honour and obey – all those actions were promised at the wedding and, I'm sure, sincerely meant at the time. But they were hardly the operative verbs of the marriage. Almost-hearing, not-quite-looking-through, leaving-the-room-without-actually-moving – nothing was said in church about any of those.

As part of my application to Cambridge I had to write an essay on any subject under the sun. Free choice, that terrifying obligation. I decided I wanted to write something which proved my mind and my character went in more than one direction, both outward and inward, so I described the various stages a flame passes through before it starves to death. Thanks to my candle-making with Mum I had a good grasp of what went on in a flame. I made it as exact and technical as I could, describing the adventures of the flame as a scientific event, a nuanced narrative of physics and chemistry, but then I changed gear and wrote, 'I am now exactly that tiny blue tongue of combustion on a cushion of gases. You, dear examiner, can snuff me out once and for all. Or you can prolong the wick of my mind's life so that I burn yellow and burn bright.' Good manipulative pyræsthetics, though it was sentimental of me to use the image of a candle flame in such a way. In Hindu mysticism it is used to represent an opposite truth, the inconstancy of personality.

Even before the interview I got the impression that Cambridge University wasn't keen on disability, not in its heart of hearts. I decided that the only way I was going to persuade them otherwise was by being very full of the old can-do. Cambridge might agree to have me as long as I made out that I hardly needed the wheelchair. Only hanging on to it for sentimental reasons, like Evelyn Waugh's silly Sebastian taking his teddy bear with him to Oxford.

Dad didn't offer to go with me this time, and anyway I thought it would be a good idea to tackle a substantial trip solo. I did ask him to draw me a map, though, one more time. 'If you're going to fly solo you must learn to navigate,' he told me. 'It's all a matter of practice.' Out of the nest pronto, my lad. Don't expect any favours. Flap those stubby wings.

Old Tin-Legs has a lot to answer for

My interviewer was called Mr A. T. Grove. He met me outside the Porter's Lodge, shook my hand and then said neutrally, 'Shall we go for a little walk?' Yes, let's! All the way to this pebble here.

It was exactly as I feared. My body would have to pass muster before my mind was even considered. 'Certainly,' I said, hoping he didn't mean more than a few steps. 'It's a lovely day, isn't it?' The surface under my shoes, however, was anything but lovely. It was gravel. There is no less coöperative material to have underneath you when you're ambulating feebly with a crutch and a cane. It's a hellish surface for me, given the small square-inchage of my feet, and my very limited bracing skills with the hand-held implements. Rudimentary implements held in deficient hands.

'How far can you go? I thought we might go to Regent Street for a cup of coffee. Is that too far for you?'

I didn't know where Regent Street was, but it seemed too much to hope that it was actually inside the college – might it perhaps be the nickname of the junior common room? I knew historic universities were full of charming bits of vocabulary. 'No, indeed,' I assured him. 'A walk in the fresh air will do me good. It'll give me an appetite for a nice cup of coffee!'

'Well, I'm not sure I can quite promise you that,' answered A. T. Grove. 'But perhaps we'll manage to choke it down.'

And so I prattled on in agony, telling myself that at least it would all be worth while if it got me away from Bourne End. After a while I realised that my conversation was beside the point – I didn't need to hold up my side of it more than notionally, as long as I kept moving. So I asked Grove about the architecture and history of the college, and nodded and smiled at a ghastly angle while he answered. If I was hoping he would be distracted then I was deceived. He shot sharp little sidelong glances at me, while I drew on the last vestiges of my CRX-and-Vulcan personality, making a final effort to pretend that ankylosed joints were quite workable, really, once I got going. Piece of cake. Lovely tasty cake. I summoned up a tutelary spirit from the past, Michael Flanders of Flanders and Swann, who had given such helpful advice in the dressing room of the Theatre Royal, Windsor, in my childhood. I imagined Flanders's rosy lips and burly beard in my ear, murmuring, 'You've got to show them the fighting spirit now and then, more's the pity,' and then, even more softly, *'Damn that fellow Bader! Old Tin-Legs has a lot to answer for!'*

The effect of this phantom pep-talk was lessened by my knowledge that Michael Flanders had himself been an able-bodied undergraduate, who contracted polio at sea during the his war service. He could still be a hero of mine, but he wasn't entitled to inspire me at this stage of a ritual ordeal he hadn't shared.

By the time we got as far as the college gates I was light-headed with pain. I suppose a Cambridge college was bound to have a more worldly attitude than a grammar school. The idea must have been that if I was going to fall down anyway, it should ideally be now, before any institutional liability had been created, rather than after I had been admitted, when litigation against the college might bloom along with my bruises. As things stood, I was an outsider, responsible for my own risk. At least the gravel didn't extend to the street – it was a strictly intramural torture. Beyond the college gates the world was stone, which wouldn't normally be reassuring.

The coffee bar was called Snax. By this stage I could hardly stand up, but I wouldn't have been surprised if A. T. Grove had expected me to carry my coffee mug to our table. Perhaps his as well. Luckily he told me to sit down. 'I'm going to have a sandwich,' he said, 'to take away the taste of the coffee. And vice versa. Can I get you something to eat?' I was hungry but couldn't see anything suitable. I asked for some chips and he looked at me rather strangely. 'Not something they usually serve in sandwich bars, but I'll make enquiries.' He came back in a few moments with a packet of something called Chiplets, which were miniature chip-shaped snacks, notionally based on the potato, greasy of feel and salty in taste. He opened the packet politely and laid it on the table in front of me. Now I was really in trouble.

By good fortune the mugs in Snax had their handles conveniently mounted, so that I could drink my coffee without drawing attention to myself. A. T. Grove, though, looked at me closely to see how I managed. I hold mugs with their handles towards me, then lift from the shoulder. It's not elegant but it gets the job done.

Eating sandwiches was quite impossible in front of a stranger, one who just happened to have the power of educational life or death over me. Chips would have been manageable with a fork. The hateful Chiplets were no sort of substitute. Throwing titbits into your mouth is a handy party trick, though I wasn't sure I could bring it off accurately with these little salted javelins as opposed to the peanuts I was used to. I would need a few undignified tries to get my hand in. Any display of the sort would have been wildly at odds with the mood of an interview, if it was ever going to start. A. T. Grove was taking an awfully long time getting round to any sort of test for this mind as opposed to this body. When would he be turning on the X-ray machine that measured the mental apparatus?

I leaned forward and sniffed the air above the packet of Chiplets, saying, 'Stale, I'm afraid. I don't think I'll bother after all. But thank you very much anyway, sir.' I had to raise the stakes with a bluff rather than admit the truth. I wasn't going to admit that I couldn't manage to eat the bloody things. The one thing I couldn't do was admit that there was anything I couldn't do. In this context it was perfectly fine to be disabled as long as you could participate fully across the board.

If I couldn't master a bag of snacks at Snax how would I be able to master a course of study at Downing? My legs were still registering aftershocks of agony, and I felt I had been humiliated enough already.

I seemed to be doomed to alternate polite and prickly patterns of behaviour, first demanding delicacies out of season and then refusing them with a hint of apology. No wonder A. T. Grove looked at me rather oddly.

He ate his sandwich with every sign of pleasure, while my tummy muttered to itself. Then he pushed his plate away and drank down the dregs of his coffee with an expression of sour determination. Now perhaps we would arrive at the intellectual portion to the day. He was nodding and murmuring, 'Mmmmm . . . Mmmmm . . . Yes I think we know where we stand now.'

Where did we stand? I hadn't the faintest idea. My interviewer had asked no relevant questions. For all he knew I had intellectual marvels up my sleeve, spanking-new proofs of the existence of God. Then he said, 'Is there anything you'd like to ask me?'

I was very thrown by this. 'Not really,' I blurted, 'but isn't there anything you want to ask *me*?'

He became vague, perhaps embarrassed. 'I don't think so, Mr Cromer. I had to see for myself what the difficulties were.' Later I discovered that he was a geographer who simply happened to be handling admissions that year. His specialism was the desert. He might have been able to ask me about Thomas Mann's prose style, but he wouldn't have been able to assess the quality of the answer (which would have been another piece of bluff, since I had got stuck on the first few pages of *Buddenbrooks*, like so many thousands before me).

By the end of our meeting, I would hardly have been surprised if A. T. Grove had said, 'I have just one more educational question to put to you,' reaching into his pocket to produce a handful of ball bearings to scatter at my feet. Then when I went arse over apex trying to leave that hellish coffee bar he could murmur sadly, 'I'm afraid you're not going to meet the academic standards for a course of study at the university. As we've always said, exams don't give the whole picture. An interview is required to plumb the candidate in depth.'

I thought that back at Downing A. T. Grove might pass me on to someone else for Assessment of Candidates' Abilities Part Two. No. The intellectual part of the interview, the part that addressed capabilities of mind, never materialised. The specialist in deserts had conducted an interview that was a desert in its own right, a place where nothing could grow. All that had been proved was that I could go for a cup of coffee on Regent Street. Just barely.

Dad debriefed me when I got home. When I told him I hadn't been asked a single question in German – or even about German – he pulled a face, which had a stiff sympathy in its composition but perhaps something else as well. Perhaps it wasn't altogether bad news that I wasn't going to overtake him educationally, after all. I too had reached a dead end on the road to learning. He didn't quite say, 'I told you so,' since in fact he hadn't told me so. He had only thought of telling me so, and his face was saying, pretty clearly, 'I thought of telling you so, and if I had actually gone through with it, "I told you so" is what I'd be saying now.'

Green fronds of calm

I wasn't hell-bent on further education, but I could think of nothing else which would get me what I actually wanted, namely a bed away from home without any nurses attached to it or hovering nearby, waiting to be summoned. So this period of waiting for news of my future would have been a tense time, if it hadn't been for Mrs Pavey. As dock-leaves never grow far from nettles, so now there were green fronds of calm pushing up beside the prickles of anxiety. Mrs Pavey came up trumps once again. In fact she came up with the ace of trumps, a spiritual bombshell.

While I was still at Burnham she had sent along another book by Mouni Sadhu, in the wake of my beloved *Tarot*, called *In Days of Great Peace*. I read it without much excitement. It was about a particular guru in India, but I can't say he made a huge impression. I was even able to read the sentence, 'He walked with difficulty, as his joints and knees were affected by acute rheumatism', without realising I had come across a spiritual leader tailor-made for me. A guru with rheumatism – wasn't that just exactly the ticket?

When you feel grace tugging at your heart and start looking for the Guru, it actually means he's already found you. He was installed in your deepest life all along. You never met him because he was never not there. Grace proceeds not by ambushes of glory but sidelong and stealthwise, in a rosy pervasion.

I don't know why I hadn't responded more strongly to that first re-fracted glimpse of my guru. Spiritually I had lain fallow for years, but now I was mysteriously cleared and ready for sowing. My mind was bringing a crop of language towards the brutal harvest of an exam, but in another way this was seed time, a season of rapid growth from nothing.

Or perhaps the comparison should be with the germination of mushroom spores – in the wider world, rather than the botched artificial version Dad and I had tried to make happen at Trees. Under the ground the mycelial threads thicken and mature, but nothing appears

207

above the surface until the right moment. Dry weather conditions impede any further progress, but when the drought breaks suddenly there are sporocarps everywhere, prodigious fruiting bodies.

The label on Mrs Pavey's bombshell was *Ramana Maharshi and the Path of Self-Knowledge* by Arthur Osborne. I expect it was the blurb which alerted her to its suitability: 'Many forms of Yoga are unsuited to the Western way of life. The Yoga of Wisdom and Understanding as taught and lived by Ramana Maharshi, however, is a point where East and West can meet, since it does not demand withdrawal from the world. Nor does its practice entail tortuous exercises or the tying of the body in knots.' Bless the blurb! And bless the librarian who popped the book into Mum's bicycle basket.

I had read about yoga, and been fascinated, though excluded from the physical practice. Yoga can give you a lovely flexible body, but only if you start off with one.

As for withdrawing from the world, it was not an attractive idea for me. I had only a toehold there and could easily lose my very marginal place. To adapt an old joke: the family is an institution – but who wants to live in an institution? Certainly not me. Even if I established some sort of independence from Mum and Dad there would always be institutions – hospitals, 'homes' – yawning to swallow me. To enter one of those would not be a way of transcending the world, only being shut out of it. That's not mystic withdrawal, that's eviction.

All my impetus was towards involvement. Between them my spiritual and pragmatic sides cooked up a rationale for this that suited them both: If you weren't really part of the world then withdrawing from it had no value. Let me get stuck in to the life people lead. *Then* I would transcend its futility. But not before.

Leisurely thunderbolt

Before I read Arthur Osborne's book I was searching at random. The fact that I didn't know what I was looking for is proved by my having read about Ramana Maharshi in Mouni Sadhu's book without really noticing. Now I was saved from any possibility of spiritual dilettantism by a leisurely thunderbolt of affinity. There's a lot of guru-hopping goes on, but I've never swerved since then from Ramana

Maharshi. Also known as Bhagavan. The change from the Maharshi as refracted by Mouni Sadhu and the robust presence in dear Arthur Osborne's book reminded me of another subtly drastic change, only in reverse – the time that my 'illuminous' watch went to Maidenhead for its thousand-day service, and came back stripped of its radioactive paint.

Mouni Sadhu's book was like my watch after its service, weakly giving back the light it had been given, soon merging with the darkness. Arthur Osborne's was like the same watch fresh from Canadian Jim's wrist, charged with every sort of potency. As I read *Ramana Maharshi and the Path of Self-Knowledge*, the part of me that had been asking *who-am-I?* for so long, since I was first ill – getting no further than the sense of a brown and waxy haze – was bombarded by illumination. Ramana Maharshi as he manifested himself in Arthur Osborne's book was an active source. His smile was powered by the radium of enlightenment.

It was all so clear, and so easy. Ramana Maharshi didn't just 'not demand' that you changed your way of life, he warned against that temptation. His principle was that if you can discover the meaning of life in the jungle you can do it just as well on a bus. You could do it even in Bourne End.

He himself led a wonderfully inactive life. As a boy in Tiruchuli in southern India, his most obvious talent was for deep sleep. Then one day he went through the experience of death, and got over it. He understood that the death of the body has no relevance to the Self. A little later, still a boy, he set off by train to the settlement of Tiruvannamalai and the holy hill Arunachala. He walked the last miles, shed his privileged status as a Brahmin without premeditation, and never left. For a long time he neglected his body, but not out of a need for mortification (the Hindu word is *tapas*). It was a profound unawareness. He didn't eat, so people assumed he was fasting. Left to himself he would have starved to death, but if food was placed in his mouth he would chew and swallow unresponsively.

He didn't speak, and people assumed he had taken a vow of silence. An ashram grew up around him but he fled it more than once. Finally he accepted that he would always be a focus of worship, and simply stipulated that there should be no restriction of access to him, no charge made. He left no gospel, though he wrote a number of poems and hymns. Sometimes he answered questions and sometimes not. His ego had fallen away. Even in the letter he left to explain his departure for Tiruvannamalai he didn't use his name. As he explained, there was nothing deliberate or conscious about this. It was simply that the ego didn't rise up to sign it. Or as he put it another time, 'After the photographic plate has been exposed to the sun, does it continue to retain images?'

He loved analogies from technology. He would certainly have kept up with developments if his body had been around now, but it didn't matter. His Grace was already inside my system like a spiritual computer virus, twining its spiderware round every function.

Despite his absence of an ego, I experienced the presence of my guru as something very unlike a blank. There's another way of referring to the status of the ego after enlightenment, apart from the photographic-plate analogy: it resembles the moon as we see it in the daytime. A minor light operating in its own sphere. Ramana Maharshi had shed his personality yet retained his character, which was a delightful one. Playful, warm and dry.

Buying knickers on the Moon

At some stage in my reading it occurred to me that if this captivatingly earthy mystic made sense to me instinctively, then I myself must be a Hindu, not a Christian nor in any meaningful sense an ex-Christian. The thought didn't trouble me unduly. Very well, I was a Hindu. There didn't seem to be any procedure for signing up – it wasn't like the Rosicrucians, the Brotherhood of the Rosy Dawn, who had so fascinated me when I saw their advertisements in *Prediction* magazine promising Cosmic Consciousness. I had only been held back by the necessity of sending my subscription (supposed to be a week's salary, so it would have been virtually nothing) made out to AMORC, a somehow unappealing acronym – standing for the Ancient and Mystical Order Rosæ Crucis, but still rhyming in the mind with Pork.

I seemed to have become a Hindu simply by the act of thinking so, which was marvellously simple. There's no equivalent of the Pope in

Hinduism. I don't mind hierarchies too much, but I do hate paperwork. Hindu Cosmic Consciousness had come to me free of charge and under its own power. No SAE had been required, even.

As I later learned, Hindu converts from Christianity are notoriously stroppy and intractable, so it was handy that I didn't fit the category. (They pine for their old certainties – they lay down beanbags in a church and then miss the discomfort of the pews.) If I had ever been a Christian, then that was a skin I had shed long ago. My new skin was Hindu.

I didn't have the experience of a conversion in the conventional sense, nor even the decisive moment which Quakers call 'convincement'. I treasure that word, perhaps more out of a love of technical terms in general, and a soft spot for the Quakers, who (apart from anything else) provided such a nurturing school for my brother, than because it describes anything that I felt. The rosy pervasion I was undergoing was perhaps closer to a chemical process, transformation on a molecular level like the action of yeast in dough or beer-making.

The great thing about this internal change was that there was nothing for anybody to notice. A carnivore turning Hindu would have to change his habits, but my vegetarianism was already in place.

Conversion doesn't always get a good press. Gandhi was opposed to the practice on principle. He felt that you should stay with the faith-structure of your upbringing, and try to fill it with your own ideals. My idea is just the reverse – every incarnation is like a treasure-hunt, and where would be the fun if the answer lay right next to the question? Going far afield for the beliefs that feel like home isn't a perverse extravagance, like buying your knickers on the Moon. The element of spiritual shopping-around is crucial, just so long as you know when to stop when you've found your bargain.

Those who content themselves with the faith of their parents aren't really playing the game. And I'm sure that the faith I inhaled, those hymns and that yawning, the earnest irrelevancies of the pulpit, would be an answer to prayer for someone brought up in another faith, even if I can't quite see how.

The letters from Keele and Cambridge arrived the same day. Mum hurried off to fetch Dad's letter-opener, samurai sword of the stationery drawer. I didn't know why it wasn't in my possession anyway. I was the only one in the house who actually needed a weapon to tackle his scanty postbag. Dad had a lovely long finger fit for the purpose. Mum had once explained that Dad's letter-knife was an heirloom, and I managed not to say, 'Yes, and I'm the heir apparent!'

Mum slid the opener across to me. She was as nervous as I was. 'Which are you going to open first?'

The one I cared about, obviously. The one from Keele.

It was a rejection, and I took it hard. I'd set my forks on the red-brick campus, the grown-up Toytown. 'Set my forks on' – that was a phrase from a television quiz show of the time – *Take Your Pick*, compèred by Michael Miles. When a new contestant came on Michael Miles would tend to ask, 'Any prize you have forks on tonight?' Reluctantly I withdrew my forks from Keele.

Perhaps Dad had been right – they already had a disabled person and weren't in any hurry to acquire another. Disabled students were like hermits on country estates in the eighteenth century, very fashionable but one is enough. In fact to have two rather than one would spoil the whole effect.

I held out no hope for Cambridge's letter. I thought I knew what it said. The atmosphere at Keele had been much more welcoming, and if Cambridge hadn't bothered to ask me any proper questions it was because they'd already decided my fate before they laid eyes on me. No one had any obligation to accept me, after all. And that was me dished, educationally. I had the car and the driving skills, but nowhere to drive away to in the Mini.

I told myself that at least Cambridge University wasn't being hypocritical. There was no pretence that I was being rejected for academic reasons. It was a nice straightforward slap in the face. My thinking hadn't been tested – I had failed in the practical, by not walking well enough to a snack bar. My intelligence wasn't being denied, just my right to develop it.

Despite my alleged cleverness, I had failed to notice a crucial detail. The Keele envelope was skinny, and the other one was not. The envelope from Cambridge was positively fat. It bulged.

That's because when they say No, that's all they need to say. Big fat no – it doesn't take up much space. If they say Yes, they have to explain the fine print, as I found out when I picked up my borrowed blade and prised open the flap. The one big Yes was hedged about with a thousand niggling Thou Shalt Nots.

The thing that Hitler stole from Dad

The bye-laws and regulations went on for page after page. They had said Yes. Yes, but . . . Yes, as long as . . . Yes, unless . . .

But still Yes, though it was slow to sink in. The Yes was so greatly outnumbered by the Nos, it hardly seemed to have a chance. The level of detail was astonishing. *Undergraduates are permitted to boil eggs on hobs and in their kitchens. More adventurous culinary efforts, especially those involving frying, are strictly prohibited.* It was easy to lose sight of the favourable verdict in the haze of caveats and prohibitions.

It took me quite a while to get it into my head that I'd been accepted – and even then Mum wasn't convinced. I had told her about not really being interviewed, just made to walk to a coffee bar. They'd only stopped short of putting me in the stocks, why would they be giving me the key to the city? She couldn't believe I was really being offered a place at Cambridge – the very thing that Hitler had stolen from Dad – just like that, with no questions asked, or no relevant questions at least.

So as to satisfy Mum, and to quiet my own unworthy doubts, I rang up the Admissions Board for confirmation. I said quite clearly, 'We just had a walk and a cup of coffee. He didn't test me at all. There must be more to it than that!' The secretary went away for a few minutes, and when she came back she said, 'Yes, he did. He did test you, and he passed you, and we've accepted you.' Apparently A. T. Grove had a portable X-ray machine with him all along, and had peered inside my mind when I wasn't looking.

It's funny that it should have been so hard, after all the to-ing and fro-ing, to take Yes for an answer. I'd won, and I demanded a recount. The doors had opened, and somehow I kept banging on them with my stick and my puny fists.

Of course there was a catch. To satisfy Cambridge I only had to get two Es in my A-levels, English and German, but if I was going to read Modern Languages (which was the whole idea), then I had to take another modern language at A-level. It couldn't be a subject that was already part of my course of study. In other words, it couldn't be French.

This was actually something of a relief, since I'd always disliked the language, or at least the chasm between what was written and what was said. Every ending in French seemed to sound like *eh*, but the spellings proliferated wildly. That had always been one of German's trump cards, the precision of its notation.

My extra language would have to be Spanish, which I'd barely started to learn. The strategy of early application had been a success, though, and I had time in hand, if I could only muster the patience. Eckstein had already got me started. I was well on my way with *Nos ponemos en camino. We put ourselves on the path.* We were picking up speed. There were three books in the series, and I sailed through the first two. Admittedly the third gave me a bit of trouble.

I would skip the O-level and study for my Spanish A-level at High Wycombe Technical College, brushing up my German at the same time, and I would arrive in Cambridge at last in September 1970.

First, though, there was some more tinkering to be done on this body. It was as if I had got used to a perverse sort of pattern – leave a school, treat yourself to some surgery. This time it was a matter of sorting out my right leg, which pointed forward so alarmingly at the knee. The procedure wasn't medically necessary, but the leg was certainly unsightly as things stood.

Mr Arden would operate, as before. 'I don't need to explain everything to you, John,' he said, 'after what you've been through already. You know the drill.' Indeed I knew the drill. The circular saw I also knew. 'But how straight do you want it?' he asked. 'I don't want to make it *too* straight, after all.' He did a little sketch of what he proposed, to be sure of getting my approval.

The proposed operation was paradoxical. I was like a Zen koan written in surgical steel: *shortening the leg we make it longer*. Mr Arden would be shortening my leg, in the sense that a wedge of bone would be removed, but lengthening it for practical purposes. My foot would meet the ground, once he had done his work, and the finished limb would be longer because more straight. The effect, if he overdid it, would be to make the other leg, the left, shorter in relative terms. My ability to reach the pedals with both feet might be impaired. He wanted me to know what would be involved, even after I had given the go-ahead on the basis of his nifty little drawing. 'You do know, don't you,' he said, 'that you'll have to learn to drive all over again when your leg has healed? Not from scratch, exactly, but near enough. It'll take you a good while to adjust.' I told myself that it couldn't be as bad as the rehabilitation from hips.

I was promised clear benefits from the operation, in terms of my posture and physical ability to manage, but really this was cosmetic surgery. If Patrick Savage had never referred to the unearthly angle of my knee and his need for a protractor to measure it, I wouldn't have tampered with it. I had wanted to be his dear love, I hadn't wanted to be his geometry homework. But of course by this time he and I hadn't spoken for months. We were no longer even at the same institution. It was too late to make any difference, and I couldn't mend the past.

Perhaps I was hoping to get off on the right foot with a future, more available Patrick Savage. To make the best of my prospects, with someone who had lacked company in the womb and might elect to become my twin. Any streamlining that could be done on this un-coöperative body was a good idea – that's the sort of thinking that passes for rational. But yes, perhaps there was an element of scape-goating, singling out my knee for punishment when it was the whole organism which had failed to find favour.

I took Arthur Osborne's precious book with me into the hospital, but I had also put in a request for another one from Mrs Pavey at the library. Not a Hindu volume – a life of Mary Baker Eddy. Ever since I had heard of Christian Science, even before I made the connection with Nancy Astor and CRX, I felt violently attracted and repulsed. Here at last was a school of religious thought which didn't regard pain as meaningful. Just what I thought myself, and part of what drew me so strongly to Hinduism. The drawback was correspondingly massive: if illness was Error, then I had been in the wrong continu-ously since I was three. It was time to decide whether Christian Science was a sort of Western Hinduism or a mean trick.

There was a Christian Science Reading Room in Maidenhead, and I had even thought of driving over there to talk to someone. The trouble was, of course – supposing that I was convinced of Mary Baker Eddy's truth – that I couldn't imagine the next step. How can the body repent? Would my joints listen when I recanted the fantasy and folly of Still's Disease?

It stood to reason, in any case, that Christian Science Reading Rooms would be up huge flights of stairs unserved by lifts, to discourage the unbelieving, the wallowers in imperfection. The most that could be hoped for, logically, was some sort of ramp, up which the wilful outcasts could trundle in their wheelchairs, to gaze with the corruptness of envy through a hagioscope (or squint, or leper window, in descending linguistic registers) at the jovial elect of Maidenhead.

I had left the choice of a book on Mary Baker Eddy up to Mrs Pavey. She must have taken a lot of trouble over her selection. A library is a sort of public garden, and librarians themselves are gardeners, but their interventions are anything but neutral. In every garden there are delicate plants that do well, and sturdy ones which succumb to a mysterious blight.

The book which was transmitted in Mum's bicycle basket was called *Mrs. Eddy*, by Edwin Franden Dakin, but that was roughly where its conventionality ended. There was a suggestive subtitle: *The Biography of a Virginal Mind*.

The book was American, published in 1929. I knew Mrs Pavey would have good reason for supplying me with a book that was less than up to date.

It was dedicated to the author's mother, in gratitude for the diligence she had shown in 'exploring with painstaking care the obscure haunts of data'. That was a phrase like a toffee to be lingeringly chewed: the obscure haunts of data. There was also a Publishers' Note which I found extremely interesting, which described the appearance of the text in a popular edition as marking 'the failure of an organized Minority to accomplish the suppression of opinions not to its liking'.

The idea of the tyrannous Minority was new to me – any tyranny I had experienced was of another kind. The Note explained that there had been a campaign to suppress the book in America, and pressure brought to bear on bookshops (though 'in all but a few cities the book could always be bought somewhere'), until a counter-campaign in defence of free speech was mounted.

So this was obviously not a life of Mary Baker Eddy which was welcomed by the organisation she founded. Why not? Mr Dakin explained it like this: 'There undoubtedly prevails a certain notion that all those who dare to talk intimately of God should conform in character to a conventional pattern, much as the design for sacred faces on church windows must all have an orthodox stare.' Something about Mrs Eddy's particular outlook didn't suit stained-glass prose. A hunger perhaps. Her life in this version was an adventure, 'a gorgeous adventure'.

I seemed to be getting a little more control over my reactions with each operation. This time as I reassembled the world after anæsthesia I neither swore nor chanted mystical Hebrew letters. I recited German verbs ending in *-ern*.

One more time my ankylosed bones had given Mr Arden a challenge and a sense of job satisfaction. He paid my ossature more extravagant compliments. 'I break bones every day,' he said. 'It's what I do for a living. But I can tell you, John, that knee of yours was something special!' Perhaps not the most tactful thing to say to someone whose body was still reverberating with the agony of it. I'd slept through the assault, yes, but my body had to stay put. It had nowhere to go, and was visited by nightmares independent of consciousness.

After a day or two I settled down to read *The Biography of a Virginal Mind*. The author was right in his own way – Mrs Eddy's life story was indeed a glorious adventure. It was even better than *Pamela*!

Part of the adventure was becoming famous late in life. The first edition of *Science and Health* didn't appear until 1875 and was slow to make its way in the world even so. Mrs Glover (her name at the time) was fifty-five then, in an age when a woman's fortieth birthday was a sort of instantaneous autumn. She was not only a widow, with an estranged – not to mention ne'er-do-well – son, but more recently a divorcée. Neither status was desirable or promising. Soon, though, she had acquired a third husband, and the name by which she is remembered.

I longed to re-enact significant episodes of the Mary Baker Eddy story. It maddened me to be surrounded by people with (as far as I could see) nothing better to do, but with a fixed resistance to taking direction. I could just about make one flinty physio ('anything for a quiet life,' she muttered, though life in the hospital was far too quiet already) act out one side of the crucial dialogue between Asa Gilbert Eddy and the man who had seemed to have a hot line to Mrs Glover's heart, Daniel Spofford.

He was her blue-eyed boy (the colour of his eyes was intense), a dreamy sort despite his rough history of farm work and service in the Civil War. Asa Gilbert Eddy, biddable, spinsterish, wearing his hair in an eccentric rolled arrangement, was not an obvious choice of husband. Then in 1876 there came a curious conversation between the two men, on the day when the engagement was announced. I coached my pet physio intensively until she could at least deliver Mr Spofford's line clearly: 'I confess I am surprised.'

Then as Mr Eddy I simpered, 'As am I – I have only just received the news myself!'

On the marriage certificate Mrs Glover tactfully subtracted seventeen years from her age, so as to harmonise it with her groom's, though presumably at the cost of making the ceremony illegal. Lemonade and cake were served.

Mary Baker Eddy's religion was a bit of a mess in doctrinal terms. As a solo turn I practised saying Mr Dakin's description of its system of beliefs – 'a cabinet of theological bric-à-brac!' – in tones most usually associated, on the English stage, with the incredulous question, 'A *handbag?*'

Edible uncut jewels

There was one scene I was particularly keen to stage: Mrs Eddy screaming for help in the middle of the night. This happened a lot. Christian Science had disposed of the possibility of ill health to its own satisfaction, but not every part of Mrs Eddy was convinced. As a child she had been sickly and subject to fits of hysterical rage, but then in her view every symptom was psychosomatic, including obesity (no more than an 'adipose belief of yourself as a substance').

After all, 'we have no evidence of food sustaining Life, except false evidence'.

Yet she was never a peaceful person. Her fear and pain had not been abolished by the flourishing of her church. They went into hiding merely, and reappeared in ever more distorted forms. She had banished error, sickness and pain, so if she experienced anything other than full health and happiness there could only be one explanation. Hostile agents were beaming destructive energy at her. The likely culprits were Mrs Eddy's own disaffected followers. Some of those she had once most relied on were trying to destroy Her (by this time pronouns attaching to her were routinely capitalised) with 'mental malpractice'.

There were other ways of describing the same destructive force: Electricity of Mortal Mind, The Red Dragon, The Trail of the Fiend, The Sting of the Serpent. The preferred term in Christian Science publications was Malicious Animal Magnetism. The attacks would normally come at dead of night, but if the magnetic assailants expected to find Mrs Eddy undefended they were mistaken. The alarm would go up – a shriek is an effective alarm. Helpers were waiting for the call (they stayed awake in relays of two-hour watches throughout the night, keeping the mental force-field charged). They would rush to Mrs Eddy's bedside and form a ring around her, bravely facing outwards, human shields against the metaphysical malice, for as long as it took her attackers to lose their destructive concentration, to abandon yet another attempt to incinerate the Pastor Emeritus from a cowardly distance with the emanations of their loathing.

What a tableau! So much more satisfying dramatically than pressing the buzzer (if it has been left within reach) and waiting for a nurse to have a spare moment.

Animal Magnetism was a powerful force. Mrs Eddy suffered from renal calculi – kidney stones – which were really only crystallised malice (I couldn't help picturing the edible uncut jewels of crystallised ginger). Rays of metaphysical hatred had found tiny cracks in the array of mental armour raised by Mrs Eddy's helpers. She had to resort to a dentist's services on a regular basis, in the teeth of her published and preached beliefs, since her upper jaw had been poisoned by the Sting of the Serpent.

I was gradually waking up to the fact that Mary Baker Eddy, elderly, disintegrating and imperious, was exactly the sort of rôle that Dad had had in mind all those years ago, when he had suggested that I could manage rather well as an actor, by playing an old lady in a wheelchair who bossed everybody about. Unfortunately I couldn't make the rest of the company play along or acknowledge my star quality.

I had to make do with the very limited supplies of curiosity available. A nurse might say, 'And what did Mary Baker Eddy do today?' and I'd say, '*You'll never guess!*' How could they possibly? She was making it all up as she went along.

What I would really have liked was a tame Christian Scientist to *wrangle* with. Granny had introduced me to this attractive word, commenting that wrangling was certainly one of my talents, and that it was a shame I wasn't more gifted in the field of mathematics, since the top student in that subject at her beloved Cambridge University was known as the Senior Wrangler.

Even wrangling of a junior sort was in short supply during my recovery and rehabilitation. Tame Christian Scientists weren't provided free under the National Health, and unfortunately, because of the very nature of their faith, a hospital was the last place such people would come of their own accord. Perhaps they should have done. At least they wouldn't be preaching to the converted.

It's a good job I didn't come across any patients with kidney stones. I couldn't have stopped myself from asking, 'Do you have a lot of enemies? People who might wish you metaphysical harm?' I'm not that strong. *In the watches of the night, do you feel the black searchlights of your foes as they search out the chinks in your walls?*

No vapour more easily ignited

My reformulated knee wasn't supposed to move, and it didn't, but still it found inventive ways to act up. It was enclosed in a large cast running more or less from hip to ankle, inside which it swelled and gave great pain. Concentrating on Mrs Eddy's life was increasingly difficult as my own became filled with intensely erroneous sensations. I thought my knee would burst. I pleaded with Mr Arden to remove the cast so as to relieve the pressure, but he said he couldn't do that.

The leg must be held in place. He compromised by having a little window cut in the plaster where the knee was, which allowed the distressed tissue to expand without jeopardising the process of healing. Then it began to itch and I had to poke at the window with anything that came to hand.

During this (third, was it?) rehabilitation my sensitive nose noticed something different in the atmosphere of the hospital. It wasn't a new smell, exactly, it was the attenuation of an old one. Times were changing. There were fewer volatilised molecules of amylum, that white powder prepared from potato and other vegetable tissue which yields a transparent viscous fluid when boiled – laundry starch, in fact. Starch was still being used in the laundering of nurses' uniforms, but in significantly smaller quantities. Nurses gave off a less peremptory rustle when they passed. It was almost a soothing whisper.

Of course the high tradition of nursing goes back to Florence Nightingale and the Crimean War. Many of the original nurses were genteel volunteers rather than professionals. I imagine that in those days the uniforms were so stiffly starched for a definite purpose. A squeamish nurse confronted with the horrors of warfare, infection or surgery, could faint without actually falling down, propped up by her amylum-impregnated clothes long enough to be trundled unobtrusively from the scene by colleagues, without her moment of weakness having an effect on the morale of the patients.

Mrs Eddy's psychology seemed very extreme and remote, and then suddenly it came into focus and sat right next to me. This unstable woman was destined to failure, until suddenly she wasn't. What had happened?

Christian Science would have been one more fizzling firework, hardly even a footnote in the history of cultic religion of America, where there is rarely a shortage of prophets and always a surfeit of disciples, if it hadn't caught fire at a single meeting in Chicago, in June 1888. Mary Baker Eddy was sixty-six, and very hit-or-miss as a public speaker. Her belief in herself fluctuated wildly between dogged assertiveness and a querulous shrinking. Even when she was advertised as a speaker, she would often quail at the last moment and delegate the task to someone else. She rebelled against anonymity but could not fully face fame.

On this occasion the local pastor was shrewd enough to advertise Mrs Eddy as a speaker, but without telling her in case she took fright. He told her only as he escorted her to her place on the stage – too late for her to appoint a substitute.

It turned out that she was having one of her good days, though Chicago was far from the Church's roots in New England. There were three thousand in the audience, on top of the eight hundred delegates. She stood up to speak, and the whole crowd came to its feet. She exported her hysteria in grand style. She released it into the hall and licensed every emotion, every wish.

But how did she do it? What did she say? She started off with the ninety-first psalm: ¶*He that dwelleth in the secret place of the most High shall abide under the shadow of the Almighty*. Not one of David's best efforts, you'd have thought, but experienced reporters were reportedly so spellbound that they forgot to take notes. There are paraphrases, but they don't give much indication of what the fuss was all about – what it was that made the crowd surge forward, desperate to touch her hand or her dress, while some cried out that their ailments had been mysteriously cured and others that they were (less mysteriously) being crushed.

If ever the guru spoke through her, it was that day – but it isn't necessary to suppose his presence. A room containing close to four thousand people is a candidate for spontaneous combustion even without the cue of a spark (spontaneous seems the wrong word for something building up so relentlessly). Few in the audience were believers already, which sounds like a disadvantage but was actually an enormous help, since there is no vapour more easily ignited than the desire to believe.

Mrs Eddy spoke, and that was all she needed to do. Whether she was the clapper or the bell, the two parts came together and the clang was immense. There followed a 'mad rhapsody' of press coverage, and it never really died down until she died herself, which she declined to do for the next twenty-two years.

The effect of becoming a public figure on this desperately unstable woman was dramatic. She showed a sudden genius for leadership. She developed astoundingly in her ability to direct and manage, to formulate plans and carry them to successful conclusion, to analyse a problem and put her finger on the underlying difficulty.

'The psychologist holds,' according to Mr Dakin, 'that there is no more able and efficient personality than the introvert who through some change of circumstances acquires or develops some extrovert tendencies.' At first I thought there was a particular psychologist being referred to at this point, but then I realised that it was the statement of a basic principle, even a commonplace. It was still news to me.

Could it really be true? Was this something everybody knew, except the one person who needed to? That person being me. I thought of myself as an extrovert billeted on an introverted body. Introverted bones, above all. Living an introverted life despite myself. Now the possibility was being floated that I might be able to transform myself, becoming so effective in the world as to be virtually unrecognisable. This was no longer a case history of an eccentric and long-dead figure, it was virtually a manifesto. There was plenty to hold me back, but no more than there had been to block Mrs Eddy's progress. Mrs Eddy had succeeded late in life in unfurling the umbrella of her character and displaying the lurid colours of its lining, and perhaps my own umbrella only seemed to be rusted shut, the catch useless if not actually broken off. I must be prepared to wait, just as she had, and watch for my moment, which would not necessarily be dramatic in any obvious way. When the time came, perhaps all I would have to do, like her, would be to open my mouth and say what I had to say.

Mrs Eddy went on being an inspiration even while it became clear she was a total monster. The two things were logically separate. What she did with her transformed character was her own affair. The inspirational thing was that she had been able to transform it.

Mrs Eddy stood revealed as a master manipulator whose tools were bureaucracy and public relations. The new religion had a particular appeal to the well-off – to people prosperous enough to identify ageing and ill-health as their supreme enemies.

A book dictated by God needs revision

The wealth of its supporters was a great asset to Christian Science. If a newspaper carried a derogatory article, or even if it referred to 'faith healing' (though surely there was faith and there was healing?), then complaints would be laid. If apologies were slow to appear then a local advertiser would telephone the newspaper offices – at a time when the telephone was a great luxury in itself – to express disappointment at such prejudicial expressions. That usually did the trick.

At a time when the church had about sixty thousand members, there were fifty publicity men paid to keep its image gleaming. One publicity man for every twelve hundred or so believers. Quite a tally. Church members were forbidden to reveal the number of believers, so as to give the impression of a vast movement.

Mrs Eddy was in her own way an innovator and inventor – something that Ramana Maharshi never claimed to be. In Hinduism it is always a question of old wine in new bottles, except that from a non-dualistic perspective wine and bottles are necessarily of the same substance and the same age. Mrs Eddy's innovations, though, were in the field of business studies rather than spirituality.

By the end of her life Mrs Eddy was making $400,000 a year from the movement's periodicals, and she knew about the importance of revenue. She never put her own money into the church. The flow of cash was quite the other way. In the 1880s she constituted the entire teaching staff of the Massachusetts Metaphysical College, which earned her over a million and a half dollars over that decade. A book dictated by God should hardly need revision, but new editions of *Science and Health* appeared very regularly, and each time the faithful were required to buy the new and discard the old, however minor the changes. Even so Mrs Eddy came to feel jealous of the profits made by the printers, and absorbed that aspect of the business also.

When a new Mother Church was built in Boston, it was paid for before its dedication. In fact an appeal had to be made asking that no more donations be made to the building fund. The newspapers couldn't get over this. They were accustomed to the moaning and wheedling of Methodists, Baptists, Presbyterians, Congregationalists and Campbellites seeking to find enough money to pay the preacher and a janitor. They publicised continual fairs, bazaars, ladies'-aid sociables and picnics dedicated to raising funds for a parsonage roof here, a Sunday-school carpet there. And now in three short years this curious sect of Christian Science had built a domed white temple of Bedford stone and granite taller by one foot than the Bunker Hill monument. Some newspapers ran articles every day for a week.

The financial miracle, at least, was well attested. Some vocations require a vow of poverty. Mrs Eddy had made a vow of wealth, and over time poverty took on the status of original sin. When it was suggested that wearing purple velvet and diamonds hardly went with the humility of the Lord's handmaid, she knew better than to say, 'If you've got it, baby, flaunt it!' She remarked that the diamonds were a present from someone whose life she had saved, which she had worn round the house until her husband reproached her, saying she was belittling the gesture of the gift. As for the velvet, it was really only velveteen and had cost barely a dollar years and years ago but was mysteriously renewed, 'like the widow's cruse'.

Healing was the key ingredient in this new religion – nothing fills a room like the prospect of a miracle cure. It was a stroke of genius for her to make out that healing was a lowly power, and to delegate it. To be sure, Mrs Eddy claimed cures of her own, up to and sometimes including the raising of the dead, but these miracles were long ago and far away, impossible to verify.

Metaphysical obstetrics

As with money, others took the risks but the benefit went to her alone. She took the credit for successful healing, but when things went wrong she disowned the practitioner. There was an outcry in 1888 when a Mrs Corner attended her own daughter in childbirth, and both mother and baby died. Some Christian Science students tried to rally round the (doubly) bereaved woman, who had handled the accouchement in accordance with Christian Science practice, but Mrs Eddy wasn't sentimental where bad publicity was involved. A statement was issued on behalf of the church pointing out, as if in sorrow, that Mrs Corner hadn't studied obstetrics at the approved institution. Hardly surprising, since courses in metaphysical obstetrics had only recently been set up. The grieving mother was branded a quack, and the church moved on.

In her long-delayed, long-lasting heyday, Mrs Eddy was less like a person than a confluence of rivers, one of cash and one of prestige. Yet the night terrors never left her.

She depended on charismatic recruits, but was also afraid of them.

Might they not break away or seek to usurp her place? She created insurance policies against rebels and rivals. The bye-laws of the Christian Scientists' Association included this sublime combination of propositions:

'*Resolved*, That every one who wishes to withdraw without reason shall be considered to have broken his oath.

'*Resolved*, That breaking the Christian Scientist's oath is immorality.'

That took care of the rebels. In 1895 she abolished the post of pastor: instead there would be Readers, whose job was literally Reading, reading aloud from the Bible and (more importantly) from *Science and Health*. They were required to identify her by name every time they read from her Book. They were to make no explanatory remarks. Nor should there be discussion of any sort afterwards – in any case she was to be notified of any meeting of church members, just to be safe. Rather, individuals should depart 'in quiet *thought*'. She had sealed the exit doors: now she pumped all the air out of the hall. And that took care of any rivals.

I started toying, idly and then more diligently, with the idea of writing a play about Mrs Eddy. Jimmy Kettle, the pupil at Vulcan who had first sold me on the world-beating genius of Tennessee Williams, had gone on to write a play of his own (or at least to start one) based on something that had happened on school premises. Why shouldn't I have a go myself? Bearing in mind that no one would write a *tour de force* solo turn for me as an immobile actor with no experience, I would have to do it myself – and in that respect Mary Baker Eddy was a gift of a subject. Power, delusion and speaking on God's behalf. Hard to go wrong, really.

It would be awkward if my play was put on in a church hall somewhere before Jimmy Kettle's first masterpiece was presented on Broadway or the West End, but it couldn't be helped. We were all grown-ups.

It made sense to set my play in Mrs Eddy's last home, Chestnut Hill in Massachusetts. I had my title already! I wrote the words *Chestnut Hill* in different styles of handwriting, and also explored the look of it in shorthand (Pitman and Gregg). In fact her previous home, Pleasant View, would have provided a more satisfactory title, but there was no help for that. I couldn't play ducks and drakes with the facts of a life, even if the life in question was more of a cautionary tale than a template for virtue or happiness.

There was certainly plenty of material. In fact Mrs Eddy's velvet-gown-and-diamonds period hadn't lasted long, and she had begun to withdraw relatively early. She moved to Concord, Massachusetts, some way from the church's core constituency in Boston. The intention was not to consolidate her mystique by making her unavailable, but that was the happy result.

Mrs Eddy didn't altogether disappear from public view. She would take a daily drive in a carriage, whatever the weather. Except that she was often too unwell to do so. On those days she would be impersonated on her outing. A white-haired woman muffled up to the ears in fur would take her place in the carriage, unobtrusively adjusting the angle of her parasol so as to shield her face from any observers.

Even so, it seemed there was no safety to be had from malicious animal magnetism. Mailboxes were particularly easily charged with it, so letters would be bundled up for posting far from home. Pleasant View became a place of fear. Mrs Leonard, the woman who had so helpfully impersonated the Pastor Emeritus in her carriage, died of diabetes. She was sixty-nine, quite an age at the time, but living in Science with nothing to fear – and fifteen years younger than She whose place she was taking. It seemed clear that the innocent with the sunshade had paid a terrible price for the service she rendered. The decoy had put herself in the firing line, and her health had been broken by invisible rays meant for Mrs Eddy. The poisoned darts had missed their intended target, but they had landed where they were sent.

Contriving to fling mesmerised trains

Mrs Eddy took the decision to move from New Hampshire altogether. She had been disrespectfully treated by the local press in Concord, to the point where she had been required to demonstrate her mental competence in a court of law. If I had been writing a proper play, with multiple characters, this would have been a scene of wild comedy, with the omnipotent bureaucrat being dragged into court and required to prove that she was in possession of all her marbles, rather than some confused old dear being manipulated and bled white by those she trusted.

The quest for a new home was an urgent one, the need for secrecy vital. Her trustees found her a suitable nest – this was Chestnut Hill, a stone mansion of some thirty-four rooms, set in twelve acres of woodland. They set about modifying it to her requirements at extreme speed. Hundreds of labourers worked in shifts day and night, with prodigious arc-lights making good the short hours of winter sunlight. Mrs Eddy's personal chambers exactly reproduced the layout and decor of her rooms at Pleasant View. There was an electric lift to spare her the effort of stairs. Steel safes were set in the walls of the landings, for the safe storage of documents – many of them giving accounts of her past rather different from the approved version. She had steadily been acquiring these for years. In the protected spaces of Mrs Eddy's safes the urge to suppress information and the urge to preserve it reached a strange equilibrium, a sort of peace.

The actual transfer of Mrs Eddy from one place to another involved activity more appropriate to an army on manœuvres than an individual moving house. Everything was done at night and in secrecy. Only when all the baggage had been delivered and installed did the mistress of the house follow with her retinue. She travelled by train, but not in the ordinary way. One locomotive went ahead of her train, and another drew up the rear, in a sort of convoy arrangement. It isn't clear whether the extra locomotives were there to block with sheer metallic bulk the rays of malign animal magnetism, or whether they were physical barriers, shock absorbers even, in the event that mental malpracticians maddened with hate somehow contrived to fling against their target mesmerised trains of their own. The precautions were effective, and the party travelled to Chestnut Hill without incident.

When the doors of the great house closed behind Mrs Eddy, they were locked and barred from within, and six armed men kept watch that night outside the house. What they were shutting out, of course, was far less relevant than what they were shutting in – a woman who had set her face against dying, but whose body, approaching its ninetieth year, was making its own arrangements. This was the point at which my play, my monologue, my one-man-show, began.

That was the theory. In practice I couldn't make the monster come alive on the page, and it was all very well having her look back on her long and crowded life, all the way to those early years which she had largely obliterated from the record, sending her agents to buy up documentary evidence, but there was such a lot to explain and organise. And how much was she supposed to know about herself? She couldn't be a complete hypocrite (no one would invent something as zany as Christian Science for fun), but nor could she completely toe her own party's line. If she had doubts then I had to show them plausibly poking through. It was harder than any school essay. Getting under Lorca's tingling skin was a pushover by comparison.

I decided to compromise by introducing another character as a foil for Mrs Eddy. A two-hander wasn't a lot less practical to stage than a solo act, and it would be far easier to get the words flowing. The other part would be a newcomer to the set-up at Chestnut Hill, thus doing most of my work for me.

Despite all the secrecy of the organisation this could smoothly be managed, thanks to a peculiarity of the church's constitution. It was one of the bye-laws that any church member must be available to serve Mrs Eddy in her home, at ten days' notice. The membership roster was a permanent solution to the servant problem! The stipulated period was originally a year, which was then raised to three. A member conscripted to the household staff in this way but leaving before due time, 'upon Mrs. Eddy's complaint thereof, shall be excommunicated from The Mother Church'.

In practice the bye-law wasn't invoked. It was best if the actual atmosphere of the household didn't become too widely known. Those who knew Mrs Eddy day to day found it hard to hold on to their admiration. Sometimes she was serene, lovable and wholly electric with dynamic charm, and sometimes . . . sometimes she was not. There was no shortage of willing helpers, which was a mercy. In those days gossip networks were very local. As long as servants were recruited from distant towns (or preferably farms), and returned there after their term of service, then Mrs Eddy's name was likely to keep its lustre. At last Christian Science had found a purpose for the poor and the poor in heart.

Enter, in my play, farm-girl of Irish descent Ellen McAlvey, seventeen, unable to believe her luck at joining the household of a living God. A trusting girl in the house of the Most High.

My title creaked and shifted under the weight of the new character, the new situation. It became *The Prophetess and the Colleen*. I was very happy with that. I absolutely adored the word 'colleen', but it's not an easy one to bring into general conversation.

I found no difficulty in writing speeches for this subsidiary character, her elation slightly dashed by the discovery that it was part of her duties, as a member of the household, to prevent such common occurrences of Error as snowfalls and thunderstorms. Ellen fully believed that Mother could dissipate a storm-cloud simply by looking at it, but doubted her own talents in that line.

When the shrieking started in the night, and Ellen took her place among the watchers round Mother's bedside, all of them facing outwards to counter the incoming storm of malicious animal magnetism, her faith was not shaken. Indeed it was intensified by the revelation of how desperately Mother's enemies wanted to harm her and bring her ministry down.

Sleepless nights, though, began to take a toll on her emotional stability . . . All in all, Ellen's voice rather went to my head. Reading what I had set down, I kept vowing to cut down on charm and Irishry, but in practice each draft was more blarney-ridden than the last. There was an Irish nurse doing shifts at the time, who greeted the smallest deviation from routine with formulas like 'That just about put the heart across me'. Ellen picked up her bad habits and added more.

Neutralising opiates on a fantastic scale

It wasn't hard to decide on the climactic incident of the drama. Late editions of *Science and Health* took an oddly sophistical position about morphine, authorising its injection in cases of violent pain, not to relieve pain but to lull the belief in it, after which the sufferer would recover the ability to handle his or her own case mentally.

There had been reports from the 1870s of Mrs Eddy's own use of the drug. Continuing rumours prompted an article in which she acknowledged that in the distant past her regular physician had prescribed morphine, 'when he could do no more for me', but that the glorious revelations of Christian Science had made it redundant. True, she had voluntarily taken large doses at one time, but that was to ascertain whether Christian Science could block the working of the drug – 'I say with tearful thanks, "The drug has no effect upon me whatever."'

In 1906 she wrote to the directors of her board of trustees asking that three more students be taught by a doctor the technique of giving morphine by hypodermic injections (in addition to the household attendant who already had that skill). Three more students! What must the directors have thought? Perhaps only that she was exercising Mind's sovereign power as only she knew how, and neutralising opiates on a fantastic scale. She often said, 'I am working on a plane that would mean instantaneous death to any of you . . .' Perhaps this was what she meant.

At the climax of my play Ellen was present and keeping vigil when Mrs Eddy begged and pleaded for her dose of morphine. Ellen was horrified when one of her attendants seemed to be preparing an injection – clearly a traitor who was trying to poison the living God. She tried to dash the syringe out of the attendant's hands and received a slap in the face for her trouble. Ellen watched in disbelief as the injection was given and peace came to the Pastor Emeritus at last.

At this point in my thinking, I realised that this was no longer a play about Mary Baker Eddy but about Ellen McAlvey. My title gave ground reluctantly with the burden of this new emphasis, and became *The Colleen and the Prophetess*.

Then at last I realised that there was no need for Mrs Eddy to appear in the play at all, since whenever Ellen had dealings with her she was either shrieking in terror or begging for morphine. I was writing a solo drama after all, but it was a one-woman show, and it wasn't about a fascinating public figure but about a woman who didn't exist. My title became *The Colleen* just before, with a final despairing crack, it splintered to matchwood.

I abandoned my grandiose scheme, retiring hurt from the competitive world of play-writing and leaving the field to Jimmy Kettle. I had no interest in writing a play I couldn't perform. I couldn't expect literary endeavour to take me out of my wheelchair, but I could reasonably expect it to get the wheelchair on stage, with me in it. That had been the whole point.

It was a shame. I would have liked to invite Granny to my first night, so as to hear what she had to say afterward. 'What an abominable creature, and an historical personage of no interest whatever'? 'A great and misunderstood woman, John, as you have helped me to see'? It would have been instructive either way.

The play-writing fiasco left me with a feeling of disgust. I wanted all my notes destroyed, and prevailed on one of my pet nurses to feed them into the hospital incinerator. I didn't doubt that she did, although looking back I can see it as unlikely. But what I had written didn't seem like ordinary neutral rubbish but something actively contaminated, in need of special measures for disposal.

When Mrs Eddy finally died, quietly, of pneumonia, in December 1910, her attendants were not so much grief-stricken as lost. They could hardly be surprised – Mrs Eddy had been warning them for years. The malice that had stalked her for so long had pounced on her in her flannel nightgown while the sentries dozed. If the watch had been kept as it should, she would have been a well woman still.

A will like a Möbius strip

The body itself was an embarrassment, since by its existence it contradicted the whole claim of her faith. Christian Science was lacking in something which every other religion has, something close to the root of the need for religion. A set of instructions for those left behind – a funeral service. Mary Baker Eddy wasn't supposed to die. That was the whole point. But if a religion has nothing to say to the bereaved, what does it have to say to anyone?

Surprisingly the immortal one had made a will, but it was a document entirely characteristic of her. It struggled to anticipate the needs of a world in which Mrs Eddy was not alive and dominant. She left everything to her Church, which sounds splendidly sensible until you realise that she owned her Church. She had taken great care to be completely inseparable from her creation, and so in legal terms she was leaving everything to herself. There must have been quite a few furrowed brows when this fact sunk in. Individual Christian Scientists weren't allowed to use the services of lawyers without Mrs Eddy's express permission, but luckily her Church was richly supplied with them. They found a way round the little difficulty of a document that fed remorselessly into itself, a will shaped like a Möbius strip. Otherwise the institution couldn't have lasted long enough to open a branch in Maidenhead.

It may be that my interest in Christian Science outstayed its welcome as far as other people at the hospital were concerned. There may have been a certain amount of eye-rolling behind my back, or to the side of my neck, or above my head – in one of the many places where eyes without the help of a supple and obliging spine can't manage to penetrate. Perhaps I forgot that anti-proselytising becomes as oppressive as proselytising itself.

I didn't presume to proselytise for Ramana Maharshi, I didn't and I don't. These affinities are very personal. I just read Arthur Osborne's book again.

Between the hysterical millionaire, cowering in her bed and shrieking for the metaphysical Home Guard, and the beaming indifference of the pauper, the choice was not hard to make.

Christian Science is a religion defined by its attitude to the failings of the body. It didn't seem to be asking too much to expect its philosophy of suffering to hold water.

In Ramana Maharshi's teaching, like Mrs Eddy's, pain and illness were unreal – but they weren't singled out. They had no special, superior unreality. They were just part of 'everything', everything that surrounds us without being real. Christian Science actually gives pain too much credit, granting it a wrongful position of privilege.

Later, when John Lennon's song 'God' came out it gave me another way of thinking about this. 'God,' Lennon sang in that winningly raw voice of his, 'is a concept by which we measure our pain.' Not so. Speaking softly, one John to another, my Home Counties breath in your Scouse ear, which bristles with sensitivity and grievance – take it from me, John. Pain is a concept by which we measure our God, and our guru, even our businesswoman lightly disguised as a prophet.

Mary Baker Eddy was a Messiah first and foremost, it was her job and her life's work. She hardly qualifies as a religious thinker at all. To judge by her morphine habit, she wasn't much of a Christian

Scientist, but then Marx wasn't a Marxist, Freud wasn't a Freudian, even Newton wasn't a Newtonian, being far too taken up with alchemy. Ramana Maharshi, though, really did embody his own teachings, in warm indifference to his own status. The guru is no more than the tiger in an elephant's dream, making it start awake.

Outpouring of medicated hope

His teaching wasn't opposed to medicine. The principle was simple, that everything must be addressed on its level. If you're hungry in a dream, you need dream food. And if a dream appetite needs dream food, then a dream cut requires a dream bandage. Christ was offering his own version of this principle when he said that we should render unto Maya the things that are Maya's, but Ramana Maharshi went further. Render unto the National Health those things that are the National Health's.

When he became seriously ill himself, well-wishers contributed medicines of every description. To his followers' dismay he had them all poured into a bowl and mixed up. Then he would take at regular intervals a small sample of that great outpouring of medicated hope. I loved that attitude, compliance with a trace of teasing, not quite colluding with the wishful thinking of it. But when Ramana Maharshi realised that if he went on taking doses of the compendious medicine everyone would follow him and devotees might become ill, he stopped his little game.

Ramana Maharshi had suffered from arthritis for many years without complaining. He didn't have disciples, exactly, who had to be called from other walks of life, *à la* Christ, but devotees, self-appointed, some of them really only hangers-on who wouldn't take no for an answer. His attitude to them was one of tender mockery. On one occasion a devotee scolded an arthritic visitor – an American woman – for her failure to cross her legs properly. Rather than scold them in his turn, Ramana Maharshi tried to force his limbs into the prescribed position. Then of course the devotees said that the rules didn't apply to him. He replied that if there were rules, they obviously did. I paraphrase. He made the devotees look foolish without claiming the right to overrule them.

I liked this no-authority principle. It extended to exactly the sort of thing a religious leader might be expected to value. It's true that there is no equivalent of the Pope in Hinduism, but there is a sort of scattered college of cardinals, people who claim the authority to decide who has authority. The word in this context is *diksha*, 'protocol' perhaps. You can't just say 'I bagsy Enlightenment'. There's a proper procedure to be followed, a formal initiation, and Ramana Maharshi didn't seem to have followed it.

A swami came by one morning to check his spiritual paperwork. It wasn't enough for Ramana Maharshi to get the right answer, he had to show his workings. He was living in the Virupaksha Cave on Arunachala at the time. This swami (actually a Sastri, but never mind) wanted to add him officially to the line of gurus, and requested him to submit to *sannyasa*, the ancient ritual of renunciation. He wasn't asking on his own account merely, but had been deputed. The swami said that he would return at three that afternoon with everything that was needed for the ceremony. It wouldn't be necessary for Ramana Maharshi to wear the full ochre-coloured robes. A loincloth of that colour would be sufficient. He went away.

Then an elderly brahmin came along, with a bundle of books. His face looked familiar. Four or five books would be enough in this context to establish a high level of learning. Ramakrishna, for instance, was relatively ignorant in linguistic terms. Sanskrit was more or less a closed book to him, though it was a closed book he loved to carry around. There was one particular book which he carries in a number of photographs. Eventually it was pointed out to him that this was a volume of erotica. He didn't seem in the least put out, saying simply, and irrefutably, 'It is made up of the same sacred letters.'

While the brahmin went to bathe in the local water tank, Ramana Maharshi picked up one of his books. It was a Sanskrit book in Nagari characters, with the title *Arunachala Mahatmyam*. He hadn't known that this book existed in Sanskrit also. He was surprised, and opened the book on a passage saluting the greatness of the place in the words:

Those who live within the radius of three yojanas [30 miles] of this place, i.e. this Arunachala Hill, will get My Sayujyam, i.e. absorption into Me, freed from all bonds, even if they do not take any diksha. This is my order.

Living on Arunachala superseded initiation. Ramana Maharshi copied out the passage and the scriptural reference, replaced the book in the bundle and tied it up again. He closed his eyes. When he opened them again there was no sign of the bundle, and the brahmin never reappeared either. The swami returned but went away again once he had read the citation, the vital authentication which had drifted towards Ramana Maharshi like a blown wisp of wool landing on a twig.

Part of the appeal of this story was that the book in it behaved exactly as I would want it to, materialising with the crucial information and then resolving back into the void, lending the weight of its authority without the burden of its physical presence, the volume so heavy to lift, the pages so awkward to turn.

I wasn't living on the holy mountain of Shiva but in Bourne End, Buckinghamshire, and I would have loved a bit of initiation, a spiritual diploma to go with my driving licence. I longed for recognition, and if it wasn't going to take the form of worldly success then it would have to be an esoteric form of belonging. I hadn't altogether left behind the scheming child whose campaign to raise funds for the PDSA was really a bid for a mention in the *Busy Bee News*. I was still the unappeased teenager who would have joined the Rosicrucians by post if their acronym had been less ugly. Ramana Maharshi showed me that every time I sought endorsement, acknowledgement, a pat on the back from a hand in the sky, I gave away what I was hoping to be given. If you need to be admired for your independence, you're going to have to find a different name for it.

A crack in the core of that nuclear brain

Dad came to visit me in hospital a couple of times on his way to work. He would say, 'I can give you ten minutes, Chicken.' He was horrified, though, when he saw the book about Mary Baker Eddy. 'So those lot have got their claws into you, have they?'

'No, Dad,' I said, perfectly truthfully. 'Don't worry. I'm perfectly safe. I'm a Hindu.' Which only made him pull another face.

Then he said something surprising. 'Your mother went shopping yesterday. Ran into that radio man . . . Aspel. Seems they had quite a chinwag.' This was a remarkable breakthrough. Michael Aspel, teddy-bear uncle turned demon driver, wouldn't be my first choice of celebrity for her to deal with, but at least he wasn't intimidatingly clever.

Then Dad said something so surprising there had to be another word for it, a word to be kept behind glass and used only in emergencies. 'It's good to have her back.' It was like hearing a tree speak.

I hope at least he didn't say anything similar to Mum herself. There's nothing so disruptive of a fragile equilibrium than a fleeting taste of what you want.

It had been touch and go for quite a time. We weren't even sure if Mum should be going to Muriel's for the sewing circle – it was her only social outing, involving only a short exposure to harmful brain-waves. But it was at Muriel's that she was most likely to hear news of the radiant thinking machine which was stopping her from sleeping.

She kept going. Dad wouldn't escort her, but he did give her the cue to set off ('Quick march!'). And then it was at Muriel's that she had the first inkling of deliverance. The bush telegraph of Bourne End was all of a twitter. Jose Stoppard had started to behave strangely after the birth of another son. She had made rather a scene at the chemist's, shouting that it was she who had written the plays which had made her husband famous.

Mum wasn't the sort to take pleasure in another woman's troubles, and marital breakdown was still a troubling rarity in her circle. Even so she had a sense of consolation, of reprieve. It was tragic that a crack in the core of that nuclear brain, some defect in its shielding, had exposed an innocent party to toxic overdose, but at least it meant, surely, that the danger to the public would be taken seriously. Then she wouldn't be alone with her thoughts any more. This wasn't a case of estrangement but of contamination, radiation sickness in its marital form.

Later bulletins confirmed the fact of breakdown. Late in 1969 Tom Stoppard moved out, taking his sons with him, and Thatch End was put on the market. Mum began to breathe more easily. Her world returned to something like normal. She still had the rituals she needed to perform before leaving the house, rapping softly with her knuckles on either side of the hall mirror in patterns of five and eleven. But after that she could do her chores, and even get some joy out of going shopping. After a while we all relaxed, until we didn't feel we needed to hide the local paper in a panic just because it reviewed an amateur production of *The Real Inspector Hound*.

Towards the end of rehabilitation I went to a convalescent home in Bognor Regis – the local authority paid for it. I can't imagine that a great deal of creativity goes into assigning rehabilitation patient to convalescent home in the normal run of things, but perhaps on this occasion someone gave it a little extra thought, reasoning that a non-standard patient might suit a non-standard home.

It was certainly an eccentric set-up, run by a Scot called Mr Johnson. This was an establishment with a guiding principle. The guiding principle was 'næ wummen'. He wouldn't employ women because, he said, they were too bossy. If you had women around then it turned into a hospital ward in no time, and that wasn't the point, was it? So the staff were all male, all young and mostly nice to look at.

When Mr Johnson showed us round, Mum put up some token resistance. She said, 'If it's only men doing the work – and young ones at that, from the look of the ones I've seen – then surfaces won't get properly wiped and hoovered and dusted, will they? And the pee bottles won't be emptied promptly, which means they'll start to smell . . .'

Mr Johnson needed only one word for his answer. 'Exactly', he said. That was just the atmosphere he was aiming at. In a way it was surprising that Mum didn't drag me out of there right away, but she actually quite approved. If I was to be looked after by anyone else, then she would prefer it to be someone entirely her opposite. She would certainly prefer to entrust me to a sloppy man than a rival stickler of a woman. Perhaps she was hoping I'd see the merits of good housekeeping from exposure to neglect. I might come to love her on the rebound.

It's true that everything was amazingly slapdash, close to hazardous in some ways. Pee bottles sat around till they got good and pongy. The male staff just slobbed about in jeans, smoking cigarettes and drinking cups of tea. They would sit on your bed for a chat, which was still unheard-of in hospitals. I thought it was cosy. I thought it was heaven. Of course we were all young. It wouldn't have suited older, more settled people.

The rule about 'nae wummen' didn't apply to girlfriends of the in-mates or indeed the staff. There was a plentiful female presence, who were forgiven for washing up the odd plate as long as they did their fair share of the smoking and chatting. Naturally the wummen had to be 'oot' by nine o'clock in the evening, and after that it was boys and men together.

My first morning at the Home set the tone. A member of staff (he'd already told us to call him Mike) came in, clapped his hands loudly and called out, 'Right, you rabble, wake up! OK, first interrogation of the day: Who's been a good boy and who hasn't?'

Silence. What could he mean? 'What are these bits of white stuff in your bottles, eh? Been blowing your noses in the night?'

People didn't suggest such things! Surely?

'Pleading the fifth amendment, eh? Bunch of wankers! And I mean that most sincerely. You won't escape me so easily.'

He picked up my piss bottle and peered inside. 'Mmmm . . . not enough evidence. Try harder next time, John! Come clean! For the moment I have to say the verdict is Not Guilty. Not innocent, mind! What Mr Johnson would call, "*Not Prrroven*".'

He moved over to the next bed and picked up my neighbour's bot-tle. 'Aha! Just as I suspected. Lots of little white floating thingies – we have a dedicated self-abuser here!' He bent his ear over the bottle, as if listening to the whispering spermatozoa. 'What's that you say, boys? You didn't jump? You were pushed? How disgraceful. We shall have to see what Mr J has to say about all this (relax, he won't mind). Oh, and don't worry if any of you ever have trouble giving yourself a good tossing-off. Don't be shy – what do you think we're here for? Not everyone has a girlfriend, you know. We're here to help in any way we can.'

The size of a pet's gravestone

Not quite the prevailing atmosphere at Trees in Bourne End. Mum had underestimated the threat to her way of doing things presented by Mr Johnson's home. It was a revelation that men without women could create such a welcoming atmosphere, and the element of rough good humour was just what I had been missing.

There was one resident called Jack who particularly befriended me. He was in the Merchant Navy, and hated it. He was recovering, very slowly, from dysentery. He could walk a few tottery steps, but then he needed to rest. He was weak, although the signals he sent were strong. He had worked for the Palm Line, owned by Unilever, transporting palm oil from Nigeria.

I couldn't decide whether the oil they loaded for the return journey, to be processed into margarine, soap and candles, sounded disgusting or delicious. Jack explained that it was bright orange and almost solid. The local people dressed their food with it, though it had no particular taste and the sweetish smell wasn't appealing.

The crew weren't well paid, but they didn't need to be. Barter was the prevailing system, and they had the goods to exchange. A Unilever product such as Lifebuoy soap, returning to Africa after its grand tour, had gained enormously in economic buoyancy. A bar of Lifebuoy soap for a sack of pawpaws, a sack of lobsters or a woman. Admittedly these weren't the sort of soap bars we bought in shops, being the size of a pet's gravestone. 'The only trouble is,' he said, 'that I get sick of pawpaws long before I finish the sack and lobster doesn't agree with me in the first place. Women don't either.' I didn't quite know what to say, and missed the moment.

Another time he asked me if I had noticed that the staff of the home were all nutty, or queer, or both. 'Of course I'm broadminded,' he said. 'Travel does that for you, it broadens the mind. But then my mind was pretty broad before I left home.'

There was no privacy for the residents, but Jack was great pals with Mike. He told me that Mike had agreed to lend us his room when we were both a little stronger, just so we could light some joss-sticks and listen to music in peace. This was a very generous offer of Mike's. Perhaps a bar of Lifebuoy changed hands. Then in the end by the time I was strong enough to think this tender little scheme was practical, Jack was still too weak. And after that I had to leave Bognor and go back to Bourne End.

Before I left, a number of people from the Home autographed my cast. There was a lot of mischievous laughter while they worked. I inhaled the delicious stink of the felt-tip they were using, but everyone had chosen to make marks where I couldn't read them. I worried that

I was innocently carrying back into Mum's zone of power any amount of incriminating commentary.

In a way I needn't have worried. Mum inspected the cast and made a non-committal noise, a genteel grunt. She didn't read them out, so I had to wait for Peter to come home and put me out of my suspense. Jack had written DON'T DO ANYTHING I WOULDN'T DO! Mike had added IF YOU CAN'T BE GOOD AT LEAST BE CAREFUL! Mr Johnson's contribution was DON'T TAKE ANY WOODEN NICKELS, SON! There was nothing overtly objectionable about these slogans. Their mischief-making was indirect. But Mum must have realised my hair had been ruffled by a permissive breeze.

Back under her roof, I decided that 'the Home' was much homier than home proper. My descriptions made where I had been sound so warm and welcoming to Peter that he made me promise, if I ever went back there, to take him too.

I wrote a short story about my little crush on Jack, changing the genders (well, one of them anyway). It pretty much wrote itself and showed me that writing stories was a lot easier than writing plays. I called it 'And Melanie Was Pleased' and sent it to *Woman's Own*. I might be unfulfilled, but perhaps I could make unfulfilment pay. They rejected it prontissimo, and I can't say I blame them. I didn't believe my own happy ending, and if I didn't believe it how could I expect belief from anyone else?

I left Edith Piaf in the dust

After the cast had served its purpose I had to learn to walk, for the fifth time. I shouldn't exaggerate the difficulty of the rehabilitation – there was no new moving part to be coaxed into function. All the same my balance was quite different, and the muscles were required to work in a new way. Re-learning to drive was more arduous than re-learning to walk. My leg was now shorter but straighter, and I was taller by an inch and a half. I had opened up a decisive lead over Edith Piaf. These days I left her in the dust – but the leg that hadn't been tampered with was now lagging behind the other, and for driving purposes I needed it built up to compensate. Even after the new shoes arrived, I was never as comfortable in the car as I had been before the surgery.

In Mr Johnson's blessèd Home my reading had shifted away from being the centre of my life. I could even begin to imagine that under extreme circumstances (I couldn't visualise them) happiness might drive out reading.

The continuing spiritual fermentation going on inside me didn't make me any less small-minded. When my life seemed to be in a rut, I would try to change my responses to stimuli but found myself reacting exactly as before. The set patterns of mind and action inherited from past lives (those pesky *vasanas*) must be dismantled before any progress can be made, and I was grappling with them unsystematically in my own feeble way.

Peter and I had enjoyed, or endured, another meal with Granny at the Compleat Angler soon after the car arrived. In fact we triumphed over her, entirely by accident. Naturally she found a way of getting her own back.

It was well known in our household that there was one foodstuff which Granny abominated. I remember her saying, 'I hope your mother isn't serving you boys any of that dreadful slop from the tins? If I find she has, my revenge will be terrible.' Possibly she was joking, but it was never safe to make that assumption.

I wonder what she would have said, if she had known that the kitchen convenience to which she was referring with such disgust had been introduced to Britain by Fortnum and Mason, the shop for top people *par excellence*, as a prestige item. For some time they were the only stockists of . . . tinned baked beans. Considered by Granny to be the active opposite of a vegetable, a food item so vulgar and American it was practically obscene.

She was explaining, not for the first time, that one of the reasons she selected this particular Otel for her stays was the excellence of the vegetable preparation. Now that Peter had found employment in the world of catering she offered relevant instruction free of charge. In a country where greens were routinely boiled to mush, the kitchen staff at the Compleat Angler knew how to retain both vitamins and flavour. It was Granny's opinion that people shouldn't be allowed to have children unless they had proved they could cook vegetables correctly. It was hard to see how this scheme could be enforced, but that wasn't Granny's responsibility. She just had the ideas.

Of course beans-on-toast was one of our favourite meals at Trees. Mum sometimes bought cleaning products because she might win a cash prize if she produced them when the manufacturers' representative came to call, though she knew in her heart of hearts that they wouldn't displace her favourites. Those items lived at the back of a cupboard, awaiting a knock on the door. They shared the space with her Heinz baked beans, those tins glowing with an indefinable blue-green, the colour of an Amazonian parrot that never was.

The beans needed to be near enough for convenience but well out of sight in case her mother pounced for a spot inspection. It was quite normal for our treats to have a lining of shame to them in this way. We never missed Bruce Forsyth on a Saturday night, when he appeared on the Light Programme, as she perversely called ITV (once she'd stopped pretending we couldn't receive the signal at all, on account of our being so near the river). We watched 'just to see how awful it is', to be amazed at what lower people found entertaining. Our pleasures lay some distance from our principles, and often the things we said we liked did nothing for us.

Now at the Compleat Angler Granny was plumping for her main course, the lamb. There only remained the selection of a vegetable. She asked what was available. Normally the staff were chatty and personable, but our waiter must have sensed he was on dangerous ground. 'Beans, Madame,' he said.

'What sort of beans, exactly? French beans? Runner beans? Broad?'

This wasn't her Spanish pet (the one who didn't want me for a pet), who would certainly have had a shot at sweet-talking her, however hopeless the odds. This one was reduced to cowed silence and dumb show. He took the lid off the chafing dish to display the contents. It might just as well have been a kidney dish of hospital waste. Granny's face went dark – this was the scalding look occasionally visited on husband or dog – and Peter suppressed a snort. He and I were throughly enjoying the fix she was in. She who loved to put people on the spot was in a bit of a spot herself. How was she going to get out of it?

I thought I'd help the drama along. 'What sort of beans are we being served with, Granny?' I sang out. 'I can't see from here! They look all orangey.'

We watched her lips, Peter, the waiter and I, waiting to hear what words would emerge. Granny played for time, taking a good ten seconds to clear her throat. 'The item . . .' she said at last. 'The item on the menu seems to be . . . haricot beans . . . gently simmered in a piquant sauce. *A la mode de Boston.*'

'Oh,' I said. 'I know what that is! My French isn't so bad after all. That's baked beans, that is.' I saw Granny quiver, as if from pain or shock. 'Bung some on here, mate!' I said cheerily to the waiter. 'There you are, Peter! I knew Granny would never mind if we ate these. Mum must have been teasing us – or else she got the wrong end of the stick. She does that sometimes.' It was lovely to have the whip hand for once. 'You're right, Granny, they really know how to cook vegetables here. First class, tip-top!' They tasted even better than the ones we ate at home in conditions of secrecy. For once we were tasting victory, served up on fine china in tomato sauce.

Of course we pushed our luck. We tried to consolidate our advantage, and naturally we came a cropper. Granny had a natural genius for One-Upmanship, and Peter and I wouldn't remain One-Up for long. Later when I read Stephen Potter's book on *One-Upmanship* it held no surprises. The manœuvres all seemed rather tame. One of these days I'll track down a biography of the man, to see how he came up with the idea. For all I know there is a legendary figure in Stephen Potter studies, a mysterious woman he met at a party in the 1930s who showed him how to hunt the big game of the ego, someone who taught him all he knew.

Now, in the elation of the triumph we had shared, Peter was urging Granny to come with us to a film that was showing locally. An X film, a Hammer Horror. Vampires. 'Come on, Granny,' said Peter, 'let your hair down.'

'No one has yet been able to explain to me, Peter, why letting one's hair down would be a good thing. Your own hair has been let down rather far already.' He blushed but didn't give up.

'Really, Granny, you'll be quite safe. We'll look after you if you get scared. I've seen it already and I'll warn you when it's going to make you jump. John hasn't seen it, but nothing scares him.' Not entirely true (anything set in a hospital gave me a sick feeling in my stomach) but a good thing to hear your brother say.

'I very much doubt that the film you propose would make me jump. I warn you, though, that I might flinch.' Peter seemed delighted. If it wasn't for the formal surroundings he would have been whooping like mad. Granny was scared – she'd admitted it!

Then Granny went off at a tangent. 'When I was a child, there was no television and no films. We used to tell each other stories instead. One friend of my father's who used to visit was called Mr Stoker. In winter we would sit close to the fire while he told us tales that held us spellbound . . .'

Peter looked at me uncertainly. Granny was rambling, Granny seemed to be going gaga. Perhaps he thought that the shock of those beans in the chafing dish had broken her spirit. I wasn't so sure. I remembered the last time I had underestimated her, in this very room. I decided I would wait to hear the full six clicks before I was sure that Granny was out of ammunition.

Granny was scanning our faces for reaction to what she had said. Then her face hardened rather, as she added, 'Bram Stoker was the one who wrote that story, you know, the one you both seem to enjoy so much. If television had existed in his day I dare say it would never have been written . . .'

She paused to let her words sink in. We were still at sea. 'There is one point on which I must correct you, much as I hate to do so.' True enough, Granny hated to correct people almost as much as she hated to breathe. 'You have been saying *Drác-ula*' – she spat the word out as though it was a slug lurking in a bowl of consommé – 'and I have held my tongue. Now I feel it only fair to tell you that the word is properly pronounced *Dra-coóla*. That is, if Mr Stoker is allowed to know something about a personage he made up. When I told you I would wince if I went to the cinema to see your film, I was not referring to the story, with which I am thoroughly familiar, but to the pain of having to hear that ghastly and ignorant mispronunciation.'

One-Up? She was a thousand up, now. We would never catch up, not even if the Compleat Angler betrayed her all over again by serving Milky Bars on the dessert trolley. Still, it had been fun while it had lasted, our little ascendancy over the Dowager

Empress of One-Upmanship. For the rest of the evening she was in full control.

I tried to find spiritual instruction in my encounters with Granny. I even thought of telling her of my Hinduism – she was surely too much a woman of the world to be alarmed. On the other hand I'd rather she was alarmed than moved to deflate me conversationally, perhaps by remembering a hunt ball in her youth at which she had taught a dark young chap all he needed to know about what she called 'passive resistance', by the way she discouraged a persistent suitor. Mohandas Gandhi, she rather thought that was the dark young chap's name.

One of the things I loved about Ramana Maharshi from the start was the way he could use anything as a text or an example. There was no gospel as such, just the warm imperative to realise yourself, refracted through the whole range of analogies waiting to be used. His teaching might take a simple gesture or a staple food as its starting point.

The unboggled mind a great hindrance

Once a presumptuous seeker after truth made the journey to Tiru-vannamalai and insisted on seeing Ramana Maharshi, who refused, saying 'Go back the way you came.' The seeker after truth was very much put out by such uncoöperative behaviour from the guru, until his acolytes pointed out that far from being dismissed without what he had come for, he had received teaching of the richest, pithiest sort. 'Go back the way you came' – what could be more enlightening, properly understood? Retrace your footsteps, seek always the source, ask yourself not what is sought but who it is that seeks. The visitor went away greatly enlightened. Though the possibility remains that Ramana Maharshi really was saying Get lost, I can't be doing with you. It's a full-time job discouraging your own personality cult – and then the devotees did what they could to put a tactful gloss on what he said.

What instruction could I extract from this evening with Granny, on which she had got up to all her old tricks, and a few new ones? Perhaps I should be concentrating on the moment when she pounced, which always took me by surprise. At those moments I had the sensation that my thoughts had run into the buffers. When the mind boggles, enlightenment is just round the corner. If I could recreate that sensation at will, I would have made a real start. The unboggled mind is a great hindrance to self-realisation.

Simpler than stopping the mind in its tracks is unstringing it, by meditation. I was determined to open my mental apparatus to the things that underlay it, but I had no technique. I was making the usual beginner's mistake of simply instructing the mind to suspend itself. Chop chop. I don't have all day.

Meditating, at least in the noisy West, is like trying not to buy anything when you actually live in a supermarket. The trick is not to let yourself be distracted by the displays of bargains but to concentrate on your shopping list, which has THERE'S NOTHING I NEED written on it (even if the words are actually OM MANE PADME OM). With practice even these words disappear from the paper, and it becomes second nature to wander along the gleaming contemplative aisles, their shelves perfectly empty, the piped music replaced by a distillation of breathing.

My own yoga breathing was more or less instinctive, thanks to all the inadvertent practice I had put in during the bed-rest years, but I didn't know what a mantra was, or how it would help me unfocus. Or perhaps I had found my own way to the idea. It seemed to me that I had come close to meditating, as a child, when I had repeated the words from the lid of a biscuit tin, draining them of meaning, or else filling them with the radiance of not meaning anything. *Peek Frean Peek Frean*. I tried it for some time, with fair results.

There's nothing in modern life which remotely resembles meditation, except possibly making mayonnaise by hand. If you have the patient alertness to add the olive oil drop by drop in the early stages, you'll probably get the knack of meditation quite quickly. Admittedly making mayonnaise was a two-person job as far as Mum and I were concerned – she did the beating and I concentrated on precisely that aspect of the process, regulating the thin dribble of oil. I really wanted to make mayonnaise out of fascination with the scientific aspect (behaviour of emulsions). Mum asked what was wrong with Heinz salad cream, and I had to say, nothing much. On the basis of his tomato ketchup, his baked beans and his salad cream, Mr Heinz didn't miss a trick.

Heart-mortar, mind-pestle

With a little effort you could see meditation as an exercise in spiritual emulsification, suspending the ego in tiny dispersed globules. There's licence for such flights of fancy in the Hinduism I follow, and plenty of precedent in my guru's poems and conversation. In 1914 or so he wrote 'Song of the Poppadum'. What could be more down to earth? It goes like this:

> Make a batch of poppadums
> Eat them and satisfy your appetite.
> Don't roam the world disconsolate.
> Hear the word, unique, unspoken
> Taught by the true teacher who teaches
> The truth of Being-Awareness-Bliss.

> 1. Take the black-gram ego-self
> Growing in the five-fold body-field
> And grind it in the quern,
> The wisdom-quest of 'Who am I?'
> Reducing it to finest flour.
> Make a batch of poppadums . . . &c.

> 2. Mix it with *pirandai*-juice,
> Which is holy company,
> Add mind-control, the cumin-seed,
> The pepper of self-restraint,
> Salt of non-attachment,
> And asafœtida, the aroma
> Of virtuous inclination.
> Make a batch of poppadums . . . &c.

> 3. In the heart-mortar place the dough
> And with mind-pestle inward turned,
> Pound it hard with strokes of 'I', 'I',
> Then flatten it with the rolling pin

Of stillness on the level slab of Being.
Work away, untiring, steady, cheerful.
Make a batch of poppadums . . . *&c.*

4. Place the poppadum in the ghee of *Brahman*,
Held in the pan of infinite silence,
And fry it over the fire of knowledge.
Now I is transmuted into That.
Eat and taste the Self as Self,
Abiding in the Self alone.
Make a batch of poppadums . . . *&c.*

How am I supposed to resist a guru who effortlessly combines such contrary literary forms – prayer and recipe? The answer is that I'm not. I had already enjoyed the idea in *The Satipatthana Sutta and Its Application to Modern Life* that there was no special time and place that needed to be set aside for the contemplation of the non-illusory. Now I was mad for the idea that everyday life actually supplied the material for its own dismantling, so that you could be plunged into self-enquiry even while you were cooking up a batch of snacks. Everything around me was a potential trigger of enlightenment. It meant that I could lower my little bucket into the ocean of contiguous moments at any point, and be sure of bringing up a sample that would yield the whole.

Admittedly I did much better on the meditation front once I had a regular mantra, even if it was that old shop-bought standby (yes) *Om Mane Padme Om*, the Mother's-Pride-sliced-white-bread of mantras. You never lose your fondness for your first mantra, in the same way that you're always tender towards the car that let you learn to drive.

If I needed formal proof of the unreality of time, I would only need to think of the year I spent at High Wycombe Technical College after Burnham, a period which seemed purgatorial and endless but left remarkably little trace. For times that came before and after my mind is well armoured with the illusion of recall, but for that year the memory gun fires blanks. I nosed my way forward, studious mole, along the blind tunnel of language acquisition. I didn't explore High Wycombe or make friends, in or out of college. It's possible that I wasn't interested in social life, that I was saving myself, socially, for

Cambridge, but I can't imagine I would have put up much of a fight against overtures. I certainly wasn't actively saving my virginity (assuming I had left Vulcan with that strange virtue intact), but still it lingered like a fog. There were no takers.

The 'Tech' had a strong vocational aspect. Many of my fellow students were doing something called Business Studies, which meant less than nothing to me. I was only a part-time student, turning up for a couple of lessons a week. I spent a lot of my time reading, not just for my course, but various arcane treasures unearthed by Mrs Pavey. I read Arthur Osborne's *The Incredible Sai Baba* with fascination, but also relief that I had established a rapport with Ramana Maharshi before I could be tempted by such a tremendous spiritual showman. Sai Baba's miracles were full of slyness and misdirection – he slept, for instance, on a plank intricately suspended by ropes. No one ever saw him climb onto it, though plenty saw him lying there. It seems to have been levitation with a few teasing strings attached. Sai Baba's principle was that he would give people what they wanted, in the hope that they would gradually develop a hunger for what he wanted to give. One day he went to fill a jar with oil for his lamps, but was given water instead by a mischievous tradesman who followed him home to see what happened. What happened was that Sai Baba filled his oil lamps with the water he had been given, and they burned very merrily indeed. Ramana Maharshi's miracles, on the other hand, were so discreet that they hardly stood out against the natural order. They made no attempt to impress. I prefer the lighter touch, the low-key miracle.

Ageing Undine

Mrs Adcock was a neighbour of ours, though a much closer one of Jon Pertwee's. She lived in a substantial riverside house – in its basement, rather perversely, which meant that she spent her days and nights below the water level of our Thames tributary, the 'brook' of Abbotsbrook. When it rained in winter the brook rose even higher, and Mrs Adcock would get flooded. Sometimes the water seeped in at its leisure, sometimes it broke its banks and washed her out. Rescuing her was a winter ritual for the local services, who must have found it irritating since there was nothing to stop her living on the ground floor if she had wanted to, or even on a higher level. Nobody else was in residence, but everything was kept in readiness in case her son Clive ever wanted to come to stay, which he hardly ever did.

Dad described her as a witch, but I think she was more of an elderly water-sprite, an ageing Undine, perhaps not of pure descent or she would have welcomed the seasonal floods which made her phone so disconsolately for rescue.

The first communication between our households (it must have been in the late 1950s) took the form of a plague of wasps. One summer while I was away at CRX a wasps' nest had been found in the garden of Trees and Mum had been frantic about getting rid of it before I got home. I think Dad smoked them out, but Mum was terrified of vengeful survivors. She filled my mind with fear about what would happen if I was stung by even a single wasp, and hundreds might be waiting in ambush. I remember, though, that Peter had been stung a couple of times, and no great fuss was made about that. For some reason it wasn't the same thing at all.

Mum made enquiries, and found that Mrs Adcock ('that woman') had had the wasps first. Her way of tackling the infestation struck Mum as even more sinister than the wasps themselves. Mrs Adcock had taken household rags and pieces of cloth, soaked them in cyanide, and hung them round the house, much as she might have hung out her washing. As far as Mum was concerned, there was a cyanide breeze blowing through Bourne End that summer. She would sniff the air for traces of the bitter-almond odour we knew from Agatha Christie mysteries.

If Mrs Adcock had known she was already a convicted poisoner (if only in the kangaroo court of Mum's prejudices) she would hardly have sent food over from her kitchen, out of the kindness of her neighbourly heart. Clearly she loved cooking, and didn't allow living alone to deter her from catering on a grand scale. Usually she sent cakes, covered with a variety of unearthly icings. Green was her favourite colour, purple the runner-up. Perhaps she was colour-blind? Her icings were phosphorescent and alarming.

I didn't need much prompting from Mum not to eat these offerings – but she insisted I must write a note thanking her and saying it was very nice, which I did. Consequently cakes and dainties continued to issue from the Adcock kitchen in a lurid procession, until it was a real problem finding any sort of home for them. Then Mum had a brainwave. I should say I was giving up cakes for Lent, and that everybody else in the family was going along with the fast. It wouldn't be fair to sit around eating delicious things in front of someone who was abstaining for religious reasons. That bought us a reprieve of forty days and forty nights, at any rate.

Mum tried to put me off Mrs Adcock by telling me that she was not only a vegetarian but an atheist. I certainly found this a strange combination. My visceral dislike of meat seemed to be part of a reverence for life, and I didn't understand how you could revere something which just happened and had no deeper meaning. I cross-examined Mum about this atheism business. Under pressure she admitted that Mrs Adcock might actually be an agnostic. It took me quite a while to understand the difference. God was so very real to me, that I grew up thinking it was the same for everybody else. God didn't say anything, and He couldn't be tricked into revealing his secrets, but he was real all right. When I tried to find out what this 'I' of mine was and where it came from, I came up against a brown, warmly pulsating wall, and hadn't been able to go any further. And that seemed to be that. It wasn't God's job to get me behind the wall. It was mine.

The path laid with lentils and rice

I had managed not to notice that Mum had manias rather than a faith, and that Dad was only in the most token way a believer. I think of him now as a spoiled atheist as others are spoiled priests. He had no religious feeling, but the family tradition of ministry stifled any pleasure he might have taken in his unattached state.

Mum didn't hesitate to present Mrs Adcock as a warning of the dangers of vegetarianism. The path that was laid with lentils and rice led to damp basements and estrangement from God.

Mum wasn't always an effective psychologist when it came to her warnings. Mrs Adcock came to fascinate me. Despite the stories of rags dripping with cyanide and the poisonous purple cakes, I decided I would go and seek her out in her lair. Her part of the house was down about half a dozen steps. Peter carried me down and then sat discreetly on the steps to wait. He didn't want to come any closer than he had to.

She seemed to be expecting me, though she could have had no notice of my visit. It may be there was a certain amount of social spontaneity in Bourne End, just not at our address. The only neighbour I remember just calling by was Joy Payne, and she was known to be unstable – she had been locked up, she told us, for being too happy as well as not being happy enough. One winter Joy tapped on the window and handed our presents through, not wanting to bother us by ringing the doorbell. Unstable or not, the purity of Joy's impulses showed everyone else up.

Mrs Adcock was certainly very old, but not decrepit. I couldn't imagine her young, which I could normally manage, even with Granny. She must have been born old.

At that age I assumed that anyone who was uncertain about God would be in a constant state of terror, particularly as the grave came closer, but she didn't look frightened. She made coffee for us, Nescafé made with all milk. We made a little small talk about schools and hospitals, and then I did my best to rattle her by saying, 'I gather you don't believe in God. What about death?'

'What about it?' she said, and now I was the one who was rattled.

'Well,' I said, 'you are rather . . .'

'Old?' she said.

'Exactly,' I said, 'and . . .'

'And you think that because I'm old I must be afraid of dying?'

'Yes!' I said. 'That's it . . .'

'Well, so far I've asked all your questions for you. Am I expected to answer them as well? I've no intention of answering a single question more unless you have the courage to ask me directly. That will be a good lesson for you to learn . . .'

If I hadn't cut my teeth on Granny, I would certainly have been shamed into silence. In the end I managed to articulate the question as directed. 'Aren't you afraid of death, Mrs Adcock?'

Mrs A looked straight at me. 'Oh no!' she said, breaking out into a heart-warming smile. 'Why should I be? Life without death would be so dull!'

'But what happens when we die?'

'We'll find out when the time comes. Do you really want to know in advance?'

'Of course.'

'There's no "of course" about it. Are you one of those funny people who turns to the end of a book and reads the last page first?'

'No!' I said, rather shocked by an idea that had never occurred to me, though of course such criminals exist.

'Well,' she said. 'What's the difference? If you were reading a really good story book, would you thank me for telling you how it all worked out in the end?' I saw what she meant. She had a point and more than a point. Uniquely among the adults I knew, she had answered more of my questions than I'd been able to answer of hers.

After that I became a regular caller. Mrs Adcock showed me her portfolios of sketches. She had been quite an artist in her day, earning a living by doing drawings for fashion magazines and clothes catalogues. Sometimes we had coffee, and though sometimes we had tea she never made it in the samovar which she showed me as something she had 'picked up on her travels'. I wanted her to start a little fire in it.

Mrs Adcock used to set me 'Fun Homework'. She'd dish out arithmetic sums which looked awful, but the answers would come out as 44444, or maybe your very own telephone number. Seeing something so nice and familiar was my reward for working so hard at the sum. She'd play endless word games with me, and I enjoyed trying to catch her out. If I found a word which Mrs A didn't know – which wasn't easy – she was genuinely delighted rather than put out. You'd get a 'thank you' and a 'that's another one to add to my list', and even a small present. Peter was still suspicious of her, so he would deliver me and then come back for me at an agreed time. It would take more than a batty old neighbour to make him think homework was fun.

Dumplings from heaven

At one stage my vegetarianism hit something of a crisis, not a lapse of principle but an intensifying of temptation. I had weaned myself with great effort off Mum's dumplings and gravy, a dish that she made particularly well, but there were times when I came close to backsliding. The smell made my salivary glands turn traitor, drenching my mouth with pleasure in anticipation. Mum told me that if I wanted dumplings and gravy all I had to do was take them onto my plate. There would be no vulgar crowing. Not a word would be said. 'You know I can't make vegeteerian dumplings for you, John,' she said, 'because the recipe contains suet, which naturally you can't eat.' Mrs Adcock urged me to hold firm against the pounce of the inner carnivore.

A few days later a knock came at the front door. Standing in the porch was a boy carrying a plate with a metal canteen cover on it. He said this was a gift from Mrs Adcock and must be eaten straight away. Mum brought it in and set in on the kitchen table in front of me. Even before she raised the lid I could smell a warm wholesome aroma. When she did I could see fluffy dumplings smothered in a thick veg soup, lounging next to something that looked like a chop, but was actually a Granose 'steak' out of a tin.

Mum banged a fork down alongside the food and told me that I'd better get on with it. She didn't repeat her warnings about not eating anything cooked by Mrs A, but her silence was hardly neutral. I hesitated, and then I decided that if there was poison anywhere in this set-up it wasn't in the food. I took a tentative nibble at a dumpling. There was nothing wrong with it. There was nothing wrong with any of it. This was manna made manifest in farinaceous form, proof of the power of prayer. Dumplings from heaven.

Mum turned her back on me while I ate, and when I had finished she snatched the plate away from me and started scrubbing fiercely at it in the sink. It was as if she wanted to scrape away any molecular trace of Mrs Adcock's kindness. Then she sent Peter to take it back, with the canteen cover, to where it came from. It was as if she couldn't bear to have these objects in her house a moment longer than she could help. She sent no message of thanks, though I'm sure Peter was too polite not to deliver one.

Clearly it wasn't pleasant for her to have a neighbour send me a treat, on a number of levels. To have food delivered into her very kitchen, as if this was Meals on Wheels for a deprived (poor) person. To have an atheist (or agnostic) demonstrate Christian charity, not to mention imaginative sympathy. Mum had no reason to feel grateful for being multiply shown up. Yet on this question the enemies were on the same side. I was too thin for my own good, and something needed to be done about it. Oddly, being underweight only seemed to signify if you were a vegetarian. Mum was a case in point – theoretically an omnivore, but not much of a vore of any sort. A nullivore if anything, or a paucivore at best, depending on the day and her mood.

Isn't Queen Mary supposed to have given Gandhi a poke in the ribs on the occasion of their meeting, saying he needed to put some meat on his bones? All right, I'm making that up, but I had always been told by those who claimed to know – including the staff at CRX, Flanny and my parents – that those who ate no meat had feeble bodies and feebler brains. Mrs Adcock was proof to the contrary.

This lady who had been a vegetarian since her teens had also worked on magazines and made her own dress designs. She had toured the world in search of textiles, getting as far as China. Her brain fizzed with energy. She loved mathematical puzzles and word games, not only solving them but setting them. She knew every card game that had ever been invented – for heaven's sake, she was even immune to cyanide, as her wasp-killing technique proved. She had been a conscientious objector in the War, though women had to make quite a fuss about it for their objections to register, since they weren't expected to fight in the front line anyway. Mrs Adcock was that precious thing, a pacifist who likes a good dust-up.

It was never hard to rekindle my relationship with Mrs Adcock. Our rapport was never a thing of blazing glory, but there was some steady combustion going on. It was a sort of smouldering friendship. It might seem to go out altogether for months or even years, but it never needed much encouragement to break out again. Just a little fuel would make it burn brightly. I still tried to make a note of new words to pass on, even if we were neither of us as easy to impress as we had once been. When I read *Gardening for Adventure* in hospital it gave me a bright bouquet of verbal novelties to present to her, or to relay in notes delivered by Peter. Mrs Adcock was perfectly familiar with *abortifacient*, but clean bowled by *emmenagogue* (used to describe anything which promotes the menstrual flow). Peter never stayed longer than the minimum, and always turned down coffee and tea. I worried sometimes about his lack of adventurousness, which seemed partly a sort of brotherly inhibition. My rôle was to chafe against the limits of my world. He seemed to atone for his wider opportunities by not taking advantage of them.

When I started visiting Mrs Adcock again in 1968, while studying at High Wycombe Technical College, she hardly seemed any older. She had all her own teeth, she had all her own wits. By this time her vegetarianism had taken a new crusading turn. She was campaigning against factory farming, and got me to take out my own membership in the society she had joined.

The astral blood spurted green

She had stopped drinking milk, since she couldn't be sure of the well-being of the cows involved, so that the milky Nescaff she served was now based on Coffee Mate. I took a discreet look at the ingredients on the label, and wondered how long she could get by on dried glucose solids and powdered hydrogenated fats. Milk had been the core of her diet. She only picked at other things.

There was hardly a vitamin or ghost of protein in her body, but there was nothing wrong with her drive and sense of purpose. In fact she had far more of a plan to change the world than either Mum or Flanny. She was expanding her range of activities and her areas of operation. So much for the low energy levels of herbivores. Not content with opposing the cruelties of the domestic food industry she had foreign barbarism in her sights. She was revolted by bull-fighting in Spain, which she wanted banned. If the Spanish had such a taste for blood, let them jab skewers in each other, and then talk about the dark glory of the sport.

I don't think bull-fighting had many defenders in Britain at the time, but by bad luck one of them was my Spanish teacher at the college, Dawn Drummond. She had lived in Spain and explained that we had it all wrong about bull-fighting. For a Spaniard going to a bull-fight was no more exotic than going to the bingo in Britain, though a great deal more profound and poetic. She had attended many *corridas*. It was a mistake to think bull-fighting was based on cruelty. In fact it was an exquisite moment when the matador came in for the kill.

I did my best to represent the bull's point of view in class but had made no headway. Dad had been chased across a field by a bull, but

257

it didn't make him wish the animal any harm. The matadors had no such grievance.

Miss Drummond said the matador used a special knife for the job, very sharp but surprisingly small. She even told us the Spanish word for it, but my mind refused to store it. Mentally I withheld my assent from the technical vocabulary of ritual killing. She said that the bull was completely exhausted by this stage, and frankly, after all the jabs he'd received from the picadors, finishing him off so cleanly was an act of mercy.

She held an imaginary knife in her hand and plunged it into the bull's imaginary heart, from which the astral blood spurted green. A macabre glow lit up her face with momentary incandescence, right in front of the eyes of the class. I felt I had seen an appalling transformation, which turned Miss Drummond into a blood sister of Miss Mitchell-Hedges gloating over her crystal skull at Vulcan School, draining the psychic energy from the pupils to feed on.

It's only fair to say that there were other elements in Miss Drummond's portrait of Spanish culture. There was flamenco, which I dismissed from a position of total ignorance. I couldn't accord much respect to a style of movement which seemed to me to resemble bad-tempered tap-dancing, a ritual re-enactment, in frothy dress and high heels, of the stamping my sister did when she didn't get her way. A choreographed tantrum. Then there was *gazpacho*, whose praises Miss Drummond constantly trumpeted, with digressions on recipe variations permissible and impermissible.

I was the closest the Cromer family had to an adventurous palate (if you bear in mind that eating meat is not an adventure). Mum greatly disliked the taste of olive oil, which I relished. I could even enjoy, or certainly tolerate, garlic, so *gazpacho* should have been well within my experimental range.

I don't know whether the barrier was physiological or mental. It's true that my body's temperature equilibrium is easily upset. After a few minutes in the hot part of the new conservatory I would overheat and take some time to recover. I felt sure that drinking cold soup would sabotage my metabolism from within – yet I was the same John Cromer who liked to leave the bedroom door open on the coldest days.

I couldn't face the idea of ingesting the icy liquid. On a hot day I didn't want a chilled drink, though of course ice cream is in a different category. Ice cream rewrites the rules. And I take tiny bites, tiny sips, tiny slurps as it melts.

In any case I rejected the idea that Spanish culture boiled down to this – soup, stamping and savagery. What about St John of the Cross, Cervantes and Lorca? I was particularly attuned to St John of the Cross and the notion of *La Noche Oscura del Alma*. In Hindu thought, there is a dark night of the soul as wide as the cosmos which lasts a hundred thousand years. There's a special word for it.

I could find excuses for Lorca's bloodlust, but none for Miss Drummond. She never actually praised Franco in class, but said darkly that we shouldn't believe what we read in the papers. You had to live in a country to know what you were talking about.

But wasn't it on Franco's orders that Lorca was killed? I wasn't the only one in class to be horrified by Miss Drummond's enthusiasm for the bull-fight, but when there were muffled protests she told us we were making judgements in ignorance. Anyone who had the courage to attend a bull-fight with an open mind would certainly be converted.

Miss Drummond's ears and tail

When I reported all this to Mrs Adcock, she immediately pulled out her own fighting equipment. A pen and a piece of paper. An envelope and a stamp. The pen in its own way was also a specialised weapon, with a deadly edge.

'I'm going to write to the principal of your college about this,' she said. She took down the relevant names. With anyone else I might have thought I was being humoured, but I knew Mrs Adcock would make good on her promises. In fact I wasn't sure whether I wanted this hoo-hah to happen. I had been more or less tortured at CRX and at Vulcan school without mounting any sort of protest. Was I really going to take Miss Drummond to court for her perverted interest in the shedding of ruminant blood? It made more sense to keep my head down and concentrate on my A-level. Unfortunately the slogan 'anything for a quiet life' practically guarantees rebirth after rebirth, with no remission from the cycle, so I had to stick to my guns.

About a week later Mum answered the telephone. It was the principal of the college. When I next came in, would I be kind enough to report to him? He would make sure that Miss Drummond was there also.

I wasn't looking forward to the meeting. When I saw Miss Drummond in the corridor she seemed tense and looked dreadful. She had never looked exactly well, even at the beginning of term, but now she looked positively ill. There was no colour in her face at all.

'John,' she said with false warmth, 'why on earth didn't you tell me more clearly about your objections? I would have been happy to explain at greater length if only you had given me the chance. Now you've gone and upset an old lady for no reason at all. You shouldn't be sneaky, John, not go around three corners. If there's anything you have to say you should just come out with it.'

The principal behaved in a friendly manner towards me. It took me a little while to realise he wasn't greatly exercised by the dispute in front of him as a disciplinary matter. He was closer to being an amused spectator than a hanging judge. I started to consider the possibility of giving him something to see.

I said I did have one question, and the principal said, 'Go on, then, John. Ask away.'

'Would it be an act of mercy if I broke Miss Drummond's neck, providing I had been kind enough to break all her fingers and toes slowly first, and as long as thousands of people were watching? Would that be *exquisite*?'

Miss Drummond drew in her breath as if she had been slapped. It had been a bit of a mistake for her to have characterised Mrs Adcock as a frail victim. After that she could hardly denounce me as the cat's-paw and mouthpiece of a vegetarian terrorist, which would have been far more accurate. It was something of a put-up job. I had more or less been coached by Mrs A, though I hadn't been sure I'd be able to go through with it until the moment I opened my mouth. Now there was nothing very much Miss Drummond could do to regain the initiative. The principal said, 'We won't keep you, Miss Drummond. I know you have a class to teach.' Whether he was letting her off the hook or twisting the knife in the wound I really couldn't say.

He seemed quite pleased with the way the meeting had gone. 'I did

260

enjoy that, I must say, John,' he said, when we were alone. Possibly Miss Drummond's Francoist inclinations made her less than popular in the staffroom. 'It's certainly made a change from my paperwork, I can tell you. I wish the College could run to a debating team. You could be our secret weapon – though perhaps as a matter of tactics it isn't necessary to go for the jugular right away. Still, if this had been a bull-fight rather than a battle of wills, the crowd would have been in a tremendous lather and I would be awarding you Miss Drummond's ears and tail at this very moment.' This was a rather ugly way of putting it, I thought.

I'm not sure if it was quite such a brainwave to have locked horns with a teacher and to have humiliated her in front of her boss. I was going to have to turn up to her class for the rest of the year.

Conversely, she was always going to have to turn up to teach me. After our meeting in the principal's office she always looked to me as if she had a barbed ceremonial dart (¿a *banderilla*?) broken off in her shoulder bone, crusted over but throbbing with stale pain every time her heart beat. And all thanks to me. As if it had been all my idea to turn further education into a blood sport.

I had to learn a new skill as a student, the skill of learning from someone who disliked me and withheld all possibility of rapport. In those lessons I was no more than an academic barge being loaded with heavy pallets of knowledge by a dockside crane which answered in other contexts to the name of Dawn. I have to say, though, that even at her most distant Miss Drummond was a lot more polite than Klaus Eckstein at his most ingratiating. Teachers have different styles, and a casual visitor to her classroom might easily have thought that I was one of the favoured pupils, just as it would have been possible to conclude at Burnham (over hundreds of German lessons) that Eckstein considered me a hateful idiot.

Death the needful

Miss Drummond was absolutely in the wrong. I had no doubts about that. But over the course of the year I began to feel a pang of my own, not confined to the shoulder, the ache of pity which she refused to those baffled animals who bled their lives away on the public sand. Perhaps it was even guilt. Miss Drummond wouldn't stay in the pigeon-hole I assigned her, of spokesman for sadism, shamed and justly routed. She began to take on some aspects of the sacrificial victim, and if that was true then I necessarily departed from my own pigeon-hole, my idea of myself. Everyone considered me innocuous, including me, but here I seemed to have done damage. Could vegetarians really draw blood?

Mrs Adcock was very sure we had done the right thing. I wondered if there wasn't some word we could come up with, using our combined lexicographical power, to mean someone who does harm by doing the right thing, a word more nuanced than *meddler*.

The year I was studying Spanish and German at High Wycombe Technical College was also the year that Gipsy began to die. When she was a puppy filled to the bubbling brim with energy I was on the very edge of life, ready to be nudged into the next one by illness and pain. Now I was much stronger, leading something relatively close to a normal existence, and she could hardly get up from her basket. If her job was to give me a transfusion of vitality then she had done it outstandingly well, but now she was paying the price for her generosity. Her legs began to pack up.

She would bark sorrowfully in the night to be let out. In the garden, or so Mum told me, she would expel with difficulty disobliging and desiccated turds. What Mum actually said was, 'Her poo is all dry, poor love.'

Gipsy was mortified to be old and helpless. The door was left open at night anyway, except in extreme conditions, but on those stiff legs Gipsy had great difficulty making it to the garden. It went against every fibre of her fur when the next stage came, and Mum had to pick her up and carry her outside to do her unsatisfactory business. A not-large woman carrying a not-small dog. Gipsy had been bought to look after me and to keep Mum sane. She had done both things. She had been a health professional all her life – no wonder she was a bad patient, or at least a very sad one. She hated seeing dependency from the other side.

On the day of my Spanish oral, I finally said to Mum, 'It's time to give Mr Ticehurst a call. He needs to do the needful for Gipsy.' Death the needful. Vets didn't usually do home visits, even then, but Mr

Ticehurst was always happy to come. It was common knowledge that he was having an affair with Isobel Dell – knowledge not confined to that hotbed of secrets, the sewing circle. Her husband was a pilot for BOAC, which meant he was away a lot. So Mr Ticehurst was very willing to turn out on any pretext. He appreciated any legitimate excuse to be in the area, the handy alibi of a house call.

In a large veterinary practice there is a designated lethalist, and perhaps there are as many children who dream of being lethalists as ones who dream of being regular vets. Mr Ticehurst's practice wasn't a large one, and he did the needful for Gipsy. Then he took her body away with him in a carrier bag, and Mum wept. I don't know why I didn't, except that I had such a strong joyful sense of the good job Gipsy had done. There's an assumption that the last incarnation has to be human, that it isn't possible to have your last rebirth 'lower down' in the animal kingdom. I don't see why that should be set in stone. There should certainly be some exceptional mechanism, just as in sporting events it's possible in certain circumstances to skip a round. Gipsy deserved a bye, a walk-over.

I'd never go to sleep until Peter came back from work at the Spade Oak. That night, after Peter had got into bed, I heard dog contentment breathing in the room. That unmistakable grumbling sigh. 'Is that you, Peter?' I whispered. 'No, Jay,' he whispered back from his bed, 'isn't it you?' No of course it wasn't. It went on for about a week, and then it stopped, or we stopped being able to hear it. We didn't tell Mum about it. It's not as if we were frightened. R.I.P. Gipsy 1953–1970. Good girl.

Finally I decided it was time to put some more pressure on Dad to make good the promise he had never quite rescinded, the one about subsidised air travel. On previous occasions when I reminded him of his agreement to this plan he would only say, 'We'll have to see – won't we? – when the time comes.' Now the time had come.

First I had to decide whether to go through Mum or ask direct. Her Dad-handling skills weren't altogether reliable, and it wasn't even certain that she would want to throw her trifling weight behind my plan. In the end I decided to try the direct route, though nothing with Dad was ever all that direct.

He didn't deny that he'd made some sort of undertaking about helping me to fly somewhere. It was my choice of destination that brought him up short. '*Madras*, John? The place in India? Do you have a death wish? You've no idea what would be involved – it's out of the question. Negative. Can't allow it.'

I was twenty years old! It wasn't a question of his allowing the expedition or not, it was a question of his helping me to get there. Dad had been there himself, shortly after the War, flying emergency blood supplies to hospitals in special tanks in the wings. Fuel capacity had been reduced to make more room for this cargo of mercy, and he had to be careful to fly relatively low, to protect the blood from extremes of pressure and temperature. Then Dad had been an angel with blood in his wings, but with me he was playing a rôle he much preferred – devil's advocate.

He had already explained to me the way trade agreements between airlines worked. The child of a BOAC employee under twenty-nine paid only 10% of the normal fare. I knew that 10% of the price of a ticket to India was still quite a bit of money, but I had been saving and was sure I could muster the tithe required.

Dad abandoned his overall objection to my plan and started to take it apart piece by piece instead. 'There's one thing you haven't thought of, John. BOAC doesn't fly to Madras. Delhi, yes, but not Madras. So I can't help you. Too bad. Ask me another.'

I didn't see the force of his objection. 'But you told me about trade agreements . . . agreements between airlines . . . ten per cent . . . child under twenty-nine.' I could feel my voice trailing away.

'Between normal civilised airlines, yes. But I'm afraid that doesn't apply in this case. Air India is a rather nasty little airline. They haven't signed the reciprocal agreements you refer to. Any time we want something from them we have to go cap in hand, and then we get a dusty answer as often as not. Or the beggars want favours in return. So there it is. Negative. And a good thing too, if you ask me. You have no idea what you'd be letting yourself in for, John. Even a flight to Paris would put a big strain on your system.'

Begging Dad for things had never played much of a part in our relationship, if only because it had a strong tendency to blow up in my face. Now there was no other option. 'Dad,' I said, 'this is very important to me. I want to go to India. I'll never ask you for anything again.' I groped for a word that would make it possible for Dad to relent. 'Couldn't you have a word with your . . . oppo . . . at Air India, please? Perhaps those beggars aren't as bad as you think. At least give them a chance.' *Oppo* was one of Dad's favourite words. I'm not sure if it's short for *opponent* or *opposite number*, but either way it was an important building block in his mental world. *Oppo* made much more sense to him than such floating categories as *friend* or *wife*. I suppose that's the Forces mind for you.

He snorted, all the same, when I used the supposedly magic word. *Oppo Sesame* it wasn't, apparently. There was no one at Air India who he could think of in those terms. When he had been in the Air Force during the War he had had oppos in the Luftwaffe, but Air India were untouchables to a man, pi-dogs not to be petted.

'I don't suppose you've thought about who would put you up in those parts, John. What makes you think you'd be welcome in the first place?'

Like a lawyer I had prepared paperwork to support my case. I showed him a letter from the ashram saying that any devotee of Ramana Maharshi was more than welcome to stay there. Could I inform them of my dates of arrival and departure? Signed by a Mr V. Ganesan, MA. I had flung an airmail letter blindly at the subcontinent, with nothing to guide it but the words 'Ramana Maharshi's Ashram, Tiruvannamalai, Southern India'. Indian postmen were obviously mystics to a man. Theirs is an inherently contemplative occupation – postmen have so much time to think their own thoughts.

Dad must have mentioned my crazy scheme to Mum, because she told me she'd put in a good word on my behalf. With any luck Dad would talk to the relevant person at Air India, whether oppo or beggar and renegade. Mum rather spoiled the effect of her intervention by saying, 'I said to Dad, "If we don't at least try, we'll never hear the end of it – you know what he's like."' They knew what I was like! That was the whole trouble – they did and I didn't. Wanting to find out was my reason for going to India in the first place.

Dad phoned and made an appointment with a Mr Dalal, the head of the nasty little airline's beggarly London office. 'Dalal' – the name itself seemed to stick in his throat. Then Mum wanted more details. 'Why do you want to go to this place anyway? To Madras?'

'Not Madras, that's just the nearest airport. I'm going to Tiruna-vannamalai.'

'Heavens, that's a bit of a mouthful. Where's that and what's there?'

'It's a hundred or so miles from Madras, and my guru is there.'

'Is that like a Maharajah – I mean a Maharishi?'

'My guru is the path I follow.'

'But you don't have to go all the way to India, do you? I mean, the Beatles had a – a guru, didn't they? A Maharishi Yogi something. And they went to see him in Wales, I think. Bangor, wasn't it?'

'Well, yes they did. But then they went to India. And my guru has never been to Wales, or anywhere outside India, all right, Mum?'

'Keep your shirt on, John, I'm just trying to understand.' Trying to understand, possibly. Trying to suggest I was planning an unnecessarily elaborate trip, certainly. As if I was dead set on driving to John o'Groats to pick up a pint of milk.

All I could do was to impress on Mum the importance of certain words. I was sure that any right-thinking Indian would respond to my quest if it was presented in the proper language. 'Make sure that Dad says I'm a devotee making a pilgrimage. "Devotee" and "pilgrimage". Those are the words that will do the trick.'

Hearing the words *pilgrim* and *devotee* applied to me, even if it was only by my own voice, changed things for me. I grew to fit these new clothes. I liked myself in them, and seemed to recognise this person. The mental mirror showed me an image which did not estrange.

Mum wasn't sure that Dad would stick to the script, and I had doubts of my own. I'd sent him off to Palm Beach Casino with strict instructions, and what had he come back with? A weekend job driving a van, that's what.

I just had to keep my head down and hope that he would bring it off. Mum said, 'I talked to Dad and he says he'll ask nicely, but he won't do any more than that. He says he won't kowtow.'

Kowtow. Another trigger word, this one with a wartime origin. The Japanese weren't content with surrender, they demanded this humiliating gesture of submission. Unfortunately Dad's idea of kowtowing overlapped with many people's idea of being polite.

On the day of the meeting with Mr Dalal, Mum and I were both very unsettled. Peter suggested taking me for a walk before his shift at the Spade Oak, but I couldn't imagine leaving the house. I was much more tense than I had ever been waiting for exam results. This felt much more important, far more of a turning point.

What I really wanted to do was wait inside the front door, so I would know his news the moment Dad got home, but Mum wasn't having that. 'You'd better give him a moment to catch his breath, John,' she said, 'before you pounce.' We placed ourselves by the kitchen window, straining to read his face as he came up the path.

Then Mum pounced in my place. The moment we heard Dad's key in the lock she swept out to meet him. I could hear her urgently whispering, but no response from Dad. There are times, of course, when words aren't necessary and facial expression says it all.

Mum bustled back in and shook her head at me. 'I'm sorry, John – but you can't say we didn't try.'

Dad followed her in, moving as if he was exhausted. He sat down and put his hand over his face. Still he said nothing. 'For heaven's sake,' said Mum, 'put the boy out of his misery! I'm the one who'll have to make him feel better – what's the point of dragging it out?'

When Dad took his hands away from his face, I almost thought that he was hiding a smile. He was good at that. He reached into his pocket, saying, 'You can't say I didn't try,' and produced a little folder of card. An airline ticket. It was a First Class return, and in the space marked Payment Required it said NO CHARGE.

He had foxed me completely. He had also foxed Mum, who had been led up the garden path by his sombre expression when he came through the front door. She had thought his embassy among the beggars had failed, and she made a creditable job of suppressing the joy she must have felt. I lost sight of her for a minute or two – the lack of flexibility in my neck means I have to wait for faces to present themselves in their own good time. When I saw her expression again it was changed, changed utterly.

I've never seen a children's party struck by lightning, the carbon-ised cake, the birthday girl twitching in her melted frock, but I think Mum's face that afternoon was a match for that scene of celebration blasted. She had been lifted for a little moment by my good news, her joy had kept pace with mine, and then she had realised what it meant for her rather than me, and then everything was ash and sizzling hair.

I was flying away, a Peter Pan determined to grow up, leaving Wendy stranded on the ground. I was serving notice of her redundancy as a mother. The one thing that had seemed certain about her life was that I would always need her – never replace her, and certainly never manage without anyone at all.

She reached over to the Air India ticket in its little folder and looked at it, as if it was a death notice in the newspaper, perhaps her own. She frowned, as if her name had been spelled wrong, and said, 'Dennis, this can't be right.' She licked her lips. Her lips were often dry. She would pour a glass of water and then forget to drink it. Sultan the cat was just as likely to wet his whistle with it as she was. 'It says he's going over for more than a month. For five weeks.'

'Yes, m'dear. That's what he wants, and quite right too. No point in travelling all that way and then having to come back next minute, is there?'

'You can't mean that, Dennis. Who's going to look after him?'

'He'll have the time of his life. He doesn't need us, m'dear, that's what you don't understand. Why should he? That's not nature's way. He's good at getting himself looked after. First he'll sit on a plane and a lot of pretty girls will make a fuss of him, and then he'll sit under a tree shamming as a holy man, and people will be thoroughly fooled and bring him treats.' This wasn't at all how I saw my pilgrimage and my quest, but after his efforts on my behalf Dad was entitled to tease me a little. 'You'll see. He'll have a whale of a time.'

I wanted all the gory details of the negotiation. 'What did you say to Mr Dalal, Dad? Was he nice? Did you say *devotee* and *pilgrimage*?'

'He was nice enough, but I'm not sure your pi-jaw would have done the trick, John. Our Mr Dalal had both feet firmly on the ground. I did mention that you were going to Cambridge, and he said his old college was Cat's – they invite him to a summer party with straw-berries and champagne. Hoping for a donation, I expect. "Cat's" is

St Catherine's, by the way. Perhaps he hoped I wouldn't know. I explained that I'd been supposed to go to Cambridge myself, except that I was invited to a let's-beat-the-Nazis party that went on till all hours and couldn't attend. Clash of engagements. We had a bit of a chuckle over that.' All told I felt that Dad had done me proud with Mr Dalal. He had done a little kowtowing after all, a little oiling of the wheels. 'He said he and his lovely wife would be delighted to meet me and *my* lovely wife for cocktails at the Garden House Hotel. A lot of play-acting, really.'

Then his face became stern. 'It's not on, you know, to give a ticket away. A discount is one thing, a free gift is quite another. That chap broke IATA rule 151. He knows he did, he knows I know it, and he knows I can't do a damn thing about it.'

From that point on, Mum and Dad, despite their different feelings in the matter, accepted that I would be going to India. I had my doubts. I wasn't half as confident as I made out.

Flushing the ashes away

Like any competent lawyer, I had been selective in the documents I had submitted to the family court. I had exercised my discretion (exercising discretion is how lawyers lie). I had shown them the first letter from the ashram, but not what came after.

There had seemed no point in mentioning disability ahead of time, before the principle of welcome was established. After the delightful letter from Mr Ganesan had arrived, it seemed a good moment to mention such unspiritual trifles. I tried to be as casual as possible. Oh, by the way . . . did I happen to mention . . . ?

The reply came quickly and was crushing. Mr V. Ganesan said that conditions in the ashram were somewhat austere, entirely unsuitable for someone with my difficulties. I wrote back, stubborn and cheeky, expressing regret that a devotee of Ramana Maharshi should pay so much attention to this irrelevant body, this old coat we wear for a little while. In any case, he could prevent me from staying in the ashram, but not from coming to Tiruvannamalai. 'As for sleeping,' I said rather grandly, 'there is always the road, which refuses no one. And did not our Bhagavan describe the bliss he always felt while begging?' Peter pushed me to the letter box and did the actual post-ing for me, while I prayed that my bluff wouldn't blow up in my face.

It was a very hollow bluff. Certainly Bhagavan had talked about the bliss of begging, but his was a rather different case. He was a Brahmin who had cast off his privileges, a splendid spiritual moult-ing – but I couldn't help feeling that the memory of privilege is a privilege in itself. There's an afterglow of entitlement which can act to insulate the organism even while it fancies itself naked to the ele-ments. I on the other hand felt as if I had been begging since I was three, in one way or another. It was hardly likely that things would be easier for me in India.

I had been a busy correspondent. There was a third letter which I also didn't show to Mum and Dad, though this time I had a better excuse. I had destroyed it, with Peter's help. We were systematic about it – tear-ing it into small strips, which we carefully burned before flushing the ashes away. Peter didn't ask who the letter was from or what it con-tained. He could see at a glance that it had thrown me into confusion, the very state which my Indian expedition was meant to dissipate.

The letter was from Mouni Sadhu. I had written to him in care of his publishers, George Allen & Unwin – Ruskin House, Museum Street – thanking him for his books. Incantation of the Tarot had al-lowed me to ventilate pain without losing dignity (let's hope), while *In Days of Great Peace*, although its direct effect on me had been oddly muted, had led me to Arthur Osborne's book and Ramana Maharshi himself. I mentioned my visit to Tiruvannamalai and I suppose I was asking for his blessing on it. Blessing was not what came.

The air letter came from Australia, where (as it turned out) Mou-ni Sadhu made his home. He said there was no point in my going to Tiruvannamalai with the Maharshi gone. The spiritual effect had vanished, as he was in a position to know. If I went there all I'd find was greedy people after my money. Piccadilly Circus offered a better prospect of enlightenment.

Even with this terrible letter ceremonially annihilated, there was a risk that Mum (or even Dad) would notice something wrong in my demeanour. I wasn't confident that I could fend off questions without revealing my dismay. I got through the day somehow, and gave my-self a talking-to once I was safely in bed.

I had saved almost fifty pounds out of the Supplementary Benefit (a little over three pounds weekly) awarded me by a tender-hearted government. I had offered to put this little income towards my keep at Trees, but Dad had said he was sure I could find better uses for it. I had been expecting to have to stump up a certain amount for the ticket to India, but now that obligation had vanished. I wasn't rich, but I was quite rich enough to be fleeced by the money-grubbers of southern India without having cause for complaint. Even if Mouni Sadhu was right, I would cope. Hadn't I survived financial shipwreck before, when the Guardian Bank betrayed my trust, sinking without trace in a haven advertised to be safer than houses? After this internal pep talk sleep came sweetly.

A week later I had to play another charade in front of Mum and Dad, but this time in a different key of feeling. A letter arrived from the ashram to say that Mr and Mrs Osborne had been kind enough to say that I could stay with them, although Arthur was unwell and I shouldn't expect too much. Now it was relief and exhilaration that I had to mask. My bluff had been successful and my desperate gamble had come up trumps. It was Arthur Osborne who had introduced me to Ramana Maharshi in the first place (with Mouni Sadhu it was a case of mistaken identity – I had walked straight past him). Now I would be able to thank my benefactor in person. Mouni Sadhu must be wrong about the departure of spiritual aura from Tiruvannamalai if Arthur Osborne lived there still.

I didn't want to be a charity case while I was in India, and racked my brain to think of what service I could offer. I settled on cutting vegetables and binding books, since it resonated with what Arthur had written. Those were activities favoured by Ramana Maharshi during his days in the ashram which formed around him. These were not books in the Western sense but little notebooks, a few pages roughly sewn together, and I thought I could probably manage.

A great tree must attract squirrels

It would be quite wrong to say that Ramana Maharshi formed an ashram – he merely stayed where he was, and an ashram grew around him. He couldn't help sustaining a rich spiritual eco-system, any more than a great tree can avoid attracting squirrels, birds and insects. In the early days his participation was less than minimal. How could it be otherwise? He was silent, cross-legged, absorbed in the bliss of Brahman.

Of course nothing could be more alien to someone in my circumstances of life, or more inspiring, than this voluntary movelessness – if you can call something voluntary which is the product of a transcendent amnesia. He didn't even notice!

His first devotee had originally been worshipping a stone god in the town, getting money by begging so as to buy camphor, sandal paste and milk, adoring the statue with tears of love in his eyes, until someone said, 'Why do you keep worshipping this stone god? In a cave on the hill there is a live Swami. He never speaks, and there isn't anyone to look after him. Why not make your worship to him?'

At first the new love-object's similarity to the old, although it was warmed from within, must have outweighed the differences. Still, food must be offered to this human statue in more than a symbolical fashion – nourishment was required to enter the mouth. The sites of excretion must be kept in order.

The ritual attentions carried over. The devotee poured a little buttermilk over this living statue's head. Meeting no objection, he followed this up with anointings of milk and then ghee. Encouraged, if only by immobility and silence, he daubed this undissenting body with sandal paste and *kumkum*. He offered fire-oblations and chanted mantras, as priests do to the statues in temples.

Indian religious practice is a sort of calligraphy whose logic is to cover every surface with intricate patterns, and then to fill the spaces between. There would be no end to this loving and meticulous scribbling.

Then one morning when the devotee came into the cave he found a change. The Swami was in the same position as when he had been left, but there was writing on the wall. It said (I paraphrase) that the service rendered was quite enough.

Amazement in the cave. For one thing, it was news that the Swami could read and write. Literacy in God-men was not a given. It was also (briefly) baffling how the writing had been done. There was no stationery cabinet in the cave. The Swami had virtually nothing in the way of possessions, if you can even use the word 'possessions' of someone whose non-spiritual activities are in abeyance. He 'owned' a loin-cloth, though that had only recently been put on him, and a cup made of half a coconut shell.

He had made marks on the wall with a half-burnt stick from the fire. Possibly there is a subtle reference here to the part played by the ego in its own dissolution. In the process of self-enquiry, the ego is like the stick that stirs the funeral pyre to make sure that everything is consumed, and burns to nothingness in its turn.

After that, people started to ask questions, and to get them answered, either by means of a burnt stick again, or by his writing in the sand. This style of teaching (*upadesa*) was superseded when the questioners started to bring their own pieces of paper and writing instruments for him to use. Then they would take the pieces of paper away with them to make fair copies of their own.

Sometimes Ramana Maharshi composed verses, and when others gathered them together he made no objection – though the term 'necklace' used of one such collection could apply to all such, the beads being strung together by another hand than the maker's. I imagined helping the Osbornes by mending little books of this type, restringing the beads and giving them a quick buff-up in passing. I had my limits, but I was quite handy with Sellotape.

I told Mum about the new arrangement as if it was no more than an administrative detail, that I would be staying in a private house not an ashram. I thought there might be some crumb of comfort in that. By this time I wouldn't have blamed Mum for developing a hatred for Mrs Pavey, the seeming friend who had slipped into her bicycle basket a book that from her point of view might just as well have been called *How To Disown and Desert Your Loving Mother* as *Ramana Maharshi and the Path of Self-Knowledge*.

I would have liked to tell her that her case wasn't so bad. Ramana Maharshi's own mother had a lot more on her plate. After her boy had run away from home she had no news of him. When she learned he was living on the holy mountain Arunachala she sent his brother to bring him home. When that didn't work, she went herself. Seeing he was immovable, she stayed herself. She put herself in charge of feeding him, not a very satisfying position given his indifference to food.

He would refuse titbits or extra portions, saying that he ate through a thousand mouths and needed no special treatment. Mum wouldn't have enjoyed running a kitchen on that basis.

The penis which pays visits

One of the great advantages of my spiritual orientation was that I didn't have to read the newspapers. I could ignore the urgent daily shrieks which die down into the moan we call history. I made sure everyone knew that I was uninterested in politics of any stripe or spot. Dad made the point that a lot of people had gone to a lot of trouble (fighting and dying, activities along those lines) to make sure that I had the right to vote.

I refused to be manipulated by such pieties. I dare say that I confirmed the impression he had already formed, that despite my departures from statistical norms I was a typical member of my spoiled and clueless generation. He wasn't completely wrong, of course. He couldn't be expected to notice the difference between the prevailing attitude (make love not war, don't trust anyone over thirty) and mine: *Love and war, age and youth, are no more than the tricks Maya plays. Dualistic thinking is a trap, whose bait and jaws are made of the same 'substance'.*

I had never had any interest in the War as a child. Men in uniform were (and are) an entirely separate subject, objects of a feeling that was religious in its own way. War was boring. You choose the womb – the *Tibetan Book of the Dead* is clear about this – at a pinch you choose the penis which pays visits there, but you don't have to take an interest in the stories which are attached to the organ.

Indifference is the supreme goal of any sensible religion, but it certainly gets on people's nerves along the way! Dad would grit his teeth and say, 'I'll have you know that if the bulk of the population had been similarly minded, we'd now have Herr Hitler in charge, or someone even worse.' It might have given me pause to be told that Herr Hitler routinely destroyed the physically defective, but Dad didn't pass that on.

People had given their lives for me and what thanks did they get? None. If people die deluded about the way the world works they have to start all over from the beginning. Do not pass Go, though perhaps I mean Stop. Do not collect (be dissolved in) Nirvana.

The general election called for June 1970 gave Dad's grumbles a new sharpness of focus. Voting age had been lowered to eighteen as of January of that year, which meant he had not one but two sons who were entitled to enter the electoral fray for the first time. Never mind that I had indicated I was above such illusory convulsions.

'My godfathers!' I heard him saying to Mum. 'The little twit is planning to throw away his vote. But not if I can help it. The proper way to throw away your vote, m'dear, is to spoil your ballot paper in the voting booth. Nothing else shows the proper respect for the democratic process. And if he's really hell-bent on being difficult, that's what he's damn-well going to have to do.' It isn't hard to say things like that out of my earshot if that's what you want. Obviously I was meant to hear him, and to know what I was up against.

Mum gave a little sigh of exasperation at her son's intransigence or (giving her the benefit of the doubt) the intransigence her husband and her first-born seemed to share. Mum had never got round to reading the *Tibetan Book of the Dead*, or she would have realised that the resemblance was purely coincidental.

To my face Dad was more politic. 'Look here, Chicken,' he said, 'Mum and I both admire you for standing up for what you believe in. We're only asking you both to vote, to show you're adult by exercising this privilege. We would never try to tell you *how* you should vote. That's not the point. It's the voting that counts. How you vote is entirely your affair and nothing to do with either of us.

'Naturally, if you wished to show a little solidarity with your parents and the cause of common sense in the face of the current country-wide opportunity to make a stand, by voting for the Conservatives, we would feel gratified. It would also not go amiss with Muriel's sewing class. There are rumours that you're going to the bad, what with your vegetarian crusades – giving teachers at your college an earful about bull-fights and what-not – and Mum could do with something positive to report. Anyway, as I said, it's the voting that counts. Where you make your mark is entirely a matter for your conscience.'

On the day itself Dad gave me a ten-bob note, telling me that Peter could push me to the polling station, and we could stop off at Thorne's Stores in the village. I could buy a strawberry Mivvi and Peter could have some ham, freshly sliced. 'Tell him he can eat it just as it is, with no bread, no roll, nothing like that. I know he loves to eat it that way. I'd be grateful, though, if he didn't actually cram it into his mouth straight from the slicer, though I know he would given half a chance. At least let the shopkeeper put it in a bag! Otherwise it's Liberty Hall . . . just don't tell your mother.'

It was strange that Dad gave the instructions to me rather than Peter, who was so much more likely to follow them. Dad must have thought, after the procurement of a first-class return ticket to Madras, that his secular authority was beyond question, but I couldn't let even gratitude sell me down the river. I had a duty to thwart him.

The taste of corruption

Don't tell your mother. This warning didn't apply to Dad's undermining of democratic process, which was blatant and undisguised, but to his giving permission for Peter to eat ham publicly in a vulgar style, news of which might also get back to Mum's sewing circle, the way everything else in the proximate cosmos seemed to.

The Cromer brothers arrived at the polling station with the taste of corruption on their lips, animal-salty in Peter's case, dairy-sweet in mine. After we had established our identities Peter tried to push me over to the polling booth, but we were intercepted. It wouldn't be right for Peter, under cover of giving help, to see how his brother cast his vote. Inwardly I chuckled – the authorities being so concerned with the little proprieties, while substantial wrongdoing was taking place beneath their very noses! I was pushed to the booth by an official who helped me stand, so that I could reach the voting surface, where I would make my crucial mark with a stubby pencil on a string, and then turned his back theatrically, as if we were playing a children's game of some kind – Elector's Footsteps, perhaps. Pin the Tail on the Candidate.

When we got home there was no formal debriefing, though Dad certainly wanted to know how the virgin voters had 'got on'. I assured him that the day's Mivvi had been particularly delicious, and Peter loudly sang the praises of fresh-sliced ham. Thanks, Dad!

More information was required. Though Dad had announced it was none of his concern how we would vote, it was a different matter when we had actually expressed our preference in the matter of national politics. The moment the deed was done any privacy was forfeit.

'Do you want to tell me how you voted, boys? Not that it's any of my business.'

'Conservative, Dad!' sang out Peter.

'Good lad. John?'

'Labour, Dad.'

'*Labour?*'

With that stubby little pencil I had pierced him to the heart. I had refused to support the powers of light against darkness. Dad gave a sort of growl, and though he didn't lay a hand on me he came close. He grasped the handles of the wheelchair and pushed me roughly to my bedroom in disgrace, muttering, 'You can stew in your own juice, you little turncoat!' Peter had left the brakes of the wheelchair locked, and Dad had to wrestle to get it in motion. For a long moment his rage discharged electrically through the chair. It was a close thing. If the wheelchair hadn't had rubber tyres I might have been cooked by that human lightning.

The whole adventure was thoroughly satisfactory. My period of house arrest as a class traitor would have been more arduous if the side door, which had a ramp installed for my benefit, hadn't been wide open as usual throughout.

As it turned out the next day, Mr Heath turfed Mr Wilson out of Downing Street even without the help I had been supposed to give him, but that wasn't the point. The point was probity, even if Peter and I defined that notion differently. He had retained his integrity despite the ham because he had been going to vote Conservative all along, while my conscience was easy as long as I hadn't done what Dad wanted.

Our votes cancelled each other out, of course, so Dad had spent his ten shillings for nothing. If he hadn't intervened in the first place, Mr Heath (or strictly speaking our local Tory candidate) would have had one more vote under his belt. All Dad had accomplished was the transfer of a Mivvi and a few ounces of ham from a deep freeze and a fridge respectively into the digestive systems of his sons. Dad was indeed a master conjuror and manipulator, a wizard of action at a distance, but only when dealing with grocery items on a small scale.

I hadn't really changed my thinking about politics, and I wasn't entirely motivated by the desire to get one over on Dad. I merely applied the teachings of Ramana Maharshi to the question. If a dream hunger requires a dream food then a dream election deserves a dream vote, and it certainly shouldn't be a cheaply corrupt one. You couldn't accuse Dad of losing his touch with his sons, since he had never set out to cultivate such a thing. But he might have chosen slightly more adult bribes if he wanted to suborn us. Show some respect!

A few days later the precarious equilibrium of my pilgrimage arrangements was upset all over again. One morning there was a knock at the door. Mum went into the hall wearing the cat. This was a fairly new arrival, a neutered male called Sultan – Mum left females alone but had males briskly disarmed, exercising summary powers in this area uniquely. Sultan liked to drape himself round her shoulders like a stole, even while she was doing the washing-up, his tail slowly lashing with contentment. I could hear a low murmur of voices, then a double thump as Mum brushed Sultan off her shoulders. Apparently this was too serious a conversation to be shared with a living fur stole. Or with me.

Once again there was a huddle and a confab just inside the front door, whispers and mysteries. This time it wasn't Dad and Mum who were talking but I soon recognised the intonations of the new arrival. It was Pheroza Tucker, an Indian lady from the other end of the Abbotsbrook Estate.

Sultan came in to me in the kitchen, rather put out, but I set my stick at an angle to debar him from the consolation of my lap. Cats are too proud to sulk, but he wasn't pleased with the turn of the day. Meanwhle I tried to tune in to the hushed voices inside the front door.

Ominous snatches of sense

Being excluded from conversations is bad for the character. It makes you construct conversations in your mind that would justify your being excluded. Plans to put something in your tea and be shot of you for good.

The murmurs in the hall yielded ominous snatches of sense – 'What a blow for his hopes', 'How am I supposed to tell him?', 'Best just to come out with it.' 'I'd ask you in for a cup of tea, but I'll have to break the news to His Nibs.' I had a right to hear all this at first hand. It was humiliating to be on the edges of something which clearly concerned me first and foremost. I suppose I could have sidled into the hall, but sidling isn't really a strong point, and it would have been the work of a moment for Mum and her visitor to step out of the front door and frustrate me again. If I sidled implacably on, they had only to float off into the depths of the garden.

At last the front door closed, and Pheroza was gone. It seems a little strange, looking back, that I took so little interest in an Indian neighbour and family friend. But I knew that Pheroza was a Parsee – who had married out of her religion – rather than a Hindu, without knowing exactly what a Parsee was. It's almost as if I was being protected from distraction. If I'd known more about the Parsees and their rituals, who knows what might have happened? There's fire involved in much Hindu observance, but nothing that can hold a candle to Zoroastrianism, where even the place of worship is called a fire temple. My pyrolatry might have become dangerously inflamed. It's odd to think I had so little interest in India outside the life and teaching of Ramana Maharshi.

When Mum came into the kitchen I pretended to be taken up with Sultan, chiding him for the sour mood to which I had contributed. She stood behind me and I could hear the crackle of a newspaper with an unfamiliar smell. She took a breath and passed it to me at last, appropriately folded. It was the *Times of India*. The death of Arthur Osborne was announced, not in a small advertisement but in an article on the front page. The headline described him as 'a good friend of India'.

She waited for me to read it and meekly asked, 'What will you do?' If her first reaction had been relief, at the prospect of such a body blow to my trip, she was politic enough to leave it in the hall.

What would I do? I didn't know. I would go anyway and take my chances, I supposed. Or turn my face to the wall.

That evening I watched Mum as she wrote a letter on her beloved headed notepaper. Sultan was keeping to the garden, and a different animal member of the household was seizing its chance, a yellow bird without a name. I don't know why the naming mechanism broke down. Normally the name is the first thing you think of.

The bird without a name perched on the end of the pen while Mum wrote her letter. There was nothing she could do to get rid of it – she would literally throw it away, pick it up and throw it across the room, and it would always come fluttering back while she muttered 'Shoo!'

There's a lot of Mum in that sequence of actions. Who taught the bird dependence in the first place? What right did Mum have to pretend that she didn't want it hanging on her every move? She could only go through the motions of rejection because she knew the returning instinct had been instilled almost on the molecular level. Mum would only risk throwing something away that would come right back. That's where I was letting her down, but of course I was following a family pattern myself. Dad, if he needed her, never said so or showed it, which trapped her in her turn. If either of us had clung to Mum she might have found something else to do with herself than look after us. In the meantime she had Audrey, whose clinging was a stranglehold.

Seeming-I is as-it-were sorry

Vasanas to the left of us, *vasanas* to the right of us. It's hard to see the road for the ruts. Sometimes it's hard to remember that there is any road apart from the ruts.

I had a letter of my own to write, expressing my sorrow to Mrs Arthur Osborne (Lucia). I felt I had to make the effort, though there were daunting obstacles. It was a sort of triple jump of condolence. On top of the foredoomed inadequacy of any attempt to express grief on paper there was the fact of my never having met either party, neither the bereaved nor the deceased. Then there was the faith we all shared, with its withholding of importance equally from birth and death.

My first draft had no spiritual underpinning. To boil it down: I'm sorry for your loss. My second attempted to go a little deeper beneath the surfaces of things. Baldly: 'Seeming-I is as-it-were sorry for seeming-you's apparent loss.' I read over it and gave it the lowest possible marks, then went back to the first version. Again Peter escorted me to the postbox. There were some messages I didn't altogether trust Mum to transmit – at least without scrawling *Please if you have any pity in you discourage my deluded boy* on the back of the envelope. Then all I could do was wait and hope for deliverance. The time of my flight was coming near, and I didn't want to be left to the mercies of the road, which refuses no one and by the same logic welcomes no one either.

Meanwhile a window was mysteriously left open by Audrey, and that was the last we knew of the bird with no name. I suppose Audrey may have been jealous of Mum's bird, at some level, but it's also true that the namelessness didn't help. Of course we're none of us real, and names are no less unreal, but having a name does seem to keep us going, doesn't it?

With Sultan Audrey tried a charm offensive. Her philosophy was that you could make any creature love you if you set your mind to it, by grabbing and smothering if need be. Mum would sometimes give Sultan orders to stay on Audrey's bed till she fell asleep. Sultan would do it, but you could feel every feline fibre straining to be gone. Every pet we ever had was wary of Audrey, perhaps knowing things we didn't.

Two days before the date of my flight, when Mum had cried all the tears she had in her and Dad had taken to leaving travel brochures for Paris around, remarking (as if casually) that the lifts on the Eiffel Tower went right the way to the top, a letter came from Mrs Osborne. I hadn't managed to strike the right note when I tried to write a Hindu letter of condolence to Mrs Osborne, but her reply had perfect pitch. She said that she would have learned nothing from Ramana Maharshi if she let the shedding of an old coat get in the way of welcoming a fellow devotee.

The arrangements could stand. There was a place made ready for me thousands of miles from home, and I was expected by strangers I loved already. Of course if life and death don't qualify as real, then family has quite a nerve to make such claims on us,. It's only common sense that the family you choose outranks the one you were given.

3

Guest of the Mountain

I was taking a leap in the dark, the enlightening dark, in a body ill suited to any sort of run-up. A solo trip to India was a fairly adventurous thing for anyone to do in 1970, but my case was almost insanely bold. Over the years I had moved from a hospital to a special school and then to a normal one. With each successive change of address I had whittled away at the elaborateness of the infrastructure that was needed to support me. In India I would have absolutely nothing familiar to rely on. I would be travelling on a wing (two wings, thanks to Air India, and First Class wings at that) and a prayer. At Burnham Grammar School my falls had been cushioned by willing helpers, and India was even more richly supplied with personnel – but it seemed foolish to expect the entire population to act as ramshackle shock-absorbers protecting me from the impact of so much difference.

I had decided on five weeks as the right period for my pilgrimage. It was a length of time which would allow me a full month of devotion in Tamil Nadu, the Indian state where Ramana Maharshi had lived and died, with half a week at each end of that to recover from arriving, and to prepare myself for departure.

I'm good at packing. Packing for me is something that takes place on a piece of paper, where I list objects and actions as precisely as possible. The satisfaction only begins to leak out of the process when I have to pass the list over to someone else – to Mum, in this period, for the executive stage of packing, the actual gathering and encasing of possessions.

At that point you might think my involvement in packing was over, but not so. That's when I have to maintain the greatest vigilance. Otherwise when the case is opened at the other end of a journey there are extensive omissions, bonuses and maddening bits of improvisation. When my outrage is reported back to the executive I never get a more satisfactory response than *I couldn't see what you wanted with X* or *You can't have too many Ys*. I have to anticipate the perverse algebra of the proxy packer, complicated in this case by the fanciful travel priorities of a virtual agoraphobic.

There was a certain amount of worldly advice current about what to take with you to India, things which were scarce there, and consequently better than hard currency – bottles of whisky and razor blades. I wasn't going to be able to be my own porter, but even so, travelling light was part of my agenda. Travelling light was an admirable goal in itself, even if Dad, the family's supreme exponent of the art, sometimes came close to showing off. He had arrived in Tanganyika once with all his possessions (toothbrush, flannel, razor) rolled in a towel under his arm.

The bottles disqualified themselves immediately, but I dare say I could have managed some razor blades – except that a pilgrim doesn't bring contraband or even legitimate wares. A pilgrim brings only his submission to the sacred, and I refused to be canny or self-serving on this devotional journey.

Mrs Osborne had given the travelling-light agenda a wonderful boost by saying that I should bring a single change of clothes and no more. That was all I would need. There wasn't much Mum could do to overrule such a definitive pronouncement. I took with me a suitcase to go in the hold of the aeroplane, and a carrier bag which would hang on the crutch when I walked. The carrier bag held crucial objects like my flannel, tooth-cleaning equipment, bum-wiper, passport and traveller's cheques. By now I had developed considerable expertise with the bum-snorkel, to the point where I could do a better job using remote-control toilet paper origami than any nurse who had looked after me at CRX, or any helper at Hephaistos. Have snorkel, will travel. I would have hated to have to put my bum in the hands of strangers during my pilgrimage. The strangers themselves would have been less than thrilled, brahmins aghast and even pariahs not best pleased.

Marmite and Roses

Mrs Osborne had specifically asked me to bring some Marmite, as that strange substance (which I remember calling 'salty jam' as a child) wasn't available in India. Mum insisted that she'd read somewhere that the manufacturers of Marmite were so keen on their product that they would send it anywhere in the world for a modest sum of money. When I expressed doubt about this, she did one of her rare Granny impersonations, smiling sweetly and saying, 'Let's write to Marmite and find out, shall we?' She didn't veto the purchase of a large jar of Marmite for my Indian expedition, but all the same she wanted to be vindicated before I left if at all possible. Marmite replied by return of post. Mum was in the right. The company would send a large jar of Marmite anywhere on the globe for the sum of 9/6 (including postage).

'That makes sense, whichever way you look at it, doesn't it, Mum?' I said. She didn't quite get the joke at first, so I wrote '9/6' on a piece of paper and then turned it upside down to show her that it still said '9/6'. She was impressed and congratulated me on my cleverness. I didn't have the honesty to confess that the idea wasn't mine. I'd pinched it from an old advertisement for Castella cigars. I was baffled by the variability of Mum's intelligence: she could sometimes be very sharp, while other times she was like a sort of super-parrot repeating things she'd read or heard. On my side, though, there was a relentless need to impress her with my brain and the constancy of its whirring. All this knotting-up of family emotion, of dependency and resentment, was something I hoped would simply fall away when I was in India and could look at the world through other eyes, eyes freed of their Bourne End blinkers, able to see beyond the sun.

Mum said if I really wanted to travel light why didn't I send the Marmite as the company recommended instead of taking it myself? 9/6 wasn't a great deal of money, and the jar was heavy. I pointed out that I'd already bought the jar, but Mum said she would pay me back and take it off my hands. So huge a quantity of yeast extract would give depth of flavour to her soups and stews for years to come. I held firm, and finally she had to give in.

This was typical of our arbitrary wrangles at that time. If I had learned about the Marmite despatch service before Mum did, I would have been on fire to take advantage of it, while she would have poured all her energy into making the case against. No stick was too small for us to lunge at, determined to get hold of it by the wrong end. These were the sticks of disputation, which have no right end.

It bothers some people that Marmite is saline mulch thrown off in the process of beer-making, defined historically as a waste product until people could be persuaded to buy it. I think that's typical of Maya's work, which is really only advertising. I don't think there's such a thing as original sin, but I do think there's such a thing as believing your own publicity.

At this point in the drama of packing the battle of wills shifted ground. The next conflict was over confectionery. Mum had finally been gracious on the Marmite question, but she took a harder line on the issue of Cadbury's Roses. Suddenly travelling light was less of a priority. She was very insistent that I should take a tin with me to India. In fact she unilaterally packed one in my suitcase, ignoring my protests, saying, 'You never know when a box of chocolates will come in handy – you know, to say thank you to your hostess. That sort of thing.'

I managed not to point out that I was going on a pilgrimage, not a house party – you don't struggle half-way across the world hot on the heels of self-realisation only to bleat out, 'Thank you for having me.' Still, I couldn't shut up altogether. The need to have the last word in argument was as strong as ever, and serenity was well beyond the horizon. I said, 'I'll be staying at the ashram, or else with a fellow devotee, and the only person I will want to thank will be my guru, whose body died in 1950, as I'm sure I've mentioned, leaving him impervious to chocolate.'

'Don't snap at me, please, John.' With a sigh she took the offending Cadbury's Roses out of my little bag. 'I'm trying to help you as best I can. I just *wish* I knew where exactly you'll be staying – will there be running water and proper conveniences at this guest-house?'

'An ashram is a sort of monastery, not a guest-house.'

'Well, will they be giving you a proper breakfast? Who will look after you when you get ill – you will get ill, won't you? It stands to reason. So far from home, eating strange food.'

'I trust my guru that my pilgrimage is pleasing and is meant to happen. Plumbing and cooking are not interesting subjects to the evolved mind. And it's meat-eaters such as yourself who get into trouble in foreign parts, not vegeteerians. As you like to call us.'

Ramana Maharshi had also had a sticky relationship with his mother. After she had despaired of persuading him to come home and had moved to Tiruvannamalai herself, she pestered him with her attentions. First she prepared a vegetable dish, than a little soup, and soon she was wandering all over the hill gathering provisions, murmuring, 'He likes this vegetable, he likes this fruit,' entirely ignoring his remonstrations. She took silence for assent, and his in-different eating, absolved of appetite, as Thanks Mum, What Would I Do Without You?

Once he teased her while she was cooking, saying, 'Beware of those onions, Mother. They are a great obstacle to deliverance!' Onions in the Hindu classification being *tamasic*, darkness foods, though not strictly forbidden like other substances in their category (such as meat).

I was lucky that Mum's phobias would prevent her from following me to the holy mountain under any circumstances. Out of the corner of my eye I could see her sneaking the Cadbury's Roses back into my case. I made a mental note to ask Peter, when he got home from work, to remove them and hide them somewhere safe. Inside his digestive system if need be.

I was beginning to understand the spiritual value of the family as an institution, which is nil. The family stands for everything that re-ligion (properly understood) opposes – in a word, attachment. Christ showed he grasped this when he rejected his blood family in favour of something more real: ¶*Know you not I must be about my father's busi-ness?* Slyly he used the rhetoric of family while slipping out of its clutches.

Mum said that worrying over me was turning her hair white. There was no sign of that, but I did try to be sympathetic about her little obsessions. At her urging I even went to see Flanny the GP, complicit in Mum's sneering at vegeteerians, for something to take with me in case of diarrhœa. Her response was typically forthright, typically un-helpful: '*Of course* you'll get diarrhœa,' she said, as if this was the real underlying purpose of the trip. 'But I'm not allowed to prescribe for things you haven't got yet.'

I always found Flanny difficult to deal with, which may only mean that she found me difficult. Doctors like to make a difference. They don't like the patients who keep turning up when there's nothing wrong with them, and they don't enjoy the long-term cases whose lives aren't susceptible to transformation. Hypochondriacs and chronics alike undermine the self-respect of professionals. The fact that I stubbornly turned up from time to time with a new demand must have seemed like malingering of a perverse sort, as if I was playing for sympathy from the far shores of ill health. In fact I don't want sympathy from a doctor (*sympathetic* in medicine being strictly a description of one branch of the nervous system). I'd rather have a snappy diagnosis or a script made out with no questions asked.

In the end I had to fork out for some Lomotil on a private prescription, which rather rankled. 10/6 it cost me, making a considerable hole in my budget. You could send a large jar of Marmite anywhere in the world for a sum like that, and still have a shilling left over for emergencies.

Mum refused to look at Tamil Nadu on a map, though Dad took an interest in that aspect of the expedition, and insisted on referring to my whole summer of pilgrimage as 'John's trip to Timbuktu' – despite his having spent some time in those parts himself.

There was very little that reassured Mum about my five weeks of proposed self-discovery, but at least there was the late Arthur Osborne's social status. He was a graduate of Oxford University, which counted for a lot in her eyes, and he had even written a book, which I had on long loan (thanks to Mrs Pavey's good offices) from Bourne End Library. Mum would have the book to hang on to while I was away.

She was comforted, too, that I would be cared for by Mrs Osborne. Wives and mothers were the same the world over, weren't they? 'Mrs Osborne' was a name with an uncommonly reassuring cadence, suggesting Queen Victoria (wasn't Osborne the name of her house on the Isle of Wight?). Nothing would go wrong, surely, while I was in the charge of a Mrs Osborne. I don't know exactly what Mum's mental picture of Mrs Osborne amounted to, but in my eyes Mrs Osborne was a sort of anti-Mum, blonde where she was dark, perhaps a little plump, serene and indulgent, like a Roman goddess of the crops depicted in a sentimental painting – like the lady on the jar of Ovaltine, in fact, clutching to her boozie a bountiful cereal sheaf which promised restful nourishment. Realising that the late Arthur Osborne had been in his sixties, so that his wife, even if she had been (as I vaguely remembered) a student of his at one stage, couldn't be so very young, I sowed silver hairs among the imaginary gold, and adorned her face with glasses whose frames curved jauntily up at the sides.

Vomiting serenely in the bushes

In the car Mum was tense, tense even for her. When we were some way from the airport Dad pulled the car over, but it must have been a signal from Mum which made him stop. From my position in the front seat, required by the inflexibility of my legs, I dare say I missed a lot of byplay over the years. Then Mum had another go at asserting herself. When she spoke, she leaned over between the seats so that her rapid breaths sounded in my ear and buffeted against my face. In that posture she wasn't properly in my line of vision – for a true confrontation she would have had to get out of the car and face me down through the windscreen, but that would hardly fit as the setting for this little tableau, A Mother's Final Appeal, though it might have fitted with her general sense that the world was bearing down on her.

Mum's sense of drama was still rudimentary – she didn't yet feel entitled to make any sort of scene. Granny had drummed into her the idea that anyone who raised his or her voice in an argument was wrong by definition. If ever Granny broke that rule and raised her voice herself, without stopping being right, other people were normally too alarmed to find the inconsistency.

From her position in the back seat, head thrust forward and turned round, she may even have felt that I was being stubborn in not meeting her gaze – being stiff-necked, as people say. She said, 'Listen, JJ. It's not too late to call this whole trip off. There's no shame in admitting you've bitten off more than you can chew. We can just turn round and go home. No one will think the less of you. Your father and I will never mention it again. Dad can get you a ticket for somewhere nearer and just as nice.'

'It's not a trip, it's a pilgrimage. I'm not going there because it's *nice!*' Perhaps this wasn't the most tactful line to take, but I was beginning to feel genuinely claustrophobic about Mum's need to control me. How threatened she was by hints of independence on my part! And I suppose, seeing it from her point of view, she had her reasons: what was the meaning of her life, unless it was to make mine possible? She had forged an identity for herself by chaining us together.

I wonder what would have happened if I had given in to the pressure, the parental front united for once. I can imagine Mum breaking out the tin of Roses from my case right away (I'd forgotten to charge Peter with their removal), passing them round in hysterical relief and stuffing her own cheeks with sweets, tears running down her face in her gratitude for the reprieve she'd won herself, by staving off my maturity. After that, she might have signalled Dad to pull over again, and vomited serenely in the bushes. Beyond that, I can't guess. I wonder if I would even have taken up my place at Cambridge, if I'd lost the battle for India.

Before I said yes to their offer of a lift, I had made Mum and Dad promise they wouldn't wait until my plane took off. Otherwise, I told them, I would take the Mini and let it take its chances for five weeks in the car park. They hung around rather helplessly after they'd helped me check my case in until I reminded Dad of his promise, and of how much he hated goodbyes and all that emotional claptrap. After that he led Mum away, though he did explore the furthest tender reaches of his vocabulary by calling me 'Chicken' when he patted me goodbye.

In 1970 Air India advertised itself as *The Airline that Treats You Like a Maharajah*, and I can't argue with that on the basis of its performance that year. Of course I can't vouch for anything but First Class. Ladies in saris started serving me dainties almost immediately. Caviar, smoked salmon, *pâté de foie gras*, all these got the thumbs-down from me, but they did a nice line in spicy nuts, and there was pink champagne, served in proper fluty glasses, which suit my hands better than any other shape.

Pinkness was a definite theme, so that the first-class cabin had almost the feel of a boudoir. There were pretty pink tablecloths and proper napkins. Luxury seemed to be a female preoccupation, though in all those hours I only glimpsed one or two Maharanis in First Class.

The ladies in saris seemed a little disappointed that I wasn't going to order a nice juicy steak, which was what Maharajas with my skin tone normally plumped for. That must have been a major part of their training, to offer taboo fare without showing disgust, up above the clouds where the cold international air strips scruples away.

My nearest Maharajah (as pale-complected as me) was a little distance away, thanks to the luxurious width of the seats, but I could see that he was making more work for the staff than I was. They couldn't do enough for him. He had loosened his tie, a procedure I've never managed to understand. Obviously I'm not the person to ask about the finer points of formal dressing, but doesn't that produce the worst of both worlds, encumbrance without the faintest possibility of elegance?

The ladies in saris kept popping juicy things into the beak of this burly cuckoo. I suppose *pâté de foie gras* is juicy – I have no plans to find out. His fantasy of luxury was clear, that he should be catered to as intensively as possible, to get the maximum value out of every costly minute (costly to his employers, I imagined, rather than to him personally), even if the unnaturally accelerated intake of food and drink made him go very red and sweaty in the face.

My notion of luxury was very different, and I was living it out very fully. Mostly I waved the attentions of the ladies in saris away, I gave little shakes of the head. I would graciously accept snacks from time to time, perhaps a small bowl of pilaff, and a little light topping-up of my elegant glass, but I declined the immoderacy of a full meal.

The theatrical show the cabin staff put on for my neighbour began to seem actively oppressive to me. I had seen similar rituals performed at the Compleat Angler, but everything looked very different at twenty-five thousand feet and six hundred miles an hour. A steward in a tunic came pushing a trolley before him, then reverently removed its polished metal cover to reveal a slab of roasted flesh, which he then carved with the gravest ceremony on to my neighbour's plate. He made great play of tossing salad high in the air, virtually juggling it with adroit tongs, so that the dressed leaves in their tumbling came within inches of colliding with the ceiling panels (necessarily low), where they would have left faint imprints flavoured with garlic and mustard.

This should have seemed merely droll, but for me it had a nightmarish aspect. The flushed businessman being fed so relentlessly seemed to be on the receiving end of a torture rather than a treat. It was as if I was being given a vision of his karma, a terrible locked pattern like a recurring equation, in which he was alternately a goose being force-fed grain until its liver slowly exploded inside it, and a man being force-fed that liver.

My own experience of force-feeding was modest, extending only to the time at Vulcan when the demonic matron Judy Brisby had stuffed congealing pilchards into my mouth and held my nose, but it had left its mark. I felt the sort of shiver which Mum always interpreted as a goose walking over her grave – in this case a goose that wanted the return of its liver, rudely confiscated, pressed in jelly, and sold on.

All this restaurant pantomime was no more than a game of status, disconnected from any matter of appetite. The stewards might just as well have spared my neighbour the labour of greed by placing in front of him a gorgeously illuminated calligraphic parchment reading: *Mere feet behind you, screened by curtains and the impalpable screens of caste, tourists, families and lesser businessmen are wrestling with sachets of salad cream and trying to unpeel slimy layers of cold meat from the bottom of a plastic tray, or else peering with distaste at bowls of sloppy curry . . . and you, perhaps, honoured sir, would care for a cheese and pickle sandwich (freshly made of course)? We have tomatoes!*

As it was, the staff were presumably struggling in a tiny galley just out of sight, trying not to bump into each other, the steward plying a blow-torch to give the surface of the roast the appropriate savoury blisters, one of the ladies in saris pulling the leaves off a dishevelled lettuce, rinsing them over a miniature sink with water poured carefully from a bottle.

Lively molecular traffic

My fantasy, of course, was that in the middle of all this finicky drudgery one attendant would say to the other, 'If only they were all like the little chap! He's no trouble at all . . .' Only in these supremely artificial circumstances could I bask in the luxury of being 'no trouble'. Normally it isn't an option for me to be no trouble. I can only hope to be worth the trouble I cause.

I resolved to remember the name of the champagne, so that I could ask Granny if it was a good make. Moët et Chandon. It seemed nice. I'd have to ask her without any men around, otherwise she would defer to their judgement, pretend not to know the names of brands, and refer to the drink itself, so lively in its molecular traffic, simply as 'fizz'. Somebody behind me, another lucky soul reincarnated for a few hours as a Maharajah, got the hiccups. Shortly afterwards so did I, whether because of champagne, altitude, suggestibility or some combination of the three. It struck me that since the state airline was part of the government of India, the country itself had paid my travelling expenses. Not only that, India had given me the First Class treatment. I was much more than a tourist, and in a special category even as a pilgrim. I was a national guest, as I lolled above the clouds in a cloud of hiccups, nicely flustered by fizz.

For me the experience of air travel was one of a marvellous levelling. Up there in the air, as I realised, we're all the same. The plane is a big box full of people who can do nothing for themselves. It's not just me. We passengers displayed our caste marks less legibly than usual. If I needed more help than my fellows to go to the toilet, then it wasn't much. I was calm even when the plane lurched in turbulence and my fellow-travellers murmured anxiously. I was at an advantage. I'd had plenty of practice at sitting still.

The only disadvantage was visual. My eyes work reasonably well, but I'm partially sighted all the same. I'm partially sighted on planes because I don't have a view even if I have a window seat. At best, with my flexibility at its maximum, I can look out but not down, and down (when you're many thousands of Maya-feet up in the air) is where the view is.

The food came in small portions at short intervals, which is just what this body likes. Eventually the hiccups stopped and I dozed off. When I woke I was in a panic. I was convinced that the plane had landed at Bombay, and somehow I had slept through the whole thing, so that the plane had taken off again and I was now on my way somewhere else. I called the stewardess for reassurance. She managed the same beautifully measured smile as she had when she had poured my champagne. She told me there were still three hours to go.

What in a semi-conscious state I had interpreted as my missing my stop, as if this was that other exotic mode of travel, a bus, must have been our Boeing 707 landing in Bahrain, a detail of its itinerary which I had somehow forgotten. I was sorry to have missed the 'reality' of Bahrain since I liked the name so much with its diacritical fleck, the dot under the *h* like a stowaway clinging to the undercarriage of the word.

Now, suddenly, I found I had run out of patience. Those three hours were harder to live through than the years I had spent in bed forbidden to move. I thought that I would go mad, now that I was definitely moving, and still not getting where I wanted to go. I didn't enjoy the way my life seemed to offer an endless cumulative proof of Zeno's paradox, that the arrow will never reach the target, since it must cover half the distance, and then half that, then half *that* . . . Patience is only tenderness in its chronological expression. At this point I had no time-tenderness left.

In my mind I tried to knock off the *o*-apostrophe-*s* to turn what was blocking my path into a more congenial Zen paradox, the one about the Zen master who always hits the target although (*because!*) he doesn't bother to look and is wholly indifferent to the result. Then all I had to do was become indifferent, all of a sudden, to everything I'd struggled for all my life.

I didn't see my gormandising co-Maharajah again after Beirut. Perhaps that was as far as he was travelling, or perhaps he was sleeping it off. Or else vomiting it out.

Before we landed at Bombay I was told the drill. I should remain in my seat while the other passengers 'deplaned'. After I had myself deplaned, of course, I would re-emplane for Madras. I was transplaning.

On hand for the deplanement was an attractive young man in white trousers and jacket, an Air India official of some sort who was helpfully holding on to a child whose mother was struggling to organise herself. He offered to take my carrier bag for me when everything was arranged for this little family and he had a hand free.

Dad had warned me to be careful in India, in fact anywhere outside

England. In England there were rules, but anywhere else it was mayhem and anarchy. You could trust no one. At Bombay airport, in my first conversation with an unknown Indian, I was unwilling to part with the bag – which was of course open to the world and contained my passport and traveller's cheques, not to mention my wash bag, flannel and perspex bum-wiper. My doubts must have shown on my face, because the white-clothed official said sweetly that he was only trying to help. That was his job! He wasn't going to run off with my bag, and he certainly didn't want to make me uneasy. I should hold on to my bag if that made me happier. But when he was finished with his current task was there something else he could do for me?

Ramana Maharshi compared anxious seekers after self-realisation to people on a train insisting on carrying their luggage. Put everything down! It's all coming with you! I wasn't sure that a similar analogy applied to my situation, now that the plane had landed and I needed to take charge of my belongings again.

Meanwhile, what did I want this young man to do? I wanted to go on looking into his eyes, which meant I wanted him to carry me slung in his arms in the appropriate position. Not very practical. I certainly didn't want him to push me in my wheelchair – that way I wouldn't be able to see him. It would be better if he pushed someone else in a wheelchair, ahead of me, while someone else (someone less rewarding to look at) was pushing me.

My mouth tasted sour, of old champagne and bad sleep, and I realised it was high time I brushed my teeth. It was thinking about my wash bag, and whether to trust it to a stranger, which reminded me. I decided I should greet the Indian Nation with gleaming teeth and fresh minty breath, and this suddenly became a worry, that I might greet the Nation with an unworthy smile. The beautiful brown man in his white clothing had handed the toddler back to its mother, and was now turning his entire attention to helping me. I told him that I wanted to visit the lavatory and also to brush my teeth. He said 'That is very fine.' He pushed me in the wheelchair as far as the Gents, then helped me out of it.

As I went into the lavatory he first held the door for me, and then made to come in himself. This was exactly what I had wanted, but it made me nervous. Politely I tried to close the door on him, but it was necessarily an unequal struggle. He persisted, and so we were both in the cubicle together. I had some slight idea about what this would mean in the West, the taboo charge of lavatory intimacy, but no notion of how it translated here. It felt strange and exciting. I felt a little embarrassment about urinating. With that safely out of the way, I turned to brushing my teeth.

The lavatory smelled foul, but in a pleasingly exotic way. There was unfamiliar spice in the fæcal aroma and I snuffed it up excitedly. Everything was new here, even bad bathroom smells. Of course their source might have been some fresh arrival from Britain overdoing it with the in-flight curry and loosening his bowels the moment he had the chance on *terra firma*, but that didn't matter. Travel is all about first impressions – it's very much Maya's department.

Love the electromagnetic pulse

I could see the young man's face in the mirror, which again was what I had wanted, but the effect was not relaxing. I had to notice that he really was staring at me very hard, and I started to get flustered. Then he started to come over to me, before I had even had time to stow away my toothbrush properly. Then he did two overpowering things at once: he turned me towards him and hugged me, and he burst into barely coherent speech. '*I know why you have come!*' he was crooning. '*I know the reason!*' The crutch slipped from the edge of the basin, but there was no one to shout 'The ruddy crutch!' There was only love in an overwhelming surge, like the electromagnetic pulse that accompanies certain types of explosion.

Looking at me with the greatest intensity, my new friend said, 'Everything must be open and known. You must not conceal your purpose. You should not hide! Why behave as if this was cause for shame?' I could hardly breathe, not daring to believe we were thinking the same thing.

Sexual feeling and the spiritual urge, those two ways of losing selfhood, are significantly close to each other, deeply similar, vitally different, like the dispensers on a café table which it doesn't even occur to you anyone could mix up until the first mouthful proves you've sugared your tea with salt.

Now I wanted to be very sure. 'What is it that must be known and not hidden?'

'Sir, dear sir! Everyone of the airline knows your story already. You are making this journey through the grace of Sri Bhagavan Ramana Maharshi, and should be proud of your purpose. Because, you see . . . ,' he added with a bewitching shyness, 'I also am a devotee.'

At this point he burst into tears, squeezed me almost too tightly and began sobbing on my shoulder. Everything exploded in my heart. Part of the detonation was relief that I had been on the right track about this lovely man. That there was nothing carnal in our contact. In India I wanted everything to be pure, and for a long moment I had wondered whether I wasn't being offered the fulfilment of the dreams I had left behind.

Before leaving Bourne End I had taken a solemn vow of celibacy. In my benighted Western way I thought that celibacy meant abstaining from sexual acts and thoughts. I had a great deal to learn on that subject, as on so many others.

I had read but not taken in what my guru had to say on the subject. *I did not eat, so they said I was fasting. I did not speak, and they said I had taken a vow of silence.* Perversely I failed to understand, in my deluded hunger for austerity, that suppressing appetites is not the point. By the repression of appetites they are intensified and distorted, when the whole object is to facilitate an evaporation. In the narrowness of my understanding I failed to realise that celibacy is the end point of a whole series of processes and that short cuts are not possible. Will-power not being the weapon, but the target.

I hadn't yet understood that there was no contradiction between Krishna being decribed as the greatest celibate (the word used is *Brahmachari*) and his having 15,000 concubines.

Meanwhile I felt a piercing guilt that I had mistrusted this marvellous man, not trusting him with the carrier bag that held my treasures, but that emotion didn't last. It was replaced by a different feeling. In my field of vision there was only whiteness, white with a periphery of brown, white jacket, white trousers with neatly zipped-up fly now pressed more or less against my chest, and warm brown skin showing where the white ended at his collar and cuffs. He caressed me, and I caressed him back, and then he smiled and with his face still streaked with tears, he held me at a small distance away from himself (as far as the size of the cubicle would allow) and formally wished me joy on my pilgrimage. Despite my vow and my relief I found it hard to disentangle my spiritual feelings from the sensation of touch, and I didn't ask myself why it seemed so important to try. I just took that for granted and felt awkward that I wasn't able to match his religious devotion, this tender piety.

Hugs work so well on paper, and in films. People flow together, step into each other's arms, become one. That's not my experience. A standard-sized person either picks me up in his arms and embraces me in mid-air, which isn't as much fun as it sounds, or presses my head and shoulders against his middle, with more or less of the courtesy of a stoop. The other option is to kneel in front of me and start from there, but that's pretty stilted in its own right, though it gives me the pleasure (usually) of feeling breath on my face. The hoist, the squeeze with semi-stoop, the kneel – none of them quite hits the spot.

Faces and groins never match up at the same time, whichever is the chosen pose, and one or other of them always has its nose put out of joint. It's never fifty-fifty – and I imagine it was the fifty-fifty idea which made hugging catch on in the first place.

Woeful tears are viscous

The lovely man in Bombay airport explored two methods. An episode of semi-stooping (and the semi-stoop can claim to be the best of a bad bunch), then some intense moments of kneeling before me, not humbly kneeling but proudly kneeling, and shedding the tears of strength.

It was his noble weeping that affected me so profoundly. His cheeks brushed past mine and left traces. The excited particles of those tears passed rapidly into my skin, dancing through the pores. The divine pervasion took only a moment. It stands to reason that happy, holy tears are governed by a different principle and have a greater penetrating power than woeful ones, which as we know are highly viscous. There must be a subtler globulation involved. I experienced those tears passing directly into me, by an osmosis of essence which science has neglected to study.

When he had reinstalled me into the wheelchair and taken me to the check-in for Madras, this angel of the magnificent aura and the percolating tears gave me a white card with his name and rank on it. I have forgotten the rank, but his name is written on my mind in italic caps. *S. P. MUNSHI.*

In the little whirlwind of sensation and revelation that was my sojourn in Bombay airport shame played a part, but it was only a walk-on. It's true that I had experienced sexual attraction to S. P. Munshi as well as spiritual common ground. S. P. Munshi vibrated to both frequencies. But if I wasn't ashamed I was certainly a little embarrassed. Life would certainly be easier if everything kept to its category, without overlap. My murky vow of purity and self-denial (as if the Self could be denied!) had rather been shown up by the brilliant white of S. P. Munshi's uniform, as echoed by the brilliant white of his business card, still in my possession, tucked reverently into the carrier bag, jostling among the traveller's cheques and the perspex bum-snorkel.

On the plane to Madras I had much to think about, though I had hardly set foot on Indian soil. I knew that I would be met by someone at Madras Airport – Mrs Osborne had promised me that much – but she hadn't told me who. In my feebly fantasising mind it was even money whether it would be some swami or some street urchin. Brahmin or pariah.

As we descended towards Madras I could see a certain amount out of the windows of First Class if I worked myself around to face them. Even after my hip operations I don't have a lot of flexibility in my mid-section – I'd need a spine replacement for that. But I was able to manage a methodical wriggle.

Everything I could see was green. I could see cows. We seemed to be about to land in a field. I couldn't understand how the cows were going to keep away from the plane, or the plane keep away from the cows, and then the plane banked and the fields disappeared.

In those days, British citizens had no need of a visa to visit India and customs procedures were rudimentary. All that happened was that a rather sweet young customs man approached me and asked if I would please fill in a required form. After a glance at the situation he offered to fill it in for me himself. He was extremely friendly and polite, but the questions just went on and on. Why was I here? Where was I staying? Would I be going anywhere else?

There were very few of these questions to which I could supply a satisfactory answer. The customs man had no objection to writing 'Not Applicable' on his forms, in a handwriting that was certainly far superior to my best efforts, but there seemed no end to his forms. Question begat question.

Eventually I groaned and said, 'Why do there have to be all these questions? All this paperwork?' The customs man turned and gave me his brightest smile yet, saying, *'We learnt it all from you, sir!'*

It was Mr Raghu Gaitonde who met me after I had cleared customs, neither swami nor urchin but to judge by his dress and demeanour a successful businessman in his forties. While I was summing him up he was doing the same with me. I was pleased with what I saw, pleased and also disappointed, since I had my heart set on the exotic. He was less satisfied with the results of his visual survey. In fact he was fairly evidently reeling. More or less his first words were, 'Mrs Osborne sent me along with the instructions "Collect him from the airport, and bung him on a bus for Tiruvannamalai."' He made a helpless gesture with his hands. 'I don't lightly disregard Mrs Osborne's instructions, but I think in this case the proposed course of action will not do. Bunging of any sort would not be responsible. Buses are not to be thought of. Other modes must be devised. She would undoubtedly scold. I myself live in Madras. You must come to my home and meet my family.'

I felt rather seasick in Raghu's large old-fashioned car, an Ambassador. Luckily there was an absorbent canvas cover on top of the leather, or else I would have been slithering queasily across the seats. From what I could see he was the most cautious driver in those seething streets. Even so, when we turned corners I felt a little insecure, at the mercy of the superannuated suspension.

I had braced myself for the hubbub of traffic, and had more or less visualised the handcarts and street traders hawking their goods. It had never occurred to me that cows would be wandering along the streets of a major city without visible attendants. Naturally enough they had the right of way – even Michael Aspel, demon driver of Bourne End, taker of mad risks, would have thought twice before locking horns with them.

Those cows gave me my first indelible (and briefly traumatic) impression of India, an odd sort of spiritual scorching. Whenever we stopped at traffic lights, or were brought to a halt by any other wayward blockage of the traffic flow, I would close my eyes for a few moments, perhaps longer. Once, when I opened them again, I could see a pair of cows leaning against the walls of a building and giving them a good old lick, showing every sign of enjoying themselves. The walls they chose were ones where cinema posters had been stuck, gaudy in their green and orange and red. They must have found that when the posters had aged a bit and started to peel away from the wall, or else were so fresh that they were still wet, they could by dint of extra licking peel a whole strip from the wall with their lips. Hadn't I given way to the same temptation with the yellow-roses wallpaper of my room in Bathford? It must be a profound animal craving.

At first the sight was no more than a bit of exotic drollery, cattle at ease in a city, imperturbably chewing the cud of advertising images. I'd heard that Indians were cinema-mad, and the craze even affected the ruminants. I could see that some of the cows were sitting down, munching whole strips of poster in a gloriously unhurried way, wide ribbons of clashing colour. Then I realised with a flash of horror that what they were really interested in eating wasn't the paper but the glue that stuck it to the wall. And what was glue made of, if it wasn't the boiled-down bones and hooves of its own kind? Gelatine. There was a heinous meeting in those mouths, as viscous saliva softened a paste made of melted kine. The sacred animal of India was contentedly masticating a gruel made of its own kind on the streets of Madras. This baleful vision of the long-lashed vegetarian turned cannibal followed me all the way to Raghu's house.

There's something sinister about the tongue itself as a body part. It flexes and drools, helpless but implacable, a chunk of meat that we can't choke down. Without it we can't speak, though if we become too conscious of it in our mouths speech becomes impossibly paradoxical. No other muscle is tethered only at one end – perhaps that's part of its uncanniness.

In my own history it spells guilt, since as an innocent and ailing child I ate it with relish, not allowing myself to know that this silky vegetable was something quite different. The bovine tongue brings on a mood of superstitious horror, not helped by my witnessing what it got up to on the streets of Madras. This is the tissue of moral dread, flesh flap that licks and whispers – or it would be, if I didn't have non-dualist thought handy to dissolve it.

When we had reached his house Raghu left me in the car while he went inside. By now I was overheating – I can keep cool for quite a time, not by any virtue except that I move about so little, but then suddenly I'm awash with sweat. In the short time that Raghu was away, the windscreen filled up with mischievous inquisitive children's faces, more thickly plastered against the glass than leaves in an autumn gale. I beamed at them and hoped that Raghu had locked the door.

He was back remarkably quickly. In fact he had hardly spent more than thirty seconds inside the house. If I had been less preöccupied with cattle atrocities seen beside the road I would have registered that this was something altogether remarkable. I was in a very different sort of society from the one I was used to. A man enters a house and tells his wife that they are having a surprise guest, not only for dinner but overnight. He emerges half a minute later, smiling and composed. It was a sequence of actions as mysterious in its way as the riddles I had enjoyed leaving unsolved at Burnham – Antony and Cleopatra, the man who asks for a glass of water and has a gun pointed at him by the barman instead. It was completely impossible in British terms without the creation of domestic turmoil, protests and mutterings, without mollification by bribery or vows of retaliation, but here it was perfectly routine. No broken glass, not even a hiccup.

I wasn't sure that I was up to socialising of any high order, but perhaps that wouldn't be expected of me. I was exhausted, and grateful to be cared for by anyone who was willing to take me on. The house was spacious and airy, well equipped with large ceiling fans. It was furnished to allow entertaining in both the Western and Indian styles, with sofas and chairs, and also mats for those who gravitated more naturally towards the floor.

I began to sit up and take notice when I was introduced to Raghu's younger brother Kashi, a fine young man with a boyish grin who seemed to dance along the ground rather than walk on it. He looked no more than thirty – in fact he was nearer to forty. He was marvellously sleek, like a matinée idol of the sort that is out of date in the West. If his features had been blown up to vast dimensions on a poster, staring into heroic distance, it would be hard to blame any sentient creature for being mesmerised by them. I would have liked to give him a good long lick myself.

Now that I was indoors I could tell that the household wasn't absorbing the fact of my presence quite as smoothly as it seemed. The establishment had been set on its ears, in the nicest possible way, by the arrival of this visitor – this person who had come from England all on his own but couldn't cross a room, let alone continue his pilgrimage, without help. I was an astonishment and a wonder.

Next to make herself known was Raghu's daughter Chu-cha, who must have been about ten at the time. I used the technique I've evolved over time for the reassurance of children, whose curiosity is so highly developed, whose vulnerability to embarrassment follows it every step of the way. I gave a little nod at the opposite wall and said, 'Is that you in that picture?' In fact I could hardly see the photograph I was indicating, and had no evidence that the girl even spoke English.

The point was to convey that I would be fixing my attention safely on the middle distance for as long as she pleased to look at me. I was giving a sort of permission, by saying in effect, '*I'm* going to be looking in this direction for a while – where *you* look is your business.' I wouldn't embarrass her by intercepting her gaze prematurely, and our eyes would meet only when she had adjusted to what was unfamiliar about me. It was up to me to create a sort of antechamber to this first encounter, where a stranger could compose herself.

When this had all been managed I asked Chu-cha, 'Is your mother in?' and she looked rather doubtfully at her father. He explained that she was indeed in the house – where else would she be? – but it was polite, when a visitor came, for a wife to wait for twenty minutes or so until called to present herself. When the time came he called softly and Sumati appeared, bowing in the sinuous posture of Namaskaaram, which alas I had no prospect of returning properly. She had to take the thought for the deed like everyone else. Her hair had a wonderful oiled shine to it, and the fragrance she carried made English scents seem two-dimensional.

Delicate balance of hospitality

She offered refreshment before retiring gracefully to attend to her duties. This too was the proper procedure. Would I care for some sweet-lime juice? I would. I was determined to drink it slowly when it came, delicious though it was, so as to defer as long as possible the moment when I needed the lavatory and tipped the delicate balance of hospitality into something cruder and more compromised. There is such a marked social difference between intake and output in digestive matters. It was too much to hope that Tamil Nadu would be the culture that disproved that rule, with excretion and embarrassment showing no overlap.

Chu-cha settled herself on a mat near my feet so that she could examine me closely – evidence that any nervousness had been dispelled. She felt entitled to look as much as she wanted.

Sumati must have been busy in the kitchen, and before long we were summoned to the large dining table. I was offered eating implements from a little revolving canteen of knives, forks and spoons, hung up by holes in their handles. My hosts would be eating by hand, but I was a Western Guest and would be lost without cutlery (true enough in my case). In the middle of the table was a large carousel loaded with cooked food, each dish in its own compartment.

I was slightly disappointed by the look of the room, since I expected the exotic in every detail. Here there were traces of the Habitat chic of the period. Low over the dining table hung a fat purple lampshade suspended from a pulley. The Washbournes had something very like it.

Raghu took great care to explain the system to me, though I wasn't expected to use it. Sumati would serve me herself. Raghu gave the carousel a proud push, so that it rotated merrily for quite a time, diffusing the aromas of a dozen separate dishes in a centrifugal spiral. Raghu and the others had large stainless steel platters onto which they helped themselves with food from the carousel. The serving spoons in their compartments were the only utensils on the table, apart from the ones I was to use.

I was thoroughly entertained by the carousel system. It was fun to watch the wheel being given a push so that the dish in front of me was replaced by a new one. It made me want to try everything. As Sumati served me she would announce the name of the dish, and I repeated it as best I could, to show that I was more than a tourist getting his mouth burnt. I was having my first lesson in Tamil, as well as my first lesson in a cuisine of great depth and variety, not founded on animal sacrifice. So many morsels in savoury counterpoint. A banquet composed of a wide range of mini-meals – perfectly calculated to tantalise then satisfy this body's appetite. The rice wasn't offered on the carousel but came passed round from hand to hand in its own dish.

Raghu gave me a demonstration of Indian eating technique. You put small amounts of most things around the edge of the platter, leaving the centre area for the rice, of which you took a modest amount. Then you would mix with your right hand various dishes with a bit of rice in the centre, adding *sambhar* until the consistency felt right. I was reminded of a painter working with his palette, mixing pigments with white and each other until tone and tint were exactly what was needed to balance the composition.

The next trick was to mould the mix into little balls which you would pop into your mouth. To start with I found this a little bit horrifying, though I repeated to myself that nervous-genteel English mantra 'Fingers were made before forks . . .'

Even so, it was with fascination and a slight revulsion that I watched Raghu eat his meal. I didn't dare to start on mine. His fingers flashed with lightning speed, his hands whipped and swirled around the plate, and sometimes he would gather his dollop of food in the centre and then pound his hand up and down to squash everything together. It was a primitive and off-putting rigmarole. Yet during the process my attitude to what I was seeing changed completely, thanks to Raghu's grace, charm and pride in hospitality. If I started watching his performance with a feeling of disgust masked by good manners, then by the time he had finished I was fully convinced that the food must taste very good. I found I was distinctly hungry myself.

I set to work on my own behalf, rather self-consciously, using the Western utensils, wishing I made a better ambassador for British eating habits. From one compartment came *sambhar*, a spicy lentil soup. There were *batatas*, spicy chilli potatoes, and *koftas*, vegetarian dumplings in gravy. There was *usli* made with bread, chilli threads and cracked mustard seeds, there was *kattirikkaay poriyal* and *sundal*. The word I had most trouble with was *appaLam*, used to describe the crisp and crinkled discs, flavoured with seeds and spices, which made such a festive crackle between people's fingers and teeth.

The *L*-sound in the word was deceptive and complex, more like the notorious Welsh double-*l*, that daunting, darkly bubbling sound, than anything in English articulation. I wouldn't let myself try the food until my pronunciation had passed muster. There were a few false starts. Again, the business of getting my tongue round the words before it encountered the named food was palate-enlivening in some profound way. It was as if I had never tasted food before. A number of discrete areas of the brain were flashing at the same time, as on a pinball table with a wizard guiding the flippers. Palate-sensation and language learning shook hands, even did a little jig together.

When I was a bed-bound child Mum had given me her own kind of instruction in table manners, showing me that the ideal forkful represented every element that was present on the plate. This principle had its source in her social nervousness, which made her long for strict rules, but the idea appealed to the cadet scientist in me. Being identical, every forkful was an equally valid sample. My mouth was a laboratory whose experiments would yield verifiable and statistically suggestive results.

This new lesson, though, was devoted to nothing but the techniques of enjoyment. It was like being let loose with the paint box after years of dutiful copying and colouring inside the lines.

No 'curry' Mum had ever made at home prepared me for the benign blast of taste. One of my fellow patients at CRX, Sarah, claimed that curry would kill anyone who hadn't been exposed to it in infancy (as she had, having been born in India). Now, despite my wayward choice of birth-place, my palate was being naturalised.

I consoled myself for any ineptness in my eating manners with the thought that at least my hands were clean. What sort of state must Raghu's right hand be in by now! All sticky and foul. As if he was reading my mind, he said:

'Observe, John, and remember well how to tell the mark of an educated Indian. A country person will get the food smudged all over his hand but . . . Observe!' Here he flourished his hand like a magician. 'Look at my hand. The fingertips have food on them, but the palms are perfectly clean and dry. Go on, take a look . . . Feel.'

I looked. And then I felt. Raghu's palms were perfect, not only clean and dry but smooth and warm. My pleasure in the food and the way my hosts approached it was intensified by the good fortune of having Kashi sit opposite me. Raghu was distinguished, but Kashi was – the verbal chime made the assessment even more irresistible – dishy. I spent much of the meal making (I dare say) sheep's eyes at him (though the phrase in my mind, thanks to a loving German physiotherapist at CRX, was *Kuh Augen*). It doesn't count as ogling if you just look at what's in front of you. If he'd been badly placed at table I wouldn't have been able to see him at all without much furtive wriggling or manœuvring of the wheelchair.

Kashi for his part flashed his eyes at me. I don't mean that he flashed them with knowledge and purpose, but he flashed them just the same. That was the sort of eyes he had, the flashing sort. He couldn't help it, and it would hardly make him unique if he had a dash of the flirt in his make-up, and the reflex or habit of making conquests socially. His slim fingers deftly raided the carousel of delights.

I managed to notice, out of the corner of my eye, despite the visual and culinary distractions of dinner, that Sumati waited until we had finished eating before she put even the first morsel in her own mouth. I wondered whether this was a formal etiquette prompted by my presence, or if the same submissive routine governed every family meal. If so then it was part of the same etiquette that made her accept an unannounced guest without a murmur. Travellers in strange lands must take care not to end up like those cartoon characters who cheerfully saw through the tree-branch they're sitting on.

The whole exhausting, exhilarating evening made me realise that if the word 'family' was enough to describe the doings and feelings of the Cromers, then I would have to find another one to describe the Gaitondes.

I had been relieved to discover that in this mixed household the plumbing was as Westernised as Raghu, rather than as Indian as Sumati. Mum had warned me to expect nothing but holes in the ground buzzing with flies, and until I had seen for myself I couldn't altogether laugh off those baleful sanitary prophecies. I paid little visits to the lavatory with help from Kashi, who would wait tactfully outside.

I wouldn't have dreamed of going abroad without being able to administer the business of defæcation properly. By now I fancied myself something of a Zen master at the relevant origami, and I could make myself perfectly clean with a single lotus blossom of folded tissue (four leaves intertwined). If I enjoyed repeating the process with a fresh flower when I had time, it was partly because I was imagining the rapt admiration of an audience, in a bathroom version of Raghu's demonstration at the meal-table.

Now I asked if I might be given some extra help in the bathroom before I went to bed. Raghu frowned and said, 'I wonder who would be the right person to help you with that.' He seemed to be running through a list in his mind, of people whose possible duties might include helping with the bedtime preparations of a surprise guest. There were servants in the household, and I imagined one might be detailed to help me, but Raghu's hesitation made me think again.

For one heart-stopping moment I thought the choice was going to fall on Kashi. My heart would stop because we would be alone in an enclosed space, and I would be able to smell the traces of *sambhar* on his elegant fingertips. On the other hand he would be able to smell the after-odour of my bowels, perfumed by spices which my body had no history of processing.

Raghu's brow cleared and he said with great good humour, 'The right person seems to be me. It is I.' Once we were in the bathroom, he lit a joss-stick, wetting it first. When I asked why, he explained this enhanced the fragrance, made it more aromatic. The sweet smoke gave the hygienic proceedings an overtone of luxury and ritual. It had the added benefit of combining two of the smells of Dad's garden, for which I felt an unexpected pang: roses and bonfires. Then Raghu asked me what to do, and managed remarkably well. I can't think there was any area of his life in which similar chores were expected of him. I very much doubt if he had ever performed the same offices for Chu-cha.

Of course the novelty was symmetrical. I myself was used to being tended to by women. Dad didn't greatly involve himself in this aspect of my life, bodily maintenance from day to day.

Raghu washed me very tenderly. I told him I had brought a flannel, but he said very decisively, 'There is nothing filthier in the whole world than a flannel. Take my word for it. Direct washing is the only way.'

At first I was embarrassed and made small talk, very much for my benefit rather than his. At any moment I felt I was going to come out with the hoariest Queen-of-England question of all – 'And what do *you* do?' As if the Queen had ever really tried to answer that question herself.

I complimented Ragu on the excellence of his English. 'I too have travelled, you know, John, and even to England. In fact I was "pulling pints" in a pub in the North of England when you must have been a small boy. If you put a bottle of White Shield in my hand this moment, I would still know how to angle the neck in order to keep the sediment back from the glass. Some things you don't forget.' It was splendid that he knew what he was talking about, even if I didn't. 'The locals couldn't get their tongues round Raghu, so I was "Reg" for the duration. Then my father had a stroke and that was that.' He didn't go into details, and I didn't know whether to ask any further.

Did I have a defective social picture of India? Truer to admit that I had no social picture at all. For me the subcontinent held equal numbers of Maharajahs and untouchables, clustered round that single point of light which was my guru – the double star made by the guru and the mountain as they pooled their cosmic fire. Raghu and his family didn't seem to fit in with this scheme. They seemed to be prosperous merchants of some sort. I managed to cast my question in marginally more refined terms than the Queen's. 'What is the family business, if you don't mind me asking?' I was balancing against the basin at the time, while he washed me.

Raghu didn't look up. 'Naturally I don't mind. Gaitonde and Company are well-established as manufacturers of leather goods.'

It was good that Raghu was taken up with his chosen task, or he would have seen a look of utter bafflement on my face. The Indian leather manufacturer seemed the stuff of jokes, the equivalent of the contraceptive machine in the Vatican basement.

'But aren't you a Hindu?'

'I am indeed. As are you. Yet I notice you wear leather footwear.' He pointed to my shoes, where he had placed them neatly on the bathroom floor.

I blushed. It was true that I had made an uneasy peace with animal sacrifice carried out for my benefit. Useless to say that my very expensive tailor-made shoes – cobbler-made – were supplied free of charge by the National Health, and that I could hardly refuse them. Hadn't I in fact rejected the synthetic Space Shoes which Ansell had taken so much trouble to commission at CRX? I didn't have a leg to stand on. I didn't try to explain, though it was true, that I thought of my shoes as in some way continuing the cow's experience of life, taking it to places it had never been.

Tingling copper wire

Raghu's intention was not to chide me. 'You are a devotee of Bhagavan Sri Ramana, whose teaching is very exalted. My own family are devotees rather of Paramahamsa Yogananda. Many of Ramana Maharshi's sayings, however, are well known, such as this one: *Wanting to reform the world without discovering one's true self is like trying to cover the world with leather to avoid the pain of walking on stones and thorns. It is much simpler to wear shoes.*' In fact this supposedly familiar saying of my Guru was news to me. It provided much food for thought, much spiritual cud to be dwelt on. 'And now, John, I think I can honestly say that you are as clean as a whistle.'

When I complimented him he merely said, 'You are not in England any more, John – that savage land where they wipe themselves with sandpaper! Water is always best.' He teased me sweetly a little longer along the same lines, India the advanced civilisation, Britain a backwater. And of course he had a point. 'Isn't your government getting ready for decimalisation just now? But here we have already introduced our *naya paisas*. You will like your *new pence*, I dare to predict, once you are used to them.'

Then Raghu insisted on giving me a proper wash, even taking the trouble to delve into my armpits. 'You will sleep better, John,' he said, 'for being cool and clean.'

I was still thinking about his tannery revelations. Since I had taken off into the air above London Airport relatively few hours earlier I seemed to have been shown nothing but irregular behaviour on the part of *Bos taurus*, of the order *Artiodactyla* and tribe *Bovidi*. Cows lolled in slabs on trolleys in the First Class cabin of the Indian national airline, on the streets they languorously licked the mucilage made from their boiled-up relatives, they gave their hides to good Hindus to be made into shoes and jackets. I was being served notice, I felt, that Maya was feverishly at work in these territories, yet I also had the feeling – it was a distinct strand of consciousness within my fatigue, like a tingling copper wire in a skein of dull wool – that everything had changed now that I was sharing a land-mass with my guru, whose 'death' had only intensified his local presence.

I had also eaten food of an unaccustomed, revelatory spiciness. Even under temperate conditions chilli, turmeric, garam masala and their allies alter consciousness and tighten the scalp. They pinch and knead the housing of the brain, producing a benign confusion of thought. In a climate of active heat, spicy food brings about a psychological cancellation like the breaking of a fever. By the time I was ready for bed I had taken the new temperature inside myself and was part-way attuned to it.

When Raghu had settled me in a downstairs bedroom with the pee bottle within reach, I should by rights have fallen asleep in seconds. In fact I was kept awake by a pulsing node of thought and feeling – to be frank, an erection. An implacable specimen of its kind.

My celibacy vow had come under pressure from more than one flank already, before my first full day in India. The visiting card from S. P. Munshi at the airport was tucked safely away, but it was so strongly charged with spiritual-erotic impulses that I could feel it pulsating in the darkness. Temptation had opened up a second front at dinner, and I had played eye ping-pong with a charming and not obviously attached young man. Why not give up an enterprise which was obviously doomed and have a good old wank? I managed to persevere, mainly (I'm afraid) by thinking what an impression the household would get of me, and of the wicked West, when Sumati's servant changed the sheets. 'Taily' was the last part of me to go to sleep, and the first to rise in the morning. I ignored it. I would not give in to its sly throbbings. 'Taily' seemed the right, childish word for it, this gross part which proved me an adult but wouldn't let me be one.

I prayed that I would be able to withstand the temptations of spending time in Kashi's proximity. Obviously I wasn't going to molest him in any positive way, but it might already count as a betrayal of my vow to have dwelt on his image and to have become excited by it later, in private. In fact, the next morning I didn't see him at all – he'd left the house early to run errands – which left me rather disappointed. The pressure was off my self-control, and I felt almost cheated. I hadn't meant to pray quite so hard.

After he had seen to my morning needs as benignly as he had the ones of the night before, Raghu explained that Mrs Osborne's 'bung him on the bus' plan had undergone further modification. Raghu and Sumati would now be bunging me in the car and driving me to Tiruvannamalai. It wasn't very far, about a hundred miles. It was all decided. I must admit I was relieved not to have to face the bus, though I had been thinking of enquiring about trains. Perhaps going there by train would have been too presumptuous an emulation of my guru, a bit too much like feeling tired all of a sudden and hopping up on a donkey, just when you happen to reach the outskirts of Jerusalem.

Little houses overgrown with creepers

Before we set off Raghu explained one slight complication: I would be showing them the way. I tried to tell myself that he was having trouble with his English, but in my heart of hearts I knew it wasn't likely. He meant what he said. In some strange way I was to guide the party. I hoped that my adopted religion, which had called to me with its depth and subtlety, wasn't going to turn out to be full of tests and ordeals after all, like the wearying one I was born into. I didn't feel that I needed to prove myself in that sort of way.

But why, then, was it my task to show citizens of Madras the way to Tiruvannamalai? Two reasons, really. The first was that Raghu and Sumati could manage conversational Tamil, but couldn't read it. They were all at sea with the script. This was a little shock. I didn't quite assume that all Indian people spoke all Indian languages. I knew there were very many, though I didn't know enough to put them in the hundreds. But I did assume that all Indian people in Tamil Nadu would be at home with the Tamil language. Why else would they live there? In fact the families of Raghu and Sumati came originally from Kerala, and they spoke Marathi at home.

That was one part of the difficulty. The other was that signposts in Tamil Nadu were written exclusively in Tamil. In a recent access of nationalist fervour, the state government had removed the familiar ABC letters from signs. The British had packed their bags and left, but if they changed their minds and came back they would be properly baffled, just like the anticipated Nazi invaders of 1940, who would have found no signposts at all and been all at sea if they had forgotten to bring maps.

The changeover of signposts had only happened a year or two before 1970 – if I'd made my pilgrimage earlier, then the trip to Tiruvannamalai would have been a piece of cake.

The state authorities hadn't anticipated that others beside the few remaining Britishers would have trouble with the signs. Indians from other states who worked in Tamil Nadu relied on English to help them find their way, so they were running around confused as well. There were already indications that the authorities would think again – trade was beginning to suffer, and pressure was mounting to let the English alphabet return from exile. So if my pilgrimage had taken place in a later year, the last stage of the journey might well have been a simple matter again. It was only around 1970 that a devotee had an extra set of obstacles to overcome – but that was the year I had chosen for my visit. It was as if my whimsical guru had overheard me thinking about the spiritual life as a sort of treasure hunt, and was dropping in a few more puzzles for my benefit, to draw out the game and sweeten the victory, like an announcer who leaves an endless pause after the words, 'And the winner is . . .'

Raghu had asked a neighbour, a native speaker of Tamil, to write down the magic word 'Tiruvannamalai' on a piece of paper – in fact a sturdy piece of card, of the same weight and texture as the pieces of card which protected Dad's shirts (to some tiny extent) from crushing when they returned from the laundry. Tamil script is made up of lovely flowing characters, loops, swirls and emphatic dots, which had an immediate appeal, making me wonder why I had ever bothered with shorthand, whose practical utility had been more or less irrelevant to me, if not actually a drawback in my eyes.

Tamil characters display a beguiling combination of architecture and flow, grid and embroidery. A line of printed Tamil looks to Western eyes like a row of irregular little houses overgrown with rather stylised creepers. When it's written by hand, the curvaceous element predominates.

For some reason the stiffness of the card made me feel much more confident about the enterprise. Surely our plan was similarly crushproof. Raghu and Sumati could remember the first part of the journey. They could negotiate our departure from the city. It was only out in the country that they would falter. That was where I would take over, comparing the curious loops and curlicues of Tamil script with what I saw written on signposts, and directing us safely to our destination. I said with as much confidence as I could muster, 'Whenever I see a signpost, I'll try to match it with what I've got written down here. Easy!' What could go wrong?

Not quite everything, as it turned out. Raghu kindly put me in the front seat of the car, with a canvas of some sort behind me. Sumati was in the back with my things. She said something to Raghu in (I suppose) Marathi after we had set off, and I asked Raghu to translate. He seemed a bit embarrassed, but I told him it was impossible for me to be offended by hosts who were going to so much trouble to help me. Then he told me, 'Sumati said, "How can such a small person have so much luggage?" She says it's all right for us up here in the front, but she's getting squashed by your things.' I laughed and asked Raghu to translate back to Sumati, 'Please help this small person to compress his luggage by accepting the small cheese which is at the top of his case.' It was a Germanic interpretation of Edam – I'd chosen smoked so it would travel better. She ferreted out the sausage of cheese in its tight plastic skin and soon started tucking into her snack.

On our car trip I noticed that the rule of waiting until men had finished eating didn't always apply. I assume it made a difference that we weren't at table, in a formal setting, and also that the food was a gift from me. I couldn't help feeling that I was derailing Raghu's day, but Sumati gave every sign of having a fine old time. The expedition seemed to free her from the constraints of an Indian lady's home. Unable to turn round and watch her, I sent out auditory antennæ instead, turning my ears backwards like a cat's, cocked pockets of vibrating fur. I could hear the little snuffles of appreciation, almost guttural, which Sumati made while she ate.

She who handles nothingness

A little later she spoke again, at greater length, and Raghu translated for my benefit. 'Sumati is warning you against going on *pradakshina* with Mrs Osborne late in the day. You understand *pradakshina*?' I did. *Pradakshina* is the ritual clockwise circumambulation of the holy mountain Arunachala. It is to be done barefoot, and in a prescribed manner: 'like a pregnant queen in her ninth month'. I didn't know quite how I was going to manage that.

'Sumati and Mrs Osborne started their walk round the mountain at about four or five, when the worst of the sun was over. She was worried that it would not be until late that they returned home. Mrs Osborne had not told her they would be sleeping by the roadside. When they started walking, she believed they would reach home that night. However, Mrs Osborne said that it was supremely beneficial to sleep while on *pradakshina*. She was remarkably insistent and Sumati had to give in.' Here Raghu broke off his translating to make a comment of his own. 'You will discover, John, that with Mrs Osborne it is usually better to give in.'

'Sumati was terrified, because as is well known, there are snakes and scorpions on the mountain in great numbers. She mentioned this to Mrs Osborne who said that everything on the mountain was holy. She wasn't worried, and indeed she was snoring within minutes, while Sumati was unable to sleep a wink. Sumati has never seen a holy scorpion. If she did drop off then her sleep was only jerky, but Mrs Osborne slept well and woke refreshed.' He added in a tactful undertone, 'Sumati once expressed the opinion that Mrs Osborne was a *suunyakaari*. Literally it means she who manipulates nothingness – perhaps you can come up with an improved translation? I have found no English word better than *witch* . . .'

Sumati interrupted with a sharp question. It required no knowledge of Marathi to interpret it as meaning, 'What nonsense are you telling him now?'

All the time we were driving I had been inspecting road signs for their correspondence with the Tamil hieroglyph which was written on the card and also, as the journey went on, imprinted on my mind. I took a certain amount of pride in having mastered a long foreign word in its original script. Our progress seemed to be rather wayward in terms of overall direction, however, and eventually we came across a sign where both directions seemed to point to Tiruvannamalai.

Under this sign of ambiguous welcome we decided to stop for refreshment. I was grateful for the rest. My bottom had started to ache unbearably on the journey. Now that Raghu had opened the car door, I could swing my legs round with his help, so that I was sitting on the edge of the seat. As I shifted round I could see that the canvas cover on the back of the seat had become drenched with sweat. Capillary action was assisting the process of cooling, at the cost of a slight embarrassment.

Sumati had brought a picnic. I don't know where we would have got food anyway, but Raghu explained she wouldn't willingly consume any food or drink not prepared within her own house. She had brought along sandwiches and a flask of coffee. I realised that she must have shopped specially for sliced bread and perhaps for the cucumber and tomatoes. I remember Dad telling me that the tomato was actually a native of South America, but it has turned itself into an exemplary world citizen, blending in with every possible cuisine, Mediterranean, Indian, even condescending to enrobe Mr Heinz's baked beans and be rendered down for his ketchup.

I tried one of the sandwiches and pronounced it delicious. In fact it was a pretty fair imitation of a flavourless British catering sandwich. She had even cut the crusts off.

Raghu looked almost dismayed at my appreciation, and rattled off some Marathi words at Sumati. It turned out, when he translated her reply, that he was asking if she had at least put some salt and pepper on them. (She had, of course.) Even properly seasoned they tasted of little enough, he thought, but without salt and pepper it was like chewing mouthfuls of air.

'Aren't you going to try one?' I asked, and they rather despondently agreed, chewing politely and clearly despairing of understanding the insipid passions of the Raj.

Dancing on the edge of pain

It turned out that Sumati had also brought along a few samosas and *poriyal* and chapattis, in a much smaller bag. I felt almost ashamed that she had put my needs first, and also overestimated my appetite, so that the sandwich supply greatly outweighed what she had brought for her husband and herself. Politeness, though, demanded that I try a samosa when it was offered me, even though I was a sandwich millionaire and they had little of their own food to spare.

That samosa was a rite of passage in its own right. Nothing I had ever put in my mouth could have prepared me for the experience. It became painfully clear that Sumati had gone easy on me with her spices the previous evening. Now like some tribal teenager in an initiation ceremony my tongue had to run over hot coals without being blistered. My taste buds hopped and winced, dancing on the edge of pain. Even more than the night before I had the sensation of a hallucinated clarity, as my senses narrowed to a point and simultaneously opened up with an unprecedented freshness.

Yet even with the spices burning off my old habits of mind I could hardly register the landscape around us, let alone describe it. My mental vocabulary was so limited, and this country was neither lush nor bare, or else was both at once. It was green, but a green that was mostly blue and brown.

While we were eating our food, the fiery and the bland, a group of people had come up to see what we were doing. In great contrast to Mum on any comparable occasion, Raghu and Sumati seemed unperturbed by the uninvited company. The most inquisitive of the bunch was an old man with a lovely character etched into his features – his looked like a face from a documentary film. Perhaps the old superstition is true, and the camera steals the soul, just not all at once, but in tiny incremental larcenies. Certainly it's the faces that have never been photographed which have the strongest identities.

I offered him a sandwich, but he seemed afraid of it and reared back suspiciously. He started addressing words to Raghu, whose spoken Tamil was reasonably fluent. He could hardly have been able to run a business in Madras without being able to get by in conversation.

Raghu retailed the conversation to me. Apparently the old man had asked where we were from. 'He'd love to know where we're going, too, but he dare not ask that. These country people are very superstitious. It's considered very unlucky to ask anyone making a journey where they are going – if he'd done that, then according to their rules of life we would have to go back to our starting-point, drink a glass of water, and set off again! Not very up-to-date, these people. Widows also can blight a travelling party by crossing its path.'

The old man was apparently wondering if I was real. 'Why don't you tell him,' I said, 'that he is welcome to touch me, if that will help him make up his mind.' Small talk in these parts seemed to be on a satisfyingly intense philosophical level. No beating about the bush here! Heirs to a long tradition of enquiry, the locals came straight out with, 'Are you a part of Reality?'

The old man came close and put out his finger very carefully, as if prepared to jerk it back at a moment's notice. He touched my arm. I was of course very hot, but this rural Indian's flesh felt cool. I noticed the fine tanned skin on his arm, faintly reptilian in its visual texture, and I touched it in return. He pulled back for an instant, but then consented to this reciprocation of contact. A few other people in his party came forward and had a touch of me as well. I was quite the craze for a little while. It wasn't clear, though, that touching me had settled their doubts about my existence. The looks they exchanged were still puzzled.

The oldest member of the group started talking to Raghu again, and I noticed that he was now pointing up to the sky. Raghu passed on what was said without my having to ask. He seemed to be getting into the swing of this new job of translating. Raghu explained that the elder was talking about the stars which come out at night after the sun had gone down. 'He wanted to know, which of those stars was your home, and why had you decided to leave it?' At my prompting, Raghu told him that I wasn't doing interstellar travel – 'at least not at the moment,' I said, but I don't expect he passed on that silly flourish – and that I was from this very planet itself. From England in fact.

The look of puzzlement on the elder's face only deepened, and then he shrugged his shoulders decisively, and his whole little party sloped off. I waited till they were out of earshot before I pestered Raghu for translation – what had he said? What was the verdict? Raghu gave a broad smile. 'He said, "If that's what he thinks, he is mad – mad beyond prayer. Mad beyond the hope of cure."' To such a connoisseur of Maya it was more likely that I'd flown in from the Crab Nebula than from London Airport.

I'd been rather enjoying the conversation with this elder, relishing my ownership of an unfamiliar kind of strangeness, until the turn it had taken at the very end. Then it knocked me off my perch surprisingly much – being dismissed as insane. Perhaps I can blame the effects on morale of jet lag, which is only a special case of the need for sleep, brought on by the additional effort of maintaining more than one 'reality' in the course of a day.

In my history I have noticed that on the threshold of a new stage of life there is often a figure of two-faced welcome, half ushering me in, half keeping me at bay. On the way to CRX it wasn't a person but the train itself, specifically its lavatory, which first terrified and then thrilled me. On the way to Vulcan it was a yokel who was unable to give my party directions until he realised we were looking for the place for 'them plastics' (spastics).

Of course there were more formal welcoming committees at those institutions, the three fateful girls with Still's come to assess me at CRX, the Grey Lady with her terrifying rhyme come to test me at Vulcan. But the outriders were just as significant. Perhaps the old countryman who thought I was from the stars was serving the same function as the train lavatory and the sardonic yokel. The place where the encounter took place was in its own way almost excessively symbolic, under a signpost that gave too much information or too little, with samosas pointing east and sandwiches pointing west.

I hope the mountain doesn't take my shoes

My trip to India was purely volitional, unlike my moves to CRX and Vulcan (CRX for treatment, Vulcan for something approaching education), and I very much wanted good auspices and a successful outcome. Still, I don't want to make too much of the incident. I'm necessarily a sort of lightning rod for little discharges of eccentricity, even a lot closer to home.

On the other hand, the holy mountain Arunachala, towards which we were driving, has his own reputation for a certain amount of caprice. He can be downright curmudgeonly. There's a legend of a wedding party on its way to pay respects to the mountain, bearing lavish gifts, who were waylaid and robbed before they reached their destination. Even the shoes of the party were taken. The groom was a child saint, Sambandhar, who was being conveyed to his nuptials in a little chariot, adorned with bells to announce his arrival. Eventually it turned out that the thieves weren't actually human. They were emanations of the mountain, sent to teach an important lesson. Pilgrims should approach Arunachala in simplicity, and barefoot. Ideally, sky-clad – stark naked.

I could only hope the mountain would not take my shoes. Having to approach Arunachala without them would inspire dismay rather than reverence, and result in complication rather than simplicity.

When we resumed our journey again I recovered my composure and even worked out why we had been going wrong. I had been paying too much attention to the first half of the elegant arabesques on the card. In unfamiliar language and an unknown script there's no way to sift out irrelevancy. The meaningful elements don't stand out.

Now I asked Raghu if the word 'Tiru' had an actual meaning in Tamil, and he replied, 'I believe it means "Sacred".' So! In this spiritually irradiated territory I was behaving like a visitor to Cornwall confidently following any sign with 'St' written on it in expectation of reaching St Ives. Raghu and Sumati shouldn't have given me so much credit as a pathfinder, but I think in those days Westerners in general were assumed to excel in practical matters.

From this point on I started to give a more intensive attention to the right-hand portion of the place name on the card. Things started to look up. I persuaded myself that the shapes at the end of the word resembled a cobra raising its head to strike, and that I would be able to recognise it immediately the next time I saw it.

Soon we came to a town which was familiar to Raghu, which was three-quarters of the way to Tiruvannamalai. It was called Sen-Jee, though also known as 'Gingee', which was as close as the lazy British vocal apparatus could get to the Tamil name. The imperialist approximation was still current locally – not all relics of the Raj could be eradicated as easily as an alphabet from a signpost. Sen-Jee (as I tried to call it right away, anxious to show that my post-Imperial tongue was ready for any and all flexing) must once have been enclosed by its wall, and still boasted a magnificent fort, on top of a scrabble of rocks that Raghu said had been 'cast by a giant hand'.

On the way out of Sen-Jee the wall persisted across the road itself, so that we drove through a gate. It did my heart good to know that we had broken the back of the journey, and I started to scan the horizon for the shape I had seen in so many dreams. Soon I felt a jump in my heart. I sang out, 'Oh look! Arunachala . . . There it is!'

Raghu chuckled indulgently at my beginner's mistake. 'No John, that is not Arunachala. We are too far away. It is very similar, though, as a lot of these mountains are. You do not need to be on the edge of your seat just yet!'

It was a mortifying moment. I hated to be playing the part of the Credulous Tourist, who on first seeing the White Cliffs of Dover exclaims that he can make out the spires of Harrods twinkling in the distance.

Sumati said something from the back which Raghu didn't translate but which I heard as the equivalent of 'Have a heart, Arthur! Don't throw cold water on the poor boy's faith!'

I accepted in my social self that what I saw was not Arunachala, although its contour fitted my dreams so well. I believed Raghu because he was Indian and this was his country, not mine, but in spite of his authoritative Indianity, I had some irrepressible instinct of recognition.

The feeling grew as we continued our journey, and the supposed not-Arunachala grew bigger and bigger, and again I piped up: 'But it must be Arunachala! You said it wasn't, Raghu, but I've kept my eye on the outline all the time, and it got bigger and bigger and *look*!'

I had by now grown used to the strange curls which spelt out 'Tiru-vannamalai'. Three times we had gone astray to follow the will-o'-the-wisp of 'Tiru. . .', but now the '. . .vannamalai' with its rearing serpent had fully lodged itself into my brain. In front of us another signpost loomed, with the swaying cobra rising up at the end of the word, looking as if it was about to swoop down at us and spit.

When Sumati spoke again from the back of the car I felt certain that I could follow the gist of what she had been saying. I knew no Marathi but I could tune into her heart. It was something along the lines of, 'There, didn't he tell you so? True faith sees further than the eyes can . . .'

A welcome mat the size of the sky

The town was indeed Tiruvannamalai, and we had arrived at Arunachala, but I don't mean to say that Raghu was wrong. Our perspectives are perfectly compatible. Nothing could be easier for Arunachala than to project himself a little further on that day, for the benefit of a pilgrim who was beginning to despair of his welcome and, as it turned out, would still find some obstacles put in his way. The mountain can be a perfect gentleman.

Sermons in my schooldays had never satisfactorily explained the Trinity, except by way of a solar analogy (the Sun, the Sun's light, the Sun's heat, triple and indivisible). Yet I didn't have the slightest difficulty in understanding the guru, the God and the mountain, Ramana Maharshi, Shiva and Arunachala, as emanations of each other. What was true of one was true of all, and I knew that Ramana Maharshi would sometimes take great pains to offer a devotee *darshan*, the word which denotes a formal manifestation of presence, spiritual grace as it is offered to the eye.

There was one occasion, for instance, when it was noticed that Ramana Maharshi had changed his morning routine. He no longer brushed his teeth in the same place, but moved, while he agitated the appropriate twig in his mouth, a little distance away.

It was a minor mystery, with the disciples wondering why he had changed the pattern of his days. ('Disciple' seems to outrank 'devotee', but their relative status is unclear. The greater susceptibility to ego tends to mark the disciple down.) Only much later did it become known there was a devotee who had sought her guru's presence on a daily basis but was no longer able, by reason of age and bodily stiffness, to climb the mountain to where a view might easily be had. It certainly seemed to her that Ramana Maharshi took those few steps to supply the *darshan* she so much desired. He himself, as befits a mountain, made no comment.

So if Arunachala graciously bowed in my direction, it had nothing to do with merit on my part. It was the apotheosis of good manners, a welcome mat the size of the sky.

Somehow we found our way to Mrs Osborne's house, which Raghu said was called 'Aruna Giri'. There was a strange pale-skinned figure on the verandah, leaning over something with a tool in her hand. She didn't look round at the sound of the car, or even when we pulled up by the house. She seemed to be in a trance. Then a young woman ran up from the garden and pulled at her sari, and she looked round rather abstractedly.

When she came towards us it gave me a real shock. Could this really be Mrs Osborne? Surely this twisted old lady, this hunchback, must indeed be a witch rather than a beacon for spiritual travellers. She seemed better suited to manhandling lost children into ovens than helping pilgrims to their destination. She was wearing a white sari rather than a black cloak, but that seemed a minor detail, the witch's summer plumage. The servant girl ran into the house.

When the old lady spoke she made it worse. She came awkwardly down the steps of her house and peered into the car. I suppressed my fear, made myself perk up and stretched out what I could of my hand with a well-brought-up 'How do you *do?*' I was trying to mimic Granny's technique of imposing herself by manners.

She completely ignored my gesture, and then exclaimed, almost with disgust, 'But Raghu, you have brought ush a *child*! Look at him! How can I poshibly cope with a shituation like thish?' Mrs Osborne had seemed completely English on the page, in the letters she wrote to me, but when she opened her mouth she had one of the thickest accents I had ever heard. Thanks to my experience talking to Barbara Broier's gruff dad in Cookham, who pronounced *r* as *g*, I was able to work out that she was Polish, but her accent was thicker even than

Barbara's dad's. These were not by any interpretation the sounds of welcome. All those hostile sibilants, those *eshesh*, made me forget how much I actually liked snakes.

We were behaving with symmetrical shallowness, equal disgraces to our faith and the arrangements we had made. Neither of us corresponded to the other's cosy image, built up over months of letter-writing, and we reacted with horror.

Gloomily I remembered that I had written to Ganesh at the ashram that he could prevent me from coming to the ashram, but not from coming to Tiruvannamalai. If necessary I would sleep at the side of the road. Unless Mrs Osborne took me in, I would have to make good on that threat.

Feeling that Arunachala might be testing my reactions and my sincerity, I started looking at the hedges around the little house. They had prickly pear cactus mixed in. Hedges with spikes were not something I'd reckoned on. It began to look as if I should have asked Mrs Pavey at Bourne End library to find me a copy of *Hedges of India*.

Mrs Osborne motioned Raghu to climb the three steps on to the verandah, and then disappeared with him into the house. She took herself off but then raised her voice so much that she might have dispensed with the fiction of withdrawal. From my seat in the car, I could hear her shrieking to Raghu: 'Imposhible, quite imPOSHible for him to manage here!'

Behind me in the car Sumati was singing to herself in a way that I did my best to find comforting. I hadn't forgotten what Sumati had said, though, about the eight-legged and no-legged inhabitants of the region. If I slept under a hedge then scorpions also and serpents would be my portion. I would have ample opportunity to test my understanding of a classic Hindu parable: *At dusk a man sees a snake at the side of the road and is frightened. By daylight he sees that it was only a coil of rope.* The snake standing in for 'reality', dusk for perception without enlightenment.

The moment I read this parable I realised how right I was to be transfixed by Mum's description of the Indian Rope Trick while I was bedbound. Of course the business of the fakir climbing up the rope and disappearing is a fable or a misunderstanding. But properly understood, everything we see around us is an Indian Rope Trick.

Then Raghu and Mrs Osborne came out of the house, and he spoke, though it was at her dictation. He was like a politician reading a prepared statement with stiff composure, saying that war had been declared or that his wife was standing by him. 'I'm sorry, John, but it really is impossible for you to stay here. I know your ways and your needs a little by now. Even if you could manage to get through to the bathroom somehow, I don't see how you could manage there on your own. And as you can see Mrs Osborne is not hale enough to help you.'

Indeed she was not, and I felt a little betrayed by her physical state. It's true that I had delayed any revelation of my disability until I had been accepted in principle, but that was to keep the two things separate, the general possibility and the particular difficulties. Mrs Osborne hadn't said a word! She was pretty much helpless, but she had kept it to herself. She couldn't have pushed the wheelchair a yard, even on the flat. How and when had she managed to do *pradakshina* with Sumati? Even with a snoring break in the middle of the eight-mile trek, the task looked to be beyond her.

Now I broke down and wept, but only on the inside, having come all these miles and braved so many hardships only to be met by this. Yet something held this vehicle of skin and blood and bone together. The body twitched its little arms in a helpless jerky gesture, while its face put on the most appealing and childlike expression it could muster.

Mrs Osborne looked exasperatedly at Raghu, as though the whole situation was somehow his fault, and Raghu looked at me. I kept up the look of supplication in the direction of Mrs Osborne, inwardly wondering whether Mum wasn't right all along, about the entire idea being crazy from start to finish. My mother thought I was mad, and so did a nameless elder in provincial Tamil Nadu. Nobody much was standing up for my sanity.

We seemed to have reached an impasse. I could feel my supplicating look beginning to run out of steam. I had never played so nakedly on my helplessness and I was becoming horrible to myself. Was this really what the mountain required?

Raghu broke the deadlock. 'What we should do next, I think, Mrs Osborne,' he said, and I blessed him for it, 'if you agree, is to get John out of the car. His joints are playing him up. We could at least give him a good breath of Arunachala, possibly on the verandah. Would there be a possibility of rustling up a cup of tea from somewhere?'

It was wonderful to hear an Indian gentleman coming out with those magic words, 'rustle up a cup of tea'. If Raghu could be so providentially English, then there was chance of a bit of it rubbing off on Mrs Osborne. Perhaps she would pick up on the national spirit of muddling through somehow, even though I had doubts about her permeability. She'd been married to an Englishman, after all, since before the war, and she still seemed to be stubbornly Polish.

Even when she spoke Tamil she sounded Polish to my ears, and I could only imagine the impression she made on her Indian hearers. '*Avvarai jaakiradai tuukkanum!*' she said, in what was the voice of command in any language, and a dark-skinned, smiling man I hadn't seen before came towards me. He had a charmingly squashed nose. 'This is Rajah Manikkam, my gardener,' she explained. 'He will lift you on to the verandah.'

Somehow or other I was lifted up those three big steps, and found myself in the wheelchair, on Mrs Osborne's verandah in Tiruvannamalai. There was a table near me at a convenient level – just over two feet high. On it was placed the welcome cuppa, which I was determined to handle competently without help. Even if there was nobody watching, I needed to demonstrate that I was something more than a helpless, hapless pilgrim, a mere drain on hospitality, not even posh but merely imposhible.

On the table was the tool Mrs Osborne had been using when we arrived, and the tablet of stone on which she had been labouring. It seemed to be a memorial tablet for her husband. A grave marker for Arthur Osborne.

It was good to be at this elevated level, and soon I began to feel almost at home, until I looked towards the dark hole which must have been the entrance to Mrs Osborne's witch-house. Then my heart sank again. All the ingenuity in the world wouldn't help me to get inside. It was cramped and poky for an able-bodied person, and anything less Johnable could hardly be imagined.

When I had finished the tea and Raghu and Mrs Osborne appeared again, they were still shaking their heads and Mrs Osborne was murmuring, 'Imposhible – absolutely imposhible.'

After the interlude of teatime I was back on pleading duty, like a puppy in a pet-shop window after a lull in the pedestrian traffic on the street. The look I was making myself wear was beginning to hurt, but I concentrated every scrap of prayerful energy I had on Mrs Osborne. At that moment her stern strict face softened and became really rather beautiful.

Between a palace and a dolls' house

'John!' she said. It was the first time she had addressed me by name. 'It's quite imposhible for me to have you in my house. I built it myself, you know. I mean to say, I had no plans and no architect. I just told the masons what to do. Arthur said it was half-way between a palace and a dolls' house. If I build another house I will try to consider your needs, but this house for you is quite imposhible. That is perfectly clear and beyond argument. We shall discuss it no further. But let me ask you one question. Where are you now?'

I didn't quite know what she was getting at. Was this a sort of Hindu catechism? 'Well, on the mundane level I'm sitting at your table on your verandah at the moment.'

'And izh there anything *wrong* with my verandah?' she asked. 'Izh there any way in which you poshibly don't *like* my verandah?'

In fact my only knowledge of verandahs and the torrid goings-on associated with them came from watching *The Rains of Ranchipur*, starring Richard Burton and Lana Turner (*Theirs was the great sin that even the great rains could not wash away!*), but I kept that to myself. 'No,' I said, trying to sound as if I was assessing the verandah by a thousand discriminating criteria, 'I like it . . . quite a lot. As verandahs go I would say that the one you've got here is . . . distinguished. Altogether a high-class verandah.'

Privately I wasn't quite so enthusiastic. The unevenness of the floor bothered me. It had a slight slope, presumably to make it easier for water to drain off when the verandah was washed or the rains came. The wheelchair wanted to veer off towards the shrubbery in the garden, but I kept the brake lightly applied. If the wheelchair did break free, there would at least be a nice cushion of shrubbery waiting to receive me. Mercifully there was no prickly pear cactus or indeed any spiky plant in that particular bed. Jasmine was curling its way up some makeshift trellising, making its contribution to the fragrance of the air.

'*Eksh*ellent!' said Mrs Osborne. 'Then it is on my verandah that you shall spend your days here in Tiruvannamalai.' Without changing her tone of voice she stopped addressing me directly. 'Arunachala has called, so he has come and is welcome!'

Wasn't that what I'd been trying to tell her all along? Getting my message across was hard slog, always. Why did it take people so long to cotton on? If I'd known it was always going to be so hard to be recognised as a separate intelligence I wouldn't have bothered with A-levels. A few exam certificates weren't going to change things.

Was the verandah solution going to work, though? Just thinking about having a tuppenny (tuppenny bit rhymes with *shit*) gave me a twinge of panic. Even if I managed against the odds to sleep on this small verandah, I would never be able to get inside Mrs O's house, let alone manage the toilet. In tuppenny terms I was OK for now, but I was bound to need one tomorrow morning. Once I had realised that, it seemed simplest to go on a long fast. My lunch of sandwiches and samosas would keep me going without hardship for the rest of the day.

Austerity, fasting, self-deprivation – everything that goes by the name of *tapas* – is an ancient strand of Hinduism. And on the mundane level, after all: no food, no shit. One of the major reasons we eat is to maintain body temperature, and I wasn't worried about that. It was almost unbearably hot. I would need to drink a lot to replace the moisture I was losing as sweat, but I could imagine myself becoming holier and holier in this place, without ever troubling this body with solids.

Mrs O's face still bore traces of that kind and melting look, as though a truce had been signed between her brain and her heart. After a moment she announced that she had something special for me, and she disappeared with Rajah Manikkam somewhere into the garden. Not long after that I heard her calling out 'John . . . Oh Joo-o-o-hn!!'

in something close to a motherly croon. 'Will you please try zhome-how to cover your eyezh? I have a surprizhe to show you!'

Mere moments ago, I had been an impossible object of hospitality. Now it seemed to be my birthday all of a sudden. Still, I was happy to humour her, though properly blocking my vision takes a little arranging. If you simply close your eyes, quite a lot of light still filters through the thin capillaried layer of the lids, so that doesn't count. When you're asked to 'close your eyes' because someone has a surprise for you, a deeper level of darkness is required. So I closed them, then I put my right hand on top of my walking stick and pushed the stick upwards with my left foot. That's how I can push the back of my hand over my eyes. I made things go pitch black in my world, my vision blocked by bone of exemplary density, while my ears, which I hadn't been told to close, told me that there was some rather laborious shuffling and trundling going on. Then Mrs Osborne was asking me to 'open my izhe', and so I did.

What I saw before me was perhaps the most beautiful sight I have ever seen (æsthetic impact depending, naturally enough, on emotional context). It was an Edwardian commode, made out of wood, with arms and proper seating and a removable pot. I felt a ripple of joy in my chest and gave thanks in my heart to Arunachala for this gift.

'We obtained it for Arthur's use,' Mrs Osborne explained, 'since he was unable to manage . . . certain things . . . when he became ill. After he shed his body, I decided to keep it in his memory, but perhaps I was following a destined impulse all along. Arthur has no use for this seat now, and I know he's delighted for it to be used again by one in need. See how well Arunachala is looking after you! I hope you realise how lucky you are.'

How could I not? Lavatories in the Western style might have caught on in Madras, but out here in the country people would never have consented to excreting indoors. Nothing could be more unnatural or oppressive. In this culture a commode made about as much sense as – I don't know – perhaps a harpsichord gives the right idea.

What I saw when I opened my eyes at Mrs Osborne's command was indeed a magnificent present. There was just the one commode in all of Tiruvannamalai, and I had exclusive use of it. Mine, all mine!

Mrs Osborne had made a journey all the way to Bangalore to get it. I promised myself that I would think tenderly of Arthur Osborne every time I ascended his throne. Forlorn, undignified perch for him, throne of convenience and joy for me.

'I'm very sorry about your husband,' I said. 'He was a great man.'

'The body, as we know, is no more than an old coat,' said Mrs Osborne rather crisply. 'What sort of devotee would I be of Bhagavan if I mourned the shedding of an old coat?' I loved hearing the word *devotee* on another person's lips, since I so much wanted to claim it for myself, but I couldn't help feeling that there was grief still liquid beneath her no-nonsense manner. Hadn't she been chiselling a memorial tablet when we arrived, too sunk in thought to respond to our presence?

On the practical level, though, Mrs Osborne seemed more and more pleased with her solution to the problem that had been denounced so recently as *imposhible*. She oversaw the delivery of a bed-frame to the verandah near where I was installed, directing the gardener's movements.

'You know, John,' she said, 'there was a Swami once who lived on a verandah. He was known as "Bench Swami" – though it was more of an outshide shofa than an actual bench. He was looked after by the people whose verandah it was, and he wasn't even invited. They brought him food. He stayed for twenty years. So I think we can manage to look after you, invited guest as you are, for a week or two.'

Black English myrrh

I felt a rush of tiredness and relief, thinking that my visit might be a success after all, and I might even enjoy my time on Mrs Osborne's verandah. It was possible that my visit was a sort of unlooked-for blessing to her, requiring her to make decisions of an unfamiliar sort and to live in the present rather than the past.

It was time for me to ask Mrs Osborne's gardener to fetch from the car that savoury contraband, the supply of Marmite. He carried the mighty jar into the house as if he was one of the Kings in a nativity play, bearing black myrrh, salty and very English, mystical tantalising myrrhmite, while his wife looked on uncertainly.

Mrs Osborne was thinking the arrangements through. 'I assume you can make your water without excessive trouble. As for the other, Kuppu here' – indicating the gardener's wife – 'can bring you water with which to clean yourself, but her caste, though humble enough, is too high to permit her to rinse out the commode, let alone attending you more intimately than that. We will perhaps have to pay a little something to a road-sweeper to clean things up. A Colony person.' By 'Colony' she seemed to mean *pariah* or *untouchable*.

With all the arrangements made, at least in Mrs Osborne's head, she came to sit down by me. 'You did not say you were so small,' she said. It's true that I had been careful in my letters to be offhand about my disability, since the last thing I wanted to do was to give the ashram any excuse to reject me. 'Would you not rather be taller?' It was an odd question to come from someone who was small herself, a little old lady who was somehow both plump and drawn.

I assumed that this was a trick question, and formulated a neutrally humble response. 'I have learned to accept this body without mistaking its illusory nature. And as the Bible says, *Which of you by thinking can add one cubit to his stature?*'

'Very good, John, Matthew chapter 6, verse 27. If you want to quote Scripture you must hope you can keep up with me! But did I say anything about a cubit? A cubit would be an ambitious target. But if change is offered you should take advantage. I'm very sure that I can increase your height – yes, even in the limited time available. How long is it that you stay? Five weeks?'

'A little less, now. But can you really make me taller? Wouldn't that be a miracle?'

'It is only medicine. All medicine is miraculous when it works. Faith will be amply rewarded, but is not required for the efficacy of the procedure, which is entirely scientific. Are you familiar with homœopathy? We should measure you right away, and once again before you leave, and . . . we shall see what we shall see.' She gave a little chuckle.

I had heard of homœopathy. It was something that my GP Flanny denounced as culpable faddishness, just as she sneered at vegetarianism, which gave me the immediate idea that there might be something in it (whatever it was). Certainly the presence of a compound vowel in the word, drawing my attention like an insect's compound eye, spoke strongly in its favour. It was on my list of things to explore – but it was far further down the list than India.

'You should pay attention to homœopathy, young man,' she said. 'I can show you books.' One thing I didn't want was a reading holiday. I hadn't come half-way round the world to find myself in an open-air outpost of Bourne End Library, The Verandah Annexe perhaps, with someone who seemed a much less sympathetic librarian than Mrs Pavey, pushing her own interests rather than exploring selflessly on my behalf.

Perhaps she sensed my resistance, because she went on to say, 'Homœopathy is one of the few good things that the West can boast. Of course there are local equivalents, in India above all, but that is not my skill. And I have had a number of illustrious patients, who could have chosen other practitioners. Who could indeed have healed themselves if they had chosen to.' She was looking almost skittish now, and I found that I was beginning to be intrigued.

'Who do you mean?'

'I mean Sri Bhagavan.'

'Of course,' I said. 'You treated Ramana Maharshi. What ailment did you treat Bhagavan for?'

'A small growth appeared on his elbow. He submitted to my treatment, as also to others more drastic. I was unable to achieve results – the prospects had never been good. Homœopathy is better suited to prevention than cure of entrenched conditions. Others treated him with knives rather than my little pills. The ashram doctor removed the growth, but it returned and was diagnosed as a sarcoma. Three more times his flesh was gouged to the bone. Three more times the growth returned. Only when amputation was recommended did he refuse further treatment.'

I knew some of the circumstances. When asked if his arm hurt, he replied, in a gentle voice and with his distinctive radiant smile, 'If you know the pain of a scorpion bite, then imagine a thousand scorpion bites – it is somewhat like that.' He made it clear that this sort of physical collapse was only to be expected, like the blowing of a fuse when a humble appliance (in this case a human body) has been plugged into an overwhelming source of power.

I was yawning so hard it hurt my jaws. My apparatus was overwhelmed with new impressions and changes of scene. Darkness had come without my noticing. Before I went to bed Mrs Osborne summoned Rajah Manikkam one more time. He helped me stand by the wall of the house, and Mrs Osborne marked my height on the wall. I'd seen Mum do the same with Peter as he grew, in the kitchen at Trees, but of course there had been no point in wasting pencil lead by measuring me – though I had a late growth spurt during my time at Burnham Grammar School, by courtesy of the surgeon's knife, when in that mystical intervention my leg was shortened and made longer. It felt strange to be the object of so hopeful a ritual, in this unfamiliar place.

Then Rajah Manikkam helped me to take my shoes off and to lie down on the bedframe. It was still hot, but I had certainly expected some sort of blanket or even sheet. None arrived, and I didn't dare to ask for any such embodiment of Western cosseting. If Mrs Osborne thought nothing of sleeping on the road while doing *pradakshina* she would hardly be indulgent if a pilgrim wanted pillows to be plumped up for his benefit. Already I seemed to personify the folly of offering hospitality too freely to strangers. I nerved myself to ask for the pee bottle to be left within my reach. Wishing me goodnight, Mrs Osborne said, 'Tomorrow you will visit the ashram and meet Ganesh.'

'Couldn't I pay my homage to Arunachala? For so long I have seen the mountain in my dreams.'

'Young man, you must be as patient as Arunachala himself. For one thing, we must decide how someone with your limitations is to undertake the ritual circumambulation of the mountain. At the ashram you will meet fellow devotees and you will be fed. The holy mountain does not offer lunch.' She looked at me shrewdly. 'Perhaps you do not wish to meet Ganesh?' It was true that I wasn't in a hurry to make the acquaintance of the gentleman who had seemed to offer encouragement, then tried to put the kibosh on my pilgrimage before it had begun. 'He is your great friend, I assure you,' she said, and I mimed one more yawn as an alternative to answering her.

'Don't be alarmed if you hear strange cries in the morning. Peacocks live wild in this area – their cries are disturbing to those unfamiliar with them.' I was able to assure Mrs Osborne that on the contrary, peacock cries would make me feel at home, since Bourne

End was infested with them. I didn't go into the whole saga of Tom Stoppard and the Abbotsbrook Estate. It was too long a story to tell a new acquaintance.

Brusque, peremptory dawn

I slept poorly that first night, buffeted by alternating gusts of exhaustion and exhilaration. I had been provided with a bed, but none of the institutions that I had been in, not notably sybaritic, would really have called it by that name. It was only a metal frame with planks laid across it, sans mattress, sans pillow. By morning my body was as sore as it had been for many years. Snakes and scorpions had left me well alone, but I wasn't spared by mosquitoes. I let them feed with a willing heart, though I couldn't really classify them as holy just by virtue of living on the mountain. On my toes they battened especially.

There were advantages to sleeplessness in my new surroundings. I saw my first Indian dawn, which wasn't at all as I expected it. I'd begun to think that India was a country where the categories that were supposed to be separate bled into each other like bright colours in a washing-machine. Everything was true and not true at the same time, thoroughly mixed and indefinite. Airline employees threw themselves into passionate embraces with strangers, cows were vegetarian cannibals, mountains could project themselves across space. But the Indian dawn wasn't like that – it was brusque, peremptory. It took hardly a moment. The English dawn was like a whole orchestra tuning up, but here it was like a single vast gong struck with a stick. The heat which the gong released was already so intense that I doubted my body's ability to adjust.

Despite the change of scene from Madras, my half-sleep was punctuated with erections, and with burnished images of S. P. Munshi and Kashi Gaitonde flickering behind my eyes. I did nothing about them, hoping that my excitement would subside before anyone could notice. I was determined to beg a sheet for the following night, since desire seemed to be mounting a permanent ambush.

Being awake so early was also a suitable expression of eagerness for my long-awaited rendezvous with Arunachala. When Mrs Osborne appeared, I could hardly wait to pester her on the subject of the mountain, but first there were formalities to be observed as between host and guest. 'I hope you were comfortable in the night, John?'

I felt that lying would be a greater breach of manners than telling the truth. 'I'm afraid not, Mrs Osborne,' I said, aiming for chirpiness. 'Please don't think I'm spoiled, but I could hardly get a wink. Still, I'm not here for my beauty sleep.'

Mrs O looked baffled. 'I myself sleep on the floor and find it very comfortable.' From her expression you would have thought I was the princess kept awake by a pea through forty mattresses, rather than someone with fixed and swollen joints who had spent the night on a bed of planks for the first time. She hobbled off the verandah as if aggrieved by my ingratitude. The word 'impossible' hovered in my mind, given a particular pronunciation. Mrs Osborne was *imposhible*.

Her own sound sleep seemed to be a badge of virtue, and my broken night a sort of self-indulgence. It was disheartening to find the same attitude I had found so suffocating in the West repeated here virtually unchanged – that with a little thought, a little *consideration* even, I could be able-bodied like the majority.

Of course if the body is no more than an old coat, there's no point in complaining about the unflattering cut or the rips in the lining. I tried to think of a Bhagavan-esque way of reproving her, although reproval was not really Ramana Maharshi's style. The way he rebuked his sometimes small-minded followers was by following their rules, showing them to be ridiculous by his very deference to absurdity.

The only saying that came to my mind was his disclaimer of austerity in his early years. '*I did not eat, so they said I was fasting.*' Perhaps that could be turned around without impiety. 'They said I was keeping vigil, but I was just bloody uncomfortable.' I've found it a useful skill to formulate rude remarks in full, savour them on the tongue and then cleanly suppress them. I have more to lose by rudeness than most.

In earlier life I was less restrained – but then pertness, if well judged, with the right audience, can be a successful way of getting on in institutions like hospitals and schools (I can't speak for prisons and asylums). Out in the open, where people have no obligation to meet your needs, emollience is what pays off.

Raghu and Sumati took their leave early, perhaps making a quick getaway before Mrs Osborne changed her mind about the poshibility of the verandah as a place for me to stay.

My nostrils began registering a delicious aroma, quite unlike anything I had smelled before. I had given no thought to the question of what Indians ate for breakfast, but from the smell it could only be a kind of curry. Then Mrs Osborne came back with a pan containing a marvellous-smelling dish, a *poriyal* of wild green figs. If she hadn't told me what it was I would have guessed at fried mushrooms. From the finished dish you'd never guess that the main ingredient was unripe fruit.

She helped me to sit upright on the bed and then to move the wheelchair, but the effort was almost too much for her and she warned me that I would have to show Kuppu the gardener's wife how to help me in future. She noticed the bites on my toes and asked about them. She herself, she said, had never been troubled by mosquitoes. Perhaps she had a spell to keep them away.

I think I could have stuck to my vow of austerity and my fast if I had been offered Western fare, but the novelty of wild fig *poriyal* sidestepped my willpower. It was delicious. I asked Mrs Osborne who had cooked them. 'Why, I myself, of course!' she said. 'Do you think I have a cook? I have a gardener because I am not so flexible, and he has a wife who would be more use if she wasn't so nervous. Whenever she sees a stranger she is sure she has had the evil eye put on her. I spend many of my days calming her down.

'The ashram sends food every day in a tiffin carrier. As you may know, Arthur made over all his earnings from books to the ashram, which shows gratitude in this and other ways. But I am not so fond of their food. It is a little flavourless – they try not to alarm the Western palate, while I am now accustomed to spicy food.'

She mentioned without false pride that an English millionaire had once fallen in love with her *poriyal*, and wanted to have supplies of wild figs flown over to England.

'Indian puddings I do not care for,' she added, 'but I am skilled at the making of rock cakes, which are I think an English favourite.'

It seemed a good idea, now that the Gaitondes had gone, to ask about things that had puzzled me. When I asked if Sumati's hanging back rather than greeting a guest was typical, she answered that it was, except in very Westernised households. 'But don't be too quick to condemn these old styles of behaviour. In this culture there are four female virtues, to wit shyness, simplicity, timidity and delicacy. In Tamil *naanam, madam, assam, payirrpu*. However there are spiritual meanings involved. Those are the qualities with which the male devotee also will approach manifestations of the divine. There is something of this in the Bible, of course, when the soul arrays herself to greet Christ the bridegroom.'

I was almost more interested to ask about the Gaitondes' family business. Mrs Osborne said, 'You must try to understand the Indian Mind. Very little is forbidden absolutely – absolutes are instead the West's idea. In India it'sh a matter of matching the person to the act. It'sh to do with caste.' I was beginning to think that Mrs Osborne's peculiarites of diction were to do with imperfect dentures as well as perfect Polishness. 'For a Brahmin to touch the shkin of a dead animal in the process of tanning would be the greatest impurity, but an untouchable can do so with no loss of status. Obviously. I know that in Calcutta there is a population of Chinamen who, not being Indian or Hindu, can provide the labour for a substantial industry of leather-dressing and tanning.'

Celebrated prompters of evacuation

I recoiled from the idea of the Indian Mind, but I had to admit the force of what she was saying, even with my infinitesimal experience of India. When it was a matter of attending to my needs in the bathroom, Raghu had tried to think of the person whose function was to deal with such things – as if there might be a glass case in the hall with a servant inside – before he made the breakthrough of deciding that, as my host, he was in fact the person to deal with me, or at least to deputise.

My normal time for a tuppenny was before breakfast, but my system was less full than usual thanks to my having skipped food since lunch the day before. Now the time would have been upon me, even without my indulgence in figs, those celebrated prompters of evacuation. Mrs Osborne summoned Kuppu and tactfully withdrew to the house.

By the time she emerged again, a number of things had happened. I had undertaken my maiden voyage on her late husband's commode, and Kuppu, who seemed to understand me with the minimum of effort, had not only emptied the pee bottle but had removed the bowl from the commode and cleaned it. Kuppu had learned very quickly to help me up by bending down and putting her arms round me. And now the bowl of the commode was sparkling and fresh, ready for the next use, and I myself had been deftly cleaned up. Kuppu had lost her fear of me, and now her smile seemed as much a part of her as her nose-ring.

Mrs Osborne was astonished. Her face softened. I exaggerate: it was a face that clung to its hardness, but there were nuances to be read there all the same, granite nuances. 'Never would I have believed this poshible,' she said. 'Truly Arunachala blesses your presence here!' Which I devoutly hoped was true. I thought of throwing back at her the observation that absolutes are a fad of the West, but decided against it. Kuppu deserved all possible credit for quietly slipping across the boundaries of caste for my benefit.

My next question to Mrs Osborne was obvious. 'When can we go to Arunachala? Can we go soon?' Her answer was not what I expected. 'My dear child, you are already there! Did you really not know? We are at the foot of the holy mountain, and the ashram is no more than a few steps from here.' With 'ashram' she had at last found a word to whose *esh*-sound she could really do justice. 'It is merely that we are so near that we do not see the profile of Arunachala, just as a fly that has landed on your neck cannot see your eyes.'

I was already where I wanted to be. This was a great discovery and a great lesson. The mountain had stretched itself towards me the day before, so that I saw it long before Raghu thought such a thing possible, and then it had hidden in plain sight. Arunachala was playing hide and seek with me, showing me how freely He could intersect with time and space. I could even feel that my residence on the verandah was somehow significant, with no walls to block spiritual access, that it pleased Arunachala to have me near and in the open air. Perhaps I could even count him, rather than Mrs Osborne, as my host in Tamil Nadu.

I was also reminded of something that Ben Nevin, the teacher I hero-worshipped, had said at Vulcan about different religions, and how it was possible that they might all be true. He asked us to imagine a mountain, which many people are climbing. Some of them climb up in a straight line, some of them look for the less forbidding slopes, others take a spiral path. It all depends on their abilities and their maps. I had thought this was a wonderful notion even before the mountain Himself started showing me the truth of it.

'Now,' said Mrs Osborne, 'perhaps Arunachala will also smile on the bed problem.' It turned out that she wasn't leaving it up to the mountain altogether. She summoned Rajah Manikkam and gave him some instructions. When he came back with some rope I expect my face fell. I had been hoping for something fluffy, cushioned, perhaps even inflatable. But then the two of them got to work. From Mrs Osborne's disapproval of my soft, bed-loving ways, I had no reason to think that what they were doing was a routine procedure, but they behaved as a team, with a degree of coöperation which seemed downright eerie.

What they were doing, in broad terms, was wrapping the rope round the bedframe in a diagonal weave. Rajah Manikkam's job was to pull the rope tight, while Mrs O put knots in it. The knots must have been the cunning sort which tighten when pulled on. Then their working became more ambitious. Rajah Manikkam started to stand on the rope bed and to trample on it in some methodical way while Mrs Osborne refined her knot-tightening. Despite her poor posture, her fingers were deft and strong. The whole process had some mysterious logic. Rajah Manikkam's trampling started at the loose bit of the rope web and moved up towards the neck of the bed. It's hard to offer accurate descriptions of actions that you can't perform yourself – the best I can do is to describe Rajah Manikkam's actions as a sort of regulated trammelling, a spontaneous blend of weaving and hopscotch. Handiwork of any kind often seems miraculous. I don't easily distinguish between degrees of accomplishment. All I can say is that it looked pretty clever to me.

From my vantage point I could see that sometimes the rope passed between Rajah Manikkam's toes, while Mrs O exerted pressure. I'm no expert on toes, but the friction on those tissues looked alarming. Those tender pegs were surely never meant to do duty as pulleys, as tiny capstans – but when Rajah Manikkam met my eyes he gave a huge grin. Only when their methodical trampling and knotting had produced results did Mrs Osborne allow herself a sharp smile of satisfaction. In the space of a quarter of an hour they had created between them a very serviceable bed, in the form of a cat's-cradle.

They had performed the Indian Rope Trick right there on the verandah, for my benefit exclusively, only they had done something much more useful than making a man vanish, by making a bed appear from nothing.

While the white witch and her gardener had been working away for my benefit, and while I basked in the satisfaction of having opened my bowels without trauma, I had been reviewing my experiences of India so far, cannibal cows and all. The only episode that seemed wholly fantastical in retrospect was Mrs Osborne telling me that she would give me pills to make me grow. It was straight out of *Alice in Wonderland*. Had I fallen asleep, tired as I was, for a few moments at least, and dreamed this unlikely piece of wish-fulfilment?

But then Mrs O reappeared with a little container of pills, one of which she insisted on popping directly onto my tongue. As she tipped it from the lid of the container she told me that homœopathic preparations should never be touched. I have to admit that this was something which appealed, the sense of medicines as sacred. I let the tiny pill unleash its sugared potency on my tongue as I was told, without chewing. Perhaps it was Mrs Osborne's aspect as a homœopathic practitioner which had made Raghu compare her to a witchy 'handler of nothingness'. Homœopaths in their spells handle something that are almost smaller than nothings.

Change eyes with a basilisk

Under Mrs Osborne's direction, Rajah Manikkam practised the drill for getting me on and off the verandah. She was well used to correcting (without expense of tact) the shortcomings of the locals, and her analytical eye had seen that there was no point lifting me anywhere if I didn't have my shoes on. Without them I could hardly stand at all. She gave him the order to hug me and lift me up or down the three steps, and showed him which uprights were strong enough to let me lean against them while he fetched the wheelchair, and which would let me down.

Perhaps Rajah Manikkam was nervous about being entrusted with these intricate tasks. The procedure, which had gone smoothly during its first execution, became problematic the moment we started practising it. At the point when his arms were wrapped round me, he would be overwhelmed by a laughing attack. Suddenly it struck him as the funniest thing in the entire world that he should be lifting John up and down the steps to the verandah. His movements became less controlled, the functional hug developed tremors and spasms. He began to sway as if he was drunk, and there was a real possibility of him falling over or else simply dropping me.

It was in the nature of our position that he should be looking me almost directly in the face, but of course I knew not a single word of Tamil, except possibly the name of a spicy appetiser served in Madras. I never saw him with a beedie in his hand or between his lips, but at this range his was unmistakably a smoker's breath, nutty and corrupt. All I could do to steady him was to *change Eyes with a basilisk* (as described in *The Duchess of Malfi*, which I had read at Burnham), hoping to freeze the laughter at its root. Of course sometimes, although this doesn't usually happen in *The Duchess of Malfi*, the change-Eyes-with-a-basilisk routine just makes things even funnier.

Much of the day was spent in a battle of wills between me and Mrs Osborne about whether I would go to the ashram first or around the mountain. She said that Rajah Manikkam was at my disposal as wheelchair-pusher, whenever I wished to go to the ashram. To which I replied, why not then put him at my disposal to take me round the mountain? Mrs Osborne, though, was not to be got round in that way. 'He is unsuitable for that purpose, since he is no devotee and can neither identify the mountain's features nor explain their significance.' Even if he possessed such knowledge he lacked any English in which it might be embodied. As if it was the dutiful parroting of a guide for which I had travelled, and not direct contact with the mountain, the divine presence expressed in geology.

To show willing (or to protect my stubbornness from a flanking attack, which is what 'showing willing' normally means) I had let Rajah Manikkam give me a test ride for a few yards. Even then I wasn't convinced that he was up to the job. His technique was very jerky and approximate – gardeners in Tamil Nadu don't have wheelbarrows to practise on. When we came to rough terrain I would be asking for trouble.

'In that case,' I said, 'I will wait for a suitable pushing-person to become available.'

'Such people gather at the ashram. Lunch is also served. Why not make enquiries there?'

'After that delicious breakfast I am in no hurry to eat again. I will try to match my patience to the mountain, as you advise.' That was telling her, all right. I closed my eyes.

Any time I closed my eyes at home, or kept them open but withdrew into the practice of meditation, I would be accused of 'woolgathering'. It would have been handy to be able to dramatise my need for privacy by locking a door behind me, or hanging up a sign saying, SPIRITUAL EXERCISE IN PROGRESS – KEEP OUT – THIS MEANS YOU, MUM, but that wasn't a possibility. 'You were miles away,' Mum would say when I had picked up the threads of mundane life, as if holding the mind stilled in quest of itself was only a form of absent-mindedness, a failure of concentration, and I would say, 'More than miles, Mum . . . light years'.

The rope inexorably shortens

Doing *pradakshina* was of course my ambition. In Rome you are photographed standing next to the Colosseum, in Paris you climb the Eiffel Tower and in Tiruvannamalai you walk clockwise round the mountain. It's not a sacrament but a ritual stroll. The limbs move but the mind is silenced.

There are numbers of *siddhas* and sages on Arunachala even now, similarly perambulating in invisibility. It's correct to walk on the left side of the road so as not to obstruct them, thereby gathering additional blessings.

Pradakshina is beneficial even in the absence of faith. There's a lovely image used for the process: just as a cow, wandering aimlessly round the post to which it is tethered, finds that the rope inexorably shortens, so by each circuit the *sadhaka* will be drawn nearer to the

Heart-Self centre. The captivated cow is not required to understand the principle of the winch.

In my case, though, it wasn't easy to disentangle theory and practice. What constituted *pradakshina* for me? I couldn't expect to reap the spiritual benefit if someone was pushing me – going barefoot was no hardship when your feet didn't touch the ground. But if I did it myself, surely the ritual had to be scaled down in some way, and doing it without shoes wasn't an option. The last time I had done any walking without shoes had been at the bidding of a sadistic physiotherapist. My guru would not make similar demands.

In religion I seemed to be re-experiencing what I had encountered in terms of my education. It stung me with a sense of unfairness. Once again it required special measures for me to participate on equal terms, schoolboy among schoolboys, devotee among devotees. My guru had walking difficulties, as I did, though admittedly his rheumatism required the help of a stick and not a wheelchair. And still I didn't fit in here. Ramana Maharshi didn't need to walk round the mountain because, for all practical purposes, he was the mountain. There was no call for him to walk round himself, he would reap no benefit thereby, and *pradakshina* as a sacred practice had nothing to teach him. If I, on the other hand, couldn't walk round the mountain, that would knock the stuffing out of my pilgrimage and my vain discipleship. All Air India's generosity, for which Dad had done such stalwart wheedling, would be a waste of grace.

When I opened my eyes again, Mrs Osborne was sitting there in front of me, with her elbows on the table, resting her austerity of a face in her hands. She looked oddly beautiful, as if her head was a flower resting in a vase designed for the purpose.

'John,' she said, 'when I think of the difficulties your body has put in your path, I think that simply making your way to Tiruvannamalai must count for half a *pradakshina.*'

This was the kindest thing Mrs Osborne had said to date, even if the sentence began more promisingly than it ended. She seemed to be able to look into my heart more easily when my eyes were closed (and my mouth also). I wondered if I had really been meditating, or only sneaking in all innocence a restorative nap.

'I have sent Rajah Manikkam to the ashram with a note. If all goes well, a brahmin from the ashram will escort you on *pradakshina* later in the day. The brahmin will explain the spiritual significance of the mountain's features as you pass them.'

This was a good start, or so I thought while I waited for the brahmin to arrive from the ashram. In England *ashram* was a highly unusual word, like *ankylosed* and *epiphysis*, needing to be explained and apologised for. Here it was an entirely everyday word and thing, like 'school' or 'library'. I loved that.

The brahmin was a bright-eyed fellow, whose greeting was merely to fold his hands in silence. This should hardly have amounted to a greeting, yet its meaning seemed clear. There was a semaphore twinkle in his eye which transmitted the message 'I bid you welcome, pilgrim.' 'Pilgrim' was the word I was anxious to supply, since it turned my restlessness into a virtue.

This wordless welcome made a pleasant change from Mrs O's original 'Imposhible, imposhible!' But after that things didn't quite go according to plan.

It was already late in the day. The evening insects had begun their thrumming song. Before the brahmin had finally turned up I had a conversation with Mrs Osborne about them, asking whether they were actually cicadas or some other variety of insect. She said, 'Strangely enough, that was a question I once put to Arthur. My husband's general knowledge was very wide. It was his opinion that they were not "strictly" cicadas, so we always just called them Hoppy Things.'

It had not been explained to me that my first *pradakshina* was to take place in dying light, in what (given the blink-and-you've-missed-it quality of the Indian dusk) was pretty much darkness. When I protested to the brahmin about the timing of so important an event, he simply said that vision was an unimportant factor in the doing of *pradakshina*. I needn't worry about being able to see the mountain – the mountain would be able to see me without difficulty.

I felt like one of those people in Greek mythology who are granted their greatest wish, with a hidden flaw that turns it into punishment – becoming immortal, say, without having remembered to ask for eternal youth. Or like a bride on her wedding night, forbidden to set eyes on her beloved. Was it for this that I had travelled so far, a mystery tour in the dark with some parables thrown in at no extra charge?

Of course I couldn't make any real protest – my bluff had been called by the brahmin's greeting. To hang on to my status as pilgrim I had to go along with the idea that vision was an incidental part of this body's operation, of no spiritual significance. If I set too much store by actually seeing things I was pretty much begging to be reclassified as a tourist. With any luck at least we wouldn't be bivouacking on the mountain.

Once we had set off, I had to admit that the brahmin was very sure-footed. He knew exactly what he was doing. It's extraordinary how hands on the wheelchair can transmit along the handles the competence or ineptness of the pusher. I felt that I was as safe with this man as Hillary was with Sherpa Tensing, on his own rather humdrum mountain quest. The air was certainly cooler than it would have been by day. Even when my eyes had adapted to the dark, though, I couldn't make out more than the vaguest shapes.

The voice behind me murmured, in a very educated English, 'Arunachala is the oldest mountain on earth, older by far than the Himalayas . . .' I managed to keep my mouth closed and not to murmur in my turn, 'Oh I know *that*,' in a voice that would have been to all intents and purposes Granny's. Then I wondered a little uneasily if he had picked up my thoughts about Hillary and Everest, as directly as I had picked up a confidence in his wheelchair-handling. Wheelchair handles can be very good conductors.

'In spiritual terms Arunachala is the South Pole of India, Mount Kailas being the northern one. There are three main peaks to the mountain,' he went on. 'They correspond to Brahma, Vishnu and Shiva.' That was something I didn't know, so I made attentive-schoolboy clucks. If people can't read your expression they tend to repeat what they've said until they get an acknowledgement. Dealing with the disabled makes people's IQ fairly plunge. 'There is another tradition which numbers the peaks as five. Opinions vary. There is much to be said on this issue. There may be three peaks or else five – but not four. Definitely not four.' Mentally I plumped for five, not wanting to have travelled half-way across the world only to bump into the Trinity in native costume.

At one point I noticed a mysterious shape looming by the road. It looked like a bus shelter – at least that's what it would have been by a suburban road in England. 'What's that?' I asked. '*Mantapam*,' said the brahmin, and I didn't want to advertise my lack of ability to concentrate on the mountain by asking anything else. Similar shapes loomed up at intervals, and I was fairly sure that they were *mantapams* too, whatever a *mantapam* was.

Finally there was a light, and also a strange hissing-puffing noise, like something a tiny steam-engine might make. 'Perhaps you would like a cup of tea?' asked the brahmin politely. No I would not! I was scandalised that there was a tea-shop brewing up in the middle of the night on the holy mountain. I felt as if I was being nudged if not positively funnelled towards the cathedral gift kiosk, in a way that slighted my piety. Did I want to look at some postcards, perhaps a calendar? Not on your nelly. Full steam ahead, please, brahmin driver. Step on the gas.

The warm glow died away behind me. It was frustrating not to be able to see the object of my pilgrimage, when I might actually be passing right beneath the rock where Bhagavan would sit in the morning, cleaning his teeth with a twig from the toothbrush tree, as he did even in bad weather, with an arthritic lady down below drinking up the *darshan* as it splashed down the slope.

Anecdotes of that sort were rather more real to me than my closeness to the mountain which had inspired them. Perhaps that was the lesson intended behind taking me on *pradakshina* in the dark, to show me that there was still plenty of baggage to be shed, trunk after trunk of it. The mountain was blazing with realised Selfhood, and my little mind clung to its cone of dark. The dunce's cap of unenlightenment.

The brahmin told me about Parvati and her penance on Arunachala. I didn't catch exactly what she was atoning for – if I was truly attuned to sin and atonement I'd have stayed at home. 'One day,' he said, 'when Parvati went on *pradakshina*, her devotion was so strong that she simply melted into the mountain, but her shape – her bosom, in fact – can still be traced at this very point on the slope.' Not by me it couldn't. I hadn't flown above the clouds with the hiccups to end up playing I Spy with divine body parts and the local rocks.

I might as well not have been on the mountain at all. Our promenade, though sacred and circular, was unleashing no inner change. Even before I finished my first *pradakshina* I began to pin my hopes for breakthrough on the ashram rather than on the mountain. Despite the antiquity and power of the mountain, after all, it was in the ashram that the transcendent powers of Bhagavan would be at their strongest. In the Old Hall above all, which must have absorbed the purest energy from his presence, *darshan* in a concentration approaching critical mass, radiant core of spiritual fission-fusion. To that fizzing sherbet fountain of anti-matter I transferred my hopes.

When we returned to Mrs Osborne's house it was well after midnight and I was exhausted, but she still seemed to have plenty of energy. I didn't make the mistake of thinking she was waiting up for me, even worrying about me. I was in the hands of the mountain. Sleeping on the bare earth certainly seemed to suit Mrs O. Being so much less firm than her formidable personality, it must have felt actively soft beneath her.

She told me that she had left a book out for my inspection, and that she would bring me out a fruit juice to refresh me. 'The local juice is good,' she said, 'though not of course as refreshing as the sour cherry juice they make in Poland.'

Thick even in dilution

These were significant concessions, the book and the juice both delivered to me on the verandah, and I felt that my sincerity as a pilgrim was really beginning to wear down Mrs Osborne's resistance. It was with faint dismay that I noted that the book was by Somerset Maugham, in 1970 definitively out of literary fashion. It was *The Razor's Edge*. I certainly didn't expect to have anything to learn from this shallow stylist – this *storyteller*. I was going up to Cambridge in a few months, after all. I was up-to-date. I had discussed Lorca's passion for another man with a Catalonian-British housewife, in a Bourne End kitchen wreathed in the smoke of our Ducados. I was far too grown-up for Maugham. Perhaps Mrs Osborne had brought the wrong book out to the verandah? A widow for only a matter of weeks, she couldn't be quite as composed as she seemed.

But no, I was the one who was confused. When Mrs Osborne came out with the mango juice, which was thick even in dilution and extremely delicious, she set me straight about that. 'A famous English

347

writer came here to do research on a guru, a spiritual teacher who might give the hero of his next novel a smattering of an Eastern perspective. Mr Maugham came to do some research. He was neither tourist nor pilgrim, but he found something a little more real than he anticipated. He knew enough to bring a basket of fruit as an offering, but the meeting with Ramana Maharshi did not go as he had planned.

'Mr Somerset Maugham came here expecting to find a charlatan. But he fainted before he even entered the presence of Bhagavan Sri Ramana. Major Chadwick, who was his host, sent for Bhagavan rather than a doctor, and Bhagavan stroked Somerset Maugham's forehead until he came to himself. Then Bhagavan said, "It is finished. Heart talk is all talk. True talk ends in silence." Mr Maugham did not say one word, but when he wrote his book he did not describe a charlatan. I have marked the passage for your interest.'

Then Mrs Osborne asked me casually about my tour of the mountain in the dark. 'Some people find their first *pradakshina* disappointing. Perhaps this is true of you?' I could have said that I had received more in the way of enlightenment from the Ghost Train at the funfair, and that was without benefit of riding the damn thing, just from watching people's faces as the cars clattered out into daylight. I managed to say that I was too humble to expect an instant impact even from a profound experience.

'That is a healthy state of mind. *Pradakshina* is not like a lightning-bolt, but like a single mighty turn of the spiritual generator that charges one's batteries. I trust your companion was informative?' I made gracious noises. Then she sprang her trap. 'Ganesh is a fine teacher, if someone is willing to learn.'

'*Ganesh?*' I gurgled. I felt utterly mortified and outmanoeuvred. Bamboozled, even. I had known that at some stage I would be in the same room as Ganesh, since he was a luminary of the ashram, after all. Even before I left Britain I had decided on the attitude I would assume when I met the man who had tried to discourage me from making my visit. I would be friendly but distant. We were united, after all, by more things than divided us. Fellow devotees – that would be my line. I was as much a follower of Ramana Maharshi in my own way as he was in his. But now Ganesh had sneaked in under my radar by presenting himself in the guise of helper, and escorting me on my first *pradakshina*, as if he was offering a belated blessing on my presence. And all of this insidious conciliation had sneaked up on me without my knowledge.

Mrs O had a certain malicious twinkle in her eyes when she said, 'Perhaps you were not looking forward to meeting Ganesh, John. It is a mistake to waste time on such feelings. Certainly you should know that the letter Ganesh sent you in England was written in consultation with me. He did not know quite what to do, and we agreed on a course of action. Why not ask him about our discussion tomorrow? He will be coming to take you to the ashram. And now I am tired, and you must be in a similar state – except that you have a bed which tonight, I trust, will meet your exacting standards.' There were times when it would have been a relief to know, by peeping into her bedroom in a way that I never could, that she was a hypocrite about her austerity and actually rolled herself up for the night in bedding so luxurious it made my Margaret Erskine Dream-Cloud seem like wire wool.

Ganesh turned up again shortly after breakfast the next day, lively and smiling. I had wanted to approach the precincts of the ashram with an attention washed entirely clean of worldly concerns, but that really wasn't on the cards after what Mrs O had told me the previous night.

This time Rajah Manikkam did the pushing, which made me wonder why he hadn't been used on the previous occasion. I knew that Westerners were technically unclean to many Hindus, and one of the advantages of the hand-folding *namaskaaram* gesture is that it offers a polite abstention from touch. Selfishly I approved, since people who are keen to shake my hand are usually in pain socially, and likely to inflict some of their own. Now I wondered if touching the wheelchair wasn't itself under a taboo for a brahmin like Ganesh, which would mean that on our first *pradakshina*, when he told me about Parvati's penance on Arunachala, he had taken on some trifling mortification of his own.

I felt it was up to me to take the initiative, and I started the conversation formally. 'My name is John Cromer, I am a devotee from England, and you I think are Ganesh, head of the ashram.' Ideally

I would have wanted to have a proper face-to-face confrontation, to *thrash things out* in bold British style, but that wasn't possible with him walking alongside me. I would have liked to fix him hypnotically with my gaze, a weapon that can be powerful on occasion but is all too easy to dodge. The ray-gun has rusted onto its tripod.

'Indeed I am Ganesh, but I am by no means "head" of the ashram. What need of a head as long as there are hearts? After Bhagavan's *mahasamadhi* his younger brother Chinnaswami was there to oversee the ashram. Then my father T. N. Venkataraman succeeded him. I am editor of *The Mountain Path* with Mrs Osborne, which is privilege and labour enough.' Much of the labour, I imagined, had to do with keeping his collaborator sweet. 'But let there be a new beginning between us. You are here, you are welcome, you are doing *pradakshina*, perhaps it has started to take effect. You may remember that I wrote you a letter that did not encourage you to continue with your visit, and perhaps you wonder why.'

'Mrs Osborne said she had something to do with it.'

'Indeed so. Yours was an unusual case, John Cromer, both in the strength of your devotion and in the obstacles in your path. Obstacles which, as perhaps you remember, were only belatedly revealed to us. I proposed that I remind you of what Bhagavan said about internal and external change: that if you could realise yourself in the jungle, you could do so anywhere. An outward journey was not necessary, and could simply be a distraction. Mrs Osborne is – can we agree? – capable of great determination. She said instead that we should not preach, but simply be as discouraging as possible on the mundane level. Her thinking (and for this also there is much precedent) was that if your visit was meant to happen then no such strictures would have the slightest effect.'

I could hear him smile at this point. A smile is a perfectly audible aspect of conversation. It colours not only speech but silence. 'It seems that determination is not exclusively Mrs Osborne's province. I hope you understand our . . . *stratagem*, and the fact that we are very happy for its failure.'

'I promise I will try.' By this time we had reached the ashram, and Ganesh said, 'I shall take you to the Old Hall and then perhaps leave you to meditate. If you need me just mention my name to anyone you see. Ganesh, the god after whom I am named, is the god who removes obstacles, and I would be happy to live up to my name, despite your past doubts.'

I had been determined to memorise my first impressions of the ashram, but alas while Ganesh was offering ambiguous compliments on my mental powers my attention was divided, and those first impressions became lost. There's a mystical idea that everything that ever happened (and will happen) is stored in a sort of metaphysical store room called the Akasic Records, the astral equivalent of that Harrods Depository where Granny kept 'nice' (or even 'good') furniture for which she didn't have space. I suppose my lost impressions must be there, properly docketed, but they slipped away from me immediately.

It was only in the Old Hall that I began to take in my surroundings. I had approached the holy of holies without the proper preparation. I found myself about six feet from the couch on which Ramana Maharshi had spent so much of his time in the body. Ganesh had delivered me into the heart of a spiritual furnace, where everything can be consumed before the devotee hears so much as a crackle.

Snide thoughts about upholstery

A photograph of Ramana Maharshi, half life-size, was reverently propped up on the couch. My view was clear, except for a middle-aged man at the very edge of my vision. He was performing a strange sequence of actions. He would sink to his knees and then struggle upright, only to be brought to his knees again. His face was washed with ecstatic tears. It was as if he was being swept over and buoyed up, continuously, by jostling waves of devotion. Eventually he subsided into a prostrate position, with his arms outstretched and clasped in front of him. It was as if he had been swept off his feet at last by a seventh wave of self-realisation, bigger than the rest. The closeness of those holy tears vividly brought back the weeping of S. P. Munshi at Bombay airport, and the way that its electrolytic dew had seemed to percolate directly into my skin.

At this point, though, it was hard to say if the osmotic transfusion of spiritual energy from that generous liquor had made any difference. My view of the couch was clear, and yet the couch itself was an obstacle. It was undeniably gaudy, covered as it was with red brocade.

An outsider could easily think that this was a religion based on the couch – a furniture cult. Couches outnumbered gurus in the Old Hall, after all, two to one. Here was the couch itself, with a photograph of the couch displayed on it. Yes, it had Ramana Maharshi sitting on the couch in the picture, but that might just be some sort of testimonial to the excellence of the springing, as attested on a historical occasion. The guru seemed to make no attempt to match the couch. He was as plain as the furniture was fancy.

From the corded look of his neck this must be a picture from late life. His facial hair and the stubble on his head are white, but his un-presumptuous smile is ageless and the expression in the eyes quietly expectant. He is leaning against a low wall of white cushions. His right hand rests lightly on his knee, while the arm is placed a little higher up the leg. His legs are crossed, so that the sole of his right foot is presented to the camera.

The couch has no significance at all. Bhagavan's choice was to sit on the floor, until he was persuaded that he would make it easier for devotees if he adopted the traditional pose. He was indifferent to such choices on the part of his followers, and the couch was the merest prop.

Another traditional pose for the guru is sitting on a tiger skin. I had seen photographs of Bhagavan doing just that and found them very jarring. I felt queasy, not liking to be reminded that there was an overlap between spiritual leaders (or their advisers) and big-game hunters. I prefer the symbolic power of the big cats, their aura, to be kept separate from their skin, sliced from the owner – the owner-occupier – at huge karmic cost.

I did know something of the history of that particular skin, though, the one in the photographs, and how little importance it had for Ramana Maharshi himself.

One day a devotee appeared to pay his respects to the guru and left with the tiger skin rolled up under his arm. The worthies of the ashram nabbed him and asked him what he thought he was doing. He simply said, 'Swami gave it to me.' Obvious nonsense, but for form's sake they had to check with Bhagavan before turning him over to the worldly authorities. 'Yes, that's true,' he said.

But why? His answer was classic Maharshi in the gentle chiding it delivered to his followers (not that they noticed, I dare say): 'Somebody comes in and says sit on the tiger skin. I do so. Somebody else comes in and asks to keep it. I say yes.'

Later in his life Bhagavan sat in the New Hall instead. When he was sick, and Mrs Osborne and others were treating him, a sign went up: no one to enter between twelve o'clock and two. The usual well-meaning acolyte meddling. The idea was to give Bhagavan time to recover. He himself voiced no objection to the rule. In fact he took it so much to heart that he vacated the premises between those hours, so as to be freely available outside.

The couch in front of me was something that someone's tasteless auntie would sit on, something that might turn up at a flea market. I had travelled here to find out who I really was, not to think snide thoughts about upholstery, but it wasn't easy. Even at these high spiritual temperatures the asbestos of habit fought against combustion. My reflex of triviality was a stubborn *vasana*, a deep rut from a previous life needing to be raked smoothly over in the sand of the new one.

I sat in the wheelchair looking at the two couches and the single guru, but my mind was straying to other rooms, other images and times. It was almost worse to be sitting in the Old Hall thinking of the New Hall than it would have been to be thinking of Bourne End. I seemed to be more attuned to anecdotes and the past than to the numinous room in the present. My attention wandered, and my reverence had no focal depth.

If anything preöccupied me, it was some of the words Ganesh had used while we were approaching the ashram. Strength of devotion. Determination. My determination was really only passive resistance, though some people (such as Dawn Drummond) had run a finger along its militant edge and left a little trace of blood there.

Those qualities had brought me to this place, but now they were blocking my path. Passive resistance was the parachute which had allowed me to descend safely into these new surroundings, but now it was entangled in a tree and had become a threat. I must free myself.

If only there was a quick-release mechanism on the harness of the ego, one which would let me drop into freedom with a single decisive click! I had the sense that I would be dangling there for some time in the breeze, while the leaves yellowed, fell and renewed themselves, without their meaning any reproach by it.

Executive moonlight

Of course Ganesh had referred to Mrs Osborne's determination as well as my own. She was calm as well as determined, certainly calm rather than frantic, but it was a sort of steel calm, lacking flexibility. I couldn't honestly say that I thought her ego functioned as it does (by all accounts) in a realised person, persisting merely as the moon does in the daytime – the ego emeritus, performing little administrative tasks, pottering in its contented retirement.

Far from it. Her ego seemed robust, even fierce. Sometimes it positively spoiled for a fight. It was strategic even in its retreats, as when Mrs O had given way on the *pradakshina* question so as to get her own way about my meeting Ganesh. If Mrs O's ego was mere executive moonlight, then why was it so hard to look at directly? Still, the state of her ego was really none of my business. I must mind my own.

When Ganesh came back to find me, it was actually a relief to be interrupted. He had left me alone for a good stretch of time. I wasn't getting anywhere with meditation, with stilling my thoughts and holding my mind alert in quest of itself. Altogether self-enquiry seemed to have reached a dead end. The whole idea seemed impossible, like using the light of a candle to make out the silversmith's mark on the base of the candlestick. Meditation solves the problem by detaching the flame from the wick, letting its light float free, but currently I seemed to have lost that knack.

Ganesh was too tactful to ask if I had profited from my first encounter with the ashram, but I said something about finding the presence of other devotees distracting. Instead of pointing out that I was a hopeless case if I couldn't ignore such irrelevancies he offered to have me brought back at a time of day when it would be quieter.

I began to feel a little flattered qualm about Ganesh's obligingness and approachability. He was making time for me in a way which

354

could hardly be standard practice. He was certainly easier company than Mrs Osborne, though of course we only really discussed one subject, and that subject was the reason for my being in India in the first place.

His face too held a fascination, being full of light and kindness. It gave the effect of constant smiling, and yet it was hard to be sure there was a smile there at all. If it was a smile, it was as different from Western smiles as a pearl lightbulb is different from a clear one. It was all glow and no dazzle. Perhaps it was as close as I would get in mere life to Bhagavan's radiant gaze and piquant serenity, his personality the embodiment of acceptance but also an agent of change.

Then Ganesh quoted a saying of Bhagavan's to me, which was not only stirring in itself but had some sort of eerily glancing connection with my disordered thought-stream in the Old Hall: 'He who is in the jaws of the tiger cannot be rescued; so also a person who has fallen into the grace of a guru cannot escape from it . . .'

Mrs Osborne too had powerful jaws, though I suppose she was more terrier than tiger. Soon she organised a schedule for me, saying, 'I thought you might like to go to the Old Hall to meditate for an hour from nine o'clock every morning, and from five in the evening.' If Mrs Osborne thought you might like something, it was best to start liking it right away.

My second visit to the Old Hall was no more rewarding spiritually than the first. There where I had counted on coming into blossom I experienced a withering. I was forced to face the fact that my pilgrimage was deviating from its planned form. Of course if you issue enlightenment with a timetable you are asking for trouble.

As it turned out, I wasn't going to leap into self-realisation the first time I entered the sacred spaces associated with my guru. I wasn't going to spend the rest of my life there, teaching people how to meditate and realise themselves. That had been my underlying hope, that I wouldn't have to return to the West at all, to the ordeals of my independence, but could simply be absorbed into the fabric of a less material society. When I had said goodbye to Mum and Dad at the airport, it was with the feeling that I might not see them again. I was conscious during the leave-taking of a finality that I welcomed with at least half my heart. But now it was becoming clear that I would be going back to them. The spiritual pull of Arunachala was still there, it never stopped even when I was at my most frustrated, but somehow the flow was blocked. It refused me, which must mean, mustn't it, that I refused it without knowing what I was doing.

I was pushed over to the Old Hall to meditate on most days. I almost began to dread those visits, not because there was anything unpleasant about them, but because they reminded me of my failure to make progress. After the initial rush of mystic bliss, meditation had become homework. While everything else in India seemed colourful and immensely interesting, sitting in the Old Hall trying to get some self-enquiry started was distinctly depressing. My mind seemed jumpier than ever, which wasn't at all the plan.

Of course self-enquiry is a drastic exercise. To make a change in your behaviour is like grafting new fruits and flowers onto a tree, to understand why you have particular desires is to lop off a few branches, but full understanding recognises that the I-tree, stubborn bole, must be pulled up by its root. The ego is a decorative feature that passes itself off as structural. It's a pillar suspended from the roof it claims to hold up.

It was strange how much at home I came to feel on Mrs Osborne's verandah. An environment which was announced as fatally hostile turned out to be highly congenial, almost tailor-made. The smell of green breakfast figs cooking, the call of the commode, the lustre of Kuppu's smile, the tiny mystical pill dissolving on my tongue, all this made up a routine rather sweeter than any I had experienced before.

Every few days Mrs Osborne would have Rajah Manikkam carry out a wind-up gramophone to the verandah. It was like a flashback to CRX, only without the operatic arias, surplus to requirements, so kindly passed on to sick children by the Decca company. Mrs O's taste was for Bach, which she explained was the Western music which Indians liked best, especially Bach in one of his twiddly moods, where ornamentation seems to stand proud of any melody. I can't say that the expressions on the faces of Rajah Manikkam and Kuppu backed her up in any definitive way.

To follow the thread of fear

Sometimes Mrs Osborne asked me about my dreams, which I wasn't in the habit of remembering unless they forced themselves on me. 'One of Arthur's first discoveries,' she said, 'after he embarked on his Quest was to do with dreams.' It gave me an English qualm and a Hindu thrill to hear her use the word quest, with its unmistakable capital. Since she had ended up living on a holy mountain whose antiquity made the Himalayas seem like teenagers, I felt she had earned the right to the holiness of the upper case. 'He realised that whenever he had experienced fear in a dream, his instinct was to make himself wake up. As an adult he decided to override the impulse to escape which had ruled his night thoughts since he was a child. Instead of waking he decided to follow the thread of fear to its end within the dream. Invariably the source of fear when revealed lost its power over him. It was frightening only so long as it was viewed as something to run from. This was an important clue on his Path.' I wondered if I myself would ever be confident enough to capitalise 'path' in conversation.

Mrs Osborne kept a cow in the garden, and that was the milk we would drink, unboiled and unpasteurised, merely chilled in her little fridge. It makes me shiver to think about that now, the blitheness with which we drank untreated milk. One day I was about to pour some over my puffed rice, and decided to taste a bit first. Not nice. It had started to turn and I told her so.

'Absholute Nonshense!' she shrilled. 'There is nothing wrong with my milk. Nothing whatshoever!' And she looked at me so fiercely that I poured the rest of it onto my cereal and swallowed it down under her unrelenting gaze. Every taste bud in my mouth protested against her doctrinaire clean bill of health. Even so, contradicting Mrs Osborne on any sustained basis was something that called for major resources of willpower. It was necessary to throw all your resources behind your audacious tongue or be annihilated, and at that stage I didn't feel strong enough.

In the mornings fruit sellers would do the rounds selling their produce – ladies who carried it on their heads in baskets. Guavas, grapes, apples. They came to me on the verandah. At first I was alarmed by this tide of small businesses sweeping across the verandah in their bird-of-paradise colours, smiling and chattering softly to each other, but it wasn't long before I was looking forward to it. I struggled to master the currency, remembering what Raghu had said about its recent decimalisation. Of course I didn't have a word of the necessary Tamil, but that didn't mean I couldn't haggle. It's amazing how much economic leverage you can pack into a doubtful frown. I wasn't in a hurry, and I enjoyed bringing to the transaction some of the grave tempo of chess. One particular woman would call my bluff, shout scornfully, pack up her wares again and walk off across the verandah – and then slow down, shrug and return to the struggle, settling very happily for a sum that differed by a single tiny coin from the amount that she had found so insulting.

One day I heard this fruit seller talking to Mrs O. Afterwards she said that the conversation had been about me. All the time I was in India, I'm ashamed to say, I had at the back of my mind the thought that someone was bound to ask what I had done (in a previous life) to earn the body I was in. But this discussion was all compliments. 'She loves dealing with you,' Mrs O was saying, 'because you always haggle, and you know how it's done.' In other words she preferred to spend more time than she might, and to receive less money than she might, just for the tiny drama of the bargain, the human contest finally resolved in smiles.

Later in the morning Mrs Osborne might come out onto the verandah with some sweet-lime juice. She always gave the impression of being very busy – she could only spare me a moment. It's true that she had taken on co-editorship of the ashram publication *The Mountain Path* from Arthur after his death, and there were editorial duties to be performed. I remember her opening a letter and saying, 'I detesht Wei Wu Wei' – Wei Wu Wei being a contributor to *The Mountain Path* – 'I have to rewrite every shingle shentensh.' I had begun to think that Lucia Osborne enjoyed choosing words with a strong sibilant element – otherwise why not say she hated or loathed this strange being? 'Wei Wu Wei' is actually a phrase meaning 'action without action', all very Zen. She told me Wei Wu Wei was an Irish aristocrat, born Terence Gray, whose passion was the theatre until he became an eccentric sort of Buddhist. His favourite saying was that 'everything is a case of mistaken identity', but Mrs O seemed to have got his number.

Arthur Osborne had left ten editorials prepared, but Lucia was working on one of her own, about Arthur and his shedding of the old coat. She read parts of it to me as she composed them. She called it 'What is Death if Scrutinised?' I was moved by it.

Sometimes we talked about spiritual experience. Mrs Osborne told me, as if apropos of nothing, that it was very common for devotees planning to come to Arunachala to have obstacles placed in their way. Sometimes the seeker would find another person actively attempting to prevent the pilgrim from making his journey. At this point I indicated that this was true in my case. I decided to leave it at that, though, and not to go into detail.

Mrs O asked me, 'Was that person called Mouni Sadhu, by any chance?', so I saw no point in denying it. I'm sure I got Mouni Sadhu into a lot of hot water spiritually, with Mrs Osborne stoking the fire beneath the cauldron, and I can't really say I'm sorry. Was I 'telling tales', the great crime of my early schooldays? Hardly. I was only answering a question.

When Mrs Osborne sat down and kept me company, she would always let me understand that there were plenty of other things she needed to do. I was slow to detect the element of pathos behind this, that despite her daily dynamism she was a widow struggling to cope. If I was lucky that Arunachala had sent me to her, perhaps there were some fringe benefits for her. She had someone new to cater for and talk to, and isn't distraction the core of consolation? I provided my fair share of that.

More than once she promised to make me rock cakes, which seemed a baffling ambition. If I was homesick for anything it wasn't rock cakes. But then it turned out that she wanted to make them for the same reason that riders who have been thrown want to get back on the horse, as a way of defying fate. She told me she was sorry to be weak, but she didn't feel up to making them just yet. 'Arthur was so fond of them,' she said, and her voice shook while a little tear came from her eye. Although I was sorry to see her distress, I was also relieved because it was proof that she wasn't a real witch. Witches can't cry – the literature is definite about that. As a child I had loved the witches in stories and had always wanted to meet one, but now I wasn't sure I wanted to take that last step.

Gross body, causal body, subtle body

One day the weather turned so cool it felt almost English. For once there was no sign of the sun. Rajah Manikkam put a shirt on and Mrs O even wore a jersey. Over breakfast she announced that someone had died – did I want to go to the funeral? I might find it instructive. Rajah Manikkam had got used to pushing the wheelchair, though I hadn't yet got used to his style of propelling it. He would bump up and down changes of level without slowing down, having no regard for the occupant of the wheelchair, someone who might have received enough jolts in his life already. If he had been employed to push round trolleys of ripe fruit instead, his employers would have insisted on more considerate driving, or the loss of revenue would have been alarming.

Rajah's pushing became more and more tentative, and he stopped some way short. To my surprise, Ganesh came to meet me and took over. He said I must forgive the superstitiousness of the locals. Rajah's caste buried their dead, although he and his wife were terrified of corpses, ghosts and spirits, while this was a Brahmin funeral.

When we arrived, the corpse was being put on the pyre. It was all a little undignified, and not just because I could see its shrunken willy. Dried cow-pats were placed over it and then they poured on some kerosene. I say 'poured' but that sounds too reverent. Kerosene was simply sloshed over the pyre and the body. The procedure was more than undignified, it was downright unfeeling, but then people are so solemn at Western funerals because nobody actually believes in the effectiveness of the ceremony. It was because the ceremony was trusted, here, that I got the impression of unceremoniousness. There was no emotion surplus to the event. The action was adequate to what it marked.

Ganesh gave me a lesson in last things. While the fire took hold, he explained the different colours of flame which issued from the body as it burned, and what they represented in spiritual terms. Vital airs were streaming from the sutures of the skull. The various sheaths of the physical envelope, the gross body, the causal body, the subtle body, were all returning to their source. All the different elements were rejoining the void. Absence was their destination. It was fascinating to hear his description, in the way that it is fascinating to hear anyone knowledgeable discoursing on a technical subject, even sport or cars.

It was a sort of treat, though an unsettling one, to be invited to look at a corpse in its fiery transition – with roasting smells beginning to break through the stink of kerosene – rather than being told to avert your eyes from the whole subject of death. Then quite abruptly Ganesh summoned Rajah Manikkam, who grasped the handles of the wheelchair and lurched off with me. All Ganesh would say was, 'You must leave now. The next part is not suitable for you to see.' We were back in the realm of taboos without explanations. Naturally being told that it wasn't suitable made me want to see it all the more, on the same principle governing the desirability of X-certificate films back in Britain. No history of disappointment could stop me hankering after the forbidden.

There is no arguing with the pusher of a wheelchair. I tried to feel privileged by what I had seen rather than tantalised by what I had not. As we left the scene a breath of wind brought thick black smoke our way. Ganesh coughed, my eyes streamed and my clothes held the smell of the various shrivelling sheaths for the rest of the day. I felt that these mild inconveniences had a symbolic aspect, though if I was receiving spiritual instruction it was slightly disheartening. Hadn't we been scrutinising death with exemplary calmness? Yet tears pursued us, even while we strove to rise above their causes.

Installed back on the verandah, I tried to find out from Mrs O about the local funeral rites, and specifically what I had missed by being hustled away from the pyre at a crucial juncture. I got the brush-off, with Mrs O sternly saying that if Ganesh had wanted me to know he would already have told me. She wasn't going to expose me to unauthorised knowledge herself. Ladies weren't allowed to attend such events anyway – though I'd like to have seen someone try to stop her if she had put her mind to it.

I tried to generalise my line of questioning. Was it a matter of caste who was buried (like Arthur, as I didn't quite say) and who was burned, or could people exercise their own discretion?

'Are you a journalist, John? Is that why you are here, to find out about the ways of the local people, these funny Indians?'

'No, Mrs Osborne, I'm here as a devotee, to practise self-enquiry.'

'Then stop asking questions that face outwards and turn your questioning inwards, since that is what it means to be a devotee.'

I had always known I would love Mrs Osborne, but I hadn't realised how long it would take. If there is no idea more fully grasped by the Indian Mind than 'scolding', then people like Mrs Osborne are largely responsible. The scolding must be done with love or it would be easy to reject, but love is not what registers first. The love only reveals itself over time. If it was so with Sister Heel at CRX – and wasn't she one of the great love-scolders of all time? – then it was true of Mrs Osborne also. Kuppu and Rajah Manikkam were veterans of long campaigns of such scolding, who had come through with their smiles intact.

In fact Mrs Osborne rather enjoyed filling me in about Tamil culture and traditions, as long as she didn't feel pressurised, as long as it was on her own terms. She told me that Tamil was an ancient and elegant language, with structural similarities to both Latin and Welsh, although modern speakers had rather an inferiority complex about it, feeling that it was a degenerate descendant of Sanskrit.

Tamil had contributed quite a number of words to English, including cheroot, catamaran (literally 'tied trees'), mango, pariah and mulligatawny, whose literal meaning is 'pepper water'. *Curry* was another gift, even if the British had firmly seized the word by the wrong end. *Kari* means a vegetable dish, not the spicing that made it so remarkable to a sheltered palate. She taught me the proper pronunciations of the original words, *curuTTu*, *kaTTa maram*, *kari*, *mang kay*, *paRaiyaar*, *miLagu taneer*.

A whole room of rain

At night rains would sometimes crash onto the roof – rain so intense that it required the rather Biblical plural form – and drown out all other sound. At night the mewing screams of the peacocks, both eerie and homely, were replaced by the shrieks of owls. No trace of the genteel quizzical Tu-Wit Tu-Woo of the British owl. These ones sounded as if they were being done to death.

There is something oddly comforting about the acoustics of a downpour, as long as wind plays no noticeable part. It seems to confer a privacy. It builds a whole room of rain, but the effect is necessarily spoiled if the body itself becomes wet. When the rain was at its most torrential I would sometimes be splashed a little from the side, which was rather exciting, but the rain never penetrated the roof of the verandah.

On Mrs Osborne's verandah I was further from being able to summon human help than I had ever been since I became ill. Yet I wasn't anxious or afraid, even when I was very far from sleep. I was beginning to understand what it meant to be the guest of the mountain. His hospitality was very subtle. Solitude, something of which I had gone short for so many years, was somehow the cornerstone of it. He didn't overwhelm me with attention.

One night I was woken by something pulling at my finger. It was a macacque, grey-furred and frenetic, of the sort I had seen everywhere in those parts, even in the ashram. While it yanked at my knuckles it looked at me with a pleading intelligence, as if it wanted to enlist me in some public-spirited rescue like the clever dogs in old films.

If so, it had chosen the wrong chap – Lassie, move on.

No help to be had at this address.

Try the next verandah along.

It was chattering at me, not angrily in the style of its species but urgently, with a pulse of meaning, and then it scampered away. It was only after the event (if it even was an event and not a dream) that it occurred to me as strange that its fur had been quite dry despite the downpour. Even so, this could be explained if it nested somehow under the roof of Mrs Osborne's verandah, sharing with me the hospitality of the mountain.

I asked Mrs O if there were any stories about the local monkeys and their behaviour. Unhesitatingly she said there were. 'Monkeys are famously fond of tamarind, and humans prize the fruit also, although it must be cooked for their consumption. In fact it is the crucial element in a true curry. Nevertheless the tree is considered unlucky. Consequently they have been nationalised and are government property. Individuals cannot own them, and are thereby spared the attendant bad luck. Instead they pay rent on the trees to the state government. This is ingenious, I feel, and shows Indian bureaucracy in a rare positive light.' I too was impressed by authorities which accepted the irrationality of their citizens, rather than plastering every wall with posters trying to dispel the superstition. Perhaps we in the U.K. should nationalise black cats and the bits of pavement under ladders.

I had even heard of tamarind, which was an important ingredient of Lea & Perrins Worcestershire Sauce, Marmite's acrid sister in the store cupboard. During my bed years, when every other bit of print in the house had been used up, I would get Mum to read me the labels of bottles from the bathroom and pantry. That's how I know that Dettol disinfectant is one-and-a-half times stronger than pure carbolic acid (Rideal-Walker Test).

'It happened,' Mrs O went on, 'that a Muslim who had rights over one such tree used a catapult to keep the monkeys away. Monkeys value the fruit of the tamarind even more than humans. Meaning only to frighten, he killed one – the monkey king. Did you not know that the monkeys have a king? Each group has its leader. The monkeys took the body to Ramana Maharshi, and asked him to bring their king back to life. Bhagavan always made sure, when feeding his followers, that the monkeys had their share. He spoke their language, as he spoke the language of every animal, but would not undertake resurrection. Instead he comforted them and assuaged their grief.

'A little later the Muslim became fevered, and rumours of a curse put on him by Bhagavan began to circulate. In fact he treated and cured the fever with an application of *vibhuti* – the ashes of Shiva. Unfortunately the rumours of a curse did not altogether die away, but nothing could have been further from Bhagavan's practice.

'As for the modern behaviour of monkeys, I am afraid that it is less elevated. Rooms at the ashram have to be locked and the windows closed, since otherwise monkeys sneak in and pilfer. It is even possible, since visitors' rooms are particularly liable to be ransacked, that some of the monkeys are currently human in form. They are perhaps laying the foundations for a future life, in which they will be fully . . .' – she looked around for the exact adjective, and for once the Polish sibilants I had learned to filter out couldn't be ignored – '*shimian*.' For a moment I thought she had used a Tamil word.

I wasn't sure what I made of these stories. If I had wanted a guru who talked to the animals I would probably have stuck with Dr Dolittle. Still, public figures can't control how they are perceived, and it made sense that the locals would assimilate Ramana Maharshi into their folk beliefs rather than absorb the full force of his teaching.

Mrs Osborne came in one morning and said that in the night she had seen a light burning on Arthur's grave. She seemed reassured rather than upset by this manifestation.

I was sceptical about the whole thing, so I asked her to wake me if it happened again. The following night I felt her tugging at me, more roughly than was necessary, and saying '*Get up!!*' Of course from a bed that low I needed help to rise. She wrestled me into an upright position and pointed me in the right direction, towards Arthur's grave. Rain was tipping down, but sure enough a steady light was visible even through the monsoon. I felt that I should be frightened, but my nervous system wouldn't play along. It stayed stubbornly serene.

One afternoon in the third week of my stay, while Kuppu was giving me a wash, tenderly pouring jugs of sun-warmed water over myself in the wheelchair, a strange couple of figures appeared at Mrs Osborne's house. There was a tall European man leaning on the shoulder of a little middle-aged Indian, being helped to walk. I had never seen the Indian before, but the European was oddly familiar.

His news was only himself

With a shock I recognised my brother Peter. He was very thin and weak, and when he spoke his voice was little more than a croak. 'I told you I'd see you in India, Jay,' he said. Kuppu ran off.

It was true that those had been Peter's last words to me before I set off on my travels – 'See you in India, Jay' – but I hadn't taken him seriously for a moment. He was an experienced traveller and a dab hand at finding cheap tickets. He was surprisingly disciplined about saving the money he earned as a waiter to fund the journeys he enjoyed. On the other hand, he'd never expressed an actual interest in India.

The look on my face gave him a transfusion of energy for just a few moments. He basked in the triumph of having delivered a major surprise, by the brilliantly simple strategy of keeping a promise I had taken for a joke, and then his body gave way and he needed to sit down. The closest thing to a seat was Arthur Osborne's commode, mercifully closed just then.

It would be going too far to compare Peter with the ancient Athenian who ran all the way from Marathon to break the news of victory. Peter's pace was crawling, his news was only himself, and his collapse was no more than a return of weakness, a convalescent setback.

It was strange that Mum should insist on having her hair turned white by worrying over me, when Peter was the one who liked to take risks. He was always flying off somewhere, and adding another country to his itinerary probably didn't strike him as unduly capricious.

He introduced his companion as Dalton, and said that Dalton had saved his life. It was only a slight exaggeration. What had happened was that Peter was at a railway station, feeling very ill, and simply fainted. He had been lucky not to fall onto the tracks, but the wallet containing all his money and also his passport did just that. He would have been in serious difficulties if Dalton had not had the kindness to pick up this stranger and look after him, as well as the presence of mind to climb down onto the track to retrieve the wallet before he took Peter to hospital.

By now Kuppu had re-appeared on the verandah, bringing with her Mrs Osborne and also Rajah Manikkam. Everyone fussed over these two odd visitors. Peter told the whole story of his experiences in an Indian hospital, while Dalton kept saying, in tones of joy, 'Please don't mention it. I only did what anyone would have done. It has been a supreme privilege to be of help to a traveller in difficulties.' Between sentences he frowned and pushed his lips forward, turning the impulse to preen into a solemn grimace.

Up to that moment I hadn't known that Mrs Osborne spoke German, though in talking about my university future (the one I didn't believe in) I had obviously told her of my familiarity with the language. Suddenly she was saying in my ear, in German, 'What's the quickest way of keeping your brother and getting rid of the other?' Mrs O could withhold a welcome in any number of languages. I was slightly shocked at the sharply defined limits to this enlightened being's sociability, but relieved that at least Peter was on the right side of them. It wasn't as if he had any real claim. I myself was perched on a narrow ledge of hospitality, and wasn't sure if I could get away with letting him bed down in the lee of the wheelchair.

Peter went on with the story, while Dalton listened with an expression of utter fascination, not because it was unfamiliar but because the part he played in it was so dazzling that he would never get used to it.

Vistas of regurgitated picnic

When Peter woke up in hospital he was violently sick, and then fell deeply asleep again. The next time he woke the light had changed and it was many hours later. His vomit was being cleared away, in the most meticulous manner. There could be no doubt about that. He closed his eyes and counted to a hundred. When he opened them, the clearing-up was still going on but no visible progress had been made.

The process was so slow because it was being carried out by ants. They worked tirelessly to carry away crusted particles from the vistas of regurgitated picnic spread out before them, while Peter watched between dozes. Watching those ants was his only entertainment, and no other creature did any cleaning. No one brought any food to replace what his body had rejected, even many hours after the event.

Every now and then a doctor would come in and administer an injection with great efficiency or at least great force. None of them addressed a word to him. Nurses he never saw, neither by day nor by night. He saw women who might have been nurses, but all they did was stride into the ward, as if to count the number of patients, and promptly walk out again. Indian nursing seemed to be restricted to this striding and counting, without any actual aspect of care.

Poor Peter was learning the hard way about the hospital etiquette of India. The maintenance of patients, their cleaning, feeding and being assisted to perform the bodily functions, was assumed to fall on family rather than professional staff. And Peter had no family. In Indian terms, the absence of any visible family made his whole existence seem tenuous. It was a moot point whether it was even worth the trouble to aid the recovery of so uncorroborated a being.

Peter having no family, Dalton stepped in to fill the vacancy. He acted as an interpreter between Peter and the doctors, he brought home-cooked food, he took upon himself humble tasks that would otherwise have been neglected. The doctors' attitude towards Peter changed, not because of anything that was said to them but because he was no longer dangling. He became worthy of humane treatment now that he had a context, however improvised and ramshackle. Sometimes Dalton's wife sat with Peter. Her English was broken at best but there was nothing broken about her smile.

And now Dalton was escorting my brother, recovered from the worst of his illness if not completely better, to join me at Mrs Osborne's, at Aruna Giri. I had learned by now that the name meant *Aruna Hill* – I was bivouacking on the foothills of enlightenment. But where would Peter be bivouacking? I started shooting glances of mute appeal at Mrs Osborne. I could almost feel them bouncing off the toughened hide of her psyche, and yet some subatomic particle of pleading may have found a flaw in her shielding.

By now Dalton had so consistently courted and refused our gratitude that I had begun to get just a whiff of an ulterior motive. Nothing material, just a faint spiritual fluffing-up of feathers. By saying so insistently that he had only done what anyone would have done, he gave us to understand nevertheless that his actions had a special status. He was setting an example by following one. His meekness was imitation of Christ.

I don't think it was an accident that Mrs O thanked him in studiously non-Christian terms, saying that he must have been inspired by the precepts of Bhagavan Sri Ramana. A shadow passed across Dalton's face, and he swallowed audibly. On features less transfigured by a righteous deed it would have been a scowl. No religion and no sect has any sort of monopoly on virtue, but they all love a squabble. Mrs O pressed home her advantage by offering to take him to the ashram for lunch. No rudeness could have got rid of the Good Samaritan more efficiently than this offer of food served under an alien blessing. Soon he took his leave of us, with a few last flourishes of humility.

Finally Mrs Osborne turned her attention to Peter and his needs. 'One brother is on my verandah, and the newcomer must also be accommodated. Young man, brother of John, name not yet vouchsafed to me, you are not I hope expecting a commode of your own? I cannot

provide the luxury of personal sanitation for all comers.' Make a commode available in exceptional circumstances, and everyone will feel
entitled to one.

Peter looked baffled, and sent me a glance that wondered about
Mrs O's mental capacity. I did my best to reassure him with a shake
of my head, and he politely answered No. He wasn't expecting to be
greeted with a commode, though he would appreciate the chance to
lie down. And he was called Peter.

'In that case I will offer you the hoshpitality of my roof,' said Mrs
O. Her roof was reached by a flight of stairs built on the outside of
the house, and Peter, who had stood for too long and was trembling
with fatigue even sitting down, set himself to climb them. He waved
away Rajah Manikkam's offers of help, but he had overestimated his
strength. He had to sit down part-way up to recover himself. For his
weakness I felt an acute pity which was entirely new and only half
welcome. How far we had both had to travel for me to see my younger
brother helpless in the body!

Just as Mrs O had boasted about the excellence of her verandah,
so now she sang the praises of her roof as a place of habitation. She
said there was a 'Goh-taa' up there, which she explained as a kind of
hut made of bamboos and palm-fronds. It sounded like a habitable
parasol. Peter's eyes were drooping even before she had finished wax-
ing lyrical about the shelter on top of her house. Peter may not have
slept for the whole of that day, but he didn't come down again to my
level. Kuppu carried up dainties to him. Mrs Osborne delivered some
sweet-lime juice in person, a great gesture of concern, well masked by
gruffness, from someone to whom stairs did not come easily.

The roof seemed to breathe out

I had time on the verandah that night to consider the impurity of
my emotions. I felt a certain amount of annoyance at seeing Peter in
this setting. Travelling to India had been my project, and truly a vast
project it was. To achieve my spiritual objective I had been forced to
mount something like a military campaign. Now Peter seemed to
be casually horning in on my territory. What was a pilgrimage for
me wasn't much more than a lark for him. In the night I examined

369

these feelings and repented of them. Peter's constitution was perhaps not as strong as I assumed. He had always suffered from sore throats, and had been prescribed many courses of antibiotics over the years by Flanny.

The next day Peter was already amazingly better. He had slept well. The resilience of youth had done the rest. He did say, though, that the roof seemed to breathe out during the night all the heat it had absorbed by day.

Peter still didn't have the strength to lift me down the three steps from the verandah, and that remained Rajah Manikkam's job. Once I was installed in the wheelchair Peter could manage me on the level. In fact he grasped the handles as if it had only been a minute since he had last let them go, and he powered me away from Aruna Giri. There was a definite feeling of nostalgia about being pushed by Peter again, even if he couldn't keep up that initial burst of energy. It was as if we were off exploring round Bourne End again, irresistibly drawn to the woods we thought were haunted.

I was torn between shyness about my spiritual false starts and eagerness to share my experiences, not sure whether to suggest a visit to the ashram or to keep that at least for myself. Peter had his own ideas anyway.

With a tourist's hands on the handles rather than a devotee's, the wheelchair began to find its way to more secular places. I had hardly noticed that a mundane town even shared the sacred geography.

Not that Peter would have cared to be labelled a tourist, nor even a traveller. He thought of himself as an explorer, and I had my own mild claim on that title. It was a significant expedition for me to go into Bourne End to buy a clandestine tube of depilatory cream from a chemist's, and here I was sleeping on a verandah, serenaded by the anguished voices of Indian owls.

The exploring we did after Peter arrived was of a particular kind. I swear that boy had a sixth sense for snacks. He could detect the smell of garlic frying from a mile away, and track it down infallibly, although Tamil Nadu was a mass of smoke and promiscuously pungent aromas, both secular and sacred. He was a teenager, after all, voracious and splendidly undiscriminating. He liked food that was meant to be eaten with the fingers – in that respect India suited him very well.

This prejudice against knife and fork may have had something to do with his work as a waiter. A day spent reverently cradling between a pair of spoons (the absurd rigmarole of 'silver service' which boosts waiters' earnings) the very potato croquette he had seen dropped by chef, picked up and dusted off, was reason enough for preferring food that wasn't turned into a fetish. He liked food snatched on the hoof, eaten without ceremony.

We discovered a stall selling little fried dumplings, crisp on the outside but soft inside, and took some home with us. Mrs Osborne told us they were called *vadas* – she pronounced the word to rhyme with 'larders' – and that we shouldn't eat too many of them. They were made from pounded lentils, onion, and curry leaves with a bit of cumin. And garlic of course. The scolding she gave us for buying them was a gentle one by her standards, no more than Force 2 on the Osborne Scale of reproach-rockets, a very mild flare.

I don't even know whether Mrs O's warnings had to do with the Hindu dietary laws which classify onion as a *darkness food*, or with common-sense ideas about the unhealthiness of frying. Whichever it was, we disregarded her. Whether she was speaking as a Hindu or as a moderate adult, she was wasting her breath. There weren't many areas of life where I could compete on equal terms with Peter, and eating snacks was one of them. I wasn't going to give it up.

On one of our early expeditions I felt the urgent need for a pee. Peter pulled the wheelchair onto some waste ground and helped me to stand sufficiently upright to accomplish my purpose. I became aware of voices behind me, and then of a boy standing in front of me, staring. He wasn't looking at my face but at the humble piece of plumbing currently in use. Soon he was joined by others, all equally mesmerised and calling to their fellows to see the show. Peter helped to zip me up as quickly as possible and we moved on, rather shaken by the extreme response to what we had imagined to be a very minor transgression.

The excrement forest

Hadn't I seen plenty of people peeing in the street in the previous weeks, without embarrassment or much in the way of discretion? But perhaps Europeans were barred from such casual customs. 'What was that all about, Jay?' Peter asked, bewildered, but I was as much in the dark as he was. The strange thing was that the crowd didn't seem angry or disapproving, just gripped by a strange fascination.

When we had arrived back at the verandah, there was no alternative but to ask Mrs Osborne. It was either that or cling to our ignorance. I decided on a cautious approach. 'Mrs Osborne, is it taboo in these parts to urinate in the open air?'

'Not at all. Males do this freely, though it is polite to step away from the road. What makes you say so?'

'Well, I had to go by the side of the road, and for some reason we gathered quite a crowd. They were all very excited, in fact they were talking at the tops of their voices.'

Mrs Osborne's flinty face took on a look of sly amusement. 'I think I can solve the mystery. It is certainly not that they are shocked by your use of the outdoors. In fact it is indoor excretion which is a puzzling novelty in Tamil culture. Even evacuation is performed out of doors, in designated places to which Tamil gives the charming name *pii kaadu*. Meaning *excrement forest*. No, these spectators who so unsettled you were taking the opportunity to satisfy a natural curiosity about your parts.'

This was worse than anything I could have imagined. 'What about my parts?'

'They are under the impression that Europeans are only furnished with white skin on the parts that show – hands and face. This would certainly explain the white man's unwillingness to bare his skin to the sun. If he did so – what is the phrase? – the jig would be up. By producing your private parts you have provided an *exsh*ellent opportunity for them to test this theory and perhaps even to settle some long-standing bets about the pigmentation of Western anatomy.' And she produced a decidedly dirty-sounding laugh. If she gave vent to merriment on any other occasion that summer I don't remember it.

As for whether her humiliating account of what we had experienced was truthful or not I really couldn't say, since for the rest of my visit I made myself ignore the demands of the bladder until I was safely in reach of that providential piece of sanitary furnishing, the late Arthur Osborne's commode, come all the way from Bangalore.

Peter's presence transformed my relationship with Kuppu. Before he arrived she and I had enjoyed a warm friendship, as free and easy as any relationship can be that is based on one person's perpetual need to be cleared up. Often she would speak to me in Tamil, starting every speech with 'Amma, Ammaaaa!' Eventually I realised from her gestures that she meant Mrs Osborne by this, but I couldn't follow the rest of what she was whispering so urgently.

I didn't think she was telling me that pale children kept arriving at Aruna Giri in pairs, hand in hand, the boys in shorts, the girls in pigtails, while nothing ever came out of the house except the smell of roast meat. But it was worth bearing in mind.

Soon after he arrived, Peter exercised his able-bodied privileges and went through my little suitcase. He came upon the tin of Cadbury's Roses, the chocolates deformed by the heat but still viable, and started doling them out to Kuppu – one every time she freshened me up, another every time she freshened the commode. This miniature bounty was enough to transform her attitude from obligingness to stark devotion. The tin was a little pharmacopœia, full of medicinal powers individually wrapped in cellophane and foil. I had to contemplate the possibility, not quite that Mum had been right all along when it came to my packing priorities, but that her hand had been guided by the guru she so resented when she had sneaked the tin back into my luggage.

Then one day we bought a dozen bangles from a stall in the town. They were ridiculously cheap – a rupee for the dozen, at a time when there were seventeen or eighteen rupees to the pound. That evening I gave them to Kuppu, thinking she should be compensated by something more lasting than chocolate for her willingness to cross caste lines and keep me clean. Her expression was unreadable as she grabbed the bangles. She simply disappeared, as if she was running for her life. She sprinted from the verandah, and we didn't see her for the rest of the day. I tried not to be put out by the absence of a show of thanks. 'It's probably not the custom here,' I told Peter uncertainly. 'She can't be offended, can she?'

'At least she didn't leave the bangles behind, unless . . . do you think it's unlucky to give jewellery here? Perhaps that's why they were so cheap.'

It was certainly a possibility, but there were others. 'Perhaps in this culture,' I wondered aloud, 'I just proposed to her?'

'A dozen bangles – that's twelve proposals! She must think you're head over heels.'

'I don't think we're ever going to understand how things work over here.'

'How are you going to explain her to Mum? Rather you than me. But at least she's pretty.'

'She's married to the gardener already, idiot.'

The next morning, early, there was an outburst of screeching from the gardener's hut, the one which Kuppu shared with Rajah Manikkam. Peter and I were quite alarmed, until Mrs Osborne came out of her house, rolling her eyes in exasperation, as she so often did when dealing with the locals.

'Are they frightened of something again, Mrs Osborne?'

'No, John, it's not that. Kuppu has invited all her friends round to show them her new treasures. I hope you haven't spoiled her for good with your lavishness.'

Spending one rupee on someone who made a hygienic life possible didn't seem like lavishness, exactly. But at least we had our explanation for her rapid exit when I handed over the bangles. Kuppu had legged it before I had a chance to change my mind.

The behaviour of dogs after death

Peter didn't react at all to Mrs Osborne as I would have expected. He hero-worshipped her more or less from the start. He said that wherever he was in the world, he would never be afraid of anything as long as Mrs Osborne was there. This from the fearless world traveller, who collapsed on Indian railway stations just to see what would happen! He wanted to ask her advice about things that were close to his heart, things (in fact) that we had never discussed with anyone.

First on the list was what happened in our room after Gipsy died. How was it that Gipsy had breathed by my bed as usual on the night after I took my Spanish oral in 1968, though she had been lethalised earlier in the day? It was as if she had forgotten she was dead. She even gave those sighs that dogs make in their sleep, aware even in unconsciousness of a job well done, the pack protected. The same thing happened every night for a week, and then the ghost breathing had simply stopped. Now it was time to take the mystery to Mrs Osborne.

She started nodding vigorously. Almost before we had finished explaining she said, 'It was burned into her *jiva* that she must look after you. That was her purpose in life. When her body died, she had to be sure you were all right without her. I have no doubt that she will be as devoted in the next life as she was in this. May her rebirths be few!'

This wasn't the wisdom I had come to India to find, but it was a pretty good explanation all the same, of something on the borderline – the melting film – between the 'real' and the Real.

Peter wanted to ask Mrs O about Mum's increasingly erratic behaviour. She would go very barmy over the smallest thing. A dropped piece of cheese could easily lead to a major row, with no end of screaming. Sometimes Mum would be shaking with rage. Peter and I dreaded the evenings when we ate fish, because that always seemed to trigger a mighty fight afterwards. The best we could do was anticipate trouble and shelter as best we could.

I very much didn't want to consult the Osborne oracle about the mundane miseries of the Cromers. She might have special insight into the behaviour of dogs after death, but she was not the guru I had come to India for. I had come to bask in the presence of Presence, not to have my questions answered. I wanted something that was equally far from a question and an answer.

I persuaded Peter that as a good Hindu Mrs Osborne would treat family itself as a source of distraction and entanglement. She really wasn't cut out for the rôle of agony aunt – of the sort that Mum so addictively sneered at in the *Daily Mirror*. At the hairdresser's in Bourne End village she would 'tidy up' the cluttered magazine table, and somehow the problem page would always fall open in front of her eyes.

Peter was slow to recover full strength after his illness. Much as he would have loved to, he still wasn't able to lift me up or down those three steps onto Mrs O's verandah. Rajah Manikkam continued to take care of that bit. Peter's stamina was poor, and he needed a lot of sleep, some of it in the day, so we rarely stayed out late. When we did, we went to the hut that Rajah Manikkam shared with Kuppu so that he could load me into the wheelchair, now that his giggling fits had been more or less exorcised.

One day Mrs Osborne announced that there was a famous Tamil singer giving a concert in the Temple that night. We should all go (though 'all' did not include Rajah Manikkam and Kuppu). The Temple was an extraordinary setting, and the concert should have something to offer both pilgrims and tourists. She looked at Peter and me when she said this, and for a moment I wondered if she was really registering a distinction in our status as travellers.

Mrs Osborne assumed that Peter would push me, once the new Rajah Manikkam (no longer hysterical) had lifted me off the verandah, but it turned out not to be quite so simple. Peter could manage the wheelchair perfectly well on the flat. But when we got to the Inner Temple, where the performance was to take place, we were confronted with some astoundingly imposing sacred architecture, an impossibly steep set of steps. 'Let's not bother,' I whispered to Peter, knowing he was incapable of any lifting – but then I remembered Burnham Grammar School and the lesson it taught. That access transcends questions of architecture.

Lightning strikes twice – of course it does! – and then twice more. Lightning strikes in a logarithmic progression of $2 \times 2 \times 2 \times 2 \times 2 \times 2 \times 2 \times 2 \times 2$ until there is nothing but the strobe-lightning that illuminates Shiva's dance. And where would Shiva more naturally put on a show than here, where the mountain, the god and the man step in and out of time in an ecstasy of mutual personification?

Very tentatively we approached those sheer steps, and then hands simply appeared from the crowd, each one grabbing a different part of the chair, collectively imparting a strong upward impulse. The wheelchair glided up the stairs as though it was on an escalator. The movement was eerily smooth. Often in the wheelchair I'm semi-consciously anxious that the person pushing will bump me up the kerb, clip my feet when executing a turn and so on, but on this occasion I felt utterly safe. Was it Elijah in the Bible who was carried up to Heaven in a chariot? I have to say I felt pretty blessed myself during that wheelchair ascension glide. I was on my own personal hovercraft, bobbing on jets of divine enablement, puffs of holy help.

For two years at Burnham School I had been lifted upstairs and downstairs by my fellows, and every time it felt like an act of faith, my life in their rowdy hands. Now a crowd of unknown Indians, none of whom individually could have pushed the wheelchair on level ground without mishap, was collectively wafting me upwards. I think I can say with confidence that this has been a life without short cuts – and yet there was this one short cut, this human thermal which uplifted me and me alone.

I wish similar miracles had happened on a regular basis since, with the result that I positively look forward to seeing a flight of steps in front of me. But once was enough. Then, after I had been magicked up all those stairs, Peter came and sat next to Mrs O. He knew her and felt safe near her. Next minute the entire audience, all seated of course on the floor, started undulating with turbulent movement like an ominous sea. I was puzzled and couldn't see why. Some of the faces in the audience wore expressions of polite distaste, others of actual horror.

Peter had gone to sit in the ladies' section. That was all it was. There was a rope down the middle of the audience, and men had to sit strictly on one side, ladies on the other. Eventually Mrs O worked out what the trouble was and had a word with Peter. She pointed him over to the other side of the rope. At first she was as baffled by the up-roar as I was – then she suddenly remembered the Indian convention against which none of us had meant to offend. Perhaps it was quite a time since she had attended this sort of event, or she had got used to being a living breach of the rules, and thought she could spread her cloak of exemption over Peter's shoulders also.

All this time I was sitting in the ladies' section myself, on the other side of Mrs O, and not a single eyebrow was raised. No questions were asked, no orders to relocate issued. The Temple's (surely?) very first wheelchair seemed to slip through the covenants of tradition and gender. I had a cloak of my own.

Worldly veins throbbed in smugness

What with the various palavers, the communal levitation of the wheelchair followed by the transgression against seating taboos, the performance itself made relatively little impression. The singer was plump and he sang with his eyes closed most of the time. If I hadn't known the songs were spiritual I wouldn't have guessed. At the time I wasn't attuned to Indian vocal style. I just didn't get it. The singer approached the note like a bee hovering in front of a flower, instead of fixing it cleanly as singers do in the Western tradition, pinning it like a butterfly onto a cork board.

I hadn't exactly lost my pang of resentment at Peter's arrival, my sense that a spiritual quest for one Cromer had turned into an adventure for two, but it had certainly gone underground. It was fun being able to explore more easily, even if it wasn't the sort of exploration I was here for. I hadn't been able to meditate since he came, not even for a second.

Then one morning Peter announced that he was leaving. When? After breakfast. One last bumper helping of wild fig *poriyal*, and he would be off. My face must have fallen. He said, 'I thought it was best just to go without making a fuss about it. Drawn-out partings are horrible – isn't that what Granny always says?' Well, yes it was, as a way of making a brusque turning on the heel seem like the height of consideration. 'And I'll see you at home, Jay, won't I?'

Well, of course he would, but it was still a shock. Perhaps subconsciously I had been anticipating having his help with the hundred hurdles of intercontinental travel on the way home.

Peter went up the stairs to the roof and came back with his case two minutes later. Either he had already packed or he was innocently showing off the impulsive efficiency of the able-bodied.

He had withdrawn emotionally by the time we came to say our goodbyes proper. This had been his habit since he was quite a little boy. When he was about ten or eleven Mum noticed a difference in the ritual of bedtime. She came to our beds as usual to give us a hug and a goodnight kiss. He would put his arms round her as usual and he said all the usual things, but he had gone to some other place inside himself, for protection. Peter coped with his great need to belong by choosing to be alone, even in company, and so when it came time to say goodbye he made sure that to all intents and purposes he had already left.

After Peter had gone, the wheelchair resumed its sacred ruts and the *vada* stall dwindled into the distance, until it was only a memory reeking of spice, carbohydrate and deep fat. I felt Peter's absence keenly. There's nothing people miss so much as a good excuse. As long as he was there, he could take the blame for my spiritual stalemate. I could forget that I hadn't been able to meditate before his arrival either, not for a second.

The weeks had flown by, and my time of pilgrimage was nearly over. What had been accomplished? I had spent many hours in the Old Hall but had made no progress in taming my mind. What if I had moved heaven and earth to make the journey, only to find that I wasn't mature enough to benefit from it? Sleepless nights were pretty much the rule for me in Tamil Nadu, what with the unravelling bed and the shrieking owls, but I had a few around that time that were distinctly bleak in terms of the thoughts that came to me and the lack of answers I had for them.

Finally I got around to reading the passage that Mrs Osborne had marked for me in *The Razor's Edge*. It filled me with an unholy rage that seedy, hateful Somerset Maugham (about whom admittedly I didn't know a great deal) had come to Tamil Nadu to do a little light research, and had approached Ramana Maharshi bearing a basket of fruit very much as he would have sent flowers to a London hostess. Having fallen into a highly convenient faint, he had been rewarded with Bhagavan's transforming hands – *darshan* upon unparalleled *darshan* – on his unworthy forehead, where worldly veins throbbed in smugness and lassitude. Concentrated Grace had been poured out over this . . . this *storyteller!* This storyteller with the ugly, turned-down lips. And all for the sake of some local colour, a whiff of the timeless East.

I on the other hand had made a pilgrimage to Tiruvannamalai in a body that would have been taxed by a visit to Canterbury, for no other purpose than to pay my respects to my guru, and been rewarded with an unquiet mind and a craving for lentil dumplings.

Then Mrs Osborne came out with another book of Maugham's. In her way she was quite a persistent director of studies. I had done the basic reading, and was to be rewarded with an advanced text. This second book was a collection of essays called *Points of View*, actually Maugham's last book, dating from the 1950s. What she wanted to show me was the piece called 'The Saint', which was a portrait of Ramana Maharshi written long after the meeting which had fed the silly fantasies of *The Razor's Edge*. Maugham had remembered Bhagavan over all those years, and considered him a great spiritual figure. His understanding of Hinduism seemed pretty erratic to me, and a guru is not a saint, but I had to admit that he hadn't entirely missed the point. That seemed to be my privilege.

I knew that I was supposed to become a Cambridge undergraduate that September, but apart from the kick of outdoing Dad (ignoble triumph, since his chance of university was scuppered by a world convulsion) it meant nothing to me. My life as I wanted it to be went only so far as this visit to Tamil Nadu, then it became incomprehensible. I hadn't foreseen having to come home. I had planned a sort of Indian rope trick all of my own. I would climb up into union with the guru and pull the rope ladder up after me. No one I knew could follow. I would simply disappear, leaving behind the return portion of my Air India ticket and a half-smile like the Cheshire Cat's, half-way up a tamarind tree.

Now I felt I was seeking self-realisation against the clock, and finding the necessary states of mind even harder to achieve. Of course 'achieve' gives the wrong impression. There can be no question of *making* something happen. That's what makes it so hard for the Western mind, and my mind was Western to its fingertips. I had built myself a carapace of brittle willpower, laboriously secreting the chitin from which an exoskeleton is constructed, and now I wanted it cracked open, pierced and raked by the loving beak of enlightenment.

Flakes of powdered glory

One afternoon I was in the Old Hall trying to meditate, and becoming aware as usual that my attention was skittering off in all directions. Then I noticed an old man brushing Bhagavan's couch. This must have been a particular privilege, since there was a small wooden fence round the couch. Clearly he had permission to pass inside. His eyes were milky with cataracts, and he worked from very close to the fabric, using a brush that was more like a fly whisk than a serious instrument of housework. Nevertheless he kept at it, drawing the little brush down the fabric in reverent strokes, turning the chore into a ritual of sustained attention. I found myself following his movements, fascinated. It took him the best part of an hour to brush the whole upper part of the couch, and then he started on the back, with the same slow meticulous pace. Then it was the turn of the underside, though he had to lie down at odd angles to reach every square inch. Then he turned his attention to the legs of the couch.

The little brush he held was only a step up from the imaginary one which Granny had told me to use as a child to beguile insomnia, patiently cleaning the cells of a beehive which was no less imaginary.

I have to say that at the end of this old man's prodigious grooming the couch looked exactly the same as it had at the beginning. It wasn't as if anyone was going to sit on it anyway. It was no more than a stand for a portrait, and a prop from a long-ago photo session. If anyone had asked to take the couch away Ramana Maharshi would very likely have said yes, just as he had with the tiger skin. Nevertheless I was very struck by the devotion of the man with the little brush. From the eerily patient way that he coaxed notional dust from that couch, you would think that it was covered in the most fragile living tissue, like the flakes of powdered glory that make up a butterfly's wing.

It was only afterwards that I realised how far I had fallen from my own hopes of pilgrimage. The point of pressurising Dad into getting the airline ticket, the whole idea of coming all this way, was to take possession of my spiritual life, not to be impressed by someone else's. I was estranged from my own devotion. I had failed to establish a primary connection with either of the complementary entities which fed the hunger of so many, the mountain and the ashram. I was turning into a sort of spiritual parasite. I had less of a real relationship with Ramana Maharshi now that I was spending time in rooms that his body had occupied, and spending every day with people who had met him, than when I had been stuck at home in Bourne End, with no stronger inspiration than a book borrowed from the local library.

Ganesh no longer did me the honour of pushing the wheelchair from Aruna Giri to the ashram. Rajah Manikkam delivered me to the gate, and then I would be ferried to the appropriate room by an American devotee who had a sonorous, almost mantra-worthy name: Caylor Truman Wadlington. Of course Ganesh had a lot to do in terms of ashram admin, and he never saw me without giving me his full smile and bidding me once again welcome. But I was rather nostalgic for the good old days earlier in my visit to India, before we had begun to be friendly. Then the obstacles to spiritual progress seemed reassuringly external. Now the resistance was pretty clearly coming from inside me. In an analogy which Ramana Maharshi took from the movies (a particularly rich source of teaching for him), if while you are watching a film a gigantic flickering hair obscures the heroine's profile, it is futile to attempt to dislodge the monster fibre from the back wall of the cinema. It is of normal size and inside the projector. Inside you, who project so unrelentingly.

In the last week of my stay, Mrs Osborne came up with an inventive solution to one aspect of my impasse, relating specifically to *pradakshina*. Since it wasn't possible to go round the mountain under my own steam in the prescribed manner, I should be assisted to climb it. She said, 'You may not be able to climb Arunachala yourself, but that is no reason for you not to be as high up as we can possibly get you. Not as high as Brahma, I dare say, but high enough to take a small visitor's breath away.'

The story goes that Vishnu and Brahma were once quarrelling over which was the greater, until Shiva was brought in to settle the question. He appeared as an infinite column of fire, a *tejolingam*, and challenged the rival gods to find its upper or lower extremity. Vishnu became a boar and burrowed down in search of the base, while Brahma became a swan and soared up in search of the summit. Brahma tried to cheat (he caught a falling flower and claimed to have picked it on the summit) and consequently Vishnu won. The column of fire was too bright to be looked at, so in consideration of the limitations of human vision, Shiva manifested himself instead as Arunachala, on the same spot. It's the sort of lively story that monotheism rules out of bounds. I do like a large cast of characters, even if they're only there on the stage, all singing, all dancing, to tell me that existence is one and indivisible.

There may have been some religious symbolism in Mrs O's suggestion. Why are there many faiths, when there is only one truth? The mountain analogy again, with many routes to the summit, over different types of terrain. Ramana Maharshi's way has always been considered as a sort of direct ascent of a precipice, as simple as it is difficult. This accounts for the idea (mistaken, I'm sure) that the task is easier with lesser gurus – hence for instance, Raghu's family's adherence to Paramahamsa Yogananda. The *vichara* path being too 'high', too 'exalted', a 'lower path' is chosen until the disciple is ready. I'm truly sorry, but bollocks! It isn't presumption that chooses the direct approach, it's faith.

There's an English climber called George Mallory who disappeared on Everest in 1924. His body has never been found, and it isn't clear whether he got to the top or not. His is the famous remark about wanting to climb Everest 'because it's "there".' He did a celebrated bit of climbing in Wales once, nipping down a sheer rock face by the most direct route to retrieve his pipe, which he'd forgotten. And for exactly the same reason: because it was 'there', and he was desperate for a soothing puff of Mayan tobacco.

The climb is written up in all the books as Mallory's Pipe, the descent of a sheer face undertaken in fading light in front of witnesses, with a note which adds, 'This is impossible.'

Come to that, it's impossible for an Indian boy mentally to live through his own death and to understand that it is nothing, but it had happened, which was why I was here. And it was also 'impossible' for a severely disabled twenty-year-old from Buckinghamshire to be spending a month as a guest of the holy mountain, but here I was. Once you enter the realm of the impossible, every possibility is equally likely.

The only thing which really did seem to be impossible was for me to find the concentration necessary to meditate – or I suppose the disconcentration. Willpower must step back from the event. I couldn't make that direct descent into the Self, lacking the aplomb of a tweeded mountaineering genius, able to nip down and grab his favourite briar without giving it a thought.

The privileges of luggage

Mrs Osborne arranged for two men to take me up Arunachala. She called them 'coolies'. I suppose she must have paid them for their labour, though I didn't think of that at the time. One of them knelt down and carried me in a sort of fireman's lift. As he clambered up the mountain I had an excellent view of his bobbing rippling muscly back as I looked down, and if I managed to raise my sights a little I could see not where I was going, which was a total mystery, but where I had been. Maybe it was just as well, since the rocky ground dropped away so rapidly it took my breath with it. I could also glimpse the second coolie lithely ascending, carrying the folded wheelchair on his head with no apparent effort.

Those two coolies were the only Indians I met in Tiruvannamalai who didn't smile at any time. They hardly even looked at me. From their point of view I suppose I was freight rather than person, and you don't smile at a parcel. I didn't mind. I had understood on trains between Bourne End, Burnham and Slough the compensating privileges of being defined as luggage. Freight doesn't ogle the porter, no one imagines such a thing is possible, and so I was free to let my gaze rove over their sinewy bodies, heated by the sun, cooled by the outflow of sharp sweat. The beauty of one body was visual, it glistened under my eye, while the other was tactile. It glowed with heat and effort as it carried me. And if I was treating them as less than fully human, then I could honestly say that I had pinched the idea from them.

I don't know exactly what instructions the coolies had had from Mrs Osborne, but eventually they settled me on a suitable rocky ledge. They unfolded the chair and put me in it, without cosseting but with perfect efficiency. They left me pointing towards the peak rather than downhill. The only flourish was that one of them produced a handkerchief, shook it out and then draped it over my head to keep the sun off. This was clearly something that Mrs Osborne had stipulated, and I had time to notice, as the handkerchief was shaken out, the initials A. O. embroidered in red on a corner. Alpha and Omega? Arunachala Om? No, I was being shaded by Arthur Osborne's handkerchief, an honour that made me feel foolish. Commode and hanky – the late Arthur was giving me the works. The coolies even knotted the corners to keep it in place, a technique which I had always assumed evolved only once in the whole of human history and geography, among English holidaymakers at seaside resorts.

I expected these paid companions to stay while I contemplated the mountain, chatting quietly perhaps, sharing a beedie, idling like taxis between fares. Mrs Osborne's instructions had been delivered in what sounded like very peppery Tamil, but of course I couldn't really understand a word of it. I was busy wondering whether her Polish accent was as strong in other languages as it was in English, and if so, how they managed to make head or tail of it.

When I looked round the 'coolies' had disappeared. There wasn't anything supernatural, I don't think, about their vanishing. Looking round isn't something I can do in a moment – I have to wriggle round first. If they hadn't been absorbed directly back into the mountain, according to the etiquette for numinous emanations, then they had clambered down its sides as spryly as they had clambered up.

I was now in direct communion with Arunachala, while the ground dropped away behind me. There was nothing between me and the mountain. In a sense I had been riding on his back for weeks, but this was different. His eye was upon me, and though the experience was very unlike being Frodo Baggins writhing beneath the stare of Sauron it wasn't exactly comfortable. Arunachala was unhostile, still residually hostly, but not (at this altitude) particularly indulgent. All my excuses went up in smoke under that gaze, like sweet wrappers on a bonfire.

Why was I here?

One answer would be that I had followed a trail from a library book to a crazy old lady with a handy verandah, but that wasn't what the mountain meant. I tried one more time to concentrate, while the sweat started to trickle down my face. Enlightenment felt like the onset of heatstroke.

I had never to my knowledge dreamed of the mountain or the god (though who's to say – how do you know when you're dreaming of white light?), but I had experienced a puzzling dream about the man, about Ramana Maharshi. This was during my time at High Wycombe Technical College, but it was a dream entirely free of the daily grit whose rubbing sets off the nacreous secretion we call dreaming – the quotidian residues. Ramana Maharshi and I were sitting on a patch of sand, whether an area of desert or a specially contrived expanse I couldn't tell, together with an Arab whom I didn't recognise. I listened attentively to what Bhagavan was saying, but after a little while the Arab walked off in disgust, kicking sand towards us as he went.

At this Ramana Maharshi turned to me and said, 'I would rather have your love than your anger.' I woke up with a great sense of injustice, since I had been attending very humbly and hadn't been the one who had kicked up all the fuss.

It took Mrs Osborne to point out the obvious – that since it was my dream, the Arab was as much me as 'I' was. The anger displaced onto him was really mine. At some level I was seething with resentment at my need of a guru. An understandable feeling, of course, since I was so comprehensively dependent in other areas, but hard to take into your heart (the only place where things can be fully owned and finally shed).

Gruffly Mrs O consoled me, pummelling antiseptic creams into the bruise which her unwelcome insight had made. 'Progress is an illusion, my dear John. As is the absence of progress.' By this time I was so used to her way with sibilants that I would only have noticed if the hissing stopped. These strange noises were like the multifarious knocks and rattles of an old car, and oddly reassuring. Only sudden silent running would announce the imminence of collapse.

'It is disheartening for you, I know. You have brought your little radio to a new place,' she would say, 'where there is a terribly powerful transmitter. The strong signal overwhelms your little apparatus, that is all.'

My little apparatus overwhelmed

Ramana Maharshi was very fond of taking parables from the wireless as well as that other high technology of his day, the cinema. He used the example of the radio (which a devotee had turned on, rather too loud) to show that there is no time and no space – here after all is a little box that says, perfectly truthfully, 'Hello, this is Hyderabad' one minute and 'Hello, Bangalore here' the next. Yet it never moves an inch.

I can't say I was much consoled by this explanation. If my little apparatus was overwhelmed, what was I supposed to do about it?

'Perhaps your little radio will tune itself to the new signal. You must learn patience from the mountain.'

I wondered if the problem was with my mantra, my regulation-issue beginner's-level *Om-Mane-Padme-Om*, so I asked her what she used to help her meditate. She seemed rather shocked by so personal a question. It was as if I had asked for the loan of some underwear. 'If you need a new mantra one will be given to you in time, but you cannot simply borrow one from someone else on the Path.' Then she relented a little. 'You might try *Arunachala Siva* or simply *Om*. Perhaps one of those will help.' In practice I didn't get anywhere with either, and fell back on my old standby. It seemed silly to think that a mantra would need converting to cope with the vagaries of a foreign current, like an electric shaver.

Mrs Osborne must have realised that my distress was real. She unbent a bit. 'It is sometimes easier for children to give full attention than adults. My daughter Catherine – Katya – was the first of any of us to enter Bhagavan's presence, carrying the customary basket of fruit. He indicated the low table on which such things were put, but she misunderstood and hopped up there herself, cradling the basket.

'The disciples nudged each other and said that she was making an offering of herself to Bhagavan. Certainly she had no difficulty communicating with him. You yourself are no longer a child, but you are younger than I was when I came here, younger also than Arthur.

'When he came here at the end of the war, he experienced similar difficulties to yours. He said that the presence of Bhagavan was less real to him than the photograph which had given him such strength and serenity during the years of his internment.'

I perked up no end at this precedent. 'So it's a sort of test?'

'It is no sort of test. There are no tests. What is it that would be tested? It is a stage merely.' I must have looked crushed all over again, and her consoling instincts gained ascendancy. 'A schoolfriend of Ramana Maharshi, visiting him here, once said, "If you stay with the *Jñani* he gives you your cloth ready woven" – meaning that you don't have to find the thread and weave it yourself, as you do with other gurus. But that is not necessarily the case for everyone. Each has his path, but the mountain is the same goal for all.'

Drowsing beneath my folkloric hanky, I began to think that the mountain had taken his eye off me. The strangest aspect of my pilgrimage was that Arunachala, in Britain so absolutely steady a signal source, became when I was in such close proximity oddly inconstant.

Arunachala didn't altogether compel my reverence as I had assumed in advance. Ramana Maharshi wrote in an evocation of the mountain that was himself, 'Though in fact fiery, my lack-lustre appearance as a hill on this spot is an effect of grace and loving solicitude for the maintenance of the world.'

There were times when Arunachala really did look lack-lustre to me, just one more mountain, fit subject for a holiday postcard, to be sent to those people who are owed holiday postcards. Sometimes Arunachala could have been any hill that had seized my imagination when I read about it – the Wrekin, say, in the poems of *A Shropshire Lad*.

At this point it would be hard to say that I was even trying to meditate. I was engaged in a rêverie which was the exact opposite of meditation, perversely imagining the Wrekin in mid-Shropshire instead of Arunachala in mid-Tamil Nadu. Behind closed eyes I was trying to subtract from my surroundings the Indian smells, baked earth, flower perfume, and spice, not to mention the Indian heat, and to replace them with genteel transient fragrances and parochial bird-song. Insipid scents and tweetings.

I tried to imagine church bells in a peal, the jangling overlapping changes which somehow spell out the opposite – changelessness. The acoustical shimmering which is the closest our ears can come to hearing eternity. It's even possible that I was feeling homesick, though I was conjuring up a synthetic landscape rather than anything I actually knew.

It seemed to me that I could really hear bells, but not church bells – cowbells. I opened my eyes and saw, some distance away, a cowherd boy with some cattle. One of the cows wasn't tethered and seemed to be free to wander where it pleased. It also seemed to see me, and as if acting from a sociable impulse it ambled my way. The bell round its neck was massive and made of some dully shining metal. It didn't seem scared or suspicious of the wheelchair, as most livestock is (many pets have the same mistrust).

Where was the cowherd boy now? Shouldn't he be rushing up to drive his charge back towards its fellows, using a stick that would make me wince in sympathy but also thank him in my heart? I couldn't see him. With a neck properly equipped with rotational and stretching powers, I might have had a better chance of getting a glimpse, but there it was. All told I miss quite a bit from the lack of play in my neck.

On the other hand, if I had been in possession of a working neck I wouldn't have been in India in the first place, I'd have taken so different a path that the two Johns, the supple and the stiff, would long since have been invisible to each other.

The cow came nearer and nearer. I became increasingly conscious of the largeness of the cow and the smallness of me. It wasn't a sleek prize-winning English cow, but it wasn't the scrawny animal I was half-expecting as the norm in India. Nor did this animal resemble the cow in Mrs Osborne's garden, which gave us milk that could never go off.

This cow was pure white except for a streak of shit on its flank. It was strongly built, with something that was almost a hump behind its shoulder. As it came close it seemed to be bigger than any normal cow could possibly be, but then I'm not used to the looming of cattle. I had an almost intoxicating sense of my own littleness, a thrill of insignificance.

At the same time I was highly aware of the precariousness of my position. As the cow came closer I started to talk to it, saying, 'Nice cow' or some such absurdity, hoping madly that it wasn't going to butt the chair or interfere with me in any way. I tried to remember whether the brakes were on, though I knew how little difference it would make if the huge animal once made physical contact. I would either be nudged off the chair or nudged off the mountain.

The cow slowed down as it approached me but didn't actually stop. She came nearer and nearer, her eyes both empty and searching, bending her head down low in a way that didn't look particularly submissive. In an obscene reflex I could smell the meatiness of her. I suppose we all harbour some such atavistic instinct, even when as individuals we have learned to find animals' lives delicious, and not their deaths.

The cow came so near that I couldn't see both her eyes at once. There was just enough play in my neck for me to turn the angle necessary to focus on one and then the other. Her massive jaw moved to the side chewingly, and she unrolled her breath in front of me like a carpet of grasses. She nudged even further forward, so that her breath rolled over me in a cuddy plume. Eventually I was touching her nose, and speaking to her as evenly as I could. If I say I was touching her nose, it must be understood that the action was hers not mine – she presented her nose to my hand.

My terror was that she was going to reach out to me with her tongue. As long as she kept it in her mouth I could contemplate her with a sort of equanimity, under my fear. Having refused my share of a thousand Sunday roasts, I was in physical danger but not shamed. If she showed her tongue I would be morally annihilated, having eaten tongue, processed and jellied, in ignorant enjoyment as a bedridden boy. How was I supposed to live with myself after that, if she reached out that wet muscle and licked me with it? My whole pilgrimage was being dominated by the bodily not the spiritual, and by cows' bodies at that, cows and their tongues, cows in the city and cows on the mountain.

I found myself crooning, 'Avatar of the cow goddess' – in my panic I'd forgotten precisely which Hindu deity took bovine form – 'Emanation of Arunachala . . .' over and over again. I was also murmuring 'Pax, pax,' as if this was a playground dispute that could be resolved by surrender. In confrontations with cattle Pax is not an effective spell, whether you're a matador impaled in his suit of lights, repenting his cruelty with sobs of blood, or a neophyte devotee whose bluff has been called, discovering that the mountain he has adored from afar is numinous beyond all reckoning.

Locking horns with Lakshmi

I was slow to realise that this was a supernatural encounter. The mountain had given up on the project of addressing me directly and had lowered himself to incarnation, and a sort of ruminant ventriloquism. Contact on a level I could understand. My abilities had been scrutinised and revised downwards, though I think without disapproval. I have observed a similar procedure in a Chinese restaurant, when the management has smilingly brought knife and fork, without being asked, to rescue a patron defeated by chopsticks.

After that the divine cow started showing signs of what I can only call affection, rubbing and pushing lightly against me. They were slight movements for a cow, but I was rocked alarmingly by them. I had as much to fear from a friendly cow as from a mad bull, not from a charge but the delicate movement that would crush me. If all this had happened down in the plain, with the cowherd nearby, watching with an indulgent smile, I would have been in *svarga* – in heaven – or at least in the Indian equivalent of Whipsnade (remembering the time a snake had handled me there), but here I was in real danger and a real state.

Her next step was to turn her head. One huge horn came down and to the side, so that it went through the wheelchair arm-piece on the left, with a smooth grinding noise as solid bone slid on hollow metal. Another small movement and she had manœuvred her left horn under the right arm-piece, so that her head ended up in the centre of the chair's rotational axis. Precisely where a cow would position itself if it wanted to use its mighty neck muscles, and the superbly articulated bones they powered, to give my wheelchair an apocalyptic flick. The cow's friendliness continued, but I was filled with terror and awe. In a perfectly friendly way, she could have lifted her head straight up, in creaturely greeting, and the chair would either have been lifted up bodily, taking me with it, or tipped backwards off the mountain.

This wasn't a cosy creature out of A. A. Milne making butter for the royal slice of bread, this was a Hindu divinity. It was terrifying. This wasn't Daisy, this was – it came to me – Lakshmi. I was locking horns with Lakshmi. Her cud-breath engulfed me. There was a long string of saliva hanging from her mouth, a glutinous rope, but I could easily believe it would hang there for a thousand years without falling.

My body entered a state of sacred shock. I was almost weeping, and when I tried to speak to this presence, no sound came out. In fact they were all here, or at least seven out of the eight: horripilation, trembling, tears, faltering of the voice, perspiration, inability to move, holy devastation. All the physical signs of the presence of God, everything that makes up what Hindus call *nirvikalpa samadhi*. I can't vouch for the changing of my body colour in any real way, but it seems hardly likely that I would stay the same colour when every other aspect and sensation was turned upside down.

Of course any one of the signs, and even whole groups of them, could be explained by my situation. At the mercy of an immense and capricious ruminant. On a mountain that I claimed as my spiritual home, but was thousands of miles from home by every other definition. But there was no doubt in my mind, as I gazed at her, that I was in the presence of Lakshmi. She turned her head a little, so that only one eye remained in my field of vision. That eye was a glazed bulge in which all contradictions were collapsed, a radiant absence and a probing vacuum.

This turning of the head, though smoothly executed, brought a huge force to bear on the wheelchair. If it hadn't been exactly in line with the axle the chair would have been tipped over, and even so the framework juddered and one wheel lifted from the ground.

Mechanistic Western thinking was all at sea in this terrain, but still it went on offering the incantation which calls itself analysis of events. What it told me was that horn and arm-piece had meshed as a result of a series of moves on the divine cow's part. The only way the knot could be undone without capsizing me was if the same sequence was performed in reverse, lateral actions with no component of movement either forward or backwards, passes as precise as the ones required to knit together the kinked silver loops of Patrick Savage's fidelity ring in the library of Burnham Grammar School. Time would have to go backwards, the film be shown in reverse. Otherwise I would shortly be united with the mountain in a crash of silence.

If I could just have banished the final particle of fear, the ego might have melted for good, dissolving into Arunachala just as Parvati did, in the story told to me on my first walk round the mountain. I wouldn't necessarily have died, although that isn't out of the question. But the ego would certainly have burned away in its current form, persisting only as a wraith, the fabled moon in the daytime. A purely executive residue with no agenda of its own, directing my life without getting in its way, a policeman on point duty with no powers of arrest.

For a long moment, the Cow on the Mountain stayed poised in entanglement with the wheelchair. Then she gently disengaged her horns, as if she knew exactly what she was doing. The film was run backwards frame by frame, and the raised wheel renewed its contact with the ground. At this point there was a subtle molecular change in the cow's gaze. After a few moments it became clear that she was baffled by her surroundings. It wasn't hard to see her as an audience member suddenly finding herself on stage at a hypnotism show, with no memory of what has been said or done while under the influence, unreassured by the welling of applause. She was definitely a cow at this point, not a deity, and as a cow she wandered off out of my line of sight.

I was in a state somewhere between revelation and shell-shock. I remember nothing about the descent from the mountain. I assume the coolies rematerialised and carried me and the wheelchair down as briskly as they carried us up, but there is nothing in my memory to vouch for that. If I had floated down under my own power or been lowered smoothly by thousands of hands appearing out of nowhere, I hope I would remember, but I can't be certain even so.

The true mystical temperament is a well fed from springs beneath, indifferent to drought or flooding. My own state at this point was rather different – a bath so overfilled that even dropping the soap would make it slop over. The moment I had recovered my presence of mind I had to blab to somebody about the cow on the mountain. I couldn't keep the miraculous to myself. I had to parade it. And even though I was always a little afraid of her, it was Lucia Osborne I was going to tell. The witch in the white sari had a knack of drawing the strangest confessions into her gnarled and Polish ears.

She asked for a clear description of the cow, and nodded as I passed on everything that I could remember. I hesitated to mention the streak of shit on her flank, but this rather lowly detail didn't make her stop nodding. 'This is certainly a photism, a visual manifestation of Lakshmi the goddess, in fact of course – though the correspondence is not exact – of Lakshmi the disciple, an extraordinary cow who achieved enlightenment on June 18th, 1948.' I didn't quite see how Mrs Osborne could be so definite, but this was a lady pickled in certainties who could go for years without saying 'perhaps'. I would have liked to quarrel with that rather gossamer word *photism*, since the massive presence of the cow, the overwhelming likelihood that it would send me flying, were not things registered by the eye alone.

'We have no choice but to call her a disciple of Bhagavan. Even as a calf she would come and place her head at his feet. That was before I came here, of course, but I was there on the day that Sri Bhagavan held her head in his hands when she was in the throes of her death. He watched over her almost as he had done with his own mother when she shed her body. Her *samadhi* is at the ashram.'

Samadhi meaning resting-place. By etymology a putting together, joining, completion, and so either the state of bliss or a place of rest. The actual cow festival is on January 15th, but I didn't think Lakshmi should be made to wait. Taking a cue from Lewis Carroll, I would celebrate her unbirthday. Mrs Osborne helped me prepare a *puja* for Lakshmi. *Puja* is I suppose the elementary form of worship in Hinduism. Chanting is more abstract, and meditation still more so. That's the order in which they are ranked for the benefit of those who think in terms of progression. But physical *puja* has its place, there's no doubt about that.

Mrs Osborne gave me guidance about the offering I should make: a miniature meal for the god, laid out on a banana-leaf. A few grains of rice, a little pile of vegetables, a dab of *sambhar*. Mountain banana was particularly pleasing to the Lakshmi she knew, she said, the historical one. This foreshortened feast appealed to many deep memories – it was a snack of savoury reminiscence in itself. I remembered Mum's doctrine that every forkful I put in my mouth should ideally contain each element of what was on the plate, the meal in microcosm.

We discussed whether the offering should be taken to the shrine in the ashram. Eventually we decided that it should be fed to an actual cow. Mrs O brought out an image of Lakshmi onto the verandah for my benefit. An image wasn't strictly necessary, since the real shrine is in your heart. We waved joss-sticks around – always a pleasure in its own right. Then we entrusted the little meal to Rajah Manikkam, who took it away and fed it to the cow of his choice, a white cow if he could find one, shit-streak not required.

Bloated with a pilgrim's blood

At night I pondered the difficulty of my quest and prayed for softness in that awful bed. My compassion for the mosquitoes biting my toes had lasted all of a day. I had given them a good night's feed, with a willing heart, but enough was enough. There's such a thing as taking liberties. After that, I was all in favour of squashing them and bother the karma. I even wondered if we could get hold of some poison somehow. Wouldn't the mosquitoes be likely to be reborn in better lives, rewarded for dying while bloated with a pilgrim's blood?

Then when Peter came, I acquired a secret weapon in the fight for a good night's sleep. A dog followed us home from the market. We fed it on *vada* scraps and anything else that came to hand. It wasn't a house dog but a street dog, wily and craven. Peter had named him Yogi Bear, after the cartoon character, a sweetly clueless creature to whom he bore no resemblance whatever. I'm sure Peter really chose the name out of fond mockery of my religion, but it stuck even after he had gone.

The dog was skinny, he was fidgety and his fur was as coarse as a wire brush, but he was an absolute godsend in the night. I could lean on him just enough to change the position of my spine, and get a little relief from the ordeal of the bed. In the mornings he would make himself scarce, though I expect Kuppu had spotted him and was turning a blind eye.

Even with the dog in place my sleep was fitful, and I would take in impressions which fully registered only later. Sleep is a mist subject to intermittent thinning, with occasional patches of clear visibility. So I was dimly aware that in the early hours Mrs Osborne had crept out onto the verandah, carrying a kerosene lamp of some sort, and crept away again. It can't have been long after three. Time for Lucia's morning meditation, before the abrupt arrival of dawn stacked the odds against inwardness. Like any good hostess she was quietly making sure that all was well with her guest. Did I have everything I needed?

Then she crept back holding something just out of sight. In my half-sleep I registered that this hunchback was suddenly growing very tall, and then that she had produced a very nasty-looking stick. Without a word she brought it cracking down on the dog, on my innocent bedmate and physiotherapy cushion. Who yelped and ran. I was shocked, frightened and in my bleary-eyed way actually very angry that this vegetarian devotee of a religion of respect for all creation should harbour such a core of rage and cruelty. What sort of person gets up early to meditate and casually brutalises an animal before she starts?

395

This demonic incarnation of Mrs Osborne gave a nod of satisfaction and returned to the house, so that the conversation which I so badly needed to have with her about how she squared such behaviour with her faith had to wait till morning.

After those few hours' delay, though, I felt awkward raising the subject, which was dishonourable and absurd. It wasn't that my feelings had eased, but the good manners in which I had been brought up intervened, and I was very aware of feeling rude and disobliging. I gave less good an account of myself in the argument than I should have. I don't think I was ever fully rested during the entire five weeks of my stay in India, but that morning broken sleep and emotional upset conspired to make me ineffective.

I pleaded that the dog was helping me sleep, and got the usual reply of *Nonshenshe*, and the familiar boast of how well she slept, despite her age, on a bare floor. I tried to explain one more time that our situations were different, but she obviously concluded that I was a softy. Even after the initial conjuring of the bed by her and Rajah Manikkam I hadn't been satisfied – the drawback of that kind of bed being that the knots loosen unevenly, so that a few stay taut and dig into you while the others start to lower you to the ground. More than once she and the gardener had made adjustments, winding tapes round the bed to reinforce the slackened ropes and hold them in place.

I had no alternative but to bring up matters of doctrine. 'Didn't Bhagavan warn us never to abuse animals round Arunachala, since they might be *siddhas* in animal form?'

'You forget, John, that I have seen that scabby dog hanging around and scratching itself for months. A siddha might take the form of a dog' – and here her delivery became positively venomous – 'but would certainly be immune to *fleas*. On the other hand it might very well be a demon.' She regarded the matter as closed, and moved away before I could remind her that Bhagavan himself in states of extreme inwardness had been infested with worse things than fleas – his flesh had been eaten by ants.

It points to my oddly intermediate state of mind that summer that I could accept a cow on the mountainside being a goddess, but not a dog on the verandah being a demon.

I didn't mention that Peter had adopted the dog (or he had adopted Peter), that we had fed him on *vada* scraps and kept him out of sight. That we had named him in honour of an American cartoon. The scrawny dog with the sidelong grin never came back, and nor did my full fondness for Mrs Osborne. I asked myself what Peter would have made of her cruelty. Could he have hung on to his dependence on Mrs O, his sense that he was safe with her, if he had seen her as I had, as a witch with a stick?

It was a jolting experience, though it also provided a moment of breakthrough in translation from the Tamil. After seeing Mrs Osborne assault a defenceless animal, I had found what Raghu Gaitonde had asked for, a passable English translation of the word *suunyakaari*, 'she who manipulates nothingness', so meagrely rendered as 'witch'. Wielder of the Void. That was her secret identity.

The whole incident with the dog cast a pall over my relationship with Mrs Osborne and made me doubt whether we really shared a faith. If we did, she was no sort of advertisement for it. It was Ramana Maharshi's practice to feed dogs before people, and though I didn't want to be the sort of Englishman abroad who makes the treatment of pets his yardstick for everything it was certainly a point of affinity between guru and disciple. I was only a visitor but Ramana Maharshi was much more than a resident, he was the quintessence of this landscape, and between us we outnumbered the Polish *suunyakaari*.

What I had seen in Lucia Osborne as she brought the stick down on an innocent animal was exactly the sort of pattern which conditions *karma*, a *vasana*, a rut of cruelty, a stuck groove in the human record, even if she saw the action as either entirely trivial or else disinterested, as if she was only ridding my bed of a pest. She was deceived. Altruistic deeds release the Self, egotistical ones imprison it.

Later that day she came out onto the verandah with an armful of books, proper Western hardbacks even if they were falling apart and had been eaten by every kind of insect. She dumped them on the table in front of me and said she'd like me to bind them professionally for her. I was utterly dismayed. They were completely unmanageable, the sort of book I would have to wrestle with to show it who's the boss before I could read a single word. I bleated something about the small size of my arms and the large size of the books, but she said coldly, 'You told me you were a bookbinder, so I had some jobs lined up for you. Whether you keep your promise is up to you.' Then she made her exit into the house, leaving the stack of moth-eaten tomes on the table for me to look at, since there was nothing else I could do with them. I had plenty of time to regret the hollow promise I had made in the hope of making myself useful and not being a burden to the household.

Even with Yogi Bear sharing the bed, my sleep had been fitful, but after he had been driven away I had hours of that insomniac awareness that is the opposite of meditation, waiting for sunrise and the relative comfort of the wheelchair. I had plenty of time to grapple with my spiritual impasse. Willpower had brought me to a place where willpower stalled.

Pradakshina had become part of my routine without quite seeming to winch me, as planned, into the centre of my Self. It was something like a sacred constitutional. The beginning of the *pradakshina* road was remarkably peaceful. The surface of the road was mud, with an almost antique patina and a scattering of sand on top. The accumulated compressive effect of thousands of devoted bare feet on *pradakshina* had somehow lightened its texture, giving it a sort of upward spiritual thrust that could be felt unmistakably rising up through the wheels of the chair. The ground had a delightful soft feel and released a seductive sifty-tilthy sensation. It transmitted shimmering spiritual tickles.

At this point on every *pradakshina* I would feel as if I was trembling on the brink of enlightenment, as if light was being born inside my eyelids. Spores of self-realisation drifted around me like flour particles on days when Mum got busy baking. Yet however fiercely I stoked my inward fires, I couldn't burn off from the unfolding experience a certain gross residue of sight-seeing.

For one thing I had become something of a connoisseur of *mantapams*, those structures which Ganesh had identified for me on that first night. When I had mentally compared them with bus shelters I wasn't too far off the mark. A *mantapam* is no more than a consecrated roof. Ideally a *mantapam* would simply float above the heads of pilgrims, keeping the rain off. Not practical in structural terms – but that's the simplicity that *mantapams* start from.

A roof without a wall would only provide shelter from rain falling in an obliging vertical, and we know how rarely that happens. So a *mantapam* will have the concession of a back wall, and four pillars to hold the roof up. It's usually possible to find a dry spot under the roof somewhere. The sacred element in a *mantapam* is variable, but it's definitely there. A *mantapam* is the bud of a temple, which can sprout very vigorously under the right conditions. An unsponsored, unloved *mantapam* remains dormant in its shelter form. And of course the bud can be blighted. At one point on the *pradakshina* circuit was a *mantapam* whose roof was falling in. Grass and weeds were taking over underneath, and an enterprising tree was tapping into the unused vitality of the edifice by growing out of the top of the dilapidated wall. I couldn't quite see where it was getting its moisture, unless as a sapling it had sent rooting fingers into an unsuspected reservoir of nourishment, some little yolk-sac of grace.

A molten yo-yo looping

Just as a *mantapam* can blossom into a temple, I suppose a temple which fell on hard times might eventually decline into a *mantapam*. But there are more possibilities than these in *mantapam* evolution. A *mantapam* may grow at an oblique angle into a *choultry*, which is only a *mantapam* with a little kitchen attached. The presence of food, whether donated or begged for, changes everything. Once cooking has come into the picture it's only a matter of time before music gets in on the act, and soon food is being offered to hungry pilgrims at the *choultry* to the accompaniment of *bhajan*s, special songs.

I had even made my peace with the tea-shop which I had scorned so bitterly earlier on. There was no resemblance, as it turned out, to a cathedral gift shop or cafeteria, unless those places recruit their staff from the circus. There was a strong element of showmanship involved. The hissing noise I had heard (which reminded me of the auto steam-engine I wasn't allowed to have as a child because it wasn't safe) came from something that can only really be called a samovar, despite the distance from Russia. I had seen its domestic equivalent at Mrs Adcock's in Bourne End, but this one was in constant use. Next to it was another pot, one that apparently had milk in it, simmering over glowing embers of charcoal. Hot water would be dispensed from the samovar and poured through a net bag the size of a man's sock containing tea dust. Then hot milk was added with a ladle.

It was the next stage of the operation that seemed to call for a drum-roll in the background, and occasional gasps from the crowd. I made sure I had a good view. This was juggling with tea, not with cups of it but the liquid itself. The juggler would pour it from one beaker into another to cool it off to the ideal temperature. Naturally enough, he started to show off, grinning broadly, pouring the tea faster and faster from an increasing distance until it looked, as it flowed from beaker to beaker, like a molten yo-yo looping between expert hands, or a Slinky miraculously promoted from mimicking fluidity with its soft metal coils to partaking of the real thing. At last the beaker was presented to the customer ready to drink, the swirling ribbons of liquid reassembled into one, the colour of caramel and tasting as sweet as it looked.

By this time I had weaned myself off taking sugar in tea (coffee was more of a challenge), but it would have been missing the point to have clung to my preferences now. The tea flowed across my tongue differently from any Western preparation. It positively sauntered down the digestive pathway, and of course there's a reason for this. The local cows (species *Bos Indicus*, breed most likely *Kangayam*) produce a sleeker milk. There's an inverse relationship between milk yield and fat content, so Daisy (species *Bos taurus*, breed perhaps Jersey) out-produces Lakshmi in volume but can't compete in richness.

High fat is good in a treat, bad when it becomes a routine. So is Hinduism inherently a high-fat religion? Good question. After all, India has the largest population of cattle (cows and buffaloes) on earth. But actually, no. We read in the *Atharva Veda* (I do, anyway) that only cows with low levels of fat in their milk should be kept as family cows. Cows producing richer milk should be donated to the priestly castes, who require a higher percentage of fat when performing *yajñas* – offering oblations of milk (among other substances) to the sacred fire, to tickle the palates of the gods. They whose digestions can cope with any extreme of lushness.

Finally the day dawned, as abrupt as all its predecessors, when it was time for me to return to England and my mundane future. It was also time for me to be measured again. Mrs Osborne was visibly excited as she bustled about with her tape measure. She seemed to have forgiven me my limitations as a book-binder. No further jobs were lined up. She didn't need me to change a fuse or dig a trench.

Homœopathy was being put to the test. An agnostic was being provided with hard evidence, and trusted to accept the facts however disruptive of previous certainties. I lined myself up against the wall of the house. Mrs Osborne took her pencil and made a mark. She was humming under her breath. Then Rajah Manikkam helped me back to the wheelchair while Mrs O grappled with the tape measure. She made a great fuss about aligning the bottom of the tape properly, asking Rajah Manikkam to check it for her. When she was satisfied that everything was properly arranged she compared the two marks and wrote measurements on the wall.

'John, do you see what has happened? When you came here four weeks ago you measured four feet eight and five-eighths of an inch. Now you are four feet eight and seven-eighths of an inch tall. You have grown a quarter of an inch in a month! And there is nothing to say that your growth will not continue, if you go on taking the pills I have prepared.' She stopped and looked at me more closely. 'You are a very unusual young man, John. Of course I don't know many young men, certainly not young men from the West, but you are certainly a special case. Something you considered fixed is revealed to be alterable, yet you hardly react. I must wonder why.'

My answer sounded awkward to me even as it came out of my mouth. 'Mrs Osborne, I didn't come to India to change on the outside. That was never the idea. That isn't the important thing.'

'You have changed, but not in the way that you most hoped. Perhaps it is simply shock that paralyses you. You will need time to accept the fact that anything is possible. I understand and will ask no more questions.'

It wasn't like that. She was on the wrong track entirely. I had taken the little pills in good faith, and the idea of miraculous growth at the age of twenty had a certain amount of power over me. But I was also cheating.

The first time I leaned against the wall I had made sure my feet in their built-up shoes were some little distance away from the wall. It wasn't hard to make out that I had reached the limit of my flexibility. So in the weeks that intervened I had it in my mind that I could either humour Mrs O or show her up, depending on how I felt on the day. It was a strange and no doubt corrupting sensation to have so much power over someone who had so much power over me.

On the day when the measuring was done, I simply stood a little closer to the wall. I was less steady in my balance, but Rajah Manikkam was there to brace me, and Mrs O was too busy with the tape measure to notice. And as for my motives, obviously they were very far from pure. Once I'd decided to play along, I was going to get my revenge on Mrs Osborne one way or another. Either I was going to show up homœopathy as futile or I was going to humour her, and let her go to her grave believing in something that I'd faked. There was anger in both options, but one option was all anger.

If I demonstrated that her therapy had failed I was punishing her pure and simple. In the option I settled on there was at least the possibility of a more positive emotion. By assenting to the idea that I'd added something to my height I was going along with my own fond hopes as well as hers. As for why I was angry with Mrs Osborne, part of it had to do with her sudden appearance as Wielder of the Void, using her stick to beat an innocent stray dog who was helping me sleep, but I would have done the same even if that bizarre event had never happened. Fundamentally, it had to do with my coming to India hoping to find a spiritual mother, and finding something else. A Polish-born Hindu repetition of Granny, another avatar of the peremptory. A human *vasana*, from my point of view, a living rut. A repeated pattern triggering love, submission and resentment, mechanical as a recurring decimal.

It was certainly true that I had changed, but not in the way that I had most hoped. I was deeply tanned, and according to Mrs Osborne I would now be growing at the rate of three inches a year until I decided to stop taking the pills, with a control over my changing size which Lewis Carroll's Alice would have envied. I would hit six feet before I hit thirty. I wonder now what preparation it was she gave me – some sort of titration of *Sequoia*? I still thought of myself as a devotee, but I had failed in my dream of abruptly realising myself for once and for all. I wouldn't be able to skip my larval stage as a university student. There was no short cut to the shimmering imago, no special ramp up the mountain installed for my convenience.

The key to the whole problem was Ganesh, the key but not a usable one. Call it a key broken off in the lock. Not Ganesh the man, who had said his goodbyes very warmly. Ganesh the principle, the whole idea of obstacles and their removal. In Bourne End before I set off I had been wise enough to ignore all barriers, discounting the possibility that anything could block my progress, but in India I had been entirely taken up with them, by the verandah, by Peter, by Mrs O and the whole stupid growing-tall project, and by the failure of meditation. I had allowed obstacles to define me and had become bogged down, there where I had counted on being most free, preöccupied with personalities, which occupy no lofty rung of reality.

After Kuppu had helped to clean me for the last time, and Rajah Manikkam had lifted me down from the verandah, while I gave him for the last time the stern glare that cuts off giggles at their root, I thought I would have time to myself in the taxi that was taking me to Madras, time to mourn and to start recovering. I planned to wallow a little in my regrets.

I hadn't understood how Indian taxis work. For a four- or five-hour trip like that, arranged in advance (and costing me a hundred rupees, more than a fiver), there will always be company. The owner of the taxi, a Muslim wearing a round hat, accompanied the driver. There were women and children, with much kissing and cuddling.

At the last minute, Mrs Osborne herself got in. She was suffering from toothache, and had decided to make her way to Madras for an extraction. There was a dentist in the city who treated her without charge, not because he was a devotee of Ramana Maharshi but because he was impressed by Mrs Osborne personally, and her steadfast refusal of anæsthesia, both local and general. Toothache didn't deter her from chatting in Tamil for the whole of the journey, while I closed my eyes and tried to meditate. If I had been a tourist it would have been a waste not to make the most of my last sights of rural India, but I was a devotee, even if I felt further than ever from enlightenment. There was one crowning disappointment in my summer of pilgrimage. I had broken my vow. Chastity had slipped away from me when I wasn't looking.

The night before, I had dreamed of the Abominable Snowman. The dream was somehow in the style of a B-movie from the 1950s. I was being hurried to safety through snow by a group of helpers who suddenly scattered and deserted me. The dream wasn't from my point of view, exactly, but the guiding principle was film cliché rather than astral travel. If I was scared in the dream then perhaps Mrs O's remarks about the importance of following dream fear to its source remained with me on these lower levels of mental life, so that I over-rode the reflex of waking.

Now the camera craned up and looked down at me, and I saw that the wheelchair was sitting squarely in the middle of an enormous footprint in the snow. Then there was either a commentary or a caption, as if this was an episode of a serial reaching its cliff-hanger ending: IS THIS THE END FOR JOHN WALLACE CROMER, TORN APART BY A MYTHICAL MONSTER IN A PART OF INDIA WHERE HE HAS NEVER EVEN BEEN? In the interior spaces of the dream I was uneasily aware that Tibet was somehow wrong.

The fact of my being in the wheelchair in the dream already put it into a special category. I walk without difficulty in most of my dreams, I glide along, but this was either wish-fulfilment of a higher sort or something other than wish-fulfilment. Then an enormous shadow fell over the enormous footprint.

Next thing I knew the Abominable Snowman was cradling me in his arms, which were warm and very soft. I couldn't see his face, but I was swept up into an ecstasy of mammal safety and release.

I had conjured up a place of altitude and hardship which was no doubt partly a plaintive self-portrait of the modern pilgrim and his travails. It was also a fantasy of relief from the heat I had been in so constantly for a month now, a dream of snow. Yet into that imaginary cold I had smuggled warmth and comfort. The strong arms of the Abominable Snowman, densely covered with black fur, squeezed me in a surging rhythm like a global heartbeat. My bones made no protest as I was hugged to that mighty chest. My bones were glad, were only glad. I was enclosed in something like the mechanism of a cat's purr, only a million times larger. Then little by little the vision receded and I became awake. It was a little after dawn, on the last morning I would spend on Mrs Osborne's verandah, as a guest of the oldest mountain on earth.

It was an undignified ending to my Indian adventure. I had set off with hopes of celibacy and self-realisation, but all I had achieved was disappointment and distraction. Now my unconscious mind had even broken my presumptuous vow. I had wanted to pitch all my thinking at an elevated level, to soar above my limitations – but then I had to go and crash-land my own quest by having a wet-dream about the Yeti.

4

Dark Ages

I felt very low on the plane home, suffering a sense of spiritual failure that was like a hangover. This Maharajah had no desire to be served champagne in the sky as he headed wearily for home. I was on the wagon, and all the fizz had gone out of me.

Even so, my depression didn't last for the whole flight. The more distance I put between India and myself, the rosier my vision of the visit became. The grotty bits tactfully disappeared, while the good moments rooted themselves firmly in my memory and sent up tender shoots. Mrs Osborne herself started to shine like a saint in my mind, which was never an illusion that I had entertained when she was sitting opposite me, hissing her savage sibilants and grieving over rock cakes when she wasn't beating stray dogs.

I had expected too much from the huge endeavour of displacing myself to India. I had banked on apotheosis and received only a holiday, something I had no use for. I had hoped to realise my Self, but I was still trapped in the lower case, confined by the daily self which so obviously offers too little but also too much. The self of every day is like some hectoring street hawker, touting bangles and sweetmeats, guides to the museum, sexual use of his family in exhaustive combinations, trayfuls of watches but never the right time. I must still engage daily with Maya, who by pulling some sort of typographical strings has managed to become capitalised on the sly herself.

Still, I knew from Dad's horticultural lectures that if you take an established plant and transfer it to another climate it never really settles down. I needed a more realistic plan, and this is what I came up with: I would graft onto my English life all the things I had learned in India.

I felt I had understood the essence of what I should do, being deceived only about details of location. I had thought I would melt into the mountain like butter into holy toast, which was greatly presumptuous. Parvati in penitent devotion had indeed vanished into

Arunachala, leaving that single bosom behind, but that was different. It had been absurd for me to imagine I could do the same, leaving later generations of devotees to trace the shape of my McKee pins in the mystically absorptive rock.

I had set my sights too high. My job was to be more like a gardener's, taking a cutting and starting new growth in another bed, and my mission would be in Britain.

I took comfort from an old episode in the history of Arunachala. Four hundred years previously a guru had ordered his prime disciple to go away, to what is now Bangalore. It was there that he must carry the inner torch. The explanation was that two mighty trees can never thrive next to each other. This wasn't banishment but husbandry. The seeds spread and scatter, and the strength is in the distance, not the closeness. And after all, Bangalore (or whatever it was called back then) is on the Deccan plateau, well elevated and much cooler. Having to go back to England was no more than the modern equivalent of being sent to Bangalore.

In my mind I had staked everything on the transformation India was going to work on me, and I had given no thought to coming home. My previous concerns had been trumped by spiritual awareness. Making progress in the world was no longer a tempting illusion. I was too old to go through the motions. Cleverness and willpower had been my bath toys, and I had played with them very happily, until the day I looked out of the window and saw the sea.

A guinea-pig in a wheelchair

Now I had little interest in reading Modern Languages at world-famous Cambridge University, and none whatever in being a guinea-pig in a wheelchair, as Downing College's first disabled student. I had lost heart for another round of the obstacle race, but really, what was the alternative?

At Cambridge there would be people responsible for my welfare, and Mum and Dad – however little I wanted to depend on them – would be no more than a telephone call away, yet it was a far more daunting prospect than the voyage I had made to India alone, when there was a real possibility of my having to sleep by a roadside infested by brigands. I had much less to fear from going to Cambridge, but incomparably slighter grounds for hope.

Nevertheless I managed to convince myself that there was a spiritual mission involved, quite distinct from the next scheduled phase of my mundane education. My job was to plant the seeds of Self-Enquiry and Ramana Maharshi, first in the heart of Buckinghamshire, and then in Cambridge University itself. Why else would a place be waiting for me there? It came to me suddenly. I was to be a teacher disguised as a student, providing a wisdom that bubbled up from underneath, not mere knowledge filtering down from above.

Cambridge was still some weeks off in the future. What mattered during that interval was the Here and the Now: Trees, Abbotsbrook, Bourne End, Bucks. The Abbotsbrook Estate would be the nursery garden for my centre. Young shoots would be watered and protected from too much sun. Morning and evening meditation would be the order of the day. Unless Mum had anything to do with it, of course.

Her first words were 'Welcome home, JJ! My, you're brown. Have you turned into a little Indian yourself?' After that, her reaction to my project for the propagation of peace and love seemed to be anger in a hundred forms. She took my five weeks away as a rejection of her love. What stung her was that I hadn't returned chastened to her bosom. I had managed perfectly well. She listened stonily to my account of Kuppu's willingness to clean commodes and its significance in caste terms. Buttering her up a bit, I emphasised that without the Cadbury's Roses she had insisted I take there would have been no easy way to reward such exceptional helpfulness, but I needn't have bothered. She was not to be won over.

I had returned after my experiment in self-sufficiency, but while I was living in the house I was still dependent on her. She could make me pay for needing her now.

Dad, of course, was impossible to pin down, lending a hand now and then very much on his own terms, not to be counted on. At one point he mentioned that colleagues of his at work were very interested in my trip to India. They had suggested that it would make a good feature for the *Today* programme. Why not have me interviewed by Jack de Manio?

Dad had told them that I was attuned to higher priorities and wouldn't be interested in anything like that. He was a big fan of the ego-diminishment project as long as the ego in question was mine, and from the spiritual perspective which I had espoused for so long I could hardly complain about being kept out of the limelight, now could I? Dad had beaten me at my own game.

Mum had things pretty much her own way. Every helpful gesture had an overtone of reproach and injured pride, as if she was always muttering under her breath OH, YOU NEED ME NOW, DO YOU?

I had failed to follow Ramana Maharshi's example, by leaving home once and for all, making a clean break. What's the worst thing that can happen if you do? That she will follow you wherever you go, as his mother did, with her cooking-pot and her tears.

Mum kept nobbling my peace of mind. She had quite a talent for spiritual disruption. I felt dented and bruised by her angry subservience. Serenity had seemed so close, but it had slipped through my fingers, fingers with remarkably little talent for gripping.

I had been led astray by my old romantic notion of the Quest — when hadn't Ramana Maharshi always made it clear that outer trials and journeys were supremely irrelevant? Changing your life without changing your life, that was the challenge he set, and I seemed to have fallen at the first fence. Life in Bourne End, far from being transfigured, was the same only worse.

Perhaps by going to India I had committed the spiritual equivalent of the ultimate English sin, namely queue-jumping. After all, the whole universe was Bhagavan's ashram. Anyone who lived in that universe was part of it. I could claim no special preference by virtue of having travelled to Arunachala, and would have lost nothing by staying away.

The inner journey supersedes the outer one. Of course there's an element of this even in the unsatisfying Western tradition — in the story of the Knight who searches for the Grail all his long life and then, when he's dying, asks his squire for water. The squire brings it to him in the battered old cup he has used all his life, and he sees that it is the Grail . . . which couldn't be found until this moment, although it had never been lost. Because it hadn't been lost.

That's a story which communicates directly with my tear ducts, somehow, but these are not the holy tears that signal the presence of God, I don't think (only one of the eight physical signs, not representing any sort of quorum). Perhaps they're even a sign of the presence of hogwash, childish feeling that hasn't been outgrown, like the hymns that stir the blood – 'Bread of Heaven', 'To Be a Pilgrim' – almost more when the religion that underwrites them has crumbled away. The account has been closed down, but the cheques make us weep even as they bounce.

Our Bourne End neighbour Pheroza Tucker, the one who had brought round the *Times of India* with the news of Arthur Osborne's death, paid a social call, though Mum warned us she'd had it up to here with India and could we please talk about something else. While Mum was out of the room I managed to tell her about the funeral pyre on Arunachala. According to Pheroza, the reason I had been hustled away at a certain stage of the proceedings was that after a time the burning body rears up like bacon (she pronounced it 'beacon') in a frying pan.

I ran through the Hindu litany, proud of my memory, pattering through the gross body, causal body, subtle body, when she interrupted me with a laugh, saying, 'Don't forget the beacon body! It's all rather primitive to my mind. Rather peasant-y.' I suppose Parsees parse such things differently. 'Did you know, John, that the skull is always pierced before the flame is lit, to prevent it from exploding?' Then Mum came in with the tea tray and we changed the subject to fruit cake.

As a Parsee Pheroza was a worshipper of fire but not someone who would use it to do such dirty work as disposing of a corpse. To her such rituals were rather undignified. In due course her dead body would be exposed on top of a Tower of Silence for the vultures to process in their own way. She would go back to India for the purpose. Bourne End was a nice enough place to live, but she wouldn't want to die there.

Peter arrived back at Bourne End a week or so after I did, after some scenic detour of his own. It was nothing to him to add a couple of countries onto his world tour. He had with him a photograph of Ramana Maharshi which he had bought at the ashram and now offered shyly to me as a present. He hadn't been sure whether I would approve of such an object, given that my religion involved discounting the seeming reality of everyday life and aiming to grasp the truth of non-duality behind appearances.

I wasn't sure whether I approved either, but I was delighted. I had felt a strong impulse to buy just such an object, but had overruled myself on spiritual grounds. Now I was in the happy position of having a wish granted after I had (laboriously, grindingly, like the hoist that lifted me up over the bath in the house at Bourne End) risen above it.

As far as the family went, Peter fell in line right behind me. He supported me in everything I said. He was a staunch ally and a brick beyond praise, but he had his own vulnerabilities. Each of us had spent months in Mum's *karpa-paay*, her womb-bag, and she knew how to undermine us from within as well as erode us from the outside. The fraternal fortress of tranquillity was under constant attack.

I reached the point where I really didn't see how I could hold out much longer. I prayed for help – help sooner rather than later. Sri Bhagavan was the shape divinity took in my mind, but as I was back in England now, worse luck, it seemed a good idea to hedge my bets, so I prayed to my old friend Jesus Christ, and to God the Father as well. I didn't forget to add a dash of Allah to the cocktail of divine appeal. Desperation is a strongly œcumenical force.

It wasn't more than a few hours later when the phone rang. Mum answered with genteel poise and warmth ('Bourne End 21176') as she always did. The world of tele-communications was expanding convulsively around us, and we in Bourne End now had five-digit numbers.

No one could have guessed the bleakness of Mum's underlying mood from the way she crooned into the receiver. 'Oh, *hello*, Malcolm . . . how lovely to hear your voice . . . Yes . . . yes . . . yes he's back and well settled in . . . yes . . . yes . . . brown as a nut. Oh, he had a *won*derful time. He's very full of his experiences . . . No it doesn't do much for me I'm afraid, but that's really not the point, is it? My only concern is for his happiness . . . Yes, Downing College. After that, who knows? I don't think there are many vacancies these days for people to get paid for sitting around on their bottoms doing nothing, but if anyone can make a living from that I dare say John can . . .'

Mum's theory of conversation seemed to be that you could say any number of disobliging things about people as long as the last thing you said was more or less positive, so I wasn't surprised to hear her start to sign off with 'Perhaps we should all take a leaf from his book . . . wouldn't life be lovely if it all worked like that?'

Then the conversation took a new turn. Mum's voice became if anything even sweeter, but her hand tightened on the receiver and she stuck her chin out. 'What's that? . . . Oh yes, Malcolm, of *course* you can . . . You know John, he'd love it . . . But promise you'll say if you get bored? There's no kindness in humouring him. Shall we say about three? . . . Perfect! . . . bye-eee . . .'

Her obliging manner was a pale shadow of itself by the time the phone was back in its cradle. 'That was Malcolm Washbourne,' she said sourly. 'He says he's *dying* to hear all about your experiences in India, and he's coming over to see you at about three o'clock. How lovely for you.'

The last door-slam

She seemed enormously put off herself. 'Now, what do you want for lunch? If you can think of a way of getting a meal to cook by itself while you sit on your bottom, please pass it on. I'd be glad to put my feet up myself.' She went into the kitchen, slamming the door behind her, so that I ached to be back with Mrs Osborne, with her wild-fig dishes and her big dog-battering stick and the scoldings that seemed loving by comparison.

I couldn't understand why I was being reproached for needing food, while Peter was catered for as a matter of course. He could easily have managed for himself in the kitchen, and would have left enough mess to keep Mum grumbling contentedly for days. I didn't argue the toss. In theory I could always get the last word, but Mum would always have the last door-slam. Conversational manœuvres, however crushing, will always come second to repartee of that physical sort. The doors in that house must have been sturdy indeed, to survive the years of melodramatic slamming.

Still, I had resources of my own. Mrs Osborne had scared me half to death about the use of aluminium pans in cookery. We were destroying ourselves at every mealtime, as surely as the Roman patricians did with their lead plates and cutlery, poisoning their brains while the plebs ate off wooden plates with their hands. There was a book on the subject: *Aluminium: A Menace to Health* by Mark Clement.

When I got home, I got hold of a copy (it was published by Thorsons). I must have driven Mum mad by waving it under her nose, and refusing to eat anything ever again that came out of one of those sinister health-destroying pans. As if I wasn't fussy enough about food, without becoming obsessed about its preparation and accusing her of killing us all under cover of nurture. If she had beaten me about the head with an aluminium pan, screaming, 'How's your brain working now? Rotting, is it? Is it?', any decent lawyer would have got her off with probation, maybe words of praise from the judge.

Peter joined the conspiracy by looking for scratches in the pans Mum used. 'That shows the bits which came off when she slashes the potatoes with her knife,' he told me. 'And we're all eating them!' We made her buy a stainless-steel one, though on the Granny principle of balancing the books, albeit with lopsided contributions, I gave a little something towards it – ten shillings. I've stuck to my guns, though, and avoided aluminium ever since. If my brain goes bad I won't hold the kitchen cupboard responsible.

Mum hated it when we ganged up on her. Unfortunately she had a talent for uniting the opposition, and had inherited none of Granny's flair for playing people off against each other.

After that miraculous phone call I felt a deep thrill of hope within me. I had prayed to God to send reinforcements, and now Malcolm was coming to visit. He was the only one of our neighbours who seemed to enjoy spending time with me, and Mum had never really understood that. I didn't exactly understand it myself – we weren't on a wave-length, exactly, we were like two notes at opposite ends of a keyboard, so that you can't really decide whether they harmonise or clash. But Mum couldn't believe his interest in me was real, that two such different people could agree on anything. Malcolm worked in advertising, which made his spiritual interests no more than play-acting to her way of thinking.

I disagreed. The products Malcolm was called on to sell were dreams in the first place, and the slogans and campaigns he came up with were dreams about dreams. They were Maya squared, Maya rampant and in spades. Dreams were his medium and his currency, so it followed that reality must be his consolation. He must find the square root of Maya in meditation, where objects, symbols, words and ideas dissolve impartially, leaving a light that has no source and casts no shadow.

I was benefiting from the resumption of my meditation practice, now that I was no longer trying to light my little match in the up-draught of a huge conflagration.

Malcolm and I would talk for hours, on subjects literary and meta-physical. Malcolm always said we were 'crackajolking away like a hearse on fire', a splendid phrase he had picked up from *Finnegans Wake*. Like most people (not just advertising men, those great experts at making a little go a long way) he had probably read only one page, but he'd found himself a good one. I hadn't so much as looked at the book, and when I did I was disappointed to find nothing that fell under my eyes matching up to the sample.

Malcolm enjoyed banter and teasing. In fact I think he positively enjoyed being told what a hopeless case of materialism he was. I dare say the actual cultivation of his spirituality came second, though he had read almost as many of the relevant books – or book-jackets – as I had and kept up pretty well.

It was high time for some spiritual work. The hearse might be on fire, but I had a firm grip on the appropriate extinguisher. Truly our astral tongues were hanging out for water to quench the hearse-fire of the Samsara, the action-reaction Ocean of births and deaths. Now that I was fully tanked up with Indian juice, I could provide him with the first cooling drink for months. I would lead us out of the maze of misery and set us on the road to freedom.

Mum bustled about Malcolm when he arrived, exactly as if he was her guest rather than mine, plying him with tea and cakes. Malcolm asked me about what I ate in India, a subject that made Mum roll her eyes, out of his line of sight but well within mine. Shouldn't it have been the other way round, making him complicit with her exasper-ation? Mum could never quite get the hang of conspiracies.

I suggested that we go to my room (mine and Peter's) and try to meditate. Malcolm was a dab-hand at sitting with his legs crossed, in a sort of informal lotus position, although conditions on the floor weren't ideal (Mum had insisted on lino rather than carpet for fear of what the wheelchair would track in). I could just about manage a symbolic crossing of the ankles in the wheelchair. After a minute or so even this token position became painful, but I knew from the Maharshi's example that a dispensation from orthodox posture was spiritually unimportant.

From the perspective of the wheelchair I could see the zone of thinning in Malcolm's hair, where the scalp showed dimly pink. It was a joy in itself to be looking down rather than up. I felt a rush of privileged piety.

'I really don't think I need a mantra,' Malcolm said. 'After a week at work my mind goes blank of its own accord.'

The mind stops twitching

'The mantra is nothing in itself,' I cooed. 'But the mind, like the tip of an elephant's trunk, must always be grasping something. So the mahout gives the elephant a chain to hold and it loses its restlessness. Similarly when provided with a mantra the mind stops twitching.' I didn't actually claim to have seen elephants and their keepers in India, but I let it be understood. In fact I had seen elephants only at Whipsnade. In India I had seen nothing larger than water buffalo. Large enough, particularly from my low angle of vision. In worldly terms they were larger than the cow on the mountain. Her immensity was of a different kind.

Peter came to join us, slipping into the room and joining our meditation like someone sliding into still, deep water. The atmosphere was blissful, a dynamo of silence in a house too often agitated by unadmitted discord and dissension.

After a period that we could only have guessed at in our timeless state, but was certainly less than ten minutes, Mum eased the door open. She couldn't bear not knowing what we were up to. She moved like an actress tiptoeing ostentatiously on stage to do something illicit. After peering round, she retreated in the same way, closing the door with a careful quietness that was existentially much more definite than a bang.

Malcolm's eyes flew open, and mine must have been open already, to notice it happening. He frowned. 'I'm afraid my psychic capacitors aren't up to the job of absorbing Laura's surplus energies. And what a shame – meditation would do her no end of good.' He hoped she would come round to the idea of such soul-refreshment in time. I tried to imagine it.

'The world is too much with us,' I said thoughtfully, and Peter said, '*Mum* is too much with us.' We tried to be faithful to our task, but then Audrey and her friend Lorraine crept in, shushing each other, and took up enviably supple lotus positions, their bones flowing round corners, on a spare patch of floor. They started to murmur something just below the level of distinctness, so that ears which were straining to tune out had no choice but to tune back in. As the murmuring became louder, their mantra revealed itself in a storm of giggles as 'Mrs Brown went to town, With her knickers hanging down, Mrs Green saw the scene, Put it in a magazine.'

That broke the mood for good. Malcolm stretched and stood up, and Peter chased the girls out of the room, which was exactly what they wanted.

Later that evening I heard Mum complain about it to Dad. 'He's trying to turn this house into a bloody ashram,' she said, 'or whatever we're supposed to call it.' Dad's reply was him all over, changing sides to keep her guessing: 'And would it be such a bad thing if he succeeded? You've got your sewing circle, after all. Let him have his prayer meeting, and try to look on the bright side – at least they don't sing.' Dad seemed to have the knack of tossing a coin inside himself at times like these, letting Heads or Tails decide which way he would jump in an argument, so that agreement and dissent were equally disorienting for Mum.

She wasn't someone with any talent for looking on the bright side, but on this occasion Dad wanted her at least to try. At other times when Malcolm came over to meditate, she made a better job of keeping her distance. She went to the other end of the house and emitted her sighs from there, though I'm sure she knew they could find me through the walls.

I felt that a campaign of holiness had been well begun. I was quite able to overlook the hypocrisy of the whole thing. Underneath my Indian tan I was a whited sepulchre, far whiter than the Taj Mahal. I was really enjoying ruling the roost. We are always fighting back our tears at the cremation of the ego, only to find it has been throwing dust in our eyes, not ashes, all along.

I had a nerve leading a group in meditation, when I had only been able to achieve that mind-free state of mind since my return from India. I was teaching lessons that I barely knew myself. In Dad's vocabulary I was shamming and no mistake. My disciples deserved better, even if they were only an advertising man with a bad conscience and a trainee chef with an unkillable respect for his older brother. Audrey and Lorraine had pretty much the right idea.

It would have served me right to be found out, except that there were others involved. I would have betrayed my guru by allowing Malcolm and Peter to have a low opinion of him through my own bad behaviour.

Similia Similibus

I went to India a Hindu, and I returned to Bourne End a Hindu and a homœopath. Soon I had Mrs Pavey hard at work tracking down copies of *Magic of the Minimum Dose* and its indefatigable sequels, and helping me to read widely in the subject.

Finally I summoned up the courage to ask Flanny for a referral to the Royal Homœopathic Hospital, on Great Ormond Street, the institution which had achieved marvellous results in a long-ago cholera epidemic, and so given a dissident tradition a foothold in national life. Flanny snorted a bit down her horse's face, but she had learned by this time to let me go my own way.

The pretext for this visit to what I regarded as the mother church of the whole fascinating cult was to find a remedy for the dandruff that had plagued me for years. More than a pretext, really – I'd have been happy to see the back of those flakes which Mum and Dad refused to refer to except as scurf. I don't know why *scurf* is U and *dandruff* is a suburban condition. Like any euphemism it soon takes on a taint of the word that's being avoided. Call it what you like, call it seborrhœa if you must – just stop it happening to my scalp.

The hospital looked like any other, both inside and out, but I was heartened to realise the hospital smell was faint, barely detectable. The doctor asked me a whole range of wide-ranging questions. Not just the usual ones, but impressionistic ones – what did I dream about, habitually? What was my favourite, what was my least favourite type of weather? He was being unusually thorough, I thought, but perhaps some of these were trick questions.

Of course it was no more than good homœopathic practice. No symptom should be regarded as insignificant, or artificially separated from the person. There's an enormous amount of cross-referencing required for diagnosing even minor ailments – though the minor/major distinction doesn't really apply in homœopathy. Hierarchies don't really come into it, when the smallest leaf and twig can be as instructive as the trunk or roots. A headache in a redhead who has nightmares about rain and feels tired in the early afternoons may lead to a quite specific remedy, which would have no healing effect on a blonde headache with insomnia.

Then a trolley was wheeled in, and the world changed around me. I was used to instruments of various sorts being used on my body, from the needle-hook for tickling the bone at Ipswich to the drill which ground into my calcified hips at Wexham Park. It's true that the body was asleep during those latter interventions, but consciousness and unconsciousness (neither of them being real awareness) aren't such separate states as we like to think. So if I didn't look up immediately, to see what was on the trolley, it was because I had no reason to expect anything good to be brought in by such a mode of transport.

When I looked at what was on the trolley, it was something astounding. A pair of enormous books, too big to carry, and nothing else. Too big for anyone to carry, not just me. They were repertories – the technical term for the comprehensive and cross-indexed volumes of symptoms and remedies. The holy books of the cult, with the word C L A R K E faded but still visible on the spine. It felt like an annunciation, a trumpeting revelation. I had found the most divinely bookish of all therapies. This was medicine as librarianship.

I had experienced years enough of impertinent probing, the finger delving anally, accompanied by the question, 'Does this hurt? And this? How about this?' If not, why not? Whatever answer I gave seemed to lead to a healing bullet of wax being inserted into my back end . . . but now I had left the baleful land of suppositories far behind. Hello to repertory, goodbye to suppository. You won't be missed.

The homœopathic doctor who treated me becomes an angel in my memory. One moment this was a health professional, the next it was one of the seraphim or cherubim. Whichever has the six wings. It's the only piece of biblical imagery which gives the Hindu gods, with their comprehensively unorthodox anatomy, a run for their money.

I don't count the great beast in Revelation, with the seven heads and ten horns, which just sounds as if the maths has gone wrong. The angel in Great Ormond Street was definitely one of the winged horde. With twain (s)he covered her face, with twain (s)he covered her feet, and with twain – just the prehensile tips of the wings – (s)he turned the pages of the repertories.

Normally I have a good memory for doctors and their ways. Which ones make real eye-contact, and which prefer to do their business at one remove. The ones for whom medicine is a harsh crusade, the ones for whom it is a losing battle. But of this doctor, the arch-homœopath, I remember nothing, not even gender, angels being beyond such things. It's the glorious therapeutic system I remember instead, and the way it treated me.

Homœopathy sums itself up in a single Latin phrase, which exists in two versions. *Similia similibus curantur* – like cures like. *Similia similibus curentur* – let like cure like. I prefer the second version. It's the verb form that gets me. It's a jussive form, though whether 'the jussive' is a mood or a voice or a tense I couldn't say. It's the same form that exists in 'Let there be light', or *Fiat lux*, the one moment in the Bible that seems to me beyond argument, the Jewish version of the *sruti*-note. That all-powerful urging from the heart of the matter.

At the back of my mind, in all my dealings with homœopathy, lay the feeling that if orthodox medicine wasn't all that there was, then the same might be true in other departments of life. Perhaps I'm not exaggerating when I look back and remember reasoning that if homœopathy could work as a system of therapy – if not for everybody, perhaps – then perhaps homosexuality was workable also. Alternative

420

or complementary. Not wrong but right in a different way. *Similes similibus amentur.*

When my amazement subsided, I found that the angel was asking me the most novel question of all. 'Why did you think you became ill?' That was all that was said, and yet it was revolutionary. In my fifteen years and more of Still's Disease, no medical person had voiced the idea that the disease had happened to a person, who might have made sense of it in his own fashion. With the emphasis on the past. Not 'Why *do* you think you became ill?' but 'Why *did* you think –?' What was the explanation that one-time person gave himself? I hadn't thought about it for years – it had never been a worked-out thought – but I had an answer ready, as if in fact I had been waiting all this time. I answered, 'I thought it was because I had eaten a dirty red Spangle in the garden, when Mummy told me not to.' I thought I had become ill because of a sweet I'd found in the garden and recklessly eaten, in defiance of all Mum's instructions about hygiene, what was nice and what was nasty.

The angel simply wrote it down with the answers to the other questions. In homœopathic terms it wasn't pivotal, merely part of the material for diagnosis. But I felt as if an ancient cyst in my memory, a little recalcitrant bubble of crystallised toxins, something that had been part of my material being all this time, had suddenly liquefied, bobbed to the surface and silently burst. Once I'd called it to mind, it vaporised, but without being asked that question I would have carried around the husk of guilt and shame indefinitely. Now it had no more personal application than the sort of children's rhyme Audrey brought home from the school playground. *Chew, chew, chewing gum, Brought me to my grave, Mother told me not to chew, And still I disobeyed . . .*

After my visit to Great Ormond Street, I was even more of a devotee of Hahnemann and his view of life. The remedy I was given, a John-sized glass tube containing pillules of *Silicea* 30, had been lovingly chosen after the most individuated assessment of my medicalised life. It was a transcendent masterpiece of diagnosis, but it didn't make the slightest impression on my dandruff. Efficacy wasn't necessarily one of the virtues of the system I loved, and scurf would be with me for a few years yet.

Mum's packing on my behalf before I went to India had been tender as well as anguished. Before I left for Cambridge it had a definite air of last rites. She handled my unimpressive possessions as if she was clearing a dead person's room, while the corpse looked meekly on.

It was herself she was mourning, of course. If life for her had become synonymous with looking after me, then my leaving home could only be a sort of death.

Her attempts at making the best of things were almost more upsetting. 'I dare say you'll make lots of new friends who will invite you to their homes . . . but perhaps you'll spare us a couple of days at Christmas.' My dreams were indeed on that level – I would be swept into a social whirlpool and would forget family entirely, pursuing more congenial illusions. It was only when I heard Mum echoing my inmost thoughts that I realised how unlikely it all was.

On the afternoon I arrived as a student, we drove in convoy. I was at the wheel of the Mini, and Mum and Dad followed in their own car with my things. Sometimes they let me put two or three cars between us before they caught up with me.

I felt I could hear Mum and Dad wrangling in the æther, as if I was tuned in to some hellish family radio station impossible to turn off. The name of the programme would have been *Family Un-Favourites*. 'Shouldn't you catch up with him, Dennis?' 'For heaven's sake, m'dear! John knows his way around, you know. He's not going to get lost – he came here for his interview.' 'That was ages ago. Not everyone's as good with directions as you think *you* are . . .'

It turned out that the college nurse was watching out for my arrival, perched in the Porter's Lodge. She was a part of the welcoming committee. Not a welcome part, as far as I was concerned, but Mum greeted her warmly, as if a weight had been lifted off her heart.

I sulked, though the passive emotional states aren't particularly effective coming from those who are assumed to be passive by decree of fate anyway. My sulk became intense without becoming any more noticeable. Was I not a standard member of the student body? And was this standard treatment? Would she be watching over us all in the same attentive manner, tucking us in and giving us our doses of cod liver oil?

It was obvious that I didn't need nursing. After all, if I had needed nursing then Downing College would have chosen someone else – someone who didn't – to have the honour of being their first disabled undergraduate. They didn't want to make work for themselves, after all.

I can't help feeling that there's something only semi-respectable about nurses who don't work in actual hospitals or surgeries. A college nurse is like a ship's surgeon or a vet attached to a circus – the position simply reeks of dark history, of secret drinking or worse. I don't know what medical arrangements exist in a flea circus, but perhaps the same type of character is drawn to that environment too, entomologist down on his luck, whiff of formaldehyde on the clothes if not the breath.

Assuming I didn't have such a prejudice already, then this must have been the moment I acquired it. This particular college nurse wouldn't have lasted a minute under the command of Sister Heel or any other of the dragons whose nostrils I had seen shoot out jets of disciplinary flame. Not only did this person wear a cardigan, she had dropped cigarette ash on it while she waited, puffing away in the Lodge with the porters. The starch had gone out of her, or never been properly absorbed, as it must be, from the fibres of the uniform right down into the nervous system.

Once she had officially greeted me, she had two questions to put: was I on any medication? No, as she must already have known. Did I know the name and address of the GP assigned to me by the University? I did, it had been in the paperwork – Dr Buchanan at the Trinity Street practice. Then she went about her business, having accomplished precisely nothing. I thought that if she was going to be there at all, she should have the good manners to take my temperature and blood pressure, to pester me about my last bowel movement. Either do the job or don't – but don't just hover!

The porters were expecting not only me but the Mini. If there was an undertone of suspicion in their welcome, it attached to the car not the disabled student. If there's one thing that college functionaries know in their bones, it's that undergraduates don't have cars – or those who do keep very quiet about it. If I was going to have a car, then I was almost being a spoilsport by owning up to it. Much more fun for the authorities to catch me red-handed at the wheel and drag me before a disciplinary board. Still, any hard feelings didn't last. The Mini was expected just as much as I was. There was a parking space designated for it, inside a back entrance of the college, accessed by Tennis Court Road. From there it was only a few yards to my room.

The room was Kenny A6 – 6 being the room, A the staircase, Kenny the Court. If you're looking at the doorway of A staircase from Kenny Court, then my room was the one with the first window on the right. Porters and others keen on brevity could just scribble 'KA6'.

The very edge of Johnability

It was almost a suitable place for me to live. Almost. So take your pick of proverbs – beggars can't be choosers, or a miss is as good as a mile. There were a couple of steps at both the front and rear entrances, so access wasn't easy in either direction, and impossible in the wheel-chair.

The back door at least had a handle I could operate, and although there was no handrail I could lean against the wall to assist my trans-fer between levels. The front door of A staircase was impossible for me to manage unaided. It had one of those hydraulic piston arrangements at the top, a door-closer of savage power. I think I've heard that device referred to as a 'muscle', though that may not be its technical name. In any case, it outclassed anything my muscles could accomplish.

I would have to get into the habit of going in the back way, after parking the car. The proximity of the car park made it simpler to come and go by the back door and the back entrance than to pass through the heart of the college.

I might have developed more *esprit de corps* if my day-to-day deal-ings with Downing had amounted to more than refuelling trips to the Hall. *Esprit de corps!* That's one of the bits of French I do like. The spirit of the body – it's irresistible. Can it also mean the wit of the body?

The room was marginally Johnable. It was on the very edge of Johnability. I dare say it was the pick of the bunch in terms of Downing's available stock, and there was no legal obligation for the college to take me at all – it was either a social experiment or an act of academic charity – so I could hardly complain. At least it was on the ground floor. It would do. It would have to.

On that day there were hundreds of fresh undergraduates installing themselves in their rooms, and most of them had the help of their parents to settle in, whether they wanted it or not. In the weeks before term began I had been looking at the map of Cambridge that I had bought when I came for my interview, making myself familiar with the town's geography, and I knew that in hundreds of rooms from Newnham to Girton, from Clare to Jesus, fathers were looking out of the window and preparing to separate a five-pound note from its fellows in their wallets, and mothers were feeling the thinness of the sheets and inspecting the stains round the plugholes in the washbasins.

I was twenty, which made me older than my academic contemporaries. Even so, here I would have a sensation I had been deprived of and had longed for. As a freshman I would be part of a generation. The closest I had come to a generation before this was a ward, then a dormitory, then a class. This was a society on a much larger scale.

In this new place, though, it would be up to me to make my own contacts. Cambridge University was an institution, but not like any I had known before. This would be a place of elective affinities. I wouldn't have company and competition thrust on me without having to make the effort. Friends, lovers, enemies. They would be all my own work.

Mum and Dad were part of a generation, too, on this day, the generation of parents settling their children in at university. I suppose the occasion must have been clouded for Dad by the sense that I was receiving a privilege which he had been denied. I couldn't do anything about the War and the forfeiture of his further education, but I could at least include him in my privilege by letting him settle me in. If I was impatient for my new life, I was well enough brought up to humour my parents on the last day of the old one. Mum laid my clothes out in the little chest of drawers, squeezing everything into the top drawer. The lower drawers being more or less out of reach.

The small room was dominated, if not actually usurped, by a large

425

Parker-Knoll reclining chair. This wasn't college issue (anything but!) nor a surprise, since it was another manifestation of Granny's equivocal bounty. I had contributed £2 on the usual basis – this was not a present but an investment in my future.

Under normal circumstances the porters might have kicked up a fuss about the delivery of an item of furniture for a freshman's room several weeks before the beginning of term (Granny liked to get things done in good time). The circumstances were not normal, but this was no sort of concession to the needs of the disabled. Granny was the abnormality, and this was a concession to her. She rarely used 'My good man' as a form of address, but she seemed permanently capable of it, and people would do almost anything to head her off before that point was reached.

Some plush ballista

The Parker-Knoll was a greenish brown or a brownish green – very much the palette of the period, after the psychedelic patterns that hurt everyone's eyes. It was very comfortable. Dad demonstrated the action. There was a lever that triggered the mechanism so the seat back reclined smoothly or surged back to the vertical. I struggled into the chair and had a go at operating it myself. The lever was no picnic for me to operate, but I loved the lower position with its altered view. When the lever was pressed again, I returned to a position from which it was possible to lurch upright without outside help. I wasn't altogether confident of the mechanism, suspecting it of scheming to hurl me across the room like an ancient weapon, some plush ballista.

'You'll get used to it,' said Dad cheerfully, inspecting the mechanism with definite admiration. It was as if he coveted a domestic ejector seat of his own. I could imagine his hand hovering over the lever, waiting for local pressure levels to become intolerable before he pulled it and was shot high in the air above Bourne End, not much caring which way the prevailing winds took his parachute from there.

'I'll get used to it,' I said, trying to match the blitheness of his tone.

I doubt if Mum and Dad thought for a moment that I would be

able to cope on my own, but for once their doubts didn't mark them out. Every parent in Cambridge had the same misgivings. All the serried mothers were inwardly wringing their hands, and all the serried fathers were giving the mothers gruff reassuring pats that made them feel much worse. In A6 Kenny the ritual ended a little differently, that's all. Instead of the father saying, with chaffing severity, 'Well, are you going to make us a cup of tea now that we've come all this way, or are you just going to sit there?' Dad asked, 'Would you like us to make you a cup of tea before we go?'

It was Mum who would make the symbolic brew if I agreed. And so I said, 'No, thanks,' and they went, which meant that I was shot of my parents much sooner than your average fresher. Mum and Dad were well on their way back to Bourne End while the other mothers were still stressing the importance of washing whites separately, and the other fathers were explaining that buying rounds of drinks at the college bar willy-nilly was the fool's route to popularity.

I had asked Mum and Dad to leave the door open and now I punted myself out into the common spaces of the staircase. A mother came bustling down the stairs from where she had been fussing over her chick. 'He's supposed to be seeing his tutor at 3.30 – Dr Mays. I'm afraid we're totally lost. Is there anywhere we ought to be? Anything we should do?'

I raised my chin and supported it with my stick – my approximation of the stroking-chin-with-hand gesture, denoting thought. I frowned and then smiled and said Dr Mays would be along presently.

The flustered mum was enormously grateful and bustled back up the stairs to pass on these words of comfort. Of course I had no idea who Dr Mays was, but if it pleased this mother to put her trust in a stranger it pleased me to play along. It was good to know that I had the look of someone who knew things. That was a definite advantage, and I didn't have many.

That first evening in Downing I could hear the other freshmen ritually revving up their record-players. The volume rose in stealthy and then flagrant increments until the noise became outrageous. I could hear Beatles, I could hear Stones, statements of counter-cultural allegiance, though the Beatles had recently betrayed their devotees by breaking up – having found out the hard way that being a guru is an exhausting business. Not everyone can stand the pressure of other people's hopes. I could also hear something rather wild, with squawks and squeaks and a deep harsh male voice wailing.

The whole upwelling of noise was a sort of instinctual ritual of arrival. The new intake was marking its territory with music. I have no doubt that there were students on the staircase whose tastes ran to the gentler strains of folk or the singer-songwriters then coming into fashion. But first night in college is no time for the roundelay, for the ballad. What marks territory is rhythm, glandular presence, energy that explodes into a chorus.

I had a gramophone of my own – a brand-new Hacker obtained direct from the factory in Maidenhead. I had a few albums – I could contribute my pennorth of racket. The machine had been set up and plugged in by Dad before he left. Yet the labour of removing a disc from its sleeve and manœuvring it down onto the spindle was daunting. I didn't feel up to it. I was tired from the effort of keeping two illusions going in a single day, the mirages of Bourne End and Cambridge University, even if I couldn't quite claim the double-strength Maya of jet lag. I wanted to go to bed, really, but that too seemed a daunting effort. There would be a meal available in Hall in an hour or so, but it seemed more fitting to fast. Perhaps I should let the toxins of my old life drain away before I started to build a new self on new food. In other words, I was a little intimidated by my new surroundings.

My shoulder ached from the drive. The technical term is adhesive capsulitis, and it has always comforted me to know the technical terms. Yet the common description is a good one. Frozen shoulder. It sounds as if it was coined by someone who had personal experience of the condition, not just a bystander or coiner of slogans.

I used my stick to draw the curtains, by pushing with the rubber tip, sealing myself off in what was to be my nest, this educational cave. The curtains moved smoothly on their runners to shut out the outside world, so I could tell myself that at least something was working as it should.

There was no toilet *en-suite*, of course, but Dad had delivered my maroon leatherette commode to one of the cubicles of the communal toilets, so I could manage perfectly well.

428

For the first time in my life there was no one hovering to offer help, however little I wanted it. I don't mean that I didn't already perform my own chores, in terms of changing clothes and brushing teeth. My snorkel technique impeachably improved. I had managed well for years, but I had always been aware of Mum in the background, seething with the need to be needed. Even in India there was some sort of back-up – if I had dawdled beyond a certain point Mrs O would have issued gruff orders for Kuppu to assist me. Here I was really on my own, and that took a certain amount of getting used to. It would be wrong to say that I missed it, but I registered that it wasn't there, the mothering tide against which I had struggled to swim for so long, swimming until my shoulder froze from the effort of keeping afloat.

It's never easy to get to sleep in a new place, where you don't instinctively know where the pee bottle is, for instance. The Margaret Erskine Dream-Cloud provided the chief element of continuity. As I lay awake on the bed I could hear the mournful chiming of a church clock – every hour on the hour, as confirmed by the Relide watch from my childhood, still keeping good time despite the inferior glow which faded long before morning. There was something wrong with the chime of the clock, so that one strike was replaced by a muffled thud. It maddened me, as if I couldn't help making a connection between the defective chime and something inside myself. A dull thud where a clang should be.

In the morning I met my bedmaker, a thin woman of about fifty with yellow hair. Her manner was frantic motion from the moment she edged open the door, pure distilled bustle. She had knocked so quietly that I hadn't been sure there was anybody there. 'Morning, Mr Cromer,' she said. 'I've brought you a cup of tea.' She put it carefully on the desk. 'I'll just have a quick go-round and get out of your way. I'll say one thing – there's not a lot of room to man-oover.'

'To man-oover,' I suggested, 'your lovely hoover.' Her face went blank. It was a mistake to start out on a playful note, as I should certainly have known. I've learned that beginnings must be neutral. My little sally hadn't broken the ice but plunged her into terror and dismay. After that, the vacuum cleaner was a mad dodgem car of suction bumping back and forth in that confined space, her duster was a blur. I let her get on with it.

Can I really have wanted to impress her with my cleverness? If so then I was demonstrating the opposite. She didn't need to be shown I was clever – why else would I be here, unless I could manage a certain something in that line? – but human and unfrightening.

I was familiar with the spectacle taking place in front of me, of tension being discharged through the medium of housework. I was installed in the Parker-Knoll, so I just pulled the joystick to lift my legs out of her way. Her gaze kept skittering to the corners of the room as if she had spotted a spider there. After a time I realised that I had the situation reversed. If there was a spider in the room, it was me, and she was doing all she could not to stare into its arachnid eyes.

I considered the cup of tea she had brought me. Was this part of a bedder's duties, to slake the morning thirst of students? It seemed unlikely. I imagined the bedder way of life as something handed down over the years, a samurai code. So these must be weak squeezings from the re-used tea-bag of charity. I would spurn them. Special treatment was exactly what I didn't want, not noticing that it can sometimes be the product of ordinary kindness.

The patience of water

I refused to be a charity case, and so I made it my mission to turn my bedder into a sort of friend. I would have to win her over very delicately. Patience was the key. Sooner or later this woman who had been assigned to me would look me in the eye, and at that point the charm offensive proper could begin. I was used to people who stared at me, or kept their distance, but her job required her to come close. She couldn't clean the room from outside the premises, and I didn't really see why I should struggle to vacate my room for her benefit.

In the meantime I needed a neutral question. I asked her about the clock I had heard in the night. She put her head on one side and gave it some thought. When she said she thought it must be the Catholic Clock – I suppose she meant the clock from the Catholic Church – her eyes just barely grazed my face. Progress enough for one day. I didn't even know her name yet. She would tell me in her own good time. I told myself with feeble bravado that I wasn't in a hurry. Time was on my side, and I would wait it out. Her name wouldn't change between now and the time she told me what it was. I'd be seeing her often enough. I had the patience of water, and would wear her petrified face down into a smile.

The bedmaker makes the bed. That's all there is to it. She does some low-level tidying-up and some low-level snooping. She's supposed to report you if you haven't slept in the bed allotted you by the college, or if you've infringed regulations in some other way. Perhaps you have been cooking gourmet meals on your gas-ring. Traces of feathers and scales on the Formica reveal that you have been stuffing swans with sturgeons – two slaps in the face for the Queen if you've only been poaching them, a third for the college if you've gone mad with the frying pan. Your bedmaker will prepare a dossier.

The gas-ring is intended for the boiling of water – milk at a pinch. Any dish more complex or whiffy than a boiled egg amounts to infraction. Frying is a mortal sin, as I had been warned well ahead of time. Time would tell if I was capable of staying on the right side of such pettifogging regulations. Meanwhile I would try my luck in the dining hall.

Of course it wasn't easy to get into Hall, physically – there were the usual couple of massive Downing steps. It was as if the architect had wanted to set up regular barriers against me personally, ritual roadblocks in my path, to remind me I was only there on sufferance and must constantly apologise for my presence by asking for help.

There was a ticket system for Hall, with everyone being issued a little book of vouchers. Eating in Hall wasn't compulsory, but undergraduates were charged for one book of tickets a term, whether they used them or not.

The vouchers were collected when you queued for your meal, and that was where I had the advantage. I wasn't expected to queue, and the staff rarely bothered to collect my tickets. Perhaps once a week a waiter would murmur, 'Better take a ticket from you today, sir, eh?' and give me a nice wink. Outrageous, really. Quite unfair on the other students, the wheelchair-deprived.

Three of us were vegetarians, out of a student body of three hundred. Three! It's an astonishingly low figure, with all the cultural upheavals of the 1960s still echoing, but there it is. Perhaps engineering and medicine, the traditional Downing subjects, attract the deep-dyed carnivore. Any reference in conversation to Gandhi's vegetarianism would be countered by a reference to Hitler's. One-all. Student culture, wavering between ideologies of diet, was waiting for the decider.

I soon made friends with one of the other dissidents, a third-year medical student called Alan Linton, and after that he sometimes helped me up the steps to the Hall with a mighty hoick. As an able-bodied third-year he didn't live in college, or else I'm sure he would have been my mainstay in terms of getting around the college at mealtimes.

I was a rather hard-line vegetarian in those days. I would call carnivores (since flesh is flesh) cannibals by proxy. I called fish 'sea flesh' or 'meat-that-swims'. Of course as a child I myself had been fond of (whisper it) cold tongue, which I had chosen to think of as a close-textured vegetable bearing no resemblance to the talking muscle installed in my own head. Perhaps I was atoning for that now, in some contorted fashion, by being so doctrinaire. I was so much at sea in my new surroundings that I made rather a meal of the few certainties I thought I had.

The standard vegetarian meal was a cheesy ratatouille-y concoction, usually served on toast. It was tasty enough, certainly not bad. Monotonous – but I was used to monotony, having grown up in its bosom. Relentless variety would have been a more searching test of character. The college meat-eaters seemed to think that what they were served was actively inedible, so we in the grazing minority weren't badly off in relative terms.

The choice of Downing hadn't been initiated by me but by Klaus Eckstein, but I'm happy to detect a deep logic to it. Downing wasn't a glamorous college, not a Cambridge icon – not famous for age or beauty, for façade or choir, student princes or Nobel laureates. It was central but tucked away, since a hedge of shops had grown up around it. It had roughly the status of a prominent recluse. The only well-known scandal in its history was of a bursar who had run off with vast sums, requiring the college to sell off a substantial tract of its holdings to the university. Hence the Downing Site of faculty buildings just next door.

Tableaux of post-mortem dissipation

Downing was mainly a slow-working factory for turning out engineers and medics. Unforeseen side-effects of the manufacturing process seemed to be drunken shouting late at night, wild laughter and a certain amount of scuffling.

Some mornings I would see half-skeletons left out in the courtyard, suggestively posed. A little later their owners, red-eyed and stumbling – the present owners, rather than the original inhabitants – would retrieve the bones from these tableaux of post-mortem dissipation.

A good joke never grows old. I soon got used to the sight of skeletal arms waved in my line of sight by giggling students crouched below the level of my window.

On her second visit the bedmaker must have been looking about her in a more relaxed fashion than before, because she got an eyeful of something even more outlandish than me. There was a tropical millipede, a nice brownish colour and about a foot long, on the windowsill. In a plastic box, mind you, not roaming free. It had cost me £1 in Maidenhead. What with the millipede and the stereo, Maidenhead had yielded quite a trove of bargains.

Actually the reason she hadn't seen it the first time was that I had stowed it in a drawer beforehand. Just being tactful, like Bluebeard not wanting to mention the wives on a first date, knowing there would likely be complications later, and wanting to get off on a good foot. Or two feet. But no more than that.

When my millipede curled up it looked very much like a Catherine wheel, though I didn't like to see it in that position too often, curling up in such creatures being an indicator of stress. This particular morning, though, it was feeding very happily. Millipedes do very well on rotten fruit.

My bedmaker stared at it. 'What on earth is that Nasty Thing?' I tried to explain the beauties of the creature, but I could make no headway. There's something about segmented arthropod bodies, legs that dance in squadrons, that seems to upset people. Coördination which would produce wild applause in a chorus line and enthusiastic cheering at a sports ground – there's something called a Mexican

433

wave, where people raise their arms in raucous sequence – just gives people the horrors in an inoffensive giant insect.

There was only one thing my bedmaker wanted to know about this beautiful creature: whether she was expected to clean out its box. I reassured her. I myself was the millipede's bedder. She could relax.

There were no signs of relaxation as yet, but it was early days. At least she was dividing her alarm between two objects, now that she had seen the millipede, so logically she must be feeling more at ease with me. We were on our way.

I knew my millipede was bisexual and hoped it would breed, not realising that you need two of them for that – any two, but you do need two. So my knowledge was curled up round a core of ignorance. Any passing biologist (and there must have been a few such at Downing) could have put me right.

The millipede had a name, but somehow I've forgotten it, and The Nasty Thing is all that remains.

Over the railings outside the back entrance of my staircase was a building on the Downing Site labelled Department of Parapsychology, which I thought was a wonderful omen and a testimony to the open-mindedness of the university – until I realised I had been misreading *Parasitology*. Also an honourable discipline, of course.

When I arrived with Mum and Dad on that first day I had been issued with a key to the door of A6, something that presented practical problems from the start. Where was I to keep it, for one thing? Pockets and I don't get on, never have and never will. Something in a pocket is as far out of my reach as a jar on a high shelf.

I asked my bedmaker for help. By now she had a name. She hadn't volunteered it, but I had extracted it like an expert dentist while her attention was elsewhere.

I had it all planned. I let her surprise me at my typewriter, tapping cheerfully away. I called out, 'I love typing, don't you? Ten tiny tendrils tapping in tempo! I'm just writing to my mother about you, only – so embarrassing! – your name has slipped my mind. I swear, I'd forget my hips if they weren't screwed on!'

She gave a little gasp and then it came out. She was Mrs Beddoes. The reluctant stump was held safe in my pliers. And it hadn't hurt a bit. 'Beddoes by name and bedder by nature,' she said. Mrs Beddoes the bedder, next card along from Mr Carve the Butcher in the Happy Families pack.

Her fear of me was still great and it was important to be delicate in my approaches. If I could I would tempt her into making the first move, as if I was coaxing a squirrel down from its branch.

I spoke soothingly, knowing that tone of voice was more important than my choice of words. 'I wish,' I said, 'I could find some way of keeping track of my room key. Perhaps a piece of string would do the trick.' This was the equivalent of the peanut on the back of my hand, tempting the flighty creature to come close.

Mrs Beddoes frowned and produced a length of string from the pocket of her pinny. Then she came up to me of her own accord, close enough to attach it to my trousers. Her hand held the string, but in another way it was me who reeled her in.

Town full of scrappy facial hair

First we tied one end to the key and the other to a belt-loop. I could retrieve the key reasonably easily by pulling on the string, but I couldn't always tuck it away again, so the whole arrangement was a bit of a business. Eventually I realised that it was simpler to have the key on its string round my neck, even if it sometimes got tangled up with my clothes. By then Mrs Beddoes was almost tame, though still a long way from eating out of my hand. Progress enough for one day.

She had gone on bringing me cups of tea, and I had gone on not drinking them. Finally she broached the subject. 'Aren't you going to have your tea, Mr Cromer?' she asked. 'I should have asked how you take it – perhaps you need sugar? If it's cold I can make you another. It's no trouble.'

Here we were at the heart of the matter, the charity case refusing to be patronised. 'Now see here, Mrs Beddoes, why do you bring me tea?'

'I thought you could do with a cuppa.'

'But you don't bring tea to anyone else, do you?'

'Well, no.'

'Perhaps you feel sorry for me.'

'Not really, Mr Cromer. It's the others I feel sorry for.'

That stopped me in my tracks. 'How do you mean?'

'Well, you're the only one who is ever awake. The only one who doesn't groan when I knock on the door. And after all, they're missing the best part of the day, aren't they?'

After that the scales fell from my eyes, and I started taking Mrs Beddoes' cups of tea at face value, as a real privilege and quite a contribution to what was (as she said), or became, the best part of the day.

A door to close behind me and a key to lock it with. These were things I had never had until I was an undergraduate. They seemed fairytale privileges. Space and privacy were not things that had gone together in my history. My most intense previous experience of control over my surroundings was possession of the ornamental Chinese box given me by Ben Nevin at Vulcan. A precious enclosure, but not large enough to accommodate so much as a pack of playing cards or, more importantly, a full tube of depilatory cream.

Now I had room for whole vats of Immac, if I had wanted, and could have kept them safe from pilferers. The Immac, incidentally, had done its work, and more than its work. I was making no efforts to suppress the sprouting of my beard, but it was chemically damaged and never grew quite right. There were irregular patches where nothing much happened. Unfortunately they were more on one side than the other, perhaps because I laid the stuff on thick where I could reach most easily. I didn't try to shave what I had, all the same. I had enough on my plate without razor chores. My growth, however substandard, didn't draw attention to itself in a whole university town full of scrappy facial hair.

Possession of a key transformed my status. It conferred so many privileges: the knowledge that no one could enter the room in my absence (except, theoretically, the Head Porter, who had a master key). Control of any admission while I was in. Privacy and security, necessary elements of the much-touted 'peace of mind'.

All this amounted to a huge step forward. My key practically defined me as an adult – far more than my beard did. Children, invalids, prisoners, the mad. None of these gets the key to his room. Thanks to the smiling authorities of Downing College, Cambridge, I was gathered in from my life on the margins. I was not only mature and well but free to roam, and certified sane into the bargain. I was in control of my own life. I was my own doorkeeper. I had the key to freedom.

It took me a couple of weeks to realise that I didn't like it. That is, I enjoyed not having inferior status, but I didn't like locking my door, or even closing it. I hadn't come to a university to shut myself away. It was at home that I sometimes wanted to do that. It was at Trees, Bourne End, that a key to the bedroom would have come in very handy from time to time. At Trees I could have become a recluse very happily between meals, ignoring Mum's anxious knocks, thinking my own thoughts and steadily filling a whole array of urine bottles like a penniless little Howard Hughes, while my beard grew long on the one side only.

The other door to the room at Trees, the one which gave wheel-chair access to the great outdoors, would always be left open wide, unless there was a blizzard or Mum tried to sneak up and spy on me from that vantage point. Even when automatic doors *à la* Starship *Enterprise*, with their soothing whoosh, become standard, I'll be senti-mental about the peerless charm of an open door. An open door offers me my only real chance of catching someone by surprise. Leaving the door open being also my best way to arrange to be surprised myself.

In any case for me the difference between a closed door and a locked one isn't as great as all that. It's almost a technicality. I went through a brief phase of leaving my door unlocked, though I tried to remem-ber to take the key with me when I went out, in case Mrs Beddoes or some other authorised person innocently locked the door on my behalf. Then one day I came back to find a stranger dozing in the Parker-Knoll. It was the junkie who regularly fixed up in the lavator-ies. He didn't make trouble, just shambled off on command like a dog in disgrace, but after that I took security more seriously.

Every possible insult

Back in Bourne End the floor of the room I shared with Peter was bare lino. In A6 Kenny I did at last have carpet. The college author-ities were less worried about the problem of my tracking mud across internal spaces than Mum – perhaps it came under the heading, from their point of view, of fair wear and tear. For Mum, wear and tear could never be fair, since everything was part of a conspiracy to make her look slovenly in her mother's eyes. Wear and tear was always unfair.

When I took a closer look at the carpet, I saw that every possible insult that could be offered to a floor covering had already been visited on it and been (more or less) wiped, hoovered and scrubbed away, darkening the overall tone of the textile.

I was a little embarrassed about being cleaned for. It was partly that I didn't want a servant – if I was condemned to having a servant I wanted one who would be more useful to me. I tried to show Mrs Beddoes that most forms of clearing up merely made things inaccessible to me. As far as I was concerned, tidying up was only hiding with a whiff of self-righteousness. Books, for instance, needed to stay on the front section of the desk if they were to remain within my reach. She nodded uncertainly, and after that she mostly left my things where I wanted them.

What I really needed, if I had to have help of some sort, was help with washing. Dressing I could manage, and laundry wasn't too much of a problem – there was a service which collected and made deliveries. Bathing was much harder work than washing clothes. I would have been delighted if there had been a similar service operating – to send this body off for laundering and get it back neatly folded and smelling fresh.

The toilet arrangements were satisfactory – in fact, since (naturally enough) the other students tended to avoid the cubicle with my commode parked in it, it was very much the cleanest of the three, the best of a bad bunch.

Bathing was a different matter. In the bathroom of A staircase, Kenny Court, I had to run a bath and transfer myself from the wheelchair to a hoist supported by a rail on the ceiling. It was reasonably manageable. I would lay two 'canvas' (actually synthetic) straps crosswise on the seat of the wheelchair before sitting down on it. Each strap had a ring on the end, which had to be slipped over the hoist's hook. These technical descriptions are hopeless! Better to imagine the picture on the front of a standard christening card. Now substitute me for the baby in the sling of cloth, and an engine attached to the ceiling (dangling a hook) for the stork.

I would rise in my cradle into the cold air of the bathroom, negotiate myself into the right position and lower myself into the water, pulling on the appropriate strings to turn the motor on and off. Green for Go and red for Stop. Even when I was in the water I had to stay in the harness of the hoist. I would conjure some suds from the soap onto a flannel, then perch the flannel on the end of my stick and poke at the outlying parts of this body, but I was relying more on the power of hot water to magic away dirt than anything else. The bare bones of this routine were familiar from life at Trees, where the bathroom ceiling was also fitted with a rail, but I was used to having help or at least company.

I'm not usually much of a wallower in baths. Experiences at the hands of a sadistic physiotherapist employed at CRX had more or less broken any link for me between bodies of water and peace of mind, though I'd felt safe enough in the pool at Burnham, surrounded by my fellows. My 'shamming' in the bath at Trees was never very prolonged, even though I was surrounded by family. It was a sort of trance state, all the same, so much so that I wonder if a spore of language, the word *shaman*, hadn't been what originally drifted into Dad's mind. Despite his own best efforts, Dad was rather good at inklings. He preferred not to tune into other people's awareness, but sometimes he couldn't help himself.

In the tub on A staircase, Kenny Court, though, I would lie there till the water grew cold. Not wallowing so much as postponing the inevitable. I knew it was going to be such an almighty effort to heave my bones out of the soapy broth and get out again.

Lowered back into the wheelchair, I had only to detach the straps from the hook and I was free, though the overall expenditure of effort had been enormous. The whole business of taking a bath single-handed was like manning some assembly line, whose only end product was myself, wet and often shivering, but with some claim to being clean.

Help getting bathed would have changed my undergraduate life more than any other single factor, but I didn't know anyone well enough to ask and I had set myself against making friendships based on need. The most I dared do was ask a passer-by or staircase-mate to close the quarter-light window in the bathroom to keep the heat in.

A large towel is unmanageable, a small one isn't up to the job.

Towelling was rather a frustrating process altogether, and it made sense to wait for the laws of nature to finish the job. Given time, drying is something which happens on its own.

There was no point in waiting in the bathroom when my room was so much warmer, so I would set off home in the wheelchair, discreetly draped in a towel. Remembering my school science lessons I said to myself, 'This is no more than an observation of the phenomenon of the loss of latent heat of evaporation,' and my body had indeed lost a lot of heat by the time I was back in my room, thanks to the movement of air (and my own trundling) in the bathroom and corridor. If I was colder then, logically, I was also drier.

Elves with hairdryers

Being back in the warm was a great luxury. It was tropical! It wasn't long before I was almost dry. Of course my shoulders lost heat more quickly than my bottom, and my bottom was still damp when the rest of me was dry. Ideally, if my body had allowed the position, I would have lain face down on the bed while National Health elves with hairdryers played warm currents of air across my backside. As it was, I would ease myself up onto the carpet, whose traction enabled me to raise my bum from the seat of the chair, and then retrieve the still-damp straps from underneath me. Sometimes I would have to take them back into the bathroom personally, but usually I could 'volunteer' a student to take them back to the bathroom and hang them up for me ready for next time.

That sort of 'volunteering' can only be an emergency measure – language itself rebels against intransitive verbs being turned inside out like that, like umbrellas in a hurricane, and the social fabric is damaged by people's helpfulness being forced instead of being allowed to open out like a blossom in its own sweet time. But as far as I was concerned, in my Cambridge period, that was just too bad. Jump to it! I haven't got all year.

I didn't do much home-making in my new premises, but I did pamper myself with a couple of indulgences that had been forbidden at home. First I bought joss-sticks and lit them, an act banned at home. Dad explained, 'The thing about joss-sticks, incense, all that sort of stuff, is . . . you see, they can disguise all sorts of other smells . . .' And I had said, 'I know. Isn't it marvellous?' I missed the point, I failed to twig. Dad wasn't referring to the standard male fug of a shared bedroom but to the smell of cannabis. Mary Jane, goblin weed, eater of souls. No doubt cannabis made people do many strange things in those years, but one of the strangest was to make parents sniff around their children like police dogs at airports.

At Trees I had wanted a red lightbulb in my room, to make it more like a shrine, but this suggestion also created alarm. Mum and Dad didn't seem to be attuned to the effect I wanted to create, that receptive spiritual aura. The disapproving term Mum used was 'boudoir', while Dad's phrase was 'knocking-shop'. So I simply draped a piece of red cloth over an existing bulb, and gave their opposition a united front. Fire risk. Concern for safety masked something more mysterious, a moral disapproval of coloured light. In my best surly-hippy manner I muttered, 'You'd tax the ruddy rainbow if you could find its home address. You're a disgrace to the Age of Aquarius.' Not that I believed any of that guff.

Now I was free to install that questionable glow, to let my moral fibre loosen softly under its influence. Mrs Beddoes rather hesitantly installed a red bulb at my command, and soon I was happily basking in its rosy aura – the colour of life in the womb, on those sunny pre-natal days – in my boudoir in Kenny Court, my yet-to-be knocking-shop.

There were ways for undergraduates to fill their calendars, short cuts to a social life – clubs and societies. These were on display at the Freshers' Fair, to be held in the Corn Exchange. My tall staircase neighbour P. D. Hughes – Pete – said he was going, and didn't mind giving me a push. I know I say 'tall' the way some people say 'nice', but Pete really was. He was nice and tall. He sometimes had to duck while going through a doorway designed for smaller folk. He and I lived in a constant state of amazement at the size of each other's shoes.

The din at the Freshers' Fair was astounding, a physical reminder that I was part of a massive intake of student flesh, perhaps the loudest noise I'd heard since The Who took the stage at Slough. I felt correspondingly oppressed and insignificant. I was hoping there would be a Ramana Maharshi Society, since Cambridge University was alleged to be a progressive environment, but I was out of luck. The closest thing to it alphabetically was Mah-Jongg Club – not close. The closest to it in content, at least as other people were concerned, was the Transcendental Meditation Society, of which I had a holy horror. How dare this sub-guru Mahesh appropriate (and garble) the name of Maharshi?

Pete seemed not to have interests or hobbies as such. He was drawn to stalls manned by women, no matter what organisation they represented, chess club or choral society. Men outnumbered women by a factor of ten at the university, something which neither gender ever forgot. Pete, though tall and nice-looking, was awkward, conscious of the odds against his being a winner in the sweepstakes for companionship. If there was a pretty face at a stall, he asked for details of the organisation concerned. With a little encouragement he might have signed up for anything. A smile could easily have drawn him in to satanism or even stamp-collecting.

He would park me at an angle while he made a play for a young woman whose looks he liked. I wouldn't be able to see his target from my position, but I could follow the progress of the little flirtation from the behaviour of Pete's hands on the handles of the wheelchair. Unconsciously he would rock me back and forth, like a mother pacifying the baby while chatting to a neighbour, but since his physique was large and strong – not to mention gripped by sexual tension – his movements weren't as smooth as he must have imagined. They weren't at all soothing. No baby could have been lulled by such agitated pushing and pulling. It would have woken and howled. I had to bite my lip myself.

Pete accumulated a lot of leaflets and fliers, smudgily printed on rough brightly coloured paper, which he dumped in my lap while he pushed the chair. After we had left the Fair, he gathered them up and thrust them into a rubbish bin. We had been warned against the temptation, common for freshmen, of signing up for every sort of society and voluntary organisation, rather than find our own way in a relatively denuded social landscape, but we seemed in our different ways to be immune.

After a few days at Cambridge, all the same, I began to have the nagging feeling that I had missed something. When the feeling clarified itself, it turned out to be a throwback to my first reactions at CRX. Then the question had been: I can see the hospital, but where's the school? Now it was more complicated: I can see Downing College, the Senate House, King's Chapel, Heffers, Lion Yard, the Corn Exchange, the Modern Languages Department, the Blue Boar and the Round Church, even the University Library (most of them, admittedly, only on the map, or while arriving in the Mini), but where's the university? If the whole august institution had devoted itself to the *vichara*, to Self-Enquiry, asking constantly with full attention the arch- and only question *Who Am I?*, what would be its answer?

Holy tipples

The University had a motto, of course, but it was a bit on the cryptic side: *Hinc lucem et pocula sacra*. Roughly, 'This is where we receive enlightenment and imbibe holiness.' But the Latin doesn't make a complete sentence and you have to supply the missing grammar. *Hinc* means 'from here'. Good – I'm in the right place. And the next bit is about light and holy tipples (*poculum* being a diminutive meaning a goblet or the liquid it contains, so 'little drinks') and it's in the accusative, so someone is doing something to the light and holy tipples – or will do something or has done something. 'Getting them' is as good a guess as any, and I suppose it may as well be 'us' that does it. It's all rather frustrating – or to put it another way, good practice for construing Sanskrit scriptures.

Oxford has a motto, too – *Dominus Illuminatio Mea* – also with the verb missing, but this is a pretty elementary conundrum since there aren't hundreds of verbs which are followed by a noun in the nominative. Technically it's called 'taking the complement'. Verbs are shy beasts. Only a few can take a complement.

God – blank – My Light. It's more or less on the level of Spike Milligan's Crossword Puzzle for Idiots (One Across: first letter of the alphabet, One Down: the indefinite article).

Any guesses? You there, at the back. . .

And the winner is. Is.

Est. Though actually . . . why shouldn't it be *Sit*, or *Fit* or *Fiat*? Let

443

God be my light, God becomes my light, Let God become my light. Not a bad little mantra, when I think about it. But given the cultural atmosphere in 1970 I suppose *Sit* would be the obvious candidate for runner-up. Let It Be.

Perhaps there was something subtler involved in the whole elliptical-motto business than I noticed at the time. It's rather suggestive: if even the motto of the place doesn't make sense unless you supply what's missing, then perhaps this is a sort of manifesto for the education being offered, where nothing will be served up on a plate. Nothing in fact can happen until you throw yourself into the void. More things than verbs can be 'understood' even when they're not there.

Bit late to understand that now! It wasn't that I was expecting to be spoon-fed even at the time, in fact that was just what I didn't want. And I was unusual as a freshman in that I had actually spent time in (theoretically) educational institutions where some of my fellow pupils had very much needed to be spoon-fed, helped to masticate and swallow.

I didn't need a welcoming committee, but I wouldn't have minded a welcome. No doubt this is an impossibly subtle distinction, and I was just being difficult.

If you encounter difficulties for long enough, you become 'difficult' yourself. Karma-particles migrate from situations to the persons who find themselves in them, and before long people are saying, 'John's a terrific character, of course . . . but he can sometimes be *rather hard work*, don't you find?' I hadn't yet found the means to reverse the current, to install myself at a hub of radiant ease.

The first Saturday of term found me at a real loose end. I had great difficulty filling my time. Suddenly I was overwhelmed by a feeling of confinement far more intense than I had ever experienced during the years when I was kept in bed. Entrapment clamped its lid down on me and sucked out all the air. Time crashed down on me in a tidal wave of stone. I would be struggling in this room – *with* this room – for a little eternity.

According to Hindu cosmology we live in the Kali Yuga, a Dark Age many thousands of years long. I had absorbed this as an outlying part of my faith, but now I began to experience it as real.

During the Bathford years of bed rest I was isolated by a body that was turning against itself, and by doctors' orders that banned any sort of adventure – but now some more obscure force was holding me under, so that I experienced my liberty as house arrest.

At that moment there came into my mind a strangely soothing set of injunctions: *You need not leave your room. Remain sitting at your table and listen. You need not even listen, simply wait, just learn to become quiet, and still, and solitary. The world will freely offer itself to you to be unmasked. It has no choice. It will roll in ecstasy at your feet.*

It sounded like Ramana Maharshi's voice murmuring in my ear. The only thing was, I had read it and been struck by it before I had read a word of his, before I had even heard of him. It was actually Kafka, a favourite writer of Eckstein's and someone he was always quoting to baffled students at Burnham Grammar School. He had written it on the blackboard, that sentence about the world rolling *in ecstasy at your feet*. He knew how to get me intrigued.

Now, though, established as a student of German and Spanish at an ancient university, I gave the passage a fresh mental reading. It didn't sound like Kafka at all, however well attested. It sounded like the opposite of Kafka, who was so attuned to the negative. That's why it sounded like Ramana Maharshi, who was as far from Kafka in temperament and background as it was possible to be. Here was Kafka, of all people, preaching on a text of Ramana Maharshi, and expounding the liberating principle that you don't have to change your life to change your life.

Kafka's wooden head

Was it really Kafka, though? I mean, I know that passage is by Kafka *now*, but was it by Kafka before Eckstein wrote it on a school blackboard in 1968? Perhaps Ramana Maharshi had reached across time and space to send me a message of encouragement. It would be very much in his character as a worker of miracles to manage something so discreet, something which blended into its mundane surroundings. A miracle in camouflage. No commandments in skywriting for Ramana Maharshi, no burning bush, just a nudge of Eckstein's chalk. Divine intervention as sly and cryptic as the crossword clues (not for idiots) which I could never manage to crack.

'Gangster ducks five hundred and fifty in the general buzz (7)'. Answer: hoodlum, apparently. Please explain.

The question that always gets asked in such circumstances is this: how do you get the nerve to think you're worthy of a miracle, however low-key? Over time I've learned to give myself the answer: where would I get the nerve to think I'm not?

I remembered the saying of Ramana Maharshi, which Ganesh had quoted to me in India. *He who is in the jaws of the tiger cannot be rescued; so also a person who has fallen into the grace of a guru cannot escape from it . . .* Grace is a serious business. So, yes. Perhaps Ramana Maharshi turned ventriloquist on my behalf, and made comforting words emerge from Kafka's wooden head.

In any case I decided I would take the hint, whether it was transmitted from an æthereal or mundane source. I would make the experiment. I would stay in my room and see what happened. After lunch I installed myself in the Parker-Knoll, but then I mounted an expedition to the door, which I opened and left open. Nothing had been said by Ramana Maharshi / Kafka about the door, but it seemed sensible to give the world some encouragement in its unmasking of itself. Then I returned to my chair.

Every few minutes someone passed my door, but no one came in. Few even glanced inside. Perhaps I hadn't learned to be properly quiet and still.

The next day, Sunday, I left the door open all day. I was baffled by the lack of interest shown by my staircase-mates. If I myself had been free to wander at will round a building, really free, I would have investigated everything just as thoroughly as I could, but clearly I was an exception in this respect. I could only think that curiosity declines proportionately with ease of access. People to whom doors had yawned open all their lives seemed to take no interest in what lay in front of their eyes.

I fought the urge to get in the car and explore my surroundings in that way, but my mobility was more apparent than real. Either the wheelchair stayed where it was, in A6 Kenny, or it came with me in the car – in which case it needed firstly to be installed there, and then to be unfolded and put at my disposal when I had arrived wherever it was that I was actually going. The smallest trip had to be planned like a military campaign. I stayed in, waiting for the world to make its move. There was space for it, just, to roll in ecstasy in front of the Parker-Knoll. If need be I would pull the lever and lift my legs out of the way, to make sure the world had enough room to disport itself.

Finally on Sunday afternoon there came a shy tap on the open door. It was a student with creamy skin and pale splotched freckles. He looked deeply into my eyes. That's such a rare thing that it can be very stirring when it happens. His own eyes were very green.

Perhaps I really hadn't seen such colouring since my brief glimpse of one of the ambulance men who accompanied me from my Bathford home to the train that took me to CRX. Since then it had reverberated in my mind, steadily acquiring a sexual overtone, but this newcomer somehow didn't prompt sexual thoughts. He wasn't exactly beautiful, but his looks had the unreal quality that often goes with beauty. He asked if he could sit with me a bit. I said he should suit himself, and we exchanged names. His was Colin Moulton. He lived on B staircase.

Small talk could get us only so far. When he had said, 'What are you reading?' and I had said Languages, and I had asked him back (he was an engineer), there was nowhere much to go conversationally. There was no point in pretending that these disciplines reached out strong hands of greeting to each other.

We sat in silence, which I found very soothing. The world might not be rolling on the dishonoured carpet just yet, but it was sitting with me in companionable silence. Finally Colin asked, 'Shall we pray together?' It turned out that this visitor wasn't an answer to prayer after all – he was a summons to it instead. And with that the whole event went prayer-shaped.

Foolishly I avoided conflict by saying that my body did not permit kneeling, instead of coming out honestly with 'Not today, thank you.' As a result I received a long lecture on the unimportance of physical posture since God knew what was in my heart. I was exasperated to be proselytised by someone who only lived on the next staircase – I know I can be a bit fussy about mobility and its obligations, but does it really count as missionary work if you're still under the same roof as when you started out?

I couldn't help noticing, all the same, that Colin Moulton wasn't as sure of himself as a man who intends to make converts needs to be. He didn't use set prayers, and this may have been a matter of pride with his sect, to speak to God without a script, but he fumbled badly in his choice of words. 'God, whose eye is on the sparrow and the hawk, God who heareth the lion and the lamb . . . we thy unworthy . . .' His voice trailed away. He had none of the professionalism I remembered from the travelling Billy Graham spectacular I had attended as a teenager, where the acolytes had the brimstone verses ready marked up in red. He was making it up as he went along, and eloquence wasn't raining down in fat drops of grace upon his tongue.

In the matter of kneeling, though, he took unilateral action, dropping to his knees with an audible impact. This made a pious thud. He started off kneeling parallel to me in my Parker-Knoll, but from this position it hardly looked as if he was leading me in prayer. He edged round until he was facing me, but that was worse. There was no easy answer to the riddle of body language I presented. To an outsider – to anyone passing my open door – it might actually have looked as if he was worshipping me.

He stood up and placed a hand on my head instead. He must have thought this made a better picture, but still his tongue was tangled. 'Oh Lord,' he intoned, with a second-hand cadence, 'Lord who knowest every secret thought, to whom every sinning heart is as clear as . . . clear as crystal . . .' Then he took his hand off my head and prostrated himself in front of me. This was such an unusual posture that I took a mental photograph, deciding I quite liked it. I was fascinated by his hair, not blond but so pale that it seemed to avoid colour altogether. But Colin was just getting started. Now he was gazing at my ankles as soulfully as he had earlier peered into my eyes. Flat on his belly on the floor, he looked as if he was gathering himself for a holy press-up. 'Lord, turn these feet . . .' he said. 'Turn these feet . . . towards Jerusalem . . .'

That was when my patience departed, leaving me furiously angry. I did my best to give him a kick, knowing even as my brain formed the command that my legs wouldn't be up to it. I swung my feet at him.

It couldn't really be called a kick. He felt the breeze from my little lunge, and looked up wide-eyed. For a moment he must have thought that he was detecting the first stirring of a miracle cure.

This was not the world rolling in ecstasy at my feet, this was someone at least as isolated as I was, taking up space on my floor. It was time to sweep him off my carpet. I told him that I didn't need converting, that I had plenty of faith of my own, even if it wasn't the same brand as his.

He blushed fiercely as he got to his feet, but now he couldn't look me in the eye. Instead he looked at the wall and blurted out, 'You've got a lot of empty space on that wall – why don't I brighten it up with a poster?'

I had so little practice in saying No that I found myself unable to refuse. I'd rejected his religious advances, and it seemed to make sense to give him back a bit of dignity by playing along.

My nature was not yet steeled against its own obligingness. I didn't anticipate that the wretch would of course return immediately, carrying not only his gift but also a roll of Sellotape in his mouth. He set about putting his poster up on the wall. '*You can't do that!*' I squeaked, but he had already done it. That was even before I saw the message I would be broadcasting: that no one comes to God except through his son Jesus Christ. I'm afraid that's just the side of the cult I can't tolerate, that blocking off of avenues. It doesn't take much of that sort of thing to give me spiritual claustrophobia. But quite apart from religious outrage, there was the matter of adhesive. Colin Moulton had been so busy reading the Bible he had neglected more worldly rule-books, and Downing's strict ban on the use of Sellotape to fix things to walls.

'You're only supposed to use Plastitack!' I shouted. Plastitack – Blu-tack's anæmic kid brother.

His skin betrayed him with another blush (I was beginning to see the disadvantages of pale colouring, that octopus-transparency to emotion), but he managed to keep his voice even. 'That's not important, is it?' he said. 'Not when we're talking about your immortal soul.'

Nothing marked him out as a fanatic so much as this attitude to fixtures and fittings. Normally you'd be safe in saying that an English believer, however fervent, would have some respect for the bye-laws. An English Luther would have Plastitacked his 95 theses to the door of Schlosskirche in Wittenberg, out of respect for the varnish and the maintenance staff, and the Reformation would have fallen at the first fence, its founding documents effortlessly binned.

On his way out Colin Moulton said two things. First that he would pray for me. Well, I couldn't stop him from doing that. Secondly that his door was always open. That last part was rich. I decided that from then on my door had better not be. I was my own doorkeeper, and now I had better practise being my own bouncer too. The world was welcome to come and roll in ecstasy on my carpet, but from now on it would at least have to knock and identify itself, to give some sort of password.

Doors are either open or closed (don't talk to me about that 'ajar' nonsense). If doors are open anyone can come in, and if they're closed they restrict me more than anyone else. Having to choose which way to leave my door seemed to restrict my options to either defence-lessness or claustrophobia. Like most people I'm an ambivert, turned both inwards and outwards, but my door couldn't mimic that double perspective.

Clearly I was still a sad case of spiritual impatience. I had gone to India and demanded self-realisation double quick, chop chop, shine a light and make it snappy. Now I had set aside a whole weekend for the solitude and stillness which would compel the world to unmask. If the world had rolled at my feet, then the world was a freckled zealot.

I fumed when I looked at my new wall decoration. A poster of that sort on a student's wall in 1970 was about as big an attraction as a big cross on the door in a plague year, but I wasn't thinking of the possible repercussions on my social life. It wasn't clear that my status could fall any lower as a God-botherer, but I didn't want to find out. I just wanted it down sharpish.

Snails in their morning slime

Colin had cannily put the poster up on the wall beyond my reach. The only way I could get it off the wall was by slipping my stick under the edge and tearing it down in ragged stages, breathing hard with the effort and the anger, and leaving scraps of paper held by stubborn twists of sticky tape.

Mrs Beddoes tutted with disapproval and removed the remaining scraps and twists of tape on the Monday morning. I would almost have preferred to leave them there to go yellow and brittle, as a reminder of my first lesson at this new palace of learning: it was easier for people at large to get at me than for me to find my way to the company I wanted. Whatever that would turn out to be.

I've always woken up cheerful, without needing to have a particular reason. I'm sure this isn't an exclusively human privilege – I dare say snails in their morning slime feel much the same thing. I was still far from waking up depressed, but there wasn't the usual shine on my morning mood.

Monday, when it came, was better. Some sort of routine could be imposed on a Monday. There had been a brief orientation for freshmen to give us some idea of what was expected of us. There were lectures, for one thing, and it was a source of grief to me that they weren't compulsory, since that would have organised my life at a stroke. In fact there were too many lectures for any one person (and for once I mean an able-bodied person) to attend. They were listed in a special issue of the University Register, swelling its pages until it amounted to quite a little book.

It was part of university lore that lecturers were paid whether or not anyone turned up to hear them. If they were alone in the room then in theory they were expected to give the lecture just the same. In fact few of them were natural performers, and many would have been relieved to be spared the ordeal of catering to an audience.

The only compulsory academic activity was the writing of essays for your supervisors. 'Writing' at the time really meant writing – making marks by hand on paper. I pecked out my essays, though, on the trusty Smith-Corona. I was making life easier for my supervisors by not submitting anything in my dismal scrawl, but there was no doubt about typing being second best, in the Cambridge way of looking at things. Typing was the province of the subliterate or American.

In those days supervisors, like pharmacists, prided themselves on their ability to decipher illegible scrawls. If handwriting truly became

451

impossible to make out, a supervisor always had the option of getting you to read your essay aloud. This was also the choice of supervisors who hadn't found the time to give your prose even a once-over.

It wasn't a tightly policed system. As long as you kept your supervisors (and your director of studies) happy, the question of how you worked was left up to you. This was almost an academic version of Ramana Maharshi's teaching: many ways up the mountain, some steeper than others, all leading to the same peak.

I, on the other hand, didn't enjoy having the freedom to construct my own course. I wanted to be roped in with a like-minded group, climbing under escort. I had only been a schoolboy in any real sense for the two years at Burnham, and I wasn't ready to move on so soon to a more solitary version of the learning process, clambering up above the tree line where the academic air is thin.

I had wheels galore, what with the wheelchair and the Mini – nine in all, counting the spare in the boot – but mobility was still in short supply. I was snookered on a regular basis. I needed to have the wheelchair in my room, or else I would be reduced to tottering pathetically about. Without it I would have gone arse over apex before the end of the first week. The Parker-Knoll was for special occasions.

But if I left the chair in A6 Kenny and drove somewhere in the Mini, then I was helpless to go any further once I had arrived wherever the car could take me. What I lacked was regular help to load the wheelchair in and out of the car.

What would solve the problem at a stroke would be another wheelchair, one that lived in the car, so that the amount of furniture-moving could be reduced. I was too proud to spell out my needs to Granny (for instance), but I'm not sure it would have done any good even if I had nerved myself to it. No one could describe her as a soft touch, but she had stumped up the bulk of the funds for the electric wheelchair that had made life easier at Vulcan, for the car that had replaced it, and even the reclining chair now occupying pride of place in A6 Kenny. Better not to go to the well too often, or the lid would slam down and catch you a nasty biff on the way. Putting it more simply, Granny would click shut the clasp of her handbag, in a judgement against which there was no appeal.

I had already realised that the Parker-Knoll was both an amenity and an obstruction, something that clogged the wheels of daily life even as it oiled them. It was hopelessly oversized for that little room. Visitors would not rest until they had explored the mechanism, and their long legs were taking up most of the little space remaining. To prevent this I would sometimes occupy the P-K myself, but then visitors would help themselves to the wheelchair and we were only moments away from wheelchair races or attempts to use it as a sort of Jeep on the stairs. Meanwhile the little chair provided by the college, hopelessly surplus to requirements, was often placed on the bed, or outside the door, to keep it out of the way. I began to feel about the Parker-Knoll roughly what Ramana Maharshi felt about his tiger skin, and if a visitor had asked to take it away I would have been tempted to say yes.

Egos in bantam display

There was an immature side of me which was still waiting for the world to understand me, to tune in to my wave-length. Surely in this ancient university town, crammed with the best brains available, young and old, there would be somebody capable of imagining what it was like to be John, someone who would ask, 'Wouldn't it be easier to manage with another wheelchair?'

I had the wrong idea about universities. They were not institutions dedicated to the development of integrated personalities, light and holy tipples notwithstanding. They weren't even places where intellectual adventurousness was encouraged. They were forcing-houses for the ego. At Cambridge the ego was fed and watered, preened and fluffed up, and then pitted against other egos in bantam display. This was apparent even at mealtimes.

I didn't have a set place to sit in Hall. It was rather a matter of where I was plonked by whatever volunteer made himself available, though the awkwardness of the wheelchair made it easiest to put me at the head of a table. Over time I was exposed to a fair cross-section of the student population, though I listened idly more than I joined in. The simplest conversation had a competitive edge. It didn't seem possible to like a book or a record without becoming embroiled in a whole set of arbitrary alignments, empty convulsions of status. *Slaughterhouse-*

Five. A Rainbow in Curved Air. Hot Rats. The Glass Bead Game. Bitches Brew. The Wretched of the Earth. Any of these could polarise a group. These artefacts were timeless masterworks, or they were pitiful trash. Endless arguments could rage on such subjects, arbitrary disputes being much more congenial to brains inflamed by egotism than sweet admissions of indifference. Not to have an opinion was seen as a sign of personality disorder, when in fact the opposite is the case. Every opinion is a rut in the road.

The way Ramana Maharshi put it (in the supplement to the *Forty Verses on Reality*) is that for unpretentious folk there is only one family to be resisted – spouse, children, dependents. Among the learned, however, there are many other families: families of books, families of theories and opinions, all of them obstacles to understanding. 'What is the use of letters,' he goes on, 'to those lettered folk who do not seek to wipe out the letters of fate by enquiring, "Whence are we born?"? They are gramophones, Oh Lord Arunachala. What else can they be? They learn and repeat words without realising their meaning.' Cambridge was more than anything a city of human gramophones, playing the same records over and over again, mental needle in plastic groove.

I don't know if television played a major part in other undergraduates' lives. On me it hardly registered. There was a set in the Junior Common Room, theoretically available (as long as your choice of channel wasn't outvoted, presumably) but I never bothered. I can't imagine that many students watched more than half an hour a week. If someone at Hall said to a friend, 'I'll see you at the usual place,' it was likely to mean a rather shame-faced conclave convened in the JCR for *Top of the Pops* or *Doctor Who*. I hadn't come to Cambridge to be an overgrown schoolboy, so I didn't take part – which was a shame, since that lovely old ham Jon Pertwee was starting his run as the Doctor, and I'd have enjoyed dropping the name. There was something called *Monty Python's Flying Circus* which people seemed to enjoy without embarrassment (one of the performers was apparently a Downing man), but the series had finished without my seeing any of it. I lost interest when I learned that it featured no snakes.

Since I was too insecure to concoct my own course of study, I would obviously have to go to lectures, and this involved its own set of hazards. I hated the help I needed. I needed the help I hated. It wasn't much use finding somebody who would be at my lecture if they weren't also in Downing. Ideally of course they should be somebody in Kenny, though this was a bit much to hope for. Since students of Modern Languages were not a strong presence in Downing, the odds were stacked against my teaming up with a fellow freshman on any sort of regular basis.

In fact there was one suitable person on my own staircase, the same nice tall Pete – P. D. Hughes – who had escorted me to the Societies Fair. He was reading Russian, which he always pronounced Rooshian like a Smersh operative in a Bond film, and had lectures at the Sidgwick Site, where mine mostly were. He was my trump card, but then again he was my only card. Trump cards wear out when played too often.

There were other stalwarts on Kenny, but their numbers dwindled. As we all in our different ways were sucked into the university's Maya, they found they had more important things to attend to than portering around one of their fellows. When novelty wore off, only drudgery remained, and being obliging became a bit of a bore. In their place I'm sure I would have done exactly the same.

Pete was very willing – I can't fault him for that. Sometimes I would give him a lift in the Mini in exchange for help getting in and out of it. How he fitted into that car I'll never know. The distance between Downing and the Sidgwick Site wasn't even very great, and Pete thought it would be fun to push me the whole way in the chair, but of course I would have to arrange to meet up with him later for the return journey, and I didn't want to do that. It seemed vital to spread the load, to avoid a situation in which the name *Cromer, J. W.* irresistibly called up in Pete's mind the association *constant toting, in need of*.

Helpfulness becomes a chore when it is taken for granted, and I couldn't help at least seeming to take it for granted, by dint of having no other option. My needs were continuous and unvarying. What I needed one day I also needed the next. Inevitably Pete would find this oppressive. I found it oppressive myself.

There was no mistaking Pete's outsized feet on the stairs, but many times when he knocked on my door I kept mum inside, forcing myself to manage without him. It was bad enough that he felt duty-bound to knock, without making him think that I was lost without him.

If I didn't have the momentum to proceed unaided then I simply missed lectures, which weren't after all compulsory. I find it much harder to drag myself down a step than up a step, which meant that the greatest single obstacle in my whole impeded day was the one between me and the Mini. It took quite a build-up of determination (or sometimes just frustration) to wash me over that barrier and into the swim of the academic day.

If I missed a lecture sometimes people would say the next week, 'I didn't see you last time – were you sick?', and I'd say yes out of polite-ness, muttering, 'Sick to the back teeth of managing without help' under my breath.

I began to think, though, that my mild hypnotic powers were wan-ing along with my ability to meditate (better than it had been in India, but nowhere near full strength). If I found myself in a group, at Hall or in a lecture theatre or library, I learned to recruit helpers from the edges of the group, not asking those near me. I would say to someone I hadn't seen before, 'I think it's your turn to take me to the lav, don't you?'

What's the usual euphemism for excretion? Going to the toilet, or the lavatory, the crapper or the bog. That's just it: going to. The journey involved. Once I'm in place, I can perform as well as anyone. It's the journey that takes the work and the organising.

My underlying strategy in recruiting outlying helpers was a long-term one. It was actually better to recruit the mildly unwilling for toilet-portering, since they were sure to have no hidden motive darker than a wholesome need to get away. Samaritans need not apply.

I hoped that as word got round people would realise that there was no safety in hanging back. They might get off more lightly by coming up and sitting right next to me, in the eye of the storm in a teacup. In fact my victims on these occasions seemed rather to enjoy themselves. Many of them were public-school boys, fantastically es-tranged from their own bodies, who found they enjoyed the neutral physical contact of carrying another human being around for a bit, though it would never have occurred to them to volunteer. After their errand was accomplished they would be likely to sit near me, looking oddly dreamy and contented. Opiated by the combination of touch and civic virtue. I began to realise that the transaction was the opposite of what it appeared to be. I was actually doing them a favour. It was charitable work.

On days when I had done without Pete's help, I would emerge from A6 in a state of mild masochistic melancholy, and totteringly trudge towards whichever exit from the building I had decided to use. The obstacles were identical – a single step in either case. The rear entrance involved the shorter journey and a manageable door, but offered a much smaller chance of my being spotted by someone who would install me in the Mini.

If I had decided to picket the front entrance, then the tableau I presented was pretty clear: the little chap and the door he couldn't manage. The step on the other side of it a further obstacle. If I heard footsteps behind me then I would wait and see. Usually people would stop and offer help. Sometimes, it's true, people would tiptoe out the back way. I wonder what that felt like. Not very nice, I expect.

I would listen to the strange pause before they (mostly) squared their shoulders, walked up to me and asked if I needed help. In those moments my lack of mobility almost seemed to be catching. It was as if I made them think about their walking and forget how the steps went. It was a little hiatus in the dance – the hesitation tango – before conscience cut in.

If people were coming from the other direction, so that they were crossing the courtyard when they saw me, I noticed that they would look quickly around to see if we were being observed by others. I seemed to put people on the spot, so that they would lose face both by helping me and by walking on. My situation emitted vibrations of embarrassment. It was my job to damp them down with charm and personal warmth.

One way or another, on my own or handily boosted, I would make it to the Mini and drive to the Sidgwick Site. Then I would resort to a new method of transport. It's the inventor's privilege to christen his device, and I call what I learned to do *hitch-lifting*. As far as I know it was a piece of social interaction unprecedented in the West, perhaps even the world. If I was a tribe I would have much to show the anthropologists, but a one-man tribe slips through the nets of the discipline.

If I wasn't in a position to equip myself with a handful of more or less unresentful slaves, then I must learn to milk the general community of its goodwill. Hitch-lifting was a type of inverted hitch-hiking which had more than a glimmer of begging about it.

Beggars are of course resourceful people, anything but passive before their fate, but their status is not high in the eyes of the world. If I played my cards right, though, I could keep my self-respect. My poverty was poverty of movement, and my task was to wheedle some free work out of people. I asked for alms in the form of action. I was playing a new game on a blank board with no rules, until over time I developed a certain amount of expertise.

The hitch-hiking was inverted because I was the one with a car, throwing myself on the resources of passing pedestrians. There was no need for me to stick out an actual thumb – luckily enough, since my thumbs are not expressive instruments.

The working of the stratagem was as follows. First I would select a target. As in all salesmanship, the choice of a victim was crucial. The target was almost always male, since the wheelchair would have to be lifted from the car. If there were no men visible, then a vigorous and bustling woman might find herself pressed into service. I would attract attention by voice, or by tapping on the window, or if all else failed by climbing laboriously out of the car and letting my deficiencies advertise themselves. I refrained from using the car horn. It was too peremptory, too much of an emergency signal. It slighted the free will of my helpers with the imperiousness of its summons. Besides, I needed to keep something in reserve for actual crisis, as opposed to the constant, barely managed crisis that was my life as an undergraduate.

Adopted by a family of logarithms

It sometimes happened that a physically slight young woman, not perhaps weighing much more than I did, put herself forward. Then the most likely consequence was a sort of secondary hitching, with my shrimp of a St Joan rallying male troops on my behalf. This transaction, what with that one-in-ten gender ratio, would take barely a moment. Perhaps I was indirectly responsible for forging romantic connections. Perhaps there are grandchildren at this moment stifling their yawns as they hear the old tale.

If I needed to be conveyed up steps, then I wouldn't announce the fact until my victim had lifted the chair out of the car. Once that had been managed, it was a very difficult position for my victim to refuse the second-stage request. The same is true of all confidence tricks. One Yes begets another until the No reflex is bound and gagged.

Then I would ask to be lifted out of the car and into the chair. *Then* I had to have my books, and *then* I needed to be taken to where my lecture was being given. If my victim was a fellow student, then all too often he was on a tight schedule, and not likely to be going to my lecture of choice. In that case I'd hitch a lift off somebody else, which was relatively easy since I was at least on the pavement. I had hoisted my sails, at least, and could reasonably hope for a personified wind to fill them for the last stage of my journey.

It all worked reasonably well. Still, the amount of mental strain involved was considerable, the continuous effort to impose myself on others by raw force of charm. All this before I could even begin to study! By the time the first lecture of the day began, I felt I had been through a whole alphabet of effort, from A to Z (passing æ somewhere along the way), while my fellow students had barely made it as far as B. I began to feel eroded and worn down. It's not that I'm shy. Anyone who has been brought up without privacy has seen his shyness wither away for lack of nourishment. But my energy wasn't unlimited.

I was gradually discovering Cromer's Paradox of Disabled Life. This is it: greater independence means greater dependence. So easily stated, so hard to live with.

To elaborate a little: if your needs are being looked after institutionally then you don't have to ask for help. Just ring the bell or wait for the nurse to come round. But if you're managing by yourself, without being able to do everything *for* yourself, then you have to ask for help many times a day. The determination not to be defined by your needs leads directly to your having to spell them out the whole time. And so: greater independence means greater dependence. QE (alas) D.

I made myself persevere with the technique of hitch-lifting despite exhaustion. Otherwise I was afraid I would gradually become a recluse, and soon even going to lectures would be beyond me. Then the authorities would conclude that mainstream education for the disabled was a noble gesture but an educational sham, without giving a thought to the extra difficulties that had been put in my path. I wasn't going to let that happen.

It didn't take me long to realise that there were students of Modern Languages in my year who were virtually bilingual. They would mention casually that they had dreams, if you please, in Spanish or German. If I had a dream in a foreign language it was only likely to involve my shouting '*Hilfe! ¡Socorro!*' while being crushed by a giant toppling dictionary. It turned out that these prodigies had spent their childhoods (in some cases) or at least large stretches of their school holidays in Germany or Spain. And at that point my patience and sympathy rapidly became exhausted. As far as I was concerned, that wasn't studying a language. That was legitimised cheating, a flagrant abuse of the system, though no one seemed to see it but me. I mean, would we really go on admiring a mathematical prodigy after it emerged that he had been adopted by a family of logarithms?

To sprain your smile

I went hitch-lifting even when I didn't have lectures to go to. I gritted my teeth and made myself go to the Whim for a cup of coffee that tasted of nothing but scalded milk. I tried to make hitch-lifting into second nature, so that I wouldn't feel any erosive effect from all this wheedling. I'd park the car somewhere, ask a passer-by to get the chair out, thank them with brisk warmth as if I wanted to be rid of them, spot someone else walking along who looked as though they might be going where I was going, and chime in with 'Ex*cuse* me . . . Could you possibly give me a push as far as . . .?'

I learned the value in such sentences of the middle-class elaborations, the pattern of stress on the first word and the genteel adverb. I tried to convey that I was quite surprised to find myself in need of help, but there it was, it'd be a funny old world if we didn't all of us need a favour now and then. And so on and so on. People were kind, and still it was all so tiring, so very tiring.

In the daily operation of hitch-lifting, in the town rather than the university precincts, my most willing helpers were definitely good-looking boys out with their girlfriends. Nothing was too much trouble for them. They would set me down properly and make sure everything was at the right level. If we were in a pub they were likely to stand me a drink and to say, 'If you want anything, I'm right here.' A lot of this must have been for the benefit of the girlfriends, but not all – and only relatively new girlfriends would be in the market for such indirect buttering-up. Established partners wouldn't be so easily fooled, if fooling was what this was about. I think it was a very natural overflow of contentment, sexual satisfaction spilling outwards as it rarely does even in the young.

Cambridge was a large town compared to Bourne End. The streets were often crowded and so were the pavements. Bicycles were everywhere. Bicycles were the elementary particles of the Cambridge universe, but I had last reacted with one on an experimental basis in hospital at Taplow, and I couldn't get excited about them now.

I could park the Mini more or less anywhere, though I tried not to obstruct the passage of traffic. The wheelchair had its own tendency to produce clots, little embolisms in the pedestrian circulation. A surprising number of able-bodied walkers – I'd put it as high as one in a hundred – seemed bewitched by the chair, unable to step aside from its progress. This seemed to happen as often when I was being pushed as when I was punting myself along in the intervals between porters.

It seemed to be some malfunction of the decision-making apparatus, with the option of going left being cancelled out by the option of going right. There was nothing to choose between them, and the alternatives produced paralysis. The wheelchair didn't have headlights, of course, and these pedestrians weren't rabbits, but the situations were parallel. At least once a day I would find myself confronted by someone, almost invariably male, blushing and mumbling, stalled in front of my vehicle, wishing the ground would open up and swallow him. Sometimes I wished for that to happen too, though I'd smile and say, 'After you.'

Hypnosis is hard work, it drains the system, and charm is hypnosis without the handy short cut of a trance. People can't be made to do things against their will, but they can be led into a state where they don't think in terms of what they want. But now I also came to see that charm is like a muscle or a gland. It took effort to clench someone's attention in mine, or to secrete the social juices that made people play along, and at the end of a day my face would simply ache from the effort of geniality.

Is it possible to sprain your smile? If so, then I did it sometime in the second week of that first term.

I still had my photograph of Ramana Maharshi on my desk, but I could hardly bring myself to look at it. I seemed to deal with the world through a deviously grinning mask, the opposite of his smile in its piercing openness.

Of course there were brighter moments, and there were even people who would come up and ask if they could help. I had my regulars, people I came to know almost as friends, just because they had helped me out a few times. One very big and broad woman seemed to enjoy the labour of assisting me. I suppose she was in her late twenties or early thirties. She wore denim skirts of an intermediate length which seemed to limit her range of movement. At all events, when she was preparing to lift me she would plant her legs far apart and then hitch up her skirts with a great grin. She seemed to be modelling her stance on a Japanese wrestler's. Her body gave off a warm friendly smell, spiced like cloves or cinnamon. Her only conventionally feminine touch was the wearing of elaborate earrings, which must have looked discreetly decorative when she put them on, head at rest, but became downright alarming when she was out in public, thanks to the abruptness of her movements.

Then one day she happened to pass when I had already accepted assistance from someone else. Her face became fixed and she went rigid with disapproval. I hadn't seen her in time to give her priority, and it was impossible to dismiss a willing volunteer just because a more experienced porter had happened along after the fact. But after that, although I saw her passing by on a regular basis, she never offered assistance again, and this is something I have never understood, the process by which the helpful impulse shades into a sense of ownership.

This person and I had never so much as exchanged names. She had held me in her arms, yes, but she was no more than an acquaintance.

Sometimes it seems that I'm in a minority all over again, for feeling that physical intimacy shouldn't go to people's heads. Offering a service shouldn't establish a right.

The blooms from traffic islands

Still, beggars can't be choosers, eh? The status of begging was much on my mind at the time, because of a remark of Ramana Maharshi's.

Of course my begging wasn't Indian begging, stumps-and-sores begging, but it felt real enough. In Cambridge at that time there seemed to be only two real beggars, both of them shaky alcoholics. One of them made a show of selling flowers on Market Hill, but everyone knew they were stolen, or at any rate pilfered. He slept in a hostel on the outskirts of town, and would uproot the blooms from traffic islands and park plantings as he neared the centre.

What Ramana Maharshi said about begging was that it made him feel like a king and more than a king. To depend on strangers for the food he needed to live gave him the exhilaration others find in the exercise of power. I found this very hard to understand. I even put it down to his having been born a Brahmin, though he had shed his caste. As if he had kept a sense of entitlement even when the entitlement ran out.

It was almost a form of slumming, wasn't it? To treat begging as a sort of royal sport. Then I reminded myself that he was so indifferent to food, in his early days in Tiruvannamalai, that others had to place it in his mouth. Eating was optional and hunger an irrelevance.

And if he had been able to see through the game of Brahminism, why should he not do the same with begging? Yet he didn't say begging was a matter of indifference to him, he said it made him feel like a king (and more than a king). I couldn't help seeing him in a constant downpour of food and flowers, which seemed less like begging than being crowned Queen of the May. It was all a long way from my world of Supplementary Benefit and Education Authority grants, and asking people to drag me from car to wheelchair so that I could attend lectures from which my absence would not be noticed.

I was a poor student of Bhagavan, not to remember that his enthusiastic description of begging referred specifically to the beginning of his reliance on others for food. Whether he experienced the royal feeling over time isn't clear.

I was still seeing the world through Christian eyes. Admittedly Christ made a splendid remark about taking no thought for the morrow, but his teaching turns the beggar into a figure of reproach to those who have more than they need. When the privileged deal with the deprived, they are face to face with Christ's representatives and their own judges – but there's not much suggestion that the lot of the judges is a happy one. I didn't want to be a reproach to anyone. I just wanted to get to lectures.

So I tried to conform my thoughts to Ramana Maharshi's, and to feel that I was partaking in something he regarded as a privilege, and still begging did not make me feel like a king. It made me feel like a beggar.

Beggars get scraps. Begging my way to lectures was the only way I might find enough scraps fallen from the academic table to fill my mental belly.

In Christianity, of course, there's 'blessed are the meek', but even before I discovered Ramana Maharshi I had a strong feeling that by a great mercy meekness was not required of me. I don't quite know what it would mean in my case, since meekness is voluntary powerlessness and I had no power to disown in the approved manner.

I started to discard the clothes I had arrived in, like many another fresher, since they seemed dated and formal. Of course, thanks to Mum's skill with her sewing-machine – 'the Bernina' – they were also made to measure, and I had to abandon fit along with formality. Wearing a gown had traditionally been a university requirement, but recent friction between town and gown had led to its suspension. The only benefit I might have got from a gown (supposing one was tailored to my size) would have been an extra layer of protection from the chilly winds for which the city is known, the icy gusts from the Urals losing little of their cutting power on the way to slice into East Anglia. One item I did hang on to was a sort of cape she had made for me, which I could drape round myself with the minimum of difficulty to keep the wind off.

Mostly the gradient of university life was against me, but there were occasions when the playing field was level, or even had a tilt in my favour. It's only fair that they should get a mention. Those were days like the ones I remembered (as a spectator, of course) from Vulcan, when an able-bodied local team was unnerved by the home side's competitiveness or was undone by its own chivalry. Either way, it got thrashed.

Fascinating elastic bread

One triumph had its roots in a moment of outrage. As I was working my knife and fork down into my plateful of food one day in Hall, they came across something which felt like a special sort of bread, resistant but also squishy. I was intrigued. Evidently Chef had excelled himself, and all for the benefit of the little Modern Languages student in the wheelchair. I thought that before I took a bite I would just peek under the topping to see what this fascinating elastic bread was. It was a steak. It was an animal slab, and I went berserk. I'm sorry (very slightly sorry) to say that I howled for this heinous object to be taken out of my sight.

The massed carnivores of the college watched it go, incredulous with sorrow. They mourned its passing, except that mourners don't usually lick their lips. Even I could see that this was a shining specimen of the flesh feast, succulent, cooked to perfection – I hadn't eaten at the Compleat Angler all those times without knowing what steak should be like. Granny might make a little road across her plate, but Peter laid down a four-lane highway over as many plates as were put in front of him. I imagine this superb atrocity was destined for High Table and had been blown off course. No wonder my fellow students looked on in such anguish. They would never see such a meal in their academic lifetimes, and I was sending it back with shrill squeals of protest.

Next day the college Chef came to interview me about my preferences. 'I'd like to make a special list of what you can and can't eat, sir!' This was a diplomatic breakthrough, this embassy to the untouchables. The outcastes were being wooed. Nato was reaching out a tentative hand to the Warsaw Pact.

The 'special list' was simple enough. *Can eat: non-meat. Can't eat: meat.* That was it, essentially, but it seemed best to go into detail and make positive suggestions. Just to be on the safe side I mentioned that vegetarians couldn't eat anything which had been in contact with aluminium, and he gravely wrote down this also.

From then on Chef paid special attention to the herbivores. The other two got the benefit without the shock of being ambushed by that steak, buried like a landmine of animal tissue beneath the innocent tomato topping. In a college of notoriously awful food, the three of us – the one per cent – dined in something like luxury. The minority is always right, of course, but rightness doesn't usually tingle in the tastebuds as it did in ours then.

It wasn't long before the carnivores noticed the general superiority of our rations. A deputation approached the Bursary to request vegetarian food. Request refused – if they had wanted to register as vegetarians they needed to do so before arriving in college. This was entirely unfair and very pleasing. On the one hand, every new vegetarian is a gift to the world. If there's one religion that should be allowed to proselytise, it's vegetarianism. On the other hand, the deputation didn't represent a change of heart but a sly bid for better grub.

We lonely three were conscientious objectors who had faced down the stigma of refusal, while they were like volunteers who wanted to desert now that they had seen what life was like in the trenches of institutional catering. They were sent smartly back to the front, and we conchies held steady at one per cent.

Mum wasn't much of a letter writer by this stage of our lives, but she did send on to me a note from Mrs Osborne. Apparently Kuppu had wished me to be informed that if I ever returned to Tamil Nadu she would look after me for the rest of her life.

This was a sweetly shocking thing to hear. The contrast with Cambridge life was very great. A gardener's wife in India could pledge herself, after a few short weeks of acquaintance, to serving me as long as she had breath. In the West my value to anyone else was not high, and my needs were strictly my own.

Dad was never much of a correspondent either. A letter from him was always something of an event, and his first letter to me at Cambridge was by his standards a hysterical document. *A bit of a facer, frankly . . . timing could be better . . . not as if they're short of a bob or two.*

He had received a bill from Downing. He sent it along for me to look at. Should he pay it? Why should he? But how could he not? Little ripples of alarm churned up the preferred flatness of his letter-writing manner.

The bill was for the expense of fitting a rail over the bath on my staircase. It was accompanied by a compliments slip from the Bursar, but no refinement of stationery could soften the blow. The bill was for ninety-two pounds. Dad didn't know whether to pay it, to refuse point-blank or to challenge the amount. And neither did I. None of the alternatives had the slightest appeal for Dad: being taken for a fool, defying authority and waiting for the bailiffs, or haggling like a carpet-seller in the souk.

Even so, this was a thunderbolt which was in some ways almost re-freshing – an antidote to brooding, something out there in the world that damanded immediate attention.

Ninety-two pounds! It was an outrageous sum of money, as Dad knew very well since he had paid for the very similar (if not identi-cal) over-bath rail at Trees. It was clear that Downing had given the work to some top-drawer contractor, then passed the mark-up on to us. It wasn't even as though the college had been required to provide a hoist. I had brought my own. Technically I suppose it was Dad who had brought it along, loading it in the back of the car that had escorted me to Cambridge. It was made by the same Everest and Jen-nings who had made my first electric wheelchair, inferior predecessor of the Wrigley, and it wasn't anything fancy. It was really only the motor from one of their chairs, lightly modified. Instead of the relays required to power a chair, there were two strings, a green and a red. Green for Go and red for Stop. Heaven help you if you're colour-blind – but not in itself an elaborate piece of equipment.

The Cromer family rail

I didn't even understand the principle behind sending Dad a bill. Was the idea that we would sell the rail back to the college when I left, minus depreciation calculated on some standard basis, or were we entitled (perhaps required by law) to rip it out and take it with us out into the wider world? Would we be sued for negligence at a later date if we left the Cromer family rail – a horizontal funicular only suited to the most unadventurous sightseer – disfiguring Downing's handsome bathroom ceiling?

Dad had no one to ask, but I did. Every Cambridge college assigns to its students an official whose job is to defend their interests, against the college itself if need be. This is their tutor. I was up against exactly the sort of situation for which the tutor system was designed, so I went and complained to mine.

When I say 'I went and complained', of course it wasn't as simple as that. Nothing is ever that simple. To get help from my tutor I needed an appointment with him, and to get an appointment I needed help from someone else, someone to carry notes back and forth on my behalf. The system was essentially the same as what Mrs Osborne used to send messages in Tiruvannamalai, except that she had the benefit of a large stock of boys clamouring to be chosen. Perhaps the simplest method in Cambridge would have been to send someone with a message to my tutor's pigeon-hole in the Porter's Lodge, but there was no guarantee of a swift response and I felt that this was an emergency of some diffuse sort.

I had been assigned a tutor on the same basis as everyone else, which was splendidly egalitarian but unrealistic, since what I really needed was a tutor with rooms at ground level. As it was, I had to be carried up two flights of stairs before I could begin to make my case. Each time I asked someone for such a favour of portering, I felt I was depleting my stock of social credit in the college, and well on my way to becoming a nuisance.

I was already forfeiting any possibility of getting a good review for my time as an undergraduate, the sort of favourable verdict that goes *A thoroughly successful experiment! An object lesson in how social inclusion can be made to work . . .*

We hardly knew he was there.

The physical remoteness of my tutor was another version of institutional tunnel vision, like the bellpush that Marion Wilding of Vulcan School always mentioned as an example of the thoughtlessness of the outside world, well in reach of everyone but the disabled people it was installed to help. Still, if Mohammed will not come to the mountain then the mountain must come to Mohammed. The mountain was always having to stir stumps in my Cambridge days. The mountain had a fair few miles on the clock before long.

It would have been a relatively easy matter for my tutor to descend from on high and meet me on my level, except that the thought never entered his head. Perhaps this was thin-end-of-the-wedge thinking, which I first encountered in Manor Hospital (my first hospital ever) over the contents of a cereal bowl: if John has Weetabix everyone will want it. To my mind this argument has yet to be sufficiently discredited.

If John Cromer's tutor makes an exception in his case, undergraduates will start expecting tutorial visits in the pub. Or in the bath.

Let them eat Weetabix, I say.

My tutor's name was Graëme Beamish. He didn't actually use the diæresis in the spelling of his name, but I felt it was required, to indicate that he was pronounced Graham rather than Grime. I supplied the symbol in my mind, out of typographical courtesy.

When I was finally admitted to his presence I explained about the bill and the worries it had caused. His response was drily chafing in a way that I discovered over time was characteristic of him, but was certainly a little disconcerting on first exposure. 'This seems rather a poor augury of our relationship, John, if I'm to be expected to intervene in every little dispute your family has with tradesmen. I'll give you the benefit of the doubt on this occasion, as long as you can assure me that you will notify me before you undertake any further structural alterations to the fabric of the college.'

In retrospect I think he was ill at ease with the rôle of tutor, actually rather shy in his dealings with people, and protected himself with a sort of performance. He took on the character of academic in a comedy some years out of date. It wasn't that he was old – probably not far into his thirties. Perhaps he felt that he would lack authority as a don unless he was actively, indefatigably donnish.

After he had got his little tease out of the way his advice was clear and helpful. 'Tell your father that this bill is *not*, repeat *not* to be paid. The problem will be induced to go away. Mr Gates our splendid Bursar will see to that, though it is to be admitted that he knows nothing of this as yet. Leave it to me to break the news to him.' As I came to learn over time, 'splendid' was Graëme Beamish's unvarying adjective for officers of the college and the university, and possibly for every person on earth. Like a word in classical Chinese its actual meaning in any single case had to be inferred from context and intonation.

I reported back to Dad that the bill was to be ignored. On clear nights, though, when the psychic acoustics were good, I felt I could hear between chimes of the Catholic Clock a high scratchy noise which carried on the wind all the way from Bourne End, and represented Dad's heroic efforts to wrestle with his nature and history. What a struggle it must have cost him, to disregard a clear demand from an established authority! His hand must have ached for his pen and his chequebook. Without Dr Beamish's countermanding order, he would never have ignored a bill, however unjust.

A few days after my interview with Graëme Beamish, a college porter knocked on my door and asked when it would be convenient for the Bursar to pay a call on me. This seemed a worrying development. Mohammed was coming to the mountain – quite possibly with a vengeance. I had contested a demand for payment, and now an inflamed Bursar was seeking me out in my warren to demand redress.

Ninety-two little snips in my gown

I was certain the threatened visit was about the blasted ceiling rail. I imagined I would be summonsed to some sort of disciplinary hearing of an ancient and intensely ritualised type – the Cambridge equivalent of a court-martial or a consistory court, a tribunal fiscal-academic, conducted in Latin or Norman French. No doubt the Bursar was required to attend in person to pass my doom upon me. On the day of reckoning the massed bursars of the university would make their way from their colleges to the Senate House, wearing full academic dress, carrying slide-rules in their left hands and red marker-pens in their right, with black caps or enormous bird-masks on their heads. Possibly Aldous Huxley's *The Devils of Loudun*, which I had read not long before, contributed to this rather hysterical imagery. It had certainly given me nightmares.

In the ancient heart of the university I would have my Post Office pass-book formally impounded, my wheelchair sold from under me. The Vice-Chancellor himself would draw near, to make ninety-two little snips in my gown with a tiny pair of inlaid shears. Academic gowns didn't have to be worn on a daily basis, but perhaps I would be issued with one for this single occasion, for a proper pantomime of disgrace.

Of course nothing of the sort happened. Mr Gates the Bursar had come on a different errand. The ritual that concerned him wasn't arraignment by bailiffs in regalia but matriculation, which seemed to be a sort of initiation ceremony for undergraduates. He said, 'I hear tell that you're not planning to attend matriculation . . . which would be a great pity.' I wondered how he knew. Perhaps I had failed to return some vital chit.

'Do you mind if I ask why not? I'm sure we can help you with any problems.' His voice was hoarse and rasping, oddly tender. He seemed genuinely preöccupied with his unreal ceremony, though it was even less plausible than the one I had dreamed up. As a Downing bursar he had inherited the stigma of a scandalous absconding. Through his voice the disgraced office seemed to plead to be trusted again.

As he talked his eyes ranged over the room, but I had the impression that he wasn't spying on me but rather the reverse. It was as if his eyeballs had been greased. This must have been his practice when mingling with the student body. By keeping his gaze on the move, not stopping to register any one thing, he was hoping to avoid the known horrors of undergraduate life. In this way he was able to absent himself from such sights as forgotten coffee mugs with lids of fur, resembling accidental exhibits of surrealist art. He could walk right past the extra-terrestrial's lost sock camouflaged as an oozing prophylactic.

I was taken aback, but did my best to rally. 'Well,' I said, 'it states quite clearly that matriculands − is that the word? − must wear black shoes. It says in fact that there are *no exceptions* to this rule.' I imagine there had been trouble in recent years with undergraduates expressing their contempt for the Establishment by turning up in blue suède shoes or Wellington boots, or perhaps barefoot.

I had only the dimmest idea about what matriculation actually was, but that was clearly not the point. The Bursar was nodding gravely, so I went on: 'But you see, I have only the one pair of shoes, which are brown. There they are, see?' His eyes slid past my feet as I wiggled them faintly. 'And I can't just pop into a shoe shop and pick up another pair. They take months to make.' I didn't give him all the details, the numbered lasts, the annual entitlement. 'It seems simpler not to go.'

'Oh, don't give up hope,' said Mr Gates. 'Do please attend. I can't say matriculation, though an ancient ceremony, is a very thrilling event in the life of an undergraduate – certainly it pales beside a "demo" or a "sit-in". But it is an academic milestone you have earned, so please attend. It doesn't exactly mark your birth as a student member of the university. Your academic christening, perhaps. We shall wet a great many babies' heads! But even so, yours would be sadly missed. So please attend. Pay no attention to trivial regulations. These rules were made to be broken.'

Which was a lovely thing to hear. It would be even lovelier if there was a list of the rules that were like that – which ones you could blow away with a single puff of breath, which ones would turn and sink their teeth into you.

I know we're all supposed to adore the big-hearted small-mindedness of British life – the professor's forbidden dog in his college rooms, for instance, classified by indulgent authority as 'cat'. I suppose it's easier to enjoy such things if you can be confident they will work in your favour.

It did seem strange that the phrase 'no exceptions' didn't offer any sort of guide to the breakability of the rule to which it was attached. It was like hearing that Fragile labels are attached promiscuously to packages of every type, rubber balls as well as crystal. Fascinating but unhelpful, particularly if you were a fragile package yourself.

Of course, it's possible to be too pedantic, though I can hardly believe I'm saying so. A number of times I've heard myself referred to as having brittle bone disease – I've even been told so to my face – and I've managed to stifle the urge to correct the mistake. This isn't *University Challenge*, this is daily life in the Kali Yuga, and they've grasped the essential point. Don't drop him.

While I was lucky enough to be holding a bursar captive in my room, carpeted between the Parker-Knoll and the wheelchair, I pressed my advantage and asked for exemption from another rule. I wanted a phone in my room. It was against regulations, of course, but so was having a car and wearing brown shoes to matriculate (or be matriculated?), and I had cleared those hurdles in my own athletic fashion.

It turned out that Mr Gates could stone-wall as well as coax. 'That's something you'll have to take up with your tutor,' he said, 'and I'm afraid university people get very worked up about possible precedents.' University people – as if he was some other order of creature.

Pretty *flink* myself

He seemed remarkably calm himself about the prospect that the next generation of freshmen, having learned of the trail I had blazed, would turn matriculation into an orgy of non-conformist footwear. Desert boots, flip-flops and Dunlop Green Flash tennis shoes would be flaunted without shame.

On the telephone question I felt confident about approaching Graëme Beamish for help. It seemed obvious that he would sympathise with the bind I was in. It leapt to the eyes. Consider: to request a telephone I needed an appointment with him, but without a telephone it wasn't easy to arrange one. That was just the sort of thing we could avoid in future, with a little flexibility and some installed apparatus.

I already had the support of my director of studies and German supervisor, Roy Wisbey, a good teacher and a terrific chap. He would carry me up to his rooms without any fuss and then sit next to me on a sofa while he looked over what I had done. I remember him praising me for the phrase *ein flinkes Eichhörnchen*, saying there was no better match in the world of adjective and noun – *ein Einhörnchen* being a squirrel and *flinkes* meaning 'frisky', though (his words not mine) frisky didn't capture the full sense of the German, that pert alertness, bristling junior vitality. That kind comment made me feel pretty *flink* myself.

Didn't Roy Wisbey keep urging me to phone him if I had a question of any sort? And every time I explained that this wasn't possible he asked almost testily: 'Why on earth haven't you got a phone in your room?', as if I might have thrown it out of the window in a fit of temper. 'How are you supposed to manage?' A very good question.

He suffered from tunnel vision as it strikes academics, mild mental glaucoma, so that although he didn't miss a thing in his subject area, he could be very vague about other parts of life. I kept telling him I wasn't on the phone, and he kept asking me for my extension number, undeterred.

Graëme (the academic who did academic impersonations) greeted me with great satisfaction. 'It is as I promised you, John,' he said. 'The bill that has lost you so much sleep has been magicked away. It has been legitimately settled without requiring the draining of your father's funds, which I'm sure are tied up as is proper in high-yielding bonds.' Perhaps he was misled by our address on the Abbotsbrook Estate, realm of stockbrokers and advertising executives, suggestive of top-people status. We had a home there, but nothing so secure as a niche. Mum would have liked a niche, nothing better. About Dad I'm not so sure.

I was curious about how the trick was managed.

'Ah, John, those who ask to have magic explained only guarantee themselves disappointment. The fact is, there exists a splendid organisation called the Bell, Abbott & Barnes Fund, whose help is available to undergraduates in hardship. I think there is a connection with the British Legion – at all events, when I learned of your father's history in the armed services I decided they should be our first port of call. We needed no other. They were happy to oblige.'

This was not at all what I had expected. I didn't know what to say. 'Don't thank me, John,' said Graëme with what seemed to be withering irony. 'I do these things for fun. It is my whim, my caprice, my joy, and no acknowledgement is expected.' In academic fact Graëme, as I had found out by this time, was a physicist whose work on 'lattice transformations in niobium disulphide' had important implications for electronics or (for all I know) cookery. He specialised in compounds of niobium, named after a bereaved mother who never stops crying. He knew the secret sorrows of the periodic table. Why should he want to put on such a show of stuffiness in his rôle as a tutor?

Actually it made perfect sense. In the lab he wore a white coat and possibly goggles. Meeting his tutees he wore a different metaphysical uniform – university fustian from head to foot, with implied spats sticking out below the hem of his gown. His rooms, of course, corresponded to his 'real' academic life rather than his persona, so there were no dusty books, wall hangings or tuns of madeira. The only thing that could be described as an ornament (though it would have drawn my eyes anyway) was an array of half-a-dozen polished globes, the size of steel marbles, suspended bilaterally from strings in a wooden framework, an executive toy designed to illustrate a physical law – to wit, the conservation of momentum. Newton's Balls, they were called. I longed to set them going, but didn't dare to ask. Silly, really. If it wasn't childish for him to have them there then it was hardly childish for me to want to play with them.

'Perhaps you have other errands for me to do, John. That would intensify the satisfactions of my job to an almost unbearable degree.'

I had come on an errand and this was an opening which could hardly be bettered, so I blundered in, not remembering that I had experienced the same sensation in a different context (with Granny) and had run into a brick wall glittering with broken glass.

There are times when the very brightness of the green light is a danger signal, but my worldly knowledge was very partial at the time. I should have cut my losses before I had any and come back another time, however foolish it would have seemed to beat a retreat just when the functionary entrusted with my welfare was advertising – however sardonically – his devotion to my cause.

Nonchalantly I laid out my case. I had decided during the negotiations about the ceiling rail that Graëme was a sensitive soul who protected himself with his stage-professorial manner. No matter – I had more than enough charm on hand to disarm him. And still the pettifogging persona adhered to the tender core. It wouldn't be peeled away, and I was stuck with the husk of this human fruit.

Graëme turned down my eminently reasonable request with what was almost satisfaction. He wouldn't even look at the note Roy Wisbey had written on my behalf, on the grounds that this was a college matter in which no faculty member should presume to meddle.

'I wonder if you realise, John,' he said, 'that it is only recently that Fellows themselves have had telephones. The telephone is the bane of modern academic life and should not be a priority for you or any other undergraduate.

'Your circumstances are not so exceptional, you know. Anyone would

475

think you were living in a croft in remotest Orkney, when in fact you will never be closer to the heart of a community than you are now. A telephone would only encourage you to withdraw from full participation in the life of the college.' He sighed. 'I wish I could get rid of my own apparatus. I would certainly get much more work done.'

As an argument this was pitiful, so the explanation of his refusal has to be sought elsewhere, in my own manner of asking. Perhaps I was simply too breezy, too sure of a positive response. It's true that I have been called cocky in my time. The words 'John' and 'bumptious' have been brought into alignment within a single sentence. Authority likes a supplicant to roll over and play dead, not to claim help on all-but-equal terms – a factor I had failed to consider.

I can't always be touching my forelock, though, can I? It's boring to do things in the same way every time, and since my life is largely made up of asking for help I amuse myself by varying the phrasing. I can't always be saying, 'Could you possibly be so kind as to pass the salt? Seasoning is the making of a meal, don't you agree? Even a little nearer, if you don't mind, so that I can actually reach it with these unsatisfactory limbs. Infinitely obliged.' Sometimes it'll be more like 'Pass the salt and make it snappy.' Perhaps with Graëme, officially on my side, I was a tiny bit brusque about the need for a telephone.

I took it for granted that he was in my corner, but after all he was *in loco parentis*, and he took that responsibility seriously. It's no small part of a parent's job to thwart the wishes of the young – certainly that was how Mum and Dad operated.

Mentally caressing my approaching phone

Perhaps unconsciously I mimicked Granny's imperious tone, asking how long it would take to install the phone, as if my time had a value in itself, a value perhaps greater than his own . . . I don't remember now. If I did, then my imitation of her methods fell sadly short of the results they consistently achieved for her. But however the responsibility should be divided between us, Graëme Beamish set his face against the idea of me being connected to the wider world by a wire. And having weakly decided, he was strongly opposed to changing his mind. Intransigent even.

Luckily I like a little intransigence now and then. It gives me something to engage with, difficulty with a human face (even if set stonily against me) rather than a hostile impersonality. I would do some research on the legal position and ride back in triumph.

In the meantime I was able to examine my feelings about the way the bill for the rail had been 'magicked away'. At the time I had been so taken up with mentally caressing my forthcoming phone that the information hardly registered. When it finally sank in I felt not just disappointment but actual resentment. This was chicanery pure and simple. I hadn't wanted the bill paid for us, on the basis that my father had been in the Air Force and money was tight. I wanted it rescinded on the basis that it was unfair. I wanted it absorbed by the devious authorities who had secreted it in the first place, not mopped up by a bloody Fund. Dad too would far rather have settled an oppressive debt than be classified as a defaulting pauper. And now a sum intended for a poor student had been swallowed up by a rich college.

Of the two theories that could explain my presence at Downing, social experiment or academic charity, the social experiment theory seemed to be losing ground. Evidence was mounting that I was a charity case, and one that needed a special subsidy if he was to keep himself clean. I seemed to balance on a knife-edge between the deserving and undeserving (the deservedly grubby) poor.

I did a little research and then requested a second appointment with another flurry of intracollegial notes. I had prepared a little dossier, almost a legal case. I had mugged up on the Chronically Sick and Disabled Persons Act 1970, and was able to refer with great confidence to subsection c of section 2.1, which concerns the provision of telephones and any special equipment.

'May I ask to see your paperwork?' Graëme said firmly.

I pushed it towards him. He read it with close attention. I should have anticipated that he would be a dab hand on committees, highly sensitised to the pulling of wool over institutional eyes. He showed a quite new sharpness of style, his dusty manner being largely for undergraduate consumption. 'It appears that such responsibilities devolve on local authorities rather than lesser institutions like our own. Perhaps you would like me to put a call through on your behalf to

Cambridge Council?' I hesitated, wondering if I would be letting myself in for a long struggle. 'I should warn you, though' – and here he looked up to give me a smirk of forensic triumph – 'that as an undergraduate you are unlikely to meet the criteria for being "ordinarily resident" in Cambridge. Three terms of eight weeks amounts to less than half the year. The local authorities are likely to regard Downing College as your holiday home. Is there a telephone at your parents' house, which is I believe your ordinary residence?'

I could hardly deny it.

'Then the legislation seems to be having the desired effect. Is there anything else I can help you with?' I still don't know why he was so dead set against my having a phone, but for the time being I was stymied.

I was exempted from rules which didn't matter to me – such as the matriculation footwear protocol – and required to conform where it did. If there was a court of appeal above my tutor, then I didn't know what it was. In the meantime I girded (even girt) my loins for matriculation. Mrs Beddoes offered to give my non-conformist shoes a bit of a buff to smarten me up.

Graëme's idea that having a phone would prevent me from engaging with the world was exactly wrong. With a phone I would have been able to get out a lot more, to be emulsified into the life of the town instead of separating from it like the oil in a failed mayonnaise. I was on a phobic cusp, poised between the fear of enclosure and fear of open spaces. I dreaded staying in my room, where no one would call on me, apparently, except those sent by a God I didn't care for, but I needed to screw up all my courage to launch myself into the uncaring human currents of the town. It took real willpower to make expeditions from A6, to mingle socially more than was demanded by my coursework and the chore of eating.

I induce bees

It didn't occur to me at the time that Dr Beamish might actually have felt he had failed me in the matter of the ceiling rail. Twinges of guilt often make people behave worse rather than better, so perhaps it consoled him to be able to dismiss me as a stubborn pest – there's no pleasing John Cromer – one who deserved no more cosseting. I'll give the idea some house room now.

Time's up, and no. That theory won't wash. He just turned against me on the phone question, he got a bee in his bonnet about it and then wouldn't back down, no matter what. It's not entirely an isolated incident. I induce bees in some people's bonnets, and there's nothing I can do about it.

As the term progressed I realised something I should have understood earlier. I had one great asset which I could use as an inducement to do me favours. The Mini was a high-ranking trump card. An undergraduate who could offer his cronies a lift was the opposite of disabled.

I learned to use my leverage tactically, to broker a complex exchange. I suggested to P. D. Hughes – Pete – that he accompany me to the Botanic Garden on the next Saturday, push me round and put up with me talking about plants. In return I would then drive him to the pub of his choice – how did he feel about Grantchester, for instance?

This confirmed the wisdom of taking the weekday pressure off Pete. Now I could suggest expeditions at the weekend with a clear conscience. In my childhood Saturday had been my favourite day, with its own colour. I would shout out, '*It's Saturday today!* Saturday at last, all lovely and red.' It radiated happiness and comfort, like a brick warm from the kiln. Sunday wasn't quite such a favourite – a sunny yellow, turning to green in the evening as Monday loomed. For years I'd held on to the feeling that the weekend was special, but at Cambridge it changed its meaning for me. Now it was a two-day abyss, and I dreaded sliding down into the next one and being lost to view altogether. The best way to keep some sort of control seemed to be to plan a treat that would blot out some of the leaching gloom.

My offer to Pete obviously sounded pretty good, but I'm not persuaded he stuck to his part of the bargain. My first experience of the Cambridge Botanic Garden was of something like a cross-country wheelchair slalom. Leaves and branches appeared before my juddering eyes for the merest fraction of a second before being replaced by another turbulent vista of foliage. We didn't slow down until Pete had delivered me back to the car and it was time for our pub trip, which was much more leisurely. The pub in Grantchester was picturesque and very quiet. Perhaps it was even quiet before we came in. The giant and his familiar.

The Botanic Garden, note, not the Botanical Gardens. Cambridge has its own terminology for things. It's a point of pride. Why else was I, whose subjects were German and Spanish, technically studying Modern and Mediaeval Languages? The only wonder was that the university authorities had omitted the digraph in 'mediæval', my favourite mutated letter, Tinkerbell of the alphabet, the wayward færy whom my childhood tutor Miss Collins had refused to recognise as real. American English has long since abolished digraphs, by the brutal expedient of lopping off half their constituent letters. I'm not giving up, though. Literate children of Britain and the Commonwealth, clap your hands if you believe in digraphs! Every time you write *hæmorrhage* or *cælacanth*, *anæmic* or *fœtid*, without remembering to blend the vowels on the page, a special symbol dies.

I don't think Pete was consciously depriving me of the pleasures of the Bot, as I came to call it on closer acquaintance. It's just that he couldn't understand what there was to see in a garden, so he treated me to a lap of honour, in and out. Gardeners and non-gardeners see different things in the same view, it's as simple as that.

I'd seen enough at the Botanic Garden, despite the slewing and shaking of the wheelchair, to realise how much there was to see. Another time I would insist on a tempo rather less close to the Starship *Enterprise*'s warp speed, so that I could contemplate the vegetable kingdom at something closer to its own pace.

When I had first phoned the Botanic Garden to ask about parking, using the phone in the Porter's Lodge, the lady told me it would be fine if I tucked the Mini by the potting shed. She also asked if I needed assistance. I had said no, because I'd already arranged an escort, but after that first sprint of a visit I took advantage of their helpfulness. In practice it worked very well. Once I had been helped out of the car and installed in the wheelchair I was very happy dawdling on my own. I could do without my headlong escort.

On my first real visit, when I had time actually to see the treasures of the Bot, I also met the head gardener, Sid Glover. He was immensely welcoming, particularly when he understood that my interest in carnivorous plants wasn't based on any supposed novelty value, but on seeing them as venerable and fascinating adaptations to life. In fact he offered me, a complete stranger, a splendid specimen of *Drosera capensis* to take away with me. That's the Cape Sundew, native to South Africa. Gardeners are the most generous of people. I was tempted, but refused. I simply didn't have the right conditions to do it justice, though as carnivorous plants go *Drosera capensis* isn't too much of a challenge to grow. Instead he gave me 'a few little things' in a bag. A little treasure trove.

In new surroundings, it's normally my instinct to get something growing as soon as possible, but I had decided before I arrived at Downing not to grow anything while I was a student. One more vow of chastity! My reasoning was that I would have enough to do maintaining my own organism, without lavishing care on other beings, however undemanding. The millipede was a different case. Dad was the only one in the house who liked it, and even so I couldn't be sure he would remember to meet its modest needs.

It wasn't easy to uproot the drive to keep something alive other than myself, an impulse which I'd say is part of a dialogue with a person's own vitality. And now I was in the happy position of having my mind changed for me without conflict, soul-searching or loss of face. I had already noticed a shop on Regent Street which sold gardening supplies. The lovely name alone drew the eye – Cramphorn's. There I bought a seed propagator with a big plastic dome, which lived on the windowsill in my room. The college radiator system supplied dry heat, but sphagnum moss in the sealed dome sent out puffs of humid air which condensed out as water droplets on the lid, then ran down the plastic sides of the tank like rain driving a perpetual-motion machine.

Eaten alive by a poisonous shirt

Meanwhile the millipede was failing to thrive. One morning Mrs Beddoes tapped me on the shoulder and said, 'That Nasty Thing – the thing in the box. Much as I don't like it, I don't think it's very well. You can always tell, can't you? You should take a look. I don't think it's long for this world.'

She wasn't wrong. My tropical millipede, also known as the Nasty Thing, was sick unto death, and lived only a few more minutes, writhing horribly. It was only afterwards that I realised that it was all my fault. The Nasty Thing's end was like something out of Greek tragedy. Wasn't it Hercules who was eaten alive by a poisonous shirt given to him in all innocence?

Something broadly similar had happened in A6, Kenny Court. I had renewed my millipede's sawdust from a bag bought from a pet-shop (I've never been able to keep out of pet-shops), not realising that the new batch, being intended for hamsters and other small game, had been discreetly scented. The impregnation of deodorant turned out to have a corrosive effect on millipede tissue. R.I.P. the Nasty Thing, born and died 1970, down in the depths of the Kali Yuga. May his-and-her rebirths be few.

Yet it was Mrs Beddoes rather than me who seemed genuinely sad. I was more preöccupied with the loss of the quid I had paid for the creature. She took the body away, with less reluctance than I expected. I wasn't happy to dispose of it without ceremony, but what choice did I have? With my low standing at Downing (both as a freshman and as someone whose tutor had taken against him) I could hardly apply for a burial plot in the Master's Garden.

Now that my private zoo, with its single arthropod exhibit, had closed because of a death in the family, I had to find other ways of feeling at home. I fell back on my old hobby of yoghurt-making. Busying myself with measures, timings and temperatures helped me pass the time without trauma, even at weekends. For me, yoghurt-making was an occupational therapy rather than a statement of counter-cultural allegiance.

It was also easy, and almost legal in college terms. All I had to do was boil the milk, let it cool, add the culture, mix it in and leave it in a warm cupboard. I experimented with a technique that eliminated the cupboard stage of yoghurt-making, which was always the most awkward part for me. I used a thermos to maintain the temperature of the mixture. It worked very well, though it had one drawback. Anyone who visited me in my room would ask about the thermos, unscrew the top out of curiosity and then put it back on with so much strength that I'd never be able to open it myself. Eventually I prepared a label that said *Stop and Think! Fingertight for You Is Plain ImPOSSible for Me! Leave Me Loose!* And still I had to remind people.

I love the idea of 'fingertight' – an unscientific but perfectly intelligible description of a degree of mechanical closure – but I live well outside the standard range (normal variation between individual grips) on which it is based.

Once I'd started using the gas-ring I began to itch for more complex acts of cooking. Hall food even at its best was bland, so in a mood of nostalgia for the food at Mrs Osborne's I started making curries. On Mum's kitchen bookshelf at Trees there was a book of International Cookery which included some timid versions of Indian dishes, though she had only indulged me with them before I actually went to India. At the time she must have thought a plateful of tentatively spiced rice was the nearest I was going to get to the subcontinent.

It happened that the nearest shop to me geographically, on Regent Street, had a fair range of spices. It was essentially Indian, despite bearing the name of Harold T. Cox. I could get all sorts of exotic treats there.

The A-staircase kitchen was the scene of frenzied frying, making nonsense of the ban on this most alluring of cooking methods. We simply washed out our fragrant pans the moment we had finished using them, hiding them where they would never be found.

Even in the rebellious 1970s this struck me as an unsatisfactory solution. I didn't want to get away with things – I wanted to be vindicated. So I 'hid' my frying pan where Mrs Beddoes was bound to discover it. She looked at me sorrowfully and said she would have to confiscate it. Nothing personal, Mr Crow-*maire*, but rules were rules.

'Just so, Mrs Beddoes. So why don't we have a cuppa together and take a look at the book of rules?'

Of course I had given this document at least as much attention as any piece of coursework. I waited for her to find the relevant passage. '. . . *Cooking activities involving frying are strictly prohibited.* You see? I'm afraid I must take away that pan.'

I let her take the first few steps with my pan towards whatever pantry Valhalla she commanded, and then said, 'Not so fast, Mrs Beddoes. Have you ever seen me frying anything in that pan?'

'No, Mr Crow-maire, but rules are rules.'

'Then show me where in the rules it says *frying pan*. I believe this college specialises in Law in a small way. It shouldn't be difficult to get a professional opinion on the interpretation of these rules.'

'Well, what else is a frying pan for, if not frying? Tell me that!'

'For boiling, for poaching, for sousing in a maize-flour sauce, for simmering, for warming through. Do you not see, Mrs Beddoes, that this pan is the only one that is perfectly suited to the unfortunate shortness and curvature of my arms?' I laid it on thick till she was thoroughly flustered. By and large it's easy to create a misleading impression of exactly what I can or can't do. No one likes to question my say-so.

Tomorrow on Wittering Sunday

So I got my pan a reprieve, and my revenge on the rules. Revenge, despite the proverb, not best served cold but sautéed, and so hot it burns the tongue.

In a certain sense I got my come-uppance shortly afterward. There was no carpet on the common spaces of Kenny staircase and the parquet was slick. One day I had fried up a storm and then washed up as usual. I was scooting briskly along with the incriminating pan when I must have fallen forwards. I say 'must have' because a blow to the head interferes with the sorting office – the mechanism which processes short-term memories into long. My brain hadn't yet decanted that thimbleful of information into the proper tank, and so it spilled.

It was hardly surprising that I should have fallen out of the wheelchair. If your knees have no play in them you must punt yourself forwards in a precarious position, and if your arms aren't very good at their job then you have very little chance of breaking your fall. My little frying pan was light, but it didn't help.

So the college legend goes that I was found with my head in a frying pan of blood. This sounds wildly exaggerated, but then the blood vessels in the scalp can put on quite an alarming show. Scale down the horror, and it's still a fairly startling sight to greet an inexperienced Spanish doctor assigned to Addenbrookes Hospital. It was a short ride in the ambulance. Old Addenbrookes was just the other side of the wall from A staircase, Kenny Court, Downing. Plans were well advanced to transfer it to a new site further out, but for the time being I had a hospital more or less *en-suite*.

Having seen the state of his patient, the doctor prepared a syringe of local anæsthetic. At this point I rejoin the narrative, speaking volubly. Consciousness resumed with a swirl of departing images. All I saw was a nice dark man with a hypodermic. I lunged for it to the best of my ability. He said, with the most enchanting accent, 'You have had a fall. I am a doctor. This will make you feel better.' I said, 'I know all that. Hand it over.' I hadn't given up on grabbing the hypodermic, and made some sort of impaired dive for it.

The doctor was inhibited as we tussled, by the knowledge of his greater strength. He was shy of pressing his advantage.

He said, 'Please let me do my job.'

'But I know just what to do. This is Lignocaine, isn't it? Just the right stuff to use. Well done. Are you Spanish?'

'I am. Hold still, please.'

There are as many types of concussion as there are of consciousness. Mine was bossy and high-spirited. I didn't want this handsome foreigner to think he was dealing with a standard-issue pig-ignorant xenophobic Brit. Even a university town is not free of such folk.

I spoke the first Spanish words that came into my head. '*Mañana Domingo de Pipiripingo*,' I sang out, taking great care with the pronunciation, '*Se case Juanito con una mujer que no tiene manos y sabe coser . . .*'

I could have done better with a bit of planning, but who plans for concussion? Telling a stranger that *tomorrow on Wittering Sunday Juanito is marrying a woman with no hands who's good at sewing*, was no way to prove my command of my faculties.

I fell back on English. 'Please give me the hypodermic. I'm quite capable of anæsthetising myself. I know where the pain is, don't I? It's my body, not yours.'

'I'm not allowed. It breaks the rules.'

'I won't tell.'

He was being very unreasonable. He wanted to play doctor even more than I did. I won't say he botched the injection, but it's a fact that a local anæsthetic depends for its effectiveness on the concentration achieved at the nerve fibre. That's why it's called a local, for heaven's sake! If he had let me do it I'm sure I would have scored a bull's-eye. He was shaking his head so fiercely to discourage me that he didn't quite get the needle in the right place, and a shed tear of Lignocaine dribbled its cold way down the side of my head. Spanish body language has its drawbacks.

After that my mood of omnipotence passed and I was content to let someone else put in the stitches. I've still got a little scar over one eyebrow, but I can't say it bothers me particularly. Nor did I give up the unauthorised frying after my little mishap, though I was more careful when bowling along with an incriminating pan.

Anyway, that's the story behind the legend which attached to me after that (The Hard-Core 'Vegetarian' Who Tried to Sneak a Black-Pudding Fry-Up When No One Was Looking). As if the blood in the pan had been on the menu all along.

As for other appetites, well . . . in some ways the twenty-year-old Cambridge undergraduate was very different from the twenty-year-old who had gone to India the previous summer, hell-bent on celibacy. I had learned that suppressing desires only leads to explosions lacking in any possible dignity. My new watchword was moderation rather than abstinence, but I had stumbled on to a rather promising definition of true moderation.

The old man must resort to the poker

Klaus Eckstein, all-round man that he was, was always going on about the essays of Montaigne, writing *Que scais-je?*, his motto, on the blackboard for us to ponder. What do I know? Not a bad slogan, though I was more interested in the question of who wanted to do the knowing in the first place. Still, according to Eckstein, Michel de Montaigne had known himself as well as anyone ever had. I told him how much I disliked French as a language, and he told me there was a famous early translation, enjoyable in its own right. John Florio, contemporary of Shakespeare. Eckstein was probably thinking of my essay on Lorca when he added that strangely enough, this nobleman with a wife and family had in his writings expressed the deepest feelings not for them, but for another man. His best friend Etienne de La Boétie.

Grudgingly I got hold of the book, through Mrs Pavey of course. Almost the first thing that my eyes fell on was this marvellous sentence: 'One should (saieth Aristotle) touch his wife soberly, discreetly and severely, lest that tickling-too-deliciously pleasure transport her beyond the bounds of reason.' There was plenty more in that vein, but what struck me with great force was something that Montaigne expounds elsewhere, viz. that the ideal of moderation should work in both directions, not only lessening what is excessive but amplifying what is insufficient. Moderation should be both curb and whip, as circumstances dictate. Montaigne could be very matter-of-fact about sexual activity, defining it as the 'tickling delight of emptying one's seminary vessels' which becomes faulty only by immoderation. He was very big on the tickling, was dear old Montaigne, but also on the moderation.

So what was my position in his scheme? Well, I didn't need to push suitors away with my crutch and my cane. If as Montaigne suggested, *An unattempted Lady could not vaunt of her chastitie*, then nor could I. If I wasn't an unattempted Lady, then I was pretty much an unattempted Lad.

Montaigne was particularly eloquent when addressing the subject of old age and the waning of the powers. The young man should damp down the blaze of his ardour, the old man must resort to the poker to get a blaze going. Young men should control their desires, old men should cultivate them. The imperative of moderation, though, underlies both cases. It is just as much a virtue for an old man to ginger up his appetites as it is for a young man to rein them in.

In this context, I was at twenty an honorary codger. Youth was no part of my portfolio. My birth year was relatively recent, but that wasn't enough by itself to make me young. As a man in a wheelchair my desires were everywhere an embarrassment and an inconvenience. I was expected to behave decorously, miming impotence, tactfully impersonating a pensioner in glandular terms, passions safely in the past. But moderation required the opposite. Moderation required excess for the proper balance.

So I took the opposite vow from the one I had taken before I visited India, the vow of celibacy that had ended with such a disconcerting burst of imagery. I vowed non-celibacy, sexual exploration in any direction that opened itself to me. Systematic debauchery on principle, whether I felt like it or not. This was at least a vow that might yield some fun along the way. The times were right for exploration rather than for abstinence. People had a new dread of being thought to be narrow-minded, which might serve my purpose. I had more to fear from not trying than from taking every chance that was offered, and making chances where there were none.

At Cambridge I saw more films than ever before or since. There were many cinemas, and most colleges had a film society of some sort. It may even be that my cinema-going in those years had a spiritual dimension, though it was hidden from me at the time. I was struggling with a sense of spiritual dryness, and it seemed ridiculous that I had ever thought of being on a Quest. That capital letter had suffered a dwindling along the way. The word itself had lost its vivid promise, the sense of illumination being just around the corner. My sense of discipleship often seemed to be unravelling, though the guru never let me go.

In his teachings Ramana Maharshi used the cinema as a source of images even more than the radio. The spectators of a film, for instance, attend to the images which replace themselves on the screen with such deceptive smoothness. No one gives a thought to the screen, although without it there could be no projection of the film. The screen is the same whether or not a film is being shown, just as the self is the same in sleep and waking. It is unchanged by what flickers across it – a filmed flood has no power to wet it. A filmed conflagration does not scorch.

A few years later, as if going out of their way to contradict this strain of Hindu mystical thought, the makers of *Earthquake* came up with a film about an earthquake which actually shook its spectators, at least in cinemas equipped with the Sensurround system, whose speakers emitted low-frequency vibrations so as to produce real tremors. But that was just showing off.

Of course when I had paid my money to get into the Arts Cinema, or the Victoria or the ABC, I was watching the projected pictures like everyone else, letting my mind be ruled by images and ignoring the screen itself. But at some level I was keeping faith with the idea of self-enquiry, even so.

It was important for me to make it a habit of going out, not to surrender to blank evenings in A6. As a schoolboy I had gone to films as part of a group, coasting along with the social momentum. Now I had to plan expeditions on my own, but I was nevertheless drawn to the cinema.

The leather belt of office

One evening I went to see *Wild Strawberries* at the Arts Cinema with a boy I knew slightly from German lectures. Noel was an angelic little blond, if angels can have snub noses. His was a type I don't much care for but he was presentable, undeniably.

He seemed very young, even for those days, when freshers arrived with their mothers' kisses still evaporating from their cheeks, and the scarves their aunts had knitted wound tightly round their necks.

I liked the way that, after a lecture, he just watched with amusement as our fellow students either made themselves scarce or squared up to volunteering to help me, as if they were signing up for years of military service. Noel seemed to find this comical, which was very much the perspective I aspired to myself.

There was no real significance to our going out together. We just arranged, after a lecture, to meet at the cinema. The choice of film was an accident from my point of view – Noel had mentioned in conversation that he would be going, and I had asked to tag along. I knew that without a definite social obligation I would back out of the expedition and all its uncertainties.

I had the sneaky feeling that our arrangement was asymmetrical. If I didn't turn up Noel would have no difficulty proceeding with his evening, but if he didn't turn up I was stymied. Before I set out I did what students so often did at the time, when puzzled over questions great or small. I would consult the Book of Changes, the yarrow-stalk oracle – the *I Ching*. I used the Westernised coin-throwing option rather than the traditional version with the yarrow stalks, although with my contacts at the Bot I should have been able to come up with the authentic flora. My question, of course, was 'How am I to dissolve myself into the life of this indifferent city while continuing to ask "Who am I?"?' The reading that came up always seemed to be *The leather belt of office will be given and taken away three times in one day*. Lovely, poetic, highly suggestive, but what I wanted was more along the lines of *Go to the flicks with someone you hardly know – make it something arty*.

I could have asked Noel to collect me from Downing, but that wasn't the point. The point was that I was forcing myself to put in the effort, hoping that there would come a moment when I stopped noticing all the hard work I was doing. That was the moment I would find my place among the mobile.

The Arts Cinema lay down its own little passage off Market Hill (a hill which isn't a hill at all, thank God, but a square with a slight tilt), so it was particularly unhandy for me to get to, even in a city of awkward access. Cambridge and above all its university is strongly fortified even against the able-bodied – the grass is always greener in the Fellows' Garden, and that's out of bounds to students except for the occasional summer party.

I hitch-lifted my way out of the car and into the wheelchair, but no one seemed to be going my way, and I ended up having to punt myself laboriously down Arts Cinema Passage.

When I arrived, Noel was looking at the showcases of stills from forthcoming attractions. Rather daunting attractions: troubled Nordic eyes and stern cheekbones gazed out of the cases. It must have been a Bergman season. Noel turned to greet me with a dazzling smile, as if he too was about to be photographed, wanting his expression to be at its peak of bloom when flashbulbs exploded to record it.

The ushers at the Arts were normally students themselves, friendly rather than businesslike. They watched with interest as I gave Noel instructions about propping me against the wall while he collapsed the wheelchair, then toting me into the cinema. Noel seemed happy to be observed coping so splendidly. Good luck to him! He might not enjoy the same level of attention if it came along every minute of the day.

When we were in the modest little auditorium I indicated a couple of empty seats in the middle of a row. That's where I wanted us to sit. Why should I have a sidelong view just to save him a little trouble? Let him earn his keep. 'They're numbered seats, John,' he whispered, 'and ours are here.'

'Tell you what, then,' I said. 'We'll move if we're asked.' I wasn't normally so bolshie, but I wanted to make clear that I wasn't just a charity parcel. You like being conspicuous? I'll give you conspicuous.

As Noel carried me along the row of seats I could feel little extra movements in his arms, which made me suspect that he was shrugging every few feet, to convey an apology to the people we were disturbing. Terribly sorry. This is what he's like.

He needn't have bothered. The people in those seats couldn't do enough to oblige us. They were practically hurling themselves out of our way. They'd have lain flat on the floor if they'd thought it would help, they would have stood on the backs of their chairs. It's wonderful what a little embarrassment can do. Most of the time I work hard to put people at their ease, but once in a while it's good to let rip and have everyone cower in their Englishness.

Then in the dark I had to revert to a meeker style. I found that I couldn't see the bottom of the screen – and consequently the subtitles – so I had to ask Noel to improvise a cushion for me out of his rolled-up coat. I certainly wasn't going to allow him to ask for one of the cushions they keep for children's screenings. Before I had new hips installed my position in a cinema seat was more upright, since I wasn't actually sitting. It was more that I was leant against the seat like an umbrella. Still, it's not something you can expect to find in even the smallest print, is it? *Warning: artificial hips may limit your enjoyment of foreign-language films.*

As the film got into its dour stride I realised that there were compensations to having company. Noel had brought along some butterscotch. Not just any butterscotch but the good stuff, Callard & Bowser's, which came in an oddly fortified packet, braced with cardboard, wrapped first in paper and then cellophane. Perhaps it still does. In those innocent days of packaging, it was a very distinctive product. It suggested a childish treat that was only accessible to deft and determined adult fingers. The sweet itself came in double tablets, wrapped one more time in a sturdy lined silver paper which retained traces of the sticky virtue it had wrapped and kept safe.

The double shape of the sweet suggested that a mother might snap it in two where the brittle toffee narrowed, before popping one tablet in her child's mouth and one in her own. Personally I had always favoured sucking the sweet entire, though the double tablet would hardly fit in my mouth. The opposite ends of the flat finger of burnt sugar poked at the insides of my cheeks in a way that was almost painful, until the oral solvents had done their leisurely work.

Noel asked in a whisper if I wanted him to unwrap the butterscotch for me. Why ever not? I wasn't in the mood for handicraft. He got points for treating me as his equal in greed – it didn't seem to occur to him to snap the tablet in two. He posted the naked butterscotch into my mouth, his fingers brushing past my lips in a way that I didn't find presumptuous or unpleasant. Then my consciousness slid back into the film and all its radiant gloom.

At the end of the showing I stayed put, and not only because it would be foolish to make a move immediately, before the lights were put on, and be jostled in the crush. It was still my habit to watch the screen till the very last credit.

To me it was a tiny crime not to finish a film or a book or even a record. I stood firm even on the issue of 'Within You Without You' at the beginning of Side Two of *Sergeant Pepper*, when everyone else wanted to plunge the needle straight into 'When I'm Sixty-Four'. I fought many battles on behalf of George Harrison's rotten pseudo-Indian song.

Swedish end-credits were no less entitled to sympathetic vibration than English ones, sympathy being distinct from understanding, and many of the names were beguiling in their own right. After *Wild Strawberries*, Noel had the sense to humour me, perhaps seeing from the set of my body that I wasn't prepared to budge just yet. He set off to retrieve the wheelchair, which had been tucked in the box office for safe-keeping.

As we left the Arts, Noel scanned the dispersing crowd while remaining attached to me. 'Are you looking for someone?' I asked, but he said no, he was all mine. When we reached the car, I asked if there was somewhere I could drop him – an absurd idea, since he lived in

Christ's, barely a hundred yards away. Even I could walk that distance, though perhaps not in one go. 'Do you want me to see you home?' he asked, as if I was a debutante at a dance. I was going to tell him not to bother – how did he think I coped on a daily basis? – when I realised that by this time the Tennis Court Road gate would be closed. I would need to get someone to open up, and I might as well take Noel along. He could scamper into the Porter's Lodge and make the request on my behalf. It isn't easy to summon people with a toot on your horn without seeming lordly.

The colleges were still officially sealed by a ten o'clock curfew, but in practical terms they were porous. Authority was crumbling of its own accord, without needing to be actively overthrown. It was common knowledge which sets of railings offered easy informal access to the various colleges. Monumental architecture offered any number of handholds to youth and recklessness stoked by beer. The back streets of the town were full of excited young men, clambering up and sliding down. Some stretches of railing saw heavy traffic even on weeknights.

If men were reckless mountaineers of the railings after dark, then women still liked to be climbed up to, rather than doing the climbing themselves. They had a rooted preference for Juliet's rôle in the balcony scene, looking down on her swain as he ascended, sweating and cursing, with a bottle of rock-bottom Hirondelle from his college buttery sticking precariously out of his jacket pocket.

The women's colleges made an effort to discourage such overnight visitors, but it was no more than a show of discipline. One second-year in my college spent most nights in New Hall. While his girlfriend dutifully entered by way of the Porter's Lodge he would shin up the wall (the modernist architecture of the college offering as many aids to climbing as the Gothic) and in through her window. His route was much quicker than hers – he boasted that by the time she reached her room he would be waiting for her in bed, wearing her nightie for that androgynous 1970 frisson, and with the kettle sighing its way to the boil.

There were times when it seemed as if I was the only one to whom a curfew still applied, though any number of undergraduates solemnly assured me that I could safely be transferred by a chain of hands over the railings in Trinity Lane, the wheelchair following, into Bishop's Hostel in Trinity and out again whenever I wanted. I never dared to accept such offers. To be transported by many hands, like a crumb at a picnic being carried off by a thousand ants, was a frightening prospect. People seemed keener to convey me over the railings of colleges after hours than to help me get to lectures in the mornings, which would have made far more difference to my university life.

The ascension glide which had conveyed me up the steps of the temple in Tiruvannamalai, a hundred hands in mystical unison, didn't seem likely to be duplicated on a secular climb in Cambridgeshire. The young men who made the offer were really only paying lip service to a favourite notion of the period, that everything was always possible for everyone without exception, with no clear idea of how it might be done.

I remember the Mistress of Girton (I think it was Muriel Bradbrook) defending the exclusion of men from the college after ten at night, though it was pointed out to her that anything men could do after ten o'clock they could also do before. 'Oh yes,' she replied, 'but if they stay after ten they may do it again.' One testy don was reported as describing this as shutting the stable door after the mare has been mounted. In circumstances like these the don being quoted was invariably from Peterhouse.

I let Noel take charge of me. My need of help was a sore point, of course, but then by this time I was mainly sore points. I do more than my fair share of sitting and my bum was sore from the pressure of the Arts Cinema's worn-down plush upholstery. If he didn't help to transfer me from car to room and wheelchair then I'd only have to hitch a carry from someone else.

In the car, Noel started to talk about how terrifying he had found *Wild Strawberries*. He didn't see how he was going to sleep that night. I was puzzled. 'But I thought you'd seen it before.'

He opened his eyes very wide. 'What makes you think that?'

I said I must have got the wrong end of the stick, but I was sure he had referred to the film as one of his favourites.

Apparently it was the dream sequence at the beginning of the film which had done for him – a famous example in that line, virtually an encyclopædia of oppressive imagery. Clocks without hands, runaway

494

hearses. The face appearing from between the boards of the shattered coffin turning out to be the dreamer's own.

I had enjoyed the film, but I can't say it touched any particular nerve. It wasn't even an X-certificate, for Heaven's sake! Still, it made sense to assume that my history had left me with off-kilter fears and immunities. Perhaps Noel's upbringing had left him unusually vulnerable to the Gothic in some way. At the same time, I was thinking back to that part of the film. At the moment when the professor in his dream sees his own body in the coffin, I could swear that I had heard a distinctive sound from my neighbour's mouth. I could have sworn it was the juice-muffled snap of a tablet of butterscotch being divided in two by a rooting tongue unable to defer the pleasure any longer.

No epidermis off my proboscis

Of course existential dread and greedy sweet-sucking can occupy a single individual simultaneously, but I had to wonder if Noel wasn't putting it on. The *Angst*, I mean. My own tablet of butterscotch was still fat in my mouth at that stage of the film, only just beginning its dwindling to a brittle blade of sweetness.

When the porters had been sweet-talked and I had safely parked the car at the back of A staircase, Kenny Court, I was in a little quandary. I didn't particularly want to invite this person in, but I needed a certain amount of assistance to get back into my room. Those two steps in my path had social repercussions. I couldn't dismiss Noel after letting him install me in the wheelchair, because it would then be obvious that I was stuck on the lower level. But if I let him help me up those steps then it would be impossible not to invite him in.

Those steps had a lot to answer for, but if ever I mentioned them to someone sensible – such as Alan Linton while we savoured the excellent vegetarian fare in Hall – he didn't seem to know what I was talking about. Steps? What steps?

I've noticed that steps have an almost evanescent quality. Are they there or are they not? It seems to be a moot point. They evaporate and then condense once more. As stone and brick they should have got the knack of seeming substantial, but they're hard to see and hard to hold in the memory.

I phone you up in advance of a visit, and I ask, are there any steps where you live? And you say, 'Steps? No, no steps.' As if it was an outlandish question. Obscurely insulting, even. Except that when I arrive, there are little steps, one, two, even three. Multiple changes of level between the street and the path, the path and the door surround, the surround and the door itself. Very real obstructions, all of them. You scratch your head, as if you have never seen them before, or as if they've only just appeared. Earthquakes aren't common in these parts, and even the ones that happen at night make a bit of noise. They're not usually so tidy either, simply extruding a building a few inches up from the ground. We stare at your puzzling steps, you and I. I'm the one who doesn't subscribe to the doctrines of materialism, and you're the one who thinks the external world is constant and consistent, but perhaps this is not the best time for either of us to draw attention to the fact that we're dressed in each other's clothes.

When I ask if there are steps, I don't necessarily mean a grand staircase leading up to the entrance. I rather hope you'd tell me about that without being prompted. I'm talking about the little changes of level that your legs take in their stride – and that your automatic pilot negotiates without your needing to switch to manual control. I suppose it all comes down to maths, to rounding up and rounding down. If there are fewer than five steps people round down and say there aren't any. If there are more than five, that counts as a flight. That's makes a quorum and can't be ignored. But fewer than five doesn't count, apparently. It's only me that feels excluded, and I apologise for being small-minded. It's actually this body that is small-minded, and can't get over the fact of your steps.

I imagine the little meeting at which rooms were assigned to the incoming freshers of Downing. Someone would be sure to say, '*Cromer, J.*, uses a wheelchair, poor beggar, so we'd better give him a room on the ground floor, don't you think?' And somebody else would say, 'How about A6 Kenny, that's just the ticket.' I realise that university business in 1970 was not conducted by World War II personnel, but I can't help that. That's how it plays out in my mind. Then the pretty WAAF comes in with the tea, and says, 'But aren't there steps outside A staircase Kenny? That'll be jolly awkward.' Everyone looks at her as if she was mad, and someone says, 'I say, little girl, you'd better not

496

poke your nose in where it's not wanted. We're not fools, you know. We've put him on the ground floor, haven't we? He'll be rocketing about, you'll see. There'll be no stopping him.' And the WAAF sniffs and says, 'No epidermis off my proboscis, I'm sure.'

With those steps taking his side, Noel simply assumed that he was coming in with me, and then something happened that took the initiative away from me for the duration. It wasn't anything in the least dramatic – it was just that I had a bit of trouble opening the door. It was locked (I had learned my lesson) and I could manage perfectly well, as long as I wasn't hurried. I could refuse Noel's help in opening the door, and I did. But I couldn't prevent cutting a figure of bravery and pathos in the eyes of a spectator, and then the drama took on its own meaning and momentum. On an ordinary night the scene would have been one of serene difficulty unobserved, but not now. I could send Noel smartly away, but that would only emphasise my bloody bravery and the sodding pathos of it all. Better to let him come in and hope to get rid of him soon.

After that Noel pretty much had his own way. I said as nonchalantly as I could, 'Perhaps you'd make me a coffee – and one for yourself, of course, if you'd like.'

Noel went on and on about the haunting power of Ingmar Bergman's images. They had bored into his head. They had tapped into his darkest dreams. He wouldn't be able to sleep, unless . . . Unless what? Unless he stayed the night with me. All Ingmar's fault, of course. Noel wouldn't be able to close his eyes for existential terror unless I was there to comfort him. I had been chosen (chosen from a list of one) to keep the Scandinavian demons at bay in A6 Kenny.

As Granny would have said, it was all very inconvenient, but I could hardly chuck him out, could I? Even if I had a phone in my room, I couldn't quite see myself using it to call the Porter's Lodge and asking them to repatriate a stray blond.

Once I had resigned myself to my fate, there was no further mention of Noel's fears. He was obviously shamming, but why should he bother to tell untruths? Perhaps he really was suffering from angst – angst in his pants, that is. And he was presentable enough, but was he my type?

I wasn't sure I could afford to have a type. There wasn't enough

497

traffic for me to risk putting up road blocks. That would lead me right back to celibacy without even needing to take a vow.

The best approach seemed to be this: anyone who fetched up in my bed for whatever reason, including sham fears of clocks without hands, was my type until proved otherwise. Of course there was a snag when I considered my romantic prospects. It seemed unrealistic to expect anyone to help me go to bed and then enjoy my company once I was in it. I couldn't quite visualise that. The waiter doesn't sit down as guest of honour – though actually it's an awkwardness that has come to pass often enough, when I have guests to a meal and then expect them to do a certain amount of fetching and carrying.

In my daydreams things were different. One person prepared me for bed and a quite different one joined me between the sheets, which is an arrangement reserved for the wedding nights of royalty. As a commoner I couldn't see how Noel was going to combine the rôles. Still, rules were made to be broken. I had college authority for that.

Noel seemed rather fidgety as he boiled the kettle to make coffee. He asked if I had anything to eat and I reluctantly revealed a cache of biscuits. He looked through my record collection but found nothing that matched his mood, or perhaps his taste.

He couldn't keep his hands away from his hair, smoothing it down far more, surely, than ordinary narcissism demanded. It made me grateful for my own narrow vocabulary of body language. What a waste of nervous energy, to thrash your hands about so! Every now and then he gave a little cat's yawn, rolling his shoulders and even sticking out his tongue, as if he was poking fun at the idea of sleep as it slyly advanced on him.

I was ensconced in the Parker-Knoll with my drawbridge raised so that I was poised and nearly horizontal. Noel couldn't seem to settle. He sat on the edge of the built-in desk, pushing back books and papers to make room for his narrow bum. I tried to protest, and then decided that I would make sure to ask him to reinstate everything in the morning. Unless things are near the front of a desk they're not much use to me.

'That's a wonderful chair you've got there,' he said. 'I didn't even see you get into it. How do you manage?' There is occasionally something quite refreshing about unembarrassed curiosity, and I ended up giving a repeat performance, struggling slowly to my feet and then relapsing onto the Granny-subsidised upholstery. It seemed unlikely that Noel had missed the first show, all the same, which must have taken perhaps two minutes from beginning to end. 'Thanks – I feel privileged to see that,' said my uninvited visitor. 'You've really got your life worked out, haven't you? Well done you!' If I had really got my life worked out, I would have been alone in my room at this point, wouldn't I? And spared this whole conversation.

Impotent mandrake

Yawns are catching, alertness is not. By this time I was unconsciously copying Noel's spasms of tiredness, and agreed that it was time for bed. Then Noel wanted to see how I managed in the bathroom. You would have thought, from his reaction, that he was positively jealous of my trolley commode, as if it was something he had wanted all his life. Finally he wanted to see how I used a flannel. Not very easily, would have been the short answer. I demonstrated, inwardly protesting. I used a table knife to bring the cloth within range of my face, and the whole operation was rather approximate. By this time I was feeling that naked curiosity wasn't so very charming after all. Perhaps it should put on some clothes like the rest of us. Noel's desire to know everything about my adaptation to life was beginning to seem rather oppressive. Of course he was just a little academic blob trying to rustle up a personality at short notice, like every other fresher, but I had stopped enjoying my part in the process.

'You aren't going to write an article about me, are you?' I asked, realising as I spoke that this was a dreadful possibility. 'I'm not going to be on the front page of *Varsity*, am I?' To hold back from Jack de Manio and the *Today* programme only to end up as an item in *Varsity*! Quite a coup for the ego-diminishment project.

'Of course not, I'm just interested. But you have to admit you're one of a kind.'

'Aren't we all?'

'You know what I mean.'

By now I was uneasy about the sharing of a bed. What if Noel did want to undertake the activity decriminalised by both the lower chamber and the Lords Spiritual and Temporal? How could I refuse? It would be no earthly use squeaking 'Stop what you're doing at once! I won't be of legal age till after Christmas!', since he was clearly younger than me. If he wanted something to happen then happen it would.

Consent and refusal in my case were abstract notions. My Yes was taken as read, and my No was a silent scream that no one would hear, impotent mandrake struck dumb at the moment of its uprooting.

It was too late for second thoughts. I hadn't made my bed, and now I would have to lie in it. Noel sat on the bed and supported me between his knees while he took my clothes off. His touch was awkward but not incompetent. This was the moment I must get through without my self-confidence shrivelling, buoyed up by nothing more than the habit of buoyancy.

Noel didn't ask me what I wore at night. It would have been a polite enquiry to make, unless naked intimacy was on the menu. If he had asked me, I would have said 'Nothing', not because I had read the James Bond books and knew that a real man sleeps in the buff, but because it was enough trouble taking off one lot of clothes without having to struggle into another. Deprived of the Margaret Erskine Dream-Cloud I dare say I would have frozen to death in my undergraduate years.

He helped me onto the bed and then undressed himself. He kept on his singlet and Y-fronts. He even looked doubtfully at his socks for a moment before taking them off. This disparity in our costumes didn't seem promising, but who was I to know what was promising? Perhaps there was striptease to come.

My sexual experiences had been fleeting, though rich in their way, and they had rarely been connected with beds. I had spent too long trapped in one to expect to discover much novelty on that terrain. A bed was far less promising a venue for me than a music room, a dark lane or a nice public lavatory.

He turned the light off and climbed into bed, moving carefully to avoid squashing me. He had a faint nutty smell, which started to interest me all over again. In the dark my nose came alive and had a sniff of something it liked. Free of visual reality, I could idealise his features. My third eye took a good look round and my third leg flexed.

I wondered if we were about to have carnal congress, and if so how much I really wanted it to happen. My consent and refusal had become elusive even to me. This was all so entirely different from any script I had ever imagined. All those back roads and lanes I had driven down, looking for the person who would inflict his secrets on me!

Was it possible to be sought out in my own bed, and be shown the skeleton key to intimate behaviour there? The thing that can happen between people who lie down together, the shiver of what is possible.

Then it turned out that Noel had no such plans, or if he had ever had them they had been overtaken by sleep. Angst or no Angst, he was well away. There would be no tickling-too-deliciously pleasure for me that night, and my reason was safe from being derailed by a landslide of bliss. Every fifteen minutes the Catholic Clock with its defective mechanism ironically saluted the protraction of my virginity. Unless I had lost it to the Yeti. Though I have to say, going by my shreds of memory about our encounter, that the Abominable Snowman behaved like a perfect gentleman.

It was strange that I regarded myself as a virgin despite having been superbly fellated more than once by the depraved and accomplished Luke Squires at Vulcan. Somehow that didn't seem to count.

Having someone sleeping so near to me was a novelty, even without the active sensuality of touch. Peter's life had been warm in our bedroom at Trees, but Noel's life was warm in my actual bed – yet I got little joy from his presence. At one point I became so overheated that I had to nudge the Dream-Cloud aside.

Unconsciousness dissolved any pact between us, in terms of my separate space, which he invaded. In sleep he was all bones and angles. Bones and angles and rapt little snores. A hot hand inched between my legs, but it was innocent of any impulse to grope.

In the night I needed a pee. I lay there wishing my bladder could sit tight for the whole night – life would be so much easier if it could. There was nothing to stop me from using the pee bottle as usual, except that it wasn't in its usual place. In the flurry of going to bed in company, I hadn't left it within reach, so I gave Noel quite a bolshie nudge. Since he was here by his own wish, he might as well be useful. He groaned as he woke and went like a sleepwalker to fetch the pee bottle.

Then I must have slept more heavily. When I awoke I was alone in the bed. Then I started to hear strange grunting from floor level. When I wriggled myself round I could see Noel doing photogenic little press-ups. He grinned at me when he caught me looking. 'I made you a cup of tea,' he said.

I took it for granted that Noel would be on his way as soon as he could. No such luck. He seemed annoyingly refreshed, and in a mood to be further entertained. He had exhausted his curiosity about me, but had apparently promised himself the treat of meeting my bedder.

His smile was on full disarming power from the moment Mrs Beddoes arrived. She'd barely had time to say, 'Hello, and who are you?' than he'd offered her a cup of coffee. My coffee, not actually a plentiful resource. Reluctantly I introduced them. From nowhere Mrs Beddoes produced something which she'd been keeping dark, a Christian name. 'Jean Beddoes.'

Noel said, 'John kindly let me stay last night after I had a fit of the heebie-jeebies from a film we saw. Have you ever had a fit of the heebie-jeebies from watching a film, Mrs Beddoes?'

She hardly hesitated. 'There was one . . . what was it called? Gravestones, and a man pouncing on a boy. Staring eyes. I couldn't sleep for weeks after that.'

Noel raised his hands in front of him and gave a theatrical shudder. He even closed his eyes. '*Magwitch!*' he whispered, in reverent horror, and then they were away, fast friends already on the basis of *Great Expectations*. At that moment, peeking out at Mrs Beddoes from behind a finger fence of artificial surprise, he looked like a minor Dickensian character himself. Minutes later he was helping her to make the bed.

Since I slept wrapped up in a cloud of dreams there was actually no need to do any such thing, but Mrs Beddoes would not be deflected from her professional code. There was no question of slackening off even when rigour was nonsensical. So every day she would unmake the bed and remake it, tucking the coverlet in with brisk determined movements so there was no possibility of the pillow making a run for it. I had shown her once that this technique would have made it hard for me to get into bed, if I hadn't preferred the Dream-Cloud. I had slid my stick in and then yanked sideways to open a usable gateway to the sheets, like Dad using his paperknife on a letter, to show her how preposterous she was being. She stuck to her principles.

In the shock of rapport with Noel her cheeks were now quite pink. Somehow they had got on to the subject of favourite pieces of music. Mrs Beddoes was saying, 'It's my husband who knows about things. Alf's favourite piece is classical music, and I really like it too. It's by Beethoven.'

'Really, Mrs Beddoes? One of the symphonies?' He thought for a moment. 'Perhaps the *Pastoral*? You may know it from *Fantasia* – the Disney film.'

'Oh no,' she said, 'It's not from a film.' I was delighted that Noel's patronising suggestion had fallen flat. 'It's called . . . it's gone out of my mind. It's called . . . that's right, "Wellington's Victory". It's on the same record as the "1812", but it's even better.' She clapped her hands together on either side of the pillow, to plump it up, but almost as if she was playing the cymbals. 'Even more cannons and whatnot!!'

Which made Noel's day, perhaps even his term. I had hoped he would leave before Mrs Beddoes did, so I could be spared the inevitable sneer about her musical taste, but he stayed on to round off the lovely morning he was having. I didn't know 'Wellington's Victory', but it seemed strange that liking Beethoven could be such a *faux pas*. Wasn't Beethoven supposed to be the tops?

It was perfectly possible that Mrs Beddoes knew more of Beethoven's music than I did. Once you'd mentioned *Moonlight*, *Für Elise* and *Da-da-da-Dum*, you'd just about exhausted my expertise on the subject. I wasn't in a position to call Noel's bluff, but I wished someody would.

What he said when we were alone was, I suppose, quite a mild exercise in contempt. 'Good for Madame Beddoes,' he said. 'If you're tone-deaf and pig-ignorant, you might as well go for the piece with the loudest bangs.'

Watching the way Noel played along with innocent Mrs Beddoes, I realised that my social skills were very partial. I needed to develop new ones. All this time I had been thinking in terms of bringing people within the orbit of my personality, entirely overlooking the fact that they were always going to be people, like the blond germ working his 'fluence on Mrs Beddoes, who badly needed to be kept at a distance. Poor mobility meant poor avoiding skills, so I would need to add an annexe to my laboratory of personal accomplishments. It wasn't enough to have charm, I needed antidotes to the charm of others. Countercharm. Even the Everest & Jennings hoist I had brought from Bourne End had a red control as well as a green one.

I wanted to be able to accept the world's butterscotch with the proper appreciation, while refusing its helping hand on my shoulder, its shallow fascination with the details of my daily life, its snores in my bed. I must learn the technique of ruling these things out of court so crisply that the offer never came again. There must be an end to haggling with the well-intentioned, the clueless and the plain invasive.

If I had liked Noel I might have crowned his name with a sparkly diæresis, so: Noël. As things stood, I stripped him mentally of any such insignia. He didn't deserve them.

I was offended by Noel's manner with Mrs Beddoes, but I also envied it. It obviously didn't strike him as unnatural that he should be looked after at his college by a sort of servant, well on his way to adulthood. Perhaps he didn't notice his dependence, but mine was highly visible to me. My independence was opening up by the slowest possible stages, and the leisure of the process maddened me. With every emancipation I became more chafed by the restrictions remaining.

Certainly Noel was a great hit with the woman he had taken so much trouble to mock. For weeks after his overnight stay, she would ask, 'And how is Mr Noel? Sleeping again at nights, I hope?' She would obviously have enjoyed a repetition of his visit. It had slipped her mind that one of her purposes, according to the university's administration, was to make sure that the students in her charge spent the stipulated number of nights a term within a one-mile radius of Great St Mary's, unless they had their tutor's permission, in their own beds and alone.

Austere brickwork *lingam*

What lay outside that magic circle was off the map and off the radar. As far as the rule was concerned, the university might be surrounded, like the earth in Hindu cosmology, by concentric oceans of (in order) brine, sugar-cane juice, wine, *ghee*, milk, whey and fresh water.

To me the University Library was far more plausible as the centre of student life than Great St Mary's. People were always complaining that it looked like a power station, as if they had spotted a flaw in the design, when that industrial imagery was exactly what the architect intended. The UL was a mighty pulsing electromagnet, which drew towards it with implacable force two copies of every book published in the country, on the very day it appeared. It was a royal engine of bibliophilia, it was an austere brickwork *lingam* throbbing with imaginative power. What it wasn't – with its staircase upon staircase – was a place I could go. The front entrance crowned a flight of steps with that abomination, a revolving door, hateful symbol of my banishment from the engine room of learning. No one has ever been able to explain to me why the trivial advantages of the revolving door are held to outweigh its obvious defects. Yes, it excludes draughts. It also excludes me.

I made one forlorn attempt at entering the premises by another avenue. There was a goods entrance at the back, where crates of books could be wheeled in. I would explore the possibilities there. Of course I had to make an appointment (more phone calls from the Porter's Lodge) to be shown the ropes – the ramps, the lifts. Of course a ramp isn't much use to a wheelchair-user unless he has a motorised chair or strong arms, and the lifts were pretty much hopeless, hardly larger than the ones at Vulcan, being designed in the first place for books and not people. All in all, the prospect of being an honorary book-crate in the UL was a lot less fun than being an honorary suitcase on trains leaving Bourne End station. It wasn't a solution. I would have to find other means of gaining access to the treasure-house of books.

Luckily my status as a second-class citizen wasn't a simple thing. It was speckled with exemptions and concessions. With a little cajoling on my part, there was a system in place. All I had to do was toot the Mini's horn outside the Library at a prearranged time and the books I wanted would be brought down to me. The able-bodied undergraduates of the university, the hale and the hearty – they were the underprivileged ones. At the feast of learning offered in that rather

sombre-looking building, they had to eat on the premises. I was entitled to take-away.

The library's statutes allowed for special arrangements to be made
at the discretion of the Librarian, but in practice it was only necessary
to adapt the mechanism which allowed third-year undergraduates to
borrow books. My Tutor became my proxy – so technically he was
the one who borrowed up to five volumes on my behalf, and incurred
any penalties also. There was a certain amount of paperwork, since
Graëme Beamish had to give his authorisation. He had a supply of
forms already printed up (normally for the use of those lucky third-
years), but he did need to sign them. 'I must say, John,' he remarked
once, 'that I never dreamed that writer's cramp would be part of the
price I pay – with joy in my heart, I assure you – for the pleasure of
acting as a moral tutor.'

Wheelchair access to libraries is a major cultural advance, but there's
no doubt about the greater poetry of the old arrangement. The boy at
the foot of the steps whistles a special signal, and the books he wants
come fluttering down from the roof of the building, birds of knowledge which alight on his fingertips. It's all very Omar Khayyam.

I don't have a nostalgic bone in my body, and I wouldn't willingly
go back to any day gone by. Adhesion to the past is as bad as wanting to sew yourself into your old clothes. I can't help it if my times of
waiting for books to be ferried down the steps are among the brighter
spots in an overcast time.

Of course the real difficulty in the library lay in locating the books
in the catalogues, writing down the relevant class-marks and placing
my order. I made another attempt to sell Beamish on the idea that a
telephone in Kenny A6 was the final element required to make the
whole system workable. The staff of the Library wouldn't mind my
ordering books by phone. They might even look things up in the
catalogue for me.

The Beamish wasn't having it. 'I'm beginning to see, John,' he
told me, 'that you have quite a talent for sweet talk. It's a fact that
the Library and indeed the whole university is full of pussycats who
could easily be talked into anything by someone with your wheedling
skills. But at the moment our splendid Bursar is under the impression that disabled students are rather expensive to run, something of

an extravagance in administrative terms. If I tell him you now need a phone in your room, he'll be absolutely sure of it. So don't over-play your hand. Put that honeyed tongue away.'

He seemed to have a very precise idea of his rôle: to make my life possible but not easy. 'As I may have mentioned,' he went on, 'it was only quite recently that the colleges began installing telephones for their Fellows. I'm not sure it counts as progress. It makes it much harder to get work done when the phone keeps ringing. Forgive me if I am repeating myself. A repetitious demand deserves a repetitious answer.'

The lowest vesicle of the *lingam*

This was a bit much to swallow, the physicist as Luddite, and I'd only just explained that having a phone would actually help me with my work. Still, I had to knuckle under. Technically, under Regulation 8(a) of the University Statutes, it was my Tutor who was held hostage when books were entrusted to me by the Library. He was responsible for any penalties incurred, as if he had borrowed them himself.

So I had to put up with a rather unsatisfactory system, relying on other people to chase up the catalogue, dropping off notes with my requirements or taking my turn on the long-suffering phone in the Porter's Lodge. All too often a porter would come down the steps to me at the agreed time, in response to my horn signal, with fewer books than I had hoped, or even none, saying cheerfully, 'I'm afraid we've run into some problems, sir!' And of course there was no possibility of appeal, to see where the system had failed.

Still, I now had at my disposal one of the great libraries in the country, stuffed with treasures Mrs Pavey could only dream of. I was determined to exploit it, and I wasn't going to wait for an academic emergency which might never arise. I was determined to dredge up a wriggling rarity from the depths of the *lingam*, from its lowest possible vesicle.

It was Mrs Pavey who gave me the idea, when she was looking into different systems of shorthand at my request. I had acquired a competence in Pitman, but then become disillusioned with it because it was so angular. On the rebound I fell into the arms of Gregg, with which

I was very happy for a while before I had to admit that it was simply too curvy. I gave up for a while, without altogether abandoning the hope that out there somewhere there was a baby bear of a shorthand system, neither too curvy nor too angular but just right. And I had never forgotten Mrs Pavey saying, 'I did come across a reference to a book based on another system, John, but it's impossibly rare. Still, it might be just what you're looking for – it's called *Brachystography*. Not just shorthand, which would be *brachygraphy*, but the shortest short-hand of all. From the Greek *brachistos*, shortest.' And I had almost-nodded, as if I had been born knowing Greek.

So that was my choice. J. A. A. Percebois's *Brachystography*, from 1898. At first the omens were good. The book had been located, in a sub-basement. There was a label on it saying NOT TO BE LENT OUT UNDER ANY CIRCUMSTANCES. Just the sort of prize I was after. There was a waiting period, while the case was referred indefinitely upwards for judgement, and then finally I received a note saying the book was ready for collection.

It was all terribly disappointing. The moment the glassy-eyed cœlacanth was in my fishing-net I realised I'd have had more fun with a goldfish in a plastic bag from the fair.

I shouldn't have been expecting a *little* book, just because it was about a system of extreme abbreviation, and anyway my love of such things should have been exhausted a long time ago, when I was in CRX and Mum gave me the World's Smallest Bible and a tiny Web-ster's Dictionary. More to the point, Percebois's system was about as sensible a way of representing the sounds of words as pictures of birds' feet. No wonder it hadn't caught on! I was reduced to my least fa-vourite position, of agreeing with what everyone has always thought. That's guaranteed to put my teeth on edge.

My status as Downing's first disabled student wasn't clear-cut. It turned out that there was another already, a blind student called Kevin who was reading Law. I would see him around the college, laden with textbooks in Braille. He was very popular, both in his own right and because he had somehow landed a job writing record reviews for the *Melody Maker*. LPs arrived for him by every post, and he was generous in passing them on. I wondered darkly whether he had a phone in his room. He seemed very favoured – and of course he hadn't needed to have a rail fitted in the college bathroom he used. He represented a modest institutional investment. Unlike some people. Mentioning no names.

The college had assigned me a room that was accessible, give or take, to someone with my poor mobility, but had overlooked the need to make a similar arrangement for my pigeon-hole, where mail would be distributed. The alphabetical run was maintained, with the result that *Cromer, J.*'s pigeon-hole was set at a height which Cromer, J. would never be able to reach. I considered protesting, in the hope of being granted a more convenient slot roughly two feet off the floor, but I was learning to ration my appeals for special treatment. Wheedling was apt to blow up in my face, and the honeyed tongue was beginning to receive caustic answers.

It would have been futile in any case, since I couldn't get into the Porter's Lodge unaided. When I needed to use their phone, I took the porters on a trip back in time, to the etymological roots of their calling. If they had been able to vote on the phone-in-John's-room question, they would have been solidly behind me, for the sake of equal rights and their backs. As for mail, they delivered it direct to my room.

The UL staff would only convey books to the bottom of the steps outside the front entrance, or a few paces further, to the door of the Mini. The personnel at Heffers, the university's foremost bookshop, would come much closer to home. They matched the efforts of the college porters. In an attempt to fight off the challenge of rival businesses such as Bowes & Bowes and (who knows?) even W. H. Smith, Heffers would deliver books to undergraduates at no charge. What an enlightened gimmick! The books came to my door.

If I had only had a phone in my room the whole book-buying transaction could have been accomplished without labour on my part, and I would have become an early example of the stay-at-home shopper. Even allowing for bookshop visits to place my order, it was a lot better than nothing.

I'm happier with hardbacks than soft covers, which isn't snobbery but pure practicality. With a paperback the only way you can avoid breaking the spine is to cradle it with your outstretched fingers. My fingers won't reach that far, so it's a matter of either balancing the book on the backs of my hands or going ahead and breaking the book's back, flattening it against the table-top. There's no room for sentiment when it comes to something as important as reading. Tender-hearted book-lovers wince when they see me in action, and I don't care.

The first book I asked about that wasn't on a course reading list was *Ramana Maharshi and the Path of Self-Knowledge*. After some inner wrestling I had finally surrendered 'my' copy, the Bourne End Library's copy, back to Mrs Pavey, though she would have been happy to go on renewing it indefinitely. Holding on to it would be wrong – a small civic crime, like wearing the life-belt that has been used to drag you out of the Slough of Despond on a permanent basis, though it is clearly marked *Property of Slough Borough Council*.

Heffers told me that the hardback was long out of print, but there was a paperback available. My heart sank at the news, though it's no secret that bibliophilia is only fetishism of self-righteous form, and a sly perversion of the longing for knowledge. Book-collecting magnifies the differences between copies of the same work until they are overwhelming, when it's the essential sameness of every copy which allows a book to make its impact.

A book is a book is a book. After lecturing myself in these terms, I ordered the paperback, which was priced at 18/6. While I waited for it to arrive, I tried to convince myself that it would connect me to my guru in exactly the same way the library copy had. In fact it would have the advantage of being fresh, free of associations – a new beginning for an established devotion. Looking at it in gardening terms, my devotion would be re-potted, with room to grow.

New improved whoopee cushion

Then when the book finally arrived, announced by a knock on the door of A6, it was the hardback after all! Still the first edition, a full fifteen years after publication, and in theory long exhausted and out of print. I made the trip to Heffers and cross-examined the staff about this miraculous mistake, but they weren't helpful, simply saying that there must have been a leftover copy at the warehouse. The word 'warehouse' indicated a place of decisions beyond the possibility of appeal, like 'Providence' or 'the Government'. They hardly noticed that I was thrilled rather than bitterly complaining. My bliss knocked them off kilter.

I was deeply moved by this godsend, this gurusend. There was no rational explanation for the appearance of the book – but nothing is impossible for the guru. It was a time when I was feeling only tenuously attached to the reality I had tried to find in India. This gesture of continued good faith from the non-dualist cosmos was all the more welcome and sustaining. If it was a miracle, it was a miracle well spent. And only twenty-five shillings.

My new copy even had the same tender blurb on the dust-jacket that had drawn Mum's eye in Bourne End Library, about the practice not entailing tortuous exercises or the tying of the body in knots. Words not holy in themselves but perfectly chosen as bait for the holy fishing-rod, making me fall for my guru hook, line and sinker.

Now I had a familiar book in my room. I also had my framed picture of Maharshi, but when Mrs Beddoes tidied it away out of sight I didn't protest. No picture of the Maharshi shows him as anything but benign, his smile a constant while his body ages, and yet sometimes I found it hard to meet his eyes.

My vow of gardening chastity had been overridden by the generosity of the Bot, and now I was making some experiments with an old friend. I bought a bulb from Sanders Seed Merchants in Regent Street, which I placed on a saucerful of sand in my window. This was an experiment on a person as well as on a plant – a practical joke. The idea was irresistible, once it had occurred to me, and this new improved whoopee cushion (the original had fizzled frustratingly under my tutor's bum during the bed-rest years) would not misfire.

No doubt in their native climes such things have a modest seasonality, but under the conditions even of humble windowsill Creation (let there be light! let there be heat! let there be water!) they can't wait to grow. Soon I could see a fine stout prong rising from the centre of the bulb. It was a naughty-looking thing which did my thin social life nothing but good. Passers-by would comment on the living phallic symbol growing on my windowsill. There were even people who knocked on the door to see the plant rather than me.

One of them was a botanist called Barry, who begged me to let him know when it flowered. He was a rather ugly squat student, always bleating about having no girlfriend. He had worse odds to contend with than the famous ten-to-one ratio of student genders. Even if the disproportion between the sexes was corrected – even if it was reversed – he could have relied on finding himself alone. From the way he kept himself, or rather neglected himself, it was surprising that anyone talked to him at all. Bad breath and body odour were his calling cards. He lived within his noxiousness as innocently as the stinkhorn mushroom. Sooner or later a friend, while such things still existed, would have to nerve himself to break the news.

The sinister inflorescence in my window grew and swelled by the day. I had let Barry in on the secret that the flower when it arrived would give off a really disgusting smell. Barry was more than a bit whiffy himself, of course, but if you were in the same room with Barry and *S. guttatum* in full inflorescence, it wouldn't be him you noticed. Whiffy Barry wasn't in the same class.

Barry was mad keen to see the thing in flower so that he could give his considered opinion as a botanist. That was just what I wanted myself. I told Barry he would be the first to know when it flowered, and I tried to predict when the great event would finally happen, but these things are hard to get right. I was really only beginning to understand the species.

Mrs Beddoes had started to take a tentative motherly interest in my welfare and happiness, so I knew my little scheme was working when she relapsed into her squirrel state of being. It was almost as bad as it had been at the beginning of term. She didn't know where to look, all over again, while I stayed put in bed. This *Eichhörnchen* was anything but *flinkes*, doleful for all her twitching.

I waited her out, with a gleeful interior chuckle. Surely she wouldn't be able to keep her peace much longer? She was being ridiculously patient. Then at last it came out, so very hesitantly. 'Now, Mr Cromer,' she said, 'I don't mind looking after you, hoovering your room, even making you the odd cup of tea. I hope you don't think I'm making difficulties – but I do . . .'

She clenched and unclenched her fists in desperation, steeling herself to produce words that went against her samurai code.

'. . . I do draw the line. I have to put my foot down somewhere . . .

Now I know it's not your fault, but try to appreciate it from my point of view, Mr Cromer.' *Appreciate* came out as *appreesherate*.

Ungraduate gentlemen are full of surprises

I let her struggle on, while I put my face through as many convincing emotional permutations as I could muster. It was all working splendidly, and I had to give her as much rope as I possibly could. Meanwhile I shuffled my legs out from under the duvet and hooked them under the wheelchair seat. With the help of the McKee pins I could pivot myself up into a sitting position on the bed and lever myself, awkwardly but unaided, into the chair.

At this stage in the pantomime it was vital that she didn't come to help me. I sidled discreetly over to the window side of the room. It would be exaggerating to say that I kept her talking. She couldn't stop, knowing that sooner or later she would have to come to the point. Finally she had exhausted the family medical encyclopædia. 'The thing is, Mr Cromer' – one last gasp and she came out with it – 'I do draw the line . . . at my gentlemen wetting the bed.'

'I see, Mrs Beddoes. Your gentlemen must not wet the bed. And you think I have committed this crime against the Holy Ghost, for which there can be no forgiveness. Is that your last word?'

'I'm afraid it is.' She bristled a bit, and I loved her for that. 'It's no crime, and I don't see what it has to do with the Holy Ghost, but I shouldn't have to put up with it.'

'And what is the solution to our problem? A rubber sheet? Plastic nappies?'

'I don't . . .' She ran out of words altogether.

'How about if I went down on my knees and begged for forgiveness?'

'Don't do that, Mr Cromer. You of all people . . .'

'The terrible thing is, Mrs Beddoes, I honestly don't remember wetting the bed. Do you think I'm going out of my mind?'

'I really couldn't say, Mr Crow-maire. Ungraduate gentlemen are full of surprises. Still, I wouldn't say you're the type.'

I wanted to take pity on her, but the game had to be played out in full. 'Anyway, Mrs Beddoes, you'll be taking this further – you have no choice in the matter, I quite understand that. But perhaps you'd better inspect the bed and show me where the wetness is.'

She prodded the Dream-Cloud, gingerly at first and then more thoroughly when she found it blameless. She sniffed. Then she went down a layer, still sniffing and snuffing, to levels of bedlinen which I didn't actually use – as if I might be caught short, yet somehow burrow down to relieve myself.

She was baffled. 'There doesn't seem to be any wetness.'

'Perhaps it's dried up already.'

'I suppose.' She wasn't convinced.

'What a mystery. While we think about it, perhaps you wouldn't mind opening the window and letting in a breath of fresh air.'

'I'm with you there, Mr Crow-maire,' she said. 'The smell is making me feel quite sick!' Mrs Beddoes drew back the curtains and went to open the window catch. At that point she reeled back. 'Lord Gracious, Mr Crow-maire,' she gasped. 'It's even worse over here!'

I assumed my best Sherlock Holmes manner, and pounced. 'Precisely!' I announced. 'And there you have it, Mrs Beddoes.'

'Have what, Mr Cromer?' Perhaps she had been too hasty in dismissing the possibility of mental breakdown – that's what I read on her face.

'The answer to the entire mystery, of course!'

Somehow I persuaded her to go over to the bed, to sniff and feel that it was both dry and clean. 'Use your eyes and your nose, Mrs Beddoes! Examine the evidence!' I almost said, *Mrs Hudson*, as if I was explaining my theories of deduction to a baffled Baker Street housekeeper. 'I insist that you give my personal hygiene a clean bill of health!'

She came back, frowning, to the window side of the room. 'Well . . .' was all she could manage to say.

'Once you have eliminated the all-too-likely, Mrs Beddoes,' I said, triumphantly indicating the unprepossessing flower, 'whatever remains, however preposterous, must be the truth. May I present *Sauromatum guttatum*, also known as the Voodoo Lily? Voodoo Lily, Mrs Beddoes, Mrs Beddoes, Voodoo Lily. This flower is responsible for the sinister smell, the smell like a neglected jakes.'

I could have added that the Voodoo Lily is also known as *Sauroma-*

tum venosum, *Typhonium venosum*, and *Arum cornutum*, but not everyone finds Latin names easy to understand and remember, so I kept things simple.

Mrs Beddoes' face went entirely empty, blank as a doll's must be before the paint is applied. She just stood there. It was very disconcerting. It was as if she had entirely forgotten who she was – a potential breakthrough during meditation, since personality must dissolve before the self can be manifested, but downright disconcerting in a college room reeking like a urinal.

Flames of laughter and relief

I started to lose confidence in my joke. 'It flowers very briefly, Mrs Beddoes. It'll be gone by tomorrow.' It was as if she was having some sort of fit, a hidden convulsion which prevented her from taking in a word I was saying. Nervously I took my explanation down a few levels of complexity. 'No more stink – everything sweet.' Then the blank look she wore suddenly went away. Her face was no longer vacant premises but a full house. It was standing room only, and the whole crowd screaming with laughter.

With the release of tension she wept hysterical tears. She had to sit down to get her breath. She made several attempts to speak, saying, 'I never . . . I never . . .', before she was able to go on with her sentence. 'I never . . . in all my years at Downing, in all my puff . . . I never heard of such a thing.' Her nervousness went up in flames of laughter and relief. The conflagration was almost alarming. She wasn't producing tears enough to put it out.

Finally she got her breath back. 'But if you're thinking of playing any more tricks like that, then you'd better be careful. My health won't stand it. It's a good job it's Alf who has the heart problem and not me. If it had been me . . . then what the consequences might have been . . . well, I wouldn't like to say, Mr Crow-maire. I might have slipped away, and you without a phone in your room to call for help.'

'I would have screamed, Mrs Beddoes,' I told her. 'I can make quite a noise when I have to.'

By taking liberties with her which she might easily have resented I had made her my friend. Charm could get me only so far, but now cheekiness had worked a magic of its own. I felt the release of tension too. I had dared to make a joke about something which had once been a baleful part of my history, bedwetting, and now I was free of the fear as well as the habit.

After that everything went smoothly between me and Mrs Beddoes. Nothing was too much trouble. Now it was official. The little yellow-haired squirrel eating out of my hand.

She started washing my hair, for one thing, though she didn't exactly volunteer. I had to do some prompting before it occurred to her to make the offer. Day after day I left a bottle of shampoo out in a conspicuous place, so that she would have to move it to clean properly. Eventually the discrepancy between the constant presence of the shampoo and the actual greasiness of my locks became impossible to ignore, and she said, 'Mr Cromer, I was wondering . . . would you mind if I had a bash at washing your hair? No offence, but it could do with a wash. Not in the bathroom, mind – I could do it here, wrap a towel round you and use a bowl . . .'

And I said, 'Well . . .' rather grudgingly, as if I would try to put up with her fussing round me. Anything for a quiet life.

After that, she would even cut my hair, just 'tidying it up', which was all that I would have wanted anyway. So the Voodoo Lily was anything but an ill wind from my point of view. It blew me no end of good. Mrs Beddoes would cut my fingernails for me and even squeeze unreachable pimples on my nose or forehead. This was a service which Mum rendered with a certain amount of cooing and scolding and chafing, saying, 'You're probably not getting enough chlorophyll in your diet' or 'Have you tried rubbing in half a fresh lemon?', but it was far too intimate to be mentioned when it was performed on an undergraduate by his bedmaker. It suited us both to pretend it wasn't happening.

Once in a while Mrs Beddoes would take a piece of my clothing home with her and wash it herself, but it was always clear between us that this was a personal favour and no part of the duties she performed for the college. It was between ourselves.

The flower of *Sauromatum guttatum* only lasts for the one day, and Whiffy Barry missed the show. He came along the following day, and together we examined the shrivelled and entirely odourless stem, which offered no insight into how the mechanism of the terrible smell might actually operate. That was my real interest in the Lily, to get hard evidence for Mr Mole at CRX, porter and self-appointed gardening expert, being wrong all those years ago. Mr Menage and *Gardening for Adventure* had sided with me in classifying *S. guttatum* as non-carnivorous, but I wanted proof, and Barry as an expert witness.

I had contradictory expectations of my fellow members of the student body. Colin the evangelical engineer wanted to get a firmer grip on his own soul by gathering mine in, and Noel the film-going chancer only wanted to pose and preen. Barry was the only one of the bunch who didn't even pretend to take an interest in me personally, and he was the only one I welcomed in.

I would invite people back to my room after lunch, bribing them with better coffee than the college provided and making sure (less defensibly) that I always had cigarettes on hand. Only my neighbour P. D. Hughes ever replaced my supply, but I didn't mind being exploited. At this point what I seemed to need was a definite idea of what my guests got out of my hospitality. What I wanted from them was less definite, in fact I can own up and say that it's a complete mystery to me now. The room was far too small for ambitious entertaining, but I liked it when people were wedged in anywhere they would fit and the ceiling swirled with smoke.

Once a guest of mine brought me a present – a lava lamp. Admittedly it was defective and a cast-off, something that had been returned to Joshua Taylor and replaced. That swanky emporium had no use for the faulty product, and so it came to me. It was prematurely aged, so that it no longer quite had the effect desired, of distended yolks of wax rising and falling through excited oil. In my lava lamp the wax was tired and unresponsive, circulating in globules and clots, weary melting streamers. You're not supposed to leave lava lamps on for extended periods, but I didn't have a lot of choice – the power point not being accessible to me. Friends would drop round for coffee and turn it on for their amusement, and then it would stay on till the next morning, when I'd ask Mrs Beddoes to turn it off. It's bad for lava lamps to be left on for so long, but what could I do? It was broken already, and I became accustomed to its sour ozone smell.

Pete had started to get weekend visits from his old girlfriend, Helen. She was from his home town (Birmingham) and they had gone out together for quite a while, but then before he went up to Cambridge he told her that a clean break was best.

Now he wasn't so sure. He felt defeated by the sheer weight of numbers, the odds against finding a student girlfriend, and he was too shy to meet girls from the town, or the nurses of Addenbrookes who were in a special category, supposedly nymphomaniacs without exception. One night, tipsy and self-pitying, he had written a letter to the girl he had dumped back home, repenting of his callousness.

She took him back, but sensibly kept him on a short rein. No student girlfriend could have had him so completely under her thumb. Helen, who was crisp, organised and already in work, seemed very grown-up.

When Helen first saw me she said, 'What are you doing?' 'Making yoghurt,' I said, to which she replied with the greatest cheerfulness, 'How revolting!' We got on well from the start, though she had no plans to share the limited time she had with Pete. She pressed him to give up smoking (so that he could contribute to her travelling expenses, as was only right), which tended to prevent him from coming to my room after meals. Helen had no interest in plants, so it was handy that I had learned to dispense with Pete's services as botanical escort at weekends.

He wasn't entirely at ease with the company after meals at A6 anyway. He had acquired a nickname he disliked, and in a way it was his own fault. Like many people studying a language he was struck by the limited sounds of Russian (while of course forcing his tongue to master intricacies unknown in English). One day he happened to mention that there was no H in Rooshian, so that his own name, Hughes, would be pronounced *Gooks*. What he said wasn't exactly 'Gooks', but that was what people decided they heard, and he was Peter Gooks after that, or just 'Gooks'. I tried to set up a counter-tradition by calling him *Pyotr* or *Petrushka* instead, but no one ever used those fond forms but me.

Sites of sordid suffering

I've always been a slow eater, and always will be, but the improvement in what we ate in Hall made Alan Linton also linger over his food. Mealtimes became companionable, now that we could bask in the envious glances of our flesh-eating fellows, who would chew their corrupt rations in grim haste. Our plates were not sites of sordid suffering, and our forks were not burdened with karma.

The slow pace of eating suited rambling chat, but I was running out of subjects. I had qualms by now about turning my summer in India into a party piece. In any case it often fell flat. In practice, telling people about my sojourn as guest of the mountain only prompted questions about Indian restaurants. Which was better, the Sylhet or the Curry Centre on Castle Hill? I had no idea. I had spotted a restaurant called the Curry Queen on Mill Road, and had decided it would be my first port of call, but I hadn't got round to it yet.

In those days even educated people knew only a tiny handful of words in any Indian language, and one of them was always Sutra. Another was Karma. I spent a lot of time explaining that the Kama in Kama Sutra was not the same thing as the Karma the hippies held so dear. To make the distinction clear I would roll the *r* in Karma exaggeratedly, until my whole brain shook in its moorings from the force of the alveolar trill.

In early days there was another obvious subject of conversation. For the amusement of my fellow-students in Hall I would imitate Mrs Beddoes, giving her an exaggeratedly strangulated voice which swooped from would-be posh to common in a single sentence. I don't know how this fool's route to popularity ranked, when set beside the folly of buying rounds indiscriminately in the college bar. Rather lower, I suspect.

I was repeating past successes in the rôle of raconteur, from the times I had beguiled the dorm at Vulcan with a thousand variations on themes of sexual passion and home cooking. Bit by bit I worked Mrs Beddoes up into a character, exaggerating her very mild mispronunciations and odd patterns of stress. 'Oh Mr Crow-*maire*, if you really think my duties extend to tidying up after your friends you're very much mis-*taiken*. Alf (that's my husband) always tells me I do too much for others, but then Mr Crow-*maire* you are a child of God as good as any. Better than most.

'All well and good, Jean, says Alf-that's-my-husband, but if I've told you once I've told you times without number, your endless

519

service to others may well se-*coor* your place in the blue hereafter, but what about the here and now, eh?

'By which he generally means his tea.'

Such routines were much in demand, and if I didn't announce a performance with a single stylised sniff the cry would go up of, 'Come on John, entertain us. Do the bedder, she's priceless.'

It was reassuring to have a routine that reliably brought approval. It was only gradually that I became uncomfortable. Wasn't I traducing the person who had shown me most friendliness, an intimacy without demands? (A cup of tea freely offered is a small miracle of consideration.) I determined to stop.

I wasn't brave or self-righteous enough to lecture my faithful audience on the misrepresentation we were conspiring to perpetrate, to announce Mrs Beddoes in so many words as the salt of the earth without which there would be no savour. My conscience pushed me in the opposite direction from the one I had taken historically, not towards wilder flights but a greater fidelity. I added in more and more of the humble details – the caravan outside Beccles, the deaf sister in Waterbeach. Eventually people stopped asking me to 'do' Mrs Beddoes, and neighbours in Hall who had missed the performance for a while would receive frantic signals not to egg me on.

Ribs in the head

All in all there has been quite a lot of eye-rolling in my immediate vicinity down the years, just outside my line of sight, or just within it when people have underestimated my peripheral vision. Most of the useful information I have gathered has reached me out of the tail of my eye.

With Alan I found myself talking about homœopathy. As a medical student, he was biased against therapies not based on the Western tradition, but he wasn't entirely opposed to new ideas. His mind was neither open nor shut, but ajar. I argued that homœopathy was a Western tradition in itself.

I emphasised that homœopathy individuates, taking each person as a separate unit, while conventional science generalises and expects the same results to hold for everyone. Alan was intrigued by the unim-

portance in homœopathy of theory without result, its sheer practicality as a set of techniques.

As always when homœopathy was the subject in those years, I was
at least partly thinking about something else. *Similes similibus amentur*, if you like. I had heard of something called the Gay Liberation
Front, which sounded angry rather than loving, and in any case hadn't
yet forced itself on my attention in the university or the town.

I asked Alan if he knew the story of the 1854 cholera epidemic in
London. 'Bloody hell, John,' he said. 'I am a medical student, you
know. I know a little bit about the history of diseases and a few things
about the human body. This is my third year of study, so I even know
that the ribs aren't located in the head.' I rather enjoyed being on the
receiving end of some sarcasm. It gingered me up. Normally people
get rather mealy-mouthed in my vicinity. 'So if you're referring to
the discovery of the water-borne transmission of cholera, and how the
doughty John Snow saved lives in Soho by taking the handle off the
Broad Street pump, then yes, I know the story of the 1854 cholera
epidemic.'

He had taken the bait. 'Then you know about the report on the
epidemic prepared for Parliament by the Board of Health.'

'What about it?'

'The exclusion from it of the data from the Homœopathic Hospital
in Golden Square, which was in the middle of the outbreak.' After
my visit to Great Ormond Street I had discovered that it wasn't the
original London base of homœopathy.

He went rather quiet. 'I'm a little vague about that. Remind me.'

'The Homœopathic Hospital gave the information as requested –
names and addresses of patients, symptoms, remedies and results. The
whole hospital had been given over to victims of the epidemic. Out of
61 cases of cholera, 10 died – a mortality of 16.4%. At the Middle-
sex Hospital nearby, 123 died out of 231. A mortality of over 50%.
Under protest the Board of Health released these figures, which had
been kept out of the original tally.'

'Did they say why they had suppressed them in the first place?'

'Oh yes. First because they were so out of keeping with the other
results that they would have distorted the findings. Second because
they didn't want to lend support to "empirical practice". You weren't

supposed to cure illness without understanding its causes, and in homœopathy you just pay attention to symptoms and deal with those. Hahnemann himself, the chap who invented the system in the first place, came up with a therapy for cholera without seeing a single case, from the symptoms described by colleagues. Treatment without formal diagnosis is intolerable to the medical establishment which you're so keen on joining. Better to let people die than have cures that don't obey the formalities. But perhaps John Snow wasn't the only one saving lives in Soho that year.'

'Is this all on the record, John? I'd hate you to be pulling my leg.'

'I can't reach your leg. And yes, it's on the record. Will Hansard do? I'm afraid I don't have the exact references.'

'I'll manage.'

I'm sure I would have heard about it if Alan's researches hadn't corroborated what I had told him. His attitude towards homœopathy slowly changed. Soon he was saying that if I gave him a prescription he would take it with an open mind. I said that it would only be a fair test if some symptom was troubling him. Perhaps there was?

The mother tongue of the placebo

Apparently so. At least there was a physical condition, too trivial to be taken to the doctor, which could be examined for experimental purposes. The matter was intimate enough for him to deliver me back to A6 Kenny so that he could make his confession. It turned out that Alan was troubled by copious sweating under the arms, even in winter, and by an accompanying animal odour. In short, B.O.

He had an exaggerated idea of his case. I was well placed, after all, while he was labouring up and down steps with me, to detect any offensive aroma. He smelled like an animal, yes, of course, but only because he was one. He smelled clean, he smelled warm and alive. Barry, on the other hand, the botanist who had been a whiffy basidiomycetous saprophytic fungus in a (recent) previous life, would never be able to detect his own aroma, any more than saints can see their own haloes.

I didn't have to work very hard to select a remedy for Alan. There's a passage of *Magic of the Minimum Dose* – from which I had been freely quoting, of course, preaching in borrowed robes – which describes just such a case. I knew I should ask a full set of questions, but on this occasion I went by hunch. Chronic issues require particular attention to the *Mind* section, and I let myself be guided by my impressions (*Nervous and excitable* / '*Brain-fag*' / *Abstracted* / *Fixed Ideas*).

I took out an empty notebook and wrote *For Overactive Sweat Glands in Young Adult Male – Silicea 200* on the first page. Then I wrote *Alan Linton* / *signetur 1/1 silicea c200* / *x3 gutt. sub linguam* on a label and attached it to a vial that had come with my starter kit of remedies. I enjoyed the paperwork for once, or more exactly the methodical feeling that comes from separating and labelling, even if there was an element of the rough and ready about my Latin. Nobody really reads the Latin – I could have written *lingam* for *linguam* without making any difference to Alan – but it massively reinforces the psychological effect. Slightly bogus Latin is the mother tongue of the placebo.

When I saw him next, Alan told me that from the first moment he held the pillule on his tongue he could feel it taking effect. His sweating moderated and any odour dissipated in a few days. Certainly his self-consciousness about it rapidly became a thing of the past. Of course homœopathy normally brings about improvements over a longer period of time, but rapid cures are not unknown. One of the great virtues of the method, in fact, is that it doesn't persist with remedies that are proving ineffective. Not for the homœopath the GP's reflex of the repeat prescription, the increased dosage. If it doesn't make a difference at the first attempt, you stop and try something else.

'What did I tell you?' I crowed. Despite this I was astounded by the success of my first attempt at prescription. What had I told him, after all? Nothing that I really knew about. Could the whole pretty system possibly work?

From that moment on, Alan Linton was a believer, verging on zealotry. He started borrowing what books I had on the subject, but he soon exhausted my modest library and started researching on his own account. To some extent this played into my hands. I was someone, after all, who had special borrowing privileges from the University Library, but found it impossible to consult the catalogue so as to order books. Alan on the other hand could only consult the UL's holdings, not take them away, but was easily able to do the legwork. So it was agreed. He would use the catalogue for me, and I would borrow books for him.

I enjoyed the feeling that I had made a convert, even though it wasn't to my religious perspective, as I had hoped before I came to Cambridge. Homœopathy wasn't a core belief of mine, it hadn't even had time to bed down as an obsession. It was no more than a hobby in waiting. I had written *Homœopathic Prescriptions* on the cover of the notebook in which I had written Alan's details, but it was quite a while before there was a second prescription noted down. In Hall at Downing, in the meantime, it was now Alan who would inform me about his latest discoveries as we took our time over tomato flan and that great novelty of vegetarian cuisine, as it seemed to us then, pasta salad.

In his own way Alan was rather a tactile person. Often he would put his arms round me and give me long hugs, saying that he got a very positive energy from being with me. Sometimes our lingering over the meal meant that he came back to A6 with me on his own.

At one stage we were talking about being 'grounded', and how wrong it was for us to elevate ourselves above the ground. The starting-point of the conversation was probably the traditional Buddhist strictures against sleeping away from the ground.

I agreed in principle, but had to add, 'Yes, Alan, that's all very well but because of my legs and whatnot, I *have* to sleep off the ground!'

'Yes, but even a little time on the ground is better than nothing . . .'

'I suppose so. Not something I know much about.' It wasn't the time to mention that I had been sexually initiated in a sleeping-bag on the ground, while at Woodlarks summer camp for disabled school-boys.

'I'm sure I could get you onto the ground for a bit. Shall we give it a try?'

'If you like.'

Carefully he manœuvred me onto the ground, cradled in his arms. Then he made a disgusted face and said, 'This carpet could certainly do with a clean . . .'

I hoped all the same that the pungency of the floor-covering wouldn't lead him to break off our experiment. I was becoming excited by our entwined posture, and couldn't help myself from pushing myself against Alan in a way that wasn't particularly Buddhist.

It was a strange experience, all the same. There was so much of him. In fantasies my sexual partners – Blyton's Julian, Rollo from the *Rupert* annual – were the same size as me. They didn't extend beyond me, or protrude in awkward ways. Admittedly Julian Robinson at Vulcan was a big boy, but in our most memorable encounter, with a kindly observer providing the motive power, the feeling of a sensual pulsation was only part of the hilarity of the total event.

Alive in the groins

Now I was pressed up against a young man several inches taller even than Julian, and fully in charge of his parts. I seemed to occupy only an intermediate zone of this enormous physique. I felt cheated of the full picture – I was getting only fragmentary impressions of his body, while the warmth poured into me through his clothes.

I could hear the gurgling of Alan's stomach, as a digestion at the peak of its young powers smoothly converted pasta salad into radiant heat and the faculty of embracing. 'Just to let you know where I stand,' he told me. 'I have a strong aversion to queers and their ways. I shouldn't be prejudiced, but there it is. Any sort of poovery gives me the creeps. At least I'm honest about it.'

He told me he'd been briefly involved with an organisation called the Monarchist League, whose members were strongly in favour of the monarchy, obviously, but not the monarchy we actually had. They believed the Queen was an impostor of some sort. He had been to one of their dinners in a house in Trumpington. At the end of the meal, after elaborate toasts to the rightful royal family, he had seen a man put his hand between another man's legs. He took the only proper action available and fled the premises, quite fast I imagine since his legs were long.

I wanted to wriggle up and be close to Alan's face, and also to wriggle downwards and be aligned with his crotch. I couldn't do both, so I made my choice. I chose down. Belatedly Alan detected the erotic vibration in what we were doing. 'Now John,' he said, 'I must remind you that if I thought for *one solitary second* there was anything sexy for you in this, I'd be out of here like a shot!'

I'm fine about being sly, but flat dishonesty isn't really in my nature, so I said, 'Then I am very sorry, Alan. I have to confess that you're making me as randified as anything.' I resigned myself to the interruption of this delightful adventure, pushing myself against him one last time.

Strangely, though, just when I had come clean he started to make excuses for me. 'Yes, well, John, you should understand that you are a person who D. H. Lawrence would say is very "alive in the groins". It's nothing to worry about, nothing to worry about at all . . . Greatly to your credit, in fact. Human beings are only animals, when you get right down to it.'

I blessed the holy name of David Herbert Lawrence, about whom I had mixed feelings. On the one hand I adored *Women in Love*, particularly the wrestling scene by the fireside – unclothed apotheosis of the tender grappling I had dreamed of in my sickbed and coveted as a Burnham schoolboy. This very encounter on institutional carpet was the closest I could ever hope to come to recreating it. I had taken an oath not to see the film, because I wanted to imagine the faces of my choice on the bodies of Gerald and Birkin. Some things are sacred, and I wouldn't let Ken Russell wrestle me away from the casting couch of my fantasies.

It was *Lady Chatterley's Lover* I shied away from. Somehow I didn't think Lawrence's plan, when he put Lady C's husband in a wheelchair, was to indicate that he was alive in the groins.

Alan kept faith with our Buddhist experiment until he started to get pins and needles, and that was as close as I got to Alan on the physical plane. It turned out that a little grounding went a long way.

The consolation prize for me was news of this amazing club called the Monarchist League. I had no interest in the royalist aspect either way. For me the hand between the legs was the good bit. Surely it must be the core value of the organisation? I didn't dare to ask any more questions, but I became obsessed with the idea that hands were being thrust between legs only a couple of miles away. Once I even drove the Mini out to Trumpington and pestered innocent pedestrians, saying, 'Ex*cuse* me! Could you possibly direct me to Headquarters of the Monarchist League?' Nobody knew, or they were all in on it and weren't accepting new recruits.

The friendship didn't exactly fizzle out, in fact it flourished in its own way, but I have to own up to a little disappointment. Perhaps it was simply that the polarity of the discipleship had switched, now that the enlightenment was flowing all the other way, and Alan was delving into homœopathy with a diligence I couldn't match.

I didn't consciously take credit for inspiring him, any more than I would have congratulated myself, after introducing bacillus culture into milk of the correct temperature, on having invented yoghurt, but isn't that always the way? The cry goes up of 'The ego is dead!', but when you look around it is the ego which has shouted the words, and is even now measuring itself for coronation robes. Perhaps there was pique at the way my small expertise had been superseded. I had yet to learn the deep spiritual significance of disappointment.

I felt sadness at the defeat which was thrown into relief by this small triumph. The real discipleship was my relationship with my guru, and however exciting and revelatory I managed to make my reminiscences of India, I knew that some longed-for process of kindling, of catching fire at last, had not in fact taken place despite my conviction of flammability. The quest and its goal seemed further away than ever.

I almost longed to be proselytised by those of other religions, so that I could have my convictions honed by the abrasion of alien creeds. In fact I didn't suffer unduly from the attentions of the God Squad – it was as if I had been inoculated by that clumsy first approach from the apostle Colin. Others weren't so lucky. One lovely gentle student called Chris Charnock, reading English, who had religious feelings that weren't fully formed, felt so persecuted by the evangelical wing of the university that he had a sort of nervous breakdown. I didn't know him very well, but we had enjoyed some vague spiritual chats, and he had lent me his copy of Aldous Huxley's *The Perennial Philosophy*. Now he couldn't stop weeping and had to be sent home. He didn't come back the next term. I felt sorry to lose an ally, someone with whom in time I might have shared my own feelings of falsity and strain, but I was glad for him that he was away from what had been for him a place of torment. Nothing could have been more damaging to this shy mystic, feeling his way towards his inklings, than to be lectured on hell and its fires.

Downing had a chaplain, but I had little contact with him. He was very tactile, and I don't mean anything sinister by that. It's just he was very keen on the hugs and pats, which I don't find it easy to discourage (there's never an electric fence around when you need one), and on one occasion he took a small liberty. He ran his hand over my starveling and lop-sided beard, saying with a twinkle, 'John Cromer, you're only half a man, aren't you?', which I found rather wounding. I should have stood up for my peculiarity and my faith both, by saying, 'I take that as a compliment, chaplain. Ardhanishvara is Lord Shiva represented as half man and half woman. It's your loss that callow Christianity has no time for such subtleties of incarnation. The interest is all in the half-tones.'

Nelson never ordered pizza

Sometimes I missed the evening meal in Hall and went out to eat with a group. The favoured destination was a cheap place called the Eros on Petty Cury. One reason for the low prices was that it occupied relatively undesirable premises on the first floor, which necessitated much human machinery to get me upstairs and downstairs again at the end of the meal. The descent was frightening since cheap wine was likely to have boosted the confidence of my porters at the expense of their coördination. The staple dish was moussaka (can it really have cost only six shillings, thirty new pee as we practised saying?), but the Eros also offered a 'Florentine' pizza, topped with spinach and a rather sinister, glistening fried egg.

That wasn't the reason, though, for my never ordering it. I have nothing against pizza beyond the fact of its being unitary. Admiral Nelson never ordered pizza either, and the reason is obvious. Two good arms are required to dismantle the savoury disc. Of course Nelson had Emma Hamilton, but for once she was no substitute. There's no getting around it – having your food cut up for you beyond the age of five is bearable only in surroundings of relaxed intimacy, and not always then. A plate of pasta, on the other hand, by the generosity of its composite nature, offers tendrils to the questing fork. Even to the fork that twirls ineptly in slow motion.

The restaurant was hardly one which Granny would have recognised as such, what with the chipped plates and the unmatched cutlery. But there was one little waiter, from the Philippines I think, who was vaguely reminiscent of the waiter at the Compleat Angler, so expert at buttering up a woman who prided herself on immunity to flattery.

This Filipino would sometimes ask an undergraduate for a phone number as well as his address on the back of a cheque. This was in the days before cheque guarantee cards, when no pledge more formal than an address was required. He certainly took the name of the establishment at face value. The god of boyish desire threw arrow after arrow into his heart, till it must have had the pitted texture of a pub dartboard.

I was the only one who seemed to notice the glaring inappropriateness of the extra request. This waiter only asked the pretty ones for this detail, and was perhaps shrewd enough to ask only parties whom wine had fuddled. Not shrewd enough, though, to realise that the numbers he was given were never more intimate than those of the public phones on some privileged staircases, which took incoming calls. The best he could hope for was pot luck. Perhaps the right person would pick up the phone and hear the plaintive murmur of 'Here is Eros boy. You are nice James?'

Some of the letters which the porters kindly delivered to A6 were government circulars to do with decimal currency, which would be introduced in February of 1971. These circulars with their jaunty tone nevertheless managed to suggest that decimal currency was an impossibly difficult challenge for young, old and everyone in between. I determined to master it. Time is an illusion, absolutely right – but that's no excuse for being stuck in the past.

By the time my Heffers bill for the term arrived I was well ahead of the game. Laboriously I converted all the sums from pounds shillings and pence into New Pennies, and wrote out a cheque accordingly. There's a thin line between being cheeky-charming and getting people's backs up, and I don't always know which side I'm on. Heffers returned the cheque, with a wry covering letter saying they were impressed by my preparedness for change, not to mention my computational skills, but would I mind replacing the old cheque drawn on the new system with a new one drawn on the old?

The tides of history were rising over Britannia's knees on the big old dirty copper penny, but she hadn't been swept away just yet. I can't help feeling it would have been more fun if Heffers had given me credit as a pioneer of the new world of sensibly divisible money, by holding on to the cheque for a couple of months, till it ripened into legal validity.

When I went home for the Christmas vacation I didn't know what sort of welcome I would get from the family. By the family I mean Mum. The others were dependable in their ways. Peter would be quietly happy, Audrey would blow hot and cold, and Dad would greet me absently, as if he was pretty sure he knew me but couldn't remember the context.

I even considered staying in Cambridge over the vacation, though Hall would close down and I would have to cater for myself. I would also need my Tutor's permission, which pretty much ruled it out. Graëme Beamish had obviously made a resolution, well ahead of the New Year, to refuse any further requests from the occupant of A6 Kenny. I made a resolution not to put his resolution to the test.

In the event Mum was warm and gracious, very much on best behaviour. It seemed that at last she accepted me having a home elsewhere. I wouldn't keep coming home if she made it an ordeal when I did. It made a difference that she was having great trouble with Audrey.

Audrey was hardly more than ten, but her wilfulness was phenomenal. She would never back down. Sometimes I think she was frightened by her own anger. She wasn't alone in that.

The present I remember most fondly from my twenty-first birthday (it did for Christmas as well) was a purse containing twenty-one fiftypence pieces. The coins were legal tender already, as ten shillingses, though I felt honour-bound to wait until decimalisation dawned to spend them. This was from my other grandmother, Dad's mother. We hardly ever saw her. By this time she was retired, living in a part of Edinburgh called Hunters Tryst, which I loved even before I learned that it was pronounced to rhyme with 'Christ'. She was a rather childlike creature who had spent most of her life running her own little gift shop, specialising in glass animals. She was always feeling sorry for people and giving them ridiculous discounts. Not much of a businesswoman. Eventually the shop burned down, and we learned that it had never been insured. She seemed remarkably calm about it, saying that she had had fun out of it for years and years without doing anyone any harm, and that was the main thing, wasn't it?

Freshly minted heptagons

Perhaps no one can watch everything they care about going up in flames without feeling a certain lifting of the spirits. Few of us get the chance to find out, and so we pay lip-service to the notion of catastrophe.

She said she would have liked to send me the full twenty-one pounds, but her funds wouldn't stretch so far. I was very pleased with my stack of coins. Peter too was impressed by my new purse bursting with freshly minted heptagons, and asked who had given it to me. 'Granny,' I said, and then, seeing his incredulous expression, 'The other one. Nice Granny.' There was no implied criticism of the one who came first in our minds, the ur-Granny, who wouldn't have thought much of an unconditional gift. For her, presents came into the same category as kites, balloons and aprons, having strings attached by definition.

Dad's mum loved animals even when they weren't made of glass. As a child I asked her, where do the animals go? Go after death. And she said, 'I'm sure there's a little corner of heaven God keeps for animals.' A paddock in paradise – why not? It's what Nice Granny would have provided herself.

The only limit on her niceness was that she didn't love her children. Nature and strangers but not her own children. A worm in a jar was 'a perfect lamb' (as she had said once), but her own children were perfect nuisances. When children got to be about eight years old they began to be bearable to her – they were allowed to say goodbye to her then, gently clasping the tip of her outstretched finger.

Luckily there was Midge to bring them up, a local girl who had joined Nice Granny's household when she was twelve and never left. When Nice Granny was getting old Midge said she wanted the house, and Nice Granny said, Then you'd better have it.

Understandably Dad had no more than a pained fondness for his mother, and a deep though resentful bond with Midge. If it turned out that his mother hadn't put anything in the will about Midge getting the house, he would certainly have seen her right.

I spent a lot of time getting my thanks about my birthday down on paper, which was probably wasted effort. There's nothing that introduces a false note into a thank-you letter more reliably than actual gratitude. It's a container that can accommodate almost anything more easily than what it was specifically designed to hold. A sincere thank-you letter is a live chick pecking its way out of a dyed egg on an Easter table-decoration, and giving everyone a turn.

Returning to Cambridge after Christmas didn't exactly feel like a home-coming, but there were fewer possibilities for explosion and upset on Kenny A staircase than in Bourne End. It was too peaceful to feel like home. I almost felt I was getting to know the ropes.

Jean Beddoes had started to confide in me – not about private matters, though I could have compiled a fair-sized dossier on her husband's health from what she let slip on the subject, and I picked up a certain amount of information about her money worries. It was more when she felt out of her depth as a bedmaker that she would come to me for advice. One day, for instance, she told me that she didn't know what to do about a student on my staircase. Should she report him to the college authorities, or was it none of her business? She couldn't make up her mind.

The student in question, Dexter Hoffman, was known to me, since he would stay talking over coffee and cigarettes when everyone else had gone. At last I would simply tell him to go. He was impervious to hints, but oddly docile when given a clear directive.

Hoff was reading philosophy, though our discussions were not philosophical in any obvious sense. Dexter (always known as 'Hoff') was known as a conversationalist, meaning that he paid only the slightest attention to what anyone else said, just enough to turn the talk back to the rut of his preference when it deviated.

Hoff was a college character whose foibles were much discussed. He filed his collection of albums by an esoteric system which remained mysterious in its details even when the general principle became known. The record at the extreme left was Love's *Forever Changes*, while the one at the other extreme was *An Electric Storm* by White Noise, a group known only to Hoff, or so it seemed.

Privileged guests would be challenged to put the record on Hoff's turntable back where it belonged in the ranking. It was considered a triumph to be only ten places off. The criterion was 'heaviness', a quality which obsessed the student population but had never before been systematically considered. The Vietnam War was *heavy*, Blind Faith were *heavy*, the prospect of getting a job and joining an oppressive Establishment was undeniably *heavy*, but no one before Hoff had even attempted to rank them comparatively.

It wasn't clear if he was serious about this, or making one of his jokes. Since he rarely laughed at other people's jokes, and never at his own, it was hard to tell. About his albums he seemed to be serious. *Forever Changes* earned its place by being 'deep' but not *heavy*. *An Electric Storm*, on the other hand, was absolute heaviness, a sort of Kelvin zero. As he put it, 'If you listen to the last track late at night and you've *smoked some shit*, you can think that it's you that's dying.' And this was not a dreadful warning but a recommendation.

Our conversations, though, were about sex. He was a ladies' man of some obsessiveness, though his preferred term was 'girls'. He was always smuggling girls into his room at night and sneaking them out again in the morning. He strongly opposed co-education (technically, co-residence), and thought it would never come to pass in Downing.

From his philanderer's perspective, co-residence would take all the excitement out of his conquests. As he explained it to me, 'If you can just click with the girl in the next room, well – where's the challenge in that?' It was a question of sportsmanship. When the grouse moor is right next to the gun room then there's nothing to brag about in bagging a huge tally.

If there had been women on the premises, he would still insist on hunting abroad, on principle. Well, partly on principle – it was also a lot easier to stop girls hanging around after he lost interest if they didn't live there in the first place.

I did wonder whether Hoff was really the womanising sensation he claimed, but his word was broadly accepted on the matter. Some dissidents suggested that girls took their clothes off just to get him to stop talking, though others questioned whether even such a drastic measure would necessarily shut him up. 'They expect me to try it on,' he would say. 'They'd never forgive me if I didn't. They'd take it personally.' He took his rôle very seriously, though I didn't think it was strictly necessary for the smooth running of the town, or even the nurses' hostel.

He had a strange hairstyle, though it was probably more of a refusal to have a hairstyle. His hair was naturally frizzy, and he both let it grow and tamed it with a savage parting, so that the ensemble looked like a cottage loaf which has risen unevenly. Of course women often like an element of helplessness in men, but I doubt if that was part of the plan.

Basilisk of the bedroom

Most of our conversations were about women's thoughts and feelings, which might seem an unlikely interest for a womaniser. But think about it: at a conference of safe-breakers the subject of discussion wouldn't be money, bullion and booty but rather tumblers, alarms and time-locks. In the same way Hoff was preöccupied with women's emotions and ideas – everything he had to get past before the marvellous mechanism swung open at last, and he glimpsed the ingots of shining pleasure stacked high on the shelves.

Hoff had an elaborate typology of women (girls). There were virgins, there were half-virgins and according to him there were some girls who had never been virgins at all. There were Clean Dirty Girls and Dirty Clean Girls (his particular pets), but there were no Dirty Dirty Girls. He explained: the Dirty Dirty Girl, the girl who matched a man in appetite and even outstripped him, was no more than a legend or fabulous beast, the unicorn of sex.

Charm played no part in his technique. He stunned women with a bolt of indifference, and after that he could do what he liked with them. According to Hoff, there was nothing a girl found more reassuring in a man than absolute unreliability. But it did have to be absolute. Mere dithering wasn't enough. She had to be able to count on his unreliability, and there Hoff had never been a disappointment. I don't know whether all women fitted this pattern, or the ones who interested him.

There are other fabulous beasts than unicorns, of course, and I began to wonder if the Dirty Dirty Girl, if she ever actually turned up with her cornucopia of desires, might not be the sort who turns men to stone, basilisk of the bedroom. If Hoff ever met her, would he tell us about it? Would he be allowed to keep the power of speech after that encounter?

I was fascinated to be having such technical discussions with an unashamed sexual predator, of a breed that was coming to be labelled the Male Chauvinist Pig, which didn't die out but certainly changed its spots, finding new ways of presenting bad behaviour.

I noticed how clean Hoff was, on the occasions when he carried me, still talking, to the lavatory (where he would raise his voice a little so as to be sure of reaching me in my stall). He was at least as clean as Alan Linton, but while Alan would certainly have given his armpits priority Hoff paid attention also to fingernails and (most likely) toes. Perhaps his secret was nothing more than the combination of low morals and good hygiene – hardly the secret of life or anything else, though admittedly unusual in that place and at that time. It was, additionally, a combination which might attract those fabled Addenbrookes nurses.

Hoff was a philosopher as a matter of academic fact, but economics loomed more largely in his daily life. He ate only the statutory minimum of meals in Hall, but liked company while he ate, so he would call in on me in A6. I don't know if he was rich or poor, but he was certainly thrifty to the point of madness. His diet was carefully calculated, made up not of the cheapest foods in absolute terms but the ones which met his body's needs most efficiently. Everything was calculated down to the last penny-calorie.

He had established to his own satisfaction that tinned cod's roe represented the best investment in terms of protein. He called it *prole caviar*, and would eat it straight from the tin so as to save on washing up. The proteinous beige-pink slab in the tin, or the lump of it in his spoon, had the visual texture of soft wet brick and a faint meaty smell.

I didn't mention that I had been to a school where actual posh caviar was delivered at intervals, thanks to the Queen Mother's interest and bounty, and later fed to pigs. I had started to clam up about my past. Every little incident seemed to need so much explaining, and I could hardly keep trotting out the whole saga. No one at Cambridge was curious about how I had got there anyway. I might just as well have been some sort of life-form cooked up in the Cavendish Laboratory and stored in A6 Kenny to await testing.

Hoff also favoured tinned ham risotto, not necessarily a dish which Italians would recognise or claim credit for. This too he ate from the tin, unheated, gaining access with a small opener, no more than a blade with a flange, which he worked round the edge of the tin with a vigorous rocking motion. Under the jagged lid, when at last he lifted it, were yellowed grains of rice and reddish cubes of ham. Among them nestled amber pearls of fat.

All these tins, heavy with karma even when empty, went into my waste-paper basket. Mrs Beddoes would frown as she retrieved them, though she must have known without needing to ask that these were not relics of binges on my part.

Girlfriends weren't exempt from Hoff's mathematical calculations, though in that department of economic affairs I think the unit was the pound-orgasm rather than the penny-calorie. A girl who gave him the full penile thrill for less than fifteen shillings (though no doubt he was learning to say 'seventy-five new pence' like everyone else) would stay on his books.

Not necessary to celebrate Hitler's birthday

So when Jean Beddoes expressed worry about Hoff I thought that perhaps a conquest of his had left some incriminating item in his room – panties in the bed, perhaps, at the least. Perhaps a number of pairs. Then she said, 'I think Mr Hoffman must be a fascist. A proper fascist.'

This was a startling thing for a bedmaker to say in 1971. It wasn't a startling thing for an undergraduate to say, of course. By this time the word was an entirely unspecific term of disapproval – it wasn't necessary to wear jackboots in the street or celebrate Hitler's birthday to earn the label. Jumping the meal queue in Hall was quite enough.

Mrs Beddoes, though, must mean something different. 'What makes you think so?' I asked. Miserably she produced something from her pinny pocket. It was an item of clothing – I'd got that right. Not panties, though, or anything else belonging to a girl. It was a bundled pair of socks. I turned them over awkwardly in my hands, completely baffled. Mrs Beddoes reached over to unroll them and exposed the shocking truth. The socks – black, nylon – were neatly labelled with blue Cash's name-tapes, and the name they carried was BENITO MUSSOLINI.

'It isn't just his socks,' she whispered. '*That name* is on everything he wears.'

Mrs Beddoes didn't actually think that Hoff was wearing a dead dictator's nylon socks, but she certainly thought the name-tapes represented a homage to sinister politics. I tried to talk her round.

I explained that it wasn't any more ominous that he had the Duce's name on all his things than that he had it in his socks. It only meant that the minimum order for Cash's name-tapes was a hundred, and that he was a dab hand with a sewing-machine, no doubt smirking as he stitched smugly away.

I managed to persuade Mrs Beddoes that it was just the sort of silly thing Hoff would do, a stupid prank that only a clever person would dream up. I think I did her a favour by persuading her that this wasn't a matter for the college authorities. Any investigation would show Hoff up as an idiot, nothing worse, but it would make her known as an oppressive snoop, and the word 'fascist' would settle on her for good.

I tackled Hoff directly about the name-tapes, the next time he sat near me in Hall. He seemed delighted to have caused so much confusion and distress, but also made out that he was making a serious philosophical point. If labels served the purpose of distinguishing one person's property from anyone else's, then Mussolini name-tapes would do the job just as well on A staircase as Hoffman ones.

He boasted of other footling projects. He had posed as Joseph Stalin to procure library tickets and opened a Post Office account in the name of Karl Marx. His long-term goal was to persuade a bank to set up an account for himself as Mussolini, without changing his name by Deed Poll or Statutory Declaration, which he regarded as an inadmissible short cut.

Hoff was above such fetishes (and extravagances) as Christmas presents, but others were more sentimental. I was clearly making an impact on Downing, to judge by the fact of receiving as presents not one but two copies of Christy Brown's *Down All The Days*, an autobiographical novel by an Irish spastic whose condition (doubly athetoid) was particularly severe. I suppose one could have been for Christmas, the other for the birthday which trailed along behind Jesus's.

I don't think they were telling me to count my blessings, exactly, though Brown's disability certainly put mine in the shade – this was cerebral palsy beyond anything I saw at Vulcan.

I tried to like the book, at least I think I did. I didn't care for the style, though, which was all rather clottedly poetic, as if the poor man was afflicted by an inflamed blarney duct on top of his other troubles. My reservations about the book must have made me seem churlish and hard to please. It was as if I'd been served the vegetarian option in a restaurant, and had sent it back just to be difficult. Bad John, wicked John. So ungrateful, after all the trouble people have gone to. A wicked part of me speculated that if they'd met Christy Brown in person, rather than through a book, they wouldn't have been able to understand a word he tried to say. And perhaps that was the way they preferred it.

I didn't need to wait till spring to get started on another Voodoo Lily. Providentially the bulbs were available at the seed merchants. The bulbs were as eager as I was. They were even attractively priced, perhaps because they were so ready for planting they were jumping the gun. The protuberance on one had already started to seek the light. I bought that one in preference to any other, knowing there wouldn't be so long to wait. Next time Whiffy Barry wouldn't miss his inflorescent cousin. He promised to come at a moment's notice.

When the day of the second Voodoo Lily's flowering arrived I sent Whiffy Barry a message to come at once. Mrs Beddoes took a keen interest in what was going on, and was very willing to run the errand for me. Like any victim of a practical joke, she couldn't wait to see it played on someone else, not realising that Barry as a botanist was well prepared for what had caused her so much dismay.

She returned to tell me that Mr Barry would be along soon. 'Today of all days,' she said, 'he's taking a bath.' She hoovered the room, then settled down in the Parker-Knoll with a cup of tea. She was enjoying herself. It wasn't every day she could eavesdrop on a miniature botanical congress, convened to inspect the plant which had played such a mean trick on her.

I took another look at the star of the show. *Sauromatum*'s purple-and-brown-spotted hood reared up like a cobra behind the glistening spadix. The smell was entirely disgusting, but there was a deep spiritual message latent here. If I had described the smell to Bhagavan as disgusting, he would certainly have replied, 'Disgusting for whom?' Then I would have had to enter the deepest sanctum of awareness, embarking on the *vichara* (Self-Enquiry). The answer was that it was disgusting for me. And who am I?

His date with Voodoo Lily

It wasn't disgusting if you were a fly, that was for certain. I pretended to be a fly and tried to tell myself that the smell was beautiful, but still I felt sick. I asked Mrs Beddoes to open the windows to their widest, which she did rather unwillingly – there had been no such concession when she was the one being tested – but the smell was still overpowering. It took a lot of determination to stay in the room.

Then there was a knock at the door and Barry came in. Mrs Beddoes was so much at home by now that she gave a happy little yawn and a wave of the hand. Barry had done more than just take a bath. He had smartened himself up considerably for his date with Voodoo Lily. He was wearing tight (and crisply ironed) black flannel trousers and a white shirt. He had the instruments of dissection in one hand and a clipboard in the other.

He grinned and shifted his legs a bit, making the rough shape of his genitals materialise and then disappear in a way which would have been irresistible if I had found him the slightest bit attractive. I may live my life at what is cock level for most people but still I have my standards.

He put his things on my cluttered table, while I made my way over to the window-sill. From there I invited him to join me. Not only was he clean, but he was wearing some sort of perfume or cologne which I found tantalising. The high notes were flirty and fleeting, but the bass notes were deep shadows, like a grotto cool with ferns on a hot summer's day. If I closed my eyes and let my nose stand in for all the other senses, I might even begin to be aroused by the information it passed on. Perhaps I had been too hasty in dismissing this lonely botanist as 'Whiffy Barry'.

Suddenly there was a connection between us. I was susceptible to him in ways I hadn't expected, yes, but I also had the sense that he was susceptible to me, as if he was in a mild hypnotic trance. An astral umbilical seemed to link us on this malodorous morning, threading through our navels and groins, weaving a cat's-cradle of chakras.

Patrly this had to do with the psychology of touch. Young English men of the period were so unaccustomed to touch, ordinary non-sensual human contact, that when it happened – and with me it had to happen – they were oddly disoriented, lightly bewitched. It was as if I had flown under their radar and disarmed them. I could give a young man's hand and arm a tug in a certain direction, and it would follow my lead. It had nothing to do with a dormant attraction to other men – in fact I suspect it worked best with those who, like Barry, had never had such thoughts. If this was voodoo then it was quite ordinary everyday voodoo. It functioned perfectly well without the help of the lily whose foulness we were gathered to analyse.

I did realise, though, that however many times I went to Sanders Seed Merchants in Regent Street Cambridge, and however many *Sauromata guttata* I paid for and set a-growing, I would never happen on anything as promising as this delightful situation again.

What had started out as a simple project of botanical research had forked deliciously. Now I had two experiments on the go simultaneously. I was confident I had enough mental power to be able to divide my attention cleanly in two. Yes, I would examine the anatomy of this araceous species, but I would also do what I could to satisfy my curiosity about the lie of the land in Barry's trousers.

All the time we probed *S. guttatum* I would be pumping power into my personality-magnet, which had seemed so defective these last few months. I would tug him about into any position I wanted. It would be child's play to come up with any number of creative adjustments of posture – because 'my arms can't reach that far'. I could do the heavy lean against his leg, mentioning that it was vital for me not to lose my balance. Of course there was no real coercion involved. Whenever he wanted to, Barry could wriggle out of any entanglement, but I had the sense that my little magnet was working again at full power, and today he would go along with anything I suggested.

After a while, as he became more deeply hypnotised, a Gulliver immobilised by the thousand tiny threads of my suggestion, we would enter into Union. Barry was already intoxicated with touch, his whole body reverberating with longing. He was only a whisker away from swimming with me in the Ocean of Desire.

I knew my magic would only work if I was alone with the hypnotic subject, and here was Mrs Beddoes sitting in my Parker-Knoll savouring the last gulps of her tea and perhaps even contemplating the making of another cup. I asked her if she hadn't got more rooms to clean, and she said no, she'd got an early start and cleaned out the other students' rooms while I was sleeping. She batted away every hint I could come up with that we should be left alone together to do our research.

'I wouldn't miss this for worlds,' she said. I was sure she was innocent of any byplay, but it was almost as if she knew exactly what was going on, and was having a rare old time thwarting me. 'You've got me so curious about this plant, Mr Cromer. I can't wait to see what it is that makes it pong so.'

From the Parker-Knoll where Mrs Beddoes was sitting with her tea she had a direct view of Barry's legs and everything that lived between them. If I was to make any real progress, I must come up with a way of blocking her view.

Barry was ready to make the first incision into the inflorescence, but he hesitated and deferred to me. After all it was technically my *Sauromatum*. He offered me the scalpel and asked if I would care to dissect the flower according to his instructions. This was good manners and the answer was actually yes – I desperately wanted to do it, to feel what a surgeon feels. But my mind was grappling with the question of what to do about Mrs Beddoes.

A very delicate and sensitive thing

I said, 'No, that's all right, Barry. Things like this should be left to the expert – which is clearly you in this case. But let's think clearly here. We must ensure that conditions for the experiment are optimal. You had better stand exactly where you are. Make sure that you hold the bulb in your left hand and cut the flower with your right. We had better stay here right near the window, because we're going to need a strong light. Don't move, because I'm leaning against you and I shall lose my balance otherwise. Wait a minute . . . if I put my hand on your leg like this, the position is perfect.

'Now then . . . it's going to be vital that we take notes during this operation, so I'll hold your clipboard in my right hand . . .'

From my contorted position, holding a clipboard at the required angle was nearly impossible, but somehow I managed to prop it against the window shelf.

With the crucial equipment in place (the clipboard, angled just so) both experiments could proceed as planned. I gave thanks for the human inability to see round corners. Mrs Beddoes made a half-hearted attempt to raise herself and come over for a better view, but I told her to stay exactly where she was. 'This is a very delicate and sensitive thing we are doing here,' I said, with an authority which surprised me. 'You stay put. I don't want you upsetting the experiment. Besides, didn't you say yourself that you got up early and did all those rooms? Take some rest, enjoy your cup of tea, and leave us to work. It's our turn!'

So that was the set-up. With the Beddoes blocked by the clipboard in my right hand, I was half leaning out of the wheelchair. The araceous flower was winking luridly up at us, cradled in Barry's left hand, while he held the scalpel in his right. My left hand was putting significant pressure on his right leg, and the black-trousered mystery between his legs was looking up at me invitingly. Just a short distance more, and both probes, the coldly metallic and the blood-hot, would be gathering data.

With my attention deliciously divided between the two explorations, I took the calculated risk of trifurcation. Mrs Beddoes used to tell me that I had a real way with people, and now was the time to put it to the test. I stretched out a mental finger to soothe her forehead and persuade her to relax. I sent a subliminal whisper across those few feet to lull her into a timely snooze.

As Barry slit the inflorescence with his scalpel I shifted myself into a better position (better in every way) by cupping my left hand over his crotch. His groin came up to meet my palm of its own accord, and fascination froze us in that position. His hand too froze as the blade went in. We might have been carved in stone, except that two hearts were pumping away inside the double statue, and Barry's stone penis throbbed inside his taut and freshly ironed slacks, tugging the creases out of alignment.

Mrs Beddoes must have dozed off in her armchair as instructed. She was snoring softly. I hoped that at least she had put her mug down.

Barry's vocabulary became technical as he cut into the vegetable flesh. Most of the Latin terms eluded me. Still, I could see for myself that the entrance to the flower was like the opening to a cave. The inside was black and mysterious. The only way we could get a proper look was by cutting a cross-section. Once this was done, I could see that the entrance was lined with cells which were waxy in character and pointed only in one direction.

Voodoo Lily certainly gave the illusion of being carnivorous. She reminded me very much of my old friend the pitcher plant. There was also a series of jagged spikes just inside the cave entrance. Barry explained that this was the secret of the seeming 'bad smell'. All it took was the swapping over of a single molecule. The spiky configuration presented the greatest possible surface area so as to maximise the efficiency of the process. As the original odour passed over these keys, the molecular exchange converted its perfume into the smell of carrion or stale urine, giving Mrs Beddoes every excuse for thinking that one of her 'gentlemen' was a bed-wetter.

Barry held *S. guttatum* up to my nose and gave it a gentle squeeze to diffuse the foul fragrance. For a few seconds there was perfect symmetry in Creation, with squeezes above and squeezes below. 'Go on,' he said, 'Have a good sniff . . .' He didn't say, 'Give me a good squeeze while you're at it,' but by that stage it could be taken as read.

I was as nauseated as ever by the stench of the flower but thrilled by the extra squeeze I was licensed to give with my left hand. 'Now,' he said, putting the bulb down again, 'if I'm not very much mistaken. . .' – deftly he cut away the spiky keys – 'deep down this flower doesn't have a bad smell at all. With the pheromone-exchange matrix out of the picture, I think you'll find that the object of our study plays a different tune . . .' He held it up again, squeeze upon squeeze. 'Go on . . . inhale deeply. Take your time.'

This time my olfactory brain was flooded with heavenly scent, and all the richness that the word *lily* conveys. My head reeled and I experienced God, but my hand didn't forget its lower business. Barry seemed entirely caught up with the respectable side of our scientific project, or perhaps he too had the knack of processing different streams of information separately.

Like a baker in a hurry

Mrs Beddoes began to stir from her rêverie. I could hear the soft thump of her mug being returned to the table. At last she came over to take a look, and this time I didn't try to stop her. My cock dwindled back to an unembarrassing size, and Barry and I moved smoothly on to erudite botanical niceties.

'So, Barry, to sum up – can you understand how a lay person might think of the flower as carnivorous?' I asked, borrowing the manner of a television interviewer, as if I hadn't been kneading his privates mere seconds before like a baker in a hurry. We played out the scene in full, jointly explaining the mystery to an amazed bed-maker.

'Oh yes,' he replied. 'It's an elementary mistake, but very understandable. The essential oil manufactured by the plant is sweet and alluring, but not to a fly. So the plant needs to use a trick to make the fly believe that there is rotting flesh nearby. As I told you, it's a very simple molecular switch to make the conversion to this odour. The flower's only interest is in getting itself pollinated. It just so happens that a trapped fly struggling to get out provides just the right amount of jiggling to attach the pollen. There are species native to Britain which use the same sort of technique – lords-and-ladies, for instance.'

'That's cuckoo-pint, isn't it?'

'That's right. *Arum maculatum*. Just like this exotic beauty here, the flower isn't equipped to eat the fly, but sometimes the fly dies of exhaustion before it can escape. If it just stayed where it was and bided its time, it could escape later on, once the flower had slackened its grip. But flies don't think of that!' In fact the whole procedure seems to be an evolutionary dead-end. Dead flies don't pollinate – unless the system depends on a super-fly with greater endurance, which subsequently spreads the pollen further than its inferior siblings would have managed.

'Well at least the fly died happy,' mused Mrs Beddoes who had become thoroughly fascinated with the proceedings by this time.

'Oh no, dear lady,' Barry said sharply, in a way that was almost rude. 'We humans may find the carrion smell disgusting, but it's nectar to a fly. The fly imagines that it's going to fulfil its own desire by following the "stink" – its drive to reproduce itself by laying its eggs. However, once past the matrix, the entrance, it finds there is nothing rotting there at all, only a sweet smell. And since the plant's real perfume is not so nice for the fly, we could say rather that the fly died in Hell!'

This was quite enough for Mrs Beddoes in the way of botanical lecturing. She produced her duster from an apron pocket. If she had really done all her housework early, then this was a little piece of theatre. I'm not sure she ever did anything that would have qualified in Granny's view as dusting. The worn yellow duster was as symbolic in its own way as a freemason's trowel.

'I mustn't let the whole day run away from me, must I?' she said, and took from another of her apron pockets an item much more central to her practice as a cleaner, an aerosol of air freshener. Her fondness for it was natural, considering that she cleaned the rooms of young men with hardly the faintest idea of how to maintain themselves. She gave the room a parting squirt with the aerosol, moving her arm in a large half-circle, then a series of loops in our direction, or towards the stench that had already been dissected out of existence. She was so generous with the volatilisation of industrial fragrance that she walked through a cloud of it on the way out, and set herself coughing. Perhaps the coughing prevented a strange thought from coming any further forward than the back of her mind: *If I didn't know better, I'd think Mr Crow-maire was giving the other chap a thorough squeeze of the privates* . . .

It was only after she had gone, as Barry began to pack up his equipment, that we stopped being at ease with each other. Mrs Beddoes hadn't been an impediment to the scene between us, as I had thought at first, but an essential ingredient in our tiny erotic drama, the spectator who didn't see a thing. In those days my sexual imagination was at least as attuned to the creation of a tableau as to any actual intimacy.

Of course eroticism is only the Ego's vain attempt to unite with the Self. The ego itself is a paradoxical amalgam of inert body and the true Self. The aim is admirable, but the ego gets it all wrong. Watching the ego try to wrestle reality into submission is like watching Laurel and Hardy move a piano. They'll move it all right, but you won't be able to get much of a tune out of it afterwards.

As for the scene with Barry, I didn't regret that it had lacked an actual sexual climax. Release of that sort would have taken away from an excitement that remained infinite because it never toppled over into the reality that is all illusion and disappointment. It was a wave that never needed to break.

I might imagine in those days that I wanted openness of expression, closeness of rapport and meaningful glandular release. What I actually enjoyed was this sort of mixture, hiding and flaunting simultaneously, which was only a new twist on being invisible and incredibly conspicuous at the same time, my normal state.

Although I saw Barry around, and we talked very happily about our common interests, I never had the faintest whiff of desire for him thereafter. The beauty of Whiffy Barry — that too was an inflorescence which blossomed and shrivelled in a single day.

I was especially in need of diversions like the dissection of Voodoo Lily, since I already knew that my field of study was a dead end. Not a dead end in general terms but a dead end in my particular case. Underneath gruffness a mile deep Eckstein had been too excited by my academic prospects to give me the guidance I needed. He passed the buck. Perhaps he was relying on my chosen university to warn me of the disillusionment that lay in store.

A. T. Grove had been so exclusively interested in my mobility that he hadn't offered me the benefit of his advice about my course. I ended up having to learn the hard way that disability debarred me from making real progress in the study of my chosen languages.

I was able to reconstruct the way my interview should have gone, if it had been designed to lay the foundations for an undergraduate career rather than to assess my ability to go for a coffee at Snax on Regent Street without depending on the wheelchair. Because a wheelchair saps independence of outlook (as everyone knows who doesn't need one), without which the human spirit withers away.

What A. T. Grove should have said was this: 'John, you need to be aware that certain courses of study presuppose certain abilities that are not merely intellectual. Your chosen subject, Modern and Mediaeval Languages, is intended to immerse you in a foreign culture, so that you end up being able to spend large parts of your mental life in Spanish or German. The finishing touch applied to this process is a period of residence abroad.

'Klaus Eckstein strongly champions your cause, in a way that hardly chimes with his continued insistence that your German accent is terrible. But I suspect that even he has not looked far enough ahead. Your independence of mind is a condition that does not extend to your body.

'How will you be able to manage abroad, when that time comes? It is difficult enough for us to place students in suitable households without the additional burden of meeting your special needs. You are hardly in a position to risk immersion in a foreign culture, when you can hardly keep your head above water in your own.

'If you do try to live abroad, you will be living in a bubble of artificial behaviour. Your exposure to a foreign culture will be for practical purposes nil. A genuine traveller can take a cable car to a beauty spot in the mountains without a second thought, while the only cable car with which you are likely to be familiar while you study for a degree will be the one, whirring and trundling, which conveys you from your wheelchair to the bath on A staircase, Kenny Court, Downing. I do not say this to be cruel but to save you time.

'Klaus Eckstein has painted a vivid picture of the hazards of travel on Spanish trains, warning you that it is polite, just as it would be in Britain, to offer to share any food you produce – but that you must be prepared, as you need not be in Britain, for people to accept your offer with alacrity, producing forks and spoons from their pockets and having a good old tuck-in. But how will you be able to experience this for yourself?

'Consider. A language student with what we consider satisfactory conversational skills in German goes to stay in a family-run Gasthaus in Thuringia. He explores his surroundings, which means in practice that he becomes familiar with the excellence of German beer, thanks to the *Reinheitsgebot*, the purity laws of 1516, which prohibit adulteration of any kind. He has more than enough German to keep on ordering more beer.

A higher presence of offal

'In the mornings his head is full of hammers, and he can hardly dare to look at the lavish breakfast his solicitous landlady brings to his room. He drinks the coffee gingerly, and takes a few tentative nibbles at a sort of roll which crumbles to dryness in his mouth.

'The breakfast tray, however, holds far more than merely coffee and rolls. It is as if his landlady is trying to save him the expense of eating for the rest of the day. There are hard-boiled eggs. There are slabs of pale cheese the size of small books, if the books were pale and sweaty. There are churned and rendered meats – swollen sausages and motley slices. There is a higher presence of offal in these productions than he would welcome even without the hammers in his head. The purity laws in Germany seem to stop with the irreproachable beer. In the butcher's shop anything goes.

'He can face none of it, not even the second half of his roll. But it's out of the question, the height of rudeness, to reject so lavish and considerate a morning offering (the rates of the Gasthaus are extremely reasonable). So he stows the food away in his suitcase, planning to dispose of it in some better place at a more convenient time.

'The next morning the hammers in his head are if anything heavier and more efficient at blotting out thought with their crashing. The breakfast tray presented to him with a flourish is even more disheartening, because he is feeling yet worse than he did the day before – and because there is even more food this time. The landlady has taken his tray-clearing performance of the day before as a challenge. In retrospect he has miscalculated by not leaving at least some of the eggs on the tray, the cheese perhaps, certainly the meats of ill omen. Too late now, though. He has no alternative but to repeat his breakfast-hiding trick. Day after day the problem recurs, but the time when he might empty his suitcase never presents itself.

'In the common spaces of the Gasthaus, as the week goes on, the landlady becomes both glowing and skittish, a preening *hausfrau*, making admiring comments about the healthy appetites of the English, comments which his better-than-average conversational skills enable him to acknowledge gracefully, and to deflect.

'It is at the beginning of the second week that a reek from the cupboard draws the landlady, while cleaning her charming young guest's room, to the cupboard and the suitcase it contains. Opening the case, she is confronted with a black museum of the previous week's breakfasts. All her thoughtful kitchen gestures are mashed together in various states of decomposition. The delicacies she had prepared to sustain this cherished guest on his explorations of her beloved locality have been dumped into the vastly inferior digestion, assisted only by flies, of his *luggage*.

'The student is out all day, which leaves the landlady many hours to perfect the outburst of grievance with which she will greet the guest who has insulted her hospitality. When he returns, dog-tired after a day of hiking, he will be faced with a problem for which no primer nor phrase book could prepare him. The words pour out of her like the waters of the Rhine in spate.

'It is now his task to find the words to explain to his landlady why he has disposed of her breakfasts as if they were sordid secrets. Only the right words will stop this solid lady, steaming with rage, from knocking him down her front steps. A large vocabulary and a secure grasp of tone will be required. A good accent will help, to be sure, but only if every other element is in place.

'We are worlds away here from such rudiments as "Can you tell me please the way to the station?" or indeed "'Brecht's genius is to make an *élite feel like the rabble, and a rabble like the élite.' Discuss.*"

'*That*, my dear John, is why we send students abroad to perfect their language skills. They must learn to manage with no protective barrier between them and the local inhabitants. You can never be in that situation. You must take that protective barrier wherever you go. You cannot expect to plumb the depths of another culture when you need a rubber ring to keep afloat in your own.

'My advice is that you should consider applying to the college and the university, but with the intention of reading English. Then there need be no delay in admitting you, since a year at High Wycombe Technical College slaving over Spanish will not be required of you.'

And while he was at it, the A. T. Grove in my fantasy might have saved me from another poor decision. He might have added, so softly that I wouldn't quite be sure he had really said it, 'Please don't have a bone cut as a way of pleasing others. Your knee already does the job adequately – the job is only part-time – and your friend either loves you or does not. Love is not fussy about knees. That is the truth of it.' Fatherly.

When I realised that it was pointless to pursue my course to the bitter end of a degree, I felt let down to a certain extent. False hopes had been encouraged. I would have to finish Part One just the same, and satisfy the examiners at the end of the year. It was hard to see this as a purposeful endeavour, or a meaningful use of my time.

The analogy is pure swank

But at least (I thought) I would be able to conclude my under-graduate career in record time. Modern and Mediæval Languages was a one-year Part I, English a one-year Part II – so I would get my degree in two years flat.

I had mixed feelings about this truncated course. I wasn't happy enough at Cambridge to want to stay any longer, but what came after Cambridge? In any case I had paid too little attention to etymology for once. The course for a Cambridge degree is called the Tripos, which derives from the Greek word meaning *three-legged*. A two-year degree, apparently, would be an absurdity exactly equivalent to a two-legged stool. So I would have to spend two years on Part II of the English course.

I could see that it would have to be English. I had grown to love both Spanish and German. They were strong flavours, Rioja and Ries-ling exploding on the palate, though the analogy is pure swank since I had tasted neither, and my inability to drop into a *bodega* or *Weinlokal* to remedy my ignorance was very much to the point.

Now I would have to wean myself back onto the small beer of my native tongue. The mild and bitter.

I had always been a literary reader. My mind was retentive, particu-larly of poetry, though I can't really take the credit for that. My child-hood tutor Miss Collins gave me a real incentive, when she restricted my reading time and took the books away. After that, my memory worked overtime, in case it happened again. I could recite reams by heart.

I didn't anticipate much of an academic challenge. English was widely regarded as a soft option. My broader European perspective would give me a significant advantage. In the Tragedy paper, for instance, which was compulsory, I would ramble on about Büchner. I'd always had a soft spot for Büchner.

I had made a head start by having a poem published in an undergraduate literary magazine. It was called 'Fourteen Ways of Looking at a Wheelchair'. The title went Wallace Stevens one better. I had loved his poetry since Klaus Eckstein had thrillingly recited, 'Let be be finale of seem / The only emperor is the emperor of ice cream.' I probably make too much of the parallels to Hindu thought in Stevens's metaphysics, but they exist. They're real. Or at least 'real', which is as much as any of us can hope for.

There may never have been a time when it was possible for a poem, legibly written or competently typed, to be rejected by an undergraduate magazine – with or without modernist flourishes and a disability-pathos undertone. If there was such a time it certainly wasn't the early 1970s. Standards were much lower than those on *Woman's Own*. I make no claims for the quality of my poem. I hope no one is ever mischievous enough to disinter it.

The magazine was called *Freeze Peach*. I don't think the editors wanted to produce a magazine and then devised a suitably clever name. More likely that they thought *Freeze Peach* too good a name not to have a magazine attached to it. The originators of *Woman's Own*, their eyes less clouded by Maya, avoided this mistake. *Freeze Peach* stumbled on as far as a third issue, then died in a ditch. I take no responsibility for that, though my contribution probably didn't help. If the magazine had kept going a little longer, I would have tried to lumber it with another opus (in the same vein of manipulative pluck) entitled 'Not Waving but Downing'. One more case of the title coming first, the actual artefact being an optional afterthought. I was getting on the magazine's wave-length, by writing a poem that was entirely parasitic on its title.

My taste was more adventurous in poetry than in prose. If I had been asked then what was the most important book published in the twentieth century, I would have answered 'Ficcíones', in unison with every other self-respecting Cambridge undergraduate of the period – and Borges's Spanish is indeed crisp and fine. But the books I read more than any others were Roald Dahl's collections of admirably sick short stories. Books have always been awkward objects to me without exception, but I managed to tuck my copies of *Kiss Kiss* and *Someone Like You* out of sight behind more impressive-looking volumes, just like everyone else.

Theoretically the person to consult in my perplexity was my tutor Graëme, but that was obviously not going to do any good with the way things stood between us, and I wasn't going to grovel. Humble pie is no dish for vegetarians (historically, *numble pie*). The filling is deer guts, if you really want to know. I didn't consult Graëme, just told him what I had decided. He gave a mannered little sigh and said that it was a matter of statistical fact that English students were more prone to nervous breakdowns than those who read Modern Languages. He hoped that my change of academic direction didn't qualify as a cry for help in its own right.

I didn't anticipate that the change of subjects would be too jarring. I was better integrated into the life of the college than I was with my department, though that wasn't saying much. Still, the Mini had become almost the Downing taxi. I was often being asked to ferry people around, and I enjoyed doing it.

The risky parts of air travel are take-off and landing. The dangerous moments when conveying bone china by hot-air balloon are loading and unloading. Why should wheelchair-based car trips be any different? I was vulnerable while my helpers were conveying me from room to car, and much more so on the return journey, at the end of the day above all, when alcohol had a bit part in the drama, and sometimes the leading rôle.

It vexed me that Downing was a castle of learning strongly fortified against its own residents. Returning from an evening out, early enough for the back gate to be open, I was faced with a barrier, a vertical stanchion blocking access for cars. Dons with parking privileges were issued with keys which let them unlock it and hinge it down out of the way, this lone fat prison bar blocking the Mini's liberty. I shared their parking privileges but not their right to a key, without which parking privileges didn't amount to much.

Until I was vandalised myself

I asked for a key at the Porter's Lodge and was told that I should apply through my tutor. Did I imagine the look of wry amusement which ricocheted around the room, bouncing off the notice boards and arrays of pigeonholes? They might have had the manners to wait until I had gone, my tail between my legs, and then they could have murmured quite audibly, 'And a fat lot of good that will do you, as everyone knows!' The nicest of the porters said that a key wouldn't make all that much difference anyway, since I couldn't manhandle the post myself – which made me wonder why I had ever thought him the nicest. If I had a key then my passengers would do the physical work for me, and the social bubble would be preserved that much longer. When I had to go by way of the Porter's Lodge people tended to mooch off, and then I would have to recruit someone to return the key anyway.

One evening I came home late with a slightly rowdy party. We had made a ritual journey across the modest urban lawn of Parker's Piece to pay our respects to Reality Checkpoint – no more than an elaborate Victorian lamp-post, really, ornamented with a motif of dolphins, but universally known by the phrase painted on its plinth. By common consent Reality Checkpoint offered reassurance to those who got lost while voyaging strange seas of thought alone and artificially bewildered by drugs. It was a pilot light to rekindle the snuffed spirits of those trapped between dimensions.

Then nothing would content the group but to play games with the traffic lights, or rather with the mechanism that made them change. There was some sort of sensor buried under a heavyweight rubber strip, which counted the cars passing over it and triggered the lights to change when a predetermined number had been reached. This seemed to the group an astoundingly sophisticated piece of technology and also (here I parted company from the general mood) something that cried out for a bit of tampering.

A lot of good my dissidence did me. The idea was to bounce the wheelchair back and forth on the decision-making flange, persuading it that cars were massing in large numbers and that the lights must therefore change. There was no logic to the use of the wheelchair, since weight was the issue and John plus wheelchair was lighter than any one of my companions, but then the logic of the group was purely alcoholic. The evening had been alcohological for some time, and I looked up at the events unfolding around me with a sour sobriety.

Returning to college had an edge of melancholy and resentment for me. My passengers didn't necessarily share this mood, and would get up to pranks and high jinks. All very amusing, until someone fell over my foot.

Someone. Mentioning no names. You know who you are – don't you, Stephen Morris?

All right, it wasn't quite as innocent as all that. My pals were busy uprooting the stanchion, and though I hadn't exactly put them up to it I was silently cheering them on. The stanchion was quite feebly rooted in concrete, like an ailing tooth, and it came out quite suddenly, which was when Stephen stumbled backwards and fell over my foot.

I had been all in favour of vandalism until I was vandalised myself. Still, I had a couple of weeks of significantly easier access to my room until the repairs were done. By then my foot had stopped hurting quite so much, and the world and I were back at our usual loggerheads.

Even so the Mini brought more joy than anything else. There were many trips in that little car which resembled rehearsals for world record attempts in the human compression category. Only the observers from the *Guinness Book of Records* were missing. We were always fitting one more person in. And then one more.

If the Mini was 120 inches long, 55 wide and 53 high (though obviously you have to discount the distance between the ground and the bottom of the car), then you subtract the measurements of the boot and the engine and you get . . . my maths isn't what it was, but I'd estimate the interior volume as being between 127 and 134 cubic feet. Call it 130. Not a lot when, like most of my passengers, you're built like a Greek god, except for your English inability to look people in the eye, or anywhere near it.

There might be as many as four outsized knees jammed up against my back in the driver's seat, so close that I could feel the freckles on them. If ever I did take the Mini for a drive on my own, it seemed to ride unnaturally high on its axles. When the suspension didn't bump it felt as if there was something wrong.

All this driving placed a lot of strain on my shoulder, which could freeze even in the warmest weather. Three-point turns were my nightmare – despite Dad's best drilling, they tended to have five or seven points. So one summer evening my passengers sweetly relieved me of the need to perform them.

There were four of them, strapping boys who had been playing cricket on Parker's Piece before I drove us all to Midsummer Common for a pint in a pub they liked. They wore their hair at a timidly daring length, creeping down over the collar, enough to needle their parents when they visited Cambridge for the ritual of Sunday lunch at the Blue Boar – roast flesh carved from the trolley, and is it so hard to find a proper tie? – but far too short to impress their contemporaries.

The pub was popular, and parking spaces were very limited. 'Just stop here,' said one of the party, and they all got out, innocently slamming the doors with a force driven from the shoulder and suited to flinging a ball or wielding a bat. If the windows had been closed I imagine my eardrums would have burst. There's an anvil in the ear, you know, and those doors banged like hammers.

After a little chat in murmurs the lads took up positions round the car and simply picked it up, taking advantage of those open windows to get a good grip.

They lifted the Mini as if it weighed nothing at all. It wasn't a heavyweight among cars, admittedly, and now it was transfigured and airborne, levitated into the balmy Cambridge evening by eight beefy arms. I'm a leg man myself, a leg man to my fingertips, but I have to say that I enjoyed watching the arms I could see from the driving seat, the tanned ones and the pale with freckles. I could see white shirts with rolled-up sleeves, and summer sweat staining the armpits. There are days when the world seems entirely peopled with giants, but this was an evening when I felt I could meet anyone's eye and hold anyone's gaze.

After they had parked the car and I had struggled out of it they picked me up in a compact version of the same formation and conveyed me in state to the outside seating area of the pub. It was like riding in some human sedan chair.

Local people had grazing rights on the Common, and while we sipped our drinks we could hear horses tearing up mouthfuls of grass, that placid ripping. I like the way horses' eyes are set in their heads, on a soft edge in a long skull. That's a particularly pleasing touch.

These young men were cider drinkers, leaving me with my half of bitter to claim maturity of taste. Their green palates preferred apple sweetness to the truthful bitterness of hops. I spent most of the evening perched on one broad knee or other. I would have one sturdy arm wrapped round me while the other hand took care of the precious pint of cider. Dandled by the group I listened to the conversation with abstract rapture.

Young people at university at that time behaved as if they spent their days in the underground youth culture of resistance and revolution, surfacing only rarely to deal with The Man (by attending a lecture or supervision). Every now and then they might have to have lunch with those aliens their parents. Asked what they were going to do with their lives, students would give rambling answers in which the words 'kibbutz', 'start a band' and 'underground newspaper' stood out.

Lads like these cider drinkers, sons of doctors and solicitors in county towns, mumbled less convincingly than most. Their hearts weren't in it. The turmoil of youth and social upheaval would pass like the measles, leaving most of them unchanged, without even a scar. What's that folksy saying? The apple doesn't fall far from the tree (unless it's wrenched tenderly off the branch to make cider). This was a period when the apple was determined to turn into an orange or a pomegranate. I loved this attitude all the more because I couldn't share it. This banana doesn't change his spots.

Even among themselves these young men stuck devotedly to the generational clichés. Asked why he had turned up late to play cricket, one of them said, 'I couldn't get my act together.' 'And what act was that, pray?' I wondered to myself dreamily. 'Billy Smart's Circus?

The Mormon Tabernacle Choir? Is it too much to expect that you be punctual, since you're installed in a body that anticipates your every wish?' I've always been slightly cracked on the subject of timekeeping. I admit it.

In fact I was enjoying myself too much to make trouble. As I was passed from lap to lap over the course of the evening, I tried to see if there was even one of these young groins that didn't stir when sat upon at the proper angle. In every lap there was a hydraulic response ignored by its owner. Young flesh salutes a change of pressure. It's a purely barometric pleasure.

Meanwhile I enjoyed their stoical conventionality, their casual social weight. These were men as reliable as the rhythms of a hymn, sung by a congregation with most of its mind on Sunday lunch. Was there also something left over from public-school loneliness, the residue of tears after lights-out? I like stolidity and stolid men, the slow processing of emotions. It's a great luxury not to respond right away. The redhead of the group must have been told three times a week since he went to kindergarten that his colouring gave him an ungovernable temper, and he was still stupendously phlegmatic.

At the end of the evening I was carried back to the car in the same processional fashion as I had been delivered to the pub. I loved being so high above the ground yet feeling so safe. Even if one of my bearers stumbled the others would keep their footing. When I was at school at Vulcan, one of the boys had tried to run away to be a truck driver's mate – perhaps this was really what he wanted, not just rough company and the dream of sounding the horn, but the elevation of the cab.

The Mini certainly had a comical aspect to eyes enlightened by drink, hemmed in so snugly by its neighbours. It looked like something dropped from the sky, or else thrust up by stage machinery. After I had been slid tenderly into the driving seat, my four porters picked up the car again, disengaging it from its narrow space and then serenely rotating it in the middle of the road, to save me the trouble of making the turn myself. The evening was still light, and there was no real need to turn the headlights on, but I did it for the sense of occasion.

Why is this memory so radiant, verging on the radioactive? It wasn't just the beauty of the young men which powered my joy. Of course mammals spend a lot of their energy trying either to generate heat or to lose it, and there's something peculiarly inviting to happiness about those moments when we are at one with our surroundings without having to work to make it so. Our bodies can turn off the fans and radiators for a while. We stop squandering energy to maintain the status quo. Summer night a case in point, bringing the human body close to the bliss of the reptile, organism which submits without a struggle to the conditions in which it finds itself.

Those tiny spasms

There were more specific inducements to happiness. The smell of earlier sweat, relatively fresh but dried in, voluptuously blended with grass smells, released and combined with new secretions as the young men exerted themselves in an improvised sport calling for a different sort of teamwork. The slightly laboured breathing of healthy young people, within earshot of each other, trying to pretend to be that little bit fitter than they were. The sound of cricket boots on road metal, long paces, regular gait, the crunch of the little nails on their soles, ominous, military, but also like little boys wearing Dad's shoes and wanting to sound just like him, striding with a manliness maintained by conscious effort. There's so much poignancy in the state of trying to be a man, nothing remotely comparable about being one.

The boy nearest to me outside the driver's window, the stolid redhead, was suffering from *singultus*. In Latin a sob, in English no more than a hiccup. He had the hiccups, and those tiny spasms translated into a strangely seductive rhythmic lurch of the whole vehicle. The involuntary movement hiccups gave his arm had a knock-on effect on his neighbour, the lad outside the passenger window. Their positions made eye contact hard to avoid, and then other factors entered in, cider and laughter. The cider caused the hiccups, it amplified and distorted the laughter, and soon the whole body of the car was faintly vibrating with the hilarity of those who carried it. The infinitesimal rocking that comes from being slightly out of step in a concerted task was subjected to an interference pattern of hiccups and laughter. Waves rippled back and forth, disrupting themselves and each other, complex functions on a graph of exhilaration.

I was whispering 'Mush!' to a team of very English huskies, on eight strong laughing arms, eight cider-drunk hiccupping legs, as if I would never need to deal with life on the flat, and yet I didn't really want to linger. I enjoyed a brief swirl of people in carbonated moments, as long as the bubbles were guaranteed to burst. I liked to be held and then passed on.

I was still dictating terms to Maya, and she always agreed to them, but she does that, doesn't she? She gets you caught in her trap by letting you design it yourself. She gives you a free hand. She plays along.

Mum and Dad were only mildly disturbed by my proposed change of subject. Of course I didn't present it as any sort of defeat. I could tell them perfectly sincerely that Cambridge had enjoyed a glorious history in English studies for much of the twentieth century, and Downing had been near the centre of all that. It was Downing, after all, that had given F. R. Leavis a professorship. Leavis, the heretic guru of English letters, who had founded and edited a massively influential magazine. That magazine had been called *Scrutiny* – the Cambridge word above all others. The unscrutinised life was not worth living and the unscrutinised text had no place on a serious person's shelves. Vast and merrily crackling was the critical bonfire of the deficient.

At that time Leavis was in retirement but could still be glimpsed occasionally. I didn't mention that the one time I had seen Leavis he was walking briskly down Senate House Passage on a chilly day with fanatical vigour and remoteness, wearing a sports jacket and an open-necked shirt. He picked up his feet like an aggrieved heron, and I was sure he would spear me if I got in his way, wheelchair or no wheelchair. Anyone less life-enhancing would be hard to imagine, but naturally I didn't pass that impression on to Mum and Dad. I simply said I would be in safe hands, experiencing the full flow of a great tradition. Of course, Leavis had eventually severed his links with Downing in the usual austere huff, scattering excommunications in all directions like black and baleful confetti, but again, there seemed no need to relay such a minor detail.

My proposed academic trajectory – from Modern Languages Part I to English Part II – felt disjointed, a wrong turn in a life that couldn't afford one. It seemed absurd that I could travel single-handed across the world (though I don't wish to slight the many strong arms and lifting hands which helped me on my way) to pay my respects to my guru in India, but not pursue my studies as I wished at an educational institution that recognised me as worthy to attend. It was absurd but there seemed to be no way round it. Trudge on, pilgrim.

The exams for Part I, when they came, felt anything but momentous. I sat the papers in a sort of academic quarantine (the same drill as for my A-levels) with an invigilator for my own exclusive use. I was segregated from my fellow examinees because of the clacking disturbance of the typewriter and also because of my privilege of extra time – bags of it. I was allowed 50 per cent more time than my fellows because of the physical inconvenience of the process, though I never used anything like that much. I'd call out 'I've finished' as soon as I properly could.

It seemed only fair that I should have a bit more time, but all the same I chafed against the extravagant allowance. It seemed so imprecisely worked out, as if the authorities were really saying, 'Give the little chap an easy ride – he doesn't get many of those.' I would have preferred a more precise system, with observers making the calculations on a case-by-case basis, so that I would be allowed, say, 3 hours and 13 minutes, *and not a second more*. I didn't want favours – I wanted a time-and-motion-study man to follow me around for a week, and then to stand sternly over me during the exam with a stopwatch. I mean, are we taking this seriously, or are we just amusing ourselves?

I imagine that standard invigilators survey the room with an impartial sternness. My personal invigilator would tend to give me encouraging smiles, which I didn't enjoy. I was afraid that this goodwill might escalate into actual patronage, that he might fetch me a cup of coffee and a sticky bun to keep me going, and then slide across specimen answers to the questions or correct my grammar.

Towards the end of that summer term Alan Linton brought me a present. He kept telling me that discovering homœopathy had changed his life and given him a direction. He was in my debt. I was rather prickly about friendship at that period, not wanting people to get too close in case I ended up relying on them, and if Alan hadn't been safely leaving Cambridge I dare say I would have bristled.

He delivered his present to A6 after Hall one evening. It was a piece of cake. 'It's a *funny* cake,' he said, making his eyebrows shoot up and down *à la* Groucho Marx, twitching, 'if you get my drift. Very funny indeed.' Meaning that it was made with marijuana. I felt very alienated by the general drug culture of the time, but this was an irresistible offer. I turned down joints with the excuse that I only smoked Spanish cigarettes (and not just any Spanish cigarette either), feeling that *Cannabis sativa* was rather dragged down by its association with *Nicotiana tabacum*. Now I could have a transgressive nibble on the sly, and no one would be any the wiser.

'And this is to go with it,' Alan said, reverently producing a record from a plastic bag. It was his treasured copy of Van Morrison's *Astral Weeks*. If albums were as good as their titles, it was already my favourite record. He made clear that the dope cake was a gift, but the record was only a loan. He must have realised that an album was a difficult object for me to manage – tape cassettes, reliable and easy to handle, would soon replace them, and I for one couldn't wait – so he put it on my stereo, perched on top of the spindle, ready to go.

He also left me something called a Dust Bug, a perspex lath with a sort of toothbrush and a miniature plush roller mounted on it, which was supposed to sit on a little rod, held in place on the surround of my turntable with a little rubber sucker, but I decided not to bother with that.

I set up the turntable with the arm that steadies records on the spindle over to the right, so that when the side had been played the needle would return to the beginning. I knew that marijuana distorted the sense of time, and I wanted to make sure that the music would last for the whole of the experience.

It made sense to eat the cake before I sat down. I was pleased to see that it was moist. I broke it into pieces which would sit snugly on the fork. I closed my eyes while I chewed the cake, savouring the slightly dusty flavour, trying to decide where spice ended and cannabis began. I got the stereo under way and was settled in the Parker-Knoll by the time the second track started. The album was famously profound and poetic. Now I would make up my own mind.

By the time the needle reached the end of the side I had remembered that I was likely, in the course of the coming intoxication, to become atrociously hungry. That much I had learned about the effects of the drug. It would make me into a monster of appetite, and all I had to appease the monster was a Mars bar tucked away in a desk drawer. I should really have been keeping it in a fridge anyway, as a homage to the Mars bars of my childhood, but there were no fridges for students then. I decided not to wait until the eating mania struck before I fetched it. I should make the trip while I was still Mr Jekyll, more or less in charge of my faculties, before Mr Hyde took over and started bellowing for ratatouille.

Even as Mr Jekyll I had trouble foraging for the hidden snack. The Mars bar felt oddly springy in my hand, like something made of an elastic syrup, or as if there were a thousand Mars bars in a loose association, so that I picked up just the first one, and there was an appreciable delay before the others caught up with it – and then of course there's always a straggler.

Finally I was back in the Parker-Knoll in the relaxed position. I had pulled up my drawbridge and was alone on the ramparts with the phenomenon of tender howling (against jazzy strings) that was *Astral Weeks*. I already knew this was the record I had been waiting for all my life. It blue my mind. It blew *through* my mind. It blew my mind.

I didn't know how many times the needle had traversed this amazing music. I had no idea what time it was anywhere on earth. I only knew it was time to eat the Mars bar.

If I'd given it more thought, I would have cut the bar into chunks or slices and used a fork. As things stood, with my arm extended to its maximum and my teeth angled forward (it certainly felt as if my teeth were angled forward) I could just about nibble the front quarter-inch of the Mars bar. I got the giggles, remembering something that I'd heard a girl asking rather coquettishly in the Whim on Trinity Street – 'Why do Mars bars have veins?' I suddenly saw that this was a question that needed to be asked.

A Mars bar does indeed have veins, chocolate tubes breaking the surface of the bar, as if caramel was circulating through them, supplying the nougat core with vital nutrients and access to unthinkable sensations. The whole ridiculously penile confection was alive. It was a soft hard-on. It was Cadbury's Flake that had the fast reputation, and its adverts always portrayed Flake-eaters as oral nymphomaniacs, but the Mars bar was every bit as concupiscent. It was shameless, and it knew what it wanted.

What a tease it was! But two could play at that game. By now I'd eaten as much as I could reach of the bar. It would have to wait for its consummation. I decided to put the rest of it down while I worked out how to convey it to my mouth. My coördination must have been affected by the action of the drug, because I immediately managed to nudge it off the arm of the Parker-Knoll and onto the floor. It annoyed me that I had been so clumsy, but there seemed no point in mounting a rescue expedition just then. The Mars bar wasn't going anywhere.

Now my thoughts were tending in a different direction. It was time to masturbate. It wasn't really my idea, and it certainly wasn't Van Morrison's. I felt it was the Mars bar's idea. Those five inches of chewy sweetness had put ideas in my head.

With a little effort I retrieved my own organ from my flies. In the position I was in I could just about flick my fingers against the glans. My mind wandered, though, and I kept losing the thread of arousal. Then suddenly I was ejaculating, without the usual run-up, and with the pleasure oddly scattered and silvery. It was the anagram of an orgasm. A *morgaso*, perhaps, or (stroke of genius, this, I thought) *Om ragas*! I suddenly wished I had one of Dad's crossword puzzles within reach. In this state, surely, I would be unstoppable – though of course, since I'd added extra letters in my anagrams, I was only on my normal dismal form.

I sat there for a few seconds, then decided that I shouldn't put off the cleaning-up operation any longer. I wriggled to make contact with the lever of the Parker-Knoll. Nothing happened. It wouldn't budge. That's when I realised that the drawbridge had malfunctioned and I was trapped in my plushly upholstered castle. The Mars bar on the floor wasn't going anywhere, and nor was I.

I began to get cold, particularly in the groin area, where I was slick with genetic information, the signed confession of my self-abuse. I tried to doze. It was hopeless. The Dream-Cloud was out of reach.

Van Morrison burbled lyrically on, unperturbed by my desperate situation. He kept on singing at me that he was beside me ('and I'm – beside – you –') with the most extraordinary intensity, but that was no real consolation. I was beside myself. My fear, of course, was that I'd still be marooned in the Parker-Knoll, pubes crackling with my own dried seed, Mars bar skulking on the carpet like a bowel movement, when Mrs Beddoes arrived to do her morning rounds.

I must have slept. I woke up in the early morning chilled to the bone. I gave the lever of the chair one last try and it yielded. The drawbridge swung smoothly down and I was free. It was as if I had been applying pressure in the wrong direction. I suppose that's possible.

The first thing I did was to turn the stereo off. Then I had hell's own job cleaning myself up. Finally I wriggled under the Dream-Cloud to get warm.

And that was pretty much the beginning and end of my student experience of *C. sativa*. It was also the beginning and the end of my Van Morrison phase. I had listened to Side One of *Astral Weeks* ('In The Beginning') non-stop between about 8.30 and 5.15 the next morning. I never got as far as Side Two ('Afterwards'). 'In the beginning' was more than enough. In the beginning just about finished me.

When Mrs Beddoes came I groaned, and she cleaned round me with theatrical tact. She asked if I needed the doctor and I made stoical noises. When I woke up again it was after eleven.

Like every other undergraduate I had formally been assigned a doctor, in my case one at a medical practice in Trinity Street. I can't say I was impressed. He didn't know anything about Still's Disease, and by now I suppose I was used to doctors who had the good manners to pretend they knew more than me.

Slowly rolling goosebumps

I was used to Flanny's little ways by now, and whatever her other shortcomings she was a good sport when it came to prescribing drugs. So I let her do the donkey-work of writing my scripts. There was no point spending the time it would take me to break in a new medical professional just for term-times, when I had Flanny so well trained.

During the summer holidays of 1971, though, Flanny took a holiday of her own, so I saw another doctor in the same practice, Dr Bailey. The summer break was the 'long vac' in Cambridge parlance, and certainly I anticipated a long vacuum which medication might help to fill. I thought this new chap might not be so biddable, so I decided to play safe.

What I wanted was a prescription for Mandrax, a widely prescribed drug of the period, much maligned since then. I still give it high marks. To me it's pretty much the Jesus Christ of prescription drugs (meaning no offence, or not much). Mild and loving, but reviled and rejected, and all for trying to help.

The name, granted, isn't well chosen. Whoever came up with it must have had *mandrake* in mind, which isn't reassuring, and then finished off with a Bond-villain flourish (isn't Drax the baddie in *Moonraker*?). Give a drug a bad name.

It's not actually one of the barbiturates, though it shares some of their properties. The great thing about Mandrax is that you can take an awful lot of it with very little in the way of side-effects. Naturally the question of 'side' effects is wholly subjective. What's at the side depends on your angle of vision. Some people lead decidely off-centre lives, and a side-effect can be right up their alley.

Above a certain dosage I might get a sort of nomadic paræsthesia, with tingles and patches of numbness lazily playing over my body. To tell the truth I rather enjoyed that. It was like having slowly rolling goosebumps, and goosebumps are only a mild case of horripilation, which is one of the signs testifying to the presence of God. Mandrax offered no more than a simulation, but I enjoyed the experience anyway, this synthetic merry-go-round of skin sensation, a slow swirling where my body met the world. Emotionally it detached me from a world that was only posing as real. Since the body is no more than a screen, it makes sense to project onto it something you enjoy.

But don't just shuffle down to the local fleapit without checking what's on! It shocked me that young people would smoke, sniff or inject anything they could get their hands on, taking untested substances into their bodies with total abandon. I found the general drug culture of the time very alienating because it was so different from my own. Didn't they have any standards, any finesse? Even in terms of transgression I preferred the drama of the subverted prescription to the flat illegality of hashish. And I always liked the reliability of standard strengths and dosages. None of the uncertainty you get with your street muck.

When I was preparing for my appointment with Dr Bailey I decided I would take no chances. I didn't write down Mandrax as such on my list of requirements. I didn't even use its generic name of Methaqualone. This was a time for heavier disguise. By now I knew my way around the *Monthly Index of Medical Specialities*, the *MIMS*, pretty well. It's pretty much a GP's Bible. I'd seen it on Flanny's shelves, and noticed how well-thumbed it always was, though of course it's not for sale to the general public. Gamekeepers do like to keep ahead of poachers, don't they? But it's better sport if both groups are well-informed.

A nurse at Addenbrookes had given me an old copy, and sometimes I'd scrounge one from my GP when I needed to check dosages. There could be no better way of keeping tabs on the profession with which this body has linked my destiny, and I didn't need to be madly up to date. The rate of change wasn't so very frantic then, and I could keep pace with the professionals without too much trouble.

Ever since CRX, where Ansell had laid aside her tenderness to reel off technical terms to her colleagues, I had coveted the medical manner. Knowledge isn't power, whatever people say. Knowledge is power's poor relation, at best. It's the consolation, if not the booby prize. Still, it was all I could aim at. I might never become a doctor, but I could reasonably hope to sound like one. I could mimic the preoccupied expression, the technical drone.

I knew from my studies of *MIMS* that Boots the Chemist had its own private version of the drug, in two fractionally different formulations called Melsedin and Melsed, so I plumped for one of those instead.

Melsedin and Melsed. They haunted me, that pair of near-identicals. I knew from experience that it was perfectly possible to be in love with just one of a pair of twins, feeling no more than warm indifference to the other – and people seemed to have strong preferences as between Pepsi and Coca-Cola, though to the outsider's eye and palate it's all just treacly carbonated water. Melsed or Melsedin? I tossed a coin.

It seemed to me, as I looked at my little slip of paper, that the Mandrax, even wearing its carnival mask as Melsedin, looked a little suspect, so I added Dexedrine in first place on the list. Dexedrine I cared less about but still enjoyed. I had moved on since the days of involuntary binges on amphetamine-tinged hundreds and thousands. I could say no, and I could do without perfectly easily. I was confident in my willpower. I was struggling to do without sugar at the time, no easy thing for vegetarians, who tend to have a weakness for sweet things.

Torpid heat-bumps

Dr Bailey might baulk at either the Dexedrine or the disguised Mandrax, but he was unlikely to withhold them both. Finally, as a gesture towards clean living, I put down 'Redoxon 1000 mg' – a gram of effervescent Vitamin C, a good all-round tonic for the system. Now there were two guilty faces in the line-up of medication, one un-disguised and the other masquerading, along with a radiant innocent included to raise the general tone of the group.

In person Dr Bailey seemed more like a handler of animals than a human doctor. He was very burly, ripe for the wrestling of steers. He can't literally have worn a butcher's apron, though that's how I pic-ture him. There was an oar hung up on the wall in his surgery, trophy of a university past. When he learned I was at Cambridge he asked which college, and then 'How's their rowing?' He seemed shocked that I had no idea. As far as he was concerned, there was no excuse for not knowing about torpid heat-bumps, times and regattas. All that nonsense – he did go on.

Then Dr Bailey saw my little manifest of pharmaceuticals and his face went long. He was troubled by what he saw. Finally he laid his pencil against one of the items on my list and said, 'Are you sure you know what you're doing? Someone with your low body weight needs to be extra-careful about dosages.'

The 1970s was the golden age of prescribing, as far as I'm con-cerned. It was all downhill after that. Dr Bailey was like the man in the Australian beer advert, who blames the bottle of sweet sherry (the ladies' choice) for the collapse of his truck's axles, after he has loaded it to the gunwales with crates of lager. Dr Bailey was an Australian at heart. The toy truck of this body was due to be fully loaded with Mandrax, but that didn't worry him. It was going to be supercharged with Dexedrine, which would set the engine pounding, but that too was fine. He worried that I might be overdoing it with the Vitamin C. It turned out that it was the only innocent in the line-up who had no alibi. A whole gram of Redoxon? Was that wise?

I promised I would be careful. Scout's honour.

The summer passed in tingling and numbness. The summer passed. Peter was off on his travels, and the Washbournes were on a Greek island. I imagined them in adjacent deck-chairs, him reading about Buddhism, her engrossed in a Regency romance, highly compatible in their own syncopated way. On my own I felt shadowy and fraudu-lent. I seemed only to be able to meditate with an audience.

I remember at one point Audrey poking me quite hard with a ruler, just to get a reaction. I didn't give her the satisfaction, and she went away. I was expecting her to return with something else from her pencil-case, the compasses perhaps. I thought I would probably react to them.

Insects and other small deer had made no inroads into my flesh. Not only did I chew my food without prompting, I put it in my mouth myself. It seemed foolish to imagine that I was travelling so far inwards, à la Maharshi, that my surroundings had become a matter of indifference to me. I was just Mandied up.

She must have found some other distraction, because she didn't come back. Mum never acquired the knack of withholding a reaction, so she was probably Audrey's next port of call. There was a sort of hysterical escalation to their confrontations, which would only end when Mum said, 'You leave me no choice,' picking up the phone and asking the operator to connect her with the Remand Home.

Then Audrey would go down on her knees pleading not to be sent away, and after a proper interval Mum would think better of it and put the phone down. It was always very melodramatic. Obviously Mum didn't mean it (children don't vanish into the disciplinary sys-tem quite so smoothly, and anyway isn't eleven a little young?), and I don't think that Audrey believed for one moment that she did. It was more that the charade of an ultimatum allowed her to back down without loss of face. It was only after exhaustive exploration of anguish and disgrace that she could find any sort of calm.

Distillation of goodwill

I had the same college room for all three years of my undergraduate life. I stayed put in A6 Kenny. This was a significant concession. Other students were shunted all over the place during their time at the university, while I only needed to get used to one set of arrangements. Even so, of course, the human context changed around me, and I was deprived of the little arrangements that had grown up with the people I knew. P. D. Hughes, for instance, went to Lensfield Road, which was very sad. My set of immediate connections was destroyed as decisively as if a child had swept a cobweb away with a stick, and I had to start spinning the old charm-threads from scratch.

Still, there were compensations to the process of starting all over again. I was an initiate, an adept, and could often answer freshmen's questions. I learned to presume on my seniority when it came to asking for little bits of portering. I told myself it was the new-bugs' privilege to oblige me. I owed them nothing for their trouble. I cultivated mild insensitivity, a much healthier thing than spending your whole time conscious of being in the world's debt.

Belatedly I was beginning to find my feet. With my change of course I could tell myself I was a freshman all over again, only this time I could play the system a lot better. I attended the Societies Fair on my own. Second-years normally gave the whole jamboree a miss, since their social lives needed less propping up, but I threw myself confidently into the mælstrøm of the Corn Exchange. I hitch-lifted without any trouble. In fact it was intoxicatingly easy. Why wasn't it always like this? I suppose because this was a meandering and a milling crowd, rather than a bustling one. I tried different approaches. Everything seemed to work. I felt like a gambler on a winning streak.

For a short time even the corniest lines brought me a smile and a hand on the tiller. 'Hey, man, can you help me keep on truckin' to the next stall but one?' That worked more than once, on those with hippy pretentions. Drawling 'Sister, Do You Know the Way to San José?'

produced as much of a beam on one young woman's face (oddly red-
dened, a drinker's face on someone who was little more than a girl) as
if I'd stuffed a handful of fivers into the pocket of her coat, a military
coat which was far too big for her. She pushed me where I wanted to
go and then took my name and college address. She said she'd be in
touch. The wheelchair ran perfectly without the need for a motor,
chugging smoothly on a distillation of goodwill.

I made a beeline for the Zoology Club, which I was charmed to
learn held 'conversaziones' rather than meetings as such. That was
what was missing from my Cambridge life – conversaziones. Then,
as I negotiated the loudly echoing spaces of the Corn Exchange, idly
wondering which human ripple I would graciously allow to carry me
forward, I could hear a subdued rhythmic chanting. It struck me immediately as ominous, before I could make out a word.

Eventually I could make out the slogan being broadcast: *Two Four
Six Eight – Gay Is Just as Good as Straight*. Crazily I thought that
everyone would look at me, that my blushing in that confined space
would spark an explosion. It wasn't so much a blush, more of a heart
attack displaced on to my face. And so soon after I had mentally disparaged another human being for undue redness of complexion!

I experienced horripilation, yes, and lowered body temperature,
but none of the other classic signs of the proximity of God. What I
felt was the proximity of terrible fear. I couldn't wait to get out of
there.

Every now and then the chant was replaced by another, which went
Three Five Seven Nine – Lesbians Are Mighty Fine. This was much less
threatening to my peace of mind. In any case, since it was uttered
by male voices exclusively, the slogan gave the impression of hearsay
rather than any great conviction.

I can't explain my panic flight. I seemed to have lost a lot of confidence. As a Vulcan schoolboy I had been positively cheeky when
confronted with evangelicals, taunting Billy Graham's minions with
their gnawed fingernails and penchant for hell-fire. As a freshman I
had groped a botanist in the presence of my bedmaker. Now I had
relapsed. I had become re-infected with depressive strains of narrow-
mindedness, guilt and shame. Perhaps it's an indication of how low
my state of being actually was, during this my higher education.

With a heavy heart I realised that sooner or later I would have to come to terms with the Cambridge Wing of the Gay Liberation Front, or CHAP, as it was actually called, rather than drive round Trumpington looking for the Monarchist League. But not just yet. Perhaps my dread was based, deep down, on something quite simple. This was one group whose rejection I wouldn't be able to shrug off. If they wouldn't have me, who would? If these untouchables refused any contact with me then there was no further to fall.

Didn't have the hips for the job

In the meantime, their slogan echoed in my head for the rest of the day. The trouble with such ear-catching formulations is that they're so vulnerable to rewording. After *Two Four Six Eight* my mind kept supplying starker conclusions for the couplet.

Cheery Chants Won't Change Your Fate.

Join and Feel the Force of Hate.

Not to mention: *John Will Never Find a Mate.*

The red-faced young woman who had taken my address at the Societies Fair tracked me down in my Kenny lair a few days later. She was tiny and elfin, with masses of red hair and many scarves. She wore glasses with octagonal lenses, which were fashionable at the time. I dare say she was modelling her style on Janis Joplin, as so many women did in those days, except that she didn't have the hips for the job, and somehow I doubted that she'd ever drunk anything stronger than Earl Grey. She did have a lot of vitality, though. She lit up my room like a little auburn bonfire.

'Oh, hello,' she said, as if we'd bumped into each other on the street. 'Good to see you again. I was just wondering – would you like to be part of a Day of Action for disabled people?'

Would I? I didn't know. What would it involve? I played for time, saying, 'I really don't know – some of my best friends were disabled, of course.' This wasn't even true, not since the day I had left Vulcan School and started to sink slowly into the mainstream.

She said, 'You might enjoy it. We're planning a consciousness-raising event, though actually it may turn into a zap.'

'Very good. What is a zap?'

'You really don't know? Oh, *man* . . . a zap is a piece of direct action intended to open people's eyes and bring about radical change.'

'Can you give me an example?'

'Easy. You know the drinks containers there used to be deposits on, so that you could return them and get a refund? Big business wants you to throw away your bottles and buy new ones. So consciousness-raising would be getting everyone to realise that this is wasteful and stupid, and zapping would be dumping, let's say, a million bottles outside the headquarters of Coca-Cola.'

'I see.' The idea of being dumped outside an uncaring institution had a certain appeal. Perhaps this dynamic waif would chain me to the railings outside Downing and set in motion some very overdue radical change. 'Can you give me some more details?'

'We plan to do a comprehensive survey of facilities in Cambridge – shop, restaurants, pubs. To see whether disabled people are fairly treated. Whether they can get into those places, for a start.'

I was impressed. It was the first time in Cambridge I'd had any inkling of social consciousness along these lines. 'And when is it, this day of action?' I asked.

'Well, let's see,' she said. 'When are you free?'

That was her way of letting me know another important detail: between us, we were the Day of Action. There was no one else, but I didn't think that was necessarily a bad thing. It made choosing our Day relatively easy and unbureaucratic. We settled on the next Saturday. She thought a busy day in the shops and the streets made the point about the exclusion of people like me more vividly, and I'd always had trouble solving the problem of the Cambridge Saturday.

Her name was Rebecca. She said she was reading Sociology, and perhaps this was her fieldwork, but that didn't put me off. I was raring to go, impatient to be excluded from shops I had no interest in entering.

Our first port of call on the Day of Action was W. H. Smith's in Market Hill. Rebecca wanted to buy a clipboard, to lend a more formal edge to our inspections, but it made sense to treat the shop as our first official port of call. Someone held the door open for us, and Rebecca did her best to get me inside, but the task was beyond her. There wasn't really a step, more of a ridge, but she was too little and too light to nudge me over. 'Looks as if we've got our first failure to record,' she said. 'Wait here.' What else was I going to do?

By the time Rebecca came back with her clipboard, an assistant from the shop had come over to me. 'What's the matter?' he asked, and Rebecca answered for me. 'This young man can't get into your shop.'

'Well, that's easily taken care of, miss. I'll give him a hand.'

'And what's supposed to happen if he doesn't have a friend with him? How's he supposed to get help when he's stranded outside the shop?'

'I don't know, miss. He could shout, or ask someone passing by to alert a member of staff.'

'And how is that supposed to make him feel, when he has to go to such trouble even to get inside?'

How was it supposed to make me feel, come to that, being used as an object lesson in this way? I felt a warm and nasty glow. Shouldn't I being doing some of the talking? But Rebecca was in full spate. 'Do you want this young man's custom or not?'

'We want it, I expect, up to a point. What is it he wants to buy?'

'Nothing at the moment, thank you. But I've bought one of your sturdy and economical clipboards, and I'm writing down what you say about your disabled customers.'

'Are you from a newspaper?'

'No. Why? Do you only care about disadvantaged members of the public when a reporter takes an interest?'

'Not at all,' said the assistant, beginning to get angry at last. 'When this young man wants to make purchase – which isn't today, apparently – he can rely on our most devoted attention. Thank you!'

'Thank *you*!' barked Rebecca, grabbing the handle of the wheel-chair and giving me rather a jolt as we set off to our next targeted business. 'What a lackey! What a running dog! The sooner everyone like that gets stood up in front of a wall the better for the rest of us!' She seemed to be in a high good humour, all the same, and looking forward to the next ideological scrap on my behalf.

As we went from place to place we started to vary our approach. Sometimes I would get up out of the wheelchair, with her help, and try to totter in to premises that resisted me with every blue line on the architect's plans. We got a lot more attention after Rebecca started to mention that she was writing a piece for *Broadsheet*. It wasn't much of a lie – it was as hard in those days to get an article rejected by a student newspaper as a poem. If she had ever written such a thing up it would certainly have appeared.

I tried to get a look at Rebecca's face whenever she was in my line of sight, which was usually at times when she was using me as a reproach to a heartless world of business. I had decided that my first interpretation of her facial redness (the demon drink) had been prejudiced and wrong. Some redheads do have rather brickish complexions, of course, but I was working on a different theory. My diagnostic nose twitched and my pencil burned to label a vial of pillules.

Cashmere tufts of ideology

After a few more skirmishes with lackeys and running dogs I was beginning to get hungry. I wondered which restaurant or café we were going to patronise and upbraid. It seemed fairer, somehow, to be pointing out the defects of establishments we actually wanted to attend, though embarrassment would run much higher in a place that offered atmosphere as much as food and drink.

There was also a budgetary element involved. We couldn't afford the Blue Boar. In fact we settled for the Corner House on King Street. Rebecca seemed much less committed to the struggle than she had been in the shops that morning, which was partly explained when she said that there was nothing on the menu she could eat, since she was a vegan.

'Oh, I'm a vegetarian too,' I said, 'but I'm sure we can find something.' I had misheard her, and now she misheard me in her turn.

'You're really a vegan?' she asked. 'I thought I was the only one in Cambridge. I'm certainly the only one in Newnham.'

'Really? There are three of us in Downing, and I thought that was a pretty feeble showing!' Then the word she had used finally sank in. 'Hold on – what was it you said? You're a vegan? What's that?'

'I thought you said that's what you were!'

'I'm a vegetarian. What's a vegan?'

'A vegan is a vegetarian with a bit of backbone. Sorry, that's what

574

my parents say but it's true, isn't it? Good luck being high and mighty about your lifestyle when you keep cows and hens as your slaves.'

I'd never thought about it in quite those terms, and it was a novel sensation having the ethical rug pulled from under me, when I had become spoiled by the feel of those cashmere tufts of ideology between my toes. Rebecca abandoned the disabled-access project for the time being, sitting me down to instruct me in living without cruelty instead. She took only a contemptuous glance at the menu, which was laminated and greasy. Even licking the menu at the Corner House could make you complicit in what she explained was called zooicide, the killing of living things.

'Vegetarians are really fifth columnists, aren't they? They commit zooicide just as much as the outright flesh-munchers. Where do you think the milk you drink comes from? Do you think the cows had no other plans for it? That they sent their calves away to school, perhaps, and had a surplus? Wake up! And how about cheese? Don't you know what rennet is? It's used to coagulate cheese, and it comes from a calf's stomach! Isn't that disgusting? Calves don't give it away out of charity, they only want to use it to digest their own food, but then they're killed and the lining is scraped out of their stomachs. S-c-r-a-p-e-d out. And all so that you can order a cheese omelette and feel pure. Slavery and slaughter on a single plate! Meaning no offence.'

'Taking none,' I said, through gritted teeth. I had indeed been about to plump for the cheese omelette. It was as if she could read my hungry mind. Admittedly the rennet question had bothered me from the moment I had heard about it. In those days vegetarian cheese seemed a purely theoretical possibility, like the eternal light-bulb and the razor blade that never lost its edge, neither of which big business would let us buy. I couldn't find it in shops and I couldn't expect even the most punctilious college kitchen to track it down.

Rebecca explained that her parents had been 'almost' founder-members of the Vegan Society, certainly among the first hundred to sign up. Her parents were Welsh speakers who had met, classically enough, at an eisteddfod. She herself had been brought up avoiding dairy produce as well as meat. Her body was uncontaminated with the pain of other species. In that respect she was like the hero of Roald Dahl's story 'Pig', except of course that he ends up hanging from a hook on a conveyor belt in an abattoir with his throat slit open. I hope I haven't spoiled the story for you.

The moment she mentioned her parents, Rebecca's voice started to betray the Celtic lilt for ever associated with Dylan Thomas. Perhaps it was true that she had avoided all dairy products from birth, but she hadn't altogether been able to steer clear of *Under Milk Wood*.

I had to ask Rebecca to attract a waitress's attention so that I could order my fifth columnist's lunch, my feast of indirect animal suffering. The waitress was trying so hard to treat me like everyone else, not staring or anything, that I could have set fire to my hair and she wouldn't have looked my way, telling herself it was all part of my unfortunate condition. 'Plain omelette, chips and salad, please,' I said, my voice a chastened whisper. I was still abusing the chicken, but cow and calf had a provisional reprieve.

Part of me, the part that loved rigour and clarity, found this new doctrine of eating very appealing. What a shock it would give Mum and Flanny if I returned to Bourne End saying No to a whole new range of foods! What consternation in the kitchen and the surgery. At the same time I had to acknowledge that as a vegan child in the bed-rest years, refusing to embark on Mum's scrambled-egg boats, I would simply have faded away, my precious Christmas-present watch dangling loosely from my shrivelled wrist.

Perhaps I would stay where I was in the pecking order of eating after all, dismissed by one camp as a faddist and by the other as a gutless fellow-traveller of slaughter.

When my omelette arrived, Rebecca graciously consented to share my salad. She even helped herself to a few chips, after sniffing one to assure herself that it hadn't been fried in an animal fat. Her nose could infallibly settle that question. After the main course she produced something she described as a carob bar from her pocket, some innocent treat which she understandably didn't offer to share. I asked her the Latin name, which she didn't know. That was a relief (it's *Ceratonia siliqua*, for the record). I was feeling oddly competitive.

I had expected to discuss Rebecca's symptoms over the lunch table. Did the red patches on her face itch or perhaps throb? Were they hot or cold, even numb? Did the sensations vary with the time of day? Each answer would narrow down the possible diagnosis until a remedy was found, as in a classic detective story – except that there would be no need to finger a culprit or even name the crime. I wouldn't have to use the (admittedly pretty) word 'Rosacea'.

M. L. Tyler in *Homœopathic Drug Pictures* uses a lovely quotation from Robert Louis Stevenson to explain the method: 'I only saw the things you did / But always you yourself you hid.' Seeing the symptoms is plenty, as long as you see them clearly enough, and learn to make the crucial distinctions between apparent similarities. Colonel Mustard in the Library is given the relevant pillule, dusted off and helped to his feet. It's not a dramatic story, granted, but something much more worthwhile, a happy ending. All friends again.

Rebecca addressed herself to the carob bar as if she was eating a shaft of sweetened sunlight. Was she more self-righteous than me? Not necessarily. Was she making a better job of it? Definitely.

Petticoats over their working clothes

I went on the offensive in a slightly indirect way. 'Rebecca isn't a very Welsh name, is it?' She seemed very pleased with the question. 'If you mean it sounds Jewish, then perhaps you're referring to the theory that the Welsh are the lost twelfth tribe of Israel.'

Are they, by Jove!

I couldn't begin to explain why I was so preöccupied with her ethnic identity. If it turned out that she put on a pointy hat between lectures and used her spinning-wheel to make the strings for harps why should I care?

'In any case I'm not sure you know what you're talking about. Rebecca and her daughters are important figures in Welsh history. They rioted against the English oppressor in the 1840s. They burned down toll-houses and terrorised the gate-keepers.'

'And what did the men do while the women ran wild?'

She looked at me rather pityingly. 'It was the men doing the rioting.'

'But I thought you said . . .'

'"Rebecca and her daughters" were men. They wore bonnets and petticoats over their working clothes. They took their name from Genesis – something about "possessing the gates of those which hate them". Farmers taking cattle to a nearby market town might have to pay six tolls. It was a group identity. They were all "Rebecca". Have you seen *Spartacus*?'

'No.'

'Never mind, then.'

'And did the brutal Establishment crack down as it always does?'

'Not really. A commission was set up which was more sympathetic to local people and established County Roads Boards instead.'

'Power to the people,' I said hopefully, but I think Rebecca had realised that my political consciousness didn't run either broad or deep.

Her carob bar was more or less Rebecca's lunch, while if I was still hungry I could always order (for instance) an ice cream – even if it was little better in the moral scheme of things than a candied pig's trotter, or a bunch of South African grapes visibly dripping with the blood of the oppressed.

Rebecca's exposition of dietary virtue had distracted us from the main thrust of our Saturday, but in the afternoon we got back into our stride. In fact we made so much of a splash at Joshua Taylor, Cambridge's poshest department store (universally known as Josh Tosh), that we came rather unstuck. By now our approach had become very slick. Perhaps our lunchtime conversation had put Rebecca back in touch with the preaching intonations of her forebears (though there must be a few Welsh folk without the pulpit in their veins). Meanwhile I had acquired the knack of helplessness – and it's definitely a knack, whatever anyone tells you. It was only in the afternoon that I got the hang of it. It felt like filling my nappies on principle, long after I'd mastered potty-training. I just looked around as if I'd never seen a door before, as if I'd been protected from the harsh truths of the entrance-way.

Meanwhile Rebecca's journalistic credentials had escalated from *Broadsheet* by way of *Varsity* to the *Cambridge Evening News*. As she helped me ostentatiously into the trendy-young-man section of the shop, which had a dandyish name all its own – 'The Peacock', the shop's bold response to the vibrant and trendsetting 'Way In' men's department of Harrods – we caused consternation. I don't think it was because there was nothing in the shop I could conceivably wear, bar a few scarves. Perhaps word had gone round the retailers of Cambridge city centre that a man in a wheelchair and a reporter were asking embarrassing questions.

We didn't look like what we were, ill-assorted acquaintances enjoying an odd sort of day out under the umbrella of idealistic agitation. We looked like the advance party of a journalistic exposé, preparing the ground for the camera crew. We caused alarm, but it wasn't too late. We could still be bought off.

A swarm of smart and rather flustered young men surged towards us. This was customer service at the highest pitch of professionalism and nervousness. By the time we left the premises, barely two minutes later, I was clutching in my hand a Joshua Taylor credit note for twenty pounds.

We had set out to make people more aware of the difficulties faced by people in wheelchairs, and ended up doing rather well out of it ourselves. Accidentally we became a protection racket. Up to the very moment the credit note was pressed into my hands, I had no idea we were in the extortion business, and nor (I'm sure) did Rebecca.

I let her keep the credit note. I didn't feel I had any right to share it – it was like her carob bar. The Day of Action had been her idea, after all. She was much more likely to find something she wanted to buy at Josh Tosh than I was, and when she did she would be able to carry it home with her to Newnham. It cost me a small pang, all the same, to say goodbye to it. It was only money, of course – in fact it wasn't even money, being a credit note. But twenty pounds went a long, long way in 1971.

When Rebecca had delivered me back to A6 Kenny I didn't know what I felt, not just about our windfall but about the whole Day of Action. Day of inaction, more like. It was the only day in my life when being disabled was my job, no more and no less. At first this was embarrassing for me, but I grew to enjoy the feeling of being the advance guard of an army of wheelchairs which would trundle smoothly into every last cubicle of the city, glide up every stairwell.

My exclusion gave me a strange sort of authority, and no one thought to ask, 'What good would ramps do you anyway, John? Unless the gradient is undetectable you're no good on a slope – you'll always need assistance anyway. So why all this fuss?' Now my hectic day of employment was over. I had clocked off, and the difficulties of my daily life no longer stood for anything outside themselves. They lost their audience and their power to stir the soul.

Looking back on it, the strangest part of the day was the little squabble over Rebecca's name at lunch. It was as if I felt threatened in my niche (what niche? I didn't have any such thing!). Some part of me seemed to think that a gay occidental Hindu with Still's Disease was beaten at his own game by a Welsh-speaking vegan named after transvestite rioters, soundly thrashed in the struggle for supremely specialised status.

We're all in the same minority. Minority of one. That's what Maya tells us, anyway.

I tried to keep in touch with Rebecca. It would have been nice if she had kept in touch with me, but perhaps the credit note stood between us. I couldn't do anything about that. All I could do was invite her to dinner, though it meant taking a lot of trouble. I had to find a non-dairy meal which was worth eating, for one thing, and that could be assembled using no more elaborate equipment than the frying pan banned in Kenny. The most alluring dish I could come up with was *imam bayildi*, or 'the imam swooned' – an aubergine stew with a lot of garlic in it, so fragrant that the imam (the legend has it) swooned when he opened the lid of the pot. I would have loved to see what effect it had on a vegan sociologist. It wasn't a practical meal, though – it needed more than a frying pan.

My major discoveries at Cambridge were Thomas Mann and the aubergine. Hard to estimate their relative importance, but I think the aubergine wins on points. Only a madman would read *Buddenbrooks* every day, or even every month, while a regular intake of aubergine is entirely sane.

I decided on a rice-and-aubergine improvisation with some cashew nuts in it for the contrast of crunch, stained the dish with tomatoes, turmeric and chilli (the purple-grey of cooked aubergine is its least attractive feature), a sort of Indo-paella or Ibero-biryani, and I invited Rebecca by way of the college post, giving her a choice of dates and times.

Other people's social lives, I can see, involve the fluent exchange of little favours. Come to dinner – no, we came to you last time, come to us. Fine as long as the difficulties are equal for both parties. It seems natural that I should always be the guest, but only to other people. This body is a bad host, but I'm not. So I periodically move mountains to set a modest plateful before an acquaintance. It's either that or break off the friendship before it has a chance to get established.

Not bleeding intracranially the slightest bit

If I'm only ever a guest then I'm a charity case, and I won't have that. Why shouldn't I be charitable too? Let's forget for a moment that from another perspective 'I' am as unreal as the body whose limitations I disparage. A dream hunger requires dream food – a dream cut requires a dream bandage – dream sociability requires a dream party. Still, at this time I sometimes felt like the social equivalent of a Doodlemaster machine, trying to construct the flowing shapes of a connected life out of the bare straight lines of what was possible for me, the fiddly intractable knobs that leave only horizontal and vertical traces.

Then on the appointed day Rebecca didn't turn up. I waited an hour and a half, and then mounted an expedition to the Porter's Lodge to phone Newnham. I said it was an emergency, which it could easily have been. It seemed perfectly likely that Rebecca had tripped in the bathroom and was lying there on the floor with a subdural hæmatoma, leaking her life away. Why else would she miss her appointment with a vegan paella? A Newnham porter was sent to rout her out. Eventually she came to the phone herself, not bleeding intracranially in the slightest bit. 'Sorry sorry sorry,' she said in a tone of voice that carried more exasperation than regret.

There was nothing irretrievable about the situation, or there wouldn't have been if she hadn't gone on to say, in the same grudging tone of voice, 'I knew there was something I had to do.' That tore it. That ripped up the social contract and threw the scraps in my face with a sneer. It turned out that having dinner with me was something Rebecca 'had to do', like getting vaccinated or going to the dentist. From her point of view my paella, so carefully considered that it was like thought itself on a plate, tender thought sending up its fragrant steam, was no more than a chore. And that was really the end of Rebecca as far as I was concerned, and veganism was tainted by association. I might reap the benefit of a calf's stomach-scrapings from time to time, and indeed I eat honey without giving much thought to the sorrows of the bees who made it, but at least if you invite me to dinner I turn up.

It was her loss – particularly as I'd done a little research into the homœopathic remedies for facial reddening. I could have worked wonders, and now we'll never know.

The Day of Action for disabled people was the high point of my political involvement as an undergraduate. It's true that I signed a petition of protest when it turned out that the college kitchen was serving South African cling peaches, supposedly blacklisted at the docks but brought into the country hugger-mugger by scab labour on barges, but that was about as engaged as I got.

Those were great years for revolutionary behaviour by students, for demos and sit-ins, but I was largely a spectator. I didn't really subscribe to the reality of the world we were supposed to be changing. I wasn't profoundly opposed, either, just unconvinced that there was any point in using Maya to fight Maya. On one occasion, though, I got caught up in quite a dust-up.

I don't even remember what the issue was. I may never have known, and I dare say I wasn't the only one to be storming the barricades without much clue about the nature of our cause. In the wheelchair I was a fellow-traveller by definition. Oh, we were against oppression, against discrimination, for liberty and the people, but as for what it was actually about, well, search me.

All I knew was that without any active decision I was being pushed along Kings Parade as part of a large and vocal crowd. We were shouting, 'Down with –' something. We were strongly opposed to something. And we wanted something too. When did we want it? We wanted it now. We were all agreed on that.

Then the crowd parted in front of me to reveal Graëme Beamish, looking distinctly anxious, asking if he could have a word. He was wearing a gown but it hung down unevenly from his shoulders. I imagine there's just the one size. I was startled, but had no control over the momentum of the group. Graëme had to keep up with us as best he could, shouting in my ear as we trundled along in our cavalcade of slogans. 'I wonder if you realise, John,' he shouted, 'that you make rather a potent mascot for any cause that chooses to brandish you? I would take it as a personal favour if you took no further part in this "demo". Just say the word and I will deliver you back to your room.'

He maintained the charade of fuddy-duddy. He was getting out of breath, but still he managed to generate a little bubble of personalised heckling within the ideological fervour of the event. 'You are being exploited. Your companions do not have your interests at heart. If you oblige me in this matter it will greatly strengthen our working relationship – I should say, our *connection* . . .'

He didn't need to spell out what he meant by that. He would approve the installation of a telephone in my room, despite his heel-dragging in the past.

'I'm not a child, Dr Beamish,' I said sternly, as I was wheeled willy-nilly towards the Senate House in my pram. 'There are political matters at stake here.' Still, it was an astute choice of bribe.

'I'm sure there are, John, and I'm also sure there are better ways to resolve them than rash action. At least give me your word that you won't go through those doors. I must insist on extracting your promise. Nothing else will satisfy me.'

'Very well. I promise not to go through the Senate House doors.'

'Very good, John. I'm glad we understand each other.' He peeled off from the group at that, saying, 'I'll be speaking to you soon.' He made a fleeting gesture with his hand by his head which could have represented the holding of a telephone receiver, before he changed it into a genial wave with no specific meaning.

It cost me nothing to make my promise. My party was visiting the Senate House more or less in a tourist capacity. It seemed possible that a few acrobatic activists might breach the defences of the university's symbolic centre, but the rest of us would entertain ourselves, as was the way with student politics, by chanting and shouting catch-phrases about our vast power and the imminent collapse of the establishment.

The revolution awaited our next move

When the Senate House came into view we saw that this was not going to happen. An occupation was in full swing. It turned out, as

583

a barrage of murmurs instantly informed us, that the authorities had forestalled destruction of property by leaving the doors open. They had borrowed drastic tactics that might be thought of as historically Russian, evacuating their capital city and leaving it hollowly in the possession of the invading hordes.

We were actually singing 'We Shall Overcome' as we rounded the corner. The song died in our throats when we saw that there was a real chance that we would. It was a terrific disappointment. We had banked on being thwarted, and being back in our rooms in time for tea, seething with a gratified discontent. Now the revolution we had pressed for so blindly was awaiting our next move.

It's true that one functionary had been left behind, but his rôle wasn't to fall under bayonets but to ask us politely not to walk on the grass. Most of us obeyed, but I didn't, or rather the person pushing the wheelchair didn't. I was familiar with the way those handles could sometimes transmit a subtle libertine impulse.

Now there was nothing to stop me entering the Senate House except the promise I had given only minutes before. It had cost me nothing to make that promise, but now it would cost me something to keep it. I was very much caught up in Maya at this point, unwilling to go down in history as someone unworthy of the moment, someone who had missed the storming of the Bastille by popping into the shop for a pastry. Dramatic events like this were rare in any case, and normally excluded me as a matter of course.

I put the brakes on – not literally. I called out 'Wait!' and our little cavalry charge pulled up short while I pondered the options. How was I going to reconcile conscience with the need to satisfy my curiosity?

Easy. You don't have to be a lawyer, a Jesuit or a diplomat to wriggle out of commitments that don't suit you. I had given my word that I wouldn't pass through the doors of the Senate House. I would use the windows instead. Not a very elaborate bit of wriggling, as wriggling goes.

My party took no persuading. A scout went into the building to prepare the way. Soon a window was opened from inside and I was hoisted up bodily and passed in. It wasn't a relaxing experience, since the windows of such a grand ceremonial building were large and high off the ground. Even on the way up I wasn't sure that there were reliable hands ready to receive me. I had a long moment of queasiness suspended over the window-sill, being transferred between teams of supporters. Then the thing was done. I had kept my narrow promise while disregarding its broader meaning.

While I was teetering over the sill I experienced a biblical twinge. The whole scene was full of New Testament echoes. Was it when one meeting was so crowded that Christ had to enter by this unorthodox route? Or did a sick man's family resort to extreme measures to get their kinsman to the top of the queue? Either way, I was a bit shaken by the parallel, once I'd detected it. If your initials are J and C, it's just the sort of thing you need to be on your guard against.

Inside, there was an atmosphere of celebration. People smoked dope and played guitars in the academic holy of holies, where students were admitted only for rites of passage, matriculation and graduation. But there was also an earnest side to the occupation. I remember a board being put up with a list of teach-ins and debates, from 'By Any Means Necessary – How to Make a Molotov Cocktail Without Blowing Yourself Up' to 'Sister Power – The Lessons of Radical Feminism'. A crèche was signposted, though there wasn't a child in sight.

There was also a tremendous sense of anticlimax and loss of purpose. We had made our point, hadn't we? Whatever it was. Couldn't we go now? No, we had to stay put indefinitely, or the whole event would fizzle.

Perhaps I was a mascot, but I was also a nuisance, bleating for veggie food when there were other priorities. I said I couldn't be expected to live on chips indefinitely. The idea seemed to be that it was a privilege to make sacrifices for the Revolution, and mine was eating Wimpys. I wished I had a book with me, and wondered if I could come up with a medical excuse for leaving in the morning. I could say there was medicine in my room which I needed to take (but what if someone offered to fetch it?).

Early the next morning the proctors arrived and drove us from the building. We hadn't done much to barricade doors that had been left open in the first place, and were dazed by sleep and cheap wine. It was a textbook bit of tactics – wait until the enemy is off his guard, and then scour him from the city you have pretended to cede to him. I do seriously wonder if the Vice-Chancellor at the time wasn't in fact a military historian, seizing the chance to demonstrate the eternal relevance of his speciality.

I was asleep on the floor in the library, with someone's coat as a mattress, when the cry went up of 'It's the pigs!' Someone blearily picked me up and ran with me. Neither of us had time to put on our shoes. It didn't matter that I was barefoot. It mattered rather a lot that he was wearing only socks, since he slipped on the staircase and dropped me.

This time there was no human providential mattress to break my fall, as at Burnham, no stoutly built Marion Wilding to absorb the impact as at Vulcan. I gave up the effort of constructing the illusion of time and space. I dropped my knitting needles, and the skein of consciousness bounced softly across a cold hard floor, unwinding as it went.

The next time I was up to the chore of creating my surroundings, I was in Addenbrookes Hospital with an unfamiliar man, formally dressed, sitting on a chair by my bed.

I don't remember the fall itself, nothing from the moment of being routed out of the library and heading towards the stairs. If I try to force my memory all I get is an academic version of the Odessa Steps sequence from *Battleship Potemkin*, with the shiny shoes of faceless proctors replacing the implacable boots of the Tsar's soldiers, the wheelchair standing in for the baby-carriage as it bounces helplessly down. Of course it didn't happen that way – I wasn't in the wheelchair, and there was no massacre on the Senate House steps. There was no massacre on the Odessa Steps either, for that matter, but there is now. That's just the way Maya works.

My heart was on its last legs

The slightly daunting man by my bed introduced himself by saying, 'I'm one of your nasty proctors.' Which made me feel a little queasy and a little guilty too. My voice sounded very tinny when I answered, as protocol demanded, 'And I'm one of your revolting students.' Was he a guard or an interrogator-in-waiting? Perhaps my tutor had told him to hold me fast until he came in wrath.

My next concern was for the wheelchair and what had happened to it, but there it was beside my bed. This was a lesson in itself: the wheelchair had followed me to my new address like a faithful pet. My shoes too had made their own way. It all went to prove one of Ramana Maharshi's favourite teachings, that self-enquiry is the only priority. Everything else takes care of itself.

They wanted to keep me in Addenbrookes for a night or two, under observation, but I didn't see the fun in that. They did an ECG, which I consented to – for all the good it would do them. An ECG is all very fine, but it's a standard procedure designed to measure a standard organ. What else could it be? But my heart is not standard. My heart is my own. Under my first diagnosis, of rheumatic fever, there was worry that my heart would be permanently damaged by the infection I was supposed to have.

Under my second diagnosis that worry was made moot. As my joints began to follow new laws during the ill-advised period of bed-rest, the chest cavity was squeezed and skewed, and the heart followed suit. My heart has adjusted to new conditions, but it's anyone's guess how well it has maintained its functions. My diaphragm, the heart's body habitus, is irregularly shaped, which makes the echoes hard to interpret. I have yet to meet a specialist who could decide from my ECG readings whether my heart was on its last legs or likely to beat its little drum another billion times. We'll just have to wait and see, won't we? Household items seem to know when their guarantees run out. Perhaps I'll feel the existential twinge which in a washing-machine immediately precedes the outpour of dirty water onto the kitchen floor.

I couldn't wait to get out of Addenbrookes, mainly because my digestion demanded it. The wheelchair had followed me to hospital, not so the loo chair, and I badly needed to defæcate. Nurses are all very well, some of them even know their business, but I'd rather do *my* business in my own way.

The disturbances were serious enough for the university to commission a report into them. It commented with displeasure on disorder 'during which a student was injured'. That's me. If you can't make the headlines, at least make the footnotes. It's my only real presence in the official record between the rites of passage of matriculation and graduation, and I'm being used as a stick to beat my radical generation. No mention of the fact that it was the university's own crackdown which caused the incident. We were snoozing happily in the library before then, safe and sound. Even without the report, though, my telephone would have been back in its original category, as far as Graëme Beamish was concerned. A lost cause. And Cambridge is not the natural home of lost causes – Oxford claims that distinction.

During the Easter holidays, in consultation with Peter, I decided it was time to try the substance which had fascinated me for so long, mescaline, which was on offer in a local pub. It would be silly to have my heart conk out with my curiosity still unsatisfied.

We had done a lot of research, one way or another. Peter wasn't much of a reader, but I had read bits of *The Doors of Perception* to him, and he had spent the previous summer hitch-hiking round California and asking a lot of questions. He volunteered to be my psychedelic chaperone, and I could think of no one better for the job. I felt entirely safe with Peter, and it made sense for him to see the effects of the drug at close hand before he slipped into the unknown himself.

We decided to avoid Easter week itself. Even if you think you're not a believer, that story is so strong that it's bound to percolate into your opened mind, even if you avoid, say, Good Friday and Easter Sunday. You'd better not be playing on the railway when the express comes through, or your consciousness will be flattened like the pennies we used to leave on the tracks.

We secured our supply well ahead of time. It was mescaline I was after. LSD-25 sounded exactly like what it was, something made in a laboratory, lacking any tradition of use, an industrial product originally intended for a different purpose and opportunistically diverted when it turned out to have surprising properties. This hardly corresponded to my sense of the sacred. I wanted a proper rite of passage, dissolving the appearances and inducting me into a higher order of meaning, not some brute of a rocket which would twang me up into the mental sky to find my own way home.

Luckily there was a dealer at the Castle pub in Windsor who supposedly sometimes had mescaline. I didn't have a sense of wrong-doing, so there was no *frisson* about being a stone's throw away from the Queen's residence. I would have liked her blessing on the enterprise.

The dealer in the pub was rather ratty-looking and couldn't keep his eyes still. 'Not here, not here,' he muttered, and led the way to the lavs. Peter had spoken a lot about the importance of setting for the encounter with hallucinatory reality, but the same rules applied, I felt, more generally. My ingrained sense of the integrity of an event made me sit through all the end-titles of films. Why would it be content with a drug experience that began in furtiveness and indignity? I wanted solemnity, if not priests in robes then some closer approximation to masonic regalia than a greatcoat with some buttons missing.

I had to generate the sense of sacrament more or less single-handed, though Peter was sympathetic from behind the handles of the wheelchair. 'What do you have for me?' I asked gravely, but the only answer I got was 'Two for a pound.'

'Is this mescaline?'

'Yeah, yeah, good stuff. How many d'you want? Two for a pound.'

'Two doses, please.'

'Is that two or four, then?'

'Er . . . two, please. Pay the gentleman, Peter.' The moment the money had changed hands, our friend grabbed a piece of hard Izal toilet paper from the cubicle and screwed it up round two little pills. Then he shoved the tawdry little packet into Peter's hand and scarpered. It was all a far cry from the enlightened heyday of the Catholic church in Mexico, the slices of peyote button offered up in all reverence at Communion long ago.

Peripheral swirling

On the day itself I would trust Peter to choose a suitable spot, scenic and not too frequented. He was the one in the family who was best at buying birthday cards – from a young age he had been able to match the image to the person perfectly, and this was really only an extension of that. We had decided that the Tan-Sad was the suitable vehicle. It was better suited than a wheelchair to rough ground, and we were mindful of all the horror stories about people having 'trips' who thought they could fly and threw themselves off buildings. Once I was in the Tan-Sad I wasn't going to throw myself anywhere.

The timetable of the psychedelic event took some working out. We knew the whole experience could last many hours, and we wouldn't necessarily find it easy, living at home as we were, to hide the signs of my derangement. Since the earlier stages were the most intense, it made sense to spend them away from Trees. The later stages would be less conspicuous. On the other hand, it would be an inefficient way to make use of our time away from home if we waited to be out of the house before starting things off. So it was agreed that I should take the pill after breakfast. Half-pill, rather. We had decided on the basis of my body weight that a half would be plenty. Peter was confident that he would be able to read the signs of the drug taking effect, and would whisk me away before my behaviour made it obvious to the untrained observer.

Peter hustled me into the Tan-Sad and had me out of the house in ten minutes flat. I didn't know what signals I had given off, and was rather startled. Apparently I had been making the shapes of words but not saying them, even when Mum wasn't nearby. I wasn't convinced that there was anything so very odd about this, and Peter himself had noticed that Mum could every now and then (less as we got older) work out exactly what we were thinking.

Still, it did no harm to be careful, and there was some watery sunshine. The place Peter had chosen was next to a pond near a sort of miniature weir, but well away from home and also Mrs Adcock's. While we were on the move I experienced a certain amount of peripheral swirling, but when I was installed by the pond nothing seemed changed. Of course the picture-postcard prettiness which Bourne End possessed in such large measure is always an unstable quality. There's always a bit of the postcard that seems to show where a body has been buried with a bone sticking out. After a while I said, 'That's a pound down the drain, Peter. I honestly think it was a dud. People are such twisters . . .'

Peter wasn't so sure, but he was getting a little bit bored and he wanted to go and buy a bag of sweets from Mr White's. I said I'd be fine.

The ducks on the pond were very talkative that day. One in particular kept making very meaningful quacks. I quacked back – but then I always do. Seconds later everything had changed and I was in the middle of a distinctly tetchy conversation. I was speaking Duck! An instant later, I was corrected. I was speaking Drake. The languages diverge in the matter of verbs, with females using entirely different forms.

What I was being told was that stale bread was a very poor food for any bird. I was being given instructions for wrapping up worms in leaves and tying them securely with knots of grass. I was trying to explain that this level of preparation was beyond me when a hand came round from behind the Tan-Sad and clamped down on my mouth.

I thought I was being kidnapped. I could almost smell the chloroform. Of course it was only Peter, back from Mr White's with his sweets, trying to stop me from quacking at the top of my voice.

I calmed down then, and realised that the mescaline had come on very strongly. I made an effort to relax, and waited for the optical effects to die down. There was a sort of shimmer sweeping back and forward, an effect of tessellation as if small units were trying to assemble themselves into bigger ones, and sometimes the sunshine made everything unbearably spangly. Then as I tried to tune in to the deeper patterns of creation the distractions died away.

I tried to focus on Mescalito, the spiritual embodiment of the mescal plant (*Lophophora williamsii*). I don't know if it was Mescalito – I assume so – but the god came out of a tree and started saying, 'If you want to prove yourself, I have some friends here who I can't do any more for. They need help with some simple things, answers to basic questions. How to carry on. Will you help them?' I said I would, honoured to be trusted with such a responsibility.

I could communicate with the god's friends at once, though perhaps not entirely in language. The first one I spoke to was called Sally – but then it turned out that they all were. She was very agitated, but I managed to calm her down. I had to explain about grafting and propagation, and there wasn't much time. These creatures, whatever they were, needed help to reproduce, though it wasn't clear that childbirth was involved. I saw four or five generations come into existence, and the elders die. Over time I was venerated for the help I brought and after four hundred years they wove me a crown of wisdom.

My awareness changed character when Peter started to push the Tan-Sad again. It was getting cold, and he had covered me up with his windcheater. It was time to go home.

Back at Trees Peter carried out the really clever part of our plan, borrowing a record of Mum's and putting it on the old player we had in our room (when Audrey didn't borrow it, that is). I lay there peacefully as the music turned to sculptures of perfume in my head, sifting through the events of the day.

My mind received in drips what would have swamped it at a greater rate of flow. I understood now who the Sallys or Sallies were. There were personifications of the willow, also known as the sallow or salley (I knew a Yeats poem about the Salley Gardens) – in fact the weeping willows round the pond where I had been reclining in porous rapture that day. *Salix sepulcralis.*

Why those particular willows should have difficulty propagating themselves I didn't know, since under normal circumstances they take root readily from cuttings and indeed anywhere that broken branches lie on the ground. But there it was. Mescalito had been concerned for them. It suddenly struck me as wonderful that the cactus god should reach out in fellow feeling to the willow, despite the remoteness of their families and the huge disparity of habitat.

I had a sense of the willow as a somehow œcumenical tree, contributing impartially to conventional and alternative medicine. The sap is heavily charged with the salicylic acid which gives us aspirin, grand-daddy of the non-steroidal anti-inflammatory. But why would anyone seek a remedy for colds and fevers in the willow to start with? Because it grew, as was symbolically appropriate, in cool damp places. That was before the two branches of medicine separated, and started to pretend that they didn't share a root.

Peter had left the record sleeve propped up where I could see it. The photograph showed water in movement over a riverbed of large stones. The music expressed a serene turbulence of its own, if I'm any judge of these things. Moura Lympany playing Rachmaninoff's Second Piano Concerto. Nicolai Malko waving his willow wand in front of the Philharmonia Orchestra.

It was our idea that classical music and illegal drugs couldn't both be present in the same room, at least in Mum's view of the world, and so that Rachmaninoff would wash all suspicion away. An inspired notion, as long as it didn't catch on too widely and become discredited. *Dear Marje, I'm at my wits' end about my teenaged son. He's started listening to Beethoven. Is he taking drugs?*

The soloist's name was a magic spell in its own right, whether I was in my right mind or the righter one brought on by the drug. Moura Lympany. Those syllables struck my mental membranes with the rippled impacts of liquid timpani.

Over time I had to modify my ideas about the drug I had ingested. It was a matter of simple mathematics. It would have needed 500 milligrams or so of the active ingredient of *Lophophora williamsii* to deliver the organic version of such an experience. It would have been a substantial tablet, and not the little pill I had bought, which must therefore have been LSD. I had a moment of hallucinated insight, connecting the synthesising of salicylic acid in 1897 by Felix Hoffmann with the synthesising of lysergic acid by Albert Hoffmann in 1943. Might not the Hoffmanns be father and son? Well, no they couldn't, since in reality Albert's surname has only the one *n*. I was reluctant to leave the domain of the drug, where everything links up and nothing is superfluous, nothing dangles.

It wasn't sensible to regret my change of subject. The results from my Part I exams had told their own story: a First for my German oral, an Upper Second for my spoken Spanish. A Lower Second overall. Reading Modern Languages had indeed been a lost cause, while reading English was merely a losing battle. Even my strengths (as I saw them) did me no good. An American lecturer came to lead a seminar on Thomas Mann, which I attended. The professor made a meal of the last sentence of Mann's story *Mario and the Magician*, saying it was a wonderful ending and the key to the meaning of the whole. Fine, but make sure you're using an accurate translation. The last sentence in German contains the clause 'ich konnte und kann nicht umhin', meaning 'I can't think otherwise', or simply 'I have to agree'. The translation on which the prof was placing so much weight said the opposite – 'I don't think so', or something of the sort.

I put up my hand to explain that the translation was defective, and the prof just said again, 'Such a wonderful ending.'

'It can't mean what you want it to mean. It's not possible in the German.'

'Uh-huh,' was the best he could manage at short notice. Then he re-grouped his forces and said, 'Literature can accommodate any amount of ambiguity. That's a great thing. We must agree to disagree. There's no dishonour in that. And I thank you for your contribution.'

Deputising for the tide

We didn't agree to disagree. We disagreed about our disagree-ment. Ambiguity is one thing, ignorance is another. He couldn't admit to being wrong on the facts of language. He was reduced to pretending that his interpretation could overrule the text, and there was dishonour in that. When he said, 'Thank you for your contribu-tion,' it was another twisting of language, this time of the English language (so he had fewer excuses). What he meant was closer to 'Piss off, you little wretch, and next time you have a bright idea keep it to yourself.'

I was rather disillusioned about the way the academic world worked. I was naïve. Small boys don't enjoy it when their sandcastles are swept away by the tide, particularly when an even smaller boy deputises for the tide, on his first day at the beach.

Not everything in the English department was so uninspiring. I attended some of Muriel Bradbrook's lectures on Ibsen. She was the Mistress of Girton who had wanted to protect her charges, if not from sex then at least from its repetition, by locking the doors at ten o'clock. As a lecturer she insisted that we couldn't understand the plays unless we understood the geography of Norway. She would rather we looked at pictures of fjords than volumes of criticism.

I found this exhilarating, until I started to think it was just another version of what I had heard in the Faculty of Modern (and Mediaeval) Languages. Nothing short of total immersion is any good.

One German word which had the power to reproach me was a fash-ionable one in English at the time, *gestalt*. All I had in the way of a life was a series of interlocking routines – bedder, Hall, lectures, yoghurt manufacture – with none of the feeling of an organic whole. My summer enlightenment had faded like a tan.

Perhaps I had as strong a claim as anyone to the word *gestalt*, since I at least knew its derivation from the Old High German *stellen*, meaning (to locate the core of a cluster of ideas) to shape. My life had no controlling shape.

Still, there were pockets in my week that gave me pleasure and some small sense of belonging. I had got into the habit, for instance, of drinking a half-pint of beer at the Cambridge Arms on a fairly regular basis. Perhaps as often as twice a week. It was my first experiment in having a 'local', a step on the way to the stranger state of actually being a local. The Cambridge Arms, on King Street, was pleasantly nondescript. The public bar at least didn't attract much of a university crowd. King Street itself was modest, not exactly a back street but mainly used by university people as a short cut, or for sheer relief when the glory of the colleges became too much to bear.

Adjusting my bow tie

The public bar of the Cambridge Arms had the advantage, from my point of view, of an outstandingly friendly and coöperative Australian barman. He was called Kerry Bashford, and after a while we evolved a routine. I would park outside and sound the horn in my trademark pattern, the series of blasts which spelled out *Om Mane Padme Om*, and Kerry would come out and help me get into the wheelchair, after lifting it out of the boot of the car. He lifted the chair one-handed, swinging it in an effortless arc. He was quite unselfconscious about his strength and the grace it produced. I liked the fact that he didn't suddenly freeze up with the realisation that he could do such a lot with his body that I couldn't. Why is it supposed to please me when people hunch their shoulders to atone for being tall, or restrict their movements to apologise for being flexible? There's nothing wrong with enjoying your body. I would if I could. I do when I can. It's much easier to see that the body is an illusion if you've actually spent some time there.

Kerry always insisted on fitting the wheelchair with its footplates. I didn't usually bother asking people to do this – say what you like about ankylosed joints, but at least they don't need support. There was something motherly about Kerry's attention to detail in this, as if he wanted me to be turned out at my best, the equivalent in wheel-chair terms of adjusting my bow tie.

Kerry was a Jehovah's Witness from Newcastle, New South Wales. My first tame Jehovah's Witness, though he'd more or less grown out of that strange faith. He had fair skin and a big broad face, with a scrawny beard more or less holding the whole unstable *gestalt* togeth-er. He told me of a time when he'd gone to an open-air pop concert back home and been so sunburned he went a sort of purple. To finance his European adventure he had worked on a gang repairing railway track. His was the sort of skin that will never take a tan, wrapped round an antipodean boy slow to take the hint that peeling is not how epithelial cells say Thank you, we enjoyed that.

Kerry would always be reading *Howards End* out of sight behind the bar, but he wasn't exactly spoiling for literary chat. If I asked whether he was enjoying the book, he'd just say, 'Bloke can write,' sometimes with neutral appreciation, sometimes dogmatically. Once he even struck the closed book lightly with his fist, but the verdict was always the same. Bloke can write. He wouldn't be coaxed into detail. He'd said all he had to say.

Kerry was very good at anticipating my needs without making me feel like part of a social worker's caseload. Even on my first visit he didn't need to be told that I needed my half of Abbot in a glass with a stem or a handle. Not a straight glass which calls for a capacious fist.

On subsequent visits he came up with the game of giving me a free half of Abbot on the basis that I was required to declare it fit for drinking. I would take a slow suspicious sniff of the bouquet of esters, then a small sip, which I swilled around my mouth. I pushed my lips forward like someone trying to kiss himself on each cheek in turn. Then I would pass judgement, as if I was an itinerant palate retained by Greene King to check on the standard of their products, a roving taster. There are worse jobs.

The real-ale movement was in its cradle in those days, but it was possible to pick up a few technical terms and use them knowingly. I would praise the maltiness and depth of the brew, but wonder politely if the original gravity of this batch was really the stipulated 1048.

Gaining confidence, I would announce that I could detect the cannabinoids in the brew, explaining that hops are after all members of the lovely hemp family, the cannabinaceæ.

Playing to the balcony to some extent, I might point out that cannabinoids were not illegal as such, the legal maximum for possession being twenty microgrammes. This enlightened legislation was to protect real ales, and it showed admirable consideration on the part of the Government.

Perhaps Kerry and I were flirting with each other in some way. It isn't always easy to tell. Usually we respected each other's boundaries, though one day he surprised me by asking if I had a spare key for the car. I agreed that I had, and he asked me to bring it along on my next visit and lend it to him for a few days. I agreed, but I must have looked unhappy because he said, 'Relax, mate – no offence, but if I was going to swipe a car I'd swipe a nice one.' The next time I saw him he gave the keys back, but with a difference. Now there was a sort of amateurish welded flange extending the body of the key sideways by a couple of inches.

I was very touched. Kerry had seen that it was difficult for me to turn the key in the lock, and had made modifications for my benefit. Over the years lots of people had seen me struggling with the car keys, but he had actually done something about it. Many had observed but only one had undertaken an empathetic metalwork project.

Then early one evening, one spring Monday, the whole modest idyll unravelled. Half-way through the half-pint that I had (after much ritual gargling) pronounced fit for drinking, I became aware that the pub was getting crowded. It began to smell much more like a pub, as if a huge disembodied tongue of beer-breath and ashtrays was lapping our faces. A bunch of students had come in, animated though not quite rowdy. They were all talking at once, but I didn't take too much notice of that. In any university town there are more talkers than listeners.

Alcohol the pickpocket

One of them plonked himself on the other side of my table, and then set a pint glass in front of me with a crash. 'We've ordered one too many . . .' he said. 'You have it.' His face was flushed and there was something not right about his eyes. He had trouble focusing. His hair was dark, but his skin was almost eerily pale and shiny. Like the others, he was wearing a scarf, in fact they all wore the same scarf, but I didn't pay much attention to their tribal insignia. Their tweed sports jackets were enough to make them stand out in the public bar of the Cambridge Arms.

I tried to say that I didn't need any more beer, since my small body weight made half a pint a sufficiently intoxicating dose for one session – and I wouldn't be able to lift such an awkward glass to my lips in any case. The newcomer didn't seem to be listening, though, so I stopped trying. I shot a glance over to Kerry at the bar. He was picking the appropriate coins from the helpless thrust-out hands of one of the recent invaders. Alcohol is a compulsive pickpocket, and from these lads it had already filched arithmetic, or else the ability to recognise the coins of the realm.

The man at my table took a huge gulp of his beer and frowned. 'Haven't seen you on the river . . . perhaps you're not a wet-bob?' To this day I don't know the meaning and derivation of *wet-bob*. It may have been a specialised Cambridge word, but not one that was used in my little circles. 'With your build you'd make a decent cox.' My jaw has a certain amount of mobility, though dentists are always complaining, and I'm sure it dropped. It must have. He called out, 'Benny! Come here! I've found us a cox!'

Benny turned out to be the helpless payer at the bar. He wore his hair in a centre parting. Choose this style and you are more or less insisting that spectators assess your degree of facial symmetry. Barely one face in a thousand is regular enough to pass such a test – this wasn't one of the privileged few. As he came over, he was bellowing, 'Two and tenpence a pint, Wop! Not a bad price!' He was still thinking in shillings and pence, after more than a year of decimal currency. Perhaps the new system would always elude this group.

Benny slammed his glass down onto the table with even more force than his friend had, following it with a packet of cigarettes. The general level of noise was becoming hard to bear. He thrust his face into mine. 'Is this your cox, Wop? I'm not sure he's got the lungs for it. Give us a sample, why don't you? Sing out STROKE . . . STROKE! . . .

STROKE!!' I begin to detect a whisper of sense under all the bellowing. In rowing, wasn't the cox the compact lightweight person who sat at the end of the boat and shouted? So I was clearly in no possible sense a cox.

I didn't sing out as directed. I made my position clear. Actually I was having a quiet drink. For all the notice they took I needn't have gone to the trouble of speaking aloud. The one called Benny took from his pocket a stopwatch on a loop of dirty string and hung it around my neck. 'Now you've got the tools of the trade at least. But you need to work on the voice projection or no one will hear a bloody word you're saying.'

Then it was the other's turn to speak. 'Perhaps we should introduce you to your eight. But first, what's your name? John? Very good, but we'll mostly call you Cox. This is Benny – Benny the Dick. Christened Benedict, hence Benny the Dictator.' He put on an ingratiating ecclesiastical singsong. *'Benedicite benedicatur, Benny's a benevolent dictator.'*

This was a baffling change of gears. Might they be a gang of rogue classicists on the razzle? 'And I'm Thomas da Silva, known as Wop on account of my dago name, at your service. Delighted.' I wasn't delighted but dismayed. They weren't at my service, in fact I seemed to be at theirs.

'Have you explained the rules to your man, Wop?'

'No Benny, I thought you'd like to do that.'

'Fine.' He took a cigarette from the packet on the table, but instead of smoking it he tucked it horizontally under his nose, holding it in place by curling his lip upwards in a way that suggested hours of practice. Then he started to rattle off information at amazing speed. The restrictions placed on his vocal apparatus by the prehensile-lip trick made him sound like what Dad would have called a silly ass, giving the noun a long vowel as service protocol demanded.

'The King Street Run. Classic university tradition. Bit of fun. Separates boys from girls, boys from men, sheep from goats, your top Wop from the regular dagoes. Basic idea: eight pubs, eight pints. Easy as pissing off a log. Refinement: time limit. Eight pubs, eight pints – in an hour. Rate of one pint every seven minutes and thirty seconds. I know – sounds easy. Reward: special tie, respect of peers

599

and inferiors. Complication: eight separate pubs, so journey time to be factored in. Seven journeys of, say, two minutes each – fourteen minutes in all. Leaving in fact . . . forty-six for drinking proper. Eights into forty-six: no idea. Five and a bit, maybe. Hence importance of stopwatch. Your department.' Effortlessly he overrode my protests, my footling squawks.

'Further complication: peeing forbidden during event. Penalty: letter P embroidered on trophy tie. Humiliation. One chap went to the other extreme, peed almost continuously, tie almost invisible beneath embroidered Ps, comic effect. Great success. Sort of trick only works once.' I suppose he was doing a compound *Monty Python* impersonation, combining every mad major and silly-walks minister from that programme. With my lack of up-to-date television awareness I thought of the *Pickwick Papers*.

As I watched Benedict's little act, my own upper lip curled spontaneously upwards. It's possible I looked mildly demented. Then he gave a sharp upward nod which dislodged the cigarette. He caught it smoothly in his mouth and lit it.

'Don't worry, we're only doing a practice run today. Peeing permitted.' I was glad of that, since the half-pint of Abbot had run swiftly through my system and was now anxious to move on.

A citizen's arrest had already taken place

I watched his smoking style admiringly. Benedict caught my eye, smiled, and then ran the lighted tip of his cigarette, with agonising slowness, across the palm of his hand, just where it met the bottom of his fingers. He never stopped smiling. Then he winked at me.

Thomas da Silva leant towards me and breathed admiringly, 'Benny has the hardest calluses on the river. Isn't he remarkable?' No doubt, but this was not a party trick I coveted.

'To be frank,' Benedict went on, 'we've done a certain amount of practice in private before this dummy run. Don't expect too much from us. We're not after a record time.' He lifted the stopwatch from my chest and took a look at it. '*Tempus fuckit*, men! Time to go!' He left the watch where it was, though, around my neck. He seemed to have forgotten it.

Thomas da Silva had finished his pint and now pointed a finger at mine, which of course I hadn't touched. 'Have you finished with that, old man?' I nodded and he picked it up. 'You're sure?' He drank it in one long gulp while Benny looked on admiringly. 'Our secret weapon,' he said proudly.

'Don't forget your stopwatch,' I said. 'How do you mean?' he said. Then they were off.

We were off, rather. Of course they hadn't forgotten the stopwatch. They hadn't left anything behind. They were taking the stopwatch (and me) with them. I barely managed to grab the crutch and the cane.

'You chose the cox, Wop,' said Benedict. 'You can drive him.'

Thomas da Silva wasn't in a fit state to drive anything. He was young and strong and clueless, 'unsafe at any speed' as a famous book title of the time put it. He was topping up his bloodstream with alcohol faster than a dozen livers plumbed in parallel could have hoped to clear it. He pulled the wheelchair roughly free of the pub's furniture and charged the door with it.

From behind me came a muffled cry of 'Oi! What the hell are you doing?' Kerry was registering a protest. But what could he do – leave his post at the bar to give chase? Make a citizen's arrest of the whole bladdered squad? A citizen's arrest had already taken place on those premises, and I was the party apprehended.

Pushing a wheelchair isn't much of a knack – say I, who have never done it – but it does require two things that Thomas was past managing. One: coördination. Two: attentiveness to the mental state of the passenger. Within seconds of propelling me on to the street, he gave the wheelchair a wild turn and came within an inch of ramming my car with my ankylosed feet. Mine! My car! My car as well as my feet.

Though there were footplates on the chair for once, my feet projected beyond them, and my own bodywork would have sustained as much damage as the Mini's panels. I shouted out 'That's my car!', but already Thomas was bouncing me at speed down King Street. He pressed down on the handles, with the result that the small front wheels reared up, and I reared up with them. Not for the first time, I thought of Luke Squires's wheelchair at Vulcan, and the great advantages of having the small wheels at the back. From Thomas da Silva's point of view, our progress may only have been a disorderly trot. From mine it was a boneshaking slalom.

When we came to the next pub – I never saw its name – Thomas da Silva would have used me as a battering ram on the door if I hadn't screamed to alert him. He seemed to think that every pub door in Cambridge, however solidly built and firmly closed, was actually one of those hinged-slat arrangements you see in saloons in Westerns. He was in a Wild West of the mind, striding towards the high noon of alcoholic meltdown, but it was my feet that would have bitten the dust if he had gone through with his original plan. My hips had been operated on, but my knees still had no play in them, so my feet led the whole demented parade. They had no choice. There was nowhere I could stow them out of harm's reach. It wasn't much of a help that I had managed to grab the crutch and the cane. There was no point in me using them to guard my feet. In the event of an impact they would simply be rammed into my upper body.

Write Off Tuesday

Luckily the rest of the disordered group caught up with us, and Benedict opened the pub door courteously enough to admit the wheelchair. Of the group he was the one who still seemed on speaking terms with his wits. I decided it was him I must cajole and address if I had any hope of release.

The air in the new pub was sour. Emptying the ashtrays was clearly a chore that was left till after closing time. It was more crowded, and our erratic group ended up being crushed in a corner. I cringed as Thomas pushed me across the space, cheerfully calling out, 'Mind your backs!' The tables didn't sit true, so that when Benedict plonked a fresh round of monstrous pints in front of me, beer slopped over and dripped onto my lap. There would only have been a few drops if I had been able to get out of the way, but I had to sit there while the rest of the little puddle followed at its leisure. Even a fair-minded person glancing at my trouser-front would assume I had lost control of my bladder.

I tried a sidelong whisper at the member of the group who seemed marginally the most trustworthy. '*Benedict . . . ?*'

'Yes, Mr Cox.'

'Who are you? I mean, who are you, as a group?'

'We're Write Off Tuesday.'

'And Write Off Tuesday is what?'

'All the splendid intellectual specimens you see around you. A total of eight.'

'Aren't you seven?'

'Really? Then we've lost one. Explains why there keeps on being one pint left over. Not that Wop minds. He'll always tidy up. He's good that way. Tidy boy.'

'Yes, but who are you all? What is the nature of your group?'

'Well, we were recently described, by the Master of Peterhouse no less, as a right-wing think-tank . . .' I knew just enough about politics to understand that this was quite an accolade. In any assessment of academic figures at the time the Master of Peterhouse would rank as an exemplary figure, a reactionary's reactionary. Then Benedict seemed to reconsider, almost going cross-eyed from the effort of dredging up the memory, and corrected himself: 'Hold on. Not a think-tank . . . a right-wing *drink*-tank.'

'And what does it mean, to "write off" a day of the week?'

'You skip it altogether. You make sure it leaves no trace on the memory. Don't you agree that Tuesday is an inherently boring day?'

I thought I had found a flaw in his argument, and asked as gently as I could, 'You do know today is Monday?'

'Yes. Another culpably drab day.'

'So you're writing off Monday?'

'No, my dear Cox, you've missed the point completely. Try to pay attention. It's all to do with preparation. Preparation is the key. To write off Tuesday effectively you have to start the day before. If Monday is properly squashed Tuesday doesn't even begin.'

'I see.' By this time Thomas da Silva had moved off, perhaps to visit the Gents – a place I myself needed to visit – so I was able to concentrate hypnotically on Benedict. 'Would you mind moving that ashtray away from me? The smell makes me feel rather sick.' It seemed to make sense to impose my will on him in small matters before brokering my separation from the group, just as a conjuror will make coins disappear before tackling doves or elephants.

'Of course, old fellow, old boy, old man, cox of the good ship Write Off Tuesday.' The hypnotic experiment was successful as far as it went, but it didn't go far. Yes, Benedict moved the ashtray away from me, then the next moment he took a cigarette from his packet, lit it up and moved the ashtray smoothly back into range, without giving it a thought.

It was time to change up a gear, in terms of the hypnotic mechanism. 'Would you be kind enough to take me for a pee? I can't manage on my own.'

'Can't you? What a pisser that must be! Very bad luck. Of course I'll lend a hand.' I tried to hold his eyes steady by fixing them with mine, but they kept slipping sideways. I felt as if I was losing my touch. He made no move to get up. Then, just as I was getting a grip on his eyes with mine, Thomas came back from the Gents. He shouted out, 'Cox! What time for this leg?' I told him I had no idea and he laughed wildly, saying, 'You're a write-off as timekeeper, Cox, which makes you perfect for the job!' He grabbed the handles of the wheelchair. We seemed to be off again. I hissed at Benedict, 'Can't you push me? Thomas isn't exactly in charge of his faculties.'

'Of course he's not! That's the whole point. Haven't you been listening? Wop, are you going to be especially careful with our cox here?'

'Of course I am.'

Of course he was not. As we left the pub, Thomas da Silva was shouting, 'Those ties are as good as ours. In the bag! Hardly a challenge for drinkers of our stature.'

Benedict sounded a marginally adult, cautionary note.

'Men, we must avoid at all costs pre-incubatory gallinumeration.'

'Yes, Benny, we know,' replied Thomas da Silva. '*Hatching cunts* . . . I beg your pardon, *Counting chickens before they're hatched.*'

'Exactly so.' The rogue-classicists theory was gaining ground in my mind.

As we turned towards the next pub, Thomas manœuvred the wheelchair – I assume by accident – so that one wheel was in the road while the other remained on the pavement. Then he started to push me at great speed in that precarious position, with the wheelchair straddling the kerb. If the footplates hadn't been on, thanks to Kerry, my feet would have been receiving the savage scraping in their place.

604

As it was, there was a tremendous noise of metal in agony, and I'm sure there was a fine display of sparks for the benefit of the people behind.

A titillating cloud

I closed my eyes and tried to recite *Om Mane Padme Om* in my deepest interior spaces. It seemed such a long time since I had sounded the mini's horn in that mantric rhythm to summon Kerry Bashford. My rickety old mantra was supposed to act as a brake on my engagement with spurious reality, or at least a clutch to disconnect me from the apparent impulses of the world. Now it was acting as an accelerator if anything, intensifying my mundane feelings of anxiety and alarm. Om-Mane-Padme-Om, OM-MANE-PADME-OM . . . OM-MANE-OH MY GOD! . . . What happens if Thomas notices the way the wheelchair is tilted and tries to put things right without stopping? I'll be pitched out of the wheelchair, that's what, old Uncle Tom Mantra and all.

My nose registered at one point that we were passing the coffee shop (in fact The Coffee Shop) on King Street. The caffeinated aroma hung around like a titillating cloud. I concentrated on the traces of a drug which seemed entirely benign compared with alcohol, in whose stupefying distortions I was so hopelessly embroiled. Like many another student in those years, I had met coffee-lovers of both the jug and filter factions, devotees of both Java and exorbitant Blue Mountain. My own favourite was Kenya Peaberry. Even the name was satisfying. It had a leguminous twang. In those years the caffeine god made at least as many converts as the marijuana god.

Then we were past the coffee shop and the vivifying aroma disappeared. I had nothing to cling to but the shreds of my mantra. I couldn't reach the armrests, to hold on to those. The stopwatch bumped painfully against my chest. At last I managed to grab it with one hand, to stop it knocking against my racing heart.

Exasperation is a rather junior emotion, a secondary impulse, but even so it is possible to feel it on a vast scale. That was what was happening with me at this point. I wasn't a child. I was a grown-up. I was of drinking age. As it happened, I even wanted to be in a pub. But I wanted to be in the pub of my choice, the Cambridge Arms, not a

sordid den chosen by cretinous carousers. I was a consenting adult – I
could even have relations with my own sex under certain conditions.
I did not consent to having my day written off by dipsomaniac louts,
however steeped in the classical languages. What made these clods
think they could override my wishes?

The fact that they could. The fact that they had.

There were shouts behind us, and a yelping sound nearer home,
which turned out to come from my own throat. We had nearly over-
shot the next pub on the via dolorosa of the King Street Run. At least
the rest of the party mucked in to rescue the wheelchair from its unstable footing, though so many hands pressing down on the handles
made it buck like a rearing horse. I couldn't hang on to anything. I
just clenched my teeth, so hard that I thought I must be shedding
flakes of enamel.

I have no memories of the next pub we visited. That's not exactly
a failure of memory, more a refusal to register anything in the first
place. I closed my eyes before we entered the place, and I kept them
shut. This was my shot at passive resistance to the absurd caravan that
had swept me up into its pilgrimage of intoxication. I couldn't veto
the proceedings, I couldn't even register a protest vote. All I could
do was abstain. Of course I wasn't paying a special tribute to Gandhi
– all my resistance is passive. All I have is my small No. No to pilchards, No to Billy Graham. No to Write Off Tuesday.

I kept my eyes closed and took no part in conversation, if the mass
of cross-purpose non-sequiturs endlessly being repeated around me
could count as conversation. Since no one was willing to take me to
the toilet, I concentrated my mental powers on reversing the normal
renal function, so that urine was driven back into the kidneys which
had distilled it, and then back into the bloodstream. Better poisoned
blood than soaked trouser. There was a jukebox in this pub. A vintage
song was playing. 'All Right Now'. By Free. Perhaps that was a good
omen. Free *right now*. But when does Maya ever play fair?

There was the usual interminable routine of getting beers. From
the muffled thud at close quarters I could deduce that once again
I had been included in the round. Beer I didn't want in a glass I
couldn't lift. Then Thomas da Silva and Benedict sat down, one on
each side of me.

'Cox? Cox?'

'What's his name? His actual name?'

'Never caught it, Benny.'

'Do you think he's asleep?'

'Might be faking.'

'Why?'

'To get out of buying a round?'

'Don't judge him by your own low standards, Wop. I think he's really asleep.'

'Maybe the poor little chap can't hold his drink. Maybe that's it. We should wake him up. COX! COX!! What a terrible thing to have to live with. Imagine not being able to hold your drink! Another thing, Benny. Have you noticed? There's something not quite right with his legs. It's more than just being small.'

'Car crash?'

'I expect so. Hurt his arms too, poor bugger.'

'I'm not sure we should wake him. Maybe he's better off as he is.'

'Don't be stupid. We have a certain responsibility here.' This was Thomas da Silva talking – my abductor-in-chief.

'Nothing'll happen to him if we just leave him be. Someone will look after him.'

'We can't take that chance. And how will he feel if he wakes up and finds we've abandoned him? We don't want to perform auto-prosopectomy thingummy . . . sorry, vocab all gone. It's all Etruscan to me . . . Don't want to cut off our nose to spite our face.'

Give the man his dignity

'Good point. He wouldn't want to miss being there when we cross the finishing line. In fact . . . do you think we could apply for him to do the Run with us, on the actual day, and get a proper tie on half-pints? Maybe a half-sized tie. Seeing as he's so small?'

'Dunno. It's always a pint for him, isn't it? I suppose he doesn't want to get special treatment. Give the man his dignity, Benny. Leave him some pride. Let him make his own choices.'

'No, think about it, Wop. This is serious. You and I weigh, what, fourteen and a half stone the day of a regatta? Fifteen stone the next

607

day, obviously . . .' These figures seemed fantastic. Is it possible for hefty but not freakish-looking youths to weigh so much, or were they joking? 'And Cox is going to weigh no more than, what, two stone?'

'*Two stone?* Are you sure? He has to be heavier than that!'

'All right, three at the outside. Call it three. So for every pint we drink he can drink . . . a lot less. Try it the other way round. For every pints *he* drinks, we can drink, what, ten? Five, anyway. We can't let him go on drinking pints just to keep up with us. He's going to kill himself. He may be in a coma already.'

Then they were both shaking me and roaring 'COX! COX!' There was nothing much I could do but open bleary eyes before their shaking became too painful on my shoulders. Then we were off to the final stages of the King Street Run.

Pubs that hosted the early pints of the Run might be reasonably grateful for the custom involved. Pubs towards the end of King Street, and the Run, had drawn short straws. They might value Varsity trade, but not the sort represented by Write Off Tuesday, sozzled and more than likely to puke. There were no longer a full eight pubs on King Street, so the Zebra, round the corner on Maids Causeway, had been requisitioned for the last two pints. Its publican was less than thrilled.

He intercepted us. He was a large, imposing man, wearing a V-necked pullover with a shirt and tie underneath it. The voice that emerged from his large neck was soft and deep, perfectly friendly but not to be trifled with. 'Are you on a bender, lads? Some sort of competition? If so I don't want your business. I don't want your mess. I've seen enough sick at this address. If you throw up I'll give you a mop, but that's my limit.'

The assembled members of Write Off Tuesday tried to head off resistance with a synchronised display of undergraduate arrogance. They didn't do a bad job, considering. They squared their shoulders and drew on surprising reserves of physical control. Benny said, 'By no means, landlord.' He indicated me. 'Our handicapped friend here requires a pint of your best bitter. We will keep him company out of good manners, but we are hardly in any sort of competition.' This I suppose was strictly true, if the whole appalling expedition was a rehearsal. And they weren't in competition with me.

I wondered, after what had been said in the last pub, when it was that Benny had noticed that I was disabled. Perhaps it was a wild guess, a piece of pure bluff. It was just my luck that this new insight gained us admission to yet another pub. The landlord hesitated, then stepped aside. 'Just one pint, mind.'

Perhaps trade was bad enough for him to fear being put on a black-list. Certainly there were fewer than a dozen drinkers present. Unless placated, I might put the word out on the disabled grapevine that these were premises which could usefully be fire-bombed come the next Day of Action.

I clung to the idea, despite everything that had happened, that given time I would be able to impose my will on my kidnappers. All I needed was a quiet moment to get the psychic electromagnets going and work my personality magic. But the quiet moment never came.

Any sobriety the group had been able to muster on their way into the pub soon deserted them once we were inside and had been served. Thomas da Silva's face was now by turns red and sweaty-white, at the mercy of the swilling beer inside him. Every few moments he would fill his cheeks with air and breathe out unhappily. He looked like someone with numbed lips trying to whistle. He whispered loudly to Benedict, 'We need to have two pints here, Benny. This is only pub number seven, and we need to tot up the full eight pints. It's the magic number. The full gallon, or no dice. No dice, no tie.'

Benedict shushed him. 'We'll have to play it by ear. Maybe if Cox orders the next round the landlord will oblige. I don't know why he's being so snot-nosed. With a shabby place like this you'd think he'd be grateful for the business.'

'About time Cox paid his whack anyway. I don't approve of free-loaders, do you?'

That was it. I could endure no longer. My small No was suddenly too big to be contained. They'd been going too far from the moment they had entered the Cambridge Arms, but now they were beyond the pale in absolute terms. I pitched my voice at a level that a cox would only need on a windy river with a flight of jet planes roaring overhead, and I bellowed, 'Shut up this instant! I NEED TO PEE!! *Right now!*'

'All right, little man, no need to shout,' said da Silva. 'You're quite right, though, we should attend to our cox. *Our cox!!*' Finally there it was, out in the open, the double meaning that had been hovering over the conversation for so long. He fought off an attack of the giggles. 'I could do with a bit of a slash myself.'

As he was clearly the most unstable of the group, I tried to head him off. 'Perhaps Benedict could oblige . . .?'

'He has better things to do, my lightweight friend. He has important cigarettes to buy.'

'I can wait.'

'I thought you couldn't. Isn't that what you were just saying?' He looked hurt. 'Don't you trust me?'

'Your driving can be a bit erratic, if you don't mind me saying so.'

'I've got the hang of your buggy now. I'm sure of it.'

I broadcast a general appeal. 'Anybody care to give me a hand to the Gents?' But Thomas da Silva had already grasped the handles, and we were off. The door to the Gents swung freely, or else it would have been agonising when he used my feet to push it open. I started panicking the moment I saw the wet floor of the Gents. A slippery floor is a death-trap in my book, much more so when I'm landed with an assistant who can hardly stand up himself.

Pure jets of desperation

'Do you mind if I go first?' he said. 'It turns out the need is rather urgent.' He unzipped his trousers without waiting for an answer. I gritted my teeth somehow as a fierce bolt of liquid escaped him, bouncing noisily against the porcelain of the urinal. 'I know, I know . . . not a good lookout for a tie with no Ps on it. But I expect it'll be all right on the night.'

The pressure of the urine-stream was so intense that like any other substantial fall of water it created a drifting veil of moisture, a fine mist which stung my eyes but cooled the backs of my hands. For a second I was transported back to the sea front at Bognor Regis, on a walk from Mr Johnson's Home, safe in the care of people who knew what they were doing.

I was so frantic to urinate myself that I had something close to an out-of-the-body experience. I felt I could see myself from above thrashing miserably about in the wheelchair, flailing my arms through their limited arc like a defective clockwork toy, a drummer whose sticks have been taken away. My mundane bladder was churning, and suddenly my astral body leapt upwards. Normally this can only happen in unconsciousness, with the arrival of a dream of knowledge, but I soared above the body on pure jets of desperation.

Then Thomas da Silva finished his business and it was my turn. He came round to the front of the wheelchair, stooped and grabbed me. It's not a good lifting position. It squashes me, it's bad for the lifter's back, there's nothing to be said in its favour. I never allowed it in normal life, but then I had been not allowing things for almost an hour now without making the slightest impact on what is alleged to be reality. More frightening than being lifted in this way was the prospect of being dumped back in a chair that could easily roll backwards. There was some hope of a safe splashdown if I could at least get him to put the brakes on.

'Put the Brakes On, Please! . . . BRAKES! . . .BRAKES!!' I bellowed. I tried to pattern my intonation on the nurses at CRX, whose capitals and exclamation marks were palpable in their delivery.

Thomas da Silva didn't understand, or at least paid no attention. He lifted me roughly, agonisingly, by my armpits and yanked me towards him. There was a moment when his balance faltered, and the wheelchair (with the brakes disengaged) slid sharply backwards away from me. I had a limited choice: either to lean backwards, on the off-chance that the wheelchair, sentimental about our long association, would wait for me, or forward, into the grip of a tottering unmindful drunk. I leant forward with my full two or three stone (which at this stage of my life even Maya assessed at four-and-a-half), and Thomas fell backwards.

This was both a lucky and an unlucky fall, depending on who you were. If you were Thomas da Silva, unlucky, since he fell on his back (unable to break his fall with hands that were fully occupied with me), with his head unpleasantly close to the trough of the urinal. Lucky if you were me, since I landed on top of him. Otherwise I could have been badly injured or even killed. It wouldn't have taken much to break my neck.

Landing on top of Thomas da Silva's stomach was like doing a belly-flop onto that fantasy item of the time, a water-bed. The pressurised liquid with which my landing-cushion was filled was beer, of course, and not water, but the same hydrostatic laws applied. We were both winded for the moment, so there was no interference from breathing. The liquid was driven out to the edges of the organism, then surged back rebounding.

My luck was about to change. Thomas took a slow rasping intake of breath, then his insides gave up its struggle to contain what in his folly he had taken in. He gave a groan, and the groan became torrential.

Obviously the jet of vomit didn't reach the wheelchair, far across the room, and slam it against the opposite wall. That was only the picture in my mind. Now I was experiencing something that was as far from my circumscribed reality as a water-bed. I was riding a roller-coaster. I didn't like it. I wanted to get off. Though Thomas politely turned his head away from me, I was perched on a set of abdominal muscles which were being trodden on by a huge internal foot, and the violence of the ejection, its muzzle velocity so to speak, was awe-inspiring. From my skewed point of view he was a geyser rather than a human being, a personified hydrant of swill.

I thought it would never stop, and then it did. He was sobbing with the effort of it. Otherwise there was silence, apart from the drip of cisterns refilling. My arms were hurting. I can't lie flat on my front, the joints don't permit it.

Up to this point the evening had been a disaster in every way, but now it became something worse. A disgrace. I urinated on Thomas da Silva. There was no element of retaliation involved. I wasn't saying, *You soil me, I soil you*. I just couldn't hold it in. For so long I had been engaged in a battle of wills with my bladder, while no one helped or listened. Now this body had its triumph and my bladder won. Thomas's vomit had sprayed far and wide, but he had been considerate enough to turn his head away from me. My released urine had nowhere to go but downwards, though capillary action ensured that the cloth of my trousers absorbed its fair share.

And to think I had been worried that the beer-drips on my trousers in the Cambridge Arms would make people think I had pissed myself!

Thomas didn't move while my bladder added the finishing touches to the tableau of degradation. It seemed highly likely that he had passed out. My mantra flowed more cleanly in my head now that the tempo of events had slowed.

The landlord came wearily into the toilet where the two of us were wallowing in the failure of our bodies to contain themselves. He asked, between his teeth, *'Gentlemen, may I have the telephone numbers of your tutors?'* Then he said, 'I thought I'd seen everything there was to see in these four fucking walls. But I was wrong about that, wasn't I, gentlemen?' The expletive was painful to listen to, since it seemed unhabitual.

A basset-hound with a secret sorrow

He picked me up from the stinking cushion that was Thomas da Silva and propped me competently against a wall. Unfortunately he didn't hand me my crutch and cane, which would have made me feel less helpless. Was it really likely that I would make a dash for it, if my utensils were left within reach?

The landlord looked from Thomas to me, directing his remarks in my direction, where they might have some effect. 'If you find you have somehow forgotten those telephone numbers, gentlemen, I'm sure your colleges will be happy to supply them.' He looked like a man who had come to a decision. To retire from the publican's dismal trade, perhaps, to sell at a loss or simply walk away. He looked like a basset-hound with a secret sorrow. His breathing was the very respiration of exasperated reproach. Then he stood up and walked out of the urinal. He left us to think about our shortcomings as human beings, though Thomas wasn't doing much thinking. It wasn't his style.

The landlord had done me a service by picking me up off the floor, but I was in a very awkward position. Leaning against a wall without crutch or cane I was as helpless as a beetle on its back. In fact I had time to think, as urine seeped downwards from my crotch, that even after his traumatic metamorphosis Gregor Samsa could have run rings round me.

It seemed that the other members of Write Off Tuesday, prudently treacherous, had disappeared. They weren't far behind Thomas in terms of drunkenness, but some profound wastrels' instinct must have enabled them to leave the premises while his vomit was still actually airborne. Benny had seemed to be the conscience of the group, but not every group has a conscience.

To my astonishment Thomas opened his eyes and got to his feet. I could have sworn he was in a coma. He didn't look at me, propped up against the wall as I was like a rank-smelling broom. He didn't look around him at all. His eyes were entirely blank, but there was a lurking awareness in there somewhere, and a furtive purpose. I swear that he *shook* the worst of the mess off himself, the ejecta and excreta. Like a dog, more or less, except that he bounced feebly on the balls of his feet to start the dislodging process. Perhaps rough tweed, the material of his sports jacket, is especially prized for this resistance to defilement. Then he lurched with grim concentration towards the door and left.

This was one more betrayal, of course. Leaving me in the hands of the enemy was as bad as abducting me in the first place, but I was fully compensated by the joy of being alone, however uncomfortable, ashamed and malodorous. The landlord might never be the president of my fan club, but he was certain to be better company than the polyglot hearties who had just absconded.

Even so, Thomas as he left reminded me sharply of Julian Robinson from Vulcan. There was no physical resemblance, and loyal Julian would never have walked out on anyone. But Thomas walked out with a tottering stiffness, as if he didn't trust what might happen if he allowed his knees to bend. It looked for all the world as if he was wearing calipers.

A plump trout on the scales

Left on my own in the squalor of the Zebra's toilet, I cheered myself up with memories of Julian. We had ended up as good friends in the school, to the point where we had pet names for each other. Despite my childish gloating over the superiority of my chemistry set (Fun With Gilbert) over his (Lotts for Tiny Tots), the human chemistry between us was good. Julian and John became Tooley and Tonny. We were sublimely innocent of the overtone of *tool*.

I don't know why we didn't go into the toilet cubicles, which were distinctly roomy, being designed to accommodate a wheelchair plus a person, but we didn't. Perhaps we relied on the sliding doors in the toilet block, which weren't lockable, to give our explorations the tension they lacked. Julian would lean against the wheelchair for balance and unzip himself, plonking his prize member onto the armrest like a fishmonger slapping a plump trout on the scales. I would squeeze it and prod it for a few minutes in the interests of science and then say, 'Now put it away. I've seen plenty.' Unresentfully Julian would return his parts to privacy.

Then we would discuss how best to leave the toilet block without arousing suspicion. This seemed to be a friendship rooted in fantasy, and our solution was a rather far-fetched one. We decided that the best alibi for our risky intimacy would be to stage a fight in the corridor. I'd say, 'Look here, I'd better knock you over when we're in the hall.' And he'd say, 'Good idea.' So I would steer the Wrigley so as to graze him, and he would cannon into the wall, shouting with outrage. Then I would cruise away at high speed, leaving him to shake his fist in my wake. I'd steam off as if I couldn't care less what happened to him. This routine became slick with much practice – you go that way and I'll go this – but I don't see that it can ever have fooled anyone. Nothing could be fishier, in fact, than these aggressive displays of indifference.

I was left, though, with a certain fondness for the atmosphere of urinals, which came in handy in the public lavatory of the Zebra pub. It can't have been long before the landlord came back. Self-pity had yet to become entrenched. He was carrying cloths and towels, and a hose, which he attached to a tap in the basin. He had his sleeves rolled up. He was wearing Wellington boots and an apron. Seeing that I was alone, he let out a disgusted sigh, but set to work on cleaning up as best he could. Sensibly he started with the wheelchair, whose wheels had been well sprayed by Thomas da Silva's own hose of second-hand beer. It wasn't as vile as it might have been. The vomit was really only beer, though tainted by digestion. Still, a little of that gastric-juice smell goes a long way.

I hoped he would come to me quickly, before I started sliding down the wall and had to scream for help.

'I wouldn't mind,' he said wearily, 'if this only happened once a

615

year, say. But these days hardly a month goes by without something like this. When I took on this place I was told all this drinking-club rubbish was dying out, but I've seen no sign. Aren't you all supposed to be smoking pot? Shouldn't you be on a demo?' It was soothing to be addressed in generational terms, to be treated as a standard aberration.

At last it was my turn. He dried the wheelchair off roughly and sat me in it. I thought he might be tempted to use the hose on me too, in the manner of riot police, but he changed over to cloths and warm water.

'I have to admit you're a novelty, though . . .' he said. There was a curious intimacy to those moments, intensified by the lack of eye contact. 'I thought I'd seen most of the gimmicks. There's a pack of toffs who do the Run on pints of champagne. The Pitt Club, they're called. Champagne makes a bit of a change from beer when it's puked up . . . but not as much as you'd think. Tell me, do you think this sort of thing happens a lot in, say, Ely? Do you think it happens at all? It's just I've had my eye on a pub there. Perhaps now's the time . . . Those lads aren't your friends, you know.'

At last I had my chance to explain. 'I know they're not my friends. That's what I've been trying to say the whole time. I've never met them before.'

He frowned as he went about his work. 'I see.' I found the deliberate tempo of his actions soothing. Most people who get that close to me are flustered and fidgety. All his movements had the buffered ease of a strong arm pulling pints. 'And because you've never met them before you obviously can't give me any of their names.'

He assumed I was subscribing to the Colditz code of old-style undergraduates in trouble in the town, who would volunteer only name, college and tutor's phone number, however gruelling the interrogation. Everyone knew that the police had little authority over university affairs, and couldn't even enter the colleges without permission. 'I hoped you weren't going to be so loyal. Loyal and stupid. What's your college, sir?'

'Downing.'

'But the missing gentlemen aren't from there?'

'Not that I know of. Never saw them before.'

616

He shrugged but didn't press the point. Nor did he make any comment about an idiosyncrasy of the way I dressed in those days. Having my laundry done and taking regular baths made the basics of hygiene simple in certain respects. I economised on others, because of the great awkwardness of dressing and undressing unaided. I solved the problem of vests by not wearing vests. I solved the problem of underpants by not wearing underpants. I solved the problem of socks by not wearing socks – since I walk relatively little, my shoes don't have much chance to rub. I had pared my costume down to shirt, trousers and shoes. In winter I didn't go out much.

432,000 years in the dark

'Did they shout out *"Dead ants!"* every now and then? And then lie flat on the floor?'

'No, that's about the only thing they didn't do. What would that mean?'

'Fitzwilliam. Never mind.' His manner had a cosy gloom to it, as if he was an undertaker from a family firm. 'Look, I haven't any clothes for you to change into. You're about three times too small. Best I can do is wipe you up, then stuff some toilet paper into your trousers to keep you dry.'

'That seems more than fair, landlord.'

'Don't call me that. Arthur Burgess. Call me Arthur. Is that enough toilet paper?'

'Yes, thank you. Arthur. I think it is. By the way, I don't want anything to do with that stopwatch' – whose case he had wiped, whose string he had rinsed – 'please keep it.' What did I want with a stopwatch? As Hindus know, we're in the depths of the Dark Age, the Kali Yuga, set to last 432,000 years. Time is going quite slowly enough.

Arthur hesitated, until I added, 'Perhaps they'll come back for it. Perhaps that's how you'll nab 'em.'

Arthur Burgess put no pressure on me for my tutor's phone number. Unfortunately there was no one else I could call for help. The Mini was a good distance away, and I wasn't in a strong position to ask favours from someone who had already cleaned me up.

I had made no special effort to remember the number, but after my childhood tutor Miss Collins restricted my access to books I had come to rely more and more on memory, just in case I had to manage without books again. By my Cambridge days, it required an act of will for me to forget a phone number. I was half hoping Graëme would be out, though I had no idea what I'd do if he was.

He was in. There are probably better times to be told that you need to retrieve a soiled student from a pub urinal than when you have just finished dressing for a formal college dinner, but the timing was not of my choice. It wasn't long after 7.30, though to me it felt like midnight.

Graëme turned up wearing evening dress, though the trousers had a hint of a flare and the lapels of the jacket were broad and edged with velvet. Fashion was involved, in some tentative professorial way. I could almost hear Mrs Beamish cooing, 'Even academics can make a bit of an effort, you know, darling!' as she lured him (without benefit of a credit note) into The Peacock, the dandy-magnet cradled inside Cambridge's own little department store, Josh Tosh, foreshortened Harrods of the Fens.

By mutual instinct, Arthur Burgess and I retreated from first-name terms the moment Graëme made his appearance. The situation was unsavoury enough without being overlaid by an element of collusion or practical joke. As he wheeled me out of the Zebra, I called out politely, 'Thank you, landlord,' as if the whole evening had gone as planned. A refreshing half-pint in my local. Arthur for his part greeted Graëme with the words, 'A student of the old school, sir. Won't peach on his fellow sinners,' in the tone of voice of someone offering professional condolences.

Arthur had thoughtfully overlapped some bar-towels over my legs and lower body, to hide the damp patches. Thanks to these I had an almost festive aspect as we trundled back down King Street. They were brightly coloured, in red and green. We might have been doing something for charity – we might have been sponsored by the brewery. In November rather than April, I might have been a Guy in effigy being pushed to Parker's Piece for burning, particularly since loose strips of toilet tissue were escaping from my waistband, touch paper waiting for a match.

From behind me, as he pushed, Graëme Beamish was saying, 'I'm disappointed that you're taking this attitude, John.'

My free will had still not been returned to me. I seemed to be stuck with other people's scripts, this new one an especially dull affair of the solidarity of miscreants.

I came close to biting my tongue. 'What attitude is that, Dr Beamish?'

'This Bridge-on-the-River-Kwai not-telling-tales attitude. It's rather old-fashioned, isn't it? Rather . . . *square.*'

I was longing to tell tales for once. What did I care if Thomas da Silva and Benedict Whoever were thrown in the river, or put in the pillory and pelted with fruit? But I was unable to retreat from the uncompromising stance that had been foisted on me. I had missed my moment, and now I was stuck with being loyal to the disloyal. My arms still ached from my brief sojourn on Thomas da Silva's belly.

A spent blob in my mouth

In my frustration at being taken for a martyr, I started rolling my eyes and sticking my tongue out, in a way I would never have done if Beamish and I could see each other's faces. For all I know he was doing the same thing himself, in annoyance at the disruption of his evening, which would have added an extra fillip to the entertainment value of our progress down King Street. It's not considered polite for wheelchair-users to install wing mirrors, attached by stems to the armrests, so that they can monitor the expressions of those who push them, but really I don't see why.

My mantra had lost all its stabilising power. It was like a piece of chewing gum so long masticated it had turned into a spent blob in my mouth. No point in thinking of that. Instead I took a symbolic revenge on Beamish for his lack of understanding by visualising the bottom of his kitchen cabinets, seen on my only visit to his lovely home in Barton. I have my own point of view, and can witness any number of flaws that are hidden from the taller world. It's one of the little privileges of wheelchair travel, to be underlooking at the over-looked. The paintwork under those cabinets was pockled and peeling.

Steam from a thousand boilings of the kettle had left it looking shabby and leprous. Shame on you, Beamish.

It's well known that the disabled are compensated for their losses, in the currency of another sense. The blind have particularly acute hearing – though, oddly, as experiments have proved, they hear less well in the dark. As for me, I have a photographic memory for the undersides of kitchen cabinets.

When we were back at the Mini, once he had helped me in and loaded the wheelchair in the boot, Dr Beamish disappeared in his turn. His duties were over. He could get to his college dinner only a little late, with a story to tell if he cared to, ready to worship the little divinities of his academic cosmos, the sherry god and the claret god, madeira god and port god.

I felt the stigma of my incontinence very keenly, despite being a victim of circumstance. A disabled person can't have a moment of weakness in that department without it becoming a permanent part of the picture. It's a character flaw in waiting. If I'd been able to, I would simply have disposed of the evidence and thrown the soiled items away, but trousers were not things I owned in mad profusion.

It wasn't so very long since I had dared to defuse Mrs Beddoes's fears about my leaky self by turning them into a joke. The game with the Voodoo Lily didn't seem quite so funny any more. Perhaps I had been tempting fate, giving Maya a poke in the ribs.

In fact Mrs Beddoes took my emergency laundry in her stride, returning the bar towels (those flags of my disgrace) neatly folded, along with my trousers clean and fresh.

One comfort was that my relationship with my tutor was so poor that nothing could damage it. When I had paid that visit to his home in Barton, and the secrets of his kitchen's undersurfaces were laid bare to me, we had been on better terms. This was statutory university hospitality, and a group of us had been invited. I had been hoping for a spot of sherry myself. As holy water to the baby's head, so sherry to the undergraduate throat. It is the sacramentally required liquid. What hope for the christening when the font is full of Lucozade?

It wasn't Lucozade that Dr Beamish had provided for his moral tutees but something just as inappropriate. Tinned beer. That's no *poculum sacrum*! That doesn't begin to qualify as a holy tipple.

He had chosen a strange moment to drop the mask of fuddy-duddydom. Perhaps the charade was harder to keep up on his home turf, with his baby daughter screaming heartily from upstairs.

He was a besotted father, as well as perhaps a sleepless one, which would explain why he failed to censor himself while rhapsodising about the joys of fatherhood. 'It's the most amazing thing,' he said, 'not something I expected at all. Maybe with a boy but not a girl. She plays with herself the whole time. She never stops! It's wonderful the way she fiddles with herself, just strumming away day and night!' His voice had all the dry wonder of Patrick Moore's on *The Sky At Night* describing a new constellation.

There was silence sudden and total. The professor's dry-as-dust mask had dropped good and proper, and all parties were immediately frantic for it to be back in place again. We wanted freeze peach, but only for our generation. Graëme faltered, but made a noble attempt at recovery by saying, 'As a scientist I'm fascinated . . . there's more to life than crystalline solids, after all!' Then he started refilling people's glasses. Normal service of bufferdom resumed as if nothing had happened.

It had been his one experiment in talking to a group of students as if they were adults and equals. He didn't make that mistake again. His donnish persona had its disadvantages, but at least it saved him from enthusing in public over the fiddling habits of his little girl.

Regimental goat

After the evening of Write Off Tuesday, I never parked the Mini in that favoured spot again. I never crossed the pub's doors, nor sounded my horn for admission in the ceremonial style that had become customary. I dropped Kerry Bashford a postcard thanking him for his many kindnesses, but I never learned whether he was working his slow and appreciative way through the whole canon, or had special reasons for choosing *Howards End*. I never deepened my knowledge of the effects of a Jehovah's Witness upbringing on the resilient young, because I never saw him again. I forfeited the precious sense of welcome I had when Kerry settled me at a table and went to pour the half of Abbot Ale with the proper solemnity.

I had been a well-known figure in my way at the Cambridge Arms, pontificating about cannabinoids, hops and the Houses of Parliament, but I had been press-ganged into a lunatic troop under everyone's nose. This was my fault. Had Write Off Tuesday even noticed that they were kidnapping me? They simply didn't classify me as a creature that might have ideas of its own, and yes, I was responsible. I had made it happen. Yes, they had been drunk and out of control, but I had conspired with them against myself.

That was the point. Brooding on the incident afterwards, long after any taint had cleared from the wheelchair, I had to see their side of things. They hadn't turned me into a mascot. I was a mascot already. I had volunteered. I had turned myself into a character in the Cambridge Arms public bar, pronouncing on the quality of the ale while people tried not to look at the way I ate peanuts.

The answer was in my hands. No more pretence of belonging to a place or an institution. I would have to change my ways. I must refuse the rôle of mascot. Once you've accepted mascot status no later refusal is possible. I must find a part to play less demeaning than the gonk on a teenaged girl's counterpane, or the regimental goat trotted out on parade, presiding ceremonially over rituals in which it has no part.

Perversely, the incident pushed me in a direction that I had refused for a long time. It made no sense to be living in fear of attending a Gay Liberation meeting, when a quiet half-pint in a familiar pub could lead inexorably to incontinence, social disgrace and vomit in the treads of my tyres. I wasn't safe anywhere, so I had no excuse for not living dangerously.

Since I had been unable to locate the Monarchist League, with its promise of groping without slogans, I would have to make my peace with CHAPs. The organisation's contact details were given in many student magazines, and even the Varsity Handbook. There was a telephone number, but I couldn't imagine explaining my history and situation down a wire to a stranger in the exposed acoustic of the Porter's Lodge. There was an address also, in Glisson Road, where a meeting was held on alternate Tuesdays.

I made myself ready to attend my first gay group meeting like someone preparing a suicide, making sure the garage is airtight or that the beam will bear a noose. I looked up the address on the map, and made a few recces and dummy runs. I realised that there could be no question of hitch-lifting on this occasion. I could just about face an appointment with my unknown peers, but I couldn't imagine hijacking a passer-by to help me make the transfer from car to wheelchair to front door, and then having to explain everyone to everyone else. Sexual panic was plenty without social embarrassment on top.

On this occasion I would have to make my own way from car to front door. It followed that I would be dispensing with the wheelchair and proceeding under my own power, with crutch and cane. It was just about possible that I would be swept along on a tide of arriving Uranians, frolicsome intermediates with jewels in their hair who would swirl me up the steps and into the premises without me having to say a single word, but it made sense not to bank on it.

In fact when I arrived in the car there was no one on the street. I was able to park only a few feet from the house, and made my way laboriously out of the car and on to the pavement. While I was struggling, a pedestrian appeared, a woman pulling a shopping trolley. She stopped and peered into the Mini's interior, almost leaning over me in her desire to inspect the coachwork. I imagine she had been brought up with the idea that it was rude to stare at people, and was desperately trying to find an innocent object for her curiosity. Not finding one, she smiled uncertainly and went on her way.

It took me a little time to reach the door. There was a bell-push. Should I use it, or rap on the door with my cane? Which was it to be? *Rat-a-tat-tat* or *Rrring rrring*? I hadn't considered these options in advance. If I used the cane on the door perhaps the assembled inverts would panic, suspecting a police raid, and escape round the back. I decided on the bell, but couldn't get a sound out of it with the tip of the cane. Perhaps its mechanism required greater force or a better angle. I would have to climb up. There was only a low step leading up to the front door, but that was enough to make the attempt a bit of an expedition. This felt appropriate. It seemed to fit. The hero confronts his fears and enters the lions' den unarmed. He shouldn't expect a butler with a ramp or a block and tackle.

I decided that my ascent of the step was best managed with my back to the wall. That felt safest – falling backwards is a frightening prospect. I would turn round again when I had reached the proper level. I approached the step from the side. By leaning away I might be able to raise my foot to the right level. My new hips were splendid pieces of equipment. They would surely power this contortion. It more or less worked. I got one foot up onto the step. It was the next move that defeated me. The angle between my legs was already at its maximum. How was I going to shuffle along until I could (somehow) hoick up the other foot?

I was standing there, unstable and stranded, when a man approached the doorway from the street. There was something ghostly about his appearance. He was wearing a white suit, and there was hardly more colour in his face than in his costume. He departed from the human norms in other ways. If he was ghostly, then he also seemed mechanical. He was like a dapper robot. This apparition looked at me entirely blankly, then turned the door-knob and walked in. He didn't slam the door, but it closed against me with what felt like a click of ultimate exclusion. So much for the welcome of my peers.

Had he really not seen me? Had he mistaken me for an architectural feature? Perhaps he thought I was some wonky and misplaced caryatid. Actually there's a word for a male caryatid. I may as well assign myself the right gender. A wonky and misplaced *atlas* or *telamon*.

Half a minute later, the man was back. In that short interval he had regained some human faculties, a little facial colour and freedom of movement. The robot had been oiled, the zombie had been warmed to room temperature. He asked if I needed a hand.

I did.

I didn't need to be carried over the threshold, just steadied over the small step. His grip on me was uncertain, as if he had just laid down a mighty weight, so that his whole body was still twanging with the relief of tension. I can tell a lot about a person from the way he or she holds me – even if I'm always half-consciously hoping for the physical assurance of the motorcycle policeman who carried me to my seat at the Royal Tournament on an expedition from Vulcan, the one who was warm steel. This one was overstretched elastic.

An emergency siesta

The man in the white suit set me down reasonably gently on a sofa in a spacious room, with the kitchen and living room knocked together in the way that was beginning to be standard. He sat down next to me and whispered, 'My name's George.' 'John.' 'I'm sorry I walked past you earlier on, but . . .' Then someone shushed him, and his explanation had to wait. There were perhaps fifteen people in the room, only two of them women.

One man, sitting at the kitchen table, was saying: 'What happened was this. My dad and I went to the cinema and saw *The Music Lovers* – you know, the one about Tchaikovsky? Ken Russell. Anyway, the film brought a lot of things to a head for me, and after we'd gone home I said to Dad, "You know the man in the film? I'm like that. He's like me." By which I didn't mean that I had a big tune in my head at all times, though God knows that's also true. I meant I didn't love women. I loved men. Glenda Jackson would be a huge mistake.'

Between every phrase he made eye contact with a different person round the table, drawing out a thread of sympathetic attention.

'Anyway, Dad didn't know what to say or do. So what he said and did was to yawn in an exaggerated way, and to say he was tired and was going straight to bed.'

By now we were all nodding our endorsement of his story, making little encouraging noises at regular intervals.

'He wanted to end the conversation, but he didn't want to reject me. He didn't throw me out of the house. He didn't stalk out of the house himself either, slamming the door behind him. He managed to find somewhere else to go, even if it was only his bedroom, and he shut the door very gently behind him. He needed to give himself some breathing space. The only thing was . . . the funny thing was that we'd been to an afternoon showing, and it was still only about five . . . He'd come over all Spanish all of a sudden, and taken an emergency siesta. He went to bed in the middle of the afternoon just to get a little breathing space . . .'

There was a silence. I wasn't altogether sure whether I'd been trusted with a traumatic experience or entertained with a droll anecdote. I wanted to say, 'So what happened next? Did you talk about it the next day? Is everything all talked out now? What about your Mum?', but as a new arrival I thought I'd better wait to see how everyone else responded.

I think my instinct was sound. There was a concealed sort of etiquette in operation. The person who seemed to be in charge of the meeting was an upright man in a houndstooth jacket, in his late twenties perhaps. He thanked the speaker and said he was delighted to see a few new faces at the meeting. He brought a tray with mugs of tea on it over to where I was sitting next to George, and introduced himself as Tony. Addressing himself to George, he asked if he'd like to say something himself. George swallowed hard and said he'd rather just listen if that was all right. 'Of course, of course – get your bearings,' said Tony and went back to the kitchen side of the room, where a man in a yellow T-shirt was sitting. This man reached up inside Tony's jacket and stroked him softly on the belly. Granny was always stressing the importance for men of leaving the bottom button of their jackets undone, but I'd never seen the point till now.

George had taken two cups of tea, one on my behalf, and was looking around for somewhere to put them. He whispered, 'That's what I was trying to tell you. I was so nervous coming here that I hardly even saw you out in the street. I'm so sorry. I'd decided I would go through that door if it was the last thing I ever did. Then when I got inside and found I was still alive, I realised I'd left you out there. I went out again saying I'd be back in a moment, but I think our host thought I'd lost my nerve. I wonder how long he'd have waited before sending out a rescue party?'

Another voice spoke up from the group round the table. 'I'll tell you what happened to me,' it said. The new speaker had a much more confident delivery, an almost actorly confidence. George put both mugs down on the floor at our feet.

'I'd given myself a deadline to tell my mother I was gay. This was a few years ago. I wasn't living at home, but I was staying with her for a few days. I'd decided that this was going to be it. Time for revelation. Zero hour. I had no reason to think she was prejudiced. She had a couple of friends who were in the theatre, and as if that wasn't enough they worked for an antique dealer when they were between acting jobs. She was always saying how terribly amusing they were, what great fun, and I thought that was probably a good sign. It's just . . . with her own little boy – the little prince – it might not be quite so much fun.'

As if to emphasise the difference between himself and the previous speaker, he kept his gaze fixed on the mug in his hands, not looking up at any of us, confident of his ability to hold us without the assistance of eye contact. It was like an audition piece. And he meant to get the part.

'I get terrible fits of cowardice, you know, but I was determined to see this through to the end. To make sure that I didn't back out, I'd written my mother a letter and sent it, so I knew I would have to speak out before it arrived. I couldn't just go on putting things off. I'd decided that to leave myself no escape hatch I would send it by recorded delivery. That was the only sensible thing to do. Otherwise I'd be tempted to hang around the front door and pounce on the letter, and then I'd have put everything off again, which I was beginning to find unbearable. I was getting so tired of not being able to respect myself.

'The morning arrived for the letter to be delivered. I'd been awake since the early hours. I could hear Mother move around the kitchen, and still I couldn't get up. I felt as if I was paralysed. I'd been doing a bit of drinking, and I was hungover, but there was more to it than that. There was a weight on my chest and I couldn't stir from the bed. Mum was doing some ironing, for some reason, and I felt as if her iron was going back and forth on my chest, and scalding me with the knowledge of my own worthlessness. And Mother was singing as she did the ironing. *Singing!* She was cheerful, innocently happy, on a day that I was going to turn into blackness for her. Total eclipse. The light of her life was going to go out. And what was she singing, I ask you? She was singing "Everything's Coming Up Roses", that's what . . .

'I forced myself to rise from the horizontal. I swear it took as much effort as actually levitating. I forced myself up from the bed, by raw willpower, making myself confront my doom. To cast the shadow that would blight her happy song.'

By this time he had started swirling his coffee mug, gently at first and then more decisively, so that the brown liquid in it began to rise up in a slurring tongue, coming just to the lip of the mug. Theatrical *tour de force*. If his control of his movements lapsed, even for a moment, then coffee would slop onto the table and perhaps the floor. We were all spellbound, host Tony's hand tightening anxiously on a dishcloth.

'And then the doorbell rang. I shouted out "I'll get that," and started across the floor of my bedroom. But exactly at that moment I was laid low by a violent access of diarrhœa. Imperative diarrhœa – the runs at their most runny. I'm not exaggerating when I say that if I'd gone to answer the door I would have shat myself, and that is really *not* how you want to start an intense family conversation.

'So I had an ignominious session on the lav, where all the tension I'd been forcing myself not to feel expressed itself in the most rudimentary terms. And then I stumbled into the kitchen, where Mum was frowning as she took a piece of paper out of its envelope. . .

'What I'd planned to send her was the baldest possible statement. Fifteen words. IF YOU'RE READING THIS THEN YOUR SON IS A COWARD AS WELL AS A BUGGER. But then I thought that was a little crude, really. Dear Noël would have winced a bit, wouldn't he? It wouldn't do any harm if I took a little trouble over expressing myself elegantly, though the whole idea was that she would never have to read it. It wouldn't make any difference, but it would be good for my self-respect. The plan was that I'd speak out like a man before the letter was delivered, and sign for the recorded-delivery packet with a virile and unshaking hand while Mother screamed the place down in the middle distance. I would exchange a glance with the postman, that glance that all men use to mean *Women . . . how can we hope to understand them when they don't understand themselves?*

'So what Mother was reading was just a teeny bit less direct. I swear her lips were moving as she read out loud,

> MY FIRST IS IN QUEST BUT NOT IN GRAIL,
> MY SECOND IS IN DUGONG BUT ISN'T IN WHALE,
> MY THIRD IS IN ERIC AND ALSO IN ERNIE,
> MY FOURTH IS IN VOYAGE AND ALSO IN JOURNEY,
> MY LAST IS IN TROUSERS AND ALSO IN TEARS . . .'

He looked around expectantly, raising his eyebrows, but his audience didn't catch on quickly enough for his liking. 'I'll give you another ten seconds, shall I? Oh, for God's sake – *Queer*! I was giving her the clues for Queer. MY WHOLE MEANS YOUR SON IS ONE OF

THOSE QUEERS.' His eyes went back to the contents of the mug. 'As I say, I'd been drinking *rather a lot* . . . I'm not sure there was alcohol of any description left in the house by this time.

'So I finally open my mouth and hear myself coming out with the words I've longed to say (and dreaded to hear) for so long: "*Mother, there's something I have to tell you . . .*" Only she says, "Shhh! dear, I'm concentrating." She doesn't take her eyes off the piece of paper in her hand. "Can't it wait? Someone's sent me a word puzzle and there must be a prize for it – why else would they go to the trouble of sending it registered? I wonder what the prize is! Don't just stare, darling, give me a hand . . ."'

At this point he looked up from the swirling coffee in his mug and winked at me, with such precision that it was like watching the interior workings of a camera, the shutter flashing down and back. The wink seemed to be saying, 'That's the way to do it. *That's* how you do a telling-your-parents story.' As if the proper delivery of the anecdote was all that concerned him.

This time there were follow-up questions: 'So what did she say? Did she work out the riddle? Or did you manage to tell her first?' But he seemed to have lost interest in his life history now that the performance aspect was over. He said matter-of-factly, 'Oh, I told her myself. It turned out she was relieved if anything. From the way I'd demolished the drinks cupboard she was afraid I was going to tell her I was a dipso . . .'

This wasn't remotely how I had visualised my first gay meeting, but really I shouldn't have been surprised. I should have anticipated something of the sort. What I'd expected was somewhere between an orgy and a prayer meeting (with readings from Oscar Wilde). But if I'd used my common sense I would have realised that in a university town there was likely to be an element of performance in people's testimony, a certain amount of showing off. The bantam displays of the ego weren't going to be suspended just because people were exploring a taboo identity. Rather the reverse. In some people it went into overdrive. Sexual self-disclosure was something of a competitive event.

'What do you make of that?' George whispered.

'Dunno,' I said. 'I'm just going to keep very quiet and hope nobody asks me any questions.'

629

'Same here.'

In fact testimony hour seemed to be over. Our host Tony stood up again. 'Apologies for repeating myself, but not everyone was here when I did the welcome.' This was for our benefit, for George and me. 'So here goes again: Welcome to CHAPs. This is an independent forum where issues of sexual and political liberation can be freely discussed and worked through. We're not affiliated with CHE or with GLF. I can't emphasise enough that this is *not* a university organisation. Gay people in all Cambridge are invited to attend and challenge our prejudices if they feel excluded in any way. Of course Tony and I met when we were students – my lifemate is also called Tony, which is handy because he's not very good with names – but if we wanted to stay in our own little world we would never have founded CHAPs. I'm the Co-ordinator, by the way, and Tony is the Secretary. This is our house, and I hope you feel welcome. Tony, are the snacks ready?'

The Tonys were home-makers, and their kitchen turned out wonders. Grisly wonders, on this occasion, laced with blood – pâtés and terrines. I nibbled awkwardly at some crisp curling sheets of Melba toast, to show willing.

George and I made small talk for half an hour. He worked for Eaden Lilley, Cambridge's less glamorous department store, in China and Glass. If Joshua Taylor was the Harrods of Cambridge, Eaden Lilley was its Bourne and Hollingsworth. He thought everyone at the meeting was a bit young. There only seemed to be one person in his own age group, mid-thirties.

Music Lovers man and Recorded Delivery man held court at opposite ends of the kitchen space. No one came to talk to us. There was no welcome apart from the statement of welcome. Welcome was a policy rather than a fact at that address – or perhaps the snacks were supposed to do most of the work. One or other Tony kept offering us snacks until George got tired of eating them (and flicking the crumbs from his white suit) and I got tired of waving them away.

George lived in Chesterton, and would have driven to the meeting if he hadn't been so nervous he was sure he would crash. He had walked instead. 'Will you be coming back?' I asked.

'Will *you*?'

'I will if you will.'

So it was agreed. I'd give him a lift to the bus station, but in the future he would pick me up from Downing. In the Mini George said, 'Meetings like that are all right for a student like you, you're a brain-box. I'm different. I don't want to talk about issues of sexual and political liberation. I want to find a nice boyfriend, someone calm and sensible and nicely dressed, and I want my mother to ask us to dinner after the first few years, when she's got over the shock.'

I was in no great hurry to go public with my own fantasies of fulfil-ment. I suppose I wanted a boyfriend. Calm and sensible – why not? Nicely dressed – I didn't care one way or the other. As far as Mum went, fine by me if the shock never wore off. No dinner invitations wished for in either direction.

I didn't want to lose my heart to a straight man if I could help it, and I certainly didn't want a beauty, of whom in any case only one or two ever showed their faces at CHAPs meetings. I didn't want to go down Cyrano de Bergerac's road. I know everybody is supposed to love Cyrano de Bergerac, but I don't. What a fraud! As far as I'm con-cerned, he's just Pinocchio gone to the bad. His nose is so swollen that no one notices the effects of yet another lie, and it's so long since he's told the truth that he doesn't remember what it feels like. If there was ever a talking cricket to give him sound advice, he's long since ground it beneath his riding boot or skewered it with his sword.

Cyrano is brave, honourable and unsightly. He isn't desirable, and this is horribly unfair because he is beautiful where it really matters, on the inside. External beauty isn't the real thing. It's a distraction.

With whom I shared my liver

So does he fall in love with a woman with a club foot or a boss eye? Does he even fall in love with a flawed paragon – the woman who would be lovely if her ears were a little smaller, her ankles less thick? No, he falls in love with an acknowledged beauty, the hypocrite, and of course it's taken as read that her inside is as beautiful as her outside. Because her outside is beautiful. Cyrano doesn't want a fairer world, he wants an unfair world that lets him in, but he blackmails the world into sobbing on his behalf. Well, my eyes are dry.

The alliance of cowards I made with George to go to CHAPs

meetings had obvious advantages, but there were also some draw-backs. We were treated as a sort of couple. Once a Tony came over and said, 'Tell me, where did you two meet?' And I said, 'Here – the first time either of us came to a meeting.' The Tony almost purred, as if he couldn't be happier about us. There was occasional mild pressure on George to offer some personal testimony, but I was exempt. Everyone could see that I had nothing to say.

In theory there was no age discrimination at CHAPs meetings, in fact there were constant tirades against its evils, but the subtle fan of wrinkles round George's eyes and the slight thinning of his hair dis-qualified him from full participation in the life of the group. In the same way, the group's goal of reaching out to the town and not just the university didn't stop him from being patronised somewhat, as if he might need subtitles during discussions.

It suited everyone to think of the two of us as an indivisible subsec-tion of CHAPs, a sort of internal splinter group. This was disconcert-ing for both of us. He wasn't used to the full blinding spotlight of invisibility, and I wasn't used to sharing it.

We were a couple without ever having been an item. The group invented a closeness for us, though I doubt if anyone wanted to think about how we fitted together. We were a sort of Darby and Joan couple. Or I might have been the rather withdrawn fellow, yawn-ing and grumbling, who always seemed to tag along when one of the original Siamese twins (Was it Eng or Chang? I should really look it up) wanted to play billiards. If ever I ran into a CHAPs member in town he'd be sure to ask, 'Where's George?', as if I'd unaccountably mislaid the twin with whom I shared my liver.

It helped to establish this coupled image that on our second visit George said, 'John had tea in the yellow mug last time – can he have it again?' So someone nicely ensconced on the sofa went bright red and surrendered the mug for my use. There was nothing special about the mug, though it wasn't too big and the handle was a good shape for me. I could have made do with most of the others, but I didn't want to correct George when he was going to so much trouble on my behalf.

But after that the yellow mug loomed larger and larger. It was absurd. There was any amount of chafing along the lines of 'Use any mug but the yellow one, that's John's, you'd better not get on his bad side.' Once the yellow mug couldn't be located right away, and the place was pandæmonium. I said I didn't mind, any mug would do. Finally it was found lurking in the sink with the rest of the washing-up. The blessèd mug was given a priority cleaning, polished with a tea towel until it squeaked. Then it was filled with tea and offered to me with a triumphant smile, as if some desperate disaster had been headed off at the last possible moment. All the people in the group seemed to compress their sense of my singularity and then stuff it into the ruddy mug. As if what made me different wasn't *John needs a wheelchair to get around*, but *John's very particular about his favourite yellow mug. Bit of a prima donna, you know.*

I even managed to drop the yellow mug once, though I was solici-tous of the Tonys' floor and waited until the mug was empty. Unfor-tunately I'm not far enough off the ground to break crockery reliably. I dare say Edith Piaf had the same problem, but her flinging talents were far beyond mine.

At our second meeting we made the acquaintance of Ken, the group's one-man intellectual vanguard and ideologue. It was obvious from the first glance that he had been typecast in the rôle by his looks. He was squat and entirely bald, which was not then a possible avenue to attractiveness, being only voluntary among the fearsome tribe of skinheads. In Ken's case it was beyond his control, thanks to child-hood alopecia after measles. Without his glasses he might have been able to lead a normal life, but baldness plus strong glasses, strong enough to make his eyes look small, could only mean one thing – fer-ocious intellectualism.

It didn't matter that he wasn't necessarily the cleverest person in the group. A style of combative extremist theory became his life-line, the vindication of his off-putting appearance. He spoke at length about sexual evolution, about unstoppable changes in society which would lead to heterosexuality, poverty and war becoming obsolete. We were the first wave of a new creation.

There was a certain amount of mismatch between the jaunty acronym of CHAPs and its rather hard-line name, the Cambridge Homosexual Activism Project. It was no secret that the name had been hammered out to justify a desirable set of initials. If anyone had been able to come up with a better name for the group then it would generally have been accepted, as long as the acronym could stay. I thought 'homophilic' might do for the H and 'assimilation' for the A, but hesitated to make the suggestion. Only Ken liked the austere ring of the name, and would have liked to use it in full on every occasion. There were frivolous elements in the group that sometimes seemed close to sniggering at him.

I had more or less crawled on hands and knees to my first meeting, as to a place of healing or punishment, Lourdes or Golgotha. What I had found, as I gradually realised, was closer to Mum's sewing circle in Bourne End, although no single stitch was sewn. I suppose it was more of an unpicking circle than a sewing circle. I tell a lie – a few stitches were sewn. I had a Greek tapestry shoulder-bag which I had bought in the market, like a huge external pocket marginally easier for me to rummage through than anything actually attached to my clothes, and a member of the group sewed a discreet lambda onto that.

Thread of exasperated fondness

Our leader Ken seemed to have a nickname, though people were careful not to use it in his hearing. At first I thought it was Sarge, which didn't seem quite right since his manner, even at its most dogmatic, was more pleading than authoritative. It turned out to be Serge, still puzzling although his earnestness might have seemed a Russian quality.

Finally it was explained to me – Serge meant Blue Serge. The material used to make certain uniforms. Our doctrinal leader had a thing about policemen. This explained a number of references that had been unclear to me, murmurs of 'Evening all' and 'What's all this, then?' when Ken turned up or launched into an aria of dialectic.

There was a certain amount of whispering behind the Tonys' backs also, though their crime wasn't ideology nor a taste for the constabulary but a more sinister sort of backsliding. George and I had been elected as a couple, we were a couple designed by a committee, while the Tonys were something much more threatening. They were an exclusive couple, exclusively composed of Tonys. Tony sports-jacket and Tony Jesus-sandals. Tony corduroy and Tony denim. Tony economist and Tony piano teacher (ex-organ scholar). I don't shine at this sort of description. The truth is that I resent having to do it. Why should I sift through the various individuating traits – precise shade of eye colour, stature, mannerisms – to convey a vivid impression when all anyone needs to say to pick me out, apparently, is 'John' and then 'You know, John in a wheelchair.'

The Tonys would sit on the sofa sometimes holding hands, not just one hand each, but doubly grasping, softly squeezing. Theirs was not an open relationship, which might have muted the criticism. Their relationship was air-tight, and no draught of eroticism from outside could flutter its curtains. This counted as degraded imitation of the heterosexual couple, itself degraded, and might easily have led to censure if it wasn't that the group had nowhere half so convenient to meet.

Never mind that this level of domestic devotion didn't actually remind us of any heterosexuals we'd ever come across. Certainly nothing I had experienced of the heterosexual tyranny corresponded to what I witnessed between the Tonys. Mum and Dad never held hands or stared into each other's eyes. Even their neighbours in what seemed better marriages didn't moon over each other in the slightest bit. They would give the lovey-dovey a wide berth, occupying their separate corners at the Black Lion. It would have been a canny observer who could pick out the couples, following the thread of exasperated fondness to predict who would drive home with whom.

It's true that there was an irritating element to the Tonys' togetherness, an unstated refrain of *What would have become of me, if I hadn't found you?* We were all aware of it, but our objections were probably not political.

They were houseproud, they made quiche. Quite apart from the fact that men didn't cook back then, quiche at the time was far from being a cliché, it was something of a showpiece of kitchen skills. Larks' tongues in aspic would hardly have caused more wonderment. People at meetings stuffed themselves, but still I think the Tonys' kitchen skills counted against them. Equal rights for sexual minorities and the search for a perfect savoury custard flan were seen, back then, as incompatible goals in life.

Eventually I summoned up the courage to tell the Tonys that their quiche smelled rather good, and was there any chance of their making a vegetarian one every now and then? After that my attendance became devoted. I didn't want to risk missing one of their meat-free evenings, but didn't quite have the nerve to phone up in advance to check.

I resolved not to join in the ritual slander of our hosts. The gossipy members tended to be young and flighty, often making little experiments in effeminacy. Ken himself was always talking about revolutionary androgyny, but the idea seemed very theoretical as it emerged from his thick neck. The flibbertigibbets of the group had their own idiosyncratic ideas about defying the patriarchy. Their revolutionary programme involved shop-lifting make-up from Josh Tosh. If there were other aspects I never heard about them.

I'm not a gossip and I don't enjoy tittle-tattle. It's not a moral position so much as a physical fact. Having an inflexible neck cuts me off from that whole aspect of the world. Gossip is only a pleasure if you've got supple vertebrae. I don't find it easy to follow the social mechanics of a group. I can't turn my head to deliver an aside, or catch the fleeting expressions on people's faces when they think they're not being observed. Peripheral vision isn't enough unless you can keep it moving, pouncing on all the giveaway nuances at the edge of events.

An appropriate punishment for gossips might be blinkers or some sort of neck-brace arrangement, inhibiting the flow of information, though the effect might be paranoiac delusions. Certainly if I try to imagine what goes on around me, socially, in any sort of detail, I inevitably imagine people whispering against me. It's a direct consequence of lack of mobility, and there's not a lot to be done about it.

If people were considerate enough to arrange themselves in front of me like a group photograph, tallest in the back row or else crouching in the front, looking only at me, not exchanging signals among themselves in any sidelong manner, then I dare say I'd enjoy parties as much as everyone else does. It doesn't seem a lot to ask. Perhaps we could arrange things on a rota basis – social life the majority way for fifty-five minutes an hour, then everyone adopting their positions at a given signal to arrange things to suit me. I could blow a little whistle. In the meantime, the simplest way for me to be part of a conversation is to rule it.

Sometimes there were guest speakers at CHAPs meetings. One was an anthropology graduate who gave a presentation about the very warlike Sambia tribe of Papua New Guinea. According to this noble tribe, semen should never be wasted. Even such rituals as rubbing it into one's hands or capturing it in an old Redoxon bottle would be unacceptable by their standards. These ways of cleaning up would qualify as dirty in their own right.

The student who told us about the Sambia wore a scarf so long that it fell below his knees, despite being coiled twice around his neck. The ends were bedraggled from being trodden on, by his own feet and those of others. He hunched his shoulders and held his elbows back while he spoke, as if he was longing to drive his hands into the pockets his jumper lacked. He was clean-shaven, except for little patches of whiskers high up on his cheekbones. He looked like a woodland creature from an early draft of *The Wind in the Willows*.

He started off by explaining that among the Sambia the transfer of semen to ladies' vaginas was extremely limited and hedged about with taboos. The main sexual practice, crucial for the initiation of young males, was fellatio.

When Christians arrived, they were unenthusiastic about this tradition. They regarded the older members of the tribe as beyond help, but succeeded in building a chapel and enticing quite a number of young boys away from the Sambia and into their own curious practices. This process continued to the point where the existence of the tribe itself was in danger.

Our little radical Rat or Mole had our attention by now. He ended by quoting the defiant words of the headman of the Sambia:

'These Christians are taking away our culture by building a chapel and converting our males.

'It is a sin for my semen to be wasted. Women can only be approached at prescribed times and in the correct manner.

'We will never defy our culture and waste our sperm. When the missionaries take our young men away, what are we to do? The only thing we can do after that is make a hole in the ground and go and fuck that when we need to have release. Tell me, is that all they will leave for us?

'I tell you, these Christians make out they are so god-like. Accordingly to them we are only primitive savages who cannot be saved, but shall I tell you something?

'One of our boys went over to these Christians and consequently never learned our initiations and our ways. Do you know what? A year or two after he had defected, a girl in that compound was raped . . . That is unthinkable amongst our peoples. All our women are loved and cherished here. They do not even know what rape is. No atrocity like that happens here. If it were ever committed, the punishment would be death. What is so "civilised" about those people?

'In our tribe we fully know and understand the way we are made by the gods. If that boy had been here, he would have been initiated into drinking the semen of his elders. When he reached puberty and started to make his own sperm, he would have a younger boy to drink his semen for him, and when the younger boy grew older he would have another boy to service him, and so on. Thus the sacred fluids are kept in trust among our peoples . . . To this degree we respect the gods and all our wonderful life.'

Despite his diffidence, our guest speaker held us spellbound. Even the ping of the timer on the Tonys' electric oven, arriving in the middle of the lecture, had no power to break our concentration.

I dare say that like most of the life-changing texts of the 1960s and '70s – *Desiderata* ('Go softly', and so forth) or the 'Cree Indian proverb' ('Only when the last tree has died and / The last river has been poisoned and / The last fish has been caught, / Will we realise that / We cannot eat money') – this plea was more or less made up. It doesn't even matter. The text changes your life not by virtue of being true but because you are ready for the transformation it announces.

In Hall, as the academic year wound down, I heard people talking about their plans for the summer. One person was going to work in a pub in Argyll, another had found work repairing slate roofs on a farm in Cornwall. And what were my plans? Not quite in that class, though ambitious enough in their way. I would be spending the long vacation in the bosom of my family, trying not to choke on the bullying nipple of Mum's need to look after me despite all protests.

There was a rather hectic atmosphere as May Week approached. I had already noticed that students made a point of breaking up their love affairs near the end of a term. A little wave of tears would break over the undergraduate population just before Christmas and Easter, and then the heartbroken would go home to mope with their families, casting a pall on the celebrations. May Week, though (which lasted more than a week and took place in June), was high jilting season, particularly for third-years, many of whom seemed determined to wipe the emotional slate clean before they moved on into the 'world' and the next stage of their lives.

I dare say there were a few women who called the shots, but it was more of a female fate in those days to start May Week as the corner-stone of your boyfriend's existence, and to end it more in the rôle of a stepping-stone, one on which he had wiped his shoes in passing.

Tickets for May Balls were very expensive, since they included food, drink and entertainment from mid-evening till dawn. Many couples had bought tickets well in advance, deposits had been paid for the hire of evening dress, so they went through the festivities de-spite the fact of rupture. Champagne, Pimm's No. 1 cup, whole roast boar, smoked salmon, all to be endured rather than enjoyed, at a som-bre carnival that was like a wake without a body (unless you count the boar). I heard enough accounts of these events to be able to build up a composite picture. Couples would hang on grimly till dawn, danc-ing with eyes averted, then trudge away from the pleasure-grounds through a tide of plastic glasses and discarded kebabs. Really it was a relief not to be going. I counted my blessings. I don't like tears and don't like silences that seethe with reproach.

Not that there was much silence on the night. If the Nasty Thing had survived so long, the ambient vibrations would surely have done it in. I remember a slow blues that seemed to have twelve hundred bars rather than the specified twelve. Sometimes between numbers I could hear a more distant uproar, presumably Pembroke's Ball or perhaps even Emmanuel's, according to the dictates of the breeze. Homerton was also a possibility, I suppose, though the Balls at wom-en's colleges had the reputation of being a little more restrained, even staid. They were rumoured to serve vegetarian food and hire trad jazz bands. These were highly effective passion-killing measures even when imposed separately. In combination they made the successful production and maintenance of an erection, its shepherding to a climax, a practical impossibility.

Finally the echoes of sobbing died away from the courtyards of the golden colleges. Spilt emotion evaporated relatively quickly from ancient flagstones, but for quite a while many undergraduate hearts would feel an affinity with the lawns where marquees had stood, drained to yellowness and marked by the sharp heels of hollow revelry.

I stayed in A6 just as long as I could. I would have loved to convalesce at Mr Johnson's Home in Bognor, but from health there can be no convalescence. Any other sort of institution might take me in but wasn't guaranteed to let me out. Finally there was nothing for it but to face the family, with nothing to shield me but a thick sheaf of the strongest prescriptions I could think of, endorsed with the autographs which Flanny distributed so freely.

Peter was away on holiday. He took a train to Inverness and spent the summer hitch-hiking round the Highlands. Audrey was in residence, but we had never really been friends. She was in a state of wildly excited transition, spending most of the time with her best friend Lorraine Leeming. They would walk around with rolled-up tights stuffed into their tops, modelling the soft shapeliness to come. They would shout, 'What God has forgotten we stuff with cotton!' then roll on the floor shrieking with laughter, till their makeshift busts were squashed flat.

Looked good in a kaftan

The rest of the time they would write cheques in each other's favour. Pay Audrey Cromer Two Million Pounds. Pay Lorraine Leeming Two Million Pounds. It was always two. A single million wasn't enough for these plutocrats in the making. They were too young to have chequebooks so they drew their own from scratch. Freed from the constraints of plausibly representing legal instruments of exchange their cheques grew physically large, sometimes made up of several pieces of cardboard taped together.

The closest thing I had to allies in Bourne End were the Washbournes, Malcolm who shared my spiritual interests and his wife Priscilla who warmly mocked them. 'Call me Prissie,' Priscilla said from the first, meaning I suppose that she wasn't. Wasn't prissy, that is.

Mum seemed to think that the Washbournes were only trying to be youthful and trendy by being friendly to me, sucking up to the young, as if I was obviously a waste of an older person's time. I said to Dad once, I don't think Mum is very keen on the Washbournes, and Dad said, 'Let's face it, John, your mother isn't very keen on anybody.' Which was true enough but didn't help in the short term.

The women were different types, and had no use for each other. Everyone always complimented Mum on how thin she was – how did she manage it? What was her secret?

Her secret was not eating. No great mystery. And to Prissie's eyes Mum was actually too thin, a monument to appetite repressed. 'You need some meat on your bones, Laura dear,' she said once, which I think Mum never forgave. In her own eyes, if she wasn't thin, she wasn't anything.

Prissie for her part made her mark in the short period, a half-decade perhaps of heyday, when undernourishment was not quite compulsory and the phrase *earth mother* had an edge of awe rather than disdain. She looked good in a kaftan, the only one I ever saw (in that age of kaftans) who did. She could carry herself.

Prissie lived in bare feet – I don't know why that way of putting it sounds so strange – though she would reluctantly put on shoes to go to the pub, slipping them off the moment she was ensconced with a drink.

From Mum's point of view, of course, she was simply obese. I heard her mutter once, 'That woman! Even her earrings are fat.' She particularly disapproved of Prissie's love of going barefoot. Mum seemed to think that shoes were necessary, like moulds for jelly, to stop the feet from spreading. Prissie would find, when she finally acknowledged the need for shoes, that she couldn't force her feet back inside them.

I would often go out to the pub with the Washbournes. In fact I'd give them a lift. Prissie would be terribly appreciative, saying what a relief it was to be able to drink and not worry, since I was so responsible. She would keep up a running commentary in the car, saying, 'John, you are miraculous. You must be the best driver in the world, that's all I can say. I mean, there hasn't been a peep out of Malcolm all this time' – perhaps two minutes – 'but when I'm driving he winces and groans the whole time. And now look at him – he's blushing. Rather sweet. That must be your doing. I haven't been able to get a blush out of him for years.'

'How marvellous,' she went on, 'that you can park anywhere you like!' – since I had the benefit of my parking permit from the council, an orange card with a revolving indicator inside, on which I could show how long I expected to be away from the car.

'How long do you think we'll be?' I asked. 'Not long,' said Prissie, 'we're just having a drink or two,' and I told her to set the clock for four hours, just to be on the safe side. The joke of the whole rigmarole being that the Black Lion was only walking distance from home, for them anyway, and there were no restrictions on parking in any case.

The comedy continued inside the pub. Malcolm would install me on one of the high bar stools. I was conserving my funds, which meant I would order water with a dash of lime cordial, costing all of 4p, and nurse it all evening if need be. I'd buy a packet of peanuts for entertainment value. At one time peanuts had been provided free in a dish (a powerful dehydrating agent, and so hardly an unselfish gesture from the management), but people had been seen wrapping some up in a napkin for later, and that was that.

Rather than treating me to round after round, the Washbournes thought it was better sport to encourage me to do my party trick with the peanuts, flicking them into my mouth. Then they'd egg someone on to betting that I couldn't still do it – and stay on the stool – if I had 'a proper drink'. In this way I got a certain amount of free alcohol and became discreetly merry. When the second packet of peanuts arrived I might eat them out of Malcolm's hand, funnelling my lips forward in a delicate trumpet, leaving his hand completely dry. Prissie, drinking her Campari, would say to no one in particular, 'Really it's just the other way about, you know. It's Malcolm who eats out of John's hand. Almost sinister, but what's a girl to do?' She sounded supremely unbothered, but then it took a lot to bother her.

She was affectionate to Malcolm but didn't in the least defer to him. There was sarcasm there, which he accepted and even seemed to enjoy. He was the breadwinner and she didn't work, though the description 'housewife' didn't remotely suit her. Their twins Joss and Alex were about to start at a fashionably progressive secondary school, and they had long been encouraged to explore other social contexts, or – as Mum would have it – 'farmed out' on the slightest pretext. Prissie was like a rich field lying fallow after her single (double) crop, not in the least beholden or unfulfilled, an earth mother who wasn't unduly addicted to the presence of her children. She certainly didn't mother Malcolm. I suppose she mainly mothered herself.

Eventually Prissie Washbourne played a walk-on part in the big drama of that summer, the family crisis which was all about me, though I hardly noticed it at first. When I say that she had a walk-on part, I mean a little more than that. She walked up the drive, she knocked on the French windows and she shouted a bit, refusing to go away. But her appearance on the scene, her splendid interference, made everything move up a gear and become more colourful, positively psychedelic in its emotional hues.

Dimly I had noticed that Mum and Dad were having one of their rows, which could simmer on for days. I also registered that every now and then they would seem to address me as much as each other. In some strange way they seemed to take it in turns to badger me. Could this really be happening? It was unlike them to coöperate so smoothly on any enterprise. I wondered vaguely what it was all about. Sometimes, of course, they sent messages to each other through me, bouncing messages off my bonce like schoolboys flicking paper pellets. I let them get on with it.

I had the good sense to absent myself mentally. There's some debate about whether you should have your eyes open or closed when you're meditating. It's a question that often came up among Bhagavan's adherents and disciples. His answer was that it didn't matter – should you even know whether your eyes are open or not? That's just the sort of Western binary opposition that Bhagavan is so good at dissolving.

Who is that wants to know? Trace that impostor to his lair. Is it even fair to describe your eyes as 'open' when they are absorbing the infinite deceptive variety of Maya, and 'closed' when you are perceiving the world in its reality?

Still, it seems very likely that during those days at home a lot of my meditating was done behind open eyes. Even when I wasn't meditating my attention wasn't completely attuned to the externals. Whenever I drifted back into my alleged body and took up the reins of mundane vision things looked very much the same. Mum and Dad might have changed places, but they were still taking turns to badger me. The sun might have moved round a fraction, the shadows might fall a little differently, but really that was all.

At one point the pot plant on the table seemed to blossom with a sudden movement, almost a lunge. The great red trumpets of its blooms seemed abruptly larger and more lustrous, which suggested that I had dropped a stitch, or even a whole row, in my knitting together of time and space. The plant itself had featured in earlier disputes between Mum and Dad, with her calling it an amaryllis and him insisting it was technically a *Hippeastrum*. Mum said he was being 'predantic', a mistake which set Dad off on a fresh bout of correction. I'm my father's son in these matters, which is no doubt why I chose Mum's womb, wanting to be brought up in a properly pedantic environment, among precise taxonomies and word-use sanctioned by dictionary. I vote for *Hippeastrum*.

I seemed to have regressed, to the point of needing to be taken to the loo, though it had been second nature for me to manage by myself for years. Mum would escort me and wait in the background while I performed, but there was a sort of truce until she pushed me back into the sitting room. Then it would start all over again – whatever it was.

I knew that there had been a knocking at the door earlier on, and even that it had gone on for some time, while Mum and Dad stopped talking and more or less stayed rigidly in their places. I even knew that the phone had rung a few times, and that Mum and Dad hadn't answered it. Again they had stopped talking and stayed frozen where they were, as if the phone could detect movement even without being picked up. Then they started right up again the moment it stopped ringing.

I was being asked a lot of questions, or else being asked the same question many times, in slightly different forms. In the course of my engagement with the *vichara*, the self-enquiry, I'd decided that if you were a non-dualist, resisting the division of reality into This and That, body and soul, real and unreal, then it followed that you couldn't answer any questions that were put to you, which always rested on assumptions of that kind. I'd read in a book the suggestion that when confronted with a false set of alternatives, you should reply simply 'Mu', meaning 'Your question cannot be meaningfully answered, since it is the product of a misconception. Please examine your premises afresh.'

So when Mum said, 'Is it your bag or not, John? We need to know,' I giggled and answered 'Mu.'

The giggle was there because when anyone of my generation, however estranged from the groovy, asked if something was your bag, it meant 'Do you like it?' Is Acid Rock your bag? Is *Buddenbrooks* your bag? Is the *vichara* your bag? From my point of view the *vichara* was the bag in which all other bags could be stored without taking up any room.

The *vichara* – the only question. Who am I? (Who is it that asks this?) I understood now why I had gone to see The Who in Slough and not some other group. I needed to devote myself to the question of The Who.

And when Dad said, 'It's a simple enough question, John. Don't be mulish. For the last time, is it your bag?' – the giggle was no longer a temptation but the answer was still Mu. With another annoying giggle because saying Mu got me called Mulish.

At some stage Mum asked me what I wanted for supper, as if this was an ordinary day, which it obviously wasn't. She put the question in an exasperated voice, admittedly, but that wasn't such a rare event. And perhaps this time I didn't answer 'Mu', because she said, 'Better not have eggs again, John, you know how binding they are.' Om Mane Padme Om. Om Mane Padme Om-pa-pah. I kept losing the thread of my threadlessness, my immersion in blissful absence. I wished Mum and Dad would let me be. I wish they'd let me Be.

'If it's your bag, John, then what's in it is also yours, isn't it?' Mu –
Mu – Mu. 'That's only logical.' Exactly. Logic based on false premises
can only generate nonsense.

Everything happened that day in stages which didn't quite follow
on from what had gone before. They were like reels from different
films. I wondered idly if Bhagavan had ever used that analogy. Or
they were like different versions of the same scene, not properly edited for continuity.

At some stage Audrey came back from a friend's birthday party.
A twelfth birthday, I expect. We heard her being dropped off in the
drive, saying her goodbyes and thank-yous as nicely as Mum could
wish. As she let herself in, Mum and Dad greeted her with 'Nice
party, dear?' Anyone could tell that they weren't really interested,
they were only marking time. They were waiting for her to go to her
room, so that they could carry on whatever business was being trans-
acted where I was.

Reels that don't match

Audrey didn't go to her room just yet. She went into the kitchen,
and then she came to have a little chat with me. Meanwhile Mum
and Dad busied themselves nonsensically. Mum started picking up
magazines and putting them away in the rack where they lived. The
moment she had finished, Dad started searching through it, as if
suddenly he couldn't live without reading a particular article. Mum
made one of her many noises of exasperation and went over to fiddle
with the telephone. It vexed her that the cord was always getting
snarled up – she thought that Dad gave the receiver a half-turn when
he answered the phone, and another half-turn in the same direction
when he returned it to its cradle. She blamed him for charging the
cord with kinks, even if she could never catch him at it. She knew full
well that at her mother's house the flex wouldn't dare to stray from
its spiral.

I roused myself a little and agreed to participate in the illusion of
time, out of politeness to Audrey, but strictly on a trial basis. She was
wearing a purple party dress, and had been allowed to put on nail
polish. Her movements were smooth and assured. Quite a little pile of

books, placed on her head, would have stayed there safely in balance.

I hardly recognised her. I had missed a few stages. Of course I hadn't been paying much attention, to her or to anyone else at that address. In any case girls between about eleven and sixteen always resemble films like the one I seemed to be in, made up of reels that don't match. The genre switches from fairy tale to love story, and sometimes to horror movie. A world of princes and ponies can suddenly be filled with screaming banshees.

I remembered that in the past she had hated party games, and asked if there had been any.

'A few specially horrible ones,' she said over her shoulder as she went to the kitchen.

'None that involved kissing, I hope?' She made an odd stylised sound, which I took a few seconds to understand without benefit of visual clues. I imagine she was miming a retch, with or without the embellishment of a finger pointing down her throat, though the whole display was as far removed from what it represented, human emesis, as something in classical Japanese drama.

Actually she sounded less disgusted than she would have done the previous year. She was going through the motions a little bit. It wouldn't be all that long before the kissing games were the only ones that interested her. I imagined she would play them as ruthlessly as she did all the others.

'Sally's mum made her invite all the boys from our class,' she said, 'but only three of them came.' I could hear the clatter of a plate. 'The really pathetic ones.'

Audrey was reading from her own little script while Mum and Dad took a reluctant break from their interrogation of me. The noises from the kitchen continued as she went about some mysterious domestic business. There was the sound of her pushing a chair against the kitchen counter so she could reach something from a high cupboard. Then I heard a familiar scrape as she pulled a particular tray out from beside the fridge, where it lived.

When she came into the sitting room, she was carrying a tray of treats for me. She had taken her party trophy, a slice of chocolate cake, and cut it into cubes, pushing a cocktail stick into each cube. It must have been the little box of cocktail sticks which was kept in the high cupbard. She set down the tray in front of me, where it rested snugly across the side-pieces of the wheelchair. All this was done with the grace of a hostess rather than the conflicted sweetness of a sister. She was growing up.

She was playing a part, of course, but so were Mum and Dad, and at the moment I preferred Audrey's.

As she came out of the kitchen with her tray of cubed cake, I saw her in a new light, despite the Mayan darkness of that afternoon. As she moved through the sitting room to the wheelchair, threading her way through the distortions of family life in her party dress, bearing her tray of John-adapted cake, I began to think for the first time that perhaps she had known, better than any of us, what she was doing when she chose the womb. Perhaps she would pick her way through everything that was wrong and out of kilter with the family. The gala purple nail-polish lent her gestures a self-conscious overtone – a finishing-school or ladies'-academy touch. She looked like the serene housewife in a television advert serving canapés to her guests. Her hands were going before her into adulthood. They were leading the way. Their movements were taking on the sophistication of things practised in front of the mirror, time after time, until they were effortless.

She gave me a smile which changed in mid-flight, becoming gravely enchanting, an expression with two distinct phases like a two-stage rocket – as if an air hostess had suddenly thought of Grace Kelly. She was growing up more or less as I watched.

My mouth was dry. My lips were sticky as I tried to mumble the chunks of cake. Audrey fetched me a glass of water and then, great refinement of refreshment, a damp flannel. She wiped my mouth with it.

Lemon juice in her eye

I don't mean to idealise Audrey's performance too much. She knew perfectly well that Mum didn't want her around, though she can't have had much clue about the interrogation that was taking place (I certainly didn't). Audrey was giving comfort to the accused in a way that was guaranteed to cause irritation.

Mum said, 'Audrey, your room is like a pigsty. You promised me you'd tidy it up the moment you got in from your party, remember? Now's the time.' Audrey said, 'Yes, Mum,' very demurely, but she gave me a wink. I think it was a wink – she hadn't quite got the knack as yet, not quite in control of the facial machinery, so it was a rather wild spasm and she looked as if she'd got some lemon juice in her eye.

My habit was to hoard my various tablets in term-time so I had plenty when I went home. Alertness seemed a waste of time at that address. To be *compos mentis* was a mug's game, or so I thought, and exposes you to all sorts of nonsense. Well, yes, but the same is true of a medicated doze.

Audrey went upstairs to her room at last. She put a record on the record-player and played it eleven times in a row. It was David Bowie's maddeningly catchy and childlike 'Starman'. She was playing it louder than she was allowed, but I fancy she had a canny sense of the disruption in the household, and what it enabled her to get away with.

Or she may simply have been trying to blot us all out, or even sending a message to the starman in the song, who was supposed to be waiting in the sky after all, to say that she needed immediate rescue. The last record she had played so many times on the trot had been 'When You Wish upon a Star'. Or perhaps 'Would You Like to Swing on a Star?' I see now that the star theme was a constant.

The interrogation began again. The bust-up of summer 1972 was about what all proper family rows are about – sex and drugs. In that respect it was exemplary. And still Mum and Dad got completely the wrong end of the stick. They could have got the wrong end of a marble. They were going by what they had found in my Greek tapestry shoulder-bag, with its discreet embroidered lambda, hanging invitingly from the handles of the wheelchair, not what they would have learned if they'd talked to me.

They thought I was on dope, simply because they had found a couple of roaches in the tapestry shoulder-bag. Pitiful stubs of joints long gone. Fossils – antiques. They should have been in the Fitzwilliam Museum, properly docketed: *Marijuana leavings of the Unknown Student, early 1970s. Private collection.* My collection, though, was no longer private.

Mum and Dad wanted to know how long I'd been using reefers. The demon weed, wrecker of young lives, bringer to its knees of the undergraduate brain. *Cannabis sativa*, a plant I respect for its hardiness, but not one that has ever done much for my consciousness.

They didn't actually bother to ask if the joints had anything to do with me. Even a policeman would have done that, just for form's sake. Mum and Dad jumped to conclusions instead. They jumped to their own confusions.

They really were the leavings of the Unknown Student, if he (conceivably she) was even a student. How much control did I have over the Greek tapestry shoulder-bag, really? It was anything but a private preserve. Friends thought nothing of using it as a communal asset, a shared pocket, even a portable dustbin. What were their reasons? Laziness, disorganisation, reluctance to spoil the line of their trousers by putting things in pockets of their own. So there was nothing unusual about people slipping their joints into my bag for safe-keeping, or their roaches for eventual disposal (which of course they never got round to).

If I had no control over what went inside the bag, the same was true of what went on it. Members of CHAPs who lost their nerve in mixed company, for instance, would slyly pin their more confrontational badges to its unprotesting weave. After a while it was almost armour-plated with revolutionary slogans, GAY IS GOOD, SAPPHO WAS A RIGHT-ON WOMAN and, more mysteriously, THE ENGLISH THINK LIBERTY IS A SHOP ON REGENT STREET.

I hadn't much enjoyed my bag becoming a dumping-ground for the flotsam of the counter-culture. I particularly resented the one that said HOW DARE YOU ASSUME I'M HETEROSEXUAL? being transferred from the denim of my colleagues to the faintly stinky wool of my bag. In common with the world at large, no one in the CHAPs revolutionary echelon assumed I was sexual in any way whatever. That was one issue of exclusion that was never going to be freely discussed and worked through in our little independent forum on Glisson Road. No one ever asked about my erotic past, or imagined that I might run to such a thing as a present, perhaps even a future.

The pin fastenings on the backs of the badges were well beyond my powers to undo. When I arrived home for the summer it was a priority to have them removed, but Peter, the obvious choice of helper, had already left on his travels. I had to draft Audrey in for the job, though I wondered what she made of the slogans. She didn't need telling that this was something to be kept quiet. That didn't worry her – she liked a secret, did Audrey.

Looking back, of course, I would have done well to ask her to sanitise the contents of the bag as well, but I hadn't realised there was anything in the bag that might cause embarrassment. I had forgotten my lack of privacy, on two fronts. It didn't occur to me that Mum and Dad would search through my reticule with their prehensile digits, screeching and tut-tutting as they went, like moralising spider-monkeys.

'Are you on drugs, John?'

Mu. 'Just tell us. We want to help.'

Mind your own Mu.

'Are you on drugs?'

Well, *of course* I was on drugs. Ask a silly question! The only question was what kind. I had steered clear of hallucinogens since my trip to the Salley gardens, and I wouldn't have considered indulging without Peter there to lean on. But I was self-medicating as if there was no tomorrow. I was self-medicating because there was a tomorrow, and I wanted to take a short cut, avoiding today, even if tomorrow turned out to be no better. There was always the day after tomorrow, and the day after that.

The black dot marks the tree line

I had learned my lesson from Write Off Tuesday, to the point where I was able to write off whole clumps of days, and all without a drop of liquor passing my lips. Everything that was entering my system was legitimate and prescribed, but those are judgements which are subject to revision, and in any case, legitimate and prescribed can be very different from sane and sensible.

When Flanny first took charge of me she put me on mefenamic acid, trade name Ponstan. It's a member of the aspirin family – call it the family's rich eccentric uncle. She also tried me on Doloxene, which is the trade name for dextropropoxyphene. That was all very well for a while, but then I was in the market for something stronger. So she moved me up to Fortral (pentazocine), which has been a controlled drug for ages now but wasn't then. In that innocent time there was no warning black dot against such things in *MIMS*, meaning 're-stricted'. It had an unblemished reputation. It was freely prescribed, and no one ever said it wasn't good at its job.

In those days the *MIMS* was very straightforward about side-effects. It didn't hesitate to spell them out. The *Monthly Index* was lagging behind the times. There were a good few toxicomanes out there (apart from me) for whom the desired effects were only part of the story.

These days the *MIMS* is very cagey about (for instance) hallucinations, for fear of tipping the wink to people who are actively seeking them out, homing in on the extras and indifferent to the main thrust of the drug. One man's poison is another man's meat. One man's side-effect is another man's illicit buzz.

These were perhaps no longer the nursery slopes of analgesia, more like the middling pistes, but still far below the dizzy peaks of Mount Morphine. The black dot in *MIMS* marks the tree line, if you like, the point where the chill becomes permanent and life approaches the point of no return.

If the phrase 'a cocktail of drugs' had been invented by this time, I hadn't heard it, but I was already a dab hand with the shaker. While I was playing doctor with myself in this wholly irresponsible fashion Audrey would sometimes pester me to let her play nurse. She was a good girl. She wanted to help. In fact earlier in the day I had let her help me get my tablets out of their bottles.

Medicine bottles weren't childproof in those days, they were only John-proof. My hands can't easily deal with any assignment much more challenging that manipulating a snapdragon. Pressing the cheeks of the flower, making its jaws close and then open again. That's my style. Audrey helped me to line up the numerous antidotes to the day, Maya's little cancellations of herself. Her expression was solemn and eager, as if she was concentrating on a tricky exam question.

There was a mocking symmetry about the whole operation, all the same. Maya was having fun at my expense. In the past I had dosed Audrey, when she was a fractious child, with hundreds and thousands, sorted by colour and consequently charged with magical power. Now she was lining up the medication for me in her turn. The drugs weren't sweeties any more, though I was wolfing them down no differently. I was treating the medicine cupboard, lavishly stocked from the local pharmacy, as if it was the Pick'n'Mix counter at Woolworths.

Analgesics kill pain, and any excess of such drugs performs a function that can be every bit as valuable, mopping up consciousness, promoting oblivion. By this stage I couldn't honestly have said which part of its operations was the more precious to me, suspension of joint pain or of the poisonous boredom of home.

My drug use could slide in a single dose from the medical to the slyly recreational. In terms of pain I had my good days and my bad days. That summer I preferred the bad days. On my bad days I could gobble down the hundreds and thousands of nothingness with a clear conscience.

A great advantage of the wheelchair was that it masked many of the effects. If my movements were poorly coördinated, who would ever know? Not everyone expected prodigies of mental alertness from me either. At home with Mum and Dad, ritual exchanges were the norm. I could fit in perfectly well while being, to be blunt about it, off my head half the time.

So much for drugs. There was also a sex-scandal component to the family bust-up of summer '72, and again it had its origins in the tapestry shoulder-bag. That bag grassed me up pretty thoroughly. It provided the authorities with evidence of more than one kind. There were any number of occasions in which my CHAPs acquaintances could have availed themselves of the convenient storage I innocently provided. Josh Tosh had entrances on more than one street, and could be used as a short cut. This short cut would inevitably turn into a long one, since we would end up dawdling by the perfume counter to try out fragrances from sample spray bottles. If I tried to hurry the party up, I too would receive squirts of clashing fragrances, asked which I liked best. There was sometimes a certain amount of rummaging in my bag, which meant that I was being used as a sort of mule in a narcissistic, mercifully small-scale shoplifting operation, smuggling an expensive bottle of *Eau Sauvage* or some such elixir past the gates of the shop and into the street.

There was no cologne forgotten in the Greek tapestry shoulder-bag, but it turned out to contain, along with the ancient roaches, a magazine. It was a picture magazine, and the pictures were of young men arranged in dreamy poses on piles of cushions, wearing socks and not a lot else. Looking sultry, if thumb-sucking strikes you as a maddening come-on. Some CHAPs fellow or other, some friend of a friend of a friend, had slipped this tentative smut into the community pocket and forgotten to retrieve it. So there I was, delivered into my parents' hysteria by a stray copy of *Nigel*. Or was it *Rupert*?

I can remember only too well. It was *Jeremy*. Mum brandished it at me often enough, waving it in my face as if she was a street-hawker trying to get me to buy the bloody thing rather than a mother losing her always elusive sense of proportion. 'Where did you get this? Who else knows about it? Who sold you the drugs? Who sold you this filth?'

I wasn't going to admit to them that the magazine wasn't mine. I refused to be ashamed. Of course it was stupid that Mum and Dad would think I had a secret life based round those insipid images. If I was going to overcome all the practical obstacles in the way of getting hold of a dirty magazine, I'd want something properly vile for my trouble. And someone who looked as if he'd been shaving for more than a week. Mum and Dad were both angry and upset, but through the chinks in the oblivion I had so patiently contrived for myself I could detect a complicating emotion. In some way Mum was partly blaming him for the rotten way I was turning out.

Once again the Inquisition was on the wrong track. If Mum and Dad had wanted a sex scandal, they could have had one, and it would have been a little bit spicier than a few pictures of dreary ephebes languid on the pillows. I'd broken the law in a public toilet on the A505 outside Royston, on the way home from Cambridge. It wasn't a private place, and still I had dared to have carnal congress with another man. No one had interrupted us, so my exhibitionistic streak was mildly frustrated. I wanted to shout out to the shocked air of Trees, Abbotsbrook Estate, Bourne End, 'It only lasted a few minutes and it happened in a public bog, but it was bloody beautiful!' Knowing that the words 'bog' and 'bloody' would have as much impact as the deed itself.

The man who was my first real sexual partner said something wonderful to me. It wasn't wonderful in a conventional way. He didn't say, for instance, 'People fear you and turn away from you, yes, and they are right to do so, since love flows in implacable streams from your eyes and loins alike. Your gaze and your desire pierce the fogs of matter. You must forgive people for feeling inadequate to such splendour.' What he said was a thousand times better. He said, 'If anyone comes in, I'm helping you out, okay, mate?' Mate! We mated and he called me *mate*. He certainly was helping me out, though no one disturbed us so I couldn't pass this revelation on. He was helping me out and no mistake. Afterwards he helped me to wash my hands. I let him, though I didn't feel the need of any cleaning up. I didn't feel soiled. I felt elevated, charged up. This too I would have liked to pass on to Mum and Dad, not in a spirit of boasting, but humbly wishing to share.

About the time that even the most ardent fan of androgynous pop might have been becoming sick of 'Starman', Maya took a surprising turn. The scene that I was absorbing through drifts of medicated meditation suddenly shifted in a way that made me sit up and take notice.

My dud of a mantra froze in mid-repetition. It had never been a really effective transcendental tool since India – it had developed a slow puncture, but now it just went phut. Prissie Washbourne was shouting through the French windows, 'Laura? Dennis? Is John all right? I'd like to see him, please.' She wasn't shouting out of rudeness, but because the music from Audrey's room was so loud.

Mum went to the windows to block any possible view into the room, and called out sharply through the French windows, 'He's fine,' adding in an undertone, 'Though I can't see that it's any of your business.' Perhaps it occurred to her that Prissie might have heard this comment, despite the lowering of her voice. She sang out more sweetly, 'Prissie dear, why don't you come to tea tomorrow? Or at the weekend?' Upstairs, Audrey must have realised that something out of the ordinary was happening. She took the needle off the record at last, and the sudden silence made the adults self-conscious.

Prissie carried it off well, though. Her voice was firm as she said,

'I'd like to see John now, Laura. I'd like to know what has happened to him. In fact I think I'll just sit here on the lawn until I'm satisfied he's all right.' At this point Dad cantered to the French windows and roared, 'Go away! You're not wanted here!' through the gap. Then he slammed the windows and locked them.

He and Mum bundled me out of the room, charging into my bedroom with the wheelchair, then hauling me roughly out of it and laying me on the bed. They seemed possessed. The arrival of an external threat intensified the sinister impression of teamwork. It didn't seem right that they were working so smoothly together. It was unprecedented. The soothing deadlock of their marriage had been violently broken, and the combination of drug scandal, sexual delinquency and an interfering neighbour had turned them into pantomime villains.

They actually hissed 'We'll deal with you later', before they rushed back to the sitting room. If the railway track had been any nearer I dare say they would have tied me to it. Perhaps they were saving that for later. I could hear them opening up the French windows again to shout at Prissie. Then the needle returned to its groove upstairs and David Bowie took up his invocations of the starman in the sky all over again.

As I lay on the bed I tried to grasp what was happening, working from first principles. For Prissie to intervene so forcefully she must have grounds for worry. So how long had it been since I had left the house? Prissie wasn't the hysterical type, and she wasn't used to seeing me every day. This pointed to a long absence from the world. Had I been indoors being harangued for days on end, while I wrapped myself in the shawl of my drug use and the tatters of my mantra, trying ineffectively to concentrate on the blooming pangs of an amaryllidaceous plant?

Calligraphy in the sky

It was only then that it occurred to me that I might have been held hostage for quite a few days. This nuance of life in Bourne End might have escaped me, disguised by a madness that had become familiar.

While the shouting continued, 'Starman' maintained its monopoly of the turntable, but Audrey came downstairs to find me. If it was

Audrey. It seemed not to be wholly Audrey. The girl who had geo-metrically modified some left-over party cake for my benefit was al-ready somewhat different from the girl I was used to, but the one who came into my room was different again. She was determined and full of purpose. Her purpose was to help me escape. She would help me get to the garage and into the car.

I can't explain the change in her, except in terms of the song she'd been playing so loudly upstairs. Not the song in itself but the message that rode on those frequencies, the signal below the signal. Ramana Maharshi had exerted himself once again for my benefit. The guru acts with obliquity and tact, and Bhagavan's miracles in his lifetime were always discreet. They didn't draw attention to themselves but shaded in with their surroundings. If there was a storm, for instance, and anxious devotees asked when it would stop, Bhagavan didn't go out and shout down the elements in the style of certain spiritual showmen (such as Sai Baba, a holy man with a streak of ham a mile wide), he would just say, 'I think it's clearing up now,' as anybody might, but those who were waiting to embark on journeys could pick up their luggage with confidence. The magic of the smallest interven-tion – homœopathy all over again.

The reason for this is actually expressed in the lyric of 'Starman': a personage from another dimension would like to meet us *but he thinks he'd blow our minds*. A very elegant exposition of the guru's polite use of a screen, a filter to protect us from rays too strong. When he was communicating with me in one of my dark times at Cambridge, the guru had tenderly ventriloquised Kafka. Now, with Audrey as his instrument, he was vibrating in sympathy with the voice of David Bowie, singing from the inmost marrow of the song, the core, where neither writer nor performer had ever been.

I tried to gather my wits. I asked her how long I'd been stuck in-side the house, but all she said was 'Far too long. It's time we got you out of here.'

Before I could ask her to be more specific (had it been three days? more?), she had picked me up and carried me to the garage. She didn't look strong, but she managed. The last time I could remember her trying to pick me up was when she was about five. She had gone through a phase of wanting to lift me because she saw Peter doing it (very put out when she was told she was too young). Now she had her moment of heroic porterage – for a few steps, and then our mode of motion became the conjoined stagger-hobble.

It would have been easier for us to take the wheelchair, but Audrey seemed to know exactly what she was doing. It's more common for the guru to speak through a person than physically to take over, but perhaps that's what was happening. It's true that Audrey was soon breathing heavily and making little grunts of effort, but the presence of the guru is also a great strain on the organism that houses it.

I prayed fervently that Mum and Dad would keep on bawling at Prissie, and that she went on answering back. If the showdown played out too quickly they would see that I was gone and intercept me double quick. I thought that Prissie's earth-mother persistence, once roused, would see me right. Failing that, I prayed that Mum would wail, 'I'm at my wits' end' and rush upstairs. The stair carpet was worn thin by the scuffing of hysterical feet.

Audrey helped me out of the kitchen by the rear door and round the side of the house. There was a side-door there leading to the garage. Of course there were stops along the way for changes of grip. She had to prop me up against the wall while she opened the back door, and again when we came to the garage. One more time when she opened the door of the car. But the moment we were in was so concentrated that everything seemed to happen in a single breath. To me that's supporting evidence for this being actual intervention – not to minimise Audrey's bravery and desire to help. Godhead itself is content to take the line of least resistance. Even Sai Baba didn't make the lightning do calligraphy in the sky or dance in lazy loops. He worked in the grain of the wood.

In normal life Audrey wasn't afraid of the garage, but she was certainly afraid of the creatures that lived there. Spiders. Never before had she been so blithely indifferent to the presence of arachnid arthropods. Proof positive, as far as I'm concerned, that she wasn't at the controls. She was growing up fast, but it's a slow business overcoming phobias or (more likely) becoming more skilled at hiding them, better at coming up with cover stories.

Audrey slipped me smoothly into the blessed Mini and whispered, 'Good luck, Godspeed.' Except it wasn't going to be quite as simple as that. I had to break it to her that I didn't have the car keys. They would be on the hall table, where Mum put them in her periodic fits of confiscation.

The car keys were one of our little battlegrounds, cause of many a tussle. I liked to leave them in the ignition of the Mini in the unlocked garage, but she was all against it. I reminded her that she was always saying that one of the reasons we had moved to the Abbotsbrook Estate that it was safe from thieves − unlike the long-ago married quarters they had lived in when I was a baby, where her wedding-ring had been stolen from the sink where she had been doing the washing-up when she looked in on me for *five seconds* to make sure I was all right . . .

Mum said that leaving the keys in the car was asking for trouble, but how was it any riskier than Peter and me sleeping with the door open? Not that I said so, for fear that she would act against that privilege also, in the name of consistency.

So the hall table was where the keys would be, and Audrey must go back for them. She swallowed once or twice at that, but she was still game and guru-guided. For the two short minutes she was away, I tried the worn-out syllables of *Om Mane Padme Om* one more time, but they did nothing to slow my racing heartbeat. My mantra was like a tyre worn smooth. It had no grip. Really, I would have done just as well with 'Starman', or indeed 'When You Wish upon a Star'.

Contrary to Dad's precept in his guise as my driving instructor, I hadn't backed the Mini in. I had been lazy and would have to take the consequences. I was facing the rear wall of the garage. I would have to back my way out. This would be a type of manœuvre that doesn't feature in any driving test that I know of − the emergency start.

Audrey was frankly panting when she came back from the house. She'd been running. She thrust the keys into my hands. 'Hurry up,' she wailed. 'They saw me. Go! Go now! They're going mad in there . . .' I had the sense that things had returned to normal. The divine whisper had said what it had to say, and we were on our own now. At any moment Audrey's eyes might slide towards the dark corners of the garage and she would start to hug herself nervously.

That was when we heard the gravel smartly crunching, and Dad closed the garage door. I could see his sports jacket in the mirror of the Mini, the triangle of neat hanky in his breast pocket, before the daylight was cut off. Of course it hadn't been very bright inside the garage before, but the sudden darkness made Audrey whimper. I started the engine, blessing the general reliability of Maestro Issigoni's economical masterpiece, and switched on the headlights. Audrey wasn't comforted by the brightness. It made her cower in a corner of the garage. The divine wind which had filled her sails had well and truly blown itself out. I shouted 'WATCH YOURSELVES OUTSIDE!' as loud as I could over the sound of the engine and waited five seconds, as timed by two breakneck Om-Mane-Padme-Oms, so that Mum and Dad at least had time to act on the warning. Then I found reverse and backed out of the garage.

Warmed his astral cockles

I didn't smash the doors open, but of course 'John nudged the garage doors open at quite a speed' has as little prospect of finding an ecological niche in family history as 'John nearly scorched the greenhouse.' John smashed, John burned – that's the official version.

I admit that the doors swung open pretty briskly. I was far more afraid of losing momentum than of doing damage to fixtures and fittings. The doors swung open as far as the hinges allowed then rebounded. As they closed again, they feebly retaliated for the initial impact by scraping the sides of the Mini. Between the first and second impacts I had a glimpse in the mirror of Mum and Dad reeling backwards. Rage was still ruling Dad's facial muscles, but Mum's expression held a sort of agony of worry. It was too late to build on that.

I had always coveted the ability to slam a door at the climax of an argument, and now I had my wish. It's true I slammed the garage doors open rather than shut, but that's a technicality. It was well worth waiting for. The noise was marvellous.

In the exhilaration of the moment, the terrible longed-for moment of breaking with my family, I did the finest three-point turn of my driving career. It was textbook. It would have cheered the shade of John Griffiths himself, patron saint of the disabled driver. Not the ghost of a graze on the garden gate or posts. It would have warmed his astral cockles.

As I turned the car I could see Audrey slinking out of the garage and back to the house. Mum and Dad kept pace with the Mini but didn't get too close, as if they were trying to herd some unfamiliar beast back to its cage, not sure whether it would actually charge them. As I came round the side of the house I saw that Prissie was still sitting on the lawn. She stood up and brushed the grass stems off herself, smiling at me incredulously. I stopped the car by her. The passenger door wasn't properly closed, so I was able to push it open with my stick. As I did so I barked, yes I *barked* a magnificent cliché out of the window. I had earned it. I for whom drawing the curtains in the morning was quite an enterprise had taken part in a scene of action. There had been shouting, threats, divine intervention and a getaway car. I had also, whether or not Dad noticed, performed a driving manœuvre that would have met his highest standards.

I barked: 'Let's get out of this madhouse, Prissie!' No guru was needed to give the script any polishing at that point. Of course Prissie lived only down the road, she came on foot and could have left the same way, but she scrambled in, sitting awkwardly on my cane and gleefully shouting '*Fuck*, what fun!', and we were off.

I'd have had a go at spinning my wheels and giving the gravel a good scatter if I hadn't been afraid of spoiling our exit by stalling or running the Mini into a wall.

Suddenly Prissie said, 'Stop, John! Stop the car!'

'I'm not going back there, Prissie,' I said grimly.

'Of course you're not. Better stop now, all the same.'

Turning round to observe the Cromers frozen in their tableau of conflict, she had seen Audrey running after us, pushing the wheelchair. Clever girl! I wouldn't have managed very well with that particular hostage left in enemy hands.

I don't have enough experience of intensely dramatic scenes to know if anti-climax always comes along for the ride. Perhaps Mum shared my feeling, and did what she could with the modest resources at her disposal to keep the emotional temperature high. She threw one of her shoes at us. I'm not sure if it had slipped off her foot or if she had taken it off expressly. It was one of those funny summer shoes with rope soles. Mum had displaced all her griefs and furies onto the flinging of an espadrille. In my memory of that afternoon it bears the perfume of solar amber as it describes its modest arc from Mum's infuriated hand, the *Ambre Solaire* sun-cream she rubbed into herself while she basked in the filtered sunshine of the conservatory.

When Audrey had caught up with us, I said to Prissie, 'Can't we take her with us?'

'Not unless you want to see me in jail.' I knew she was right, but it was important that she said it out loud. I wanted Audrey to understand that my hands were tied. I couldn't return the favour of rescue.

Prissie got out and loaded the chair in the boot, leaving us to say our goodbyes. I might not see Audrey again until she came of age and could make her own decisions. When there's a decade's worth of age-gap between siblings, conversation doesn't often run smoothly. She looked now like a tired and frightened child. I wondered how much she remembered of what had gone on in the last fifteen minutes, hoping that there would be some balm left behind by the guru when he departed. It wouldn't be fair if she suffered after-shocks of intervention.

Then I realised that I had been given a cue, the same cue as hers, and from the same benign source. Ramana Maharshi's influence persisted like the Cheshire Cat's discarnate smile. This was the twinkle without the guru, the starman remotely beaming.

'Let the children use it . . .' I said gently. 'Let the children lose it . . .'

I waited for her to finish the refrain. Her eyes went very wide, so that she seemed to be regressing after so much precocious growing-up. 'Let . . . all the children boogie?' she said at last, with an upward intonation, as if after all those listenings she still wasn't sure of the words.

If Prissie had second thoughts about being the catalyst of my freedom, she didn't admit it on the (ridiculously short) drive to her house. I asked, 'Will Malcolm mind if I stay at your house for a night or two?'

'Stay as long as you like,' she said. 'He'll be thrilled.' This hardly seemed possible, though she didn't seem to be joking. With her I never quite knew. 'He's always saying he needs someone to talk to. Listen, John, do you love your mother very much?'

I did my best to be honest. 'I try not to.'

A suitably plumbed bolt-hole

'I think that's sensible. Best to get along without her. She doesn't really want you to have a life of your own.' It was shocking to hear something like that, something I had come to believe, stated so calmly by someone outside the family. 'I do feel sorry for Laura,' Prissie went on, 'but she doesn't own you and she shouldn't try. I've learned the hard way with the twins – *your children are not your children*, and all that – *they are the sons and daughters of life's longing for itself*. Kahlil Gibran, you know. Preachy stuff and no mistake, but Malcolm adores it. So be warned. If you get him started on the glories of *The Prophet* I'll phone Laura to come and pick you up. Understood?'

I thought I could abide by this condition of residence. When we got in, Prissie couldn't wait to get unshod. She had been wearing stout walking shoes which looked particularly wrong on someone almost caricaturally free-spirited. I imagine she had chosen them as much to cope with the formality of confrontation as for the discomfort of gravel.

The twins Joss and Alex, now twelve, had been farmed out in France, spending the summer in France to improve their language skills, so there was room to spare *chez* Washbourne. In her own way Prissie seemed to share Dad's idea of the importance of pushing chicks out of the nest, though she made sure that they had a parachute of money and some useful addresses.

Chez Washbourne was relatively similar to Trees, though the downstairs facilities only ran to a lavatory, not a bathroom. Granny had missed a trick by omitting to fund an extension at a neighbour's house, so as to provide me with a suitably plumbed bolt-hole in case of family crisis.

Malcolm came home from work on his usual train to find a house-guest installed, a house-guest who was both easy and difficult. Easy in himself (let's hope), difficult by virtue of his needs. Without the bum-snorkel the lavatory would be a bit of a challenge. I decided to go easy on the Washbournes' food, at least until my indispensable utensil had been restored to me. I envy the hauteur of cats at stool, the way they dissociate themselves so successfully from basic acts. By that reckoning my experience is canine. With me it's all shameful straining, wagging my tail and hoping to be forgiven for being such a dirty dog. I would also need to be helped upstairs every now and then to bathe unless I was to smell like a young goat.

Prissie hadn't bothered to alert her husband by phone of the dramatic changes in Cromer family life. 'Malcolm, darling,' she said, 'Laura and Dennis have completely lost their senses. There was nothing else I could do. They've always been, shall we say, remarkably *uptight*, but this time they were downright crazed.' That was as close as she got to explaining herself to the man of the house. He took it completely in his stride. I thought this rather splendid, coming as I did from a household where Mum forgetting to warm the plates before a meal could cast a pall that might not lift for days, even if no word of reproach was uttered.

The rest of the conversation was equally off-hand.

Malcolm: 'Is there a chance of their coming to their senses any time in the foreseeable future?'

Prissie: 'Not really.'

Malcolm: 'That's all right, then.'

I thought that was splendid too.

My full-blooded participation in a family showdown (once I'd actually worked out that I was being held against my will) came at a certain price. My shoulder froze after all that driving out of garages and down driveways, that adrenalin-boosted three-point turn. I would have been happy to be excused driving for a few days while my shoulder loosened up, but I was determined not to cut a helpless figure in this new household. The Washbournes for their part were anxious to reassure me I wasn't being a burden, so there were all sorts of errands cheerfully suggested and accepted that both parties could happily, I dare say, have done without.

I was in pain and I was separated from my supplies of Fortral. It would be exaggerating to say that I was in withdrawal, but I certainly missed my pharmaceutical crutch, the crutch that formed a sturdy enough tripod with my actual crutch and cane.

Prissie treated the whole situation as an adventure and a joke. She looked out some paper knickers for me, which she'd bought for a holiday in Greece to save the trouble of laundry, though Malcolm in a rare assertive moment had refused to wear them. Sniffing a pair, she claimed that they had absorbed the aroma of olives, even a distant whiff of retsina.

I couldn't expect to go on with my dissolute Cambridge ways, doing without socks and underpants, while I was a guest in someone's home, but my heart sank at the prospect of those disposables, with their thin thread of elastic and doubtful absorbency. Still, I had company. Prissie insisted that Malcolm wear the paper pants too – this was her revenge for his lack of coöperation on the Greek holiday. If they were good enough for me, she said, they were certainly good enough for him, and this time he didn't put up a fight.

By now I had given an account of the row over the contents of my shoulder-bag, feeling that those who were offering me sanctuary had a right to know the crimes of which I stood accused.

Prissie said, 'Malcolm can go up to Soho at the weekend and pick up some queer filth for you. You can wait that long, can't you, John? But he's not normally a very inspired shopper. Best to give him an exact title, or else give him a general subject area and sort through his haul later on. As for the cannabis, we're very moderate users here. A few puffs every month or so. I'm sorry we're so unadventurous. Tell us what you need and we'll try to get it.'

I could never quite make up my mind whether she was telling the simple truth, cracking jokes or engaged on some sort of double bluff. No more was said about Malcolm's proposed Soho pornography trawl, and nothing was smoked in my presence that would have shocked the author of *Gardening for Adventure*. The household's actual level of taboo-breaking was low. Malcolm's bookmark seemed stuck in the early pages of *Last Exit To Brooklyn*, a landmark work, an earthquake of the mind guaranteed to shock and horrify, but not necessarily to hold the attention.

The next morning a letter arrived for me, in the early hours, with the words BY HAND written on the envelope. It's a phrase that has always puzzled me. Could people not have worked out by themselves that an unstamped envelope had not been delivered by the postman? And doesn't the postman deliver by hand too?

The letter was from Dad. He took me to task about how much I had hurt Mum by my bad behaviour, Mum who had devoted *her entire life* to me. The phrase was doubly underlined. Of course that was the whole trouble, as Dad could see in more lucid moods – devotion (as she interpreted devotion) inflamed and corroded her character.

The lair he shared with her

Dad's letter gave offence in its turn. He must have got out his ruler to make those double underlinings under '*her entire life*'. Truly I knew the depth of my disgrace when I saw that the full panoply of the family stationery was ranged against me: best notepaper, fountain pen and ruler – the bell, book and candle of the writing-desk. Another passage showed a complete refusal to accept reality: 'I don't know what you said to Audrey to get her to help you, but I hope you're ashamed of yourself.' Even he had seen there was something mysterious about Audrey's participation, but he was temperamentally inclined to look for the working of sinister rather than radiant forces.

Worldly powers rule by consent, and I didn't consent to these rulings. Nor did I take kindly to being told I should buck up my ideas and apologise to Mum, or else everything I had left behind would be 'put in sequestration'. Dad seemed to savour the legal formula with a bailiff's solemn gloating.

I showed the letter to Prissie. Her reaction was to send Malcolm round to Trees in the car, to beard Dad in his lair and 'thrash things out' with him man to man. Malcolm had instructions to demand the return of my possessions (that's why he was to go by car, to carry off my reclaimed goods). I wasn't at all keen on this line of approach, and Malcolm certainly flinched from the mission proposed for him. Eventually, though, he realised that bearding Dad in his lair presented fewer risks than thwarting Prissie in the lair he shared with her.

He came back with my things, seeming faintly stunned by the success of the project – and rightly so, since thrashing things out man to man is one of the least successful courses of action ever devised. Prissie seemed almost disappointed, though she rallied and teased Malcolm about his great bravery. He wouldn't go into detail about the encounter, but said that Dad hadn't made difficulties. He was reasonable in the end – and I don't think divine intervention has to be dragged in for everything mildly surprising, only the epic departures from precedent.

It's unlikely the guru was working overtime. Normal service had resumed. It was probably enough for Mum to be out at the shops, or at her sewing circle, for Dad to come to his senses and side against her, with almost anyone.

If she was at the sewing circle she wouldn't be mentioning the recent traumas. She was in no hurry to join their troubled ranks, the parents whose children drank till they passed out, or went through handbags for money to buy drugs.

I was glad to have my books restored to me, but the bum-snorkel had been top of the list of my needs. Its return was particularly welcome. I hadn't been looking forward to an extended period of bathroom wheedling in that house of wayward welcome.

I was fascinated by the workings of the Washbournes' marriage. Prissie didn't believe in giving Malcolm too many choices. In the matter of their children's names, for instance, he had been given free rein, but within a very restricted area. It was Prissie who had selected the names Jocelyn and Alex for the twins, with her stubborn jokiness persisting at the most serious moments. It was up to him to attach these ambivalent tags to the children when they arrived (a boy and a girl, as it happened). The names were like strips of litmus paper which only turned pink or blue when touched to an actual child.

Malcolm never seemed to feel undermined or embarrassed by Prissie's bossiness. I felt that this was a healthy marriage despite the lopsided distribution of power, much healthier than Mum's and Dad's, where the rôles were conventionally assigned but eaten away from inside. In practical terms Dad had no more assertiveness than Malcolm did, but he spent a lot more time and energy simulating the proper male behaviour.

I suppose Malcolm and I, kitted out in our disposable knickers, were Prissie's babies that summer, in the absence of Joss and Al. In fact things worked out pretty well. She sent Malcolm on a second expedition to Trees, since some clothes and medication hadn't found their way to my new address. This time his reception was distinctly frosty, since it was Mum who answered the door. She told him that family life had been quite tricky enough before he put his oar in. His 'oar' presumably being Prissie! It was a bit much to blame him for her actions, since she was so obviously an oar unto herself. Still, nothing was said about refusing me my things, nothing about sequestration or distraint of goods.

One morning the postman knocked on the door, not because he had a parcel to deliver but because he wanted to know why my car was parked outside, four doors from home. This sort of thing is the reason people want to live in small communities, until they do. Prissie said brightly that I was having a change of scene. A rest cure.

I wouldn't put it past the postman to have knocked on the door of Trees for more information, which would have been a bad moment for Mum and no mistake. But what was I supposed to do – cover the Mini with turves and branches?

At first I tried to keep my distance from Prissie. My emotional distance, of course – there wasn't much I could do to avoid her physically. Better the mother you know than the mother you don't. I was afraid I would turn into her confidant willy-nilly, going from being a captive at Trees to being a captive audience at Heron's Gate.

While she painted her toenails

In fact Prissie was a fairly undemanding companion. She read the romantic-historical novels of Georgette Heyer much of the time, so she didn't pester me with conversation. Of her chosen author she would say, 'Georgette Heyer really does write wonderfully well, and you can usually tell quite early on (not that I mind) if it's one that you've read before . . .' She really enjoyed buying a more serious novel, something by William Golding or Margaret Drabble, and then going right on reading Georgette Heyer instead. Playing truant from a real engagement with life, like someone keeping an important visitor waiting while she painted her toenails.

You could often catch her looking with simple pleasure at her own pink feet. I say you could catch her at it, but there was nothing furtive about her appreciation of herself. If she became conscious of my gaze she would meet it, with a further flowering of her smile. She would lean her head back and stroke her own plump throat in the same admiring spirit. This was all rather disconcerting – we're all so used to people who are on bad terms with their bodies that anything

668

else comes to seem slightly mad. Of course the body is unreal, but you really sit up and take notice when someone wears it well.

Prissie told me about a famous flight of fancy – that Heaven would be like eating *foie gras* to the sound of trumpets. Her own equivalent of this, she said, was reading Georgette Heyer to the sound of the Jacques Loussier Trio playing Bach. It wasn't extravagant. Those who couldn't afford her modest Heaven could easily order its ingredients from the local library.

The weather was fine, and she'd often take me out into the garden with her. That was a little odd, being so like the garden at Trees and so very unlike it. I'd be trying to meditate, or perhaps simply dozing, and I'd hear scraps of conversation that might have been Mum and Audrey in the garden of Trees, and echoes of 'Starman' (now charged with purely human meanings) carried on the breeze.

In its way this was an idyllic period. The Washbournes weren't vegetarians or anything like it, but they catered to me without fuss. Their loose hippie allegiance tended to exclude meat from their table, at least in blatant slabs, though mince might pass muster (flesh once safely granulated dips below the ethical radar of so many). From that summer I remember avocado pears (which we ate, I think, every day) and the deliciousness of French bread, the surprise of French cheese, the revelation of olives both black and green.

Prissie had been the first person in our social circle to risk the technical marvel of Gold Blend (freeze-dried granules, imagine!). Later, Muriel Foot got in on the act on behalf of the sewing circle, joining the Licensed Victuallers' association for the sake of wholesale prices and buying tins of Gold Blend the size of waste-paper bins, despite the palaver required to decant granules from the tin into manageable jars.

At Downing I practised a little religion of 'proper coffee', but the Gold Blend at Prissie's, made with hot milk, offered its own pleasures.

I felt guilty to have left Audrey vulnerable in Trees, house of misrule, but hadn't she always known how to wind Mum round her little finger? Surely she wouldn't have lost that skill. Perhaps things would be easier for her in my absence. It was perfectly possible that Audrey had on some level wanted me out of the house, which wouldn't in the least invalidate the miraculousness of her intervention.

Peter came back from his travels to find a home transformed. He hated it. He would call in morosely on Prissie's house on his way to or from work, and begged me to ask her to take him in also. I had to explain it wasn't on. This was a sanctuary for one, rather than a mass adoption programme. There wasn't a vacancy in the Paper Pants Club.

The household in Trees now contained two males who hated scenes in their different ways and two females who, in their different ways, required them, Audrey hell-bent on winning (unless the guru in passing had changed her habits), Mum bagsy-ing the rôle of tragic victim. The emotional barometer of the household would be stuck on Stormy for some time.

Up to this point Peter's plan in life had been summed up by Granny (who was baffled by it) as: Earn some money. Get on a train or a plane until it's gone. Start again.

But now he made the decision to move out himself and find somewhere else to live. So perhaps I can take credit, by leaving the house under such a cloud, for clearing the skies for Peter and letting him escape his rut of travel and return. Unless my long residence in the house is to blame for his slowness in taking up his birth-right of independence – so deep and foundational was fraternal loyalty in his make-up.

When Malcolm came home from work he'd usually sit with me rather than his wife. He'd even hold my hand and close his eyes, while Prissie idly mustered food in the kitchen. Mum had never got to grips with avocado pears. Of course we'd seen them in shops. They had been talked about. They were even on the menu at the Compleat Angler where Granny stayed, but how to manage them at home was beyond Mum. I had tried to reassure her that it couldn't be hard to know when the enigmatic objects were ripe, but Mum was convinced that there were tenderising protocols withheld from laymen outside the restaurant trade, and that Peter wasn't telling.

Prissie, on the other hand, actually had bowls in avocado colours, a darker green on the outside, creamy-pale within. When she came back in to the dining room where Malcolm was holding my hand she'd ask sweetly, 'Is this homosexuality, Malcolm?' He'd simply say, 'You don't understand, darling. I get such pure energy from John.'

'Don't mind me,' she said, with the same large calm. 'Just carry on with your canoodling. The wife is always the last to know, of course. And it serves her right.'

What went on between me and Malcolm wasn't canoodling so much as low-level mystical chat. Perhaps Malcolm felt piqued that I had gone to India, where my guru was, and talked about his plans to visit his own inspiration, Don Juan, in Mexico. He had read Carlos Castaneda's books, which Penguin published and which adorned almost every student's shelves those days. Later they were exposed as 'fakes' – the inverted commas seem appropriate because it's a hard position for someone like me to defend, that time and space, life and death, are all unreal, but Carlos Castaneda is more unreal than any of these and must therefore be shunned. If you're not careful you can end up saying that the unreality of Carlos Castaneda's mystical claptrap is the only real thing in the whole of Maya.

Finch, Pearsall & Mephistopheles

I'm afraid we got into something that was almost an enlightenment competition. I'd quote something Ramana Maharshi had said, and he'd quote something that Castaneda's Don Juan had said, though we were neither of us tremendously up on our subjects. Under the influence of peyote Castaneda had a vision of Mescalito, seeing him as a green man with a pointed hat. I decided not to mention that I had gone him one better by being granted an interview with Mescalito, and had been trusted with some important dendrological work.

At one stage I remember intoning, *'Those who know do not speak;'* and while I was taking a breath at that semi-colon, he completed the aphorism with *'those who speak do not know.'* Then we smiled enigmatically at each other.

This was the shallowest of profundities, filched from Alan Watts's *Zen Flesh, Zen Bones*, also published by Penguin – worse still, filched from the blurb about that book printed at the back of another one. Prissie looked up from her Heyer and gave us her own little smile, which recognised us as spiritually pretentious fakes, bluffers to our very souls. Certainly her relationship with Georgette Heyer was more authentic than ours with Alan Watts. We didn't even realise, while we parroted Zen quotes, how neatly they summed us up.

If Prissie overheard Malcolm telling me, not for the first time, that advertising was killing his soul, she would say, 'Malcolm, darling, that's the whole point of the enterprise. Why do you think your firm is called Finch Pearsall & *Mephistopheles*, for heaven's sake? If you haven't sold your soul yet, it's because nobody wants it. Face it, Malcolm, you're a lost soul, you're not damned at all. Only lost souls wear Hush Puppies. The damned have a lot more style.' These, though, were tender squabbles, quite outside my experience, with all the rancour on the surface.

While I stayed *chez* Washbourne I tried to ration my intake of liquids, so as not to have to go to the toilet too often. I didn't overdo it. There was no virtue in dehydrating myself in a warm season, parching my kidneys just to avoid embarrassment. It made sense to discipline my bladder so that I could last the night, like a well-trained dog, to spare the household the duty of emptying a pee bottle. Gradually I worked up to a steely continence. In fact I may as well admit that since then I have often used the call of the bathroom as a way of getting some good earthed contact, whether with strangers or old friends. Nothing breaks the ice like embarrassment in a bathroom.

I could hardly expect there to be no repercussions from the rupture with Mum and Dad, but I hoped not to have to deal with them until after the vacation. No such luck. One day the phone rang and Prissie told me it was for me. Her voice was rather hushed. 'Who is it?' I mouthed, and she answered in a whisper, 'Perhaps a bishop?'

It was Graëme Beamish, my tutor.

'John,' he said, 'please find it in your heart to forgive me for disturbing you in the well-earned rest of your vacation. Then I will try to find it in mine to forgive your mother for disturbing the peace of mine.

'I would have left her letter unanswered were it not for the fact that I am taking next term as a sabbatical. It didn't seem fair to pass on to my replacement the obligation of dealing with as tricky a customer as I have come across in my experience as a tutor.'

I could hear regular metallic impacts in the background, from which I deduced that Dr Beamish was finding amusement in setting Newton's Balls a-clack.

'I'm not referring to you, John, though you yourself do not offer the authorities the easiest of rides. I mean your mother.

'As you may not know, your mother has written to me roughly every two weeks of university term since you first came up.

'John? Are you there?'

'Yes, Dr Beamish.' I was very shocked to learn that Mum had been so hideously active on what she imagined to be my behalf. Knowing that my tutor had been screening me from her interference for the last two years felt almost as bad as being pushed down King Street by him with a stranger's sick caking my wheels.

'Shall I continue? I hope I'm not interrupting any important activity. The file on *Cromer, Mrs L* is even larger than the one on *Cromer, J*. For some time her idea was that I should forbid you from changing your course of study. Now it seems that your family has exploded in some way. I have to say I have no interest in how you all get on with each other. I propose simply to read you my reply to your mother's latest letter so that you know where you stand. Is that agreed?'

'Agreed.'

'"*Dear Mrs Cromer, I am sorry to learn that John has fallen victim to sexual deviance and drug addiction. These scourges do unfortunately claim a small proportion of undergraduates, and not always the unpromising ones, during their years of study. The evidences of wrongdoing which you mention, however, came to light during the vacation and on private property: as such they cannot be said directly to involve the College or indeed the University. If John is found in possession of further caches of smut or illegal narcotics I will, of course, inform you at once. I myself had always imagined that his temptations were the more traditional ones of strong drink and bad company.*"'

I could hear a self-satisfied smile in his voice, and could imagine him looking at me over the tops of imaginary half-moon glasses, while he congratulated himself on the neatness of this oblique reference to my kidnap at the hands of Write Off Tuesday.

He was certainly getting his pennyworth of revenge for an evening when he was made to feel uncomfortable in the Senior Common Room, sniffing the air from time to time and checking his smart shoes for traces of undergraduate vomit.

"'*As for your suggestion that he should receive medical treatment, although it is true that the University has access to the 'top men' in many fields, most of them indeed the products of our system of education, it is my impression that John knows almost as much as any of the health professionals with whom his difficult history has brought him into contact. Some say that he eats doctors for breakfast, others that he merely chews them and spits them out, without going to the trouble of swallowing.*'" It is perhaps true that I was impatient with the general practitioner assigned by the university to preside over my health. Dr Beamish paused, as if trying to detect down the telephone wire whether his bufferish persiflage was succeeding in making me squirm.

"'*There seems no pressing need to add to the list of casualties, unless of course John's academic progress begins to suffer. If and when that happens, we will certainly seek medical help.*'"

'Does this reply seem satisfactory to you, John?'

'Perfectly satisfactory, Dr Beamish. Thank you.'

'Not at all, John. I shall see you in the new year, after my sabbatical term. But please go easy on my replacement. Not everyone has my inner strength.'

All in all it was a fine show of donnish humour, in a style which I imagine has changed little over the decades, even the centuries. I had to be grateful to Beamish for fobbing off Mum and Dad with his elegant mockery, even if it did sting me a little in the process. To judge from his sardonic references to drink and so on he regarded me as having good character more or less by default. Mechanically unable to sin rather than either virtuous or vicious on the level of morals.

With the Washbournes' permission I phoned Granny. I wasn't sure which way she would jump, which was of course just the way she liked it. Her tone was predictably crisp from the word go. 'Halnaker 226.'

'Hello, Granny, this is John.'

'Good morning, John.'

'Have you heard from Mum lately?'

'Indeed I have not. We are not in morbidly regular communication. Laura seeks to shield me from good and bad news alike. Luckily Peter retains some dim memory of his grandmother.'

'Well, Granny, the thing is, we had a row and I've moved out.'

'So I hear. People are always saying that blood is thicker than water but I can't say I've noticed.' Wonderful Granny, so unsuspectingly Hindu in her instincts! So right in thinking that the fluids of kinship have no metaphysical claim to viscosity. 'Are you well placed where you are staying now?'

'Very well placed, Granny.'

'I am pleased to hear it. I take it your allowance has been discontinued?'

'I'm afraid so.'

'What sums were involved?'

'Dad gave me £10 a month.'

'I will maintain that level of stipend. Were there other expenses met by your parents?'

'Only books.'

'I see. I will carry that burden also, though I shall expect scrupulous accounts. Goodbye, John.'

'Of course, Granny. Thank –'

But she had already put down the receiver at the Tangmere end. It's true she was of a generation that didn't necessarily perform expansively on the phone, but I think her brusqueness was more idiosyncratic. Granny just got a kick out of hanging up, without footling politesse. And for all the terseness of the conversation, that was my finances fixed, for the time being, without opposition or even haggling. It's true that Granny liked any such arrangement to be provisional, renewed or withdrawn as she pleased.

In her financial conversations she could be oddly playful, even skittish. She might say, 'I had a little investment, John, and nothing would it bear – not even a silver nutmeg or a golden pear, I'm afraid, though that would have been charming. But now the King of Spain's daughter has paid me a rather nice dividend after all, and I thought I would send you some of it – not all the fruit from my little nut tree, but enough I hope to give you a pleasant taste.' Or else: 'I'm afraid my portfolio has caught rather a bad cold, John – it may even be 'flu – so we must both tighten our belts for the time being and hope for improvement. Portfolios are particularly susceptible to coughs and sneezes at this time of year, as perhaps you know.

675

Cases of pneumonia have been reported in the Square Mile. We must watch and wait.'

I returned to Cambridge for the academic year 1972–3 as an honorary orphan (at least in my own mind), and deprived of the tutor who had protected me in previous years.

It was my chance to get a telephone installed. I seized it. I got to work right away. I wasn't confident of putting one over on his replacement – I could all too easily imagine Graëme leaving a note saying THE ENDLESSLY PESTERING JOHN CROMER IS NOT TO HAVE A TELEPHONE HOWEVER ELOQUENTLY HE PLEADS HIS SPECIOUS CASE – but it was worth a go. And then it went like a dream. I had my paperwork with me: the original note from Roy Wisbey proposing it, not to mention my photocopy of the relevant section of the Disabled Persons Act 1971. The tender-hearted substitute asked for no documentation (locums are usually pushovers). My case spoke for itself. I should have asked for a fridge and a shower in my room while the going was good.

I remember nothing about Beamish's temporary replacement except that he was a historian. As he opened my file and then Mum's a look of amazement spread across his face. What a teeming archive of pathology he had in his hand! Such bad luck that it wasn't from the formative years of a Beethoven or a Churchill.

'How is your relationship with your parents?' he asked.

'Non-existent.'

'Well, you're already getting the maximum grant, so that won't change. Do you have resources of your own?'

'My Granny helps out.' These few words painted a wonderfully pathetic picture. Granny would have given an elegant snort of glee at it.

'I see that the Bell Abbot & Barnes Fund helped out in another . . . emergency. Do you want me to try them again?'

'I suppose so.' Said with the right amount of swallowed pride. In fact it was resentment I was swallowing, at the way the college had used an outside agency to reward its own greed, in the matter of the ceiling rail. And indeed Bell Abbot & Barnes came up trumps, matching Granny's £10 monthly. I was now better off than I was before the bust-up, though I had to budget very carefully if I was to get through the vacations (and I had no idea where I would be spending them). God bless Bell, God bless Abbot and God bless Barnes. Bless their cotton-rich socks. Bless every fibre.

The *Zeitgeist* had me fooled

I was now an undergraduate of means. I was more or less flush. So when an English student called Robin Baines-Johnson I met at a Tragedy lecture asked to borrow £5, I gave it to him. He was already known to me at second-hand, since his uncle was the Governor of the Bank of England. He was a mini-celebrity of the student body. I hardly hesitated. If anyone in Cambridge – anyone in the whole world – was good for a loan, then surely it was the nephew of the Governor of the Bank of England! I entirely misunderstood the mood of the times. The *Zeitgeist* had me fooled good and proper. This was a period when all institutions were considered evil by student culture, above all those which were explicitly capitalist, and personal responsibility was felt to be a bourgeois perversion. I should have understood. The nephew of the Governor of the Bank of England was the last person in the country who would risk repaying a debt. Existentially it would be a disaster. It would strip him of his last shred of authenticity. At all events I never got my fiver back.

I didn't really relax until my phone connection was installed. It didn't seem impossible that Graëme would reappear from wherever he had gone, with a tan and a straw hat, a suitcase in each hand, specifically to hiss at the engineers, 'Kindly disconnect that phone!' In the event he stayed away, and at last I had a proper link with the world.

In one respect the timing was perfect. In previous years I would have had to tell Mum about the phone sooner or later, and then she'd have been calling me the whole time, sparing Dr Beamish and putting pressure on me direct.

I had some enjoyable little chats with the operator. In those days the telephone wire went straight into the wall, and if you put the phone off the hook you could be reported. They would put the howler on to get your attention. I used to enjoy teasing the operator, saying I had sabotaged the bell with a wire so I didn't hear the bell if I didn't want to. Technically this would have been tampering, and a punishable offence. I was living dangerously.

As a third-year I had lost some of my social fear. I was beginning to be anxious about the future rather than the present, wondering what life after Cambridge would be like. I couldn't imagine it. Clearly, though, it was a good thing that returning to the bosom of the family was no longer an option. The family bosom was off limits and out of bounds. Family and I were giving each other the cold, the frozen shoulder.

One worthwhile 'side-effect' was that there was no need to worry about my reputation any more. I had nothing to lose. My parents already thought I derived sexual pleasure from pictures of youngsters lolling in socks.

Still, when someone at a CHAPs meeting first disparagingly mentioned the 'meat market' I thought, as a long-serving vegetarian, that these gloating carnivores were referring to an actual market where carcases were displayed, all the marvellous machinery of life impaled on a hook and cut up to be sold. In fact the reference was to the Stable Bar, off Trinity Street, a narrow premises where homosexuals not enlightened enough to attend meetings might be found. It had the look of a hotel bar, with plenty of red plush and folksy bits of beaming which looked fake even if they weren't, and plenty of horse brasses to back up the name, though there would only have been the space to accommodate a single horse.

I never heard anyone refer to the Stable Bar in anything but damning terms, yet everyone turned up there at some stage, even Ken, though he looked rather lost. I saw the Tonys there once or twice, although they hardly noticed strangers and were the only people present whose motives were blamelessly social.

Ken only visited the meat market to spread the word about the group, to tell those writhing in the coils of the patriarchy the good news that there existed an independent forum, not far away, where issues of sexual and political liberation could be freely discussed and worked through. He would nerve himself with a couple of pints then spread the word from table to table. His reception from groups was sometimes mildly abusive, so he tended to gravitate towards single strangers, less prompt to defend themselves. There was something

about him, as he advanced heavily towards people who often edged
away or tried to avoid his eyes, reminiscent of Gladstone scouring Piccadilly for loose women to coax back to Downing Street for soup and
Bible-reading. He had the same admirable and slightly suspect motives, even if his success rate in these mercy swoops couldn't compete.

On Saturday nights George took to pushing me up to the street
entrance to the Stable, then over its awkward threshold. He would
pause outside the door of the bar to take a deep breath. Entering the
premises with a wheelchair required careful choreography: a vigorous
push to the door followed immediately by a judicious pressing down
on the handles so as to clear the change of level before the door came
back and bashed me, while also swinging the chair round to negotiate
the cramped space inside the doorway.

Practical criticism

There was another reason for George's intake of breath, every bit
as understandable. The mass turning of heads was unnerving, though
conversation didn't stop. Nor did the jukebox stop playing, but its
music seemed to be replaced for those crucial moments of appraisal by
a drum-roll, the ominous linked paradiddles that precede a star turn
or a public execution.

George pushed me ahead of him in the wheelchair like a hostage-
taker advancing into police spotlights behind a human shield. I could
hardly blame him for that, but my invisibility despite its impressive
candle-power was only enough for one.

He shrivelled under the fusillade of judging eyes. *This* was scrutiny, if you like. This was practical criticism. No Leavisite concentrating the intellectual X-rays onto a page of *Our Mutual Friend* or *Sons
and Lovers* could send out a beam of comparable intensity.

Of course George wasn't particularly informed about the Cambridge tradition of English Studies. Nothing in his life of genteel re-
tail had prepared him for this raking blast of icy assessment. Then its
wave-length shifted as we were classified as unattractive and (worse)
familiar. I can't say I was too bothered, but then for me it was much
of a muchness, more or less business as usual. It cost me nothing to
absorb some of the impact, and I was happy to screen him from the

worst of the mutagenic exposure, the crossfire from whole emplacements of appraising eyes.

When I wasn't actually in the firing line, there was some fun to be had from noticing the nuances of the examination. Some people only looked at the bottoms of people with nice faces. Others only looked at the faces of people with nice bottoms.

I don't remember making any new acquaintances at the Stable Bar, except when one man came over to me and said he worked in the University Library. He was good enough to tell me that I had a nickname at the UL. Toad of Toad Hall (*Poop! poop!*). Not the worst nickname in the world and yes, I dare say I could seem a little imperious when I sounded the car horn, to signal that the books I had ordered should be toted down to me.

While the leaves were still on the trees I began to be preöccupied with the ritual midwinter festival. Over the years I had borne various grudges against Christmas. First because it came round so slowly. Then that it crowded out my birthday by being so close to it. Next that it was too commercial. Then that it was too Christian. Now I felt that it came round too quickly. The Christ Child seemed to be bearing down on me at the wheel of his holly-trimmed steamroller, and this was the first year that he would find me out in the open, with nowhere to hide.

If I had been able to send a message about what I wanted for Christmas using Granny's special system of chimney semaphore, a slip of paper burnt in the fireplace to give Santa his cue, mine would have been along the lines of *Yule! Yule! Steer well clear! Come again another year!*

Peter had found a job at a hotel near Bristol, an old coaching inn. He had accommodation there and gamely offered to play host, but I couldn't quite see that as a practical proposition. So what were my options, realistically? Well, now that I no longer had a home, there was always a Home. A referral from my GP would be child's play. No exaggeration would be necessary. It was a perfectly routine request. Still, I was in no hurry to meet the Ghost of Christmas Future, the many Ghosts of Christmases to come. What sort of person ends up in a Home at the time of year when even the most abject orphans are taken in? I wasn't in any hurry to find out.

I decided that I would put myself about, socially, and accept the first offer I got, no questions asked. Call it Russian roulette, only played with Christmas crackers rather than the customary revolver. The trouble being that if ever I pull a cracker and win, it's because someone is being kind and would like me to have a tie-pin.

Socially the hot spot of the moment was something called King's Bop, that is, a disco in the cellar of a modern building in King's College. Downing could offer no comparable attraction. King's was ever a trendy hotbed. Girls had been sighted there, rare girls, girls never seen elsewhere. A different species from those who manifested themselves in common room and lecture hall, shop and street.

I had already experienced the event. Part of its fashionability lay in its unpredictable disc-jockey and part in its exclusiveness, since there were people at the door who were supposed to make sure that only students of King's were admitted.

The policing of King's Bop was hardly rigorous – someone at the door would politely ask for your locker number – but surely no one would question the right of the chap in the wheelchair to attend?

This was a reasonable hypothesis. It reached me, though, not as an abstract proposition or social experiment but in the form of an ambush after Hall one Wednesday evening. A little party wanted to make an attempt on King's Bop, using the wheelchair's magical powers as a pass-key, or else an enchanted textile, not so much a cloak of invisibility as a small trundling marquee.

I was a good sport about it. I would have screamed bloody murder if I had known I would be carried downstairs by people I hardly knew, but the trauma was well under way before I had any idea. The word 'cellar' had not been part of the approach that was made to me.

At the door we were waved through with smiles of embarrassment. The hypothesis was confirmed. The wheelchair belonged everywhere as well as nowhere.

The noise was extreme and made conversation difficult. There's a limit to how far I can stretch to bring my ear close to someone's mouth, and if all the bending is done by others then they must feel they're part of something more like limbo dancing than chat. As for whether there were any rare girls in attendance, I really couldn't say.

I wasn't expected to buy drinks since I had made the whole expedition possible, which I took as no more than my due. The beer was from kegs and served in plastic glasses, either to save washing-up or from fear of rowdiness. A glass without a handle or a stem is pretty much useless to me, and I was reduced (if I really wanted to wet my whistle) to having people hold up to my mouth the nasty beer in its nasty plastic glass.

The Mini was always an asset, but it turned out that the wheelchair had an indoor magnetism of its own. It stimulated and intoxified. People too awkward or shy to dance by themselves would grab hold of the wheelchair and push it about in rhythm, swinging me around with sickening force.

There were also people who would prise me out of the wheelchair and hug me to themselves while they danced. It seemed to be their feeling that the main deprivation in a life of restricted mobility was the experience of centrifugal force in raw form. My value to these dance partners may partly have been the low risk of treading on my toes. There was no factor working to reduce the speed and recklessness of our whirling.

I learned to spot the type. When I saw someone approach me with a particular look of glazed joy, I would start reeling off excuses, saying 'I'm afraid I've got a cold,' or even 'I've eaten a bad mushroom and I'm going to be sick,' though no threat of mucus, virus, even vomit in the pipeline had a reliably deterrent effect.

After that visit I had refused to consider a return, but now I had an agenda of my own. I volunteered, and though there was obviously something fishy about my change of heart no one worried too much. My fear of Christmas outweighed, just about, my fear of being dropped downstairs in a slapdash re-enactment of the Senate House occupation.

Almost the moment we arrived I was caught up in a piece of musical torture. The disc-jockey put on something which wasn't even a single but an album track, and it wasn't a recent release, but it had a stubborn popularity in student circles as a stereo showpiece. People used the song to make sure that their speakers were wired the right way round. It was a track called 'Industrial-Military-Complex Hex' from the Steve Miller Band's album *No. 5*. The song had outlasted the album, which had been controversial when new (in 1969, I think), not because of any musical content but something written in small print inside the gatefold for the sharp-eyed to discover. It was dedicated to President Richard Nixon, a betrayal of hippy ideals only partly excused by the infantile phrasing. *We luv you cuz you need it.*

'Industrial-Military-Complex Hex' starts with a sombre atmosphere rather than a tune as such. Then an electric guitar makes its entrance. The sound is supercharged with reverberation and echo. It's also strongly directional. This golden noise is flung from left to right of the stereo picture. It's an acoustic projectile which finds the target and hangs there for a moment, pulsing. Then the pattern repeats with the polarity reversed, the note catapulting back from the right to the left. Two more convulsions of the guitar and the song itself gets under way, murkier and less dramatic, less memorable in every respect.

In those days records were supposed to contain subliminal messages, Satanic commands played backwards – *God is dead, Paul is dead, Kill the piggies till the piggies are dead.* Thousands of undergraduate hours were spent dragging gramophone needles backwards through the final grooves of 'A Day In The Life', to yield everything from 'We'll fuck you like supermen' to 'The gardener was hellish unmathematical'.

No one ever implicated the Steve Miller Band in this practice, as far as I know, yet the opening of 'Industrial-Military-Complex Hex' sent a strong message to a number of people at King's Bop. The song told them *Commandeer John's wheelchair and propel it at high speed from one side of the stereo image to the other. Grant him the joy of embodying this king among riffs.*

If I had known what was coming, I would have put on the wheelchair's brakes, so it's a good job I didn't, because that would have made things worse. We were off.

Be careful of what you wish for – I had wished to ride the Ghost Train, and my wish was coming true in debased form as I was flung about in deafening darkness, all the more alarmed because no conscious attempt was being made to scare me.

After the performance there was an outburst of applause, which wasn't really for John the human riff, the riff on wheels, though some came my way in the form of rough handshakes and shoulder-pats, but for whoever had abducted me. Nobody seemed to find it strange that I had so little say in my part of the floor show.

The disc-jockey responded to the happy hubbub by encoring the beginning of the song. Apparently I hadn't been shaken up enough yet.

There was a scuffle behind me, presumably for control of the wheel-chair. Everyone wanted a turn. Some beer slopped down my back. The worst part of the ordeal was the instant U-turn required to reposition me for the next guitar entry, and then the next. The wheelchair slewed sideways, as the struggle for control became more heated. I don't know who won, I only know it wasn't me. The blast-off to accompany the final guitar note was delayed by several seconds.

Now there was a concerted call for the song to be played a third time, insistent shouts of 'Again! Again! Once more from the top!' This time, though, I was spared. I think the disc-jockey must have seen the horror on my face and perhaps even regretted his part in a joyride with the joy taken out. I could hear people grumbling 'Unfair!', which seemed a bit much. What was so unfair about giving me a reprieve from being shaken to pieces?

No diamonds at all

Then the disc-jockey soothed the mood of the room by playing a single, and one that was even in the charts at the time. John Lennon's 'Happy Xmas (War Is Over)', that rather tentative anthem. 'War is over', yes, but only 'if you want it'. A man and a woman danced together for a few moments, and then the man said, rather roguishly, 'May we?' Meaning, include me in the dance. I said, 'Why not?' and then they did. They really did include me. They pushed the wheel-chair back and forth between them, but always smoothly, always with consideration for what it was like to be sitting in it. They didn't seem quite student-y, though I don't know in what way, exactly. They seemed like a proper couple. Then the man whispered in the woman's ear, she shrugged and nodded, and then he was asking, 'So what are you doing for Christmas, little man?'

'Little man' isn't a phrase I'm any too fond of, but they seemed nice, and if it wasn't for rough diamonds I wouldn't have any diamonds at all. Sometimes the wheelchair acts as a lie-detector, and I certainly didn't think they were messing me about. 'Nothing much,' I said, not thinking anything of it. 'Come to ours, then,' he said. 'I'm Frank and this is Shirley. It'll be a laugh.' As I say, I didn't take it seriously in the slightest bit, but Frank was very insistent, asking for my phone number (and getting Shirley to write it down on her hand). He said, 'I know I've had a drink, mate, but I mean it. Come to ours for Christmas. That's twice I've asked you drunk, and I'll phone tomorrow to ask you sober. That'll make it official.' Just then a groan went up, not from me but from the whole packed room. The disc-jockey had followed 'Happy Xmas (War Is Over)' with Little Jimmy Osmond's 'Long-Haired Lover from Liverpool'. Frank didn't seem surprised, saying, 'Bill said he'd do that, but I didn't think he'd see it through.'

It was a minor outrage in relative terms. One legendary night 'Bill', assuming it was the same character, played Velvet Underground's 'The Murder Mystery' (an evocation of a bad trip generally agreed to be more damaging than the real thing) four times in a row, then followed it with 'Rudolph the Red-Nosed Reindeer', which by all accounts began to sound equally sinister.

People groaned at the Osmond song partly because they knew there was a fair chance they would wake up the next morning with that tune in their heads, and would have to be vigilant and avoid humming for the rest of the day.

Blow me down if Frank didn't phone the next day and repeat the invitation, and by this time I was beginning to take him seriously. He said he and Shirley lived in a basement flat on Victoria Avenue, but we'd all manage somehow.

And in fact my first experience of a family festival without a family was a fair success, though once was probably enough for all parties.

Frank and Shirley's basement was below a barber's (Alley Barber's, if you must know). I was expecting it to be dark, but hadn't entirely reckoned on the cold and the damp. There was only an outside lavatory, across a little yard, which was a bit of a shock to the system. There had been indoor plumbing on *Coronation Street* for years. Frank's record collection was enormous, though I wouldn't have been surprised to see moss growing on the vinyl of records he hadn't played for a while.

He worked in the record department of Miller's music shop on King Street, an old-fashioned sort of business which sold instruments and hired pianos to students. He was in charge of the pop record section, which was smaller than the classical one, and his real interest was the even smaller section labelled New Wave & Progressive. There were only two racks, *New Wave & Progressive A–L* and *New Wave & Progressive M–Z*, though he was hoping they would expand to three.

The discount he got as a Miller's employee explained the size of his collection. 'I like a good beat,' he told me, 'but why settle for one when you can have two or three, all going on at the same time?' We listened to Gentle Giant, to Caravan, to Gong, and of course to Frank Zappa, not only my host's namesake but the uncrowned king of *New Wave & Progressive M–Z*.

The only sentimental moment of my stay came on Christmas Eve, when Frank played 'Lucky Man', a track from Emerson Lake & Palmer's first LP. It was a sort of soulful folk song, with an anti-war message, and it acted on him like a thousand Christmas carols rendered down. He had been rolling a joint when the song started and he froze, though he must have known what was coming since he had just put it on. He wept openly all the way through and then sat still, wiped clean of emotion. If he had wanted to give that joint a festive touch he could have moistened the edge of the rolling paper with tears rather than the traditional saliva.

Shirley worked as a secretary at a firm of solicitors. I told her she should become a lawyer herself, but she just laughed. It seemed to me that once you got a foothold in the world of work there was nothing to stop you, but that wasn't how Shirley saw it. She was very sure she wasn't clever. 'I'm hopeless,' she said. 'Frank bought me *The Naked Eunuch* for my birthday in June, and I still haven't got past Chapter One.' It was tantalising not knowing which of two famous books of the period she actually meant.

Shibboleth nut roast

Frank did most of the cooking, and came up with plenty of vegetarian basics. I had told him in advance that he should stick to his normal style of eating, and for form's sake he had decided to roast a bird on the day. I was really agitating against that strange shibboleth nut roast, something that nobody much likes, a misunderstanding that has turned into an iron-clad ritual, with each party convinced of making a concession to the other.

And what could possibly be wrong with a plate of sprouts, carrots and bread sauce?

Everything went swimmingly until Shirley asked me, while Frank was making our omelettes, if I wanted to come with her to Midnight Mass. She said she was as lapsed a Catholic as it was possible to be, but she didn't feel right not going on Christmas Eve, and I agreed. She warned me that Frank wouldn't come.

I don't think she'd realised that there was a difference between her going to Midnight Mass on her own and her saying that 'we' were going to Midnight Mass. He was obviously put out about it, though he wouldn't own up. We begged him to come along, but of course that wasn't the point. He should have been asked first. Finally he said he was going for a training run. Never mind that he'd been half asleep over his beer half an hour earlier.

It turned out that Frank was an exercise nut in between attempts to drink and smoke his way to oblivion. Now he pulled on his Dunlop Green Flash tennis shoes, which everyone understood in those days were the mark of the committed athlete, did a couple of stretches and toe-touches, and went out into the night. This was apparently his favourite way of working off a hangover, just as a joint was part of his winding-down routine. Smoking and drinking were known to be unhealthy, but the experiments that young people conduct on themselves are invariably designed to prove the immortality they assumed as first premise. What's a flawed methodology between friends?

It was strange to be joining a congregation at the very Catholic Church whose off-kilter bells had haunted my insomnia from the first week of my first term. I might have enjoyed it if I hadn't been worrying about the domestic tensions of the household I was installed in.

I had Frank and Shirley's bed, while they slept on a pile of cushions. For extra warmth they zipped me up in a sleeping bag. Just as I was slipping off to sleep I thought there was a moment when the silence between them lost its sharp edges and became tender, but I didn't have a lot to go on.

Shirley brought me breakfast in bed on Christmas morning. Hot chocolate followed by tomato soup – a rather harrowing transition for the taste buds, but effective in boosting body heat. I particularly remember from that morning a gesture Shirley made with her hand, like the one furtive smokers use to hide their cigarettes, except that (unflappable hostess) she was unobtrusively plucking from my sleeping bag a wandering slug, cupping it out of sight in her palm. I realised that this gastropod was a bit of a rarity, since the ones that don't die in the autumn usually hibernate, but even so it didn't rank highly as a Christmas present, despite the trail of mucous tinsel it left behind on the nylon facing of the sleeping-bag. Oh Maya, you shouldn't have!

We had a no-presents pact, though in the manner of such things it involved a certain element of suspense. Only at the last moment of the day would it become clear if we had held our nerve. I had some globes of bath oil in reserve, in case she reneged, just as Shirley kept a box of Maltesers handy. In the end we were doomed, for all our good intentions, to exchange small spheres.

Frank seemed depressed, not by the mild upsets of the night before but by something that had been announced on the radio. Clumsily I tried to cheer him up, and Shirley didn't make a much better job of it. It doesn't mean anything, we tried to tell him. It's of no consequence. He thought the world was being overwhelmed by commercialism and bubble-gum. What chance was there for a third rack of *New Wave & Progressive* at Miller's?

What caused all this soul-searching was the announcement on the radio that 'Long-Haired Lover from Liverpool' was Britain's Christmas Number One. I thought it was par for the course, the world being what it is, Christmas being what it is, Little Jimmy Osmond being what he was. But Frank took it hard.

After lunch I proposed a visit to the Bot, knowing full well that it would be closed on Christmas Day, but needing to mount some sort of expedition. Frank came along, as I had guessed he would (unless perhaps I asked him to). He was fascinated by the orange cardboard indicator which went with my parking privileges. 'That's dead handy, that is,' he said. 'Everyone should have one of those.' Rather missing the point, I felt, of the civic concession. 'What do you call that? Your cripple clock?' Well, no, I called it my orange thingy. I flinched at his phrase, though I don't think it was meant aggressively. It was just the least attractive facet of a rough diamond catching the dim light of a winter's day. I said those words to myself a few times, trying to neutralise them, cripple clock, cripple clock, but they were like a mantra in reverse, they refused to shed their meaning. 'No,' I said, 'I call it the time machine.' Hoping to override the appalling catchiness of his formula.

While Shirley and I went on our walk, Frank stayed in the car to have a smoke. It wasn't immediately obvious why he couldn't have done that while he walked with us, but it's no news that men (in particular), though they hate to be excluded, prefer not to participate fully in other people's lives.

For all the vividness of what I could show Shirley of the splendours of the Bot at that distance and in that season it would have been simpler to stay at home, ask her to close her eyes, and fearlessly describe. I was reduced to pointing vaguely with the stick, indicating the place where the Bot grew cannabis as an attractive herbaceous annual, with no sense of playing with fire.

When we came back there seemed to be a grin on Frank's face, or somewhere near it. There was a preening twinkle that couldn't be pinned to any individual feature but belonged only to the collective. He seemed to have cheered up in some way.

It was days before I noticed that he had embellished the orange thingy, the time machine, using a ball-point pen to change the units of measurement from hours to thousands of years. In all innocence he had recalibrated the instrument to help me navigate in the depths of the Dark Ages. Without in the least knowing what he was doing, he was reminding me that I was in it for the long haul. I was no time lord, but serving my time like everyone else in the Kali Yuga, unless my guru laid on a Tardis for my benefit, with modified controls.

Apricocks out of season

New Year was actually more traumatic than Christmas, not as an event but as a symbol. 1973 was the year in which my undergraduate exemption from life's real demands lapsed and all bills fell due. I felt like Faustus towards the end of Marlowe's play, when the soul on which he has borrowed so heavily must be repossessed. The bailiffs are on their way. *O lente, lente currite noctis equi*. In preparation for the Tragedy paper I had learned to admire the metrical skill of that interpolated Latin line, the dragging hooves of the first half while the reins are pulled back, the helter-skelter careering of the second. It wasn't so enjoyable to be caught up in the same terrible rhythm, without having had any of Faustus's fun. I hadn't enjoyed legendary beauties or apricocks out of season, just a few fumbles. Nobody had even wanted me to sign on the dotted line in the first place. Slow down, my nightmares, galloping, galloping on.

Everyone else seemed remarkably calm about the end of their student lives, the deepening shadows in the academic grove. In my third undergraduate year I still took what everyone said at face value. It's a good job I wasn't reading philosophy, or this would have counted as an academic failing as well as a personal one.

An odd masquerade was going on as my contemporaries faced up to the end of their student lives. Academic work itself had been out of fashion for some time, thanks to the lingering effects of the '60s. Application to books on any more than a casual basis went by the unsavoury name of 'gnoming'. Everyone claimed to be aiming for a Third Class degree, though it was understood as a matter of brute mathematics that there weren't enough of them to go around. Some unlucky folk would end up with Firsts. Life could be very unfair.

The incorrigibly interested or slyly ambitious would study in secret, working their way through books that they would defensively insist they had shoplifted. Everyone spoke the language of anarchistic disaffection in a cryptic counter-cultural Esperanto. Fashion demanded that those who had splashed out on tickets for a May Ball should claim to have gatecrashed the event by some providential set of circumstances, such as a stacked pile of chairs found by the river, handy stepping stones into the college grounds, while heavily armed porters patrolled elsewhere.

Any talk of jobs was disparaged, even by those who had quietly been making plans. At that period of all but full employment, when a Cambridge degree gave potential employers a throb of desire, any actual plan to enter the world of work was seen as a great betrayal. It meant selling out your dreams, giving in to what was variously called the System, the Machine, the Man, even (by those who imported their radical reading matter, buying it from an eccentric bookshop in town calling itself Cockaygne) Straightsville or Amerika.

As far as the rival party lines went, I was necessarily a dissident. I didn't think that it would be a betrayal of counter-cultural values if I got a job. Nor did I think that it was my duty to make a contribution to the economic functioning of the country. I just thought it would be a bloody miracle.

My tutor, though returned from sabbatical, was aggressively neutral where my welfare was concerned, but I don't mean to suggest that there was nobody paying me any mind. There was a definite sense of rallying round. Some of my supervisors started coming to A6 Kenny, rather than expecting me to toil over to their rooms. Not only that, a handful of fellow-students had mercy on me and started to take notes on my behalf (for the Tragedy paper, for instance) so that I was spared the ordeal of hitch-lifting to lectures. The only trouble was that there seemed to be an inverse relation between people's helpfulness and the legibility of their handwriting. Often the simplest solution was to ask my helpers to read out their notes, and to make my own record of the re-enactment.

At the library I had those take-away privileges, while everyone else had to eat on the premises. Now I was benefiting from the academic equivalent of room service. It might seem that after three years the world had finally showed up in my room as promised, helpless to resist me, wanting its belly tickled. In fact these were emergency measures undertaken by kind people who rightly suspected I was close to throwing in the towel.

My levels of disposable energy had greatly diminished, though there was nothing obscure about how this had come about. For reasons of economy I had dropped first breakfast and then dinner from my schedule. Lunch became my only real meal, and that is not a regime on which the body thrives. I lost weight, and gained a certain perverse satisfaction from being in full charge of my appetite, if of nothing else.

Wealth is relative, wealth is subjective, and I felt poor. In strict monetary terms I was better off than I had been at the start of my university life, but my predicament was much more intractable. My only guarantor was Granny, and she wasn't reliable in that rôle. She enjoyed having beneficiaries but soon got bored of dependents and was likely to punish them.

There was a recession going on, even if it was only in my head. I was no longer pushing the boat out. I was pulling the boat in. No more fancy cigarettes from Bacon's to beguile my guests, and no more snacks to fill the metabolic crannies left empty by the catering in Hall.

In better times I had provided a finger buffet – slivers of Ry-King crispbread spread with cashew-nut butter from the Health Food Shop in Rose Crescent. This was hugely popular. I got through so much Ry-King that I could send off the required number of coupons for the clear-top plastic holder for their product which the manufacturers dangled as a temptation in front of eager consumers. It gave me pleasure to arrange the crisp rectangles in their tailor-made vivarium, and even got me thinking that I should collect the coupons for another and relaunch my menagerie with a new millipede to revolt Jean Beddoes – Son of Nasty Thing. Son and daughter in one.

A sizeable whack of my income in this period went on cashew-nut butter, which has never been cheap, but I considered it an expense well justified. I imagined that every savoury nutritious bite I provided was making converts to vegetarianism, lessening the demand for animal slaughter, when I was only pandering to the outrageous calorific demands of active healthy bodies.

I clung to the totem of 'proper coffee', despite the expense, preferring to limit my intake than permit a return to granule or powder. Real coffee was a currency I could use to repay those who came to share their lecture notes.

One of my helpers had hair of a strange dark blond and lips so absurdly full even an angel would want to bite them. He turned out to be half-Spanish, and so I ventured into his mother's tongue if only to brush up my accent. That sort of brushing-up always feels rather fierce, less like grooming of any sort than scrubbing rust off metal using bristles of wire.

I enjoyed it, and was pleased when this young man mentioned a Spanish-language film that was playing at the weekend and had become some sort of underground hit. *El Topo*, 'The Mole' – could an underground film possibly have a better title? The director was Mexican, so the delivery of the dialogue wouldn't be what we were used to, but we thought we could survive for a couple of hours without the 'Castilian lisp'.

Strange film. It turned out to be an existential Western or something of the sort, perhaps an allegory, with lashings of startling imagery. Pretentious? Of course. I tried to keep my eyes away from the bottom of the screen so as to take in the dialogue without help, but I couldn't altogether manage. In any case, *El Topo* can boast one of the great subtitles of all times – 'When you came within 250 yards of my boundary fence, my rabbits started dying.' That has to rank with the all-time greats. I'm thinking of the neighbour saying, 'Look what eating nettles has done for her' after the maid has started to levitate in *Theorem*, or the hero of *Hour of the Wolf* saying, as he (literally) walks up the wall, 'Don't mind me, it's only my jealousy.' The acknowledged classics, the ones on everybody's list.

I sat tight while the film meandered luridly on. Of course I noticed that there was a lot of symbolic deformity involved, and that there was a strong element of brutality meted out to the wrongly shaped or oddly sized. I took it in my stride. I'm all for hostility against the disabled coming into the open. Let it show itself. It's not me that's going to be shocked by it. I signed up for normal life, and I don't expect to be feather-bedded. I didn't find it all that hard to disconnect from my everyday responses, and to take pleasure in this welter of punitive glory.

My escort, though, wasn't just trying to blot out the subtitles but the whole of the screen. I could feel the misery pouring out of him. He winced and gave a little moan at the cruelty of each fresh tableau. In the darkness his lips were being chewed without outside assistance. Cruelly he raked the plump tissues with his teeth. I don't know why he took it quite so personally – did he think I'd suspect him of dragging me to see this film specifically to cause me pain? Paranoia was mother's milk in those days, but it was hard to believe that anyone had supped so deep. Perhaps it made things worse for him that (in a spirit of gratitude) I had paid for the tickets. The Spanish side of him had shrivelled away to nothing, and he was Englishness itself in his experience of social pain. The English feel embarrassment the way other peoples experience anger or desire.

So in a spirit of charity I groped him, leaning precariously over to interfere with his person. Anything to take his mind off his discomfort. More than discomfort – agony, really. Now if he wanted to cling to his paranoia he would have to suspect me of dragging him to see this film specifically so that I could knead his private parts. I confronted taboo with taboo, then we were quits. I'd rather take advantage, however feebly, than be lumbered with the rôle of injured party. It's not natural casting.

It lets you cry

I began to think I had been slow to notice the way that invisibility could work in my favour. Spectators chose not to notice the most outrageous groping liberties being taken, when the groper was me. So after that, I started to become more reckless. It was hardly likely there would be any drastic consequences. What were the authorities going to do – send me down, rusticate me? It was much too late for disciplinary measures. And if I didn't know where I would be living in a few short months' time, then the authorities would have to hew out my place of exile first, before they could send me there.

It was already established that I had a certain amount of hypnotic talent, a personality magnet or minor force-field which could work wonders when properly aligned. The hypothesis was confirmed on a daily basis. I had a way with young males particularly. By this time I had found that I could use a little tug on a metaphysical sleeve to get a young man moving in the desired direction. Sometimes there would be no resistance at all, sometimes just a little, but no one was ever moved to say, 'What on earth do you think you're doing?' It's a spell, of an elementary sort. Most people can work small enchantments, it's just that they don't know it, or they have more direct ways of getting what they want.

My method worked best with emotionally withdrawn ex-public-schoolboys ill at ease with their bodies, hungering for touch but powerfully estranged from it. There was no shortage of such in the Cambridge of the time – in fact this was a thumbnail sketch of the bulk of the student body. Changing my subject of study brought me in contact with a new crop of such young men. The English Faculty turned out to be a brimming reservoir of the susceptible, as far as I was concerned. Public schools were very much over-represented in the group, though not the household names, more the minor ones. Places with a little bit of history but not too much, a handful of eminent old boys to point to, rather than a lengthy roll-call of cabinet ministers, laureates galore.

I don't know what these schools had done to their new old boys, but they emerged blinking into the world (or at least into Cambridge) almost wholly estranged from their own impulses, their emotions not even distinct enough to be called confused. I began to recognise the tribe. Undergraduates, often physically big and actively sporty, who hadn't been keen to take me on my little trips to the lavatory found it in some strange way liberating. They would come back from our little expedition quietly thrilled, and would settle next to me, holding my hand and mooning at me with a blush of joy.

I seemed to be a specific trigger, like the music that 'makes people cry'. It doesn't make you cry, it lets you cry. But what was stopping you from crying in the first place, if you had some crying that needed doing?

I suppose it was no more than the famous 'grounding', a rush of reconnection with the species after being called upon to help a fellow being on a basic errand. Looking down at those big hands tenderly squeezing mine, their huge paws all warm, it was a shock to realise the fullness of their surrender. They were putty in my hands. For the time being they were under a spell. I began to see how much further I could take it. Under my ever-expanding cloak of invisibility a remarkable amount could be accomplished. I was a naughty Frodo Baggins who didn't need to fear the searing eye of Sauron on him.

At some point it became hard to tell my advantages from my disadvantages. They tended to blend. It helps that in these matters keeping my distance has never been an option. Anyone who has dealings with me must get close, and physical proximity puts many of my countrymen into a light trance. By the time either party is fully aware of it, foreplay may have begun.

It's true I never managed to coax a startled penis out into the open, while sitting in a pub or college bar, but I wasn't far off. It was lack of dexterity that stopped me rather than a failure of nerve, but I didn't deeply mind. An exhibitionist doesn't really thrive in a setting where the most lurid transgressions attract no attention whatever.

Geoff. Keith. Simon. Charles. Hugh. It was surprising how many young men were interested in having a lie down at some stage, and a little genteel exploration. I would try to persuade them to leave the door open or at least unlocked. I was always keen to have a witness. I don't think I ever actually made a dive at a person's cock, but I'm sure I startled a few folk. When you're dealing with someone whose very identity is supposed to be the Limited-Mobility Man, then the last thing you expect is a surge of randy purpose.

I can reach my cock when I really want to. It isn't comfortable – if God had meant me to lean over, he wouldn't have given me infantile rheumatoid arthritis – but I can certainly do it. If my organ of pleasure was as remote as my toes I'd be in a bad way, very much in need of acts of corporal charity. It's just that, all things considered, if I'm going to make the effort, I'd rather touch someone else's than my own. So it makes sense to wait for some susceptible person to have a kindly impulse and put his hand on my groin. Then I return the favour, groping happily away.

Perhaps some of these young men felt sorry for me. I felt sorry for them, come to that, if they needed to go to such lengths to gather up the scattered parts of their personalities. Obviously they weren't virgins, but they had managed to become sexually experienced without developing the slightest emotional expressiveness. D. H. Lawrence would have understood perfectly. They were Gerald Criches to a man, even if one or two of them had probably read every word Lawrence ever wrote. As a minor university Birkin, I sometimes seemed to have my work cut out to make them whole.

After our little bit of fumbling, my playmates couldn't wait to be gone, babbling excuses as they beat their retreat. It was sweet that they imagined I wanted them to stay.

Once and only once I was able to play out a romantic scene in full, though it was necessarily of an unorthodox sort. I was sitting sideways in this young man's lap, and both of us were cradled by the Parker-Knoll in its lowered configuration. In itself this didn't count as an especially intimate position. It was comfortable. Geoff and I had been discussing (in anticipation of the Tragedy paper) the idea of dual determination, whereby people freely choose what has been laid down for them, so that there is no conflict between fate and free will. I had been wondering whether to mention my own conviction (gleaned from *The Tibetan Book of the Dead*, an otherwise unenlightening read) that I had chosen Mum's womb in the endless moment of clarity between lives, so that I had accepted in advance what I would freely choose. It seemed better to keep quiet about that, both during the exam and in casual conversation.

I was paying a lot of attention to Geoff's shirt, though no more than it deserved. It was made of cheesecloth, in a pattern of tiny blue houndstooth checks. It was cut loosely, in emulation of a peasant smock. The collar was soft, and softly rounded. The material was held together under his Adam's apple by a row of little buttons, miniature discs with a granular shine – not so much mother-of-pearl as mother-of-plastic. They were set so closely that each disc almost touched the next.

I fiddled with his buttons, those many buttons, and I talked as I fiddled. He watched me with a warm wariness through glasses that made his eyes seem oddly defenceless behind that corrective barrier. I could smell his long hair, no longer clean but faintly musky.

I had time to consider the buttons closely. They fastened the shirt not by going through a buttonhole but by being lassoed instead, with a little noose of thread. That was what my fingers were trying to do, to slip the little cotton nooses from round the buttons and release them. 'Do you know which is older,' I murmured, 'buttons or buttonholes?'

'How do you mean?' he said, after a pause. 'Is it a riddle?'

'Well, it's not like chickens and eggs. We come to university in search of knowledge, but how rarely do we get it, eh? There's a definite answer here, and the answer is this: buttons are thousands of years older than buttonholes.'

'Thousands of years? How is that possible? I don't get it.'

Buttons and buttonholes seem so obviously designed for each other that Geoff can't really be blamed for being puzzled. It must have sounded as if I was saying there was a time when there were men and no women. 'It's a fact of textile history. There's no serious disagreement among the experts.' I'd listened to enough second-rate lecturers doing their stuff to be able to assume their flatly intense manner. 'The button comes relatively early in the history of clothing. The first button was probably a piece of bone. Buttons don't have to be regular in shape, you know. The wooden toggles on a duffel coat work perfectly well without being symmetrical. In fact you could say that the toggle is the most atavistic form of button, the fastening that keeps alive the deep memory of clothing, all the way back to the Ur-button. The primordial toggle.'

All this time I was working away at the ridiculous task of undoing the numberless buttons on his shirt. For me it was an enterprise on the scale of a fairy-tale task, counting all the leaves in the forest, say, plucking a scale from every fish in the sea.

He didn't reply immediately, and his voice was oddly thick when he did. It had changed in character and also somehow in texture – no longer single cream, now double and potentially even clotted. 'And how . . . how did buttons work before there were buttonholes?' My personality magnet had mysteriously come into play.

'That's what makes the shirt you're wearing so educational. It's a history lesson in itself. The first buttonhole wasn't a buttonhole as we understand it at all, merely a slit in an animal skin, then (with the invention of sewing) a loop at the edge of a piece of cloth. To make an actual buttonhole requires a much higher level of needle-work, as I'm sure you understand. Nowadays buttonholes are sewn by machines, but your garment with these excessively numerous loops – which are giving me a lot of trouble, incidentally – is a throwback in its own way. Just as cheesecloth is a peasant fabric enjoying a vogue among those who are not peasants, so these button-loops, sewn perhaps by small children, represent for the customer the dream of escaping from an industrialised present.'

'And all for £1.25 from the market,' he said. He was playing along wonderfully well.

'For you, the dream. For little children, the nightmare – the pricked fingers, the education forfeited, the eyesight that fails . . .'

As I fiddled and talked, sexual excitement became as real as cloth and as elusive as tiny buttons. There is no task to which my fingers are less suited than the undoing of tiny buttons. Since I was sitting in Geoff's lap, he had the position of control, and my explorings were only under licence. I couldn't have undertaken this rare dalliance against his wishes.

I wonder where I learned all that about buttons. I can't have been making it all up, can I?

He had started rocking me on his hips – it's an action deeply engraved in the nature of hips, and not hugely compromising. Being rocked might make me into a baby, I suppose. He might not even have been aware of the movement he was making.

Mole stable

The ridiculous glory of the scene was summed up by one silly fact, that the buttons were essentially ornamental. They didn't go all the way down but ended in a placket. So however many buttons I undid, this shirt would never lie open before me. I could hope to unveil him as far as the breastbone, but actually taking the shirt off would involve lifting it over his head, something that was far beyond my powers. For all my studious fiddling, this manly boy or boyish man would have to undress himself without my help, or stay inside his clothes.

The vocabulary of sexual attraction is on the narrow side, and was even narrower then. At CHAPs meetings no one admitted to anything as flighty as 'fancying' anyone else. Everything seemed fraught and problematic, the acts, the feelings and the words. Sex seemed to be some sort of duty, either sacred or grim. George and I had evolved a code word for those we found attractive: *mole stable*. Not much of a code word, I grant you, since it was really only the word 'molestable', rather arch in itself, split into two parts and jocularly pronounced, in the same silly spirit that makes people say picture skew for picturesque. Geoff in the cheesecloth shirt was definitely *mole stable*.

His sexual availability was more or less a fiction, thanks to the limited coöperation offered by his cheesecloth shirt. But it wasn't a fixed quantity. We had arrived at a finely balanced moment in psychological terms, and a balance can always be upset. His shirt was now sufficiently open for one nipple to be on show. It was less than a foot away from me.

Gently I blew onto it from my little distance. I sent out a column of air to do my caressing for me. The air was warmed from being taken inside me, though it must have felt cool on Geoff's chest. The centre of his nipple raised itself above the surface. It puckered into life under the influence of exhaled desire.

Geoff's eyebrows went sharply up, and then slowly settled back down. The pucker in his nipple, too, slowly subsided. He had kept his balance, and it was time to raise the stakes.

I launched myself forward, in what was the equivalent in my range of motion of a trapeze artist swinging into the void, and made a grab for his glasses. For an instant Geoff could do either of two things, either defend his glasses and risk me falling, or reach to hold me safe. He had to choose, and he chose to hold me.

His legs were suddenly rigid with tension, now that I had made a decisive move. His eyes, naked without glasses, registered the depths of his dismay, the wavering of male privilege. He was no longer in charge of what was happening.

But was I? I was holding his glasses, that was all. He had only to take them back. But the balance had tipped just the same, and he badly needed to take back the initiative with a new action of his own. And so he did the only thing he could, by lifting me up and carrying me to the bed, as if that was what he had been planning all along. He lost face if he let me seduce him, but there was no embarrassment about being the seducer. And how could I resist him? He was lovely.

But was he free at the moment he made his choice? Here was dual determination all over again, but with a slight difference. I was determined enough for both of us.

It would have been nice to talk such things over with my peers at a CHAPs meeting, but it was never on the cards. Sex with straight men was an issue with more than its fair share of disquiet attached. On the one hand we maintained that there was no such thing as a straight man, and it was part of the revolutionary agenda to overthrow the ramparts of the patriarchy with cannonades of pleasure. On the other hand, anyone with an actual preference for heterosexual partners had internalised a lot of self-hatred and was thoroughly suspect. In any case nobody ever asked me at meetings if I had ever had anything in the way of a sex life, and it was simpler not to speak up. In fact, the single institution which has come closest to making me shut up was Cambridge's independent forum where issues of sexual and political liberation could be freely discussed and worked through.

Cheshire Far from Home

In the Easter vacation of 1973, with very mixed feelings, I went to the Cheshire Home in Gerrards Cross for a respite visit. The name was mildly appealing, since 'Cheshire' had been one of the candidates for my middle name, because of exactly the Leonard Cheshire, veteran of the Battle of Britain, who had founded the Homes. The first Cheshire Home was actually Leonard Cheshire's home – he lived there. He wasn't disabled himself but was concerned for friends who were, and wanted them to have all possible control over their lives. I had a little fantasy about becoming something of a pet in the Home he had set up.

Gerrards Cross was only a few miles from Bourne End. It was strange to drive so nearly home, and then to stay away. My only previous experience of *respite* had been the gloriously ramshackle all-male nursing home ('næ wummen') in Bognor, where I had gone after my knee operation. Clearly that establishment was an oddity, and more likely to be closed down double-quick than taken as a model anywhere else.

Leonard Cheshire had been a Group-Captain. He would expect a certain amount of order and decorum. He wouldn't want half-empty cups of tea or coffee left uncollected, let alone half-full pee-bottles. I couldn't hope for ribald raillery. But a breeze seemed to be blowing through so many stuffy institutions, even Cambridge University, and I didn't anticipate the Cheshire Homes would have double-glazed every window against every faintest zephyr of permissiveness.

When I arrived, there was a sort of interview. It wasn't called that, it was called an Informal Welcome, but I decided it was really an interview, and a proper interview at that. The 'inter' part of the word meaning mutuality. Back and forth. Exchange of views. I would expect to ask questions as well as to answer them.

Mr Giles the Director told me what a privilege it was to be responsible for my well-being, which is just the sort of thing that puts my back up. I don't believe it, and don't see how they could expect me to. I don't regard it as a privilege to look after me, so why should he?

He went on with a nice flourish: 'What I say to all our residents – I say "resident" however short their stay may happen to be – is that this is not *a* home, this is *your* home. You are what we exist for. You are our whole purpose. I may be called the Director, but I too buckle down and have been known to help with the washing-up!'

As he spoke he held a propelling pencil over a printed form. I've always coveted propelling pencils but can't properly manage the rotating mechanism that extrudes the lead. I have something of a talent for breaking them. The rotation factor does for me every time.

Mr Giles asked for my name and address. 'Which address?' I asked. 'Bourne End or Downing College, Cambridge?'

This wasn't very coöperative of me, since Gerrards Cross wasn't near Cambridge and I had applied through the good offices of the High Wycombe local authority.

'The permanent one, please.'

'They're both of them temporary, but I'll give you my parents' permanent address.'

'If you don't mind.'

Mr Giles gave the hand holding the propelling pencil a soft shake, to disengage the cuff-link which was snagging the sleeve of his jacket. He asked for the details of what I could and could not manage without assistance. Did I have any special dietary needs? I said I had a very ordinary dietary need, which was that blood should not be shed in the process of feeding me. I pointed out that someone with my physical limitations would be much more likely to need help if he ate meat, hacking at the fibres of tissue as tightly knit as our own. He pursed his lips but made no reply.

Then I started on my own questions. 'Thank you, Mr Director, for making me welcome. Perhaps you can tell me where my locker is.'

'Your locker?'

'Where I can keep private things safe and secure.'

He looked doubtful. 'If there's anything special I suppose I could keep it for you.'

'So residents have no privacy?'

'People come here for respite. For comfort and quality of life, not for privacy as a be-all and end-all.'

'I can't help feeling that privacy is part of the quality of life. Are the bathrooms lockable?'

'That wouldn't be appropriate. It is in the bathroom that many of our residents need most help.'

'Well, I don't.' It was true that I didn't need help to go to the lavatory as long as I could use my bum-snorkel, though bath-times were a different matter. I wasn't planning solo acts of dunking with the help of a hoist. I was expecting full use of the facilities, viz. nurses on tap to make bathing a smooth and convenient process. Leonard Cheshire would expect no less. That was his whole idea, to have certain things taken for granted – and why shouldn't privacy be one of them?

The fuss I was making about this issue was purely symbolic, in the sense that I had brought nothing with me that needed protecting. But I had got used to the idea of a lockable door. There was a principle involved – why shouldn't another inmate, less accustomed than me to standing up for himself, have somewhere to stow his girly magazines or the diary in which he vented his loathing of the staff? 'I'm confident that you have a lock on the bathroom in *your* home, to prevent Mrs Director from trotting in at a moment that would not be appropriate. This office, too, seems to have a lock . . .'

'You've made your point, John.' I don't know why people say that, when all it means is that you have articulated very clearly into an ear which is sealed against you. 'We can't hope to provide an environment tailor-made to suit every individual, however much we pride ourselves on our quality of care. You have high standards, which is all to the good, but perhaps there should be a certain amount of adult compromise. Of give and take. You should take us as you find us.' Another vapid formula.

'Certainly, Mr Director. And perhaps you will take me as you find me.'

It was intoxicating, it aroused my baser nature, to be dealing again with people who had undertaken an obligation, after so long negotiating daily life in an undergraduate setting where nobody owed me anything. Finally I could let it out, without too much fear of the consequences, the rancour of dependence.

The Director's propelling pencil descended again on his form. There was still a lot of blank space on it – I didn't need 'toilet attendance' and I could eat for myself. Staff weren't even expected to administer medication in my case. In those respects I was a model of the undemanding resident. Yet the pencil descended on a box near the bottom of the form and wrote a single word.

In CRX days I had taught myself to read upside down. It was far the best way of keeping track of what was going on – the medical staff played their cards very close to their chests. I hardly needed that skill, here in the Director's office, to pinpoint the word he was writing down as a summary of my character and attitude. He wasn't writing down, 'An admirable resistance to institutional conformity', or even 'What an abrasive little charmer!' but simply 'Difficult.'

Presumably all the residents had been given roughly the same speech of welcome. They hadn't been tempted to take it at face value. If they thought of themselves as being at home they kept it to themselves. They behaved like prisoners who had been told that if they behaved themselves they wouldn't actually have to slop out their cells.

I was shocked by the cowed atmosphere at meal-times. I know male undergraduates are boisterous and no reasonable point of comparison for a dining room full of disabled people, whether fully resident or in need of respite. I felt I could screen out the variables. This was different. This was a roomful of people, most of whom couldn't walk, trying to live on tiptoe. This was numb despair, chewed thirty-two times and mechanically swallowed down.

If the Director called in on the dining room people would actually eat faster (both those who needed help and those who could manage by themselves) as if to ingratiate themselves with him with a show of appetite.

Early on in my stay I was trying to strike up some conversation when everyone went quiet. 'What's the matter?' I said. 'Why the two minutes' silence? Armistice Day isn't for months.'

'Shh! Mr Giles is walking past.'

'Yes I see that. So what?'

'It's not respectful to talk when he's doing his rounds.' Apparently we were supposed to be good little girls and boys, however grown-up we were.

'I see. We have to KEEP QUIET! when the director WALKS PAST!' Intentionally I raised my voice, so that everyone winced. 'So much for the home from home.' As far as I was concerned this was a Cheshire Far From Home. A Cheshire un-Home.

What the establishment needed was to have all its moral windows opened, every cobwebbed corner swept with a dynamic broom. I volunteered. Since the prevailing mood was of cringing, I set myself to swagger. Let everyone else impersonate refugees if that's what they wanted. I would behave as if I owned the place. Obviously I had advantages – I was just passing through, and I had more mobility than some. It seemed worthwhile to show them that abasement wasn't a necessary condition of life.

I wasn't trying to be popular. It was fine by me if I was hated by the other residents, just as long as I got the message across that we were worms by consent, and could just as easily choose to be pests.

The Director wasn't actively a bully, but his régime inflamed those who were. One cleaner called Molly had the knack of looking as wholesome as a pear on a dish as long as there were other staff members around, but came nastily alive when she was on her own. She carried the shark gene, the one that delivers sure knowledge of what can be got away with.

She had no more right to tell people what to do than the postman, though I suppose she could legitimately ask someone to move so that she could clean where they were. Everyone lived in fear, though, and she took full advantage. She would hiss to some rather faded lady with multiple sclerosis, 'I don't want you talking to *him*. I won't tell you again.' *Him* being me.

If I ignored her she would hoover immediately behind the wheelchair for an exaggeratedly long time, so that it was impossible to think of anything but the grimaces she must be making, or the passes with an imaginary knife.

Everyone let her walk all over them, saying 'Anything for a quiet life' to themselves until they had no life left. Louise, the woman with multiple sclerosis, would wait until Molly was long gone from the day-room before she dared to whisper, 'You know what? I wish I could whack her on that bum of hers.'

'It's a big enough target. Would you like me to do it for you? Save you the trouble?'

'You . . . wouldn't . . . dare!'

'I think you know that I would. I will. Shall we sell tickets? Everyone will want a ringside seat.'

'No. Just do it for me. Make sure I have a good view.'

'Agreed. It will be a royal command performance, just for you.'

So the next time Molly was in range (and bending over) I whacked her with my stick. Louise watched goggle-eyed as I undertook my little swing. The impact was less than mighty, and not only because of the padded nature of the target. My arms can only describe a brief arc, and to land the blow at all I had to lean over at a precarious angle. There was a muffled thwack, though I tried to convey by way of a certain solemnity that this was a community reprisal rather than an act of individual impulse.

Weakness is not a weakness. Lack of physical force is not a character flaw. These formulas need work before they can turn into inspiring slogans, though on some deep level they are so clearly true. Till then, the strong must be whacked whenever the opportunity arises.

Molly spat with rage, but I stood my ground. 'There's more where that came from,' I told her. 'I'm not afraid of you, and I'm only doing what everyone here would like to.'

The ladder of pain relief

Which was true, though my status as a visitor protected me. If I made a bad smell I didn't have to sit in it indefinitely. I could trundle away, drive away if necessary, from any repercussions. The difference between me and most of the inmates made me feel virtually able-bodied, which was almost intoxicating. As long as I played the part of the resident vigilante I could forget that I was a resident at all.

It was perversely invigorating to encounter actual opposition rather than passive difficulty. A level of energy which was hardly enough to meet the challenges of student life seemed prodigious in this setting. I fizzed with it. By my standards the inmates had hardly stuck their heads over the parapet of the day before they began to shrink back down towards sleep.

The doctors attached to the Home earnestly collaborated on the goal of a quiet life. They prescribed with a free hand. I clambered up quite a few of the rungs on the ladder of pain relief in my time at the Cheshire Home.

Under Flanny's guidance I had broken with Ponstan and Doloxene, and had struck up a rewarding relationship with Fortral (pentazocine). She wasn't trigger-happy with her scripts, though, and she knew what she was dealing with. She said, 'We'll try you on this stuff but you'll need to be a bit careful. It's not quite DDA but it's not far off.' DDA meaning Dangerous Drugs Act. That worked fine for quite a while, but now I needed something stronger.

At the Cheshire Home Dr Pye started me on Omnopon (papaveretum) after I'd sweet-talked him a bit. Any gardener will tell you that the *papaver-* bit means poppy. You're homing in on an opiate.

Under Dr Pye's guidance I learned to inject an ampoule of Fortral intramuscularly. I'd do it in the top of the leg. That provided exemplary pain relief, and even the ghost of a buzz. *Ampoule* – is there a more seductive word in the language?

The nurse said, 'He seems to manage it quite well,' and Dr Pye said, 'Let him have one whenever he wants.' I became quite a dab hand with the needle. There was definite satisfaction in doing a neat job. I was making great strides in my effort to play doctor as well as patient, the worm Ouroboros medicating his own tail.

The other inmates had their routines, and I had mine. On the first evening, after supper, I sang out, 'So who's for the pub?' I didn't really expect an answer, though I wasn't quite prepared for the shocked quality of the silence that followed. It's true that I would have been stymied if some of the residents had taken up the suggestion (Louise, for instance) but some of the cerebral palsy cases were more or less roadworthy. Their paralysis was largely psychological.

I dare say that from the point of view of the more settled residents I seemed to be carving out a syndrome of my own, as a florid psychotic with delusions of invulnerability.

My show of initiative shocked the staff as much as the residents. A nurse asked timidly, 'When will you be back?' To which I replied with enormous satisfaction, 'Don't know. Late. I don't see that it matters. There's a night nurse, isn't there?'

'Well, yes.'

'There you are, then. *Don't wait up!*'

My exit would have been even more impressive if I hadn't needed a certain amount of help to get into the car, but after that I was launched on the open road, destination the Black Lion in Bourne End.

I was pretty sure that Malcolm and Prissie Washbourne, veterans of the Battle of Trees, would be there. If they weren't I would chivvy the barman to roust them out with a phone call. They were there. Perhaps because they were already a few drinks to the good, they greeted me entirely without surprise. That's the whole virtue of a local – people are always popping in. I ordered my usual lime juice cordial and mounted (with help) the stool next to Prissie's. From that narrow throne I started to pontificate in the style which the elevation of the furniture seemed to demand.

Prissie said I should write up my experiences for the local papers – or the national press, why not? It was hard to imagine that such an exposé of low-level misery would find much of a readership. Better, really, from a journalistic point of view, if the inmates were being starved and brutally bludgeoned rather than bossed about and subjected to ominous hoovering.

After the pub closed we went back to the Washbournes' for a nightcap and to listen to some music. It amused them to be driven home the tiny distance in the Mini. It's possible that Mum, putting out the bottles for the milkman, could have heard us talking as we left the car, or caught raucous laughter of a familiar timbre wafting over from the open windows four doors down. Neighbours might have asked her if that wasn't my car parked outside the pub the night before, and seen later at the Washbournes'. Any of this would have given her pain, but there was no remedy for that. The Black Lion was the only pub where there was a welcome for me, and I certainly wasn't going to stay in the Home in the evenings communing with the zombies.

I didn't leave the Washbournes' that night until nearly one in the morning. Despite my bravado I wasn't sure how I would be received back at Gerrards Cross. I could see no lights from the road. Perhaps I'd been locked out as a way of teaching me a lesson. Even Mr Toad has his moments of doubt, before he sounds the horn – *poop! poop!* – that summons his welcome.

I needn't have worried. Out swept a large and very capable woman, very Irish, who introduced herself as Eileen. She had hair dyed black and a face that was dark pink, almost the colour of blackcurrant fool. She looked at me merrily and said, 'And you must be the bad boy John.' She was in a high good humour, not in any hurry to have me go to bed. She was happy for me to sit up with her and keep her company.

This was the first time I had properly understood that day staff and night staff are different. They're as different as night and day. Day staff have too much to do, night staff have too little. Day staff want compliance, but night staff enjoy stimulation. Eileen wanted to know which pub I'd been to, who my friends were, my history and plans (precious few) . She didn't pry. She just wanted to know everything.

Astringent, anti-tussive and vulnerary

During my time in the Cheshire Home the nights gave back what the days took away, what with the Black Lion and the warmth of Eileen's welcome. She taught me to play backgammon, and also to keep a keen eye on the pieces in case they moved of their own accord, which sometimes happened. We didn't play for money but for sweets, Maltesers at first and then Smarties for preference since they were less given to rolling.

Eileen couldn't digest milk properly, or so she said, and would make up mugs of something called Slippery Elm Food. This was a powder which she added to a pan of milk to thicken it, making it porridgy and easier to absorb. It was like glue, in fact – it even said 'mucilage' on the packet. She told me she got it from Boots the Chemist. That too became part of our ritual, the sharing of Slippery Elm Food, that potable glue. We bonded.

In our late-night sessions Eileen passed on the lessons which life had taught her. Her habit on holiday, in Ireland and elsewhere, was to look at the local paper and find out the times and places of funerals. She'd made many good friends that way over the years, going to the funerals of strangers, starting off with 'I'm sorry for your loss', playing it by ear after that. It sounds rather a splendid exercise, a sort of spiritual party game. Gatecrash the funerals of strangers, and end up recruiting them for your own. Not many funerals are standing-room-only, after all.

She said I should try it myself, though I think she underestimated my personal distinctiveness, my sore-thumb tendency. That was the great thing about Eileen. She would come and help me out of the Mini and into the Home, but nurse-Eileen and chatterbox-Eileen seemed to be separate agents, and she would talk to me about anything. I told her that the only stranger's funeral I had attended was in India, the pyre on Arunachala. I told her about the necessary piercing of the skull and the rearing-up of the body once combustion was established.

Eileen took in the grisly details without dismay. From the look of her face it was unlikely that she was contemplating the end of human existence. She was probably wondering whether I'd complain if she started frying some rashers. Irish people never seem to say bacon. It's always rashers.

That first night I didn't go to bed until well after two, and bedtime could be even later than that on the nights which followed. Then in the morning I'd give breakfast a miss, and not roll out of bed properly until ten or even eleven. This was more than respite, it was close to paradise.

I would probably have met a certain amount of resistance during the day, but luckily Martha Green, who was in charge of the office, turned out to have a soft spot for me. She always wore gypsy scarves, advertising the free spirit within the administrator, and she knew how to keep everyone sweet. I'd call her a breath of fresh air except for her chain-smoking. Her cigarette consumption was conspicuous even at a time when smoking was seen as a human right, and faculty libraries at Cambridge still had designated tables for smokers.

Martha wouldn't be able to defend me in frontal conflicts with our dear Director, but she could certainly block any complaints that came from Molly. Quite often there's someone tucked away in the middle of an organisation who quite likes troublemakers, as long as the conflict is amusing and can be contained.

Meanwhile I benefited from what the establishment offered without needing to feel either respect or gratitude. I had a friend at night and a nice balance of forces during the day: an ally in the office and an enemy cleaning the floors.

Molly hadn't retaliated in any real way for her humiliation at my hands, or so I thought. Just the once she hissed, 'You think you can live by your own rules, don't you? You'll find out soon enough.' It seemed logical that she would keep her counsel about the incident with the stick and not make waves. There were only two witnesses, Louise and me. It made sense that Molly would keep quiet.

I'm glad I didn't know that she was phoning Mum up and telling her that I was upsetting everybody in the Home. That I was evil. She must have broken quite a few of the rules of the establishment to get hold of the number. The Director's office certainly had a lock, as I had pointed out in our interview, but perhaps it wasn't used very often. Or she had got hold of a copy somehow.

If Dad had happened to pick up the phone, he might have enjoyed the conversation in his own perverse way. I can imagine him hearing this stranger's voice describe his son as evil, and coming back with something quite unexpected, along the lines of:

'You don't have to tell *me*! I've had years of it. What with one thing or another you'd think John would have learned to fit in by now, but that's not the way he does things. Gets it from his grandmother, I dare say. Count yourself lucky *she's* not in residence where you are! Thank you for bringing me up to date about his activities, my dear. I might have guessed he'd not lose his gift for rubbing people up the wrong way. What did you say your name was?'

But no – she had to get through to Mum. That was bad luck. It could never be that way with Mum, the taking things lightly, making a joke of it. She didn't have any equivalent of Dad's oddly slippery character armour. I wonder if Molly called in the evening, when I was actually in the pub down the road from Trees, when Mum might be able to hear me laugh, or the drone of my pontificating on the breeze. Molly had only made the call in the hope of making mischief – she wasn't to know that the mischief had already been done. You might say it had been done before I made Mum's acquaintance.

These were not good times for her. Sooner or later it was inevitable that word of my banishment or apostasy would reach the sewing circle, and then the joy must have gone out of Mum's needlework.

It's not something I particularly want to think about. I was lucky in the Washbournes, luckier yet in Eileen. The conspiratorial late-night atmosphere of our chats seemed to put Slippery Elm in the category of bootleg liquor, moonshine whisky, though it tasted much like oatmeal.

Some people like to sniff glue, apparently. I'd rather drink it. Ten grains of the powdered bark will make a thick potion with an ounce of water. *Ulmus fulva*, as I didn't then know to call it, of the family *Ulmaceæ*. Also known as the Red Elm, the Moose Elm, the Indian Elm, its virtues well known to the American aborigines, who used it as the basis of a healing salve. Demulcent, emollient, expectorant, diuretic, nutritive, astringent, anti-tussive and vulnerary, it is altogether a boon to the herbalist or freelance practitioner, not to mention the tireless self-medicator and respite-home rebel, returning back to base half-cut. It is tolerated by the stomach when all other foods fail, provides unfailing respite for a digestion in disarray.

The knife of advertising

After my stay in the Cheshire Home I didn't write an article for the *News of the World*. Instead I wrote to the magazine of the parent organisation, delightfully called the *Cheshire Smile*. Perhaps my letter was too literary, too steeped in the imagery of the *Alice* books. I told them that while I was staying in the Home I felt I'd fallen down the rabbit-hole and ended up in a topsy-turvy world where only the Director's door had a lock and everyone was told what was best for them, by people who had no idea. Perhaps I came across as one of life's belittlers, someone whose only contribution is negative, but writing sunny letters of complaint isn't the easiest trick to bring off. They didn't print my letter, and I only got a standard acknowledgement, so from that point of view it was the *Busy Bee News* from hospital days all over again. I should really have kept on at them. Persistence pays off in these things. Rejection doesn't stand a chance in the long run.

Back at Downing after my respite at Gerrards Cross I was starting my last term as a student. Certain things had to be faced. I arranged an appointment with the department of the university which gave advice about careers, the Appointments Board (but universally known as the Disappointments Board), and had a good meeting with someone called Bill Kirkman. A delightful chap, obviously very taken with me. He kept saying that it was obvious I'd be 'quite excellent' at something, if we could only work out between us what it might be. Somewhere in the cosmos there was a jigsaw puzzle missing a piece of exactly my quite excellent shape – but not necessarily in the Cambridge area.

Bill Kirkman had obviously sat on his glasses at some stage and bent the stems out of true, because he couldn't make them sit on his face properly – one side or the other was always sticking up at an angle, however often he adjusted them. He asked me if I thought the UKAEA might be my thing. I gave it a lot of thought, tilting my head this way and that as if I was trying to make sense of the world through my own pair of lop-sided glasses.

There's no denying the glamour of a set of initials. Perhaps UKAEA was some sort of cousin organisation to AMORC, the Ancient and Mystical Order Rosae Crucis. I said it to myself: *You-Kay-A*. It sounded like the name of a Maori god. I said that I thought this might indeed be my thing, though in fairness it did rather depend what the UKAEA actually was.

'It's actually the United Kingdom Atomic Energy Authority.'

'You know,' I said, 'I don't think the UKAEA is going to be my thing after all.' The isotopes of glamour can have a short half-life.

His second suggestion seemed more promising. A firm called J. Walter Thompson was always interested in snapping up Cambridge graduates. I managed to get quite excited about that. 'Do you think they'll want me?' I asked.

'I don't see why not. Do you want me to set up an interview?'

'I don't see why not.' I had heard of J. Walter Thompson as a giant in the advertising game, but until I had phoned Malcolm Washbourne I hadn't realised quite what big boys 'JWT' were in his world.

He was impressed despite himself, even while he warned me

frantically against his whole line of business. I had no inherent interest in advertising, and Malcolm had warned me against it any number of times as a living death of the spirit – but sometimes when the inner and the outer voices coincide, it becomes a sacred duty to disregard them. Perhaps there would be a little niche for me in this baffling industry. Perhaps I would clinch the coveted Margaret Erskine Dream-Cloud account.

I would dance with the devil. I would give J. Walter Beelzebub a whirl.

On the morning of the interview, all the same, I found I wasn't looking forward to it. I popped a Fortral or two into my mouth before attending, thinking this would make it more bearable. Always a risky assumption.

The interview was held in some sort of meeting room in the Blue Boar, the town's GHQ of meat-eating on Trinity Street. The first thing I was told was that I should ignore the camera – but I'd never seen one like it before. It was an enormous piece of apparatus, hardly smaller than what they had used when they filmed *The Pumpkin Eater* in Bourne End with Peter Finch, years before. They explained that it was the newest thing, a great breakthrough, and it was called a video camera. Soon they would be used in every interview, enabling employers to make entirely objective assessments of the candidates on offer.

I managed to ignore the camera, but only by dint of staring at the lady who was doing the interview. She was American, had a pointy nose and wore a smart suit – but she had a hair-band in her hair. I hadn't seen a grown woman wear such a thing before, but perhaps she'd seen it advertised and thought it looked smart.

She started off making kneading gestures with her hands, as if there was a ball of dough on her lap, and her voice was soft and crooning. 'Our goal is to get our audience to relax . . . we massage them . . . we let them know that they're in safe hands . . . they can let down their guard . . .'

Shamanistically delving

It seemed to me while she was saying all this that her nose was getting longer (by several inches) and even more pointed. I tried to decide whether this was to do with the hallucinogenic effects of pentazocine, or if I was shamanistically delving into her inmost soul and putting together a portrait, a Photofit like the ones on the news, of the culpable demon of lies I found at her core. These are probably just two ways of looking at the same thing. It stood to reason, though, that if I got this job my shamanistic talents would be fully engaged. They'd be working overtime.

Then the lady said, 'When consumers are thoroughly at their ease, completely relaxed . . . *that's* when we Plunge in the Knife of Advertising!' She thrust her hand forward in a completely savage gesture, and I won't even begin to describe her facial contortions while she did it. It was the most vicious display imaginable, and I gave a little scream.

That wasn't technically the end of the interview, but after that there was really nothing to be said. Why did I want the job? I didn't. What did I have to offer the company that would set me apart from the other applicants? Well, let me see – I was on the phone.

Somewhere in the archives of J. Walter Thompson there may exist video footage of the Knife of Advertising being plunged into the psychic flesh of an innocent bystander. I hope my scream on the soundtrack seeps into a thousand executive nightmares.

So I declined Maya's invitation to help change the fuel rods on nuclear reactors or to perforate consumers with lies about the things they were supposed to buy. My contemporaries grappled with similar choices, though I imagine they had a wider range of possibilities open to them.

The good people of the Disappointments Board disappointed everybody impartially, of course, but I rather felt that they had saved up something special for me. A bumper setback. Ridiculous of course for me to expect third parties to find me a place in life. The *vichara* is not to be delegated.

It was fascinating to see that people went on asserting the values of the counter-culture right up to the moment they betrayed it. I have known students who talked about the underground press, the wholefood co-operative and those blasted *kibbutzim* right up to the day of their final interview with Unilever, and then suddenly started invoking the need to grow up and make a contribution to the economy.

Youthful ideals being all very well and nothing to be ashamed of, but there being a real world out there which had to be dealt with sooner or later.

The disconcerting thing was not how abrupt the transition was but how smooth, not how much people had changed but how little. They behaved like actors who find, after auditioning for *Marat/Sade*, that they have been cast in *The Admirable Crichton*, but are too polite to make a fuss. Barely a shrug of the shoulders, and on with the show.

Of course change in nature can also be abrupt. The continuity between the caterpillar and the butterfly is anything but obvious. Sometimes the larva is physically bigger than the mature butterfly. Pupation, though, is a correspondingly laborious process. In these human cases pupation took no more than a moment, and the wings of the imago when they unfurled from the tie-dyed chrysalis bore pinstripes of grey.

I couldn't reasonably hope to develop wings of my own. I'd have settled for claws – anything to help me maintain my grip on my little world. At this point I was dangling desperately, a tree-shrew hanging on by its tail to the slender twig of what it knows. A cedilla clinging for dear life to the letter *c* without which it can't exist. I didn't feel as if I was writing the book of my life, I didn't even think I was reading it. I felt like an insect crawling across its pages, who would be squashed flat when the volume was shut.

I felt as necessary to the world at large as dandruff. I still had dandruff, and I knew how little I'd miss it if it went.

Of course what I was feeling wasn't unique. The heir to the throne had experienced something similar in outline three years previously, as his own graduation approached. His anguish didn't paint the air, so why should mine? We live in a democracy, after all.

Our experiences were similar in outline, very different in colour. For Prince Charles his years at Cambridge were a freer time than any he had known, or was likely to know again. Cambridge had been a sort of respite home for him. With his degree under his belt, he was back where he started, as Muggins Windsor, heir to the throne. It's well known that the great self-enquiry, the *vichara*, is particularly hard for those who have been strongly cast in a rôle by 'life'. In that respect I had all the advantages.

I slightly regretted not having overlapped at university with the Prince, though I came across quite a few people who had met him. It would have been lovely to get him to carry me to the lavatory, or up and down stairs. I'm sure I wouldn't have had to remind him that his motto was *Ich Dien*. I serve . . . We live in a democracy, after all.

It was a great thing, or so I told myself, to be able to study for my Finals without any impulse to panic, knowing that the results wouldn't make the slightest bit of difference to my future. There was a further lining (tin, perhaps, or pewter) to the dark clouds hanging over my future, namely: the answer to the question 'What will I be doing for a living?' had been answered. I would be doing nothing, supported by a State which understood that my value was not to be measured by narrow criteria. And this suggested the obvious answer to another question, 'Where will I be living?' I would be living in accommodation arranged for me by local government. There would be some paperwork to be managed, but there was a system in place to support me.

The local authorities didn't quite see it that way. Which local authority, anyway? Where did I belong? Depending on which way you looked at it, I belonged either with the other Cromers or with the other graduates of my year. Having a choice of two possible home addresses turned out to be a fancy way of being of no fixed abode, of loitering without the faintest intent. I applied to Cambridge, but the choice wasn't mine to make, apparently.

There was much correspondence on this subject. It was almost flattering. Two authorities were competing not to take responsibility for me. It certainly made me feel important.

I got hold of a copy of the Chronically Sick and Disabled Persons Act and tried to find potential leverage in that text. The most cheering thing about the whole document was that it was authorised by 'the Lords Spiritual and Temporal'. With spiritual authorities in my corner, it seemed clear that there would be a happy outcome.

I followed some of the bureaucratic tussle as if it was a tennis match in extreme slow motion. My case was bounced back and forth. Cambridge felt that I should be housed near my family (and far from Cambridge). Well played! Surely that was an ace?

Then High Wycombe argued that I should stay in Cambridge because I was more likely to get started on a career there. Brilliant return! Phenomenal racket control!

It was mentioned that High Wycombe had a very limited number of 'units' available, all of which had been allocated to applicants with needs far greater than mine. I'd driven past such units more than once. They were flimsy and draughty-looking pre-fabs, the sort of thing that gets built as a temporary measure and never demolished, unless it turns out to be crawling with asbestos.

During all these exchanges I tried to pretend I was the umpire and to forget that I was actually the bloody ball.

The only thing the two authorities were able to agree on was that it might be best for me to go back to CRX. Back into the cage of my childhood. Oh, I say! Very poor play, gentlemen. Highly unsporting. Not tennis, and not cricket.

There was another episode of sneaky manœuvring: while the two local authorities were knocking me back and forth so happily, playing their best administrative tennis for the privilege of not housing me, High Wycombe had the bright idea of applying on my behalf to the Cheshire Home in Gerrards Cross, with a view to getting me installed as a permanent resident.

The first I heard about it was when Martha Green phoned me up from the Home to break the bad news that I hadn't made the grade. Bad news. That was the way we played it. Dreadful pity. Sad turn of events. She read out the saddening verdict on my personality and its unsuitability for communal life: 'I'm afraid that John is something of a disruptive presence, rather too unconventional for the peace of mind of the other residents.'

'Oh dear,' I said.

'Yes,' she said, 'I knew you'd be disheartened.'

'It's rather a blow.'

'I wish there was something I could do.' She'd already done me the immense good turn of organising the veto, making sure the rejection wasn't scuppered by a misguided softening or any sort of plea for a second chance.

We kept up the charade of disappointment for as long as we could. Then I became aware of a dusty tinkling coming down the line. After a moment or two I realised that the bureaucrat-gypsy Martha must be wearing one of her favourite scarves, which had coins sewn into the hem, and was shaking with suppressed laughter, until a coughing fit flushed the hilarity out into the open.

It had been at the back of my mind, when I went to the Cheshire Home for my respite break, that this was a sort of trial run or probationary visit. I might be expected to live at Gerrards Cross sometime in the future. I think I can honestly say that I took no particular pains to make myself unacceptable. It was without ulterior motive that I blotted my copy-book, though the resulting disgrace certainly came in handy. My bad behaviour was disinterested and long overdue. I squeezed a lot of adolescence into a short span of days.

In terms of respite the Home gave me what I needed. If I had ended up living there I would have lost my vitality bit by bit, or else been frozen in a posture of rebellion against my surroundings, which is only another way (admittedly more seductive) of becoming institutionalised.

The pans of the scales seemed to be evenly balanced between the two authorities, so I decided I must hurl my trusty typewriter down onto the Cambridge side. I charged the ribbon of the Smith-Corona with its most irresistible ink and wrote a letter to my MP, appealing for help with my housing 'difficulties'. To prevail over Cambridge I had to appeal to High Wycombe, since that was where I was a constituent, but I couldn't be choosy about what tiny leverage I had. The MP for High Wycombe, Sir John Hall, wrote back in charming and eloquent terms, though I don't know whether he actually did anything. If he did, it amounted to foisting me definitively on Cambridge. Wearily they accepted responsibility for me, and wearily I accepted their acceptance. Then all I had to do was wait to hear the details of my new home.

It seemed to take a long time. Downing told me that it would be all right for me to stay on a bit after the end of term, which took the pressure off a little and made the waiting easier.

After I had taken my final exams, my Cambridge GP gave me a referral to be looked after. I was booked in for ten days at the Mary Marlborough Rehabilitation Lodge, part of the Nuffield Orthopaedic

Centre at Headington. This wasn't really about rehabilitation, though, it was about playing for time, though I picked up some useful kitchen skills.

I had taken some Gerard Manley Hopkins with me to read. Poetry in general has the advantage of portability, but this was a poor choice. Not because it was too remote from my experience, but too close.

> I am soft sift
> In an hourglass – at the wall
> Fast, but mined with a motion, a drift,
> And it crowds and it combs to the fall . . .

The same rhythmic trick, dragging then racing, Faustus's nightmares. Not at all reassuring to my thoughts of that season.

Mary Marlborough gave me a refresher course in the forked nature of institutions, in case I had forgotten. The establishment harboured contradictory attitudes towards its own goals. Independence was the be-all and end-all of the place, and yet a Plan B was provided at all times. You were encouraged to make a meal for yourself – but when you signed up to do it you also had to order a meal from the kitchens, in case yours was a disaster. A slightly insulting precaution. We weren't painting the Forth Bridge. This wasn't the Normandy landings. This was a lentil bake.

I was confident in my own modest culinary skills and shocked by the proposed waste of food, so I wouldn't choose from the menu. Then the staff would get quite shirty and end up ordering meals over my head, since that was the approved procedure. A very strange attitude in a place with Rehabilitation in the name. They wanted me to fend for myself and were rather put out when I did. They protected me from the possible consequences of my actions (lentil bake burned to buggery), though how this would fit me for independent living wasn't clear. Safety-nets are fine, but no one wants to be tripping over them the whole time. Is it going too far to suggest that staff felt rejected when their help wasn't needed, and were quite pleased by dehabilitation and back-sliding?

The people at Mary Marlborough kept me housed and fed. They offered me a selection of gadgets for use in the kitchen, mainly picker-uppers which my hands were too small and stiff to work. The only handy tool was a little bill-hook, which I use to this day. The most valuable lesson I learned was from a Pakistani occupational therapist called Mariam, who taught me how to skin tomatoes by scalding them. So I showed a modest profit on my stay in Headington.

Mariam was fun. She was lovely. She would always say, 'I'm just going to sneak to the fridge' or 'sneak to the bathroom', making the most wholesome activities seem unauthorised, loaded with the promise of transgression.

A ghost in hibernation

After my stint at Mary Marlborough, though, I really did feel I was sneaking back to Downing, where everyone else was getting ready to leave and I was getting ready to overstay my welcome. There was nowhere else for me to go. It wasn't as if I could go home to Mum and Dad, after everything that had happened. Of course I was glad that I had closed off that option. If further education was a dead end then 'home' was certainly another.

The examiners worked against the clock to mark our exams promptly, as if it mattered. On the day that results were posted up outside the Senate House the academic air was so tense it crackled. I stayed where I was in my room. Nothing on those lists could make a difference to me. A few times friends came to knock on my door, but I didn't answer. Eventually someone pushed a note under the door to tell me where I stood. I was in no hurry to go over and read it. The future could wait, particularly as I didn't have one.

At last I punted the wheelchair over and read the note where it lay. I had landed one of the coveted, and strictly limited, First Class degrees – the counter-cultural ones, technically known as Thirds. I had collected the whole set, and completed my downward progress from that First in spoken German. I had found my level. Still, going to Cambridge hadn't been about scholastic achievement. It had been about . . . I couldn't remember.

If the note had been pushed under the door face downwards, or folded over, I really don't know when I would have bothered to read it. My hunger for abstract knowledge seemed to have been stalled for the time being. I had no burning need to know. The ceremony of graduation, the supposed consummation of my undergraduate career, seemed so stunningly futile as to cast a favourable light backwards on the rigmarole of matriculation.

I left the note, my badge of honour, where it lay. Mrs Beddoes picked it up, glanced at it, and put it on the desk. She at least sincerely didn't care.

We parted with real emotion, she and I, when the time came. We had been 'John' and 'Jean' for ages by then. I'd taught her to make coffee the way I liked it, and she'd even started to like it that way too. I'd say we were like an old married couple, but that seems a rather slighting comparison. I'd say she loved me like a mother, though the same objection applies.

She said she would come in to college as usual during my overstay, to make sure I was all right, but I told her not to be silly. If she hadn't earned a holiday, who had?

She brought me a leaving present and helped me unwrap it. It was horrible, but it showed she had come a long way. It was a Harlequin Beetle in a little case, *Acrocinus longimanus* if memory serves, framed like a painting, something which she had found in the market. It was a great credit to her that she could see that this arthropod, at least, was beautiful – was a Nice Thing. It had a wonderful colour scheme – the camouflage pattern really did look consciously designed, as if someone like Braque had had a hand in it. I oohed and aahed like anything, and I think I convinced her I really liked it.

It was too much to expect, after all the imaginative effort she had expended, that she would realise these things stop being beautiful the moment they are killed, dried and fixed behind glass. I gritted my teeth and tried to persuade myself that in the natural course of things this lovely creature would have long died and been broken down into nothingness by now, and that it was permissible to appreciate it as being a storage system for Jean's emotional impulses, a bulb lit up by her feeling for me.

I had never been able to generate a very solid presence for myself on those premises, but now, left alone after the other students had gone, I felt so tenuous as to be positively allegorical, like the ancient servant forgotten in the great house at the end of *The Cherry Orchard*. If I did represent the passing of an old order, though, it would have been nice to know where exactly I had once fitted so snugly, what heyday I had so unwisely outlived. I felt like the shadow of a shadow, a ghost in hibernation. I almost looked forward to being exorcised. I would go quietly.

Downing didn't become deserted in vacation time, just because the students had gone away. In due course it played host to a conference of doctors. This was a godsend, and not just because the college catering system started up again for their benefit, so that I could be sneaked in, the staff turning a blind eye as usual. One waiter who had always made a bit of a pet of me even started calling me Doctor.

The medics and I had some amusing times together. I'd been reading my Martindale, so it wasn't hard for me to bustle my way into their conversations with some informed nonsense, asking for instance, 'Are you up to date about the enhancing relationship between benzodiazepenes and simple analgesics?'

I also saw something of the hazards of the profession. One delegate offered me some Pethidine as casually as if he was talking about a packet of crisps rather than a synthetic narcotic analgesic. There was something sexual about the way he slid the tube of Pethidine out of his pocket and waggled it in front of me, murmuring, 'If you like I can let you have these when I leave.'

The little sod knows too much

He also told me that Proladone was 'really nice', as if he was talking about a girl he'd just met, and not another heavyweight drug. He was obviously an addict, in the part of that trajectory where despair is still muffled by numbness and masked by nervous excitement.

Another delegate, rather handsome in a hangdog way, came to my room for coffee and sat on the bed, a promising situation until he started moaning that he'd ruined his life. 'I've got a sharp tongue,' he said, 'I can't help myself. I drive everyone away. My woman has left me and I have no friends. I have periodic incontinence of the anal sphincter and no one to love.'

I had nothing to offer him but the coffee I had promised, except for a nice yellow Valium to hold him together on a temporary basis. It was a treat to give drugs to a medic and fascinating to witness doctors at play. I saw at first hand that their lives were at least as disordered as anyone else's. I've never met a physician who could heal himself (as opposed to medicate himself). I don't think such a creature exists, which is why my medical interests can only ever be a sideline for me, not the main thrust of the journey.

I took it upon myself to inform as many of the medics as I could buttonhole over the week of the conference that it was no part of a doctor's job to tell the patient whether or not he was feeling pain. I preached this sermon on a text of my own, The Epistle to the Epiphyses, Chap. 1 verse 1. It had been simply insulting to be told that I couldn't be experiencing pain where there was no movement.

It wasn't easy for the medics to change gear from treating me as a pseudo-colleague to listening to the informed complaints of an ancient patient, but most of them seemed to manage it. There's an outside chance that I made a difference to their professional practice further along the line.

On the last night of the conference one of the delegates, a Dr Love (originally from Canada), even proposed a toast to me in Hall. He warned the others against me very charmingly, saying, 'If this little sod turns up in your area, for God's sake don't let him on to your list. He knows far too much! It's not healthy. If they were all like him, the jig would be up for the lot of us.'

It was July before I heard anything much from Cambridge Social Services. Then I was told where I would be living, in Mayflower House. I liked the sound of that. The *Mayflower* took pilgrims to a new world. When would I be moving in? When the flat was 'ready'.

My application to be a parasite had been accepted, but parasites can't dictate terms. Nothing I did could qualify as 'dropping out' because I hadn't been sufficiently 'in' to start with. My destiny seemed to be a sort of evaporation, one long exercise (a vast amplification of my sessions in the bathroom on Kenny staircase) in the loss of latent heat. Hadn't I arrived at Cambridge with a good head of spiritual steam, even a bumptious sense of my own purpose? I was now entirely cold and dried up, shivering and desiccated.

I had assumed I would be riding the Vichara Express, in the luggage compartment (but then the body is always and only luggage), but this was the stopping train at best, if it wasn't actually old rolling stock abandoned in an overgrown siding. The sense of forward motion, so precious and so hard to come by, was now too faint to be detected. Only when the metaphysical speedometer was patiently tapped and then scrutinised with the eye of faith was it possible to see that the needle wasn't stuck at zero.

Evaporation is a gradual process. When had mine started? I had felt quite monstrously present during my Cambridge years, clogging the pavements in the wheelchair, waiting hopefully to be helped through a door or up a staircase, but perhaps that wasn't the impression I made on other people. Possibly even before I started to withdraw from community life, buffeted by traumas familial and academic, the shrinkage had begun. Edith Piaf towered above me now, and I had enough regrets for the two of us.

The lessons of my university life seemed to have been overwhelmingly negative. What had I learned at Cambridge? I'd learned that a hand once placed on the handle of the wheelchair was hard to dislodge. That a bag slung over that handle, nominally mine, could be filled with things that had nothing to do with me. That a fussy manner could cloak a sensitive soul or a hard one. That once people had entered my room I couldn't actually throw them out. And once someone had lifted me up in his arms, it wasn't up to me whether we reached the bottom of the stairs in the conventional manner.

In my three years as an undergraduate I had made any number of acquaintances, but friendship was a different matter. I could lay the blame on the world at large, and say that nobody wanted to venture beyond the outskirts of intimacy in my particular case, but that's too easy. It lets me off the hook, when the truth is that I had mixed feelings about friendship myself. Of course the original plan was for me to be a beacon of enlightenment for my guru, and to fill my entire generation with his truth, but somehow that idea got lost along the way. A strong connection with other people would have been a decent consolation prize. But my experience of life from day to day over those three years made me think twice about trusting people's good intentions.

To claw back some control over my environment I had learned to take charge in psychological terms. I would requisition favours without granting any of the rights in return, having found that they were disproportionately hard to retract. In the free social setting which I had worked so hard to enter I had walled myself away from my fellows, whose freedom often seemed to be at my expense.

Emotionally I closed myself off. I didn't actively seek out situations in which I might be hurt. Why would I do such a thing? Why would I give away chances to hurt me as if they were tickets in a raffle?

There were certainly people I knew in those years who could be trusted. Alan Linton was one, who kept in touch after he left Cambridge at the end of my first year. Yet even then I responded to his letters in a rather tepid way, writing just often enough to go through the motions. Eventually he wrote saying he had the feeling that he was keeping our friendship going single-handed. He went on to say that it was quite all right if I had lost interest, such things happened, friendship had its rhythms and its seasons, but I wrote back saying no, no, it was always good to hear from him, which was great hypocrisy on my part. I let Alan dangle. I did nothing to extend the life of our friendship but wouldn't take the active responsibility of ending it. I let him strangle himself on his own goodwill. I didn't even have the good manners to behave badly, and I may have left him with a feeling of guilt rather than the proper annoyance. A few years ago I saw his name listed in Yellow Pages as a homœopath based in Saffron Walden. The alternative medicine he had resisted so fiercely when he first encountered it ended by wooing him away from his first, his conventional love. And perhaps the part I played in his life wasn't entirely ignoble, thanks to those early exchanges, conversations in which I was largely showing off.

Underlying crackle of dialectic

Hoff the Downing Casanova came to see me from time to time while he was living out of college, though we were never as intimate as when we lived on the same staircase. At some stage his cottage-loaf-made-of-wire hairstyle had been replaced by something modestly trendy, allowed to grow out without savage brushing but kept reasonably short, in a sort of home counties Afro.

For Hoff exclusively I would make coffee by the filter method, using Kenya Peaberry beans that had been ground before my eyes at the King Street coffee shop. Luckily in those glory days all my other visitors stuck to their preference, turning up their noses at the suspect brew I made in a glass vessel by a laborious technical process, boiling the kettle (filled with fresh-drawn water, of course) and then waiting two minutes for the temperature to be right. For this diehard group the filter method perverted the true taste of coffee, the powdered or granular joys of Nescafé. As far as these purists were concerned, unless it had been prepared for the jar using high-pressure industrial sprays, properly dehydrated or freeze-dried at the very moment that the flavour reached its peak, it hardly counted as coffee at all. My small-scale operation, with its plastic funnel and paper filter struck them as insultingly amateurish. Who was I to set myself up against Messrs Nestlé?

Considering the expense of Kenya Peaberry, this was handy. Of course it's when life seems to be collaborating merrily with you, supporting all your little schemes, that you have to watch out. Luckily the sensation is very fleeting.

Once, very disconcertingly, Hoff said he wished I was a girl. Or rather he wished he had met a girl he got on with as easily as he did with me. My mind in a body he fancied – but then why would we be discussing his several protocols? 'Girls are fantastic, girls are wonderful,' he told me, 'they shoot their stars across the sky and then they fizzle out. I'd never get tired of you, John.'

A mad thing to say, but touching too. And to a limited extent I could agree. My chats with Hoff were the closest I got in my Cambridge years to the university experience as promised and advertised. There was a nice Socratic feel to our conversations, an underlying crackle of dialectic, even if the subject was the sexual availability of young women. Getting into their knickers, to be perfectly frank.

Things might have worked less well if I had found Hoff the slightest bit attractive, but I didn't. I wasn't put off by the name-tapes on his socks or even the way he called ten thousand unborn cod, compressed into a tin, by the name of 'lunch'. That wave-length simply wasn't there.

On his last visit, at the very end of term, he brought me a present. It was an extremely thoughtful gift, positively disorienting in its attunement to my needs. I'm not used to people reading my mind, but if they can do it on special occasions, why not on a regular basis?

It was a simple enough piece of electrical equipment, an array of plug sockets, five of them side by side, on a short extension lead. It meant I could have all my devices on at the same time – record player, Anglepoise, electric typewriter, even my prematurely senile lava lamp – without the labour of juggling with an adaptor (itself a luxury) which would only accommodate two plugs at a time.

I don't frequent electrical stores any more than I do shoe shops, but I was pretty sure that this wasn't an item on sale to the public. It was a rather fancy piece of technology in those days. I went into raptures of entirely sincere appreciation, and managed not to mention two little details.

One was the timing. Hoff was passing on this highly desirable gadget only when he himself had no further use for it. He was leaving it with me rather than take it with him when he went down.

The other was the provenance. There was a strip of Dymotape stuck on the white plastic of the array's body.

Dymotape, sublime Dymotape! Dymotape was a lettering system which printed raised characters on a long roll of self-adhesive tape. It came as a sort of ray-gun (or so it seemed to minds formed in the '50s), with a wheel mounted on the top with which you selected the next letter, rather than ANNIHILATE or ANTI-GRAVITY, before squeezing the trigger to advance your message by a single space. The clever thing about it was that the plastic tape turned white under pressure, so that the raised letters stood out blanched and clear against the coloured ground. A final extra-strength squeeze on the trigger caused a blade to clip off the strip, while also nicking the underside so that it was easy to peel off the protective layer and expose the adhesive. I knew the pleasures of the machine only by watching, since it was no better suited to my handling than any other ray-gun (a ray-gun made to fit my grip would actually look alien), but even at second hand they were considerable.

The strip of Dymotape said PROPERTY OF THE CAVENDISH LABORATORY. By this time I knew Hoff well enough to be sure this name-tape was no joke, though Mrs Beddoes would never have suspected that this was stolen property, now that the riddle of the dictator's socks had been cleared up. There's no one so gullible as someone who's been fooled once already, as long as you don't pull the same trick twice.

University security was rudimentary in those days, and libraries suffered a steady leakage of their treasures. I imagine Hoff had crossed paths at some stage with a shopping-trolley filled with oscilloscopes, and had spotted and snaffled this humble device so well adapted to his needs (and in due course to mine).

Metaphysical oilskins

Stealing things was always described in those days as 'liberating' them, as long as the thieves were young and subscribed to a revolutionary agenda of some sort, but for once the word applied. Not having to struggle with plugs was indeed a little liberation.

It was entirely in character that Hoff should offer me a present only after getting plenty of use out of it himself, and also that he shouldn't remove the incriminating tape in order to convince me that money had been laid out on my behalf. Yet even when any generosity had been so scrupulously scrubbed from the gesture, a residue remained. By Hoff's sacred code of miserliness, passing on the socket-array at all was a sort of mad spending-spree, a morbid splurge of emotional extravagance all the more unsettling because its economic basis couldn't be mathematically established. Consequently my thanks were heartfelt.

Hoff and I 'exchanged addresses', which is a more satisfactory exercise when you have one to give out. Hoff's was 'c/o The Dean of International Students' at Harvard. He had won something called a Harkness Award to study there – a place where British plugs wouldn't go in the wall.

It seems clear that my various inadequacies in friendship were no more than the social aspect of a spiritual crisis. As Maharshi often pointed out, and had first ventriloquised for my benefit through the pages of the guru Paul Gallico's *Snow Flake*, the drop merges with the ocean, but the ocean also merges with the drop. I had tried to play my part in this merging, but my grasp on the fluid dynamics of the invisible was fatally faulty. The ocean of other people seemed to take the form of a vast waxed mackintosh, a set of metaphysical oil-skins even, from whose slick sleeves this yearning drop was doomed to drip.

There was one fact I failed to consider in my pig-headed misery – that disappointment is a form of grace. What is disappointed is always the ego, cheated of its applause. Every breakthrough for the Self is greeted by the ego's tears. When Self-realisation makes its entrance, then the jig is up with the ego, as the ego knows only too well. The ego looks forward to enlightenment the way turkeys look forward to December 25th (in Christian countries, and putting the question of nut roast to one side). And yet there is yearning underneath the dread, since despite all its fears the ego longs to be dissolved.

In those days of Cambridge summertime the grace of disappointment was poured down on me unstintingly, grace ubiquitous and grace abounding. If I wasn't at my wits' end, I was close to it. I phoned Graëme Beamish at his home, hoping he would somehow arrange for me to stay in mine – in A6 Kenny, where my Cambridge roots were if I had any. I needed just those few more days in residence, to bridge the gap until Mayflower House was ready to receive me. Otherwise I was afraid it was a gap which I would fall into, never to be seen or heard from again.

When Graëme answered the phone, there was no trace of his stuffy academic manner. Was this a delayed effect of his sabbatical? If so, it had brought about a miracle cure. He gave plain answers to plain questions. If he had appeared to me in this version from the start I would have known where I stood with him at every point. We need not have struggled to find a wave-length. Unfortunately the reason for the transformation was that he had washed his hands of me.

He listened as I started an outline of the predicament I was in and then said, 'John, I must interrupt. I'm not your moral tutor. You're no longer an undergraduate. New rules apply. Do you make this appeal as a friend?'

'Well . . . yes, Dr Beamish,' I said, suddenly stricken. 'As a friend.'

'I have some friends among my ex-tutees, but I can't honestly say you qualify as one of them. I have found you very difficult to deal with. Impossible to satisfy. It can't be such a good idea to make it so hard for people to help you. That was your choice, though, and friendship didn't come into it. I hope you find some way out of your difficulties, but I'm not the one to help you. Goodbye, John.'

At least I knew now how he explained himself to himself. I was difficult to deal with! I made it hard for people to help me!

I seemed to have very little talent as an exploiter of disability. I couldn't seem to live up to its full potential as a way of manipulating people. Almost anyone else, apparently, would have made a better job of it. I lacked talent.

In some separate, safely seething part of my brain I planned a Day of Action – Day of Inaction – when everyone who had ever told me how to live my life was strapped into the wheelchair, glued to the crutch and the cane, and given as much time as they needed to show me exactly where I was going wrong.

The college reluctantly agreed to look after my stuff – a modest hoard by most standards but still far beyond my power to move or muster. It all went into store in some Downing cellar or outbuilding until I had somewhere to put it: the Parker-Knoll, the record player, the lava lamp, my frying pan, records and books. I would have liked them to chuck the lava lamp away, to be honest, but I could hardly ask them to sort through my things as well as store them. It was a relief to feel my belongings were in safe hands. Well, safe-ish. I never saw that copy of *Kiss Kiss* again.

Dormant in the academic dark

My property had a home, even if I didn't. A couple of times in the past I had been treated as paraphernalia myself, on a par with luggage or furniture. I had travelled free of charge by train to hear The Who do their stuff, and I had been toted up Arunachala for a consultation with the Cow Goddess. I wasn't lucky this third time, otherwise I'd have been stowed below ground for a few days with no harm done, a little human mushroom dormant in the academic dark, waiting for the moment to fling its billion spores into the future.

I would have to 'manage on my own' for three days. For three nights. What did the council think I had been doing for the last three years? Living off the fat of the land?

I still had the Greek tapestry bag which had let out all the secrets and illusions, Pandora's bag with its embroidered lambda. I put in it the absolute necessities of life, pee bottle, photograph of Ramana Maharshi, wash bag. Breath mints, to make a better impression if I had to crank down the car window (it would take about ten minutes, so I'd have plenty of time to pop in a mint) in answer to a policeman's polite tap on the glass.

I had three fifty-pence coins and a pair of two-pence pieces – a grand total of £1.54.

I parked the car somewhere quiet and inconspicuous. A side road off Victoria Avenue. I draped the Dream-Cloud round me as best I could and dozed off, exhausted by the stressful efforts of the day. It was July, but I was uncomfortable and by this stage considerably underweight. I kept waking up in the night freezing cold, and I would have to turn on the engine so as to reap the benefit of the heater. The windows were steamed with my recirculating breath. All in all, it was like waking up inside the lung of someone recently dead.

Running the engine without moving an inch burned valuable petrol, but after a few minutes at least the inside of the Mini felt more welcoming, an environment marginally able to support life.

Minis aren't luxurious vehicles – they're not intended for long-term occupancy. Mr Issigonis, despite Granny's admiring comments, couldn't do everything. I ached from the restrictions of posture, and it's not as if I have a wide range of viable positions at my disposal in the first place. It would be just my luck to come through years of enforced immobility with the tissue more or less intact, and then to get bedsores from a few nights of sleeping rough. Normal life is abrasive. I don't want a cocoon but I need a cushion. I can only stand so much of what is called 'normal wear and tear'.

While I waited for the engine to warm up I would tune the radio to the World Service for a bit of company, some bulletins on fresh developments in the Kali Yuga. The car was very untidy, which is what happens when you give lifts to students, those tireless subcontractors of entropy. There were scattered sweet papers and crushed cigarette packets more or less everywhere. There was a sweet smell hinting at an abandoned apple core, but after a while the smell of urine from my pee bottle put that upstart aroma in its place.

Solitude in a cold car at night promotes introspection. I considered my progress. My life had opened up, as I had so much desired it to do, and then in just a few years it had contracted again, to what seemed to be, at this exact moment, some sort of vanishing point. I hadn't expected a degree to give me the freedom of the city, let alone the world, but there must be some advantage to having one. Nevertheless the dimensions of my living accommodation, newly graduated as I was after gaining as much education as world-famous Cambridge University was willing to dispense, had a volume amounting to something between 127 and 134 cubic feet. Call it 130. Learning to drive had always been part of my plan, and I had made it happen with help from the late John Griffiths, and despite everything my fellow road users, notably Michael Aspel (not late whatever the cost) could throw at me. It had never been part of the plan for the car to become, in this eternal interim, my only home.

Here it was

There was no bottom to the vessel of disappointment, no end to its pouring out. The fountain of disillusionment has an infinite cubic capacity, and there is no slaking the thirst for an anti-climax. I was bathed and sluiced down by living streams of negation, the metaphysical liquids freely gushing from their transfinite tank, disappointment that can never run dry, a cataract of revealed futility.

Disappointment is a form of grace, and I was blessed beyond all expectation. I was no more than a stray eyelash which the unobserving world would never know it had shed, unmissed ciliary casualty, cedilla without a *c* to hang from. In some way this must have been what I wanted. I had made it clear from the start that it was important for me to confront the world on equal terms. Nothing else would satisfy me. I had waited a long time for the day when there would be no safety-nets, and here it was.